BETH CAUSEY
7/12/77

ONE FLEW OVER THE CUCKOO'S NEST

THE VIKING CRITICAL LIBRARY

KEN KESEY

One Flew Over the
Cuckoo's Nest

TEXT AND CRITICISM

EDITED BY JOHN CLARK PRATT

COLORADO STATE UNIVERSITY

THE VIKING PRESS : NEW YORK

CONTENTS

Introduction

<hr />

> The first book one writes is a
> noisemaker, a play with no pressure,
> and it may sometimes have that free-
> swinging song of the cells.
>
> *Ken Kesey to Ken Babbs*

During the ten years that followed its publication in 1962, *One Flew Over the Cuckoo's Nest* had a sale of more than a million copies, generally increasing from year to year, and this testifies to its acceptance by readers who obviously felt the pressures of what Kesey symbolizes in his novel by "the Combine." Since World War II, many Americans have done more than merely read about the insurmountable pressures of the modern world. Some have resorted to resistance, rebellion, or, as a last expedient, retreat. A few have withdrawn in groups to neotranscendental communes, and others, perhaps the loneliest of all, have entered the reality-replacing, consciousness-expanding world of drugs. A significant number have, by society's standards, gone insane.

It is the last group, consisting of those whose consciousness is admittedly impaired in some fashion, that provides the cast of characters for Kesey's novel. For them as for Prince Hamlet, the world is indeed out of joint, but their madness is not in most cases feigned and their "antic disposition" is all too real. Men such as Harding, Ruckly, and Colonel Matterson have not the ability or even the desire to change what they cannot bear living with. Powerless, frustrated, docile, the men of Kesey's disturbed ward feel no such curse as that which impelled Hamlet "to set it right." For them any reordering must come from without, ironically from the same society that they blame for having caused their withdrawal. They must choose either the disordered world of R. P. McMurphy or the intolerably ordered world of Big Nurse Ratched, for whom no paradoxes exist. That they can unqualifiedly accept neither world, and yet must make a choice, provides the basic tension of the novel.

The characters in *One Flew Over the Cuckoo's Nest* cannot bring themselves to admit all possible points of view, an admission that Kesey regards as necessary for a truly sane existence. What he thinks is needed—according to Tom Wolfe, who wrote a widely read book about Kesey, *The Electric Kool-Aid Acid Test*—is the ability to apprehend the "synchronicity" of life, to force one's mind to "reach for connections between . . . vastly different orders of experience." But among the inmates of Nurse Ratched's ward—which stands in some measure for the world outside—most persons react with what Wolfe calls "the inevitable confusion of the unattuned."

If a person is unattuned, if his point of view differs markedly from that of persons with more power, then he risks being called insane. I think one should approach this novel by paying close attention to point of view, in life as well as in fiction. What one person accepts as reality may well be regarded as delusional and schizophrenic by another. After all the narrator, Bromden or "Chief Broom," is insane by anyone's standards. He has not always been so, but his perception has been clouded by the pressures of a hostile and changing world, much in the fashion that his fictional identity was altered as Kesey reworked the novel. Once Kesey told his friend Ken Babbs:

> I am beginning to agree with [Wallace] Stegner that [point of view] truly is the most important problem in writing. The book I have been doing on the lane [Perry Lane, in Menlo Park] is a

third-person work, but something was lacking; I was not free to impose my perception and bizarre eye on the god-author who is supposed to be viewing the scene. . . . Think of this: I, me ken kesey, is stepped back another step and am writing about a third-person author writing about something. Fair makes the mind real, don't it?

That Kesey fixed on Chief Broom as his narrator is what Wolfe says was his "great inspiration." Kesey himself finds it hard to explain how that choice was made. He says:

That the narrator happened to be an Indian, despite my never having known an Indian before, I attributed to the well-known association between peyote and certain tribes of our southwest. . . . Now I don't think so. Like if you keep thinking the Indian was your creation won't you eventually be forced to think of yourself as Tom Wolfe's creation?

Inspiration is a term that has become increasingly important to Kesey since the publication of *One Flew Over the Cuckoo's Nest*. Certain passages, he attests, were truly inspired, whether the catalyst might have been drugs, experience, or insight. He likes to offer as an example a passage beginning on page 243, reading it aloud as if it were broken into lines of verse:

We'd drove back inland instead of the coast,
to go through the town McMurphy'd lived in the most
he'd ever lived in one place.
Down the face
of the Cascade hill,
thinking we were lost till . . .
we came to a town
covered a space
about twice the size of the hospital ground.

As he reads, one becomes caught up in the sound of the words:

I was able to see a thing like a flag,
flapping high in the branches over a shed.
"The first girl ever drug me to bed
wore that very same dress.

I was about ten and she was probably less,
and at the time a lay seemed like such a big deal
I asked her if she didn't think, *feel,*
we ought to *announce* it some way? Like, say,
tell our folks, 'Mom, Judy and me got engaged today.' "

Whose rhymed verse is this? McMurphy's? Kesey's? Bromden's? After all, the Chief has just introduced his lyric reminiscence of what McMurphy told him by saying, "I was feeling better than I'd remembered feeling since I was a kid, when everything was good and the land was still singing kids' poetry to me." Inspired as he may have been, Kesey does admit that the rhymes (first noticed, he says, by Malcolm Cowley in a Stanford writing course) were made much more explicit in revision.

Whatever the sources of Kesey's inspiration in the novel, it should be seen primarily as related to point of view, not only that of the narrator but also that of the artist himself. Working "the midnight-to-eight shift . . . five days a week," Kesey endeavored to create a narrative that would be completely objective. "In the antiseptic wilderness of the Menlo Park VA Hospital," he writes, "I cleared a space and rigged a runway and waited for my muse to take the controls." What resulted is a novel that shows the author's awareness of the essentially schizophrenic nature of perceived existence—of a multifaceted, often foggy *discordia concors* that offers only occasional flashes of day-glo–painted truth. The vehicle for this awareness is the narrative of a schizophrenic American Indian.

Obviously neither this view of life nor the use of a first-person narrator to reveal it is new in American literature. In some ways Kesey's vision is not unlike that of Melville or Mark Twain or Steinbeck, the last author being one whom Kesey admires deeply, though not for what he says are "the wrong reasons—for his social commentary." He respects Steinbeck for his point of view, his synchronicity. Where Kesey differs from those others who told stories in the first person is in his use of a narrator whose own values are not only to be questioned but are often patently unreal. Unlike Melville's Ishmael, Hawthorne's Miles Coverdale, or Huckleberry Finn, Kesey's Chief Broom is obviously deforming the events that figure in the early part of his narrative. That fact distinguishes him too from Faulkner's Benjy in the first part of *The Sound and the Fury*, for Benjy sees exactly what happens, even though he doesn't connect one event with another. Chief Broom makes connections, but sees everything through a distorting haze. The fact that he is insane produces the same state of mind in him that Kesey attempted to produce in himself while writing the novel, a state in which there are no preconceptions. At times Kesey produced the state by taking drugs:

> I studied inmates as they daily wove intricate and very accurate schizophrenic commentaries of the disaster of their environment, and had found that merely by ingesting a tiny potion I could toss word salad with the nuttiest of them, had discovered that if I plied my consciousness with enough of the proper chemicals it was impossible to preconceive, and when preconception is fenced out, truth is liable to occur.

Other first-person narrators color what they perceive with their own preconceptions, their own limitations and oversights. It is only by looking behind their masks that we can glimpse the visions of their authors. No such problem is offered by *The Cuckoo's Nest* because the personality of Chief Broom is only a small factor in our judgment; it is primarily his failure to see things clearly that counts. For the Chief, reality is being transformed at every moment. While the fog swirls or the lights glare, he cannot glimpse the real outlines of his world, but the reader can. What the Chief does see is a basic struggle for survival, with McMurphy as the "good guy" on his side. "All you could do," he says, "was keep on whipping it, till you couldn't come out any more and somebody else had to take your place." But McMurphy too is a psychopath, and the Chief's "All you could do" might apply equally well to Big Nurse, who would no doubt agree with the statement from her own point of view. All McMurphy's scheming, his humor,

and his leadership serve only to delay the inevitable confrontation, in which neither side can win out completely.

One cannot say that *The Cuckoo's Nest* is altogether without preconceptions, but it is as nearly without them as any
first-person American narrative. The result is that it often plays
upon the preconceptions of its readers, a point borne out by
the critical essays reprinted in this volume. Teased by shapes
that elude him, one critic after another goes wading through
the fog and finds that it is full of allusions. Not one of them
comes back with a satisfactory discussion of the novel as a
whole, but all have interesting points to make. John A. Barsness, for example, sees a basically simple conflict, McMurphy
versus Big Nurse, as a result of which Chief Broom, the
"natural man," comes out the victor. Joseph J. Waldmeir
equates the politics of the ward with that of a "true democracy." Leslie A. Fiedler, among others, invokes Melville by
noting that it is Chief Bromden who is "left to boast: *And I
only am escaped alive to tell thee.*" The Melvillean allusion is
expanded by Waldmeir when he associates McMurphy first
with Ahab, then with Christ. But what Waldmeir will only
imply is the quite proper comparison between Big Nurse and
Melville's equally white leviathan.

That *The Cuckoo's Nest* makes its critics uneasy has become
apparent, but equally obvious is the fact that it is supposed to
do so. The echoes of Melville, Hemingway, and William
Burroughs should be recognized, but the novel's multivalent
synchronicity (elsewhere I have used the term "syncretic alle-
gory") often makes it impossible to assign a precise meaning
to any one allusion. Some critics define the world of this novel
as being absurd. I should disagree: it is all too real. As can be
seen by comparing the characters with the persons whom
Kesey actually observed, no one except Nurse Ratched is unbelievable in the same fashion as many characters in Joseph
Heller's *Catch 22*, and Big Nurse herself is a creation of the
schizophrenic Chief. What is truly absurd is usually the point
of view of the narrator.

One value of this novel is that it admits and substantiates almost any interpretation. "The Big Nurse murdered President Kennedy," Kesey said in a letter. "Check her photo in *Time* if you don't believe it." Should one question the author's own statement? With Kesey, perhaps, one should. After admitting that the name and character of Billy Bibbitt were suggested by Billy Budd, Kesey has denied remembering that the first Billy stuttered in the same fashion as the second.

To doubt the reality of the novel, as well as that of its author, is part of the game. *One Flew Over the Cuckoo's Nest*, with all its truth, is also a grand prank, an example of what Tom Wolfe records as the "ultimate fantasy," life itself. Says Kesey, "Peyote, I used to claim, inspired my chief narrator, because it was after choking down eight of the little cactus plants that I wrote the first three pages." This opening section, he adds, remained virtually unchanged in subsequent drafts. One has only to compare the early and the final version to see how much change there actually was. To conclude is folly, Kesey implies, but to doubt, divine—and doubt one must, not only the perception of the narrator but also, perhaps, the vision of the author. What one should not question is the perfectly painful reality that is depicted in precise detail by a completely believable schizophrenic.

Behind it all, somewhere, lies Kesey's own consciousness. "It's the *consciousness that the author is communicating* that I'm concerned with," Kesey has said, in reference to his reading comic strips—an important influence that Terry G. Sherwood has quite properly identified. "*Whatever* the subject matter," Kesey goes on, "or how luridly it was dealt with . . . I now read . . . first to try to plumb the *consciousness* serving as the impetus." How can we plumb Kesey's own consciousness? First, I should say, by recognizing that in addition to being the man so well described by Tom Wolfe, he is also a professed Christian who follows the *I Ching*, who has run—unsuccessfully—for the Pleasant Hill, Oregon, School Board, and who attends his children's school Christmas plays. That he lives paradoxically implies the existence of similar paradoxes in his artistic consciousness, and one should beware of absolute judgments when considering Kesey or his work.

One should avoid, for instance, referring to Kesey's belief in "the Combine." It is the Chief who defines it, with McMurphy's help. If there is a real tragedy in *One Flew Over the Cuckoo's Nest*, it may well be due to the fact that persons of different perceptive capacities believe in the real existence of the Combine. When their quixotic attacks on the monster windmill fail, they manage to blame everyone but themselves. Should we regard McMurphy's last futile attempt to impose an alternate order by force as pathetic, inevitable, or tragic? After all, his merely spontaneous disruptions—much on the order of Kesey's "merry pranks"—are the one thing that has made existence in the ward (call it the world) not only bearable but even delightful. When McMurphy stops laughing— when he attempts to fight Big Nurse on her own terms—he in effect has given up.

In the consciousness of Ken Kesey, I suspect, there is a feeling that the martyrdom of McMurphy is inevitable, but in itself not ultimately tragic. It is as inevitable as was the loss of that American safety valve, the existence of illimitable land. It is as certain as the vanishing of the Red Man as we have known him from the myths of our past. For Kesey there is obviously no going back; what counts is the point of view with which we must always go forward. Unlike Hemingway's clean, well-lighted café, Kesey's place of "a certain cleanness and order" is the disturbed ward of a mental hospital, the last refuge of those who seek an end to chaos. What Kesey suggests is that sanity is not produced by any perceived order, but by just the opposite, that is, by a recognition of disorder leading to productive change. One should not forget that most of the patients in *The Cuckoo's Nest* have committed themselves voluntarily to a world that they can most certainly not control, but one that they *might* comprehend. Whether or not they do comprehend it as a result of McMurphy's death is a question left to the awareness of the reader.

All the inmates except those who have either given up or been broken are free to go—where? To Canada, if they wish, but they do not have to go there. Kesey's Canada is not Joseph Heller's Sweden. The Chief says at the end of the novel, "I might go to Canada eventually," but not yet, not until he has looked "over the country around the gorge again, just to bring some of it clear in my mind." His own consciousness newly restored, the Chief may well see what readers of the novel can also see: the meaning-filled clutter of existence, the spontaneity of life, the multifaceted, many-colored mess which is what living is all about. Those who believe in the Combine will repeatedly fail, no matter which side they happen to be on. The struggle will continue, to be sure, but how we bring it clear in our own minds is entirely, and rightfully, up to us.

—JOHN CLARK PRATT

EDITOR'S NOTE

Although every effort has been made to reproduce Kesey's letters exactly as he wrote them, the editor has made silent emendations where obvious typographical errors or confusing misspellings exist.

CHRONOLOGY

1935   Ken Kesey born September 17 in La Junta, Colorado; after his family moved to Springfield, Oregon, Kesey attended public schools there, then the University of Oregon at Eugene. In college, writing classes from James B. Hall had a lasting influence on him. Writing included short stories, one-act plays, and poetry.

1956   Married Faye Haxby, May 20. (The Keseys have two sons and one daughter.)

1957–   Graduated from the University of Oregon, where he had been
1958   active in wrestling and drama; worked a year; wrote novel about college athletics: *End of Autumn*. Attended Stanford University as a graduate student.

1959–   At Stanford, studied with Wallace Stegner, Malcolm Cowley,
1961   Richard Scowcroft, and Frank O'Connor. While living on Perry Lane, met and learned from other writers, many of whom became long-time friends (Gurney Norman, Larry McMurtry, Ken Babbs, Bob Stone, Wendell Berry). Wrote novel about San Francisco's North Beach: *Zoo*. Volunteered for government drug experiments (Spring 1960–Spring 1961). Wrote *One Flew Over the Cuckoo's Nest* (Summer 1960–Spring 1961). In April 1961, worked as aide in Menlo Park VA Hospital. In the fall of 1961, moved to Springfield, Oregon, to help brother start Springfield Creamery.

1962   Lived on Oregon Coast, doing extensive research for *Sometimes a Great Notion*. Worked on character and plot outlines. Publication of *Cuckoo's Nest* in February. Moved back to Perry Lane in late spring, where he began writing *Sometimes a Great Notion*. In the summer, moved to La Honda.

1963   Stage version of *Cuckoo's Nest* opened in New York, starring Kirk Douglas—unfavorable reviews. Closed three months after November 14 opening.

1964   Kesey finished revisions of *Notion* just as Ken Babbs returned from Vietnam. A planned sightseeing trip for Kesey and Babbs for the New York publication of *Notion* in July snowballed into the cross-country bus trip.

1965   After return to California, worked on "The Movie," attempting to cut more than forty hours of film shot on the bus trip. Arrested in April for possession of marijuana; a year of hearings and court appearances followed.

1966   Found guilty of possession. Sentenced to six months in county jail and three years' probation. Appeal filed. Arrested again on January 19. Fled to Mexico, then returned late in the fall and was arrested by the FBI in October. Visited by Tom Wolfe while in jail. In November, a hung jury for the January arrest.

1967   In April, another hung jury. After pleading *nolo contendere* to a lesser charge, Kesey sentenced to ninety days. In June, he dropped his appeal for the January 1966 conviction and began serving both sentences at the San Mateo County Jail and later at the San Mateo County Sheriff's Honor Camp. Released in November. Letters to McMurtry from Mexico published in *Ararat*.

1968   Moved to farm in Pleasant Hill, Oregon. Wrote/drew elaborate book based on his jail journals: *Cut the Mother-Fuckers Loose*. In August, Wolfe's *Electric Kool-Aid Acid Test* published. Various Kesey letters and short pieces published in underground publications such as *The Free You*.

1969   Lived in London, England, from March to June, doing some work for *Apple*. Revised version of the *Cuckoo's Nest* play opened successfully in San Francisco.

1970   Filmed a children's movie, *Atlantis Rising*, in the spring. During the summer, Paul Newman's company shot a screen version of *Sometimes a Great Notion*. Kesey's three-year probation completed in July.

1971   Revised version of *Cuckoo's Nest* opened in New York. In the spring, Kesey coedited (with Paul Krassner) *The Last Supplement to The Whole Earth Catalogue*. Along with Ken Babbs and Paul Foster, Kesey began work on collection of short essays and prose fiction entitled *Garage Sale*. Also started a new novel based upon the jail journals. Movie of *Sometimes a Great Notion* released late in the year.

I

One Flew Over
the Cuckoo's Nest

The Text

> . . . one flew east, one flew west,
> One flew over the cuckoo's nest.
>
> —Children's folk rhyme

part 1

they're out there.

Black boys in white suits up before me to commit sex acts in the hall and get it mopped up before I can catch them.

They're mopping when I come out the dorm, all three of them sulky and hating everything, the time of day, the place they're at here, the people they got to work around. When they hate like this, better if they don't see me. I creep along the wall quiet as dust in my canvas shoes, but they got special sensitive equipment detects my fear and they all look up, all three at once, eyes glittering out of the black faces like the hard glitter of radio tubes out of the back of an old radio.

"Here's the Chief. The *soo*-pah Chief, fellas. Ol' Chief Broom. Here you go, Chief Broom. . . ."

Stick a mop in my hand and motion to the spot they aim for me to clean today, and I go. One swats the backs of my legs with a broom handle to hurry me past.

"Haw, you look at 'im shag it? Big enough to eat apples off my head an' he mine me like a baby."

They laugh and then I hear them mumbling behind me, heads close together. Hum of black machinery, humming hate and death and other hospital secrets. They don't bother not talking out loud about their hate secrets when I'm nearby because they think I'm deaf and dumb. Everybody think so. I'm cagey enough to fool them that much. If my being half Indian ever helped me in any way in this dirty life, it helped me being cagey, helped me all these years.

I'm mopping near the ward door when a key hits it from the other side and I know it's the Big Nurse by the way the lockworks cleave to the key, soft and swift and familiar she been around locks so long. She slides through the door with a gust of cold and locks the door behind her and I see her fingers trail across the polished steel—tip of each finger the same color as her lips. Funny orange. Like the tip of a soldering iron. Color so hot or so cold if she touches you with it you can't tell which.

She's carrying her woven wicker bag like the ones the Umpqua tribe sells out along the hot August highway, a bag shape of a tool box with a hemp handle. She's had it all the years I been here. It's a loose weave and I can see inside it; there's no compact or lipstick or woman stuff, she's got that bag full of a thousand parts she aims to use in her duties today—wheels and gears, cogs polished to a hard glitter, tiny pills that gleam like porcelain, needles, forceps, watchmakers' pliers, rolls of copper wire . . .

She dips a nod at me as she goes past. I let the mop push me back to the wall and smile and try to foul her equipment up as much as possible by not letting her see my eyes—they can't tell so much about you if you got your eyes closed.

In my dark I hear her rubber heels hit the tile and the stuff in her wicker bag clash with the jar of her walking as she passes me in the hall. She walks stiff. When I open my eyes she's down the hall about to turn into the glass Nurses' Station where she'll spend the day sitting at her desk and looking out her window and making notes on what goes on out in front of her in the day room during the next eight hours. Her face looks pleased and peaceful with the thought.

Then . . . she sights those black boys. They're still down there together, mumbling to one another. They didn't hear her come on the ward. They sense she's glaring down at them now, but it's too late. They should of knew better'n to group up and mumble together when she was due on the ward. Their faces bob apart, confused. She goes into a crouch and advances on where they're trapped in a huddle at the end of the corridor. She knows what they been saying, and I can see she's furious clean out of control. She's going to tear the black bastards limb from limb, she's so furious. She's swelling up, swells till her back's splitting out the white uniform and she's let her arms section out long enough to wrap around the three of them five, six times. She looks around her with a swivel of her huge head. Nobody up to see, just old Broom Bromden the half-breed Indian back there hiding behind his mop and can't talk to call for help. So she really lets herself go and her painted smile twists, stretches to an open snarl, and she blows up bigger and bigger, big as a tractor, so big I can smell the machinery inside the way you smell a motor pulling too big a load. I hold my breath and figure, My God this time they're gonna do it! This time they let the hate build up too high and overloaded and they're gonna tear one another to pieces before they realize what they're doing!

But just as she starts crooking those sectioned arms around the black boys and they go to ripping at her underside with the mop handles, all the patients start coming out of the dorms to check on what's the hullabaloo, and she has to change back before she's caught in the shape of her hideous real self. By the time the patients get their eyes rubbed to where they can halfway see what the racket's about, all they see is the head nurse, smiling and calm and cold as usual, telling the black boys they'd best not stand in a group gossiping when it *is* Monday morning and there *is* such a lot to get done on the first morning of the week. . . .

". . . mean old Monday morning, you know, boys . . ."

"Yeah, Miz Ratched . . ."

". . . and we have quite a number of appointments this morning, so perhaps, if your standing here in a group talking isn't *too* urgent . . ."

"Yeah, Miz Ratched . . ."

She stops and nods at some of the patients come to stand around and stare out of eyes all red and puffy with sleep. She nods once to each. Precise, automatic gesture. Her face is smooth, calculated, and precision-made, like an expensive baby doll, skin like flesh-colored enamel, blend of white and cream and baby-blue eyes, small nose, pink little nostrils—everything working together except the color on her lips and fingernails, and the size of her bosom. A mistake was made somehow in manufacturing, putting those big, womanly breasts on what would of otherwise been a perfect work, and you can see how bitter she is about it.

The men are still standing and waiting to see what she was onto the black boys about, so she remembers seeing me and says, "And since it *is* Monday, boys, why don't we get a good head start on the week by shaving poor Mr. Bromden first this morning, before the after-breakfast rush on the shaving room, and see if we can't avoid some of the—ah—disturbance he tends to cause, don't you think?"

Before anybody can turn to look for me I duck back in the mop closet, jerk the door shut dark after me, hold my breath. Shaving before you get breakfast is the worst time. When you got something under your belt you're stronger and more wide awake, and the bastards who work for the Combine aren't so apt to slip one of their machines in on you in place of an electric shaver. But when you shave *before* breakfast like she has me do some mornings—six-thirty in the morning in a room all white walls and white basins, and long tube-lights in the ceiling making sure there aren't any shadows, and faces all round you trapped screaming behind the mirrors—then what chance you got against one of their machines?

I hide in the mop closet and listen, my heart beating in the dark, and I try to keep from getting scared, try to get my thoughts off someplace else—try to think back and remember things about the village and the big Columbia River, think about ah one time Papa and me were hunting birds in a stand of cedar trees near The Dalles. . . . But like always when I try to place my thoughts in the past and hide there, the fear close at hand seeps in through the memory. I can feel that least black boy out there coming up the hall, smelling out for my fear. He opens out his nostrils like black funnels, his out-sized head bobbing this way and that as he sniffs, and he sucks in fear from all over the ward. He's smelling me now, I can hear him snort. He don't know where I'm hid, but he's smelling and he's hunting around. I try to keep still. . . .

(Papa tells me to keep still, tells me that the dog senses a bird somewheres right close. We borrowed a pointer dog from

a man in The Dalles. All the village dogs are no-'count mon-
grels, Papa says, fish-gut eaters and no class a-tall; this here
dog, he got *insteek!* I don't say anything, but I already see
the bird up in a scrub cedar, hunched in a gray knot of
feathers. Dog running in circles underneath, too much smell
around for him to point for sure. The bird safe as long as he
keeps still. He's holding out pretty good, but the dog keeps
sniffing and circling, louder and closer. Then the bird breaks,
feathers springing, jumps out of the cedar into the birdshot
from Papa's gun.)

The least black boy and one of the bigger ones catch me
before I get ten steps out of the mop closet, and drag me back
to the shaving room. I don't fight or make any noise. If you
yell it's just tougher on you. I hold back the yelling. I hold
back till they get to my temples. I'm not sure it's one of those
substitute machines and not a shaver till it gets to my temples;
then I can't hold back. It's not a will-power thing any more
when they get to my temples. It's a . . . *button,* pushed, says
Air Raid Air Raid, turns me on so loud it's like no sound,
everybody yelling at me hands over their ears from behind a
glass wall, faces working around in talk circles but no sound
from the mouths. My sound soaks up all other sound. They
start the fog machine again and it's snowing down cold and
white all over me like skim milk, so thick I might even be able
to hide in it if they didn't have a hold on me. I can't see six
inches in front of me through the fog and the only thing I can
hear over the wail I'm making is the Big Nurse whoop and
charge up the hall while she crashes patients outta her way
with that wicker bag. I hear her coming but I still can't hush
my hollering. I holler till she gets there. They hold me down
while she jams wicker bag and all into my mouth and shoves
it down with a mop handle.

(A bluetick hound bays out there in the fog, running scared
and lost because he can't see. No tracks on the ground but the
ones he's making, and he sniffs in every direction with his cold
red-rubber nose and picks up no scent but his own fear, fear
burning down into him like steam.) It's gonna burn me just

that way, finally telling about all this, about the hospital, and her, and the guys—and about McMurphy. I been silent so long now it's gonna roar out of me like floodwaters and you think the guy telling this is ranting and raving my *God*; you think this is too horrible to have really happened, this is too awful to be the truth! But, please. It's still hard for me to have a clear mind thinking on it. But it's the truth even if it didn't happen.

When the fog clears to where I can see, I'm sitting in the day room. They didn't take me to the Shock Shop this time. I remember they took me out of the shaving room and locked me in Seclusion. I don't remember if I got breakfast or not. Probably not. I can call to mind some mornings locked in Seclusion the black boys keep bringing seconds of everything—supposed to be for me, but they eat it instead—till all three of them get breakfast while I lie there on that pee-stinking mattress, watching them wipe up egg with toast. I can smell the grease and hear them chew the toast. Other mornings they bring me cold mush and force me to eat it without it even being salted.

This morning I plain don't remember. They got enough of those things they call pills down me so I don't know a thing till I hear the ward door open. That ward door opening means it's at least eight o'clock, means there's been maybe an hour and a half I was out cold in that Seclusion Room when the technicians could of come in and installed anything the Big

Nurse ordered and I wouldn't have the slighest notion what.

I hear noise at the ward door, off up the hall out of my sight. That ward door starts opening at eight and opens and closes a thousand times a day, kashash, *click*. Every morning we sit lined up on each side of the day room, mixing jigsaw puzzles after breakfast, listen for a key to hit the lock, and wait to see what's coming in. There's not a whole lot else to do. Sometimes, at the door, it's a young resident in early so he can watch what we're like Before Medication. BM, they call it. Sometimes it's a wife visiting there on high heels with her purse held tight over her belly. Sometimes it's a clutch of grade-school teachers being led on a tour by that fool Public Relation man who's always clapping his wet hands together and saying how overjoyed he is that mental hospitals have eliminated all the old-fashioned cruelty: "What a *cheery* atmosphere, don't you agree?" He'll bustle around the schoolteachers, who are bunched together for safety, clapping his hands together. "Oh, when I think back on the old days, on the filth, the bad food, even, yes, brutality, oh, I realize ladies that we have come a long way in our campaign!" Whoever comes in the door is usually somebody disappointing, but there's always a chance otherwise, and when a key hits the lock all the heads come up like there's strings on them.

This morning the lockworks rattle strange; it's not a regular visitor at the door. An Escort Man's voice calls down, edgy and impatient, "Admission, come sign for him," and the black boys go.

Admission. Everybody stops playing cards and Monopoly, turns toward the day-room door. Most days I'd be out sweeping the hall and see who they're signing in, but this morning, like I explain to you, the Big Nurse put a thousand pounds down me and I can't budge out of the chair. Most days I'm the first one to see the Admission, watch him creep in the door and slide along the wall and stand scared till the black boys come sign for him and take him into the shower room, where they strip him and leave him shivering with the door open while they all three run grinning up and down the halls looking for

the Vaseline. "We *need* that Vaseline," they'll tell the Big
Nurse, "for the thermometer." She looks from one to the
other: "I'm *sure* you do," and hands them a jar holds at least
a gallon, "but mind you boys don't group up in there." Then
I see two, maybe all three of them in there, in that shower
room with the Admission, running that thermometer around
in the grease till it's coated the size of your finger, crooning,
"Tha's right, mothah, tha's right," and then shut the door and
turn all the showers up to where you can't hear anything but
the vicious hiss of water on the green tile. I'm out there most
days, and I see it like that.

But this morning I have to sit in the chair and only listen
to them bring him in. Still, even though I can't see him, I
know he's no ordinary Admission. I don't hear him slide scared
along the wall, and when they tell him about the shower he
don't just submit with a weak little yes, he tells them right
back in a loud, brassy voice that he's already plenty damn
clean, thank you.

"They showered me this morning at the courthouse and last
night at the jail. And I *swear* I believe they'd of washed my
ears for me on the taxi ride over if they coulda found the
vacilities. Hoo boy, seems like everytime they ship me someplace I gotta get scrubbed down before, after, and during the
operation. I'm gettin' so the sound of water makes me start
gathering up my belongings. And *get* back away from me with
that thermometer, Sam, and give me a minute to look my new
home over; I never been in a Institute of Psychology before."

The patients look at one another's puzzled faces, then back
to the door, where his voice is still coming in. Talking louder'n
you'd think he needed to if the black boys were anywhere near
him. He sounds like he's way above them, talking down, like
he's sailing fifty yards overhead, hollering at those below on
the ground. He sounds big. I hear him coming down the hall,
and he sounds big in the way he walks, and he sure don't slide;
he's got iron on his heels and he rings it on the floor like horse-
shoes. He shows up in the door and stops and hitches his
thumbs in his pockets, boots wide apart, and stands there with
the guys looking at him.

"Good *morn*in', buddies."

There's a paper Halloween bat hanging on a string above his head; he reaches up and flicks it so it spins around.

"Mighty nice fall day."

He talks a little the way Papa used to, voice loud and full of hell, but he doesn't look like Papa; Papa was a full-blood Columbia Indian—a chief—and hard and shiny as a gunstock. This guy is redheaded with long red sideburns and a tangle of curls out from under his cap, been needing cut a long time, and he's broad as Papa was tall, broad across the jaw and shoulders and chest, a broad white devilish grin, and he's hard in a different kind of way from Papa, kind of the way a baseball is hard under the scuffed leather. A seam runs across his nose and one cheekbone where somebody laid him a good one in a fight, and the stitches are still in the seam. He stands there waiting, and when nobody makes a move to say anything to him he commences to laugh. Nobody can tell exactly why he laughs; there's nothing funny going on. But it's not the way that Public Relation laughs, it's free and loud and it comes out of his wide grinning mouth and spreads in rings bigger and bigger till it's lapping against the walls all over the ward. Not like that fat Public Relation laugh. This sounds real. I realize all of a sudden it's the first laugh I've heard in years.

He stands looking at us, rocking back in his boots, and he laughs and laughs. He laces his fingers over his belly without taking his thumbs out of his pockets. I see how big and beat up his hands are. Everybody on the ward, patients, staff, and all, is stunned dumb by him and his laughing. There's no move to stop him, no move to say anything. He laughs till he's finished for a time, and he walks on into the day room. Even when he isn't laughing, that laughing sound hovers around him, the way the sound hovers around a big bell just quit ringing—it's in his eyes, in the way he smiles and swaggers, in the way he talks.

"My name is McMurphy, buddies, R. P. McMurphy, and I'm a gambling fool." He winks and sings a little piece of a song: "'. . . and whenever I meet with a deck a cards I lays . . . my money . . . down,'" and laughs again.

He walks to one of the card games, tips an Acute's cards up

with a thick, heavy finger, and squints at the hand and shakes his head.

"Yessir, that's what I came to this establishment for, to bring you birds fun an' entertainment around the gamin' table. Nobody left in that Pendleton Work Farm to make my days interesting any more, so I requested a *transfer*, ya see. Needed some new blood. Hooee, look at the way this bird holds his cards, showin' to everybody in a block; man! I'll trim you babies like little lambs."

Cheswick gathers his cards together. The redheaded man sticks his hand out for Cheswick to shake.

"Hello, buddy; what's that you're playin'? Pinochle? Jesus, no wonder you don't care nothin' about showing your hand. Don't you have a straight deck around here? Well say, here we go, I brought along my own deck, just in case, has something in it other than face cards—and check the pictures, huh? Every one different. Fifty-two positions."

Cheswick is pop-eyed already, and what he sees on those cards don't help his condition.

"Easy now, don't smudge 'em; we got lots of time, lots of games ahead of us. I like to use my deck here because it takes at least a week for the other players to get to where they can even see the *suit*. . . ."

He's got on work-farm pants and shirt, sunned out till they're the color of watered milk. His face and neck and arms are the color of oxblood leather from working long in the fields. He's got a primer-black motorcycle cap stuck in his hair and a leather jacket over one arm, and he's got on boots gray and dusty and heavy enough to kick a man half in two. He walks away from Cheswick and takes off the cap and goes to beating a dust storm out of his thigh. One of the black boys circles him with the thermometer, but he's too quick for them; he slips in among the Acutes and starts moving around shaking hands before the black boy can take good aim. The way he talks, his wink, his loud talk, his swagger all remind me of a car salesman or a stock auctioneer—or one of those pitchmen you see on a sideshow stage, out in front of his flapping banners, standing there in a

striped shirt with yellow buttons, drawing the faces off the saw-
dust like a magnet.

"What happened, you see, was I got in a couple of hassles
at the work farm, to tell the pure truth, and the court ruled
that I'm a psychopath. And do you think I'm gonna argue with
the court? Shoo, you can bet your bottom dollar I don't. If
it gets me outta those damned pea fields I'll be whatever their
little heart desires, be it psychopath or mad dog or werewolf,
because I don't care if I never see another weedin' hoe to my
dying day. Now they tell me a psychopath's a guy fights too
much and fucks too much, but they ain't wholly right, do you
think? I mean, whoever heard tell of a man gettin' too much
poozle? Hello, buddy, what do they call you? My name's Mc-
Murphy and I'll bet you two dollars here and now that you
can't tell me how many spots are in that pinochle hand you're
holding *don't* look. Two dollars; what d'ya say? God *damn*,
Sam! can't you wait half a minute to prod me with that damn
thermometer of yours?"

he new man stands looking a minute, to get the
set-up of the day room.

One side of the room younger patients, known as Acutes because the doctors figure them still sick enough to be fixed,
practice arm wrestling and card tricks where you add and sub-
tract and count down so many and it's a certain card. Billy
Bibbit tries to learn to roll a tailormade cigarette, and Martini
walks around, discovering things under the tables and chairs.

The Acutes move around a lot. They tell jokes to each other and snicker in their fists (nobody ever dares let loose and laugh, the whole staff'd be in with notebooks and a lot of questions) and they write letters with yellow, runty, chewed pencils.

They spy on each other. Sometimes one man says something about himself that he didn't aim to let slip, and one of his buddies at the table where he said it yawns and gets up and sidles over to the big log book by the Nurses' Station and writes down the piece of information he heard—of therapeutic interest to the whole ward, is what the Big Nurse says the book is for, but I know she's just waiting to get enough evidence to have some guy reconditioned at the Main Building, overhauled in the head to straighten out the trouble.

The guy that wrote the piece of information in the log book, he gets a star by his name on the roll and gets to sleep late the next day.

Across the room from the Acutes are the culls of the Combine's product, the Chronics. Not in the hospital, these, to get fixed, but just to keep them from walking around the streets giving the product a bad name. Chronics are in for good, the staff concedes. Chronics are divided into Walkers like me, can still get around if you keep them fed, and Wheelers and Vegetables. What the Chronics are—or most of us—are machines with flaws inside that can't be repaired, flaws born in, or flaws beat in over so many years of the guy running head-on into solid things that by the time the hospital found him he was bleeding rust in some vacant lot.

But there are some of us Chronics that the staff made a couple of mistakes on years back, some of us who were Acutes when we came in, and got changed over. Ellis is a Chronic came in an Acute and got fouled up bad when they overloaded him in that filthy brain-murdering room that the black boys call the "Shock Shop." Now he's nailed against the wall in the same condition they lifted him off the table for the last time, in the same shape, arms out, palms cupped, with the same horror on his face. He's nailed like that on the wall, like a stuffed trophy. They pull the nails when it's time to eat or time to

drive him in to bed or when they want him to move so's I can
mop the puddle where he stands. At the old place he stood
so long in one spot the piss ate the floor and beams away under
him and he kept falling through to the ward below, giving them
all kinds of census headaches down there when roll check came
around.

Ruckly is another Chronic came in a few years back as an
Acute, but him they overloaded in a different way: they made
a mistake in one of their head installations. He was being a
holy nuisance all over the place, kicking the black boys and
biting the student nurses on the legs, so they took him away
to be fixed. They strapped him to that table, and the last anybody saw of him for a while was just before they shut the door
on him; he winked, just before the door closed, and told the
black boys as they backed away from him, "You'll pay for this,
you damn tarbabies."

And they brought him back to the ward two weeks later, bald
and the front of his face an oily purple bruise and two little
button-sized plugs stitched one above each eye. You can see
by his eyes how they burned him out over there; his eyes are
all smoked up and gray and deserted inside like blown fuses.
All day now he won't do a thing but hold an old photograph
up in front of that burned-out face, turning it over and over
in his cold fingers, and the picture wore gray as his eyes on
both sides with all his handling till you can't tell any more
what it used to be.

The staff, now, they consider Ruckly one of their failures,
but I'm not sure but what he's better off than if the installation had been perfect. The installations they do nowadays are
generally successful. The technicians got more skill and experience. No more of the button holes in the forehead, no cutting
at all—they go in through the eye sockets. Sometimes a guy
goes over for an installation, leaves the ward mean and mad
and snapping at the whole world and comes back a few weeks
later with black-and-blue eyes like he'd been in a fist fight, and
he's the sweetest, nicest, best-behaved thing you ever saw. He'll
maybe even go home in a month or two, a hat pulled low over

the face of a sleepwalker wandering round in a simple, happy
dream. A success, they say, but I say he's just another robot
for the Combine and might be better off as a failure, like Ruckly
sitting there fumbling and drooling over his picture. He never
does much else. The dwarf black boy gets a rise out of him
from time to time by leaning close and asking, "Say, Ruckly,
what you figure your little wife is doing in town tonight?"
Ruckly's head comes up. Memory whispers someplace in that
jumbled machinery. He turns red and his veins clog up at one
end. This puffs him up so he can just barely make a little whistling sound in his throat. Bubbles squeeze out the corner of his
mouth, he's working his jaw so hard to say something. When
he finally does get to where he can say his few words it's a
low, choking noise to make your skin crawl—"Ffffff*fuck* da
wife! Ffffff*fuck* da wife!" and passes out on the spot from the
effort.

Ellis and Ruckly are the youngest Chronics. Colonel Matterson is the oldest, an old, petrified cavalry soldier from the
First War who is given to lifting the skirts of passing nurses
with his cane, or teaching some kind of history out of the text
of his left hand to anybody that'll listen. He's the oldest on
the ward, but not the one's been here longest—his wife brought
him in only a few years back, when she got to where she wasn't
up to tending him any longer.

I'm the one been here on the ward the longest, since the
Second World War. I been here on the ward longer'n anybody.
Longer'n any of the other patients. The Big Nurse has been
here longer'n me.

The Chronics and the Acutes don't generally mingle. Each
stays on his own side of the day room the way the black boys
want it. The black boys say it's more orderly that way and let
everybody know that's the way they'd like it to stay. They move
us in after breakfast and look at the grouping and nod. "Tha's
right, gennulmen, tha's the way. Now you keep it that way."

Actually there isn't much need for them to say anything,
because, other than me, the Chronics don't move around much,
and the Acutes say they'd just as leave stay over on their own

side, give reasons like the Chronic side smells worse than a dirty diaper. But I know it isn't the stink that keeps them away from the Chronic side so much as they don't like to be reminded that here's what could happen to *them* someday. The Big Nurse recognizes this fear and knows how to put it to use; she'll point out to an Acute, whenever he goes into a sulk, that you boys be good boys and cooperate with the staff policy which is engineered for your *cure*, or you'll end up over on *that* side.

(Everybody on the ward is proud of the way the patients cooperate. We got a little brass tablet tacked to a piece of maple wood that has printed on it: CONGRATULATIONS FOR GETTING ALONG WITH THE SMALLEST NUMBER OF PERSONNEL OF ANY WARD IN THE HOSPITAL. It's a prize for cooperation. It's hung on the wall right above the log book, right square in the middle between the Chronics and Acutes.)

This new redheaded Admission, McMurphy, knows right away he's not a Chronic. After he checks the day room over a minute, he sees he's meant for the Acute side and goes right for it, grinning and shaking hands with everybody he comes to. At first I see that he's making everybody over there feel uneasy, with all his kidding and joking and with the brassy way he hollers at that black boy who's still after him with a thermometer, and especially with that big wide-open laugh of his. Dials twitch in the control panel at the sound of it. The Acutes look spooked and uneasy when he laughs, the way kids look in a schoolroom when one ornery kid is raising too much hell with the teacher out of the room and they're all scared the teacher might pop back in and take it into her head to make them all stay after. They're fidgeting and twitching, responding to the dials in the control panel; I see McMurphy notices he's making them uneasy, but he don't let it slow him down.

"Damn, what a sorry-looking outfit. You boys don't look so crazy to me." He's trying to get them to loosen up, the way you see an auctioneer spinning jokes to loosen up the crowd before the bidding starts. "Which one of you claims to be the craziest? Which one is the biggest loony? Who runs these card games? It's my first day, and what I like to do is make a good impression straight off on the right man if he can prove to me he *is* the right man. Who's the bull goose loony here?"

He's saying this directly to Billy Bibbit. He leans down and glares so hard at Billy that Billy feels compelled to stutter out that he isn't the buh-buh-buh-bull goose loony yet, though he's next in luh-luh-line for the job.

McMurphy sticks a big hand down in front of Billy, and Billy can't do a thing but shake it. "Well, buddy," he says to Billy, "I'm truly glad you're next in luh-line for the job, but since I'm thinking about taking over this whole show myself, lock, stock, and barrel, maybe I better talk with the top man." He looks round to where some of the Acutes have stopped their card-playing, covers one of his hands with the other, and cracks all his knuckles at the sight. "I figure, you see, buddy, to be sort of the gambling baron on this ward, deal a wicked game of blackjack. So you better take me to your leader and we'll get it straightened out who's gonna be boss around here."

Nobody's sure if this barrel-chested man with the scar and the wild grin is play-acting or if he's crazy enough to be just like he talks, or both, but they are all beginning to get a big kick out of going along with him. They watch as he puts that big red hand on Billy's thin arm, waiting to see what Billy will say. Billy sees how it's up to him to break the silence, so he looks around and picks out one of the pinochle-players: "Harding," Billy says, "I guess it would b-b-be you. You're p-president of Pay-Pay-Patient's Council. This m-man wants to talk to you."

The Acutes are grinning now, not so uneasy any more, and glad that something out of the ordinary's going on. They all razz Harding, ask him if he's bull goose loony. He lays down his cards.

Harding is a flat, nervous man with a face that sometimes makes you think you seen him in the movies, like it's a face too pretty to just be a guy on the street. He's got wide, thin shoulders and he curves them in around his chest when he's trying to hide inside himself. He's got hands so long and white and dainty I think they carved each other out of soap, and sometimes they get loose and glide around in front of him free as two white birds until he notices them and traps them between his knees; it bothers him that he's got pretty hands.

He's president of the Patient's Council on account of he has a paper that says he graduated from college. The paper's framed and sits on his nightstand next to a picture of a woman in a bathing suit who also looks like you've seen her in the moving pictures—she's got very big breasts and she's holding the top of the bathing suit up over them with her fingers and looking sideways at the camera. You can see Harding sitting on a towel behind her, looking skinny in his bathing suit, like he's waiting for some big guy to kick sand on him. Harding brags a lot about having such a woman for a wife, says she's the sexiest woman in the world and she can't get enough of him nights.

When Billy points him out Harding leans back in his chair and assumes an important look, speaks up at the ceiling without looking at Billy or McMurphy. "Does this . . . gentleman have an appointment, Mr. Bibbit?"

"Do you have an appointment, Mr. McM-m-murphy? Mr. Harding is a busy man, nobody sees him without an ap-ap-pointment."

"This busy man Mr. Harding, is he the bull goose loony?" He looks at Billy with one eye, and Billy nods his head up and down real fast; Billy's tickled with all the attention he's getting.

"Then you tell Bull Goose Loony Harding that R. P. McMurphy is waiting to see him and that this hospital ain't big enough for the two of us. I'm accustomed to being top man. I been a bull goose catskinner for every gyppo logging operation in the Northwest and bull goose gambler all the way from Korea, was even bull goose pea weeder on that pea farm at Pendleton—so I figure if I'm bound to be a loony, then I'm bound to be a stompdown dadgum good one. Tell this Harding that he either meets me man to man or he's a yaller skunk and better be outta town by sunset."

Harding leans farther back, hooks his thumbs in his lapels. "Bibbit, you tell this young upstart McMurphy that I'll meet him in the main hall at high noon and we'll settle this affair once and for all, libidos a-blazin'." Harding tries to drawl like McMurphy; it sounds funny with his high, breathy voice. "You might also warn him, just to be fair, that I have been bull goose loony on this ward for nigh onto two years, and that I'm crazier than any man alive."

"Mr. Bibbit, you might warn this Mr. Harding that I'm so crazy I admit to voting for Eisenhower."

"Bibbit! You tell Mr. McMurphy I'm so crazy I voted for Eisenhower *twice!*"

"And you tell Mr. Harding right back"—he puts both hands on the table and leans down, his voice getting low—"that I'm so crazy I plan to vote for Eisenhower again this *November*."

"I take off my hat," Harding says, bows his head, and shakes hands with McMurphy. There's no doubt in my mind that McMurphy's won, but I'm not sure just what.

All the other Acutes leave what they've been doing and ease up close to see what new sort this fellow is. Nobody like him's ever been on the ward before. They're asking him where he's from and what his business is in a way I've never seen them do before. He says he's a dedicated man. He says he was just a wanderer and logging bum before the Army took him and taught him what his natural bent was; just like they taught some men to goldbrick and some men to goof off, he says, they taught him to play poker. Since then he's settled down and devoted himself to gambling on all levels. Just play poker and stay single and live where and how he wants to, if people would let him, he says, "but you know how society persecutes a dedicated man. Ever since I found my callin' I done time in so many small-town jails I could write a brochure. They say I'm a habitual hassler. Like I fight some. Sheeut. They didn't mind so much when I was a dumb logger and got into a hassle; that's ex*cusable*, they say, that's a hard-workin' feller blowing off steam, they say. But if you're a gambler, if they know you to get up a back-room game now and then, all you have to do is spit slantwise and you're a goddamned criminal. Hooee, it was breaking up the budget drivin' me to and from the pokey for a while there."

He shakes his head and puffs out his cheeks.

"But that was just for a period of time. I learned the ropes. To tell the truth, this 'sault and battery I was doing in Pendleton was the first hitch in close to a year. That's why I got busted. I was outa practice; this guy was able to get up off the floor and get to the cops before I left town. A very tough individual . . ."

He laughs again and shakes hands and sits down to arm wrestle every time that black boy gets too near him with the thermometer, till he's met everybody on the Acute side. And when he finishes shaking hands with the last Acute he comes right on over to the Chronics, like we aren't no different. You can't tell if he's really this friendly or if he's got some gambler's reason for trying to get acquainted with guys so far gone a lot of them don't even know their names.

He's there pulling Ellis's hand off the wall and shaking it just like he was a politician running for something and Ellis's vote was good as anybody's. "Buddy," he says to Ellis in a solemn voice, "my name is R. P. McMurphy and I don't like to see a full-grown man sloshin' around in his own water. Whyn't you go get dried up?"

Ellis looks down at the puddle around his feet in pure surprise. "Why, I thank you," he says and even moves off a few steps toward the latrine before the nails pull his hands back to the wall.

McMurphy comes down the line of Chronics, shakes hands with Colonel Matterson and with Ruckly and with Old Pete. He shakes the hands of Wheelers and Walkers and Vegetables, shakes hands that he has to pick up out of laps like picking up dead birds, mechanical birds, wonders of tiny bones and wires that have run down and fallen. Shakes hands with everybody he comes to except Big George the water freak, who grins and shies back from that unsanitary hand, so McMurphy just salutes him and says to his own right hand as he walks away, "Hand, how do you suppose that old fellow knew all the evil you been into?"

Nobody can make out what he's driving at, or why he's making such a fuss with meeting everybody, but it's better'n mixing jigsaw puzzles. He keeps saying it's a necessary thing to get around and meet the men he'll be dealing with, part of a gambler's job. But he must know he ain't going to be dealing with no eighty-year-old organic who couldn't do any more with a playing card than put it in his mouth and gum it awhile. Yet he looks like he's enjoying himself, like he's the sort of guy that gets a laugh out of people.

I'm the last one. Still strapped in the chair in the corner. McMurphy stops when he gets to me and hooks his thumbs in his pockets again and leans back to laugh, like he sees something funnier about me than about anybody else. All of a sudden I was scared he was laughing because he knew the way I was sitting there with my knees pulled up and my arms wrapped around them, staring straight ahead as though I couldn't hear a thing, was all an act.

"Hooeee," he said, "look what we got here."

I remember all this part real clear. I remember the way he closed one eye and tipped his head back and looked down across that healing wine-colored scar on his nose, laughing at me. I thought at first that he was laughing because of how funny it looked, an Indian's face and black, oily Indian's hair on somebody like me. I thought maybe he was laughing at how weak I looked. But then's when I remember thinking that he was laughing because he wasn't fooled for one minute by my deaf-and-dumb act; it didn't make any difference *how* cagey the act was, he was onto me and was laughing and winking to let me know it.

"What's your story, Big Chief? You look like Sittin' Bull on a sitdown strike." He looked over to the Acutes to see if they might laugh about his joke; when they just sniggered he looked back to me and winked again. "What's your name, Chief?"

Billy Bibbit called across the room. "His n-n-name is Bromden. Chief Bromden. Everybody calls him Chief Buh-Broom, though, because the aides have him sweeping a l-large part of the time. There's not m-much else he can do, I guess. He's deaf." Billy put his chin in hands. "If I was d-d-deaf"—he sighed—"I would kill myself."

McMurphy kept looking at me. "He gets his growth, he'll be pretty good-sized, won't he? I wonder how tall he is."

"I think somebody m-m-measured him once at s-six feet seven; but even if he is big, he's scared of his own sh-sh-shadow. Just a bi-big deaf Indian."

"When I saw him sittin' here I *thought* he looked some Indian. But Bromden ain't an Indian name. What tribe is he?"

"I don't know," Billy said. "He was here wh-when I c-came."

"I have information from the doctor," Harding said, "that he is only half Indian, a Columbia Indian, I believe. That's a defunct Columbia Gorge tribe. The doctor said his father was the tribal leader, hence this fellow's title, 'Chief.' As to the 'Bromden' part of the name, I'm afraid my knowledge in Indian lore doesn't cover that."

McMurphy leaned his head down near mine where I had to look at him. "Is that right? You deef, Chief?"

"He's de-de-deef and dumb."

McMurphy puckered his lips and looked at my face a long time. Then he straightened back up and stuck his hand out.

"Well, what the hell, he can shake hands can't he? Deef or whatever. By God, Chief, you may be big, but you shake my hand or I'll consider it an insult. And it's not a good idea to insult the new bull goose loony of the hospital."

When he said that he looked back over to Harding and Billy and made a face, but he left that hand in front of me, big as a dinner plate.

I remember real clear the way that hand looked: there was carbon under the fingernails where he'd worked once in a garage; there was an anchor tattooed back from the knuckles; there was a dirty Band-Aid on the middle knuckle, peeling up at the edge. All the rest of the knuckles were covered with scars and cuts, old and new. I remember the palm was smooth and hard as bone from hefting the wooden handles of axes and hoes, not the hand you'd think could deal cards. The palm was callused, and the calluses were cracked, and dirt was worked in the cracks. A road map of his travels up and down the West. That palm made a scuffing sound against my hand. I remember

the fingers were thick and strong closing over mine, and my
hand commenced to feel peculiar and went to swelling up out
there on my stick of an arm, like he was transmitting his own
blood into it. It rang with blood and power. It blowed up near
as big as his, I remember. . . .

"Mr. McMurry."

It's the Big Nurse.

"Mr. McMurry, could you come here please?"

It's the Big Nurse. That black boy with the thermometer has
gone and got her. She stands there tapping that thermometer
against her wrist watch, eyes whirring while she tries to gauge
this new man. Her lips are in that triangle shape, like a doll's
lips ready for a fake nipple.

"Aide Williams tells me, Mr. McMurry, that you've been
somewhat difficult about your admission shower. Is this true?
Please understand, I appreciate the way you've taken it upon
yourself to orient with the other patients on the ward, but
everything in its own good time, Mr. McMurry. I'm sorry to interrupt you and Mr. Bromden, but you do understand: *everyone* . . . must follow the rules."

He tips his head back and gives that wink that she isn't fooling him any more than I did, that he's onto her. He looks up
at her with one eye for a minute.

"Ya know, ma'am," he says, "ya know—that is the ex-*act*
thing somebody *always* tells me about the rules . . ."

He grins. They both smile back and forth at each other, siz-
ing each other up.

". . . just when they figure I'm about to do the dead opposite."

Then he lets go my hand.

In the glass Station the Big Nurse has opened a package from a foreign address and is sucking into hypodermic needles the grass-and-milk liquid that came in vials in the package. One of the little nurses, a girl with one wandering eye that always keeps looking worried over her shoulder while the other one goes about its usual business, picks up the little tray of filled needles but doesn't carry them away just yet.

"What, Miss Ratched, is your opinion of this new patient? I mean, gee, he's good-looking and friendly and everything, but in my humble opinion he certainly takes *over.*"

The Big Nurse tests a needle against her fingertip. "I'm afraid"—she stabs the needle down in the rubber-capped vial and lifts the plunger—"that is exactly what the new patient is planning: to take over. He is what we call a 'manipulator,' Miss Flinn, a man who will use everyone and everything to his own ends."

"Oh. But. I mean, in a mental hospital? What could his ends be?"

"Any number of things." She's calm, smiling, lost in the work of loading the needles. "Comfort and an easy life, for instance; the feeling of power and respect, perhaps; monetary gain—perhaps all of these things. Sometimes a manipulator's own ends are simply the actual *disruption* of the ward for the sake of disruption. There are such people in our society. A manipulator can influence the other patients and disrupt them to such an extent that it may take months to get everything running smooth once more. With the present permissive philosophy in mental hospitals, it's easy for them to get away with it. Some years back it was quite different. I recall some years back we had a man, a Mr. Taber, on the ward, and he was an *intolerable* Ward Manipulator. For a while." She looks up from her work, needle half filled in front of her face like a little

wand. Her eyes get far-off and pleased with the memory. "Mis-
tur Tay-bur," she says.

"But, gee," the other nurse says, "what on earth would *make*
a man want to do something like disrupt the ward for, Miss
Ratched? What possible motive . . . ?"

She cuts the little nurse off by jabbing the needle back into
the vial's rubber top, fills it, jerks it out, and lays it on the tray.
I watch her hand reach for another empty needle, watch it
dart out, hinge over it, drop.

"You seem to forget, *Miss* Flinn, that this is an institution
for the insane."

The Big Nurse tends to get real put out if something keeps
her outfit from running like a smooth, accurate, precision-made
machine. The slightest thing messy or out of kilter or in the
way ties her into a little white knot of tight-smiled fury. She
walks around with that same doll smile crimped between her
chin and her nose and that same calm whir coming from her
eyes, but down inside of her she's tense as steel. I know, I can
feel it. And she don't relax a hair till she gets the nuisance
attended to—what she calls "adjusted to surroundings."

Under her rule the ward Inside is almost completely adjusted
to surroundings. But the thing is she can't be on the ward
all the time. She's got to spend some time Outside. So she
works with an eye to adjusting the Outside world too. Working alongside others like her who I call the "Combine," which
is a huge organization that aims to adjust the Outside as well
as she has the Inside, has made her a real veteran at adjusting things. She was already the Big Nurse in the old place
when I came in from the Outside so long back, and she'd been
dedicating herself to adjustment for God knows how long.

And I've watched her get more and more skillful over the
years. Practice has steadied and strengthened her until now she
wields a sure power that extends in all directions on hairlike
wires too small for anybody's eye but mine; I see her sit in the
center of this web of wires like a watchful robot, tend her network with mechanical insect skill, know every second which

wire runs where and just what current to send up to get the results she wants. I was an electrician's assistant in training camp before the Army shipped me to Germany and I had some electronics in my year in college is how I learned about the way these things can be rigged.

What she dreams of there in the center of those wires is a world of precision efficiency and tidiness like a pocket watch with a glass back, a place where the schedule is unbreakable and all the patients who aren't Outside, obedient under her beam, are wheelchair Chronics with catheter tubes run direct from every pantleg to the sewer under the floor. Year by year she accumulates her ideal staff: doctors, all ages and types, come and rise up in front of her with ideas of their own about the way a ward should be run, some with backbone enough to stand behind their ideas, and she fixes these doctors with dry-ice eyes day in, day out, until they retreat with unnatural chills. "I tell you I don't know *what* it is," they tell the guy in charge of personnel. "Since I started on that ward with that woman I feel like my veins are running ammonia. I shiver all the time, my kids won't sit in my lap, my wife won't sleep with me. I *insist* on a transfer—neurology bin, the alky tank, pediatrics, I just don't *care!*"

She keeps this up for years. The doctors last three weeks, three months. Until she finally settles for a little man with a big wide forehead and wide jowly cheeks and squeezed narrow across his tiny eyes like he once wore glasses that were way too small, wore them for so long they crimped his face in the middle, so now he has glasses on a string to his collar button; they teeter on the purple bridge of his little nose and they are always slipping one side or the other so he'll tip his head when he talks just to keep his glasses level. That's her doctor.

Her three daytime black boys she acquires after more years of testing and rejecting thousands. They come at her in a long black row of sulky, big-nosed masks, hating her and her chalk doll whiteness from the first look they get. She appraises them and their hate for a month or so, then lets them go because they don't hate enough. When she finally gets the three she wants—gets them one at a time over a number of years, weaving them into her plan and her network—she's damn positive they hate enough to be capable.

The first one she gets five years after I been on the ward, a twisted sinewy dwarf the color of cold asphalt. His mother was raped in Georgia while his papa stood by tied to the hot iron stove with plow traces, blood streaming into his shoes. The boy watched from a closet, five years old and squinting his eye to peep out the crack between the door and the jamb, and he never grew an inch after. Now his eyelids hang loose and thin from his brow like he's got a bat perched on the bridge of his nose. Eyelids like thin gray leather, he lifts them up just a bit whenever a new white man comes on the ward, peeks out from under them and studies the man up and down and nods just once like he's oh yes made positive certain of something he was already sure of. He wanted to carry a sock full of birdshot when he first came on the job, to work the patients into shape, but she told him they didn't do it that way anymore, made him leave the sap at home and taught him her own technique; taught him not to show his hate and to be calm and wait, wait for a little advantage, a little slack, then twist the rope and keep the pressure steady. All the time. That's the way you get them into shape, she taught him.

The other two black boys come two years later, coming to work only about a month apart and both looking so much alike I think she had a replica made of the one who came first. They are tall and sharp and bony and their faces are chipped into expressions that never change, like flint arrowheads. Their eyes come to points. If you brush against their hair it rasps the hide right off you.

All of them black as telephones. The blacker they are, she learned from that long dark row that came before them, the more time they are likely to devote to cleaning and scrubbing and keeping the ward in order. For instance, all three of these boys' uniforms are always spotless as snow. White and cold and stiff as her own.

All three wear starched snow-white pants and white shirts

with metal snaps down one side and white shoes polished like ice, and the shoes have red rubber soles silent as mice up and down the hall. They never make any noise when they move. They materialize in different parts of the ward every time a patient figures to check himself in private or whisper some secret to another guy. A patient'll be in a corner all by himself, when all of a sudden there's a squeak and frost forms along his cheek, and he turns in that direction and there's a cold stone mask floating above him against the wall. He just sees the black face. No body. The walls are white as the white suits, polished clean as a refrigerator door, and the black face and hands seem to float against it like a ghost.

Years of training, and all three black boys tune in closer and closer with the Big Nurse's frequency. One by one they are able to disconnect the direct wires and operate on beams. She never gives orders out loud or leaves written instructions that might be found by a visiting wife or schoolteacher. Doesn't need to any more. They are in contact on a high-voltage wave length of hate, and the black boys are out there performing her bidding before she even thinks it.

So after the nurse gets her staff, efficiency locks the ward like a watchman's clock. Everything the guys think and say and do is all worked out months in advance, based on the little notes the nurse makes during the day. This is typed and fed into the machine I hear humming behind the steel door in the rear of the Nurses' Station. A number of Order Daily Cards are returned, punched with a pattern of little square holes. At the beginning of each day the properly dated OD card is inserted in a slot in the steel door and the walls hum up: Lights flash on in the dorm at six-thirty: the Acutes up out of bed quick as the black boys can prod them out, get them to work buffing the floor, emptying ash trays, polishing the scratch marks off the wall where one old fellow shorted out a day ago, went down in an awful twist of smoke and smell of burned rubber. The Wheelers swing dead log legs out on the floor and wait like seated statues for somebody to roll chairs in to them. The Vegetables piss the bed, activating an electric shock and buz-

zer, rolls them off on the tile where the black boys can hose
them down and get them in clean greens. . . .

Six-forty-five the shavers buzz and the Acutes line up in al-
phabetic order at the mirrors, A, B, C, D. . . . The walking
Chronics like me walk in when the Acutes are done, then the
Wheelers are wheeled in. The three old guys left, a film of
yellow mold on the loose hide under their chins, they get shaved
in their lounge chairs in the day room, a leather strap across
the forehead to keep them from flopping around under the
shaver.

Some mornings—Mondays especially—I hide and try to buck
the schedule. Other mornings I figure it's cagier to step right
into place between A and C in the alphabet and move the route
like everybody else, without lifting my feet—powerful magnets
in the floor maneuver personnel through the ward like arcade
puppets. . . .

Seven o'clock the mess hall opens and the order of line-up
reverses: the Wheelers first, then the Walkers, then the Acutes
pick up trays, corn flakes, bacon and eggs, toast—and this morning a canned peach on a piece of green, torn lettuce. Some of
the Acutes bring trays to the Wheelers. Most Wheelers are
just Chronics with bad legs, they feed themselves, but there's
these three of them got no action from the neck down what-
soever, not much from the neck up. These are called Vegetables. The black boys push them in after everybody else is sat
down, wheel them against a wall, and bring them identical trays
of muddy-looking food with little white diet cards attached to
the trays. Mechanical Soft, reads the diet cards for these toothless three: eggs, ham, toast, bacon, all chewed thirty-two times
apiece by the stainless-steel machine in the kitchen. I see it
purse sectioned lips, like a vacuum-cleaner hose, and spurt a
clot of chewed-up ham onto a plate with a barnyard sound.

The black boys stoke the sucking pink mouths of the Vegetables a shade too fast for swallowing, and the Mechanical Soft
squeezes out down their little knobs of chins onto the greens.
The black boys cuss the Vegetables and ream the mouths bigger
with a twisting motion of the spoon, like coring a rotten apple:

"This ol' fart Blastic, he's comin' to pieces befo' my very eyes. I can't tell no more if I'm feeding him bacon puree or chunks of his own fuckin' tongue.". . .

Seven-thirty back to the day room. The Big Nurse looks out through her special glass, always polished till you can't tell it's there, and nods at what she sees, reaches up and tears a sheet off her calendar one day closer to the goal. She pushes a button for things to start. I hear the wharrup of a big sheet of tin being shook someplace. Everybody come to order. Acutes: sit on your side of the day room and wait for cards and Monopoly games to be brought out. Chronics: sit on your side and wait for puzzles from the Red Cross box. Ellis: go to your place at the wall, hands up to receive the nails and pee running down your leg. Pete: wag your head like a puppet. Scanlon: work your knobby hands on the table in front of you, constructing a make-believe bomb to blow up a make-believe world. Harding: begin talking, waving your dove hands in the air, then trap them under your armpits because grown men aren't supposed to wave their pretty hands that way. Sefelt: begin moaning about your teeth hurting and your hair falling out. Everybody: breath in . . . and out . . . in perfect order; hearts all beating at the rate the OD cards have ordered. Sound of matched cylinders.

Like a cartoon world, where the figures are flat and outlined in black, jerking through some kind of goofy story that might be real funny if it weren't for the cartoon figures being real guys. . . .

Seven-forty-five the black boys move down the line of Chronics taping catheters on the ones that will hold still for it. Catheters are second-hand condoms the ends clipped off and rubberbanded to tubes that run down pantlegs to a plastic sack marked DISPOSABLE NOT TO BE RE-USED, which it is my job to wash out at the end of each day. The black boys anchor the condom by taping it to the hairs; old Catheter Chronics are hairless as babies from tape removal. . . .

Eight o'clock the walls whirr and hum into full swing. The speaker in the ceiling says, "Medications," using the Big Nurse's voice. We look in the glass case where she sits, but she's no-where near the microphone; in fact, she's ten feet away from the microphone, tutoring one of the little nurses how to pre-pare a neat drug tray with pills arranged orderly. The Acutes line up at the glass door, A, B, C, D, then the Chronics, then the Wheelers (the Vegetables get theirs later, mixed in a spoon of applesauce). The guys file by and get a capsule in a paper cup—throw it to the back of the throat and get the cup filled with water by the little nurse and wash the capsule down. On rare occasions some fool might ask what he's being required to swallow.

"Wait just a shake, honey; what are these two little red capsules in here with my vitamin?"

I know him. He's a big, griping Acute, already getting the reputation of being a troublemaker.

"It's just medication, Mr. Taber, good for you. Down it goes, now."

"But I mean what *kind* of medication. Christ, I can see that they're pills—"

"Just swallow it all, shall we, Mr. Taber—just for me?" She takes a quick look at the Big Nurse to see how the little flirting technique she is using is accepted, then looks back at the Acute. He still isn't ready to swallow something he don't know what is, not even just for her.

"Miss, I don't like to create trouble. But I don't like to swal-low something without knowing what it is, neither. How do I know this isn't one of those funny pills that makes me some-thing I'm not?"

"Don't get upset, Mr. Taber—"

"Upset? All I want to *know*, for the lova Jesus—"

But the Big Nurse has come up quietly, locked her hand on his arm, paralyzes him all the way to the shoulder. "That's all right, Miss Flinn," she says. "If Mr. Taber chooses to act like a child, he may have to be treated as such. We've tried to be kind and considerate with him. Obviously, that's not the an-swer. Hostility, hostility, that's the thanks we get. You can go, Mr. Taber, if you don't wish to take your medication orally."

"All I wanted to *know*, for the—"

"You can go."

He goes off, grumbling, when she frees his arm, and spends the morning moping around the latrine, wondering about those capsules. I got away once holding one of those same red capsules under my tongue, played like I'd swallowed it, and crushed it open latter in the broom closet. For a tick of time, before it all turned into white dust, I saw it was a miniature electronic element like the ones I helped the Radar Corps work with in the Army, microscopic wires and girds and transistors, this one designed to dissolve on contact with air. . . .

Eight-twenty the cards and puzzles go out. . . .

Eight-twenty-five some Acute mentions he used to watch his sister taking her bath; the three guys at the table with him fall all over each other to see who gets to write it in the log book. . . .

Eight-thirty the ward door opens and two technicians trot in, smelling like grape wine; technicians always move at a fast walk or a trot because they're always leaning so far forward they have to move fast to keep standing. They always lean forward and they always smell like they sterilized their instruments in wine. They pull the lab door to behind them, and I sweep up close and can make out voices over the vicious zzzth-zzzth-zzzth of steel on whetstone.

"What we got already at this ungodly hour of the morning?"

"We got to install an Indwelling Curiosity Cutout in some nosy booger. Hurry-up job, she says, and I'm not even sure we got one of the gizmos in stock."

"We might have to call IBM to rush one out for us; let me check back in Supply—"

"Hey; bring out a bottle of that pure grain while you're back there: it's getting so I can't install the simplest frigging component but what I need a bracer. Well, what the hell, it's better'n garage work. . . ."

Their voices are forced and too quick on the comeback to be real talk—more like cartoon comedy speech. I sweep away before I'm caught eavesdropping.

The two big black boys catch Taber in the latrine and drag

him to the mattress room. He gets one a good kick in the
shins. He's yelling bloody murder. I'm surprised how helpless
he looks when they hold him, like he was wrapped with bands
of black iron.

They push him face down on the mattress. One sits on his
head, and the other rips his pants open in back and peels the
cloth until Taber's peach-colored rear is framed by the ragged
lettuce-green. He's smothering curses into the mattress and the
black boy sitting on his head saying, "Tha's right, Mistuh
Taber, tha's right. . . ." The nurse comes down the hall,
smearing Vaseline on a long needle, pulls the door shut so
they're out of sight for a second, then comes right back out,
wiping the needle on a shred of Taber's pants. She's left the
Vaseline jar in the room. Before the black boy can close the
door after her I see the one still sitting on Taber's head,
dabbing at him with a Kleenex. They're in there a long time
before the door opens up again and they come out, carrying
him across the hall to the lab. His greens are ripped clear off
now and he's wrapped up in a damp sheet. . . .

Nine o'clock young residents wearing leather elbows talk to
Acutes for fifty minutes about what they did when they were
little boys. The Big Nurse is suspicious of the crew-cut looks of
these residents, and that fifty minutes they are on the ward is
a tough time for her. While they are around, the machinery
goes to fumbling and she is scowling and making notes to check
the records of these boys for old traffic violations and the
like. . . .

Nine-fifty the residents leave and the machinery hums up
smooth again. The nurse watches the day room from her glass
case; the scene before her takes on that blue-steel clarity again,
that clean orderly movement of a cartoon comedy.

Taber is wheeled out of the lab on a Gurney bed.

"We had to give him another shot when he started coming
up during the spine tap," the technician tells her. "What do
you say we take him right on over to Building One and buzz
him with EST while we're at it—that way not waste the extra
Seconal?"

"I think it is an excellent suggestion. Maybe after that take him to the electroencephalograph and check his head—we may find evidence of a need for brain work."

The technicians go trotting off, pushing the man on the Gurney, like cartoon men—or like puppets, mechanical puppets in one of those Punch and Judy acts where it's supposed to be funny to see the puppet beat up by the Devil and swallowed headfirst by a smiling alligator. . . .

Ten o'clock the mail comes up. Sometimes you get the torn envelope. . . .

Ten-thirty Public Relation comes in with a ladies' club following him. He claps his fat hands at the day-room door. "Oh, hello, guys; stiff lip, stiff lip. . . . Look around, girls; isn't it so clean, so bright? This is Miss Ratched. I chose this ward because it's *her* ward. She's, girls, just like a mother. Not that I mean age, but you girls understand . . ."

Public Relation's shirt collar is so tight it bloats his face up when he laughs, and he's laughing most of the time I don't ever know what at, laughing high and fast like he wishes he could stop but can't do it. And his face bloated up red and round as a balloon with a face painted on it. He got no hair on his face and none on his head to speak of; it looks like he glued some on once but it kept slipping off and getting in his cuffs and his shirt pocket and down his collar. Maybe that's why he keeps his collar so tight, to keep the little pieces of hair out.

Maybe that's why he laughs so much, because he isn't able to keep all the pieces out.

He conducts these tours—serious women in blazer jackets, nodding to him as he points out how much things have improved over the years. He points out the TV, the big leather chairs, the sanitary drinking fountains; then they all go have coffee in the Nurses' Station. Sometimes he'll be by himself and just stand in the middle of the day room and clap his hands (you can *hear* they are wet), clap them two or three times till they stick, then hold them prayerlike together under one of his chins and start spinning. Spin round and around there in the middle of the floor, looking wild and frantic at the TV, the new pictures on the walls, the drinking fountain. And laughing.

What he sees that's so funny he don't ever let us in on, and the only thing I can see funny is him spinning round and around out there like a rubber toy—if you push him over he's weighted on the bottom and straightaway rocks back upright, goes to spinning again. He never, never looks at the men's faces. . . .

Ten-forty, -forty-five, -fifty, patients shuttle in and out to appointments in ET or OT or PT, or in queer little rooms somewhere where the walls are never the same size and the floors aren't level. The machinery sounds about you reach a steady cruising speed.

The ward hums the way I heard a cotton mill hum once when the football team played a high school in California. After a good season one year the boosters in the town were so proud and carried away that they paid to fly us to California to play a championship high-school team down there. When we flew into the town we had to go visit some local industry. Our coach was one for convincing folks that athletics was educational because of the learning afforded by travel, and every trip we took he herded the team around to creameries and beet farms and canneries before the game. In California it was the cotton mill. When we went in the mill most of the team took a look and left to go sit in the bus over stud games on suitcases, but I stayed inside over in a corner out of the way of the Negro girls running up and down the aisles of machines. The mill put me in a kind of dream, all the humming and clicking and rattling of people and machinery, jerking around in a pattern. That's why I stayed when the others left, that, and because it reminded me somehow of the men in the tribe who'd left the village in the last days to do work on the gravel crusher for the dam. The frenzied pattern, the faces hypnotized by routine . . . I wanted to go out with the team, but I couldn't.

It was morning in early winter and I still had on the jacket they'd given us when we took the championship—a red and green jacket with leather sleeves and a football-shaped emblem sewn on the back telling what we'd won—and it was making a lot of the Negro girls stare. I took it off, but they kept staring. I was a whole lot bigger in those days.

One of the girls left her machine and looked back and forth up the aisles to see if the foreman was around, then came over to where I was standing. She asked if we was going to play the high school that night and she told me she had a brother played tailback for them. We talked a piece about football and the like and I noticed how her face looked blurred, like there was a mist between me and her. It was the cotton fluff sifting from the air.

I told her about the fluff. She rolled her eyes and ducked her mouth to laugh in her fist when I told her how it was like looking at her face out on a misty morning duck-hunting. And she said, "Now what in the everlovin' world would you want with me out alone in a duck blind?" I told her she could take care of my gun, and the girls all over the mill went to giggling in their fists. I laughed a little myself, seeing how clever I'd been. We were still talking and laughing when she grabbed both my wrists and dug in. The features of her face snapped into brilliant focus; I saw she was terrified of something.

"Do," she said to me in a whisper, "do take me, big boy. Outa this here mill, outa this town, outa this life. Take me to some ol' duck blind someplace. Someplace *else*. Huh, big boy, huh?"

Her dark, pretty face glittered there in front of me. I stood with my mouth open, trying to think of some way to answer her. We were locked together this way for maybe a couple of seconds; then the sound of the mill jumped a hitch, and something commenced to draw her back away from me. A string somewhere I didn't see hooked on that flowered red skirt and was tugging her back. Her fingernails peeled down my hands and as soon as she broke contact with me her face switched out of focus again, became soft and runny like melting chocolate behind that blowing fog of cotton. She laughed and spun around and gave me a look of her yellow leg when the skirt billowed out. She threw me a wink over her shoulder as she ran back to her machine where a pile of fiber was spilling off the table to the floor; she grabbed it up and ran featherfooted down the aisle of machines to dump the fiber in a hopper; then she was out of sight around the corner.

All those spindles reeling and wheeling and shuttles jumping
around and bobbins wringing the air with string, whitewashed
walls and steel-gray machines and girls in flowered skirts skip-
ping back and forth, and the whole thing webbed with flowing
white lines stringing the factory together—it all stuck with me
and every once in a while something on the ward calls it to
mind.

Yes. This is what I know. The ward is a factory for the
Combine. It's for fixing up mistakes made in the neighborhoods and in the schools and in the churches, the hospital is.
When a completed product goes back out into society, all fixed
up good as new, *better* than new sometimes, it brings joy to
the Big Nurse's heart; something that came in all twisted different is now a functioning, adjusted component, a credit to
the whole outfit and a marvel to behold. Watch him sliding
across the land with a welded grin, fitting into some nice little
neighborhood where they're just now digging trenches along
the street to lay pipes for city water. He's happy with it. He's
adjusted to surroundings finally. . . .

"Why, I've never seen anything to beat the change in Maxwell Taber since he's got back from that hospital; a little black
and blue around the eyes, a little weight lost, and, you know
what? he's a *new man*. Gad, modern American science . . ."

And the light is on in his basement window way past midnight every night as the Delayed Reaction Elements the technicians installed lend nimble skills to his fingers as he bends over
the doped figure of his wife, his two little girls just four and
six, the neighbor he goes bowling with Mondays; he adjusts
them like he was adjusted. This is the way they spread it.

When he finally runs down after a pre-set number of years,
the town loves him dearly and the paper prints his picture
helping the Boy Scouts last year on Graveyard Cleaning Day,
and his wife gets a letter from the principal of the high school
how Maxwell Wilson Taber was an inspirational figure to the
youth of our fine community.

Even the embalmers, usually a pair of penny-pinching tight-
wads, are swayed. "Yeah, look at him there: old Max Taber,

he was a good sort. What do you say we use that expensive thirty-weight at no extra charge to his wife. No, what the dickens, let's make it on the house."

A successful Dismissal like this is a product brings joy to the Big Nurse's heart and speaks good of her craft and the whole industry in general. Everybody's happy with a Dismissal.

But an Admission is a different story. Even the best-behaved Admission is bound to need some work to swing into routine, and, also, you never can tell when just that *certain* one might come in who's free enough to foul things up right and left, really make a hell of a mess and constitute a threat to the whole smoothness of the outfit. And, like I explain, the Big Nurse gets real put out if anything keeps her outfit from running smooth.

before noontime they're at the fog machine again but they haven't got it turned up full; it's not so thick but what I can see if I strain real hard. One of these days I'll quit straining and let myself go completely, lose myself in the fog the way some of the other Chronics have, but for the time being I'm interested in this new man—I want to see how he takes to the Group Meeting coming up.

Ten minutes to one the fog dissolves completely and the black boys are telling Acutes to clear the floor for the meeting. All the tables are carried out of the day room to the tub room across the hall—leaves the floor, McMurphy says, like we was aiming to have us a little dance.

The Big Nurse watches all this through her window. She

hasn't moved from her spot in front of that one window for three solid hours, not even for lunch. The day-room floor gets cleared of tables, and at one o'clock the doctor comes out of his office down the hall, nods once at the nurse as he goes past where she's watching out her window, and sits in his chair just to the left of the door. The patients sit down when he does; then the little nurses and the residents straggle in. When everybody's down, the Big Nurse gets up from behind her window and goes back to the rear of the Nurses' Station to that steel panel with dials and buttons on it, sets some kind of automatic pilot to run things while she's away, and comes out into the day room, carrying the log book and a basketful of notes. Her uniform, even after she's been here half a day, is still starched so stiff it don't exactly bend any place; it cracks sharp at the joints with a sound like a frozen canvas being folded.

She sits just to the right of the door.

Soon as she's sat down, Old Pete Bancini sways to his feet and starts in wagging his head and wheezing. "I'm tired. Whew. O Lord. Oh, I'm *awful* tired . . ." the way he always does whenever there's a new man on the ward who might listen to him.

The Big Nurse doesn't look over at Pete. She's going through the papers in her basket. "Somebody go sit beside Mr. Bancini," she says. "Quiet him down so we can start the meeting."

Billy Bibbit goes. Pete has turned facing McMurphy and is lolling his head from side to side like a signal light at a railroad crossing. He worked on the railroad thirty years; now he's wore clean out but still's functioning on the memory.

"I'm ti-i-uhd," he says, wagging his face at McMurphy.

"Take it easy, Pete," Billy says, lays a freckled hand on Pete's knee.

". . . Awful tired . . ."

"I know, Pete"—pats the skinny knee, and Pete pulls back his face, realizes nobody is going to heed his complaint today.

The nurse takes off her wrist watch and looks at the ward clock and winds the watch and sets it face toward her in the basket. She takes a folder from the basket.

"Now. Shall we get into the meeting?"

She looks around to see if anybody else is about to interrupt her, smiling steady as her head turns in her collar. The guys won't meet her look; they're all looking for hangnails. Except McMurphy. He's got himself an armchair in the corner, sits in it like he's claimed it for good, and he's watching her every move. He's still got his cap on, jammed tight down on his red head like he's a motorcycle racer. A deck of cards in his lap opens for a one-handed cut, then clacks shut with a sound blown up loud by the silence. The nurse's swinging eyes hang on him for a second. She's been watching him play poker all morning and though she hasn't seen any money pass hands she suspects he's not exactly the type that is going to be happy with the ward rule of gambling for matches only. The deck whispers open and clacks shut again and then disappears somewhere in one of those big palms.

The nurse looks at her watch again and pulls a slip of paper out of the folder she's holding, looks at it, and returns it to the folder. She puts the folder down and picks up the log book. Ellis coughs from his place on the wall; she waits until he stops.

"Now. At the close of Friday's meeting . . . we were discussing Mr. Harding's problem . . . concerning his young wife. He had stated that his wife was extremely well endowed in the bosom and that this made him uneasy because she drew stares from men on the street." She starts opening to places in the log book; little slips of paper stick out of the top of the book to mark the pages. "According to the notes listed by various patients in the log, Mr. Harding has been heard to say that she 'damn well gives the bastards reason to stare.' He has also been heard to say that he may give *her* reason to seek further sexual attention. He has been heard to say, 'My dear sweet but illiterate wife thinks any word or gesture that does not smack of brickyard brawn and brutality is a word or gesture of weak dandyism.'"

She continues reading silently from the book for a while, then closes it.

"He has also stated that his wife's ample bosom at times

gives him a feeling of inferiority. So. Does anyone care to touch upon this subject further?"

Harding shuts his eyes, and nobody else says anything. McMurphy looks around at the other guys, waiting to see if anybody is going to answer the nurse, then holds his hand up and snaps his fingers, like a school kid in class; the nurse nods at him.

"Mr.—ah—McMurry?"

"Touch upon what?"

"What? Touch—"

"You ask, I believe, 'Does anyone care to touch upon—' "

"Touch upon the—subject, Mr. McMurry, the subject of Mr. Harding's problem with his wife."

"Oh. I thought you mean touch upon her—something else."

"Now what could you—"

But she stops. She was almost flustered for a second there. Some of the Acutes hide grins, and McMurphy takes a huge stretch, yawns, winks at Harding. Then the nurse, calm as anything, puts the log book back in the basket and takes out another folder and opens it and starts reading.

"McMurry, Randle Patrick. Committed by the state from the Pendleton Farm for Correction. For diagnosis and possible treatment. Thirty-five years old. Never married. Distinguished Service Cross in Korea, for leading an escape from a Communist prison camp. A dishonorable discharge, afterward, for insubordination. Followed by a history of street brawls and barroom fights and a series of arrests for Drunkenness, Assault and Battery, Disturbing the Peace, re*peated* gambling, and one arrest—for Rape."

"Rape?" The doctor perks up.

"Statutory, with a girl of—"

"Whoa. Couldn't make that stick," McMurphy says to the doctor. "Girl wouldn't testify."

"With a child of fifteen."

"Said she was *seven*teen, Doc, and she was *plenty* willin'."

"A court doctor's examination of the child proved entry, re*peated* entry, the record states—"

"So willin', in fact, I took to sewing my pants shut."

"The child refused to testify in spite of the doctor's findings. There seemed to be intimidation. Defendant left town shortly after the trial."

"Hoo boy, I *had* to leave. Doc, let me tell you"—he leans forward with an elbow on a knee, lowering his voice to the doctor across the room—"that little hustler would of actually burnt me to a frazzle by the time she reached legal sixteen. She got to where she was tripping me and beating me to the floor."

The nurse closes up the folder and passes it across the doorway to the doctor. "Our new Admission, Doctor Spivey," just like she's got a man folded up inside that yellow paper and can pass him on to be looked over. "I thought I might brief you on his record later today, but as he seems to insist on asserting himself in the Group Meeting, we might as well dispense with him now."

The doctor fishes his glasses from his coat pocket by pulling on the string, works them on his nose in front of his eyes. They're tipped a little to the right, but he leans his head to the left and brings them level. He's smiling a little as he turns through the folder, just as tickled by this new man's brassy way of talking right up as the rest of us, but, just like the rest of us, he's careful not to let himself come right out and laugh. The doctor closes the folder when he gets to the end, and puts his glasses back in his pocket. He looks to where McMurphy is still leaned out at him from across the day room.

"You've—it seems—no other psychiatric history, Mr. Mc-Murry?"

"McMurphy, Doc."

"Oh? But I thought—the nurse was saying—"

He opens the folder again, fishes out those glasses, looks the record over for another minute before he closes it, and puts his glasses back in his pocket. "Yes. McMurphy. That is correct. I beg your pardon."

"It's okay, Doc. It was the lady there that started it, made the mistake. I've known some people inclined to do that. I had this uncle whose name was Hallahan, and he went with a woman once who kept acting like she couldn't remember his name right and calling him Hooligan just to get his goat. It went on for months before he stopped her. Stopped her good, too."

"Oh? How did he stop her?" the doctor asks.

McMurphy grins and rubs his nose with his thumb. "Ah-ah, now, I can't be tellin' that. I keep Unk Hallahan's method a strict secret, you see, in case I need to use it myself someday."

He says it right at the nurse. She smiles right back at him, and he looks over at the doctor. "Now; what was you asking about my record, Doc?"

"Yes. I was wondering if you've any previous psychiatric history. Any analysis, any time spent in any other institution?"

"Well, counting state *and* county coolers—"

"*Mental* institutions."

"Ah. No, if that's the case. This is my first trip. But I *am* crazy, Doc. I swear I am. Well here—let me show you here. I believe that other doctor at the work farm . . ."

He gets up, slips the deck of cards in the pocket of his jacket, and comes across the room to lean over the doctor's shoulder and thumb through the folder in his lap. "Believe he wrote something, back at the back here somewhere . . ."

"Yes? I missed that. Just a moment." The doctor fishes his glasses out again and puts them on and looks to where McMurphy is pointing.

"Right here, Doc. The nurse left this part out while she was *summarizing* my record. Where it says, 'Mr. McMurphy has evidenced re*peated*'—I just want to make sure I'm understood completely, Doc—'*repeated* outbreaks of passion that suggest the possible diagnosis of psychopath.' He told me that 'psychopath' means I fight and fuh—pardon me, ladies—means I am he put it *overzealous* in my sexual relations. Doctor, is that real serious?"

He asks it with such a little-boy look of worry and concern all over his broad, tough face that the doctor can't help bending his head to hide another little snicker in his collar, and his glasses fall from his nose dead center back in his pocket. All of the Acutes are smiling too, now, and even some of the Chronics."

"I mean that overzealousness, Doc, have you ever been troubled by it?"

The doctor wipes his eyes. "No, Mr. McMurphy, I'll admit I haven't. I am interested, however, that the doctor at the work farm added this statement: 'Don't overlook the possibility that this man might be feigning psychosis to escape the drudgery of the work farm.'" He looks up at McMurphy. "And what about that, Mr. McMurphy?"

"Doctor"—he stands up to his full height, wrinkles his forehead, and holds out both arms, open and honest to all the wide world—"do I look like a sane man?"

The doctor is working so hard to keep from giggling again he can't answer. McMurphy pivots away from the doctor and asks the same thing of the Big Nurse: "*Do I?*" Instead of answering she stands up and takes the manila folder away from the doctor and puts it back in the basket under her watch. She sits back down.

"Perhaps, Doctor, you should advise Mr. McMurry on the protocol of these Group Meetings."

"Ma'am," McMurphy says, "have I told you about my uncle Hallahan and the woman who used to screw up his name?"

She looks at him for a long time without her smile. She has the ability to turn her smile into whatever expression she wants to use on somebody, but the look she turns it into is no different, just a calculated and mechanical expression to serve her purpose. Finally she says, "I beg your pardon. Mack-Murph-y." She turns back to the doctor. "Now, Doctor, if you would explain . . ."

The doctor folds his hands and leans back. "Yes. I suppose what I should do is explain the complete *theory* of our Therapeutic Community, while we're at it. Though I usually save it until later. Yes. A good idea, Miss Ratched, a fine idea."

"Certainly the theory too, doctor, but what I had in mind was the rule that the patients remain seated during the course of the meeting."

"Yes. Of course. Then I will explain the theory. Mr. Mc-

Murphy, one of the first things is that the patients remain seated during the course of the meeting. It's the only way, you see, for us to maintain order."

"Sure, Doctor. I just got up to show you that thing in my record book."

He goes over to his chair, gives another big stretch and yawn, sits down, and moves around for a while like a dog coming to rest. When he's comfortable, he looks over at the doctor, waiting.

"As to the *theory* . . ." The doctor takes a deep, happy breath.

"Ffffuck da wife," Ruckly says. McMurphy hides his mouth behind the back of his hand and calls across the ward to Ruckly in a scratchy whisper, "Whose wife?" and Martini's head snaps up, eyes wide and staring. "Yeah," he says, "whose wife? Oh. Her? Yeah, I see her. *Yeah*."

"I'd give a lot to have that man's eyes," McMurphy says of Martini and then doesn't say anything all the rest of the meeting. Just sits and watches and doesn't miss a thing that happens or a word that's said. The doctor talks about his theory until the Big Nurse finally decides he's used up time enough and asks him to hush so they can get on to Harding, and they talk the rest of the meeting about that.

McMurphy sits forward in his chair a couple of times during the meeting like he might have something to say, but he decides better and leans back. There's a puzzled expression coming over his face. Something strange is going on here, he's finding out. He can't quite put his finger on it. Like the way nobody will laugh. Now he thought sure there would be a laugh when he asked Ruckly, "Whose wife?" but there wasn't even a sign of one. The air is pressed in by the walls, too tight for laughing. There's something strange about a place where the men won't let themselves loose and laugh, something strange about the way they all knuckle under to that smiling flour-faced old mother there with the too-red lipstick and the too-big boobs. And he thinks he'll just wait a while to see what the story is in this new place before he makes any kind of play. That's a good rule for a smart gambler: look the game over awhile before you draw yourself a hand.

I've heard that theory of the Therapeutic Community enough times to repeat it forwards and backwards—how a guy has to learn to get along in a group before he'll be able to function in a normal society; how the group can help the guy by showing him where he's out of place; how society is what decides who's sane and who isn't, so you got to measure up. All that stuff. Every time we get a new patient on the ward the doctor goes into the theory with both feet; it's pretty near the only time he takes things over and runs the meeting. He tells how the goal of the Therapeutic Community is a democratic ward, run completely by the patients and their votes, working toward making worth-while citizens to turn back Outside onto the street. Any little gripe, any grievance, anything you want changed, he says, should be brought up before the group and discussed instead of letting it fester inside of you. Also you should feel at ease in your surroundings to the extent you can freely discuss emotional problems in front of patients and staff. Talk, he says, discuss, confess. And if you hear a friend say something during the course of your everyday conversation, then list it in the log book for the staff to see. It's not, as the movies call it, "squealing," it's helping your fellow. Bring these old sins into the open where they can be washed by the sight of all. And participate in Group Discussion. Help yourself and your friends probe into the secrets of the subconscious. There should be no need for secrets among friends.

Our intention, he usually ends by saying, is to make this as much like your own democratic, free neighborhoods as possible—a little world Inside that is a made-to-scale prototype of the big world Outside that you will one day be taking your place in again.

He's maybe got more to say, but about this point the Big Nurse usually hushes him, and in the lull old Pete stands up and wigwags that battered copper-pot head and tells everybody how tired he is, and the nurse tells somebody to go hush him up too, so the meeting can continue, and Pete is generally hushed and the meeting goes on.

Once, just one time that I can remember, four or five years back, did it go any different. The doctor had finished his spiel, and the nurse had opened right up with, "Now. Who will start? Let out those old secrets." And she'd put all the Acutes in a trance by sitting there in silence for twenty minutes after the question, quiet as an electric alarm about to go off, waiting for somebody to start telling something about themselves. Her eyes swept back and forth over them as steady as a turning beacon. The day room was clamped silent for twenty long minutes, with all of the patients stunned where they sat. When twenty minutes had passed, she looked at her watch and said, "Am I to take it that there's not a man among you that has committed some act that he has never admitted?" She reached in the basket for the log book. "Must we go over past history?"

That triggered something, some acoustic device in the walls, rigged to turn on at just the sound of those words coming from her mouth. The Acutes stiffened. Their mouths opened in unison. Her sweeping eyes stopped on the first man along the wall.

His mouth worked. "I robbed a cash register in a service station."

She moved to the next man.

"I tried to take my little sister to bed."

Her eyes clicked to the next man; each one jumped like a shooting-gallery target.

"I—one time—wanted to take my brother to bed."

"I killed my cat when I was six. Oh, God forgive me, I stoned her to death and said my neighbor did it."

"I lied about trying. I did take my sister!"

"So did I! So did I!"

"And me! And *me!*"

It was better than she'd dreamed. They were all shouting to outdo one another, going further and further, no way of stopping, telling things that wouldn't ever let them look one another in the eye again. The nurse nodding at each confession and saying Yes, yes, yes.

Then old Pete was on his feet. "I'm *tired!*" was what he shouted, a strong, angry copper tone to his voice that no one had ever heard before.

Everyone hushed. They were somehow ashamed. It was as if he had suddenly said something that was real and true and important and it had put all their childish hollering to shame. The Big Nurse was furious. She swiveled and glared at him, the smile dripping over her chin; she'd just had it going so good.

"Somebody see to poor Mr. Bancini," she said.

Two or three got up. They tried to soothe him, pat him on his shoulder. But Pete wasn't being hushed. "Tired! Tired!" he kept on.

Finally the nurse sent one of the black boys to take him out of the day room by force. She forgot that the black boys didn't hold any control over people like Pete.

Pete's been a Chronic all his life. Even though he didn't come into the hospital till he was better than fifty, he'd always been a Chronic. His head has two big dents, one on each side, where the doctor who was with his mother at borning time pinched his skull trying to pull him out. Pete had looked out first and seen all the delivery-room machinery waiting for him and somehow realized what he was being born into, and had grabbed on to everything handy in there to try to stave off being born. The doctor reached in and got him by the head with a set of dulled ice tongs and jerked him loose and figured everything was all right. But Pete's head was still too new, and soft as clay, and when it set, those two dents left by the tongs stayed. And this made him simple to where it took all his straining effort and concentration and will power just to do the tasks that came easy to a kid of six.

But one good thing—being simple like that put him out of the clutch of the Combine. They weren't able to mold him into a slot. So they let him get a simple job on the railroad, where all he had to do was sit in a little clapboard house way

out in the sticks on a lonely switch and wave a red lantern at
the trains if the switch was one way, and a green one if it was
the other, and a yellow one if there was a train someplace up
ahead. And he did it, with main force and a gutpower they
couldn't mash out of his head, out by himself on that switch.
And he never had any controls installed.

That's why the black boy didn't have any say over him. But
the black boy didn't think of that right off any more than the
nurse did when she ordered Pete removed from the day room.
The black boy walked right up and gave Pete's arm a jerk
toward the door, just like you'd jerk the reins on a plow horse
to turn him.

"Tha's right, Pete. Less go to the dorm. You disturbin' ever'-
body."

Pete shook his arm loose. "I'm *tired*," he warned.

"C'mon, old man, you makin' a fuss. Less us go to bed and
be still like a good boy."

"Tired . . ."

"I said you goin' to the dorm, old man!"

The black boy jerked at his arm again, and Pete stopped
wigwagging his head. He stood up straight and steady, and his
eyes snapped clear. Usually Pete's eyes are half shut and all
murked up, like there's milk in them, but this time they came
clear as blue neon. And the hand on that arm the black boy
was holding commenced to swell up. The staff and most of
the rest of the patients were talking among themselves, not
paying any attention to this old guy and his old song about
being tired, figuring he'd be quieted down as usual and the
meeting would go on. They didn't see the hand on the end of
that arm pumping bigger and bigger as he clenched and un-
clenched it. I was the only one saw it. I saw it swell and
clench shut, flow in front of my eyes, become smooth—hard.
A big rusty iron ball at the end of a chain. I stared at it and
waited, while the black boy gave Pete's arm another jerk
toward the dorm.

"Ol' man, I say you got—"

He saw the hand. He tried to edge back away from it, saying,

"You a good boy, Peter," but he was a shade too late. Pete had that big iron ball swinging all the way from his knees. The black boy whammed flat against the wall and stuck, then slid down to the floor like the wall there was greased. I heard tubes pop and short all over inside that wall, and the plaster cracked just the shape of how he hit.

The other two—the least one and the other big one—stood stunned. The nurse snapped her fingers, and they sprang into motion. Instant movement, sliding across the floor. The little one beside the other like an image in a reducing mirror. They were almost to Pete when it suddenly struck them what the other boy should of known, that Pete wasn't wired under control like the rest of us, that he wasn't about to mind just because they gave him an order or gave his arm a jerk. If they were to take him they'd have to take him like you take a wild bear or bull, and with one of their number out cold against the baseboards, the other two black boys didn't care for the odds.

This thought got them both at once and they froze, the big one and his tiny image, in exactly the same position, left foot forward, right hand out, halfway between Pete and the Big Nurse. That iron ball swinging in front of them and that snow-white anger behind them, they shook and smoked and I could hear gears grinding. I could see them twitch with confusion, like machines throttled full ahead and with the brake on.

Pete stood there in the middle of the floor, swinging that ball back and forth at his side, all leaned over to its weight. Everybody was watching him now. He looked from the big black boy to the little one, and when he saw they weren't about to come any closer he turned to the patients.

"You see—it's a lotta baloney," he told them, "it's all a lotta baloney."

The Big Nurse had slid from her chair and was working toward her wicker bag leaning at the door. "Yes, yes, Mr. Bancini," she crooned, "now if you'll just be calm—"

"That's all it is, nothin' but a lotta baloney." His voice lost

its copper strength and became strained and urgent like he
didn't have much time to finish what he had to say. "Ya see, I
can't help it, I can't—don't ya see. I was born dead. Not you.
You wasn't born dead. Ahhhh, it's been hard . . ."

He started to cry. He couldn't make the words come out
right anymore; he opened and closed his mouth to talk but
he couldn't sort the words into sentences any more. He shook
his head to clear it and blinked at the Acutes:

"Ahhhh, I . . . tell . . . ya . . . I tell *you*."

He began slumping over again, and his iron ball shrank back
to a hand. He held it cupped out in front of him like he was
offering something to the patients.

"I can't help it. I was born a miscarriage. I had so many
insults I died. I was born dead. I can't help it. I'm tired. I'm
give out trying. You got chances. I had so many insults I was
born dead. You got it easy. I was born dead an' life was hard.
I'm tired. I'm tired out talking and standing up. I been dead
fifty-five *years*."

The Big Nurse got him clear across the room, right through
his greens. She jumped back without getting the needle pulled
out after the shot and it hung there from his pants like a little
tail of glass and steel, old Pete slumping farther and farther
forward, not from the shot but from the effort; the last couple
of minutes had worn him out finally and completely, once and
for all—you could just look at him and tell he was finished.

So there wasn't really any need for the shot; his head had
already commenced to wag back and forth and his eyes were
murky. By the time the nurse eased back in to get the needle
he was bent so far forward he was crying directly on the floor
without wetting his face, tears spotting a wide area as he
swung his head back and forth, spatting, spatting, in an even
pattern on the day-room floor, like he was sowing them.
"Ahhhhh," he said. He didn't flinch when she jerked the needle
out.

He had come to life for maybe a minute to try to tell us
something, something none of us cared to listen to or tried to
understand, and the effort had drained him dry. That shot in

his hip was as wasted as if she'd squirted it in a dead man—
no heart to pump it, no vein to carry it up to his head, no brain
up there for it to mortify with its poison. She'd just as well
shot it in a dried-out old cadaver.

"I'm . . . tired . . ."

"Now. I think if you two boys are *brave* enough, Mr.
Bancini will go to bed like a good fellow."

". . . aw-ful tired."

"And Aide Williams is coming around, Doctor Spivey. See
to him, won't you. Here. His watch is broken and he's cut
his arm."

Pete never tried anything like that again, and he never will.
Now, when he starts acting up during a meeting and they
try to hush him, he always hushes. He'll still get up from time
to time and wag his head and let us know how tired he is, but
it's not a complaint or excuse or warning any more—he's finished with that; it's like an old clock that won't tell time but
won't stop neither, with the hands bent out of shape and the
face bare of numbers and the alarm bell rusted silent, an old,
worthless clock that just keeps ticking and cuckooing without
meaning nothing.

The group is still tearing into poor Harding when two
o'clock rolls around.

At two o'clock the doctor begins to squirm around in his
chair. The meetings are uncomfortable for the doctor unless
he's talking about his theory; he'd rather spend his time down
in his office, drawing on graphs. He squirms around and finally
clears his throat, and the nurse looks at her watch and tells
us to bring the tables back in from the tub room and we'll
resume this discussion again at one tomorrow. The Acutes
click out of their trance, look for an instant in Harding's direction. Their faces burn with a shame like they have just woke
up to the fact they been played for suckers again. Some of
them go to the tub room across the hall to get the tables, some
wander over to the magazine racks and show a lot of interest
in the old *McCall's* magazines, but what they're all really

doing is avoiding Harding. They've been maneuvered again into grilling one of their friends like he was a criminal and they were all prosecutors and judge and jury. For forty-five minutes they been chopping a man to pieces, almost as if they enjoyed it, shooting questions at him: What's he *think* is the matter with him that he can't please the little lady; why's he *insist* she has never had anything to do with another man; how's he expect to get well if he doesn't answer *honestly?*— questions and insinuations till now they feel bad about it and they don't want to be made more uncomfortable by being near him.

McMurphy's eyes follow all of this. He doesn't get out of his chair. He looks puzzled again. He sits in his chair for a while, watching the Acutes, scuffing that deck of cards up and down the red stubble on his chin, then finally stands up from his arm chair, yawns and stretches and scratches his belly button with a corner of a card, then puts the deck in his pocket and walks over to where Harding is off by himself, sweated to his chair.

McMurphy looks down at Harding a minute, then laps his big hand over the back of a nearby wooden chair, swings it around so the back is facing Harding, and straddles it like he'd straddle a tiny horse. Harding hasn't noticed a thing. McMurphy slaps his pockets till he finds his cigarettes, and takes one out and lights it; he holds it out in front of him and frowns at the tip, licks his thumb and finger, and arranges the fire to suit him.

Each man seems unaware of the other. I can't even tell if Harding's noticed McMurphy at all. Harding's got his thin shoulders folded nearly together around himself, like green wings, and he's sitting very straight near the edge of his chair, with his hands trapped between his knees. He's staring straight ahead, humming to himself, trying to look calm—but he's chewing at his cheeks, and this gives him a funny skull grin, not calm at all.

McMurphy puts his cigarette back between his teeth and folds his hands over the wooden chair back and leans his chin on them, squinting one eye against the smoke. He looks at Harding with his other eye a while, then starts talking with that cigarette wagging up and down in his lips.

"Well say, buddy, is this the way these leetle meetings usually go?"

"Usually go?" Harding's humming stops. He's not chewing his cheeks any more but he still stares ahead, past McMurphy's shoulder.

"Is this the usual *pro*-cedure for these Group Ther'py shindigs? Bunch of chickens at a peckin' party?"

Harding's head turns with a jerk and his eyes find Mc-Murphy, like it's the first time he knows that anybody's sitting in front of him. His face creases in the middle when he bites his cheeks again, and this makes it look like he's grinning. He pulls his shoulders back and scoots to the back of the chair and tries to look relaxed.

"A 'pecking party'? I fear your quaint down-home speech is wasted on me, my friend. I have not the slightest inclination what you're talking about."

"Why then, I'll just explain it to you." McMurphy raises his voice; though he doesn't look at the other Acutes listening behind him, it's them he's talking to. "The flock gets sight of a spot of blood on some chicken and they all go to *peckin'* at it, see, till they rip the chicken to shreds, blood and bones and feathers. But usually a couple of the *flock* gets spotted in the fracas, then it's their turn. And a few more gets spots and gets pecked to death, and more and more. Oh, a peckin' party can wipe out the whole flock in a matter of a few hours, buddy, I seen it. A mighty awesome sight. The only way to prevent it—with chickens—is to clip blinders on them. So's they can't see."

Harding laces his long fingers around a knee and draws the knee toward him, leaning back in the chair. "A pecking party. That certainly is a pleasant analogy, my friend."

"And that's just exactly what that meeting I just set through reminded me of, buddy, if you want to know the dirty truth. It reminded me of a flock of dirty chickens."

"So that makes me the chicken with the spot of blood, friend?"

"That's right, buddy."

They're still grinning at each other, but their voices have dropped so low and taut I have to sweep over closer to them with my broom to hear. The other Acutes are moving up closer too.

"And you want to know somethin' else, buddy? You want to know who pecks that first peck?"

Harding waits for him to go on.

"It's that old nurse, that's who."

There's a whine of fear over the silence. I hear the machinery in the walls catch and go on. Harding is having a tough time holding his hands still, but he keeps trying to act calm.

"So," he says, "it's as simple as that, as stupidly simple as that. You're on our ward six hours and have already simplified all the work of Freud, Jung, and Maxwell Jones and summed it up in one analogy: it's a 'peckin' party.'"

"I'm not talking about Fred Yoong and Maxwell Jones, buddy, I'm just talking about that crummy meeting and what that nurse and those other bastards did to you. Did in spades."

"*Did* to me?"

"That's right, *did*. Did you every chance they got. Did you coming and did you going. You must of done something to make a passle of enemies here in this place, buddy, because it seems there's sure a passle got it in for you."

"Why, this is incredible. You completely disregard, completely overlook and disregard the fact that what the fellows were doing today was for my own benefit? That any question or discussion raised by Miss Ratched or the rest of the staff is done solely for therapeutic reasons? You must not have heard a word of Doctor Spivey's theory of the Therapeutic Community, or not have had the education to comprehend it if you did. I'm disappointed in you, my friend, oh, very disappointed. I had judged from our encounter this morning that you were more intelligent—an illiterate clod, perhaps, certainly a backwoods braggart with no more sensitivity than a goose, but basically intelligent nevertheless. But, observant and insightful though I usually am, I still make mistakes."

"The hell with you, buddy."

"Oh yes; I forgot to add that I noticed your primitive brutality also this morning. Psychopath with definite sadistic tendencies, probably motivated by an unreasoning egomania. Yes. As you see, all these natural talents certainly qualify you as a competent therapist and render you quite capable of criticizing Miss Ratched's meeting procedure, in spite of the fact that she is a highly regarded psychiatric nurse with twenty years in the field. Yes, with your talent, my friend, you could work subconscious miracles, sooth the aching id and heal the wounded superego. You could probably bring about a cure for the whole ward, Vegetables and all, in six short months ladies and gentlemen or your money back."

Instead of rising to the argument, McMurphy just keeps on looking at Harding, finally asks in a level voice, "And you really think this crap that went on in the meeting today is bringing about some kinda cure, doing some kinda good?"

"What other reason would we have for submitting ourselves to it, my friend? The staff desires our cure as much as we do. They aren't monsters. Miss Ratched may be a strict middle-aged lady, but she's not some kind of giant monster of the poultry clan, bent on sadistically pecking out our eyes. You can't believe that of her, can you?"

"No, buddy, not that. She ain't peckin' at your *eyes*. That's not what she's peckin' at."

Harding flinches, and I see his hands begin to creep out from between his knees like white spiders from between two moss-covered tree limbs, up the limbs toward the joining at the trunk.

"Not our eyes?" he says. "Pray, then, where *is* Miss Ratched pecking, my friend?"

McMurphy grinned. "Why, don't you *know*, buddy?"

"No, of course I don't know! I mean, if you insi—"

"At your balls, buddy, at your everlovin' *balls*."

The spiders reach the joining at the trunk and settle there, twitching. Harding tries to grin, but his face and lips are so white the grin is lost. He stares at McMurphy. McMurphy takes the cigarette out of his mouth and repeats what he said.

"Right at your balls. No, that nurse ain't some kinda monster chicken, buddy, what she is is a ball-cutter. I've seen a thousand of 'em, old and young, men and women. Seen 'em all over the country and in the homes—people who try to make you weak so they can get you to toe the line, to follow their rules, to live like they want you to. And the best way to do this, to get you to knuckle under, is to weaken you by gettin' you where it hurts the worst. You ever been kneed in the nuts in a brawl, buddy? Stops you cold, don't it? There's nothing worse. It makes you sick, it saps every bit of strength you got. If you're up against a guy who wants to win by making you weaker instead of making himself stronger, then watch for his knee, he's gonna go for your vitals. And that's what that old buzzard is doing, going for your vitals."

Harding's face is still colorless, but he's got control of his hands again; they flip loosely before him, trying to toss off what McMurphy has been saying:

"Our dear Miss Ratched? Our sweet, smiling, tender angel of mercy, Mother Ratched, a ball-cutter? Why, friend, that's *most* unlikely."

"Buddy, don't give me that tender little mother crap. She may be a mother, but she's big as a damn barn and tough as knife metal. She fooled me with that kindly little old mother bit for maybe three minutes when I came in this morning, but no longer. I don't think she's really fooled any of you guys for any six months or a year, neither. Hoo*wee*, I've seen some bitches in my time, but she takes the cake."

"A bitch? But a moment ago she was a ball-cutter, then a buzzard—or was it a chicken? Your metaphors are bumping into each other, my friend."

"The hell with that; she's a bitch and a buzzard and a ball-cutter, and don't kid me, you know what I'm talking about."

Harding's face and hands are moving faster than ever now, a speeded film of gestures, grins, grimaces, sneers. The more he tries to stop it, the faster it goes. When he lets his hands and face move like they want to and doesn't try to hold them back, they flow and gesture in a way that's real pretty to watch, but when he worries about them and tries to hold back he becomes a wild, jerky puppet doing a high-strung dance. Everything is moving faster and faster, and his voice is speeding up to match.

"Why, see here, my friend Mr. McMurphy, my psychopathic sidekick, our Miss Ratched is a veritable angel of mercy and why just *every*one knows it. She's unselfish as the wind, toiling thanklessly for the good of all, day after day, five long days a week. That takes heart, my friend, heart. In fact, I have been informed by sources—I am not at liberty to disclose my sources, but I might say that Martini is in contact with the same people a good part of the time—that she even *further* serves mankind on her weekends off by doing generous volunteer work about town. Preparing a rich array of charity—canned goods, cheese for the binding effect, soap—and presenting it to some poor young couple having a difficult time financially." His hands flash in the air, molding the picture he is describing. "Ah, look: There she is, our nurse. Her gentle knock on the door. The ribboned basket. The young couple overjoyed to the point of speechlessness. The husband open-mouthed, the wife weeping openly. She appraises their dwelling. Promises to send them money for—scouring powder, yes. She places the basket in the center of the floor. And when our angel leaves—throwing kisses, smiling ethereally—she is so *intoxicated* with the sweet milk of human kindness that her deed has generated within her large bosom, that she is beside herself with generosity. Be-*side* herself, do you hear? Pausing at the door, she draws the timid young bride to one side and offers her twenty dollars of her own: 'Go, you poor unfortunate underfed child, go, and buy yourself a *decent* dress. I *realize* your husband can't afford it, but here, take this, and *go*.' And the couple is forever indebted to her benevolence."

He's been talking faster and faster, the cords stretching out in his neck. When he stops talking, the ward is completely silent. I don't hear anything but a faint reeling rhythm, what I figure is a tape recorder somewhere getting all of this.

Harding looks around, sees everybody's watching him, and he does his best to laugh. A sound comes out of his mouth like a nail being crowbarred out of a plank of green pine; Eee-eee-eee. He can't stop it. He wrings his hands like a fly and clinches his eyes at the awful sound of that squeaking. But he can't stop it. It gets higher and higher until finally, with a suck of breath, he lets his face fall into his waiting hands.

"Oh the bitch, the bitch the bitch," he whispers through his teeth.

McMurphy lights another cigarette and offers it to him; Harding takes it without a word. McMurphy is still watching Harding's face in front of him there, with a kind of puzzled wonder, looking at it like it's the first human face he ever laid eyes on. He watches while Harding's twitching and jerking slows down and the face comes up from the hands.

"You are right," Harding says, "about all of it." He looks up at the other patients who are watching him. "No one's ever dared come out and say it before, but there's not a man among us that doesn't think it, that doesn't feel just as you do about her and the whole business—feel it somewhere down deep in his scared little soul."

McMurphy frowns and asks, "What about that little fart of a doctor? He might be a little slow in the head, but not so much as not to be able to see how she's taken over and what she's doing."

Harding takes a long pull off the cigarette and lets the smoke drift out with his talk. "Doctor Spivey . . . is exactly like the rest of us, McMurphy, completely conscious of his inadaquacy. He's a frightened, desperate, ineffectual little rabbit, totally incapable of running this ward without our Miss Ratched's help, and he knows it. And, worse, she *knows* he knows it and reminds him every chance she gets. Every time she finds he's made a little slip in the bookwork or in, say, the charting you can just imagine her in there grinding his nose in it."

"That's right," Cheswick says, coming up beside McMurphy, "grinds our noses in our mistakes."

"Why don't he fire her?"

"In this hospital," Harding says, "the doctor doesn't hold the power of hiring and firing. That power goes to the supervisor, and the supervisor is a woman, a dear old friend of Miss Ratched's; they were Army nurses together in the thirties. We are victims of a matriarchy here, my friend, and the doctor is just as helpless against it as we are. He knows that all Ratched has to do is pick up that phone you see sitting at her elbow and call the supervisor and mention, oh, say, that the doctor seems to be making a *great* number of requisitions for Demerol—"

"Hold it, Harding, I'm not up on all this shop talk."

"Demerol, my friend, is a synthetic opiate, twice as addictive as heroin. Quite common for doctors to be addicted to it."

"That little fart? Is he a dope addict?"

"I'm certain I don't know."

"Then where does she get off with accusing him of—"

"Oh, you're not paying attention, my friend. She *doesn't* accuse. She merely needs to insinuate, insinuate anything, don't you see? Didn't you notice today? She'll call a man to the door of the Nurses' Station and stand there and ask him about a Kleenex found under his bed. No more, just ask. And he'll feel like he's lying to her, whatever answer he gives. If he says he was cleaning a pen with it, she'll say, 'I see, a pen,' or if he says he has a cold in his nose, she'll say, 'I see, a cold,' and she'll nod her neat little gray coiffure and smile her neat little smile and turn and go back into the Nurses' Station, leave him standing there wondering just what *did* he use that Kleenex for."

He starts to tremble again, and his shoulders fold back around him.

"No. She doesn't need to accuse. She has a genius for insinuation. Did you ever hear her, in the course of our discussion today, ever *once* hear her accuse me of anything? Yet it seems I have been accused of a multitude of things, of jealousy and paranoia, of not being man enough to satisfy my wife, of having relations with male friends of mine, of holding my cigarette in an affected manner, even—it seems to me—ac-

cused of having nothing between my legs but a patch of hair
—and *soft* and *downy* and *blond hair at that!* Ball-cutter? Oh,
you *underestimate* her!"

Harding hushes all of a sudden and leans forward to take
McMurphy's hand in both of his. His face is tilted oddly,
edged, jagged purple and gray, a busted wine bottle.

"This world . . . belongs to the strong, my friend! The ritual
of our existence is based on the strong getting stronger by de-
vouring the weak. We must face up to this. No more than right
that it should be this way. We must learn to accept it as a
law of the natural world. The rabbits accept their role in the
ritual and recognize the wolf as the strong. In defense, the
rabbit becomes sly and frightened and elusive and he digs holes
and hides when the wolf is about. And he endures, he goes on.
He knows his place. He most certainly doesn't challenge the
wolf to combat. Now, would that be wise? Would it?"

He lets go McMurphy's hand and leans back and crosses his
legs, takes another long pull off the cigarette. He pulls the
cigarette from his thin crack of a smile, and the laugh starts up
again—eee-eee-eee, like a nail coming out of a plank.

"Mr. McMurphy . . . my friend . . . I'm not a chicken,
I'm a rabbit. The doctor is a rabbit. Cheswick there is a rabbit.
Billy Bibbit is a rabbit. All of us in here are rabbits of varying
ages and degrees, hippity-hopping through our Walt Disney
world. Oh, don't misunderstand me, we're not in here *because*
we are rabbits—we'd be rabbits wherever we were—we're all
in here because we can't *adjust* to our rabbithood. We *need* a
good strong wolf like the nurse to teach us our place."

"Man, you're talkin' like a fool. You mean to tell me that
you're gonna sit back and let some old blue-haired woman talk
you into being a rabbit?"

"Not talk me into it, no. I was born a rabbit. Just look at
me. I simply need the nurse to make me *happy* with my role."

"You're no damned rabbit!"

"See the ears? the wiggly nose? the cute little button tail?"

"You're talking like a crazy ma—"

"Like a crazy man? How astute."

"Damn it, Harding, I didn't mean it like that. You ain't crazy that way. I mean—hell, I been surprised how sane you guys all are. As near as I can tell you're not any crazier than the average asshole on the street—"

"Ah yes, the asshole on the street."

"But not, you know, crazy like the movies paint crazy people. You're just hung up and—kind of—"

"Kind of rabbit-like, isn't that it?"

"Rabbits, *hell!* Not a thing like rabbits, goddammit."

"Mr. Bibbit, hop around for Mr. McMurphy here. Mr. Cheswick, show him how *furry* you are."

Billy Bibbit and Cheswick change into hunched-over white rabbits, right before my eyes, but they are too ashamed to do any of the things Harding told them to do.

"Ah, they're bashful, McMurphy. Isn't that sweet? Or, perhaps, the fellows are ill at ease because they didn't stick up for their friend. Perhaps they are feeling guilty for the way they once again let her victimize them into being her interrogators. Cheer up, friends, you've no reason to feel ashamed. It is all as it should be. It's not the rabbit's place to stick up for his fellow. That would have been foolish. No, you were wise, cowardly but wise."

"Look here, Harding," Cheswick says.

"No, no, Cheswick. Don't get irate at the truth."

"Now look here; there's been times when I've said the same things about old lady Ratched that McMurphy has been saying."

"Yes, but you said them very quietly and took them all back later. You are a rabbit too, don't try to avoid the truth. That's why I hold no grudge against you for the questions you asked me during the meeting today. You were only playing your role. If you had been on the carpet, or you Billy, or you Fredrickson, I would have attacked you just as cruelly as you attacked me. We mustn't be ashamed of our behavior; it's the way we little animals were meant to behave."

McMurphy turns in his chair and looks the other Acutes up and down. "I ain't so sure but what they should be ashamed.

Personally, I thought it was damned crummy the way they swung in on her side against you. For a minute there I thought I was back in a Red Chinese prison camp . . ."

"Now by God, McMurphy," Cheswick says, "you listen here."

McMurphy turns and listens, but Cheswick doesn't go on. Cheswick never goes on; he's one of these guys who'll make a big fuss like he's going to lead an attack, holler charge and stomp up and down a minute, take a couple steps, and quit. McMurphy looks at him where he's been caught off base again after such a tough-sounding start, and says to him, "A hell of a lot like a Chinese prison camp."

Harding holds up his hands for peace. "Oh, no, no, that isn't right. You mustn't condemn us, my friend. No. In fact . . ."

I see that sly fever come into Harding's eye again; I think he's going to start laughing, but instead he takes his cigarette out of his mouth and points it at McMurphy—in his hand it looks like one of this thin, white fingers, smoking at the end.

". . . you too, Mr. McMurphy, for all your cowboy bluster and your sideshow swagger, you too, under that crusty surface, are probably just as soft and fuzzy and rabbit-souled as we are."

"Yeah, you bet. I'm a little cottontail. Just what is it makes me a rabbit, Harding? My psychopathic tendencies? Is it my fightin' tendencies, or my fuckin' tendencies? Must be the fuckin', mustn't it? All that whambam-thank-you-ma'am. Yeah, that whambam, that's probably what makes me a rabbit—"

"Wait; I'm afraid you've raised a point that requires some deliberation. Rabbits are noted for that certain trait, aren't they? Notorious, in fact, for their whambam. Yes. Um. But in any case, the point you bring up simply indicates that you are a healthy, functioning and adequate rabbit, whereas most of us in here even lack the sexual ability to make the grade as adequate rabbits. Failures, we are—feeble, stunted, weak little creatures in a weak little race. Rabbits, *sans* whambam; a pathetic notion."

"Wait a minute; you keep twistin' what I say—"

"No. You were right. You remember, it was you that drew our attention to the place where the nurse was concentrating her pecking? That was true. There's not a man here that isn't afraid he is losing or has already lost his whambam. We comical little creatures can't even achieve masculinity in the rabbit world, that's how weak and inadequate we are. Hee. We are —the *rabbits*, one might say, of the rabbit world!"

He leans forward again, and that strained, squeaking laugh of his that I been expecting begins to rise from his mouth, his hands flipping around, his face twitching.

"Harding! Shut your damned mouth!"

It's like a slap. Harding is hushed, chopped off cold with his mouth still open in a drawn grin, his hands dangling in a cloud of blue tobacco smoke. He freezes this way a second; then his eyes narrow into sly little holes and he lets them slip over to McMurphy, speaks so soft that I have to push my broom up right next to his chair to hear what he says.

"Friend . . . *you* . . . may be a wolf."

"Goddammit, I'm no wolf and you're no rabbit. *Hoo*, I never heard such—"

"You have a very wolfy roar."

With a loud hissing of breath McMurphy turns from Harding to the rest of the Acutes standing around. "Here; all you guys. What the hell is the matter with you? You ain't as crazy as all this, thinking you're some animal."

"No," Cheswick says and steps in beside McMurphy. "No, by God, not me. I'm not any rabbit."

"That's the boy, Cheswick. And the rest of you, let's just knock it off. Look at you, talking yourself into running scared from some fifty-year-old woman. What is there she can do to you, anyway?"

"Yeah, what?" Cheswick says and glares around at the others.

"She can't have you whipped. She can't burn you with hot irons. She can't tie you to the rack. They got laws about that sort of thing nowadays; this ain't the Middle Ages. There's not a thing in the world that she can—"

"You s-s-*saw* what she c-can do to us! In the m-m-meeting today." I see Billy Bibbit has changed back from a rabbit. He leans toward McMurphy, trying to go on, his mouth wet with spit and his face red. Then he turns and walks away. "Ah, it's n-no use. I should just k-k-kill myself."

McMurphy calls after him. "Today? What did I see in the meeting today? Hell's bells, all I saw today was her asking a couple of questions, and nice, easy questions at that. Questions ain't bonebreakers, they ain't sticks and stones."

Billy turns back. "But the wuh-wuh-*way* she asks them—"

"You don't have to answer, do you?"

"If you d-don't answer she just smiles and m-m-makes a note in her little book and then she—she—oh, *hell!*"

Scanlon comes up beside Billy. "If you don't answer her questions, Mack, you *admit* it just by keeping quiet. It's the way those bastards in the government get you. You can't beat it. The only thing to do is blow the whole business off the face of the whole bleeding earth—blow it all up."

"Well, when she asks one of those questions, why don't you tell her to up and go to hell?"

"Yeah," Cheswick says, shaking his fist, "tell her to up and go to hell."

"So then what, Mack? She'd just come right back with 'Why do you seem so *upset* by that par-tick-uler question, Patient McMurphy?'"

"So, you tell her to go to hell again. Tell them all to go to hell. They still haven't hurt you."

The Acutes are crowding closer around him. Fredrickson answers this time. "Okay, you tell her that and you're listed as Potential Assaultive and shipped upstairs to the Disturbed ward. I had it happen. Three times. Those poor goofs up there don't even get off the ward to go to the Saturday afternoon movie. They don't even have a TV."

"And, my friend, if you *continue* to demonstrate such hostile tendencies, such as telling people to go to hell, you get lined up to go to the Shock Shop, perhaps even on to greater things, an operation, an—"

"Damn it, Harding, I told you I'm not up on this talk."

"The Shock Shop, Mr. McMurphy, is jargon for the EST machine, the Electro Shock Therapy. A device that might be said to do the work of the sleeping pill, the electric chair, *and* the torture rack. It's a clever little procedure, simple, quick, nearly painless it happens so fast, but no one ever wants another one. Ever."

"What's this thing do?"

"You are strapped to a table, shaped, ironically, like a cross, with a crown of electric sparks in place of thorns. You are touched on each side of the head with wires. Zap! Five cents' worth of electricity through the brain and you are jointly administered therapy and a punishment for your hostile go-to-hell behavior, on top of being put out of everyone's way for six hours to three days, depending on the individual. Even when you do regain consciousness you are in a state of disorientation for days. You are unable to think coherently. You can't recall things. Enough of these treatments and a man could turn out like Mr. Ellis you see over there against the wall. A drooling, pants-wetting idiot at thirty-five. Or turn into a mindless organism that eats and eliminates and yells 'fuck the wife,' like Ruckly. Or look at Chief Broom clutching to his namesake there beside you."

Harding points his cigarette at me, too late for me to back off. I make like I don't notice. Go on with my sweeping.

"I've heard that the Chief, years ago, received more than two hundred shock treatments when they were really the vogue. Imagine what this could do to a mind that was already slipping. Look at him: a giant janitor. There's your Vanishing American, a six-foot-eight sweeping machine, scared of its own shadow. That, my friend, is what we can be threatened with."

McMurphy looks at me a while, then turns back to Harding. "Man, I tell you, how come you stand for it? What about this democratic-ward manure that the doctor was giving me? Why don't you take a vote?"

Harding smiles at him and takes another slow drag on his cigarette. "Vote what, my friend? Vote that the nurse may not ask any more questions in Group Meeting? Vote that she shall not *look* at us in a certain way? You tell me, Mr. McMurphy, what do we vote on?"

"Hell, I don't care. Vote on anything. Don't you see you have to do something to show you still got some guts? Don't you see you can't let her take over completely? Look at you here: you say the Chief is scared of his own shadow, but I never saw a scareder-looking bunch in my life than you guys."

"Not me!" Cheswick says.

"Maybe not you, buddy, but the rest are even scared to open up and *laugh*. You know, that's the first thing that got me about this place, that there wasn't anybody laughing. I haven't heard a real laugh since I came through that door, do you know that? Man, when you lose your laugh you lose your *footing*. A man go around lettin' a woman whup him down till he can't laugh any more, and he loses one of the biggest edges he's got on his side. First thing you know he'll begin to think she's tougher than he is and—"

"Ah. I believe my friend is catching on, fellow rabbits. Tell me, Mr. McMurphy, how does one go about showing a woman who's boss, I mean other than laughing at her? How does he show her who's king of the mountain? A man like you should be able to tell us that. You don't slap her around, do you? No, then she calls the law. You don't lose your temper and shout at her; she'll win by trying to placate her big ol' angry boy: 'Is us wittle man getting *fussy*? Ahhhhh?' Have you ever tried to keep up a noble and angry front in the face of such consolation? So you see, my friend, it is somewhat as you stated: man has but *one* truly effective weapon against the juggernaut of modern matriarchy, but it certainly is not laughter. One weapon, and with every passing year in this hip, motivationally researched society, more and more people are discovering how to render that weapon useless and conquer those who have hitherto been the conquerers—"

"Lord, Harding, but you do come on," McMurphy says.

"—and do you think, for all your acclaimed psychopathic powers, that you could effectively use your weapon against our champion? Do you think you could use it against Miss Ratched, McMurphy? Ever?"

And sweeps one of his hands toward the glass case. Everybody's head turns to look. She's in there, looking out through her window, got a tape recorder hid out of sight somewhere, getting all this down—already planning how to work it into the schedule.

The nurse sees everybody looking at her and she nods and they all turn away. McMurphy takes off his cap and runs his hands into that red hair. Now everybody is looking at him; they're waiting for him to make an answer and he knows it. He feels he's been trapped some way. He puts the cap back on and rubs the stitch marks on his nose.

"Why, if you mean do I think I could get a bone up over that old buzzard, no, I don't believe I could. . . ."

"She's not all that homely, McMurphy. Her face is quite handsome and well preserved. And in spite of all her attempts to *conceal* them, in that sexless get-up, you can still make out the evidence of some rather extraordinary breasts. She must have been a rather beautiful young woman. Still—for the sake of argument, could you get it up over her even if she wasn't old, even if she was young and had the beauty of Helen?"

"I don't know Helen, but I see what you're drivin' at. And you're by God right. I couldn't get it up over old frozen face in there even if she had the beauty of Marilyn Monroe."

"There you are. She's won."

That's it. Harding leans back and everybody waits for what McMurphy's going to say next. McMurphy can see he's backed up against the wall. He looks at the faces a minute, then shrugs and stands up from his chair.

"Well, what the hell, it's no skin off my nose."

"That's true, it's no skin off your nose."

"And I damn well don't want to have some old fiend of a nurse after me with three thousand volts. Not when there's nothing in it for me but the adventure."

"No. You're right."

Harding's won the argument, but nobody looks too happy. McMurphy hooks his thumbs in his pockets and tries a laugh.

"No sir, I never heard of anybody offering a twenty-bone bounty for bagging a ball-cutter."

Everybody grins at this with him, but they're not happy. I'm glad McMurphy is going to be cagey after all and not get sucked in on something he can't whip, but I know how the guys feel; I'm not so happy myself. McMurphy lights another cigarette. Nobody's moved yet. They're all still standing there, grinning and uncomfortable. McMurphy rubs his nose again and looks away from the bunch of faces hung out there around him, looks back at the nurse and chews his lip.

"But you say . . . she don't send you up to that other ward unless she gets your goat? Unless she makes you crack in some way and you end up cussing her out or busting a window or something like that?"

"Unless you do something like that."

"You're sure of that, now? Because I'm getting just the shadiest notion of how to pick up a good purse off you birds in here. But I don't want to be a sucker about it. I had a hell of a time getting outa that other hole; I don't want to be jumping outa the fryin' pan into the fire."

"Absolutely certain. She's powerless unless you do something to honestly deserve the Disturbed Ward or EST. If you're tough enough to keep her from getting to you, she can't do a thing."

"So if I behave myself and don't cuss her out—"

"Or cuss one of the aides out."

"—or cuss one of the aides out or tear up jack some way around here, she can't do nothing to me?"

"Those are the rules we play by. Of course, she always wins, my friend, always. She's impregnable herself, and with the element of time working for her she eventually gets inside everyone. That's why the hospital regards her as its top nurse and grants her so much authority; she's a master at forcing the trembling libido out into the open—"

"The hell with that. What I want to know is am I safe to try to beat her at her own game? If I come on nice as pie to her, whatever else I in-*sinuate*, she ain't gonna get in a tizzy and have me electrocuted?"

"You're safe as long as you keep control. As long as you don't lose your temper and give her actual reason to request the restriction of the Disturbed Ward, or the therapeutic benefits of Electro Shock, you are safe. But that entails first and foremost keeping one's temper. And you? With your red hair and black record? Why delude yourself?"

"Okay. *All* right." McMurphy rubs his palms together. "Here's what I'm thinkin'. You birds seem to think you got quite the champ in there, don't you? Quite the—what did you call her?—sure, impregnable woman. What I want to know is how many of you are dead *sure* enough to put a little money on her?"

"Dead sure enough . . . ?"

"Just what I said: any of you sharpies here willing to take my five bucks that says that I can get the best of that woman —before the week's up—without her getting the best of me? One week, and if I don't have her to where she don't know whether to shit or go blind, the bet is yours."

"You're *betting* on this." Cheswick is hopping from foot to foot and rubbing his hands together like McMurphy rubs his.

"You're damned right."

Harding and some of the others say that they don't get it.

"It's simple enough. There ain't nothing noble or complicated about it. I like to gamble. And I like to win. And I think I can win this gamble, okay? It got so at Pendleton the guys wouldn't even lag pennies with me on account of I was such a winner. Why, one of the big reasons I got myself sent here was because I needed some new suckers. I'll tell you something: I found out a few things about this place before I came out here. Damn near half of you guys in here pull compensation, three, four hundred a month and not a thing in the world to do with it but let it draw dust. I thought I might take advantage of this and maybe make both our lives a little more richer. I'm starting level with you. I'm a gambler and I'm not in the habit of losing. And I've never seen a woman I thought was more man than me, I don't care whether I can get it up for her or not. She may have the element of time, but I got a pretty long winning streak goin' myself."

He pulls off his cap, spins it on his finger, and catches it behind his back in his other hand, neat as you please.

"Another thing: I'm in this place because that's the way I planned it, pure and simple, because it's a better place than a work farm. As near as I can tell I'm no loony, or never knew it if I was. Your nurse don't know this; she's not going to be looking out for somebody coming at her with a trigger-quick mind like I obviously got. These things give me an edge I like. So I'm saying five bucks to each of you that wants it if I can't put a betsy bug up that nurse's butt within a week."

"I'm still not sure I—"

"Just that. A bee in her butt, a burr in her bloomers. Get her goat. Bug her till she comes apart at those neat little seams, and shows, just one time, she ain't so unbeatable as you think. One week. I'll let you be the judge whether I win or not."

Harding takes out a pencil and writes something on the pinochle pad.

"Here. A lien on ten dollars of that money they've got drawing dust under my name over in Funds. It's worth twice that to me, my friend, to see this unlikely miracle brought off."

McMurphy looks at the paper and folds it. "Worth it to any of the rest of you birds?" Other Acutes line up now, taking turns at the pad. He takes the pieces of paper when they're finished, stacking them on his palm, pinned under a big stiff thumb. I see the pieces of paper crowd up in his hand. He looks them over.

"You trust me to hold the bets, buddies?"

"I believe we can be safe in doing that," Harding says. "You won't be going any place for a while."

One Christmas at midnight on the button, at the old place, the ward door blows open with a crash, in comes a fat man with a beard, eyes ringed red by the cold and his nose just the color of a cherry. The black boys get him cornered in the hall with flashlights. I see he's all tangled in the tinsel Public Relation has been stringing all over the place, and he's stumbling around in it in the dark. He's shading his red eyes from the flashlights and sucking on his mustache.

"Ho ho ho," he says. "I'd like to stay but I must be hurrying along. Very tight schedule, ya know. Ho ho. Must be going. . . ."

The black boys move in with the flashlights. They kept him with us six years before they discharged him, clean-shaven and skinny as a pole.

The Big Nurse is able to set the wall clock at whatever speed she wants by just turning one of those dials in the steel door; she takes a notion to hurry things up, she turns the speed up, and those hands whip around that disk like spokes in a wheel. The scene in the picture-screen windows goes through rapid changes of light to show morning, noon, and night—throb off and on furiously with day and dark, and everybody is driven like mad to keep up with that passing of fake time; awful scramble of shaves and breakfasts and appointments and lunches and medications and ten minutes of night so you barely get your eyes closed before the dorm light's screaming at you to get up and start the scramble again, go like a sonofabitch this way, going through the full schedule of a day maybe twenty times an hour, till the Big Nurse sees everybody is right up to the breaking point, and she slacks off on the throttle, eases off the pace on that clock-dial, like some kid been fooling with

the moving-picture projection machine and finally got tired
watching the film run at ten times its natural speed, got bored
with all that silly scampering and insect squeak of talk and
turned it back to normal.

She's given to turning up the speed this way on days like,
say, when you got somebody to visit you or when the VFW
brings down a smoker show from Portland—times like that,
times you'd like to hold and have stretch out. That's when she
speeds things up.

But generally it's the other way, the slow way. She'll turn
that dial to a dead stop and freeze the sun there on the screen
so it don't move a scant hair for weeks, so not a leaf on a tree
or a blade of grass in the pasture shimmers. The clock hands
hang at two minutes to three and she's liable to let them hang
there till we rust. You sit solid and you can't budge, you can't
walk or move to relieve the strain of sitting, you can't swallow
and you can't breathe. The only thing you can move is your
eyes and there's nothing to see but petrified Acutes across the
room waiting on one another to decide whose play it is. The
old Chronic next to me has been dead six days, and he's rotting
to the chair. And instead of fog sometimes she'll let a clear
chemical gas in through the vents, and the whole ward is set
solid when the gas changes into plastic.

Lord knows how long we hang this way.

Then, gradually, she'll ease the dial up a degree, and that's
worse yet. I can take hanging dead still better'n I can take that
sirup-slow hand of Scanlon across the room, taking three days
to lay down a card. My lungs pull for the thick plastic air
like getting it through a pinhole. I try to go to the latrine and
I feel buried under a ton of sand, squeezing my bladder till
green sparks flash and buzz across my forehead.

I strain with every muscle and bone to get out of that chair
and go to the latrine, work to get up till my arms and legs are
all ashake and my teeth hurt. I pull and pull and all I gain is
maybe a quarter-inch off the leather seat. So I fall back and
give up and let the pee pour out, activating a hot salt wire
down my left leg that sets off humiliating alarms, sirens,

spotlights, everybody up yelling and running around and the big black boys knocking the crowd aside right and left as the both of them rush headlong at me, waving awful mops of wet copper wires cracking and spitting as they short with the water.

About the only time we get any let-up from this time control is in the fog; then time doesn't mean anything. It's lost in the fog, like everything else. (They haven't really fogged the place full force all day today, not since McMurphy came in. I bet he'd yell like a bull if they fogged it.)

When nothing else is going on, you usually got the fog or the time control to contend with, but today something's happened: there hasn't been any of these things worked on us all day, not since shaving. This afternoon everything is matching up. When the swing shift comes on duty the clock says four-thirty, just like it should. The Big Nurse dismisses the black boys and takes a last look around the ward. She slides a long silver hatpin out of the iron-blue knot of hair back of her head, takes off her white cap and sets it careful in a cardboard box (there's mothballs in that box), and drives the hatpin back in the hair with a stab of her hand.

Behind the glass I see her tell everyone good evening. She hands the little birthmarked swing-shift nurse a note; then her hand reaches out to the control panel in the steel door, clacks on the speaker in the day room: "Good evening boys. Behave yourselves." And turns the music up louder than ever. She rubs the inside of her wrist across her window; a disgusted look shows the fat black boy who just reported on duty that he better get to cleaning it, and he's at the glass with a paper towel before she's so much as locked the ward door behind her.

The machinery in the walls whistles, sighs, drops into a lower gear.

Then, till night, we eat and shower and go back to sit in the day room. Old Blastic, the oldest Vegetable, is holding his stomach and moaning. George (the black boys call him Rub-a-dub) is washing his hands in the drinking fountain. The Acutes sit and play cards and work at getting a picture on our

TV set by carrying the set every place the cord will reach, in search of a good beam.

The speakers in the ceiling are still making music. The music from the speakers isn't transmitted in on a radio beam is why the machinery don't interfere. The music comes off a long tape from the Nurses' Station, a tape we all know so well by heart that there don't any of us consciously hear it except new men like McMurphy. He hasn't got used to it yet. He's dealing blackjack for cigarettes, and the speaker's right over the card table. He's pulled his cap way forward till he has to lean his head back and squint from under the brim to see his cards. He holds a cigarette between his teeth and talks around it like a stock auctioneer I saw once in a cattle auction in The Dalles.

". . . hey-ya, hey-ya, come on, come on," he says, high, fast; "I'm waitin' on you suckers, you hit or you sit. Hit you say? well well well and with a king up the boy wants a hit. Whaddaya know. So comin' at you and *too* bad, a little lady for the lad and he's over the wall and down the road, up the hill and dropped his load. Comin' at you Scanlon and I *wish some idiot in that nurses' hothouse would turn down that frigging music!* Hooee! Does that thing play night and day, Harding? I never heard such a driving racket in my life."

Harding gives him a blank look. "Exactly what noise is it you're referring to, Mr. McMurphy?"

"That damned *radio*. Boy. It's been going ever since I come in this morning. And don't come on with some baloney that you don't hear it."

Harding cocks his ear to the ceiling. "Oh, yes, the so-called music. Yes, I suppose we do hear it if we concentrate, but then one can hear one's own heartbeat too, if he concentrates hard enough." He grins at McMurphy. "You see, that's a recording playing up there, my friend. We seldom hear the radio. The world news might not be therapeutic. And we've all heard that recording so many times now it simply slides out of our hearing, the way the sound of a waterfall soon becomes an unheard sound to those who live near it. Do you think if you lived near a waterfall you could hear it very long?"

(I still hear the sound of the falls on the Columbia, always will—always—hear the whoop of Charley Bear Belly stabbed himself a big chinook, hear the slap of fish in the water, laughing naked kids on the bank, the women at the racks . . . from a long time ago.)

"Do they leave it on all the time, like a waterfall?" McMurphy says.

"Not when we sleep," Cheswick says, "but all the rest of the time, and that's the truth."

"The hell with that. I'll tell that coon over there to turn it off or get his fat little ass kicked!"

He starts to stand up, and Harding touches his arm. "Friend, that is exactly the kind of statement that gets one branded assaultive. Are you so eager to forfeit the bet?"

McMurphy looks at him. "That's the way it is, huh? A pressure game? Keep the old pinch on?"

"That's the way it is."

He slowly lowers himself back into his seat, saying, "Horse muh-noo-ur."

Harding looks about at the other Acutes around the card table. "Gentlemen, already I seem to detect in our redheaded challenger a most unheroic decline of his TV-cowboy stoicism."

He looks at McMurphy across the table, smiling. McMurphy nods at him and tips his head back for the wink and licks his big thumb. "Well sir, ol' Professor Harding sounds like he's getting cocky. He wins a couple of splits and he goes to comin' on like a wise guy. Well well well; there he sits with a deuce showing and here's a pack of Mar'boros says he backs down. . . . *Whups*, he sees me, okeedokee, Perfessor, here's a trey, he wants another, gets another deuce, try for the big five, Perfessor? Try for that big double pay, or play it safe? Another pack says you won't. Well well well, the Perfessor sees me, this tells the tale, *too* bad, another lady and the Perfessor flunks his exams. . . ."

The next song starts up from the speaker, loud and clangy and a lot of accordion. McMurphy takes a look up at the speaker, and his spiel gets louder and louder to match it.

". . . hey-ya hey-ya, okay, *next*, goddammit, you hit or you
sit . . . comin at ya . . . !"

Right up to the lights out at nine-thirty.

I could of watched McMurphy at that blackjack table all
night, the way he dealt and talked and roped them in and led
them smack up to the point where they were *just about* to
quit, then backed down a hand or two to give them confidence
and bring them along again. Once he took a break for a cigarette and tilted back in his chair, his hands folded behind his
head, and told the guys, "The secret of being a top-notch con
man is being able to know what the mark *wants*, and how to
make him think he's getting it. I learned that when I worked
a season on a skillo wheel in a carnival. You *fe-e-el* the sucker
over with your eyes when he comes up and you say, 'Now here's
a bird that needs to feel tough.' So every time he snaps at
you for taking him you quake in your boots, scared to death,
and tell him, 'Please, sir. No trouble. The next roll is on the
house, sir.' So the both of you are getting what you want."

He rocks forward, and the legs of his chair come down with
a crack. He picks up the deck, zips his thumb over it, knocks
the edge of it against the table top, licks his thumb and finger.

"And what I deduce you marks need is a big fat pot to
temptate you. Here's ten packages on the next deal. Hey-*yah*,
comin' at you, guts ball from here on out. . . ."

And throws back his head and laughs out loud at the way
the guys hustled to get their bets down.

That laugh banged around the day room all evening, and
all the time he was dealing he was joking and talking and trying to get the players to laugh along with him. But they were
all afraid to loosen up; it'd been too long. He gave up trying
and settled down to serious dealing. They won the deal off him
a time or two, but he always bought it back or fought it back,
and the cigarettes on each side of him grew in bigger and bigger
pyramid stacks.

Then just before nine-thirty he started letting them win,
lets them win it all back so fast they don't hardly remember

losing. He pays out the last couple of cigarettes and lays down the deck and leans back with a sigh and shoves the cap out of his eyes, and the game is done.

"Well, sir, win a few, lose the rest is what I say." He shakes his head so forlorn. "I don't know—I was always a pretty shrewd customer at twenty-one, but you birds may just be too *tough* for me. You got some kinda uncanny *knack*, makes a man leery of playing against such sharpies for real money tomorrow."

He isn't even kidding himself into thinking they fall for that. He let them win, and every one of us watching the game knows it. So do the players. But there still isn't a man raking his pile of cigarettes—cigarettes he didn't really win but only won back because they were his in the first place—that doesn't have a smirk on his face like he's the toughest gambler on the whole Mississippi.

The fat black boy and a black boy named Geever run us out of the day room and commence turning lights off with a little key on a chain, and as the ward gets dimmer and darker the eyes of the little birthmarked nurse in the station get bigger and brighter. She's at the door of the glass station, issuing nighttime pills to the men that shuffle past her in a line, and she's having a hard time keeping straight who gets poisoned with what tonight. She's not even watching where she pours the water. What has distracted her attention this way is that big redheaded man with the dreadful cap and the horrible-looking scar, coming her way. She's watching McMurphy walk away from the card table in the dark day room, his one horny hand twisting the red tuft of hair that sticks out of the little cup at the throat of his work-farm shirt, and I figure by the way she rears back when he reaches the door of the station that she's probably been warned about him beforehand by the Big Nurse. ("Oh, one more thing before I leave it in your hands tonight, Miss Pilbow; that new man sitting over there, the one with the garish red sideburns and facial lacerations—I've reason to believe he is a sex maniac.")

McMurphy sees how she's looking so scared and big-eyed at

him, so he sticks his head in the station door where she's issuing pills, and gives her a big friendly grin to get acquainted on. This flusters her so she drops the water pitcher on her foot. She gives a cry and hops on one foot, jerks her hand, and the pill she was about to give me leaps out of the little cup and right down the neck of her uniform where that birthmark stain runs like a river of wine down into a valley.

"Let me give you a hand, ma'am."

And that very hand comes through the station door, scarred and tattooed and the color of raw meat.

"Stay back! There are two aides on the ward with me!"

She rolls her eyes for the black boys, but they are off tying Chronics in bed, nowhere close enough to help in a hurry. McMurphy grins and turns the hand over so she can see he isn't holding a knife. All she can see is the light shining off the slick, waxy, callused palm.

"All I mean to *do*, miss, is to—"

"Stay back! Patients aren't allowed to enter the— Oh, stay back, I'm a *Catholic!*" and straightaway jerks at the gold chain around her neck so a cross flies out from between her bosoms, slingshots the lost pill up in the air! McMurphy strikes at the air right in front of her face. She screams and pops the cross in her mouth and clinches her eyes shut like she's about to get socked, stands like that, paper-white except for that stain which turns darker than ever, as though it sucked the blood from all the rest of her body. When she finally opens her eyes again there's that callused hand right in front of her with my little red capsule sitting in it.

"—*was* to pick up your waterin' can you dropped." He holds that out in the other hand.

Her breath comes out in a loud hiss. She takes the can from him. "Thank you. Good night, good night," and closes the door in the next man's face, no more pills tonight.

In the dorm McMurphy tosses the pill on my bed. "You want your sourball, Chief?"

I shake my head at the pill, and he flips it off the bed like it was a bug pestering him. It hops across the floor with a cricket scrabble. He goes to getting ready for bed, pulling off his clothes. The shorts under his work pants are coal black satin covered with big white whales with red eyes. He grins when he sees I'm looking at the shorts. "From a co-ed at Oregon State, Chief, a Literary major." He snaps the elastic with his thumb. "She gave them to me because she said I was a symbol."

His arms and neck and face are sunburned and bristled with curly orange hairs. He's got tattoos on each big shoulder; one says "Fighting Leathernecks" and has a devil with a red eye and red horns and an M-1 rifle, and the other is a poker hand fanned out across his muscle—aces and eights. He puts his roll of clothes on the nightstand next to my bed and goes to punching at his pillow. He's been assigned the bed right next to mine.

He gets between the sheets and tells me I better hit the sack myself, that here comes one of those black boys to douse the lights on us. I look around, and the black boy named Geever is coming, and I kick off my shoes and get in bed just as he walks up to tie a sheet across me. When he's finished with me he takes a last look around and giggles and flips the dorm lights off.

Except for the white powder of light from the Nurses' Station out in the hall, the dorm is dark. I can just make out McMurphy next to me, breathing deep and regular, the covers over him rising and falling. The breathing gets slower and slower, till I figure he's been asleep for a while. Then I hear a soft, throaty sound from his bed, like the chuckle of a horse. He's still awake and he's laughing to himself about something.

He stops laughing and whispers, "Why, you sure did give a jump when I told you that coon was coming, Chief. I thought somebody told me you was deef."

first time for a long, long time I'm in bed without taking that little red capsule (if I hide to keep from taking it, the night nurse with the birthmark sends the black boy named Geever out to hunt me down, hold me captive with his flashlight till she can get the needle ready), so I fake sleep when the black boy's coming past with his light.

When you take one of those red pills you don't just go to sleep; you're paralyzed with sleep, and all night long you can't wake, no matter what goes on around you. That's why the staff gives me the pills; at the old place I took to waking up at night and catching them performing all kinds of horrible crimes on the patients sleeping around me.

I lie still and slow my breathing, waiting to see if something is going to happen. It is dark my lord and I hear them slipping around out there in their rubber shoes; twice they peek in the dorm and run a flashlight over everybody. I keep my eyes shut and keep awake. I hear a wailing from up on Disturbed, loo loo *looo*—got some guy wired to pick up code signals.

"Oh, a beer, I think, fo' the long night ahead," I hear a black boy whisper to the other. Rubber shoes squeak off toward the Nurses' Station, where the refrigerator is. "You like a beer, sweet thing with a birthmark? Fo' the long night ahead?"

The guy upstairs hushes. The low whine of the devices in the walls gets quieter and quieter, till it hums down to nothing. Not a sound across the hospital—except for a dull, padded rumbling somewhere deep in the guts of the building, a sound that I never noticed before—a lot like the sound you hear when you're standing late at night on top of a big hydroelectric dam. Low, relentless, brute power.

The fat black boy stands out there in the hall where I can see him, looking all around and giggling. He walks toward the dorm door, slow, wiping the wet gray palms in his armpits. The light from the Nurses' Station throws his shadow on the dorm wall big as an elephant, gets smaller as he walks to the dorm door and looks in. He giggles again and unlocks the fuse box by the door and reaches in. "Tha's right, babies, sleep tight."

Twists a knob, and the whole floor goes to slipping down away from him standing in the door, lowering into the building like a platform in a grain elevator!

Not a thing but the dorm floor moves, and we're sliding away from the walls and door and the windows of the ward at a hell of a clip—beds, bedstands, and all. The machinery— probably a cog-and-track affair at each corner of the shaft—is greased silent as death. The only sound I hear is the guys breathing, and that drumming under us getting louder the farther down we go. The light of the dorm door five hundred yards back up this hole is nothing but a speck, dusting the square sides of the shaft with a dim powder. It gets dimmer and dimmer till a faraway scream comes echoing down the sides of the shaft— "Stay *back!*"—and the light goes out altogether.

The floor reaches some kind of solid bottom far down in the ground and stops with a soft jar. It's dead black, and I can feel the sheet around me choking off my wind. Just as I get the sheet untied, the floor starts sliding forward with a little jolt. Some kind of castors under it I can't hear. I can't even hear the guys around me breathing, and I realize all of a sudden it's because that drumming's gradually got so loud I can't hear anything else. We must be square in the middle of it. I go to clawing at that damned sheet tied across me and just about have it loose when a whole wall slides up, reveals a huge room of endless machines stretching clear out of sight, swarming with sweating, shirtless men running up and down catwalks, faces blank and dreamy in firelight thrown from a hundred blast furnaces.

It—everything I see—looks like it sounded, like the inside of a tremendous dam. Huge brass tubes disappear upward in the dark. Wires run to transformers out of sight. Grease and

cinders catch on everything, staining the couplings and motors
and dynamos red and coal black.

The workers all move at the same smooth sprint, an easy,
fluid stride. No one's in a hurry. One will hold up a second,
spin a dial, push a button, throw a switch, and one side of his
face flashes white like lightning from the spark of the connect-
ing switch, and run on, up steel steps and along a corrugated
iron catwalk—pass each other so smooth and close I hear the
slap of wet sides like the slap of a salmon's tail on water—stop
again, throw lightning from another switch, and run on again.
They twinkle in all directions clean on out of sight, these flash
pictures of the dreamy doll faces of the workmen.

A workman's eyes snap shut while he's going at full run, and
he drops in his tracks; two of his buddies running by grab him
up and lateral him into a furnace as they pass. The furnace
whoops a ball of fire and I hear the popping of a million tubes
like walking through a field of seed pods. This sound mixes
with the whirr and clang of the rest of the machines.

There's a rhythm to it, like a thundering pulse.

The dorm floor slides on out of the shaft and into the machine room. Right away I see what's straight above us—one of
those trestle affairs like you find in meat houses, rollers on
tracks to move carcasses from the cooler to the butcher without much lifting. Two guys in slacks, white shirts with the
sleeves turned back, and thin black ties are leaning on the catwalk above our beds, gesturing to each other as they talk,
cigarettes in long holders tracing lines of red light. They're
talking but you can't make out the words above the measured
roar rising all around them. One of the guys snaps his fingers,
and the nearest workman veers in a sharp turn and sprints to
his side. The guy points down at one of the beds with his
cigarette holder, and the worker trots off to the steel steplad-
der and runs down to our level, where he goes out of sight between two transformers huge as potato cellars.

When that worker appears again he's pulling a hook along
the trestle overhead and taking giant strides as he swings along
it. He passes my bed and a furnace whooping somewhere sud-

denly lights his face up right over mine, a face handsome and brutal and waxy like a mask, wanting nothing. I've seen a million faces like it.

He goes to the bed and with one hand grabs the old Vegetable Blastic by the heel and lifts him straight up like Blastic don't weigh more'n a few pounds; with the other hand the worker drives the hook through the tendon back of the heel, and the old guy's hanging there upside down, his moldy face blown up big, scared, the eyes scummed with mute fear. He keeps flapping both arms and the free leg till his pajama top falls around his head. The worker grabs the top and bunches and twists it like a burlap sack and pulls the trolley clicking back over the trestle to the catwalk and looks up to where those two guys in white shirts are standing. One of the guys takes a scalpel from a holster at his belt. There's a chain welded to the scalpel. The guy lowers it to the worker, loops the other end of the chain around the railing so the worker can't run off with a weapon.

The worker takes the scalpel and slices up the front of old Blastic with a clean swing and the old man stops thrashing around. I expect to be sick, but there's no blood or innards falling out like I was looking to see—just a shower of rust and ashes, and now and again a piece of wire or glass. Worker's standing there to his knees in what looks like clinkers.

A furnace got its mouth open somewhere, licks up somebody.

I think about jumping up and running around and waking up McMurphy and Harding and as many of the guys as I can, but there wouldn't be any sense in it. If I shook somebody awake he'd say, Why you crazy idiot, what the hell's eating you? And then probably help one of the workers lift me onto one of those hooks himself, saying, How about let's see what the insides of an *Indian* are like?

I hear the high, cold, whistling wet breath of the fog machine, see the first wisps of it come seeping out from under McMurphy's bed. I hope he knows enough to hide in the fog.

I hear a silly prattle reminds me of somebody familiar, and I roll enough to get a look down the other way. It's the hairless

Public Relation with the bloated face, that the patients are always arguing about why it's bloated. "I'll say he *does*," they'll argue. "Me, I'll say he doesn't; you ever hear of a guy *really* who wore one?" "Yeh, but you ever hear of a guy like *him* before?" The first patient shrugs and nods. "Interesting point."

Now he's stripped except for a long undershirt with fancy monograms sewed red on front and back. And I see once and for all (the undershirt rides up his back some as he comes walking past, giving me a peek) that he definitely *does* wear one, laced so tight it might blow up any second.

And dangling from the stays he's got half a dozen withered objects, tied by the hair like scalps.

He's carrying a little flask of something that he sips from to keep his throat open for talking, and a camphor hanky he puts in front of his nose from time to time to stop out the stink. There's a clutch of schoolteachers and college girls and the like hurrying after him. They wear blue aprons and their hair in pin curls. They are listening to him give a brief lecture on the tour.

He thinks of something funny and has to stop his lecture long enough for a swig from the flask to stop the giggling. During the pause one of his pupils stargazes around and sees the gutted Chronic dangling by his heel. She gasps and jumps back. The Public Relation turns and catches sight of the corpse and rushes to take one of those limp hands and give it a spin. The student shrinks forward for a cautious look, face in a trance.

"You *see?* You *see?*" He squeals and rolls his eyes and spews stuff from his flask he's laughing so hard. He's laughing till I think he'll explode.

When he finally drowns the laughing he starts back along the row of machines and goes into his lecture again. He stops suddenly and slaps his forehead—"Oh, scatterbrained *me!*"—and comes running back to the hanging Chronic to rip off another trophy and tie it to his girdle.

Right and left there are other things happening just as bad— crazy, horrible things too goofy and outlandish to cry about and too much true to laugh about—but the fog is getting thick enough I don't have to watch. And somebody's tugging at my arm. I know already what will happen: somebody'll drag me out of the fog and we'll be back on the ward and there won't be a sign of what went on tonight and if I was fool enough to try and tell anybody about it they'd say, Idiot, you just had a nightmare; things as crazy as a big machine room down in the bowels of a dam where people get cut up by robot workers don't exist.

But if they don't exist, how can a man see them?

It's Mr. Turkle that pulls me out of the fog by the arm, shaking me and grinning. He says, "You havin' a bad dream, Mistuh Bromden." He's the aide works the long lonely shift from 11 to 7, an old Negro man with a big sleepy grin on the end of a long wobbly neck. He smells like he's had a little to drink. "Back to sleep now, Mistuh Bromden."

Some nights he'll untie the sheet from across me if it's so tight I squirm around. He wouldn't do it if he thought the day crew knew it was him, because they'd probably fire him, but he figures the day crew will think it was me untied it. I think he really does it to be kind, to help—but he makes sure he's safe first.

This time he doesn't untie the sheet but walks away from me to help two aides I never saw before and a young doctor lift old Blastic onto the stretcher and carry him out, covered with a sheet—handle him more careful than anybody ever handled him before in all his life.

ome morning, McMurphy is up before I am, the first time anybody been up before me since Uncle Jules the Wallwalker was here. Jules was a shrewd old white-haired Negro with a theory the world was being tipped over on its side during the night by the black boys; he used to slip out in the early mornings, aiming to catch them tipping it. Like Jules, I'm up early in the mornings to watch what machinery they're sneaking onto the ward or installing in the shaving room, and usually it's just me and the black boys in the hall for fifteen minutes before the next patient is out of bed. But this morning I hear McMurphy out there in the latrine as I come out of the covers. Hear him singing! Singing so you'd think he didn't have a worry in the world. His voice is clear and strong slapping up against the cement and steel.

" 'Your horses are hungry, that's what she did say.' " He's enjoying the way the sound rings in the latrine. " 'Come sit down beside me, an' feed them some hay.' " He gets a breath, and his voice jumps a key, gaining pitch and power till it's joggling the wiring in all the walls. " 'My horses ain't hungry, they won't eat your hay-ay-aeee.' " He holds the note and plays with it, then swoops down with the rest of the verse to finish it off. " 'So fare-thee-well darlin', I'm gone on my way.' "

Singing! Everybody's thunderstruck. They haven't heard such a thing in years, not on this ward. Most of the Acutes in the dorm are up on their elbows, blinking and listening. They look at one another and raise their eyebrows. How come the black boys haven't hushed him up out there? They never let anybody raise that much racket before, did they? How come they treat this new guy different? He's a man made outa skin and bone that's due to get weak and pale and die, just like the rest of us. He lives under the same laws, gotta eat, bumps up against the same troubles; these things make him just as vulnerable to the Combine as anybody else, don't they?

But the new guy *is* different, and the Acutes can see it, different from anybody been coming on this ward for the past ten years, different from anybody they ever met outside. He's just as vulnerable, maybe, but the Combine didn't get him.

" 'My wagons are loaded,' " he sings, " 'my whip's in my hand. . . .' "

How'd he manage to slip the collar? Maybe, like old Pete, the Combine missed getting to him soon enough with controls. Maybe he growed up so wild all over the country, batting around from one place to another, never around one town longer'n a few months when he was a kid so a school never got much a hold on him, logging, gambling, running carnival wheels, traveling lightfooted and fast, keeping on the move so much that the Combine never had a chance to get anything installed. Maybe that's it, he never gave the Combine a chance, just like he never gave the black boy a chance to get to him with the thermometer yesterday morning, because a moving target is hard to hit.

No wife wanting new linoleum. No relatives pulling at him with watery old eyes. No one to *care* about, which is what makes him free enough to be a good con man. And maybe the reason the black boys don't rush into that latrine and put a stop to his singing is because they *know* he's out of control, and they remember that time with old Pete and what a man out of control can do. And they can see that McMurphy's a lot bigger than old Pete; if it comes down to getting the best of him, it's going to take all three of them and the Big Nurse waiting on the sidelines with a needle. The Acutes nod at one another; that's the reason, they figure, that the black boys haven't stopped his singing where they would stop any of the rest of us.

I come out of the dorm into the hall just as McMurphy comes out of the latrine. He's got his cap on and not much else, just a towel grabbed around his hips. He's holding a toothbrush in his other hand. He stands in the hall, looking up and down, rocking up on his toes to keep off the cold tile as much as he can. Picks him out a black boy, the least one, and walks up to him and whaps him on the shoulder just like they'd been friends all their lives.

"Hey there, old buddy, what's my chance of gettin' some toothpaste for brushin' my grinders?"

The black boy's dwarf head swivels and comes nose to knuckle with that hand. He frowns at it, then takes a quick check where's the other two black boys just in case, and tells McMurphy they don't open the cabinet till six-forty-five. "It's a policy," he says.

"Is that right? I mean, is that where they keep the toothpaste? In the cabinet?"

"Tha's right, locked in the cabinet."

The black boy tries to go back to polishing the baseboards, but that hand is still lopped over his shoulder like a big red clamp.

"Locked in the cabinet, is it? Well well well, now why do you reckon they keep the toothpaste locked up? I mean, it ain't like it's dangerous, is it? You can't poison a man with it, can you? You couldn't brain some guy with the tube, could you? What reason you suppose they have for puttin' something as harmless as a little tube of toothpaste under lock and key?"

"It's ward policy, Mr. McMurphy, tha's the reason." And when he sees that this last reason don't affect McMurphy like it should, he frowns at that hand on his shoulder and adds, "What you s'pose it'd be like if *evahbody* was to brush their teeth whenever they took a notion to brush?"

McMurphy turns loose the shoulder, tugs at that tuft of red wool at his neck, and thinks this over. "Uh-huh, uh-huh, I think I can see what you're drivin' at: ward policy is for those that can't brush after every meal."

"My *gaw*, don't you *see?*"

"Yes, now, I do. You're saying people'd be brushin' their teeth whenever the spirit moved them."

"Tha's right, tha's why we—"

"And, lordy, can you imagine? Teeth bein' brushed at six-thirty, six-twenty—who can tell? maybe even six o'clock. Yeah, I can see your point."

He winks past the black boy at me standing against the wall.

"I gotta get this baseboard cleaned, McMurphy."

"Oh. I didn't mean to keep you from your job." He starts to back away as the black boy bends to his work again. Then he comes forward and leans over to look in the can at the black boy's side. "Well, look here; what do we have here?"

The black boy peers down. "Look where?"

"Look here in this old can, Sam. What is the stuff in this old can?"

"Tha's . . . soap powder."

"Well, I generally use paste, but"— McMurphy runs his toothbrush down in the powder and swishes it around and pulls it out and taps it on the side of the can—"but this will do fine for me. I thank you. We'll look into that ward policy business later."

And he heads back to the latrine, where I can hear his singing garbled by the piston beat of his toothbrushing.

That black boy's standing there looking after him with his scrub rag hanging limp in his gray hand. After a minute he blinks and looks around and sees I been watching and comes over and drags me down the hall by the drawstring on my pajamas and pushes me to a place on the floor I just did yesterday.

"There! Damn you, right there! That's where I want you workin', not gawkin' around like some big useless cow! There! There!"

And I lean over and go to mopping with my back to him so he won't see me grin. I feel good, seeing McMurphy get that black boy's goat like not many men could. Papa used to be able to do it—spraddle-legged, dead-panned, squinting up at the sky that first time the government men showed up to negotiate about buying off the treaty. "Canada honkers up there," Papa says, squinting up. Government men look, rattling papers. "What are you—? In July? There's no—uh—geese this time of year. Uh, no geese."

They had been talking like tourists from the East who figure you've got to talk to Indians so they'll understand. Papa didn't

seem to take any notice of the way they talked. He kept looking at the sky. "Geese up there, white man. You know it. Geese
this year. And last year. And the year before and the year before."

The men looked at one another and cleared their throats.
"Yes. Maybe true, Chief Bromden. Now. Forget geese. Pay attention to contract. What we offer could greatly benefit you—
your people—change the lives of the red man."

Papa said, ". . . and the year before and the year before and
the year before . . ."

By the time it dawned on the government men that they
were being poked fun at, all the council who'd been sitting on
the porch of our shack, putting pipes in the pockets of their
red and black plaid wool shirts and taking them back out again,
grinning at one another and at Papa—they had all busted up
laughing fit to kill. Uncle R & J Wolf was rolling on the
ground, gasping with laughter and saying, "You know it, white
man."

It sure did get their goat; they turned without saying a word
and walked off toward the highway, red-necked, us laughing
behind them. I forget sometimes what laughter can do.

The Big Nurse's key hits the lock, and the black boy is up to
her soon as she's in the door, shifting from foot to foot like a
kid asking to pee. I'm close enough I hear McMurphy's name
come into his conversation a couple of times, so I know he's
telling her about McMurphy brushing his teeth, completely
forgetting to tell her about the old Vegetable who died during the night. Waving his arms and trying to tell her what that
fool redhead's been up to already, so early in the morning—
disrupting things, goin' contrary to ward policy, can't she *do*
something?

She glares at the black boy till he stops fidgeting, then looks
up the hall to where McMurphy's singing is booming out of
the latrine door louder than ever. " 'Oh, your parents don't like
me, they say I'm too po-o-or; they say I'm not worthy to enter
your door.' "

Her face is puzzled at first; like the rest of us, it's been so long since she's heard singing it takes her a second to recognize what it is.

" 'Hard livin's my pleasure, my money's my o-o-own, an' them that don't like me, they can leave me alone.' "

She listens a minute more to make sure she isn't hearing things; then she goes to puffing up. Her nostrils flare open, and every breath she draws she gets bigger, as big and tough-looking's I seen her get over a patient since Taber was here. She works the hinges in her elbows and fingers. I hear a small squeak. She starts moving, and I get back against the wall, and when she rumbles past she's already big as a truck, trailing that wicker bag behind in her exhaust like a semi behind a Jimmy Diesel. Her lips are parted, and her smile's going out before her like a radiator grill. I can smell the hot oil and magneto spark when she goes past, and every step hits the floor she blows up a size bigger, blowing and puffing, roll down anything in her path! I'm scared to think *what* she'll do.

Then, just as she's rolling along at her biggest and meanest, McMurphy steps out of the latrine door right in front of her, holding that towel around his hips—stops her *dead!* She shrinks to about head-high to where that towel covers him, and he's grinning down on her. Her own grin is giving way, sagging at the edges.

"Good morning, Miss Rat-shed! How's things on the outside?"

"You can't run around here—in a *towel!*"

"No?" He looks down at the part of the towel she's eye to eye with, and it's wet and skin tight. "Towels against ward policy too? Well, I guess there's nothin' to do exce—"

"*Stop!* don't you dare. You get back in that dorm and get your clothes on this *instant!*"

She sounds like a teacher bawling out a student, so McMurphy hangs his head like a student and says in a voice sounds like he's about to cry, "I can't do that, ma'am. I'm afraid some thief in the night boosted my clothes whilst I slept. I sleep awful sound on the mattresses you have here."

"Somebody boosted . . . ?"

"Pinched. Jobbed. Swiped. Stole," he says happily. "You know, man, like somebody boosted my threads." Saying this tickles him so he goes into a little barefooted dance before her.

"Stole your clothes?"

"That looks like the whole of it."

"But—prison clothes? Why?"

He stops jigging around and hangs his head again. "All I know is that they were there when I went to bed and gone when I got up. Gone slick as a whistle. Oh, I do *know* they were nothing but prison clothes, coarse and faded and uncouth, ma'am, well I know it—and prison clothes may not seem like much to those as has *more*. But to a nude man—"

"That outfit," she says, realizing, "was *supposed* to be picked up. You were issued a uniform of green convalescents this morning."

He shakes his head and sighs, but still don't look up. "No. No, I'm afraid I wasn't. Not a thing this morning but the cap that's on my head and—"

"Williams," she hollers down to the black boy who's still at the ward door like he might make a run for it. "Williams, can you come here a moment?"

He crawls to her like a dog to a whipping.

"Williams, why doesn't this patient have an issue of convalescents?"

The black boy is relieved. He straightens up and grins, raises that gray hand and points down the other end of the hall to one of the big ones. "Mistuh Washington over there is 'signed to the laundry duty this mornin'. Not me. No."

"Mr. *Washington!*" She nails him with his mop poised over the bucket, freezes him there. "Will you come here a moment!"

The mop slides without a sound back in the bucket, and with slow, careful movements he leans the handle against the wall. He turns around and looks down at McMurphy and the least black boy and the nurse. He looks then to his left and to his right, like she might be yelling at somebody else.

"Come down here!"

He puts his hands in his pockets and starts shuffling down the hall to her. He never walks very fast, and I can see how if he don't get a move on she might freeze him and shatter him all to hell by just looking; all the hate and fury and frustration she was planning to use on McMurphy is beaming out down the hall at the black boy, and he can feel it blast against him like a blizzard wind, slowing him more than ever. He has to lean into it, pulling his arms around him. Frost forms in his hair and eyebrows. He leans farther forward, but his steps are getting slower; he'll never make it.

Then McMurphy takes to whistling "Sweet Georgia Brown," and the nurse looks away from the black boy just in time. Now she's madder and more frustrated than ever, madder'n I ever saw her get. Her doll smile is gone, stretched tight and thin as a red-hot wire. If some of the patients could be out to see her now, McMurphy could start collecting his bets.

The black boy finally gets to her, and it took him two hours. She draws a long breath. "Washington, why wasn't this man issued a change of greens this morning? Couldn't you see he had nothing on but a towel?"

"And my cap," McMurphy whispers, tapping the brim with his finger.

"Mr. Washington?"

The big black boy looks at the little one who pointed him out, and the little black boy commences to fidget again. The big boy looks at him a long time with those radio-tube eyes, plans to square things with *him* later; then the head turns and he looks McMurphy up and down, taking in the hard, heavy shoulders, the lopsided grin, the scar on the nose, the hand clamping the towel in place, and then he looks at the nurse.

"I guess—" he starts out.

"You *guess!* You'll do more than *guess!* You'll get him a uniform this instant, Mr. Washington, or spend the next two weeks working on Geriatrics Ward! Yes. You may need a month of bedpans and slab baths to refresh your appreciation of just how little work you aides have to do on this ward. If this was one of the other wards, who do you think would be scouring the hall all day? Mr. Bromden here? No, you know who it would be. We excuse you aides from most of your house-keeping duties to enable you to see to the patients. And that means seeing that they don't parade around exposed. What do you think would have happened if one of the young nurses had come in early and found a patient running round the halls without a uniform? What do you think!"

The big black boy isn't too sure what, but he gets her drift and ambles off to the linen room to get McMurphy a set of greens—probably ten sizes too small—and ambles back and holds it out to him with a look of the clearest hate I ever saw. McMurphy just looks confused, like he don't know how to take the outfit the black boy's handing to him, what with one hand holding the toothbrush and the other hand holding up the towel. He finally winks at the nurse and shrugs and un-wraps the towel, drapes it over her shoulder like she was a wooden rack.

I see he had his shorts on under the towel all along.

I think for a fact that she'd rather he'd of been stark naked under that towel than had on those shorts. She's glaring at those big white whales leaping round on his shorts in pure wordless outrage. That's more'n she can take. It's a full minute before she can pull herself together enough to turn on the least black boy; her voice is shaking out of control, she's so mad.

"Williams . . . I believe . . . you were supposed to have the windows of the Nurses' Station polished by the time I ar-rived this morning." He scuttles off like a black and white bug. "And you, Washington—and you . . ." Washington shuffles back to his bucket in almost a trot. She looks around again, wondering who else she can light into. She spots me, but by this time some of the other patients are out of the dorm and wondering about the little clutch of us here in the hall. She closes her eyes and concentrates. She can't have them see her face like this, white and warped with fury. She uses all the power of control that's in her. Gradually the lips gather to-gether again under the little white nose, run together, like the red-hot wire had got hot enough to melt, shimmer a second, then click solid as the molten metal sets, growing cold and strangely dull. Her lips part, and her tongue comes between them, a chunk of slag. Her eyes open again, and they have that strange dull and cold and flat look the lips have, but she goes into her good-morning routine like there was nothing different about her, figuring the patients'll be too sleepy to notice.

"Good morning, Mr. Sefelt, are your teeth any better? Good morning Mr. Fredrickson, did you and Mr. Sefelt have a good night last night? You bed right next to each other, don't you? Incidentally, it's been brought to my attention that you two have made some arrangement with your medication—you are letting Bruce have your medication, aren't you, Mr. Sefelt? We'll discuss that later. Good morning, Billy; I saw your mother on the way in, and she told me to be sure to tell you she thought of you all the time and *knew* you wouldn't disappoint her. Good morning, Mr. Harding—why, look, your fingertips are red and raw. Have you been chewing your fingernails again?"

Before they could answer, even if there was some answer to make, she turns to McMurphy still standing there in his shorts. Harding looks at the shorts and whistles.

"And you, Mr. McMurphy," she says, smiling, sweet as sugar, "if you are finished showing off your manly physique and your gaudy underpants, I think you had better go back in the dorm and put on your greens."

He tips his cap to her and to the patients ogling and poking fun at his white-whale shorts, and goes to the dorm without a word. She turns and starts off in the other direction, her flat red smile going out before her; before she's got the door closed on her glass station, his singing is rolling from the dorm door into the hall again.

" 'She took me to her parlor, and coo-oo-ooled me with her fan' "—I can hear the whack as he slaps his bare belly—" 'whispered low in her mamma's ear, I luh-uhvvv that gamblin' man.' "

Sweeping the dorm soon's it's empty, I'm after dust mice under his bed when I get a smell of something that makes me realize for the first time since I been in the hospital that this big dorm full of beds, sleeps forty grown men, has always been sticky with a thousand other smells—smells of germicide, zinc ointment, and foot powder, smell of piss and sour old-man manure, of Pablum and eyewash, of musty shorts and socks musty even when they're fresh back from the laundry, the stiff odor of starch in the linen, the acid stench of morning mouths, the banana smell of machine oil, and sometimes the smell of singed hair—but never before now, before he came in, the man smell of dust and dirt from the open fields, and sweat, and work.

all through breakfast McMurphy's talking and laughing a mile a minute. After this morning he thinks the Big Nurse is going to be a snap. He don't know he just caught her off guard and, if anything, made her strengthen herself.

He's being the clown, working at getting some of the guys to laugh. It bothers him that the best they can do is grin weakly and snigger sometimes. He prods at Billy Bibbit, sitting across the table from him, says in a secret voice, "Hey, Billy boy, you remember that time in Seattle you and me picked up those two twitches? One of the best rolls I ever had."

Billy's eyes bob up from his plate. He opens his mouth but can't say a thing. McMurphy turns to Harding.

"We'd never have brought it off, neither, picking them up on the spur of the moment that way, except that they'd heard tell of Billy Bibbit. Billy 'Club' Bibbit, he was known as in

them days. Those girls were about to take off when one looked
at him and says 'Are you *the* renowned Billy Club Bibbit? Of
the famous fourteen inches?' And Billy ducked his head and
blushed—like he's doin' now—and we were a shoo-in. And I
remember, when we got them up to the hotel, there was this
woman's voice from over near Billy's bed, says, 'Mister Bibbit,
I'm disappointed in you; I heard that you had four—four—for
goodness *sakes!*' "

And whoops and slaps his leg and gooses Billy with his
thumb till I think Billy will fall in a dead faint from blushing
and grinning.

McMurphy says that as a matter of fact a couple of sweet
twitches like those two is the *only* thing this hospital does lack.
The bed they give a man here, finest he's ever slept in, and
what a fine table they do spread. He can't figure why everybody's so glum about being locked up here.

"Look at me now," he tells the guys and lifts a glass to the
light, "getting my first glass of orange juice in six months.
Hooee, that's good. I ask you, what did I get for breakfast at
that work farm? What was I served? Well, I can describe what
it *looked* like, but I sure couldn't hang a name on it; morning
noon and night it was burnt black and had potatoes in it and
looked like roofing glue. I know one thing; it wasn't orange
juice. Look at me now: bacon, toast, butter, eggs—coffee the
little honey in the kitchen even asks me if I like it black or
white thank you—and a great! big! cold glass of orange juice.
Why, you couldn't *pay* me to leave this place!"

He gets seconds on everything and makes a date with the girl
pours coffee in the kitchen for when he gets discharged, and
he compliments the Negro cook on sunnysiding the best eggs
he ever ate. There's bananas for the corn flakes, and he gets a
handful, tells the black boy that he'll filch him one 'cause he
looks so starved, and the black boy shifts his eyes to look down
the hall to where the nurse is sitting in her glass case, and says
it ain't allowed for the help to eat with the patients.

"Against ward policy?"

"Tha's right."

"Tough luck"—and peels three bananas right under the black boy's nose and eats one after the other, tells the boy that any time you want one snuck outa the mess hall for you, Sam, you just give the word.

When McMurphy finishes his last banana he slaps his belly and gets up and heads for the door, and the big black boy blocks the door and tells him the rule that patients sit in the mess hall till they all leave at seven-thirty. McMurphy stares at him like he can't believe he's hearing right, then turns and looks at Harding. Harding nods his head, so McMurphy shrugs and goes back to his chair. "I sure don't want to go against that goddamned policy."

The clock at the end of the mess hall shows it's a quarter after seven, lies about how we only been sitting here fifteen minutes when you can tell it's been at least an hour. Everybody is finished eating and leaned back, watching the big hand to move to seven-thirty. The black boys take away the Vegetables' splattered trays and wheel the two old men down to get hosed off. In the mess hall about half the guys lay their heads on their arms, figuring to get a little sleep before the black boys get back. There's nothing else to do, with no cards or magazines or picture puzzles. Just sleep or watch the clock.

But McMurphy can't keep still for that; he's got to be up to something. After about two minutes of pushing food scraps around his plate with his spoon, he's ready for more excitement. He hooks his thumbs in his pockets and tips back and one-eyes that clock up on the wall. Then he rubs his nose.

"You know—that old clock up there puts me in mind of the *targets* at the target range at Fort Riley. That's where I got my first medal, a sharpshooter medal. Dead-Eye Murphy. Who wants to lay me a pore little dollar that I can't put this dab of butter square in the center of the face of that clock up there, or at least *on* the face?"

He gets three bets and takes up his butter pat and puts it on his knife, gives it a flip. It sticks a good six inches or so to the left of the clock, and everybody kids him about it until he pays his bets. They're still riding him about did he mean

Dead-Eye or Dead-Eyes when the least black boy gets back from hosing Vegetables and everybody looks into his plate and keeps quiet. The black boy senses something is in the air, but he can't see what. And he probably never would of known except old Colonel Matterson is gazing around, and *he* sees the butter stuck up on the wall and this causes him to point up at it and go into one of his lessons, explaining to us all in his patient, rumbling voice, just like what he said made sense.

"The but-ter . . . is the Re-pub-li-can party. . . ."

The black boy looks where the colonel is pointing, and there that butter is, easing down the wall like a yellow snail. He blinks at it but he doesn't say a word, doesn't even bother looking around to make certain who flipped it up there.

McMurphy is whispering and nudging the Acutes sitting around him, and in a minute they all nod, and he lays three dollars on the table and leans back. Everybody turns in his chair and watches that butter sneak on down the wall, starting, hanging still, shooting ahead and leaving a shiny trail behind it on the paint. Nobody says a word. They look at the butter, then at the clock, then back at the butter. The clock's moving now.

The butter makes it down to the floor about a half a minute before seven-thirty, and McMurphy gets back all the money he lost.

The black boy wakes up and turns away from the greasy stripe on the wall and says we can go, and McMurphy walks out of the mess hall, folding his money in his pocket. He puts his arms around the black boy's shoulders and half walks, half carries him, down the hall toward the day room. "The day's half gone, Sam, ol' buddy, an' I'm just barely breaking even. I'll have to hustle to catch up. How about breaking out that deck of cards you got locked securely in that cabinet, and I'll see if I can make myself heard over that loudspeaker."

Spends most of that morning hustling to catch up by dealing more blackjack, playing for IOUs now instead of cigarettes. He moves the blackjack table two or three times to try to get out from under the speaker. You can tell it's getting on his nerves. Finally he goes to the Nurses' Station and raps on a pane of glass till the Big Nurse swivels in her chair and opens the door, and he asks her how about turning that infernal noise off for a while. She's calmer than ever now, back in her seat behind her pane of glass; there's no heathen running around half-naked to unbalance her. Her smile is settled and solid. She closes her eyes and shakes her head and tells McMurphy very pleasantly, No.

"Can't you even ease down on the volume? It ain't like the whole state of Oregon needed to hear Lawrence Welk play "Tea for Two" three times every hour, all day long! If it was soft enough to hear a man shout his bets across the table I might get a game of poker going—"

"You've been told, Mr. McMurphy, that it's against the policy to gamble for money on the ward."

"Okay, then down soft enough to gamble for matches, for fly buttons—just turn the damn thing down!"

"Mr. McMurphy"—she waits and lets her calm schoolteacher tone sink in before she goes on; she knows every Acute on the ward is listening to them—"do you want to know what I think? I think you are being very selfish. Haven't you noticed there are others in this hospital besides yourself? There are old men here who couldn't hear the radio at all if it were lower, old fellows who simply aren't capable of reading, or working puzzles—or playing cards to win other men's cigarettes. Old fellows like Matterson and Kittling, that music coming from the loudspeaker is all they have. And you want to take that away from them. We like to hear suggestions and requests whenever we can, but I should think you might at least give some thought to others before you make your requests."

He turns and looks over at the Chronic side and sees there's something to what she says. He takes off his cap and runs his hand in his hair, finally turns back to her. He knows as well as she does that all the Acutes are listening to everything they say.

"Okay—I never thought about that."

"I thought you hadn't."

He tugs at that little tuft of red showing out of the neck of his greens, then says. "Well, hey; what do you say to us taking the card game someplace else? Some other room? Like, say, that room you people put the tables in during that meeting. There's nothing in there all the rest of the day. You could unlock that room and let the card-players go in there, and leave the old men out here with their radio—a good deal all around."

She smiles and closes her eyes again and shakes her head gently. "Of course, you may take the suggestion up with the rest of the staff at some time, but I'm afraid everyone's feelings will correspond with mine: we do not have adequate coverage for two day rooms. There isn't enough personnel. And I wish you wouldn't lean against the glass there, please; your hands are oily and staining the window. That means extra work for some of the other men."

He jerks his hand away, and I see he starts to say something and then stops, realizing she didn't leave him anything else to say, unless he wants to start cussing at her. His face and neck are red. He draws a long breath and concentrates on his will power, the way she did this morning, and tells her that he is very sorry to have bothered her, and goes back to the card table.

Everybody on the ward can feel that it's started.

At eleven o'clock the doctor comes to the day-room door and calls over to McMurphy that he'd like to have him come down to his office for an interview. "I interview all new admissions on the second day."

McMurphy lays down his cards and stands up and walks over to the doctor. The doctor asks him how his night was, but McMurphy just mumbles an answer.

"You look deep in thought today, Mr. McMurphy."

"Oh, I'm a thinker all right," McMurphy says, and they walk off together down the hall. When they come back what seems like days later, they're both grinning and talking and happy about something. The doctor is wiping tears off his glasses and looks like he's actually been laughing, and McMurphy is back as loud and full of brass and swagger as ever. He's that way all through lunch, and at one o'clock he's the first one in his seat for the meeting, his eyes blue and ornery from his place in the corner.

The Big Nurse comes into the day room with her covey of student nurses and her basket of notes. She picks the log book up from the table and frowns into it a minute (nobody's informed on anybody all day long), then goes to her seat beside the door. She picks up some folders from the basket on her lap and riffles through them till she finds the one on Harding.

"As I recall, we were making quite a bit of headway yesterday with Mr. Harding's problem—"

"Ah—before we go into that," the doctor says, "I'd like to interrupt a moment, if I might. Concerning a talk Mr. McMurphy and I had in my office this morning. Reminiscing, actually. Talking over old times. You see Mr. McMurphy and I find we have something in common—we went to the same high school."

The nurses look at one another and wonder what's got into this man. The patients glance at McMurphy grinning from his corner and wait for the doctor to go on. He nods his head.

"Yes, the same high school. And in the course of our reminiscing we happened to bring up the carnivals the school used to sponsor—marvelous, noisy, gala occasions. Decorations, crepe streamers, booths, games—it was always one of the prime events of the year. I—as I mentioned to McMurphy—was the chairman of the high-school carnival both my junior and senior year—wonderful carefree years . . ."

It's got real quiet in the day room. The doctor raises his head, peers around to see if he's making a fool of himself. The Big Nurse is giving him a look that shouldn't leave any doubts about it, but he doesn't have on his glasses, and the look misses him.

"Anyway—to put an end to this maudlin display of nostalgia—in the course of our conversation McMurphy and I wondered what would be the attitude of some of the men toward a carnival here on the ward?"

He puts on his glasses and peers around again. Nobody's

jumping up and down at the idea. Some of us can remember Taber trying to engineer a carnival a few years back, and what happened to it. As the doctor waits, a silence rears up from out of the nurse and looms over everybody, daring anybody to challenge it. I know McMurphy can't because he was in on the planning of the carnival, and just as I'm thinking that nobody will be fool enough to break that silence, Cheswick, who sits right next to McMurphy, gives a grunt and is on his feet, rubbing his ribs, before he knows what happened.

"Uh—I personally believe, see"—he looks down at McMurphy's fist on the chair arm beside him, with that big stiff thumb sticking straight up out of it like a cow prod—"that a carnival is a real good idea. Something to break the monotony."

"That's right, Charley," the doctor says, appreciating Cheswick's support, "and not altogether without therapeutic value."

"Certainly not," Cheswick says, looking happier now. "No. Lots of therapeutics in a carnival. You bet."

"It would b-b-be fun," Billy Bibbit says.

"Yeah, that too," Cheswick says. "We could do it, Doctor Spivey, sure we could. Scanlon can do his human bomb act, and I can make a ring toss in Occupational Therapy."

"I'll tell fortunes," Martini says and squints at a spot above his head.

"I'm rather good at diagnosing pathologies from palm reading, myself," Harding says.

"Good, good," Cheswick says and claps his hands. He's never had anybody support anything he said before.

"Myself," McMurphy drawls, "I'd be honored to work a skillo wheel. Had a little experience . . ."

"Oh, there are numerous possibilities," the doctor says, sitting up straight in his chair and really warming to it. "Why, I've got a million ideas. . . ."

He talks full steam ahead for another five minutes. You can tell a lot of the ideas are ideas he's already talked over with McMurphy. He describes games, booths, talks of selling tickets, then stops as suddenly as though the Nurse's look had hit him right between the eyes. He blinks at her and asks, "What do you think of the idea, Miss Ratched? Of a carnival? Here, on the ward?"

"I agree that it may have a number of therapeutic possibilities," she says, and waits. She lets that silence rear up from her again. When she's sure nobody's going to challenge it, she goes on. "But I also believe that an idea like this should be discussed in staff meeting before a decision is reached. Wasn't that your idea, Doctor?"

"Of course. I merely thought, understand, I would feel out some of the men first. But certainly, a staff meeting first. Then we'll continue our plans."

Everybody knows that's all there is to the carnival.

The Big Nurse starts to bring things back into hand by rattling the folio she's holding. "Fine. Then if there is no other new business—and if Mr. Cheswick will be seated—I think we might go right on into the discussion. We have"— she takes her watch from the basket and looks at it—"forty-eight minutes left. So, as I—"

"Oh. Hey, wait. I remembered there is some other new business." McMurphy has his hand up, fingers snapping. She looks at the hand for a long time before she says anything.

"Yes, Mr. McMurphy?"

"Not me, Doctor Spivey has. Doc, tell 'em what you come up with about the hard-of-hearing guys and the radio."

The nurse's head gives one little jerk, barely enough to see, but my heart is suddenly roaring. She puts the folio back in the basket, turns to the doctor.

"Yes," says the doctor. "I very nearly forgot." He leans back and crosses his legs and puts his fingertips together; I can see he's still in good spirits about his carnival. "You see, McMurphy and I were talking about that age-old problem we have on this ward: the mixed population, the young and the old together. It's not the most ideal surroundings for our Therapeutic Community, but Administration says there's no helping it with the Geriatric Building overloaded the way it is. I'll be the first to admit it's not an absolutely pleasant situation for anyone concerned. In our talk, however, McMurphy and

I did happen to come up with an idea which might make things more pleasant for both age groups. McMurphy mentioned that he had noticed some of the old fellows seemed to have difficulty hearing the radio. He suggested the speaker might be turned up louder so the Chronics with auditory weaknesses could hear it. A very humane suggestion, I think."

McMurphy gives a modest wave of his hand, and the doctor nods at him and goes on.

"But I told him I had received previous complaints from some of the younger men that the radio is already so loud it hinders conversation and reading. McMurphy said he hadn't thought of this, but mentioned that it did seem a shame that those who wished to read couldn't get off by themselves where it was quiet and leave the radio for those who wished to listen. I agreed with him that it did seem a shame and was ready to drop the matter when I happened to think of the old tub room where we store the tables during the ward meeting. We don't use the room at all otherwise; there's no longer a need for the hydrotherapy it was designed for, now that we have the new drugs. So how would the group like to have that room as a sort of second day room, a *game* room, shall we say?"

The group isn't saying. They know whose play it is next. She folds Harding's folio back up and puts it on her lap and crosses her hands over it, looking around the room just like somebody might dare have something to say. When it's clear nobody's going to talk till she does, her head turns again to the doctor. "It sounds like a fine plan, Doctor Spivey, and I appreciate Mr. McMurphy's interest in the other patients, but I'm terribly afraid we don't have the personnel to cover a second day room."

And is so certain that this should be the end of it she starts to open the folio again. But the doctor has thought this through more than she figured.

"I thought of that too, Miss Ratched. But since it will be largely the Chronic patients who remain here in the day room with the speaker—most of whom are restricted to lounges or wheel chairs—one aide and one nurse in here should easily be able to put down any riots or uprisings that might occur, don't you think?"

She doesn't answer, and she doesn't care much for his joking about riots and uprisings either, but her face doesn't change. The smile stays.

"So the other two aides and nurses can cover the men in the tub room, perhaps even better than here in a larger area. What do you think, men? Is it a workable idea? I'm rather enthused about it myself, and I say we give it a try, see what it's like for a few days. If it doesn't work, well, we've still got the key to lock it back up, haven't we?"

"Right!" Cheswick says, socks his fist into his palm. He's still standing, like he's afraid to get near that thumb of Mc-Murphy's again. "Right, Doctor Spivey, if it don't work, we've still got the key to lock it back up. You bet."

The doctor looks around the room and sees all the other Acutes nodding and smiling and looking so pleased with what he takes to be him and his idea that he blushes like Billy Bibbit and has to polish his glasses a time or two before he can go on. It tickles me to see the little man so happy with himself. He looks at all the guys nodding, and nods himself and says, "Fine, fine," and settles his hands on his knees. "Very good. Now. If that's decided—I seem to have forgotten what we were planning to talk about this morning?"

The nurse's head gives that one little jerk again, and she bends over her basket, picks up a folio. She fumbles with the papers, and it looks like her hands are shaking. She draws out a paper, but once more, before she can start reading out of it, McMurphy is standing and holding up his hand and shifting from foot to foot, giving a long, thoughful, "Saaaay," and her fumbling stops, freezes as though the sound of his voice froze her just like her voice froze that black boy this morning. I get that giddy feeling inside me again when she freezes. I watch her close while McMurphy talks.

"Saaaay, Doctor, what I been dyin' to know is what did this dream I dreamt the other night mean? You see, it was like I was *me*, in the dream, and then again kind of like I *wasn't* me—like I was somebody else that looked like me—like—like my *daddy!* Yeah, that's who it was. It was my daddy because sometimes when I saw me—him—I saw there was this iron bolt through the jawbone like daddy used to have—"

"Your father has an iron *bolt* through his jawbone?"

"Well, not any more, but he did once when I was a kid. He went around for about ten months with this big metal bolt going in *here* and coming out *here!* God, he was a regular Frankenstein. He'd been clipped on the jaw with a pole ax when he got into some kinda hassle with this pond man at the logging mill— Hey! Let me tell you how *that* incident came about. . . ."

Her face is still calm, as though she had a cast made and painted to just the look she wants. Confident, patient, and un-ruffled. No more little jerk, just that terrible cold face, a calm smile stamped out of red plastic; a clean, smooth forehead, not a line in it to show weakness or worry; flat, wide, painted-on green eyes, painted on with an expression that says I can wait, I might lose a yard now and then but I can wait, and be patient and calm and confident, because I know there's no real losing for me.

I thought for a minute there I saw her whipped. Maybe I did. But I see now that it don't make any difference. One by one the patients are sneaking looks at her to see how she's taking the way McMurphy is dominating the meeting, and they see the same thing. She's too big to be beaten. She covers one whole side of the room like a Jap statue. There's no moving her and no help against her. She's lost a little battle here to-day, but it's a minor battle in a big war that she's been winning and that she'll go on winning. We mustn't let McMurphy get our hopes up any different, lure us into making some kind of dumb play. She'll go on winning, just like the Combine, be-cause she has all the power of the Combine behind her. She don't lose on her losses, but she wins on ours. To beat her you don't have to whip her two out of three or three out of five, but every time you meet. As soon as you let down your guard, as soon as you lose *once*, she's won for good. And eventually we all got to lose. Nobody can help that.

Right now, she's got the fog machine switched on, and it's

rolling in so fast I can't see a thing but her face, rolling in thicker and thicker, and I feel as hopeless and dead as I felt happy a minute ago, when she gave that little jerk—even more hopeless than ever before, on account of I know now there is no real help against her or her Combine. McMurphy can't help any more than I could. Nobody can help. And the more I think about how nothing can be helped, the faster the fog rolls in.

And I'm glad when it gets thick enough you're lost in it and can let go, and be safe again.

there's a Monopoly game going on in the day room. They've been at it for three days, houses and hotels everywhere, two tables pushed together to take care of all the deeds and stacks of play money. McMurphy talked them into making the game interesting by paying a penny for every play dollar the bank issues them; the monopoly box is loaded with change.

"It's your roll, Cheswick."

"Hold it a minute before he rolls. What's a man need to buy thum hotels?"

"You need four houses on every lot of the same color, Martini. Now let's *go*, for Christsakes."

"Hold it a minute."

There's a flurry of money from that side of the table, red and green and yellow bills blowing in every direction.

"You buying a hotel or you playing happy new year, for Christsakes?"

"It's your dirty roll, Cheswick."

"Snake eyes! Hoooeee, Cheswicker, where does that put you? That don't put you on my Marvin Gardens by any chance? That don't mean you have to pay me, let's see, three hundred and fifty dollars?"

"Boogered."

"What's thum other things? Hold it a minute. What's thum other things *all* over the board?"

"Martini, you been seeing them other things all over the board for two days. No wonder I'm losing my ass. McMurphy, I don't see how you can concentrate with Martini sitting there hallucinating a mile a minute."

"Cheswick, you never mind about Martini. He's doing real good. You just come on with that three fifty, and Martini will take care of himself; don't we get rent from him every time one of his 'things' lands on our property?"

"Hold it a minute. There's so many of thum."

"That's okay, Mart. You just keep us posted whose property they land on. You're still the man with the dice, Cheswick. You rolled a double, so you roll again. Atta boy. *Faw!* a big six."

"Takes me to . . . Chance: 'You Have Been Elected Chairman of the Board; Pay Every Player—' Boogered and double boogered!"

"Whose hotel is this here for Christsakes on the Reading Railroad?"

"My friend, that, as anyone can see, is not a hotel; it's a depot."

"Now *hold* it a minute—"

McMurphy surrounds his end of the table, moving cards, rearranging money, evening up his hotels. There's a hundred-dollar bill sticking out of the brim of his cap like a press card; mad money, he calls it.

"Scanlon? I believe it's your turn, buddy."

"Gimme those dice. I'll blow this board to pieces. Here we go. Lebenty Leben, count me over eleven, Martini."

"Why, all right."

"Not that one, you crazy bastard; that's not my piece, that's my *house*."

"It's the same color."

"What's this little house doing on the Electric Company?"

"That's a power station."

"Martini, those ain't the dice you're shaking—"

"Let him be; what's the difference?"

"Those are a couple of houses!"

"*Faw*. And Martini rolls a big, let me see, a big nineteen. Good goin', Mart; that puts you— Where's your piece, buddy?"

"Eh? Why here it is."

"He had it in his mouth, McMurphy. Excellent. That's two moves over the second and third bicuspid, four moves to the board, which takes you on to—to Baltic Avenue, Martini. Your own and only property. How fortunate can a man get, friends? Martini has been playing three days and lit on his property practically every time."

"Shut up and roll, Harding. It's your turn."

Harding gathers the dice up with his long fingers, feeling the smooth surfaces with his thumb as if he was blind. The fingers are the same color as the dice and look like they were carved by his other hand. The dice rattle in his hand as he shakes it. They tumble to a stop in front of McMurphy.

"*Faw*. Five, six, seven. Tough luck, buddy. That's another o' my vast holdin's. You owe me—oh, two hundred dollars should about cover it."

"Pity."

The game goes round and round, to the rattle of dice and the shuffle of play money.

here's long spells—three days, years—when you can't see a thing, know where you are only by the speaker sounding overhead like a bell buoy clanging in the fog. When I can see, the guys are usually moving around as unconcerned as though they didn't notice so much as a mist in the air. I believe the fog affects their memory some way it doesn't affect mine.

Even McMurphy doesn't seem to know he's been fogged in. If he does, he makes sure not to let on that he's bothered by it. He's making sure none of the staff sees him bothered by anything; he knows that there's no better way in the world to aggravate somebody who's trying to make it hard for you than by acting like you're not bothered.

He keeps up his high-class manners around the nurses and the black boys in spite of anything they might say to him, in spite of every trick they pull to get him to lose his temper. A couple of times some stupid rule gets him mad, but he just makes himself act more polite and mannerly than ever till he begins to see how funny the whole thing is—the rules, the disapproving looks they use to enforce the rules, the ways of talking to you like you're nothing but a three-year-old—and when he sees how funny it is he goes to laughing, and this aggravates them no end. He's safe as long as he can laugh, he thinks, and it works pretty fair. Just once he loses control and shows he's mad, and then it's not because of the black boys or the Big Nurse and something they did, but it's because of the patients, and something they *didn't* do.

It happened at one of the group meetings. He got mad at the guys for acting too cagey—too chicken-shit, he called it. He'd been taking bets from all of them on the World Series coming up Friday. He'd had it in mind that they would get to watch the games on TV, even though they didn't come on

during regulation TV time. During the meeting a few days before he asks if it wouldn't be okay if they did the cleaning
work at night, during TV time, and watched the games during the afternoon. The nurse tells him no, which is about what
he expected. She tells him how the schedule has been set up
for a delicately balanced reason that would be thrown into turmoil by the switch of routines.

This doesn't surprise him, coming from the nurse; what does
surprise him is how the Acutes act when he asks them what
they think of the idea. Nobody says a thing. They're all sunk
back out of sight in little pockets of fog. I can barely see them.

"Now look here," he tells them, but they don't look. He's
been waiting for somebody to say something, answer his question. Nobody acts like they've heard it. "Look here, damn it,"
he says when nobody moves, "there's at least twelve of you guys
I know of myself got a leetle personal *interest* who wins these
games. Don't you guys care to watch them?"

"I don't know, Mack," Scanlon finally says, "I'm pretty used
to seeing that six-o'clock news. And if switching times would
really mess up the schedule as bad as Miss Ratched says—"

"The hell with the schedule. You can get back to the bloody
schedule next week, when the Series is over. What do you say,
buddies? Let's take a vote on watching the TV during the afternoon instead of at night. All those in favor?"

"Ay," Cheswick calls out and gets to his feet.

"I mean all those in favor raise their hands. Okay, all those
in favor?"

Cheswick's hand comes up. Some of the other guys look
around to see if there's any other fools. McMurphy can't believe it.

"Come on now, what is this crap. I thought you guys could
vote on policy and that sort of thing. Isn't that the way it
is, Doc?"

The doctor nods without looking up.

"Okay then; now who wants to watch those games?"

Cheswick shoves his hand higher and glares around. Scanlon shakes his head and then raises his hand, keeping his elbow

on the arm of the chair. And nobody else. McMurphy can't say a word.

"If that's settled, then," the nurse says, "perhaps we should get on with the meeting."

"Yeah," he says, slides down in his chair till the brim of his cap nearly touches his chest, "Yeah, perhaps we should get on with the sonofabitchin' meeting at that."

"Yeah," Cheswick says, giving all the guys a hard look and sitting down, "yeah, get on with the godblessed meeting." He nods stiffly, then settles his chin down on his chest, scowling. He's pleased to be sitting next to McMurphy, feeling brave like this. It's the first time Cheswick ever had somebody along with him on his lost causes.

After the meeting McMurphy won't say a word to any of them, he's so mad and disgusted. It's Billy Bibbit who goes up to him.

"Some of us have b-been here for fi-fi-five years, Randle," Billy says. He's got a magazine rolled up and is twisting at it with his hands; you can see the cigarette burns on the backs of his hands. "And some of us will b-be here maybe th-that muh-muh-much longer, long after you're g-g-gone, long after this Wo-world Series is over. And . . . don't you see . . ." He throws down the magazine and walks away. "Oh, what's the use of it anyway."

McMurphy stares after him, that puzzled frown knotting his bleached eyebrows together again.

He argues for the rest of the day with some of the other guys about why they didn't vote, but they don't want to talk about it, so he seems to give up, doesn't say anything about it again till the day before the Series starts. "Here it is Thursday," he says, sadly shaking his head.

He's sitting on one of the tables in the tub room with his feet on a chair, trying to spin his cap around one finger. Other Acutes mope around the room and try not to pay any attention to him. Nobody'll play poker or blackjack with him for money any more—after the patients wouldn't vote he got mad and skinned them so bad at cards that they're all so in debt they're

scared to go any deeper—and they can't play for cigarettes because the nurse has started making the men keep their cartons
on the desk in the Nurses' Station, where she doles them out one
pack a day, says it's for their health, but everybody knows it's to
keep McMurphy from winning them all at cards. With no
poker or blackjack, it's quiet in the tub room, just the sound
of the speaker drifting in from the day room. It's so quiet you
can hear that guy upstairs in Disturbed climbing the wall,
giving out an occasional signal, loo loo *looo*, a bored, uninterested sound, like a baby yells to yell itself to sleep.

"Thursday," McMurphy says again.

"*Looooo*," yells that guy upstairs.

"That's Rawler," Scanlon says, looking up at the ceiling. He
don't want to pay any attention to McMurphy. "Rawler the
Squawler. He came through this ward a few years back.
Wouldn't keep still to suit Miss Ratched, you remember, Billy?
Loo loo loo all the time till I thought I'd go nuts. What they
should do with that whole bunch of dingbats up there is toss
a couple of grenades in the dorm. They're no use to anybody—"

"And tomorrow is Friday," McMurphy says. He won't let
Scanlon change the subject.

"Yeah," Cheswick says, scowling around the room "tomorrow
is Friday."

Harding turns a page of his magazine. "And that will make
nearly a week our friend McMurphy has been with us without
succeeding in throwing over the government, is that what you're
saying Cheswickle? Lord, to think of the chasm of apathy in
which we have fallen—a shame, a pitiful shame."

"The hell with that," McMurphy says. "What Cheswick
means is that the first Series game is gonna be played on TV
tomorrow, and what are we gonna be doin'? Mopping up this
damned nursery again."

"Yeah," Cheswick says. "Ol' Mother Ratched's Therapeutic
Nursery."

Against the wall of the tub room I get a feeling like a spy;
the mop handle in my hands is made of metal instead of wood
(metal's a better conductor) and it's hollow; there's plenty of

room inside it to hide a miniature microphone. If the Big Nurse is hearing this, she'll really get Cheswick. I take a hard ball of gum from my pocket and pick some fuzz off it and hold it in my mouth till it softens.

"Let me see again," McMurphy says. "How many of you birds will vote with me if I bring up that time switch again?"

About half the Acutes nod yes, a lot more than would really vote. He puts his hat back on his head and leans his chin in his hands.

"I tell ya, I can't figure it out. Harding, what's wrong with *you*, for crying out loud? You afraid if you raise your hand that old buzzard'll cut it off."

Harding lifts one thin eyebrow. "Perhaps I am; perhaps I *am* afraid she'll cut it off if I raise it."

"What about you, Billy? Is that what you're scared of?"

"No. I don't think she'd d-d-*do* anything, but"—he shrugs and sighs and climbs up on the big panel that controls the nozzles on the shower, perches up there like a monkey— "but I just don't think a vote wu-wu-would do any good. Not in the l-long run. It's just no use, M-Mack."

"Do any *good?* Hooee! It'd do you birds some good just to get the exercise lifting that arm."

"It's still a risk, my friend. She always has the capacity to make things worse for us. A baseball game isn't worth the risk," Harding says.

"Who the hell says so? Jesus, I haven't missed a World Series in years. Even when I was in the cooler one September they let us bring in a TV and watch the *Series*; they'd of had a riot on their hands if they hadn't. I just may have to kick that damned door down and walk to some bar downtown to see the game, just me and my buddy Cheswick."

"Now there's a suggestion with a lot of merit," Harding says, tossing down his magazine. "Why not bring that up for vote in group meeting tomorrow? 'Miss Ratched, I'd like to move that the ward be transported *en masse* to the Idle Hour for beer and television.' "

"I'd second the motion," Cheswick says. "Damn right."

"The hell with that in mass business," McMurphy says. "I'm tired of looking at you bunch of old ladies; when me and Cheswick bust outa here I think by God I'm gonna nail the door shut behind me. You guys better stay behind; your mamma probably wouldn't let you cross the street."

"Yeah? Is that it?" Fredrickson has come up behind McMurphy. "You're just going to raise one of those big he-man boots of yours and *kick* down the door? A real tough guy."

McMurphy don't hardly look at Fredrickson; he's learned that Fredrickson might act hard-boiled now and then, but it's an act that folds under the slightest scare.

"What about it, he-man," Fredrickson keeps on, "are you going to kick down that door and show us how tough you are?"

"No, Fred, I guess not. I wouldn't want to scuff up my boot."

"Yeah? Okay, you been talking so big, just how *would* you go about busting out of here?"

McMurphy takes a look around him. "Well, I guess I could knock the mesh outa one of these windows with a chair when and if I took a notion. . . ."

"Yeah? You could, could you? Knock it right out? Okay, let's see you try. Come on, he-man, I'll bet you ten dollars you can't do it."

"Don't bother trying, Mack," Cheswick says. "Fredrickson knows you'll just break a chair and end up on Disturbed. The first day we arrived over here we were given a demonstration about these screens. They're specially made. A technician picked up a chair just like that one you've got your feet on and beat the screen till the chair was no more than kindling wood. Didn't hardly dent the screen."

"Okay then," McMurphy says, taking a look around him. I can see he's getting more interested. I hope the Big Nurse isn't hearing this; he'll be up on Disturbed in an hour. "We need something heavier. How about a table?"

"Same as the chair. Same wood, same weight."

"All right, by God, let's just figure out what I'd have to toss through that screen to bust out. And if you birds don't think I'd do it if I ever got the urge, then you got another think coming. Okay—something bigger'n a table or a chair . . . Well, if it was night I might throw that fat coon through it; he's heavy enough."

"Much too soft," Harding says. "He'd hit the screen and it would dice him like an eggplant."

"How about one of the beds?"

"A bed is too big even if you could lift it. It wouldn't go through the window."

"I could lift it all right. Well, hell, right over there you are: that thing Billy's sittin' on. That big control panel with all the handles and cranks. That's hard enough, ain't it? And it damn well should be heavy enough."

"Sure," Fredrickson says. "That's the same as you kicking your foot through the steel door at the front."

"What would be wrong with using the panel? It don't look nailed down."

"No, it's not bolted—there's probably nothing holding it but a few wires—but *look* at it, for Christsakes."

Everybody looks. The panel is steel and cement, half the size of one of the tables, probably weighs four hundred pounds.

"Okay, I'm looking at it. It don't look any bigger than hay bales I've bucked up onto truck beds."

"I'm afraid, my friend, that this contrivance will weigh a bit more than your bales of hay."

"About a quarter-ton more, I'd bet," Fredrickson says.

"He's right, Mack," Cheswick says. "It'd be awful heavy."

"Hell, are you birds telling me I can't *lift* that dinky little gizmo?"

"My friend, I don't recall anything about psychopaths being able to move mountains in addition to their other noteworthy assets."

"Okay, you say I can't lift it. Well *by* God . . ."

McMurphy hops off the table and goes to peeling off his green jacket; the tattoos sticking half out of his T-shirt jump around the muscles on his arms.

"Then who's willing to lay five bucks? Nobody's gonna convince me I can't do something till I try it. Five bucks . . ."

"McMurphy, this is as foolhardy as your bet about the nurse."

"Who's got five bucks they want to lose? You hit or you sit. . . ."

The guys all go to signing liens at once; he's beat them so many times at poker and blackjack they can't wait to get back at him, and this is a certain sure thing. I don't know what he's driving at; broad and big as he is, it'd take three of him to move that panel, and he knows it. He can just look at it and see he probably couldn't even tip it, let alone lift it. It'd take a giant to lift it off the ground. But when the Acutes all get their IOUs signed, he steps up to the panel and lifts Billy Bibbit down off it and spits in his big callused palms and slaps them together, rolls his shoulders.

"Okay, stand outa the way. Sometimes when I go to exertin' myself I use up all the air nearby and grown men faint from suffocation. Stand back. There's liable to be crackin' cement and flying steel. Get the women and kids someplace safe. Stand back. . . ."

"By golly, he might do it," Cheswick mutters.

"Sure, maybe he'll talk it off the floor," Fredrickson says.

"More likely he'll acquire a beautiful hernia," Harding says. "Come now, McMurphy, quit acting like a fool; there's no man can lift that thing."

"Stand back, sissies, you're using my oxygen."

McMurphy shifts his feet a few times to get a good stance, and wipes his hands on his thighs again, then leans down and gets hold of the levers on each side of the panel. When he goes to straining, the guys go to hooting and kidding him. He turns loose and straightens up and shifts his feet around again.

"Giving up?" Fredrickson grins.

"Just *limbering* up. Here goes the real effort"—and grabs those levers again.

And suddenly nobody's hooting at him any more. His arms commence to swell, and the veins squeeze up to the surface. He clinches his eyes, and his lips draw away from his teeth. His head leans back, and tendons stand out like coiled ropes running from his heaving neck down both arms to his hands. His whole body shakes with the strain as he tries to lift something he *knows* he can't lift, something *everybody* knows he can't lift.

But, for just a second, when we hear the cement grind at our feet, we think, by golly, he might do it.

Then his breath explodes out of him, and he falls back limp against the wall. There's blood on the levers where he tore his hands. He pants for a minute against the wall with his eyes shut. There's no sound but his scraping breath; nobody's saying a thing.

He opens his eyes and looks around at us. One by one he looks at the guys—even at me—then he fishes in his pockets for all the IOUs he won the last few days at poker. He bends over the table and tries to sort them, but his hands are froze into red claws, and he can't work the fingers.

Finally he throws the whole bundle on the floor—probably forty or fifty dollars' worth from each man—and turns to walk out of the tub room. He stops at the door and looks back at everybody standing around.

"But I tried, though," he says. "Goddammit, I sure as hell did that much, now, didn't I?"

And walks out and leaves those stained pieces of paper on the floor for whoever wants to sort through them.

a visiting doctor covered with gray cobwebs on his yellow skull is addressing the resident boys in the staff room.

I come sweeping past him. "Oh, and what's this here." He

gives me a look like I'm some kind of bug. One of the residents points at his ears, signal that I'm deaf, and the visiting doctor goes on.

I push my broom up face to face with a great big picture Public Relation brought in one time when it was fogged so thick I didn't see him. The picture is a guy fly-fishing somewhere in the mountains, looks like the Ochocos near Paineville—snow on the peaks showing over the pines, long white aspen trunks lining the stream, sheep sorrel growing in sour green patches. The guy is flicking his fly in a pool behind a rock. It's no place for a fly, it's a place for a single egg on a number-six hook— he'd do better to drift the fly over those riffles downstream.

There's a path running down through the aspen, and I push my broom down the path a ways and sit down on a rock and look back out through the frame at that visiting doctor talking with the residents. I can see him stabbing some point in the palm of his hand with his finger, but I can't hear what he says because of the crash of the cold, frothy stream coming down out of the rocks. I can smell the snow in the wind where it blows down off the peaks. I can see mole burrows humping along under the grass and buffalo weed. It's a real nice place to stretch your legs and take it easy.

You forget—if you don't sit down and make the effort to think back—forget how it was at the old hospital. They didn't have nice places like this on the walls for you to climb into. They didn't have TV or swimming pools or chicken twice a month. They didn't have nothing but walls and chairs, confinement jackets it took you hours of hard work to get out of. They've learned a lot since then. "Come a long way," says fat-faced Public Relation. They've made life look very pleasant with paint and decorations and chrome bathroom fixtures. "A man that would want to run away from a place as nice as this," says fat-faced Public Relation, "why, there'd be something wrong with him."

Out in the staff room the visiting authority is hugging his elbows and shivering like he's cold while he answers questions the resident boys ask him. He's thin and meatless, and his clothes flap around his bones. He stands there, hugging his elbows and shivering. Maybe he feels the cold snow wind off the peaks too.

i t's getting hard to locate my bed at night, have to crawl around on my hands and knees feeling underneath the springs till I find my gobs of gum stuck there. Nobody complains about all the fog. I know why, now: as bad as it is, you can slip back in it and feel safe. That's what McMurphy can't understand, us wanting to be safe. He keeps trying to drag us out of the fog, out in the open where we'd be easy to get at.

t here's a shipment of frozen parts come in downstairs—hearts and kidneys and brains and the like. I can hear them rumble into cold storage down the coal chute. A guy sitting in the room someplace I can't see is talking about a guy up on Disturbed killing himself. Old Rawler. Cut both nuts off and bled to death, sitting right on the can in the latrine, half a dozen people in there with him didn't know it till he fell off to the floor, dead.

What makes people so impatient is what I can't figure; all the guy had to do was wait.

I know how they work it, the fog machine. We had a whole platoon used to operate fog machines around airfields overseas. Whenever intelligence figured there might be a bombing attack, or if the generals had something secret they wanted to pull—out of sight, hid so good that even the spies on the base couldn't see what went on—they fogged the field.

It's a simple rig: you got an ordinary compressor sucks water out of one tank and a special oil out of another tank, and compresses them together, and from the black stem at the end of the machine blooms a white cloud of fog that can cover a whole airfield in ninety seconds. The first thing I saw when I landed in Europe was the fog those machines make. There were some interceptors close after our transport, and soon as it hit ground the fog crew started up the machines. We could look out the transport's round, scratched windows and watch the jeeps draw the machines up close to the plane and watch the fog boil out till it rolled across the field and stuck against the windows like wet cotton.

You found your way off the plane by following a little referee's horn the lieutenant kept blowing, sounded like a goose honking. Soon as you were out of the hatch you couldn't see no more than maybe three feet in any direction. You felt like you were out on that airfield all by yourself. You were safe from the enemy, but you were awfully alone. Sounds died and dissolved after a few yards, and you couldn't hear any of the rest of your crew, nothing but that little horn squeaking and honking out of a soft furry whiteness so thick that your body just faded into white below the belt; other than that brown shirt and brass buckle, you couldn't see nothing but white, like from the waist down you were being dissolved by the fog too.

And then some guy wandering as lost as you would all of a sudden be right before your eyes, his face bigger and clearer than you ever saw a man's face before in your life. Your eyes were working so hard to see in that fog that when something did come in sight every detail was ten times as clear as usual, so clear both of you had to look away. When a man showed up you didn't want to look at his face and he didn't want to look at yours, because it's painful to see somebody so clear that it's like looking inside him, but then neither did you want to look away and lose him completely. You had a choice: you could either strain and look at things that appeared in front of you in the fog, painful as it might be, or you could relax and lose yourself.

When they first used that fog machine on the ward, one they bought from Army Surplus and hid in the vents in the new place before we moved in, I kept looking at anything that appeared out of the fog as long and hard as I could, to keep track of it, just like I used to do when they fogged the airfields in Europe. Nobody'd be blowing a horn to show the way, there was no rope to hold to, so fixing my eyes on something was the only way I kept from getting lost. Sometimes I got lost in it anyway, got in too deep, trying to hide, and every time I did, it seemed like I always turned up at that same place, at that same metal door with the row of rivets like eyes and no number, just like the room behind that door drew me to it, no matter how hard I tried to stay away, just like the current generated by the fiends in that room was conducted in a beam along the fog and pulled me back along it like a robot. I'd wander for days in the fog, scared I'd never see another thing, then there'd be that door, opening to show me the mattress padding on the other side to stop out the sounds, the men standing in a line like zombies among shiny copper wires and tubes pulsing light, and the bright scrape of arcing electricity. I'd take my place in the line and wait my turn at the table. The table shaped like a cross, with shadows of a thousand murdered men printed on it, silhouette wrists and ankles running under leather straps sweated green with use, a silhouette neck and head running up to a silver band goes across the forehead. And a technician at the controls beside the table looking up from his dials and down the line and pointing at me with a rubber glove. "Wait, I *know* that big bastard there—better rabbit-punch him or call for some more help or something. He's an awful case for thrashing around."

So I used to try not to get in too deep, for fear I'd get lost and turn up at the Shock Shop door. I looked hard at anything that came into sight and hung on like a man in a blizzard hangs on a fence rail. But they kept making the fog thicker and thicker, and it seemed to me that, no matter how hard I tried, two or three times a month I found myself with that door opening in front of me to the acid smell of sparks and ozone. In spite of all I could do, it was getting tough to keep from getting lost.

Then I discovered something: I don't have to end up at that door if I stay still when the fog comes over me and just keep quiet. The trouble was I'd been finding that door my own self because I got scared of being lost so long and went to hollering so they could track me. In a way, I was hollering for them *to* track me; I had figured that anything was better'n being lost for good, even the Shock Shop. Now, I don't know. Being lost isn't so bad.

All this morning I been waiting for them to fog us in again. The last few days they been doing it more and more. It's my idea they're doing it on account of McMurphy. They haven't got him fixed with controls yet, and they're trying to catch him off guard. They can see he's due to be a problem; a half a dozen times already he's roused Cheswick and Harding and some of the others to where it looked like they might actually stand up to one of the black boys—but always, just the time it looked like the patient might be helped, the fog would start, like it's starting now.

I heard the compressor start pumping in the grill a few minutes back, just as the guys went to moving tables out of the day room for the therapeutic meeting, and already the mist is oozing across the floor so thick my pants legs are wet. I'm cleaning the windows in the door of the glass station, and I hear the Big Nurse pick up the phone and call the doctor to tell him we're just about ready for the meeting, and tell him perhaps he'd best keep an hour free this afternoon for a staff meeting. "The reason being," she tells him, "I think it is past time to have a discussion of the subject of Patient Randle McMurphy and whether he should be on this ward or not." She listens a minute, then tells him, "I don't think it's wise to let him go on upsetting the patients the way he has the last few days."

That's why she's fogging the ward for the meeting. She don't usually do that. But now she's going to do something with McMurphy today, probably ship him to Disturbed. I put down my window rag and go to my chair at the end of the line of Chronics, barely able to see the guys getting into their chairs and the doctor coming through the door wiping his glasses like he thinks the blurred look comes from his steamed lenses instead of the fog.

It's rolling in thicker than I ever seen it before.

I can hear them out there, trying to go on with the meeting, talking some nonsense about Billy Bibbit's stutter and how it came about. The words come to me like through water, it's so thick. In fact it's so much like water it floats me right up out of my chair and I don't know which end is up for a while. Floating makes me a little sick to the stomach at first. I can't see a thing. I never had it so thick it floated me like this.

The words get dim and loud, off and on, as I float around, but as loud as they get, loud enough sometimes I know I'm right next to the guy that's talking, I still can't see a thing.

I recognize Billy's voice, stuttering worse than ever because

he's nervous. ". . . fuh-fuh-flunked out of college be-be-cause
I quit ROTC. I c-c-couldn't take it. Wh-wh-wh-whenever the
officer in charge of class would call roll, call 'Bibbit,' I couldn't
answer. You were s-s-supposed to say heh—heh—heh . . ."
He's choking on the word, like it's a bone in his throat. I hear
him swallow and start again. "You were supposed to say,
'Here sir,' and I never c-c-could get it out."

His voice gets dim; then the Big Nurse's voice comes cutting
from the left. "Can you recall, Billy, when you first had speech
trouble? When did you first stutter, do you remember?"

I can't tell is he laughing or what. "Fir-first stutter? First
stutter? The first word I said I st-stut-tered: m-m-m-m-mamma."

Then the talking fades out altogether; I never knew that to
happen before. Maybe Billy's hid himself in the fog too. Maybe
all the guys finally and forever crowded back into the fog.

A chair and me float past each other. It's the first thing I've
seen. It comes sifting out of the fog off to my right, and for
a few seconds it's right beside my face, just out of my reach.
I been accustomed of late to just let things alone when they
appear in the fog, sit still and not try to hang on. But this
time I'm scared, the way I used to be scared. I try with all
I got to pull myself over to the chair and get hold of it,
but there's nothing to brace against and all I can do is thrash
the air, all I can do is watch the chair come clear, clearer than
ever before to where I can even make out the fingerprint where a
worker touched the varnish before it was dry, looming out for
a few seconds, then fading on off again. I never seen it where
things floated around this way. I never seen it this thick before, thick to where I can't get down to the floor and get on
my feet if I wanted to and walk around. That's why I'm so
scared; I feel I'm going to float off someplace for good this time.

I see a Chronic float into sight a little below me. It's old
Colonel Matterson, reading from the wrinkled scripture of that
long yellow hand. I look close at him because I figure it's the
last time I'll ever see him. His face is enormous, almost more
than I can bear. Every hair and wrinkle of him is big, as though
I was looking at him with one of those microscopes. I see him

so clear I see his whole life. The face is sixty years of southwest Army camps, rutted by iron-rimmed caisson wheels, worn to the bone by thousands of feet on two-day marches.

He holds out that long hand and brings it up in front of his eyes and squints into it, brings up his other hand and underlines the words with a finger wooden and varnished the color of a gunstock by nicotine. His voice as deep and slow and patient, and I see the words come out dark and heavy over his brittle lips when he reads.

"Now . . . The flag is . . . Ah-mer-ica. America is . . . the plum. The peach. The wah-ter-mel-on. America is . . . the gumdrop. The pump-kin seed. America is . . . tell-ah-vision."

It's true. It's all wrote down on that yellow hand. I can read it along with him myself.

"Now . . . The cross is . . . Mex-i-co." He looks up to see if I'm paying attention, and when he sees I am he smiles at me and goes on. "Mexico is . . . the wal-nut. The hazelnut. The ay-corn. Mexico is . . . the rain-bow. The rain-bow is . . . wooden. Mexico is . . . woo-den."

I can see what he's driving at. He's been saying this sort of thing for the whole six years he's been here, but I never paid him any mind, figured he was no more than a talking statue, a thing made out of bone and arthritis, rambling on and on with these goofy definitions of his that didn't make a lick of sense. Now, at last, I see what he's saying. I'm trying to hold him for one last look to remember him, and that's what makes me look hard enough to understand. He pauses and peers up at me again to make sure I'm getting it, and I want to yell out to him Yes, I see: Mexico *is* like the walnut; it's brown and hard and you feel it with your eye and it *feels* like the walnut! You're making sense, old man, a sense of your own. You're not crazy the way they think. Yes . . . I see . . .

But the fog's clogged my throat to where I can't make a sound. As he sifts away I see him bend back over that hand.

"Now . . . The green sheep is . . . Can-a-da. Canada is . . . the fir tree. The wheat field. The cal-en-dar . . ."

I strain to see him drifting away. I strain so hard my eyes

ache and I have to close them, and when I open them again
the colonel is gone. I'm floating by myself again, more lost
than ever.

This is the time, I tell myself. I'm going for good.

There's old Pete, face like a searchlight. He's fifty yards off
to my left, but I can see him plain as though there wasn't any
fog at all. Or maybe he's up right close and real small, I can't
be sure. He tells me once about how tired he is, and just his
saying it makes me see his whole life on the railroad, see him
working to figure out how to read a watch, breaking a sweat
while he tries to get the right button in the right hole of his
railroad overalls, doing his absolute damnedest to keep up with
a job that comes so easy to the others they can sit back in a
chair padded with cardboard and read mystery stories and girlie
books. Not that he ever really figured to keep up—he knew
from the start he couldn't do that—but he had to try to keep
up, just to keep them in sight. So for forty years he was able
to live, if not right in the world of men, at least on the edge
of it.

I can see all that, and be hurt by it, the way I was hurt by
seeing things in the Army, in the war. The way I was hurt
by seeing what happened to Papa and the tribe. I thought I'd
got over seeing those things and fretting over them. There's no
sense in it. There's nothing to be done.

"I'm tired," is what he says.

"I know you're tired, Pete, but I can't do you no good fretting
about it. You know I can't."

Pete floats on the way of the old colonel.

Here comes Billy Bibbit, the way Pete come by. They're all
filing by for a last look. I know Billy can't be more'n a few
feet away, but he's so tiny he looks like he's a mile off. His face
is out to me like the face of a beggar, needing so much more'n
anybody can give. His mouth works like a little doll's mouth.

"And even when I pr-proposed, I flubbed it. I said 'Huh-
honey, will you muh-muh-muh-muh-muh . . . till the girl
broke out l-laughing."

Nurse's voice, I can't see where it comes from: "Your mother
has spoken to me about this girl, Billy. Apparently she was

quite a bit beneath you. What would you speculate it was about her that frightened you so, Billy?"

"I was in luh-love with her."

I can't do nothing for you either, Billy. You know that. None of us can. You got to understand that as soon as a man goes to help somebody, he leaves himself wide open. He *has* to be cagey, Billy, you should know that as well as anyone. What could I do? I can't fix your stuttering. I can't wipe the razorblade scars off your wrists or the cigarette burns off the back of your hands. I can't give you a new mother. And as far as the nurse riding you like this, rubbing your nose in your weakness till what little dignity you got left is gone and you shrink up to nothing from humiliation, I can't do anything about that, either. At Anzio, I saw a buddy of mine tied to a tree fifty yards from me, screaming for water, his face blistered in the sun. They wanted me to try to go out and help him. They'd of cut me in half from that farmhouse over there.

Put your face away, Billy.

They keep filing past.

It's like each face was a sign like one of those "I'm Blind" signs the dago accordion players in Portland hung around their necks, only these signs say "I'm tired" or "I'm scared" or "I'm dying of a bum liver" or "I'm all bound up with machinery and people *pushing* me alla time." I can read all the signs, it don't make any difference how little the print gets. Some of the faces are looking around at one another and could read the other fellow's if they would, but what's the sense? The faces blow past in the fog like confetti.

I'm further off than I've ever been. This is what it's like to be dead. I guess this is what it's like to be a Vegetable; you lose yourself in the fog. You don't move. They feed your body till it finally stops eating; then they burn it. It's not so bad. There's no pain. I don't feel much of anything other than a touch of chill I figure will pass in time.

I see my commanding officer pinning notices on the bulletin board, what we're to wear today. I see the US Department of Interior bearing down on our little tribe with a gravel-crushing machine.

I see Papa come loping out of a draw and slow up to try and take aim at a big six-point buck springing off through the cedars. Shot after shot puffs out of the barrel, knocking dust all around the buck. I come out of the draw behind Papa and bring the buck down with my second shot just as it starts climbing the rimrock. I grin at Papa.

I never knew you to miss a shot like that before, Papa.

Eye's gone, boy. Can't hold a bead. Sights on my gun just now was shakin' like a dog shittin' peach pits.

Papa, I'm telling you: that cactus moon of Sid's is gonna make you old before your time.

A man drinks that cactus moon of Sid's, boy, he's already old before his time. Let's go gut that animal out before the flies blow him.

That's not even happening now. You see? There's nothing you can do about a happening out of the past like that.

Look there, my man . . .

I hear whispers, black boys.

Look there that old fool Broom, slipped off to sleep.

Tha's right, Chief Broom, tha's right. You sleep an' keep outta trouble. Yasss.

I'm not cold any more. I think I've about made it. I'm off to where the cold can't reach me. I can stay off here for good. I'm not scared any more. They can't reach me. Just the words reach me, and those're fading.

Well . . . in as much as Billy has decided to walk out on the discussion, does anyone else have a problem to bring before the group?

As a matter of fact, ma'am, there does happen to be something . . .

That's that McMurphy. He's far away. He's still trying to pull people out of the fog. Why don't he leave me be?

". . . remember that vote we had a day or so back—about the TV time? Well, today's Friday and I thought I might just bring it up again, just to see if anybody else has picked up a little guts."

"Mr. McMurphy, the purpose of this meeting is therapy, group therapy, and I'm not certain these petty grievances—"

"Yeah, yeah, the hell with that, we've heard it before. Me and some of the rest of the guys decided—"

"One moment, Mr. McMurphy, let me pose a question to the group: do any of you feel that Mr. McMurphy is perhaps imposing his personal desires on some of you too much? I've been thinking you might be happier if he were moved to a different ward."

Nobody says anything for a minute. Then someone says, "Let him vote, why dontcha? Why ya want to ship him to Disturbed just for bringing up a vote? What's so wrong with changing time?"

"Why, Mr. Scanlon, as I recall, you refused to eat for three days until we allowed you to turn the set on at six instead of six-thirty."

"A man needs to see the world news, don't he? God, they coulda bombed Washington and it'd been a week before we'd of heard."

"Yes? And how do you feel about relinquishing your world news to watch a bunch of men play baseball?"

"We can't have both, huh? No, I suppose not. Well, what the dickens—I don't guess they'll bomb us this week."

"Let's let him have the vote, Miss Ratched."

"Very well. But I think this is ample evidence of how much he is upsetting some of you patients. What is it you are proposing Mr. McMurphy?"

"I'm proposing a revote on watching the TV in the afternoon."

"You're certain one more vote will satisfy you? We have more important things—"

"It'll satisfy me. I just'd kind of like to see which of these birds has any guts and which doesn't."

"It's that kind of talk, Doctor Spivey, that makes me wonder if the patients wouldn't be more content if Mr. McMurphy were moved."

"Let him call the vote, why dontcha?"

"Certainly, Mr. Cheswick. A vote is now before the group. Will a show of hands be adequate, Mr. McMurphy, or are you going to insist on a secret ballot?"

"I want to see the hands. I want to see the hands that don't go up, too."

"Everyone in favor of changing the television time to the afternoon, raise his hand."

The first hand that comes up, I can tell, is McMurphy's, because of the bandage where that control panel cut into him when he tried to lift it. And then off down the slope I see them, other hands coming up out of the fog. It's like . . . that big red hand of McMurphy's is reaching into the fog and dropping down and dragging the men up by their hands, dragging them blinking into the open. First one, then another, then the next. Right on down the line of Acutes, dragging them out of the fog till there they stand, all twenty of them, raising not just for watching TV, but against the Big Nurse, against her trying to send McMurphy to Disturbed, against the way she's talked and acted and beat them down for years.

Nobody says anything. I can feel how stunned everybody is, the patients as well as the staff. The nurse can't figure what happened; yesterday, before he tried lifting that panel, there wasn't but four of five men might of voted. But when she talks she don't let it show in her voice how surprised she is.

"I count only twenty, Mr. McMurphy."

"Twenty? Well, why not? Twenty is all of us there—" His voice hangs as he realizes what she means. "Now hold on just a goddamned minute, lady—"

"I'm afraid the vote is defeated."

"Hold on just one goddamned *minute!*"

"There are forty patients on the ward, Mr. McMurphy. Forty patients, and only twenty voted. You must have a majority to change the ward policy. I'm afraid the vote is closed."

The hands are coming down across the room. The guys know they're whipped, are trying to slip back into the safety of the fog. McMurphy is on his feet.

"Well, I'll be a sonofabitch. You mean to tell me that's how you're gonna pull it? Count the votes of those old birds over there too?"

"Didn't you explain the voting procedure to him, Doctor?"

"I'm afraid—a majority *is* called for, McMurphy. She's right. she's right."

"A majority, Mr. McMurphy; it's in the ward constitution."

"And I suppose the way to change the damned constitution is with a majority vote. Sure. Of all the chicken-shit things I've ever seen, this by God takes the *cake!*"

"I'm sorry, Mr. McMurphy, but you'll find it written in the policy if you'd care for me to—"

"So this's how you work this democratic bullshit—hell's bells!"

"You seem upset, Mr. McMurphy. Doesn't he seem upset, Doctor? I want you to note this."

"Don't give me that noise, lady. When a guy's getting screwed he's got a right to holler. And we've been damn well screwed."

"Perhaps, Doctor, in view of the patient's condition, we should bring this meeting to a close early today—"

"Wait! Wait a minute, let me talk to some of those old guys."

"The vote is closed, Mr. McMurphy."

"Let me talk to 'em."

He's coming across the day room at us. He gets bigger and bigger, and he's burning red in the face. He reaches into the fog and tries to drag Ruckly to the surface because Ruckly's the youngest.

"What about you, buddy? You want to watch the World Series? Baseball? Baseball games? Just raise that hand up there—"

"Fffffffuck da wife."

"All right, forget it. You, partner, how about you? What was your name—Ellis? What do you say, Ellis, to watching a ball game on TV? Just raise your hand. . . ."

Ellis's hands are nailed to the wall, can't be counted as a vote.

"I said the voting is closed, Mr. McMurphy. You're just making a spectacle of yourself."

He don't pay any attention to her. He comes on down the line of Chronics. "C'mon, c'mon, just one vote from you birds, just raise a hand. Show her you can still do it."

"I'm tired," says Pete and wags his head.

"The night is . . . the Pacific Ocean." The Colonel is reading off his hand, can't be bothered with voting.

"*One* of you guys, for cryin' out loud! This is where you get the edge, don't you see that? We have to do this—or we're *whipped!* Don't a one of you clucks know what I'm talking about enough to give us a hand? You, Gabriel? George? No? You, Chief, what about you?

He's standing over me in the mist. Why won't he leave me be?

"Chief, you're our last bet."

The Big Nurse is folding her papers; the other nurses are standing up around her. She finally gets to her feet.

"The meeting is adjourned, then," I hear her say. "And I'd like to see the staff down in the staff room in about an hour. So, if there is nothing el—"

It's too late to stop it now. McMurphy did something to it that first day, put some kind of hex on it with his hand so it won't act like I order it. There's no sense in it, any fool can see; I wouldn't do it on my own. Just by the way the nurse is staring at me with her mouth empty of words I can see I'm in for trouble, but I can't stop it. McMurphy's got hidden wires hooked to it, lifting it slow just to get me out of the fog and into the open where I'm fair game. He's doing it, wires . . .

No. That's not the truth. I lifted it myself.

McMurphy whoops and drags me standing, pounding my back.

"Twenty-one! The Chief's vote makes it twenty-one! And by God if that ain't a majority I'll eat my hat!"

"Yippee," Cheswick yells. The other Acutes are coming across toward me.

"The meeting was closed," she says. Her smile is still there, but the back of her neck as she walks out of the day room and into the Nurses' Station, is red and swelling like she'll blow apart any second.

But she don't blow up, not right off, not until about an hour later. Behind the glass her smile is twisted and queer, like we've never seen before. She just sits. I can see her shoulders rise and fall as she breathes.

McMurphy looks up at the clock and he says it's time for the game. He's over by the drinking fountain with some of the other Acutes, down on his knees scouring off the baseboard. I'm sweeping out the broom closet for the tenth time that day. Scanlon and Harding, they got the buffer going up and down the hall, polishing the new wax into shining figure eights. Mc-Murphy says again that he guesses it must be game time and he stands up, leaves the scouring rag where it lies. Nobody else stops work. McMurphy walks past the window where she's glaring out at him and grins at her like he knows he's got her whipped now. When he tips his head back and winks at her she gives that little sideways jerk of her head.

Everybody keeps on at what he's doing, but they all watch out of the corners of their eyes while he drags his armchair out to in front of the TV set, then switches on the set and sits down. A picture swirls onto the screen of a parrot out on the baseball field singing razor-blade songs. McMurphy gets up and turns up the sound to drown out the music coming down from the speaker in the ceiling, and he drags another chair in front of him and sits down and crosses his feet on the chair and leans back and lights a cigarette. He scratches his belly and yawns.

"Hoo-*weee!* Man, all I need me now is a can of beer and a red-hot."

We can see the nurse's face get red and her mouth work as she stares at him. She looks around for a second and sees everybody's watching what she's going to do—even the black boys and the little nurses sneaking looks at her, and the residents beginning to drift in for the staff meeting, they're watching. Her mouth clamps shut. She looks back at McMurphy and waits till the razor-blade song is finished; then she gets up and goes to the steel door where the controls are, and she flips a switch and the TV picture swirls back into the gray. Nothing is left on the screen but a little eye of light beading right down on McMurphy sitting there.

That eye don't faze him a bit. To tell the truth, he don't even let on he knows the picture is turned off; he puts his cigarette between his teeth and pushes his cap forward in his red hair till he has to lean back to see out from under the brim.

And sits that way, with his hands crossed behind his head and his feet stuck out in a chair, a smoking cigarette sticking out from under his hatbrim—watching the TV screen.

The nurse stands this as long as she can; then she comes to the door of the Nurses' Station and calls across to him he'd better help the men with the housework. He ignores her.

"I said, Mr. McMurphy, that you are supposed to be working during these hours." Her voice has a tight whine like an electric saw ripping through pine. "Mr. McMurphy, I'm *warning* you!"

Everybody's stopped what he was doing. She looks around her, then takes a step out of the Nurses' Station toward McMurphy.

"You're committed, you realize. You are . . . under the *jurisdiction* of me . . . the staff." She's holding up a fist, all those red-orange fingernails burning into her palm. "Under jurisdiction and *control—*"

Harding shuts off the buffer, and leaves it in the hall, and goes pulls him a chair up alongside McMurphy and sits down and lights him a cigarette too.

"Mr. Harding! You return to your scheduled duties!"

I think how her voice sounds like it hit a nail, and this strikes me so funny I almost laugh.

"Mr. Har-*ding!*"

Then Cheswick goes and gets him a chair, and then Billy Bibbit goes, and then Scanlon and then Fredrickson and Sefelt, and then we all put down our mops and brooms and scouring rags and we all go pull us chairs up.

"You *men*— Stop this. *Stop!*"

And we're all sitting there lined up in front of that blanked-out TV set, watching the gray screen just like we could see the baseball game clear as day, and she's ranting and screaming behind us.

If somebody'd of come in and took a look, men watching a blank TV, a fifty-year old woman hollering and squealing at the back of their heads about discipline and order and re-criminations, they'd of thought the whole bunch was crazy as loons.

part 2

just at the edge of my vision I can see that white enamel face in the Nurses' Station, teetering over the desk, see it warp and flow as it tries to pull back into shape. The rest of the guys are watching too, though they're trying to act like they aren't. They're trying to act like they still got their eyes on nothing but that blank TV in front of us, but anyone can see they're all sneaking looks at the Big Nurse behind her glass there, just the same as I am. For the first time she's on the other side of the glass and getting a taste of how it feels to be watched when you wish more than anything else to be able to pull a green shade between your face and all the eyes that you can't get away from.

The residents, the black boys, all the little nurses, they're watching her too, waiting for her to go down the hall where it's time for the meeting she herself called, and waiting to see how she'll act now that it's known she can be made to lose control. She knows they're watching, but she don't move. Not even when they start strolling down to the staff room without her. I notice all the machinery in the wall is quiet, like it's still waiting for her to move.

There's no more fog any place.

All of a sudden I remember I'm supposed to clean the staff room. I always go down and clean the staff room during these meetings they have, been doing it for years. But now I'm too scared to get out of my chair. The staff always let me clean the room because they didn't think I could hear, but now that they saw me lift my hand when McMurphy told me to, won't they know I can hear? Won't they figure I been hearing all these years, listening to secrets meant only for their ears? What'll they do to me in that staff room if they know that?

Still, they expect me to be in there. If I'm not, they'll know for sure that I can hear, be way ahead of me, thinking, You see?

141

He isn't in here cleaning, don't that prove it? It's obvious what's to be done. . . .

I'm just getting the full force of the dangers we let ourselves in for when we let McMurphy lure us out of the fog.

There's a black boy leaning against the wall near the door, arms crossed, pink tongue tip darting back and forth over his lips, watching us sitting in front of the TV set. His eyes dart back and forth like his tongue and stop on me, and I see his leather eyelids raise a little. He watches me for a long time, and I know he's wondering about the way I acted in the group meeting. Then he comes off the wall with a lurch, breaking contact, and goes to the broom closet and brings back a bucket of soapy water and a sponge, drags my arms up and hangs the bucket bale over it, like hanging a kettle on a fireplace boom.

"Le's go, Chief," he says. "Le's get up and get to your duties."

I don't move. The bucket rocks on my arm. I don't make a sign I heard. He's trying to trick me. He asks me again to get up, and when I don't move he rolls his eyes up to the ceiling and sighs, reaches down and takes my collar, and tugs a little, and I stand up. He stuffs the sponge in my pocket and points up the hall where the staff room is, and I go.

And while I'm walking up the hall with the bucket, zoom, the Big Nurse comes past me with all her old calm speed and power and turns into the door. That makes me wonder.

Out in the hall all by myself, I notice how clear it is—no fog any place. It's a little cold where the nurse just went past, and the white tubes in the ceiling circulate frozen light like rods of glowing ice, like frosted refrigerator coils rigged up to glow white. The rods stretch down to the staff-room door where the nurse just turned in at the end of the hall—a heavy steel door like the door of the Shock Shop in Building One, except there are numbers printed on this one, and this one has a little glass peephole up head-high to let the staff peek out at who's knocking. As I get closer I see there's light seeping out this peephole, green light, bitter as bile. The staff meeting is about to start in there, is why there's this green seepage; it'll be all over the walls and windows by the time the meeting is halfway through, for me to sponge off and squeeze in my bucket, use the water later to clear the drains in the latrine.

Cleaning the staff room is always bad. The things I've had to clean up in these meetings nobody'd believe; horrible things, poisons manufactured right out of skin pores and acids in the air strong enough to melt a man. I've seen it.

I been in some meetings where the table legs strained and contorted and the chairs knotted and the walls gritted against one another till you could of wrung sweat out the room. I been in meetings where they kept talking about a patient so long that the patient materialized in the flesh, nude on the coffee table in front of them, vulnerable to any fiendish notion they took; they'd have him smeared around in an awful mess before they were finished.

That's why they have me at the staff meetings, because they can be such a messy affair and somebody has to clean up, and since the staff room is open only during the meetings it's got to be somebody they think won't be able to spread the word what's going on. That's me. I been at it so long, sponging and dusting and mopping this staff room and the old wooden one at the other place, that the staff usually don't even notice me; I move around in my chores, and they see right through me like I wasn't there—the only thing they'd miss if I didn't show up would be the sponge and the water bucket floating around.

But this time when I tap at the door and the Big Nurse looks through the peephole she looks dead at me, and she takes longer than ordinary unlocking that door to let me in. Her face has come back into shape, strong as ever, it seems to me. Everybody else goes ahead spooning sugar in their coffee and borrowing cigarettes, the way they do before every meeting, but there's a tenseness in the air. I think it's because of me at first. Then I notice that the Big Nurse hasn't even sat down, hasn't even bothered to get herself a cup of coffee.

She lets me slip through the door and stabs me again with both eyes as I go past her, closes that door when I'm in and locks it, and pivots around and glares at me some more. I know she's suspicious. I thought she might be too upset by the way McMurphy defied her to pay any attention to me, but she don't look shook at all. She's clear-headed and wondering now just how *did* Mr. Bromden hear that Acute McMurphy asking him to raise his hand on that vote? She's wondering how did he know to lay down his mop and go sit with the Acutes in front of that TV set? None of the other Chronics did that. She's wondering if it isn't time we did some checking on our Mr. Chief Bromden.

I put my back to her and dig into the corner with my sponge. I lift the sponge up above my head so everybody in the room can see how it's covered with green slime and how hard I'm working; then I bend over and rub harder than ever. But hard as I work and hard as I try to act like I'm not aware of her back there, I can still feel her standing at the door and drilling into my skull till in a minute she's going to break through, till I'm just about to give up and yell and tell them everything if she don't take those eyes off me.

Then she realizes that she's being stared at too—by all the rest of the staff. Just like she's wondering about me, they are wondering about her and what she's planning to do about that redhead back down there in the day room. They're watching to see what she'll say about him, and they don't care anything about some fool Indian on his hands and knees in the corner. They're waiting for her so she quits looking at me and goes and draws a cup of coffee and sits down, stirs sugar in it so careful the spoon never touches the side of the cup.

It's the doctor who starts things off. "Now, people, if we can get things rolling?"

He smiles around at the residents sipping coffee. He's trying not to look at the Big Nurse. She's sitting there so silent it makes him nervous and fidgety. He grabs out his glasses and puts them on for a look at his watch, goes to winding it while he talks.

"Fifteen after. It's past time we started. Now. Miss Ratched, as most of you know, called this get-together. She phoned me before the Therapeutic Community meeting and said that in her opinion McMurphy was due to constitute a disturbance on the ward. Ever so intuitive, considering what went on a few minutes ago, don't you think?"

He stops winding his watch on account of it's tight enough another twist is going to spray it all over the place, and he sits there smiling at it, drumming the back of his hand with pink little fingers, waiting. Usually at about this point in the meeting she'll take over, but she doesn't say anything.

"After today," the doctor goes on, "no one can say that this is an ordinary man we're dealing with. No, certainly not. And he *is* a disturbing factor, that's obvious. So—ah—as I see it, our course in this discussion is to decide what action to take in dealing with him. I believe the nurse called this meeting—correct me if I'm off base here, Miss Ratched—to talk the situation out and unify the staff's opinion of what should be done about Mr. McMurphy?"

He gives her a pleading look, but she still doesn't say anything. She's lifted her face toward the ceiling, checking for dirt most likely, and doesn't appear to have heard a thing he's been saying.

The doctor turns to the line of residents across the room: all of them got the same leg crossed and coffee cup on the same knee. "You fellows," the doctor says, "I realize you haven't had adequate time to arrive at a proper diagnosis of the patient, but you *have* had a chance at observing him in action. What do *you* think?"

The question pops their heads up. Cleverly, he's put them on the carpet too. They all look from him to the Big Nurse. Some way she has regained all her old power in a few short minutes. Just sitting there, smiling up at the ceiling and not saying anything, she has taken control again and made everyone aware that she's the force in here to be dealt with. If these boys don't play it just right they're liable to finish their training up in Portland at the alky hospital. They begin to fidget around like the doctor.

"He's quite a disturbing influence, all right." The first boy plays it safe.

They all sip their coffee and think about that. Then the next one says, "And he could constitute an actual danger."

"That's true, that's true," the doctor says.

The boy thinks he may have found the key and goes on. "Quite a danger, in fact," he says and moves forward in his chair. "Keep in mind that this man performed violent acts for the sole purpose of getting away from the work farm and into the comparative luxury of this hospital."

"*Planned* violent acts," the first boy says.

And the third boy mutters, "Of course, the very nature of this plan could indicate that he is simply a shrewd con man, and not mentally ill at all."

He glances around to see how this strikes her and sees she still hasn't moved or given any sign. But the rest of the staff sits there glaring at him like he's said some awful vulgar thing. He sees how he's stepped way out of bounds and tries to bring it off as a joke by giggling and adding, "You know, like 'He Who Marches Out Of Step Hears Another Drum' "—but it's too late. The first resident turns on him after setting down his cup of coffee and reaching in his pocket for a pipe big as your fist.

"Frankly, Alvin," he says to the third boy, "I'm disappointed in you. Even if one hadn't read his history all one should need to do is pay attention to his behavior on the ward to realize how absurd the suggestion is. This man is not only very very sick, but I believe he is definitely a Potential Assaultive. I think that is what Miss Ratched was suspecting when she called this meeting. Don't you recognize the arch type of psychopath? I've never heard of a clearer case. This man is a Napoleon, a Genghis Khan, Attila the Hun."

Another one joins in. He remembers the nurse's comments about Disturbed. "Robert's right, Alvin. Didn't you see the way the man acted out there today? When one of his schemes was thwarted he was up out of his chair, on the verge of violence. You tell us, Doctor Spivey, what do his records say about violence?"

"There is a marked disregard for discipline and authority," the doctor says.

"Right. His history shows, Alvin, that time and again he has acted out his hostilities against authority figures—in school, in the service, in *jail!* And I think that his performance after the voting furor today is as conclusive an indication as we can have of what to expect in the future." He stops and frowns into his pipe, puts it back in his mouth, and strikes a match and sucks the flame into the bowl with a loud popping sound. When it's lit he sneaks a look up through the yellow cloud of smoke at the Big Nurse; he must take her silence as agreement because he goes on, more enthusiastic and certain than before.

"Pause for a minute and imagine, Alvin," he says, his words cottony with smoke, "imagine what will happen to one of us when we're alone in Individual Therapy with Mr. McMurphy. Imagine you are approaching a particularly painful break-through and he decides he's just had all he can take of your— how would he put it?—your 'damn fool collitch-kid pryin'l' You tell him he mustn't get hostile and he says 'to hell with that,' and tell him to calm down, in an authoritarian voice, of course, and here he comes, all two hundred and ten red-headed psychopathic Irishman pounds of him, right across the inter-viewing table at you. Are you—are any of us, for that matter— prepared to deal with Mr. McMurphy when these moments arise?"

He puts his size-ten pipe back in the corner of his mouth and spreads his hands on his knees and waits. Everybody's thinking about McMurphy's thick red arms and scarred hands and how his neck comes out of his T-shirt like a rusty wedge. The resident named Alvin has turned pale at the thought, like that yellow pipe smoke his buddy was blowing at him had stained his face.

"So you believe it would be wise," the doctor asks, "to send him up to Disturbed?"

"I believe it would be at the very least safe," the guy with the pipe answers, closing his eyes.

"I'm afraid I'll have to withdraw my suggestion and go along with Robert," Alvin tells them all, "if only for my own protec-tion."

They all laugh. They're all more relaxed now, certain they've come round to the plan she was wanting. They all have a sip of coffee on it except the guy with the pipe, and he has a big to-do with the thing going out all the time, goes through a lot of matches and sucking and puffing and popping of his lips. It finally smokes up again to suit him, and he says, a little proudly, "Yes, Disturbed Ward for ol' Red McMurphy, I'm afraid. You know what I think, observing him these few days?"

"Schizophrenic reaction?" Alvin asks.

Pipe shakes his head.

"Latent Homosexual with Reaction Formation?" the third one says.

Pipe shakes his head again and shuts his eyes. "No," he says and smiles round the room, "*Negative Oedipal.*"

They all congratulate him.

"Yes, I think there is a lot pointing to it," he says. "But whatever the final diagnosis is, we must keep one thing in mind: we're not dealing with an ordinary man."

"You—are very, very wrong, Mr. Gideon."

It's the Big Nurse.

Everybody's head jerks toward her—mine too, but I check myself and pass the motion off like I'm trying to scrub a speck I just discovered on the wall above my head. Everybody's confused all to hell for sure now. They figured they were proposing just what she'd want, just what she was planning to propose in the meeting herself. I thought so too. I've seen her send men half the size of McMurphy up to Disturbed for no more reason than there was a chance they might spit on somebody; now she's got this bull of a man who's bucked her and everybody else on the staff, a guy she all but said was on his way off the ward earlier this afternoon, and she says no.

"No. I don't agree. Not at all." She smiles around at all of them. "I don't agree that he should be sent up to Disturbed, which would simply be an easy way of passing our problem on to another ward, and I don't agree that he is some kind of extraordinary being—some kind of 'super' psychopath."

She waits but nobody is about to disagree. For the first time she takes a sip of her coffee; the cup comes away from her mouth with that red-orange color on it. I stare at the rim of the cup in spite of myself; she *couldn't* be wearing lipstick that color. That color on the rim of the cup must be from heat, touch of her lips set it smoldering.

"I'll admit that my first thought when I began to recognize Mr. McMurphy for the disturbing force that he is was that he should most definitely be sent up to Disturbed. But now I believe it is too late. Would removing him undo the harm that he has done to our ward? I don't believe it would, not after this afternoon. I believe if he were sent to Disturbed now it would be exactly what the patients would expect. He would be a martyr to them. They would never be given the opportunity to see that this man is not an—as you put it, Mr. Gideon— 'extraordinary person.' "

She takes another sip and sets the cup on the table; the whack of it sounds like a gavel; all three residents sit bold upright.

"No. He isn't extraordinary. He is simply a man and no more, and is subject to all the fears and all the cowardice and all the timidity that any other man is subject to. Given a few more days, I have a very strong feeling that he will prove this, to us as well as the rest of the patients. If we keep him on the ward I am certain his brashness will subside, his self-made rebellion will dwindle to nothing, and"—she smiles, knowing something nobody else does—"that our redheaded hero will cut himself down to something the patients will all recognize and lose respect for: a braggart and a blowhard of the type who may climb up on a soapbox and shout for a following, the way we've all seen Mr. Cheswick do, then back down the moment there is any real danger to him personally."

"Patient McMurphy"—the boy with the pipe feels he should try to defend his position and save face just a little bit—"does not strike me as a coward."

I expect her to get mad, but she doesn't; she just gives him that let's-wait-and-see look and says, "I didn't say he was exactly a coward, Mr. Gideon; oh, no. He's simply very fond of

someone. As a psychopath, he's much too fond of a Mr. Randle
Patrick McMurphy to subject him to any needless danger." She
gives the boy a smile that puts his pipe out for sure this time.
"If we just wait for a while, our hero will—what is it you college boys say?—give up his bit? Yes?"

"But that may take weeks—" the boy starts.

"We have weeks," she says. She stands up, looking more
pleased with herself than I've seen her look since McMurphy
came to trouble her a week ago. "We have weeks, or months,
or even years if need be. Keep in mind that Mr. McMurphy is
committed. The length of time he spends in this hospital is
entirely up to us. Now, if there is nothing else . . ."

the way the Big Nurse acted so confident in that
staff meeting, that worried me for a while, but
it didn't make any difference to McMurphy. All weekend, and
the next week, he was just as hard on her and her black boys
as he ever was, and the patients were loving it. He'd won his
bet; he'd got the nurse's goat the way he said he would, and
had collected on it, but that didn't stop him from going right
ahead and acting like he always had, hollering up and down
the hall, laughing at the black boys, frustrating the whole
staff, even going so far as to step up to the Big Nurse in the
hall one time and ask her, if she didn't mind tellin', just what
was the actual inch-by-inch measurement on them great big
ol' breasts that she did her best to conceal but never could.
She walked right on past, ignoring him just like she chose to

ignore the way nature had tagged her with those outsized
badges of femininity, just like she was above him, and sex, and
everything else that's weak and of the flesh.

When she posted work assignments on the bulletin board,
and he read that she'd given him latrine duty, he went to her
office and knocked on that window of hers and personally
thanked her for the honor, and told her he'd think of her every
time he swabbed out a urinal. She told him that wasn't necessary; just do his work and that would be sufficient, thank you.

The most work he did on them was to run a brush around
the bowls once or twice apiece, singing some song as loud as
he could in time to the swishing brush; then he'd splash in
some Clorox and he'd be through. "That's clean enough," he'd
tell the black boy who got after him for the way he hurried
through his job, "maybe not clean enough for *some* people,
but myself I plan to piss in 'em, not eat lunch out of 'em."
And when the Big Nurse gave in to the black boy's frustrated
pleading and came in to check McMurphy's cleaning assign-
ment personally, she brought a little compact mirror and she
held it under the rim of the bowls. She walked along shaking
her head and saying, "Why, this is an outrage . . . an outrage . . ." at every bowl. McMurphy sidled right along beside
her, winking down his nose and saying in answer, "No; that's a
toilet bowl . . . a *toilet* bowl."

But she didn't lose control again, or even act at all like she
might. She would get after him about the toilets, using that
same terrible, slow, patient pressure she used on everybody, as
he stood there in front of her, looking like a little kid getting
a bawling out, hanging his head, and the toe of one boot on
top of the other, saying, "I *try* and *try*, ma'am, but I'm afraid
I'll never make my mark as head man of the crappers."

Once he wrote something on a slip of paper, strange writing
that looked like a foreign alphabet, and stuck it up under one
of those toilet bowl rims with a wad of gum; when she came
to that toilet with her mirror she gave a short gasp at what she
read reflected and dropped her mirror in the toilet. But she
didn't lose control. That doll's face and that doll's smile were

forged in confidence. She stood up from the toilet bowl and gave him a look that would peel paint and told him it was his job to make the latrine *cleaner*, not dirtier.

Actually, there wasn't much cleaning of any kind getting done on the ward. As soon as it came time in the afternoon when the schedule called for house duties, it was also time for the baseball games to be on TV, and everybody went and lined the chairs up in front of the set and they didn't move out of them until dinner. It didn't make any difference that the power was shut off in the Nurses' Station and we couldn't see a thing but that blank gray screen, because McMurphy'd entertain us for hours, sit and talk and tell all kinds of stories, like how he made a thousand dollars in one month driving truck for a gyppo outfit and then lost every penny of it to some Canadian in an ax-throwing contest, or how he and a buddy slick-tongued a guy into riding a brahma bull at a rodeo in Albany, into riding him while he wore a blindfold: "Not the bull, I mean, the *guy* had on the blindfold." They told the guy that the blindfold would keep him from getting dizzy when the bull went to spinning; then, when they got a bandanna wrapped around his eyes to where he couldn't see, they set him on that bull backward. McMurphy told it a couple of times and slapped his thigh with his hat and laughed everytime he remembered it. "Blindfolded and backwards . . . And I'm a sonofagun if he didn't stay the limit and won the purse. And I was second; if he'd been throwed I'd of took first and a neat little purse. I swear the next time I pull a stunt like that I'll blindfold the damn bull instead."

Whack his leg and throw back his head and laugh and laugh, digging his thumb into the ribs of whoever was sitting next to him, trying to get him to laugh too.

There was times that week when I'd hear that full-throttled laugh, watch him scratching his belly and stretching and yawning and leaning back to wink at whoever he was joking with, everything coming to him just as natural as drawing breath, and I'd quit worrying about the Big Nurse and the Combine behind her. I'd think he was strong enough being his own self that he would never back down the way she was hoping he would. I'd think, maybe he truly is something extraordinary. He's what he is, that's it. Maybe that makes him strong enough, being what he is. The Combine hasn't got to him in all these years; what makes that nurse think she's gonna be able to do it in a few weeks? He's not gonna let them twist him and manufacture him.

And later, hiding in the latrine from the black boys, I'd take a look at my own self in the mirror and wonder how it was possible that anybody could manage such an enormous thing as being what he was. There'd be my face in the mirror, dark and hard with big, high cheekbones like the cheek underneath them had been hacked out with a hatchet, eyes all black and hard and mean-looking, just like Papa's eyes or the eyes of all those tough, mean-looking Indians you see on TV, and I'd think, That ain't me, that ain't my face. It wasn't even me when I was trying to be that face. I wasn't even really me then; I was just being the way I looked, the way people wanted. It don't seem like I ever have been me. How can McMurphy be what he is?

I was seeing him different than when he first came in; I was seeing more to him than just big hands and red sideburns and a broken-nosed grin. I'd see him do things that didn't fit with his face or hands, things like painting a picture at OT with real paints on a blank paper with no lines or numbers anywhere on it to tell him where to paint, or like writing letters to somebody in a beautiful flowing hand. How could a man who looked like him paint pictures or write letters to people, or be upset and worried like I saw him once when he got a letter back? These were the kind of things you expected from Billy Bibbit or Harding. Harding had hands that looked like they should have done paintings, though they never did; Harding trapped his hands and forced them to work sawing planks for doghouses. McMurphy wasn't like that. He hadn't let what he looked like run his life one way or the other, any more than he'd let the Combine mill him into fitting where they wanted him to fit.

I was seeing lots of things different. I figured the fog machine had broke down in the walls when they turned it up too high for that meeting on Friday, so now they weren't able to circulate fog and gas and foul up the way things looked. For the first time in years I was seeing people with none of that black outline they used to have, and one night I was even able to see out the windows.

Like I explained, most nights before they ran me to bed they gave me this pill, knocked me out and kept me out. Or if something went haywire with the dose and I woke up, my eyes were all crusted over and the dorm was full of smoke, wires in the walls loaded to the limit, twisting and sparking death and hate in the air—all too much for me to take so I'd ram my head under the pillow and try to get back to sleep. Every time I peeked back out there would be the smell of burning hair and a sound like sidemeat on a hot griddle.

But this one night, a few nights after the big meeting, I woke up and the dorm was clean and silent; except for the soft breathing of the men and the stuff rattling around loose under the brittle ribs of the two old Vegetables, it was dead quiet. A window was up, and the air in the dorm was clear and had a taste to it made me feel kind of giddy and drunk, gave me this sudden yen to get up out of bed and do something.

I slid from between the sheets and walked barefoot across the cold tile between the beds. I felt the tile with my feet and wondered how many times, how many thousand times, had I run a mop over this same tile floor and never felt it at all. That mopping seemed like a dream to me, like I couldn't exactly believe all those years of it had really happened. Only that cold linoleum under my feet was real right then, only that moment.

I walked among the guys heaped in long white rows like snowbanks, careful not to bump into somebody, till I came to the wall with the windows. I walked down the windows to one where the shade popped softly in and out with the breeze, and I pressed my forehead up against the mesh. The wire was cold and sharp, and I rolled my head against it from side to side to feel it with my cheeks, and I smelled the breeze. It's fall coming, I thought, I can smell that sour-molasses smell of silage, clanging the air like a bell—smell somebody's been burning oak leaves, left them to smolder overnight because they're too green.

It's fall coming, I kept thinking, fall coming; just like that was the strangest thing ever happened. Fall. Right outside here it was spring a while back, then it was summer, and now it's fall—that's sure a curious idea.

I realized I still had my eyes shut. I had shut them when I put my face to the screen, like I was scared to look outside. Now I had to open them. I looked out the window and saw for the first time how the hospital was out in the country. The moon was low in the sky over the pastureland; the face of it was scarred and scuffed where it had just torn up out of the snarl of scrub oak and madrone trees on the horizon. The stars up close to the moon were pale; they got brighter and braver the farther they got out of the circle of light ruled by the giant moon. It called to mind how I noticed the exact same thing when I was off on a hunt with Papa and the uncles and I lay rolled in blankets Grandma had woven, lying off a piece from where the men hunkered around the fire as they passed a quart jar of cactus liquor in a silent circle. I watched that big Oregon prairie moon above me put all the stars around it to shame. I kept awake watching, to see if the moon ever got dimmer or if the stars got brighter, till the dew commenced to drift onto my cheeks and I had to pull a blanket over my head.

Something moved on the grounds down beneath my window—cast a long spider of shadow out across the grass as it ran out of sight behind a hedge. When it ran back to where I could get a better look, I saw it was a dog, a young, gangly mongrel slipped off from home to find out about things went on after dark. He was sniffing digger squirrel holes, not with a notion to go digging after one but just to get an idea what they were up to at this hour. He'd run his muzzle down a hole, butt up in the air and tail going, then dash off to another. The moon glistened around him on the wet grass, and when he ran he left tracks like dabs of dark paint spattered across the blue shine of the lawn. Galloping from one particularly interesting hole to the next, he became so took with what was coming off—the moon up there, the night, the breeze full of smells so wild makes a young dog drunk—that he had to lie down on his back and roll. He twisted and thrashed around like a fish, back bowed and belly up, and when he got to his feet and shook himself a spray came off him in the moon like silver scales.

He sniffed all the holes over again one quick one, to get the smells down good, then suddenly froze still with one paw lifted and his head tilted, listening. I listened too, but I couldn't hear anything except the popping of the window shade. I listened for a long time. Then, from a long way off, I heard a high, laughing gabble, faint and coming closer. Canada honkers going south for the winter. I remembered all the hunting and belly-crawling I'd ever done trying to kill a honker, and that I never got one.

I tried to look where the dog was looking to see if I could find the flock, but it was too dark. The honking came closer and closer till it seemed like they must be flying right through the dorm, right over my head. Then they crossed the moon—a black, weaving necklace, drawn into a V by that lead goose. For an instant that lead goose was right in the center of that circle, bigger than the others, a black cross opening and closing, then he pulled his V out of sight into the sky once more.

I listened to them fade away till all I could hear was my memory of the sound. The dog could still hear them a long time after me. He was still standing with his paw up; he hadn't moved or barked when they flew over. When he couldn't hear them any more either, he commenced to lope off in the direction they had gone, toward the highway, loping steady and solemn like he had an appointment. I held my breath and I could hear the flap of his big paws on the grass as he loped; then I could hear a car speed up out of a turn. The headlights loomed over the rise and peered ahead down the highway. I watched the dog and the car making for the same spot of pavement.

The dog was almost to the rail fence at the edge of the grounds when I felt somebody slip up behind me. Two people. I didn't turn, but I knew it was the black boy named Geever and the nurse with the birthmark and the crucifix. I heard a whir of fear start up in my head. The black boy took my arm and pulled me around. "I'll get 'im," he says.

"It's chilly at the window there, Mr. Bromden," the nurse tells me. "Don't you think we'd better climb back into our nice toasty bed?"

"He cain't hear," the black boy tells her. "I'll take him. He's always untying his sheet and roaming 'round."

And I move and she draws back a step and says, "Yes, please do," to the black boy. She's fiddling with the chain runs down her neck. At home she locks herself in the bathroom out of sight, strips down, and rubs that crucifix all over that stain running from the corner of her mouth in a thin line down across her shoulders and breasts. She rubs and rubs and hails Mary to beat thunder, but the stain stays. She looks in the mirror, sees it's darker'n ever. Finally takes a wire brush used to take paint off boats and scrubs the stain away, puts a nightgown on over the raw, oozing hide, and crawls in bed.

But she's too full of the stuff. While she's asleep it rises in her throat and into her mouth, drains out of that corner of her mouth like purple spit and down her throat, over her body. In the morning she sees how she's stained again and somehow she figures it's not really from inside her—how could it be? a good Catholic girl like her?—and she figures it's on account of working evenings among a whole wardful of people like me. It's all our fault, and she's going to get us for it if it's the last thing she does. I wish McMurphy'd wake up and help me.

"You get him tied in bed, Mr. Geever, and I'll prepare a medication."

I n the group meetings there were gripes coming up that had been buried so long the thing being griped about had already changed. Now that McMurphy was around to back them up, the guys started letting fly at everything that had ever happened on the ward they didn't like.

"Why does the dorms have to be locked on the weekends?" Cheswick or somebody would ask. "Can't a fellow even have the weekends to himself?"

"Yeah, Miss Ratched," McMurphy would say. "Why?"

"If the dorms were left open, we have learned from past experience, you men would return to bed after breakfast."

"Is that a mortal sin? I mean, *normal* people get to sleep late on the weekends."

"You men are in this hospital," she would say like she was repeating it for the hundredth time, "because of your proven inability to adjust to society. The doctor and I believe that every minute spent in the company of others, with some exceptions, is therapeutic, while every minute spent brooding alone only increases your separation."

"Is that the reason that there has to be at least eight guys together before they can be taken off the ward to OT or PT or one of them Ts?"

"That is correct."

"You mean it's sick to want to be off by yourself?"

"I didn't say that—"

"You mean if I go into latrine to relieve myself I should take along at least seven buddies to keep me from brooding on the can?"

Before she could come up with an answer to that, Cheswick bounced to his feet and hollered at her, "Yeah, is that what you mean?" and the other Acutes sitting around the meeting would say "Yeah, yeah, is that what you mean?"

She would wait till they all died down and the meeting was quiet again, then say quietly, "If you men can calm yourself enough to act like a group of adults at a discussion instead of children on the playground, we will ask the doctor if he thinks it would be beneficial to consider a change in the ward policy at this time. Doctor?"

Everybody knew the kind of answer the doctor would make, and before he even had the chance Cheswick would be off on another complaint. "Then what about our cigarettes, Miss Ratched?"

"Yeah, what about that," the Acutes grumbled.

McMurphy turned to the doctor and put the question straight to *him* this time before the nurse had a chance to answer. "Yeah, Doc, what about our cigarettes? How does she have the right to keep the cigarettes—*our* cigarettes—piled up on her desk in there like she owned them, bleed a pack out to us now and again whenever she feels like it. I don't care much about the idea of buying a carton of cigarettes and having somebody tell me when I can smoke them."

The doctor tilted his head so he could look at the nurse through his glasses. He hadn't heard about her taking over the extra cigarettes to stop the gambling. "What's this about cigarettes, Miss Ratched? I don't believe I've heard—"

"I feel, Doctor, that three and four and sometimes five packages of cigarettes a day are entirely too many for a man to smoke. That is what seemed to be happening last week—after Mr. McMurphy's arrival—and that is why I thought it might be best to impound the cartons the men purchased at the canteen and allow each man only one pack a day."

McMurphy leaned forward and whispered loudly to Cheswick, "Hear tell her next decision is about trips to the can; not only does a guy have to take his seven buddies into the latrine with him but he's also limited to two trips a day, to be taken when she says so."

And leaned back in his chair and laughed so hard that nobody else could say anything for nearly a minute.

McMurphy was getting a lot of kick out of all the ruckus he

was raising, and I think was a little surprised that he wasn't getting a lot of pressure from the staff too, especially surprised that the Big Nurse wasn't having any more to say to him than she was. "I thought the old buzzard was tougher than this," he said to Harding after one meeting; "Maybe all she needed to straighten her out was a good bringdown. The thing is"— he frowned—"she acts like she still holds all the cards up that white sleeve of hers."

He went on getting a kick out of it till about Wednesday of the next week. Then he learned why the Big Nurse was so sure of her hand. Wednesday's the day they pack everybody up who hasn't got some kind of rot and move to the swimming pool, whether we want to go or not. When the fog was on the ward I used to hide in it to get out of going. The pool always scared me; I was always afraid I'd step in over my head and drown, be sucked off down the drain and clean out to sea. I used to be real brave around water when I was a kid on the Columbia; I'd walk the scaffolding around the falls with all the other men, scrambling around with water roaring green and white all around me and the mist making rainbows, without even any hobnails like the men wore. But when I saw my Papa start getting scared of things, I got scared too, got so I couldn't even stand a shallow pool.

We came out of the locker room and the pool was pitching and splashing and full of naked men; whooping and yelling bounced off the high ceiling the way it always does in indoor swimming pools. The black boys herded us into it. The water was a nice warm temperature but I didn't want to get away from the side (the black boys walk along the edge with long bamboo poles to shove you away from the side if you try to grab on) so I stayed close to McMurphy on account of I knew they wouldn't try to make him go into deep water if he didn't want to.

He was talking to the lifeguard, and I was standing a few feet away. McMurphy must of been standing in a hole because he was having to tread water where I was just standing on the bottom. The lifeguard was standing on the edge of the pool; he had a whistle and a T-shirt on with his ward number on it. He and McMurphy had got to talking about the difference between hospital and jail, and McMurphy was saying how much better the hospital was. The lifeguard wasn't so sure. I heard him tell McMurphy that, for one thing, being committed ain't like being sentenced. "You're sentenced in a jail, and you got a date ahead of you when you *know* you're gonna be turned loose," he said.

McMurphy stopped splashing around like he had been. He swam slowly to the edge of the pool and held there, looking up at the lifeguard. "And if you're committed?" he asked after a pause.

The lifeguard raised his shoulders in a musclebound shrug and tugged at the whistle around his neck. He was an old pro-footballer with cleat marks in his forehead, and every so often when he was off his ward a signal would click back of his eyes and his lips'd go to spitting numbers and he'd drop to all fours in a line stance and cut loose on some strolling nurse, drive a shoulder in her kidneys just in time to let the halfback shoot past through the hole behind him. That's why he was up on Disturbed; whenever he wasn't lifeguarding he was liable to do something like that.

He shrugged again at McMurphy's question, then looked back and forth to see if any black boys were around, and knelt close to the edge of the pool. He held his arm out for McMurphy to look at.

"You see this cast?"

McMurphy looked at the big arm. "You don't have a cast on that arm, buddy."

The lifeguard just grinned. "Well, that cast's on there because I got a bad fracture in the last game with the Browns. I can't get back in togs till the fracture knits and I get the cast off. The nurse on my ward tells me she's curing the arm in secret. Yeah, man, she says if I go easy on that arm, don't exert it or nothing, she'll take the cast off and I can get back with the ball club."

He put his knuckles on the wet tile, went into a three-point stance to test how the arm was coming along. McMurphy watched him a minute, then asked how long he'd been waiting for them to tell him his arm was healed so he could leave the hospital. The lifeguard raised up slowly and rubbed his arm. He acted hurt that McMurphy had asked that, like he thought he was being accused of being soft and licking his wounds. "I'm committed," he said. "I'd of left here before now if it was up to me. Maybe I couldn't play first string, with this bum arm, but I could of folded towels, couldn't I? I could of done *something*. That nurse on my ward, she keeps telling the doctor I ain't ready. Not even to fold towels in the crummy old locker room, I ain't ready."

He turned and walked over to his lifeguard chair, climbed up the chair ladder like a drugged gorilla, and peered down at us, his lower lip pushed way out. "I was picked up for drunk and disorderly, and I been here eight years and eight months," he said.

McMurphy pushed backward from the edge of the pool and trod water and thought this over: he'd had a six months' sentence at the work farm with two months finished, four more to go—and four more months was the most he wanted to spend locked up any place. He'd been close to a month in this nuthouse and it might be a lot better than a work farm, what with good beds and orange juice for breakfast, but it wasn't better to the point that he'd want to spend a couple of years here.

He swam over to the steps at the shallow end of the pool and sat there the rest of the period, tugging that little tuft of wool at his throat and frowning. Watching him sitting there frowning all to himself, I remembered what the Big Nurse had said in the meeting, and I began to feel afraid.

When they blew the whistle for us to leave the pool and we all were straggling toward the locker room, we ran into this other ward coming into the swimming pool for their period, and in the footbath at the shower you had to go through was this one kid from the other ward. He had a big spongy pink head and bulgy hips and legs—like somebody'd grabbed a

balloon full of water and squeezed it in the middle—and he
was lying on his side in the footbath, making noises like a
sleepy seal. Cheswick and Harding helped him stand up, and
he lay right back down in the footbath. The head bobbed
around in the disinfectant. McMurphy watched them lift him
standing again.

"What the devil is he?" he asked.

"He has hydrocephalus," Harding told him; "Some manner
of lymph disorder, I believe. Head fills up with liquid. Give us
a hand helping him stand up."

They turned the kid loose, and he lay back down in the
footbath again; the look on his face was patient and helpless
and stubborn; his mouth sputtered and blew bubbles in the
milky-looking water. Harding repeated his request to Mc-
Murphy to give them a hand, and he and Cheswick bent down
to the kid again. McMurphy pushed past them and stepped
across the kid into the shower.

"Let him lay," he said, washing himself down in the shower.
"Maybe he don't like deep water."

I could see it coming. The next day he surprised everybody
on the ward by getting up early and polishing that latrine till
it sparkled, and then went to work on the hall floors when the
black boys asked him to. Surprised everybody but the Big
Nurse; she acted like it was nothing surprising at all.

And that afternoon in the meeting when Cheswick said that
everybody'd agreed that there should be some kind of showdown on the cigarette situation, saying, "I ain't no little kid
to have cigarettes kept from me like cookies! We want something done about it, ain't that right, Mack?" and waited for
McMurphy to back him up, all he got was silence.

He looked over at McMurphy's corner. Everybody did. Mc-
Murphy was there, studying the deck of cards that slid in and
out of sight in his hands. He didn't even look up. It was
awfully quiet; there was just that slap of greasy cards and Cheswick's heavy breathing.

"I want something *done!*" Cheswick suddenly yelled again.
"I ain't no little kid!" He stamped his foot and looked around

him like he was lost and might break out crying any minute.
He clenched both fists and held them at his chubby round
chest. His fists made little pink balls against the green, and
they were clenched so hard he was shaking.

He never had looked big; he was short and too fat and had a
bald spot in the back of his head that showed like a pink dollar, but standing there by himself in the center of the day
room like that he looked tiny. He looked at McMurphy and got
no look back, and went down the line of Acutes looking for
help. Each time a man looked away and refused to back him
up, and the panic on his face doubled. His looking finally came
to a stop at the Big Nurse. He stamped his foot again.

"I want something *done!* Hear me? I want *something* done!
Something! Something! Some—"

The two big black boys clamped his arms from behind, and
the least one threw a strap around him. He sagged like he'd
been punctured, and the two big ones dragged him up to Disturbed; you could hear the soggy bounce of him going up the
steps. When they came back and sat down, the Big Nurse
turned to the line of Acutes across the room and looked at
them. Nothing had been said since Cheswick left.

"Is there any more discussion," she said, "on the rationing of
cigarettes?"

Looking down the canceled row of faces hanging against the
wall across the room from me, my eyes finally came to Mc-
Murphy in his chair in the corner, concentrating on improving
his one-handed card cut . . . and the white tubes in the
ceiling begin to pump their refrigerated light again . . . I
can feel it, beams all the way into my stomach.

After McMurphy doesn't stand up for us any longer, some
of the Acutes talk and say he's still outsmarting the Big Nurse,
say that he got word she was about to send him to Disturbed
and decided to toe the line a while, not give her any reason.
Others figure he's letting her relax, then he's going to spring
something new on her, something wilder and more ornery than
ever. You can hear them talking in groups, wondering.

But me, I *know* why. I heard him talk to the lifeguard. He's finally getting cagey, is all. The way Papa finally did when he came to realize that he couldn't beat that group from town who wanted the government to put in the dam because of the money and the work it would bring, and because it would get rid of the village: Let that tribe of fish Injuns take their stink and their two hundred thousand dollars the government is paying them and go some place else with it! Papa had done the smart thing signing the papers; there wasn't anything to gain by bucking it. The government would of got it anyhow, sooner or later; this way the tribe would get paid good. It was the smart thing. McMurphy was doing the smart thing. I could see that. He was giving in because it was the smartest thing to do, not because of any of these other reasons the Acutes were making up. He didn't say so, but I knew and I told myself it was the smart thing to do. I told myself that over and over: It's safe. Like hiding. It's the smart thing to do, nobody could say any different. I know what he's doing.

Then one morning all the Acutes know too, know his real reason for backing down and that the reasons they been making up were just lies to kid themselves. He never says a thing about the talk he had with the lifeguard, but they know. I figure the nurse broadcast this during the night along all the little lines in the dorm floor, because they know all at once. I can tell by the way they look at McMurphy that morning when he comes in to the day room. Not looking like they're mad with him, or even disappointed, because they can understand as well as I can that the only way he's going to get the Big Nurse to lift his commitment is by acting like she wants, but still looking at him like they wished things didn't have to be this way.

Even Cheswick could understand it and didn't hold anything against McMurphy for not going ahead and making a big fuss over the cigarettes. He came back down from Disturbed on the same day that the nurse broadcast the information to the beds, and he told McMurphy himself that he could understand how he acted and that it was surely the sharpest thing to do, considering, and that if he'd thought about Mack being committed he'd never have put him on the spot like he had the other day. He told McMurphy this while we were all being taken over to the swimming pool. But just as soon as we got to the pool he said he did wish *something* mighta been done, though, and dove into the water. And got his fingers stuck some way in the grate that's over the drain at the bottom of the pool, and neither the big lifeguard nor McMurphy nor the two black boys could pry him loose, and by the time they got a screwdriver and undid the grate and brought Cheswick up, with the grate still clutched by his chubby pink and blue fingers, he was drowned.

U p ahead of me in the lunch line I see a tray sling in the air, a green plastic cloud raining milk and peas and vegetable soup. Sefelt's jittering out of the line on one foot with his arms both up in the air, falls backward in a stiff arch, and the whites of his eyes come by me upside down. His head hits the tile with a crack like rocks under water, and he holds the arch, like a twitching, jerking bridge. Fredrickson and Scanlon make a jump to help, but the big black boy shoves them back and grabs a flat stick out of his back pocket, got tape wrapped around it and covered with a brown stain. He pries Sefelt's mouth open and shoves the stick between his teeth, and I hear the stick splinter with Sefelt's bite. I can taste the slivers. Sefelt's jerks slow down and get more powerful, working and building up to big stiff kicks that lift him to a bridge, then falling—lifting and falling, slower and slower, till the Big Nurse comes in and stands over him and he melts limp all over the floor in a gray puddle.

She folds her hands in front of her, might hold a candle, and looks down at what's left of him oozing out of the cuffs of his pants and shirt. "Mr. Sefelt?" she says to the black boy.

"Tha's right—*uhn.*" The black boy is jerking to get his stick back. "Mistuh *See*-fel'."

"And Mr. Sefelt has been asserting he needs *no more medication.*" She nods her head, steps back a step out of the way of him spreading toward her white shoes. She raises her head and looks round her at the circle of Acutes that've come up to see. She nods again and repeats, ". . . needs *no more medication.*" Her face is smiling, pitying, patient, and disgusted all at once —a trained expression.

McMurphy's never seen such a thing. "What's he got wrong with him?" he asks.

She keeps her eye on the puddle, not turning to McMurphy. "Mr. Sefelt is an epileptic, Mr. McMurphy. This means he may be subject to seizures like this at any time if he doesn't follow medical advice. He knows better. We'd told him this would happen when he didn't take his medication. Still, he will insist on acting foolish."

Fredrickson comes out of the line with his eyebrows bristling. He's a sinewy, bloodless guy with blond hair and stringy blond eyebrows and a long jaw, and he acts tough every so often the way Cheswick used to try to do—roar and rant and cuss out one of the nurses, say he's gonna *leave* this stinkin' place! They always let him yell and shake his fist till he quiets down, then ask him if you are *through,* Mr. Fredrickson, we'll go start typing the release—then make book in the Nurses' Station how long it'll be till he's tapping at the glass with a guilty look and asking to apologize and how about just *forgetting* those hotheaded things he said, just pigeonhole those old forms for a day or so, okay?

He steps up to the nurse, shaking his fist at her. "Oh, is that it? Is that it, huh? You gonna crucify old Seef just as if he was doing it to *spite* you or something?"

She lays a comforting hand on his arm, and his fist unrolls. "It's okay, Bruce. Your friend will be all right. Apparently he hasn't been swallowing his Dilantin. I simply don't know what he is doing with it."

She knows as well as anybody; Sefelt holds the capsules in his mouth and gives them to Fredrickson later. Sefelt doesn't like to take them because of what he calls "disastrous side effects," and Fredrickson likes a double dose because he's scared to death of having a fit. The nurse knows this, you can tell by her voice, but to look at her there, so sympathetic and kind, you'd think she was ignorant of anything at all between Fredrickson and Sefelt.

"Yeahhh," says Fredrickson, but he can't work his attack up again. "Yeah, well, you don't need to act like it was as simple as just take the stuff or don't take it. You know how Seef worries about what he looks like and how women think he's ugly and all that, and you know how he thinks the Dilantin—"

"I know," she says and touches his arm again. "He also blames his falling hair on the drug. Poor old fellow."

"He's not that old!"

"I know, Bruce. Why do you get so *upset?* I've never understood what went on between you and your friend that made you get so *defensive!*"

"Well, heck, anyway!" he says and jams his fists in his pockets.

The nurse bends over and brushes a little place clean on the floor and puts her knee on it and starts kneading Sefelt back to some shape. She tells the black boy to stay with the poor old fellow and she'll go send a Gurney down for him; wheel him into the dorm and let him sleep the rest of the day. When she stands she gives Fredrickson a pat on the arm, and he grumbles, "Yeah, I have to take Dilantin too, you know. That's why I know what Seef has to face. I mean, that's why I—well, heck—"

"I understand, Bruce, what *both* of you must go through, but don't you think anything is better than *that?*"

Fredrickson looks where she points. Sefelt has pulled back halfway normal, swelling up and down with big wet, rattling breaths. There's a punk-knot rising on the side of his head where he landed, and a red foam around the black boy's stick where it goes into his mouth, and his eyes are beginning to roll back into the whites. His hands are nailed out to each side with the palms up and the fingers jerking open and shut, just the way I've watched men jerk at the Shock Shop strapped to the crossed table, smoke curling up out of the palms from the current. Sefelt and Fredrickson never been to the Shock Shop. They're manufactured to generate their own voltage, store it in their spines and can be turned on remote from the steel door in the Nurses' Station if they get out of line—be right in the best part of a dirty joke and stiffen like the jolt hit square in the small of the back. It saves the trouble of taking them over to that room.

The nurse gives Fredrickson's arm a little shake like he'd gone to sleep, and repeats, "Even if you take into consideration the harmful effects of the medicine, don't you think it's better than *that?*"

As he stares down at the floor, Fredrickson's blond eyebrows are raised like he's seeing for the first time just how *he* looks at least once a month. The nurse smiles and pats his arm and heads for the door, glares at the Acutes to shame them for gathering around watching such a thing; when she's gone, Fredrickson shivers and tries to smile.

"I don't know *what* I got mad at the old girl about—I mean, she didn't do anything to give me a reason to blow up like that, did she?"

It isn't like he wants an answer; it's more sort of realizing that he can't put his finger on a reason. He shivers again and starts to slip back away from the group. McMurphy comes up and asks him in a low voice what *is* it they take?

"Dilantin, McMurphy, an anti-convulsant, if you must know."

"Don't it work or something?"

"Yeah, I guess it works all right—if you take it."

"Then what's the sweat about taking it or not?"

"Look, if you must know! Here's the dirty sweat about taking it." Fredrickson reaches up and grabs his lower lip between his thumb and finger, pulls it down to show gums ragged and pink and bloodless around long shiny teeth. "Your *gungs*," he says, hanging onto the lip. "Dilantin gnakes your gungs rot. And a seizure gnakes you grit your teeth. And you—"

There's a noise on the floor. They look to where Sefelt is moaning and wheezing, just as the black boy draws two teeth out with his taped stick.

Scanlon takes his tray and walks away from the bunch, saying, "Hell of a life. Damned if you do and damned if you don't. Puts a man in one confounded *bind*, I'd say."

McMurphy says, "Yeah, I see what you mean," looking down into Sefelt's gathering face. His face has commenced to take on that same haggard, puzzled look of pressure that the face on the floor has.

Whatever it was went haywire in the mechanism, they've just about got it fixed again. The clean, calculated arcade movement is coming back: six-thirty out of bed, seven into the mess hall, eight the puzzles come out for the Chronics and the cards for the Acutes . . . in the Nurses' Station I can see the white hands of the Big Nurse float over the controls.

hey take me with the Acutes sometimes, and sometimes they don't. They take me once with them over to the library and I walk over to the technical section, stand there looking at the titles of books on electronics, books I recognize from that year I went to college; I remember inside the books are full of schematic drawings and equations and theories—hard, sure, safe things.

I want to look at one of the books, but I'm scared to. I'm scared to do anything. I feel like I'm floating in the dusty yellow air of the library, halfway to the bottom, halfway to the top. The stacks of books teeter above me, crazy, zig-zagging, running all different angles to one another. One shelf bends a little to the left, one to the right. Some of them are leaning over me, and I don't see how the books keep from falling out. It goes up and up this way, clear out of sight, the rickety stacks nailed together with slats and two-by-fours, propped up with poles, leaning against ladders, on all sides of me. If I pulled one book out, lord knows what awful thing might result.

I hear somebody walk in, and it's one of the black boys from our ward and he's got Harding's wife with him. They're talking and grinning to each other as they come into the library.

"See here, Dale," the black boy calls over to Harding where he's reading a book, "look here who come to visit you. I tole her it wun't visitin' hours but you know she jus' sweet-talk me into bringin' her right on over here anyhow." He leaves her standing in front of Harding and goes off, saying mysteriously "Don't you forget now, you hear?"

She blows the black boy a kiss, then turns to Harding, slinging her hips forward. "Hello, Dale."

"Honey," he says, but he doesn't make any move to take the couple of steps to her. He looks around him at everybody watching.

She's as tall as he is. She's got on high-heeled shoes and is carrying a black purse, not by the strap, but holding it the way you hold a book. Her fingernails are red as drops of blood against the shiny black patent-leather purse.

"Hey, Mack," Harding calls to McMurphy, who's sitting across the room, looking at a book of cartoons. "If you'll curtail your literary pursuits a moment I'll introduce you to my counterpart and Nemesis; I would be trite and say, 'to my better half,' but I think that phrase indicates some kind of basically equal division, don't you?"

He tries to laugh, and his two slim ivory fingers dip into his shirt pocket for cigarettes, fidget around getting the last one from the package. The cigarette shakes as he places it between his lips. He and his wife haven't moved toward each other yet.

McMurphy heaves up out of his chair and pulls his cap off as he walks over. Harding's wife looks at him and smiles, lifting one of her eyebrows. "Afternoon, Miz Harding," McMurphy says.

She smiles back bigger than before and says, "I hate Mrs. Harding, Mack; why don't you call me Vera?"

They all three sit back down on the couch where Harding was sitting, and he tells his wife about McMurphy and how McMurphy got the best of the Big Nurse, and she smiles and says that it doesn't surprise her a bit. While Harding's telling the story he gets enthusiastic and forgets about his hands, and they weave the air in front of him into a picture clear enough to see, dancing the story to the tune of his voice like two beautiful ballet women in white. His hands can be anything. But as soon as the story's finished he notices McMurphy and his wife are watching the hands, and he traps them between his knees. He laughs about this, and his wife says to him, "Dale, when are you going to learn to laugh instead of making that mousy little squeak?"

It's the same thing that McMurphy said about Harding's laugh on that first day, but it's different somehow; where McMurphy saying it calmed Harding down, her saying it makes him more nervous than ever.

She asks for a cigarette, and Harding dips his fingers in his pocket again and it's empty. "We've been rationed," he says, folding his thin shoulders forward like he was trying to hide the half-smoked cigarette he was holding, "to one pack a day. That doesn't seem to leave a man any margin for chivalry, Vera my dearest."

"Oh Dale, you never do have enough, do you?"

His eyes take on that sly, fevered skittishness as he looks at her and smiles. "Are we speaking symbolically, or are we still dealing with the concrete here-and-now cigarettes? No matter; you know the answer to the question, whichever way you intended it."

"I didn't intend nothing by it except what I said, Dale—"

"You didn't intend *any*thing by it, sweetest; your use of 'didn't' and 'nothing' constitutes a double negative. McMurphy, Vera's English rivals yours for illiteracy. Look, honey, you understand that between 'no' and 'any' there is—"

"All right! That's enough! I meant it both ways. I meant it any way you want to take it. I meant you don't have enough of nothing *period!*"

"Enough of *anything*, my bright little child."

She glares at Harding a second, then turns to McMurphy sitting beside her. "You, Mack, what about you. Can you handle a simple little thing like offering a girl a cigarette?"

His package is already lying in his lap. He looks down at it like he wishes it wasn't, then says, "Sure, I always got cigarettes. Reason is, I'm a bum. I bum them whenever I get the chance is why my pack lasts longer than Harding's here. He smokes only his own. So you can see he's more likely to run out than—"

"You don't have to apologize for my inadequacies, my friend. It neither fits your character nor complements mine."

"No, it doesn't," the girl says. "All you have to do is light my cigarette."

And she leans so far forward to his match that even clear across the room I could see down her blouse.

She talks some more about some of Harding's friends who she wishes would quit dropping around the house looking for him. "You know the type, don't you, Mack?" she says. "The hoity-toity boys with the nice long hair combed so perfectly and the limp little wrists that flip so nice." Harding asks her if it was only him that they were dropping around to see, and she says any man that drops around to see her flips more than his damned limp wrists.

She stands suddenly and says it's time for her to go. She takes McMurphy's hand and tells him she hopes she sees him again sometime and she walks out of the library. McMurphy can't say a word. At the clack of her high heels everybody's head comes up again, and they watch her walk down the hall till she turns out of sight.

"What do you think?" Harding says.

McMurphy starts. "She's got one hell of a set of chabobs," is all he can think of. "Big as Old Lady Ratched's."

"I didn't mean physically, my friend, I mean what do you—"

"Hell's bells, Harding!" McMurphy yells suddenly. "I don't know what to think! What do you want out of me? A marriage counsellor? All I know is this: nobody's very big in the first place, and it looks to me like everybody spends their whole life tearing everybody else down. I know what you want me to think; you want me to feel sorry for you, to think she's a real bitch. Well, you didn't make her feel like any queen either. Well, screw you and 'what do you think?' I've got worries of my own without getting hooked with yours. So just quit!" He glares around the library at the other patients. "Alla you! Quit *bugging* me, goddammit!"

And sticks his cap back on his head and walks back to his cartoon magazine across the room. All the Acutes are looking at each other with their mouths open. What's he hollering at *them* about? Nobody's been bugging him. Nobody's asked him for a thing since they found out that he was trying to behave to keep his commitment from being extended. Now they're surprised at the way he just blew up at Harding and can't figure the way he grabs the book up from the chair and sits down and holds it up close in front of his face—either to keep people from looking at him or to keep from having to look at people.

That night at supper he apologizes to Harding and says he don't know what hung him up so at the library. Harding says perhaps it was his wife; she frequently hangs people up. McMurphy sits staring into his coffee and says, "I don't know, man. I just met her this afternoon. So she sure the hell isn't the one's been giving me bad dreams this last miserable week."

"Why, Mis-tur McMurphy," Harding cries, trying to talk like the little resident boy who comes to the meetings, "you simply must tell us about these dreams. Ah, wait until I get my pencil and pad." Harding is trying to be funny to relieve the strain of the apology. He picks up a napkin and a spoon and acts like he's going to take notes. "Now. Pre-cisely, what was it you saw in these—ah—dreams?"

McMurphy don't crack a smile. "I don't know, man. Nothing but faces, I guess—just faces."

The next morning Martini is behind the control panel in the tub room, playing like he's a jet pilot. The poker game stops to grin at his act.

"EeeeeeaahHOOoomeerrr. Ground to air, ground to air: object sighted four-oh-sixteen-hundred—appears to be enemy missile. Proceed at once! EeeahhOOOmmmm."

Spins a dial, shoves a lever forward and leans with the bank of the ship. He cranks a needle to "ON FULL" at the side of the panel, but no water comes out of the nozzles set around the square tile booth in front of him. They don't use hydrotherapy any more, and nobody's turned the water on. Brand-new chrome equipment and steel panel never been used. Except for the chrome the panel and shower look just like the hydrotherapy outfits they used at the old hospital fifteen years ago: nozzles capable of reaching parts of the body from every angle, a technician in a rubber apron standing on the other side of the room manipulating the controls on that panel, dictating which nozzles squirt where, how hard, how hot—spray opened soft and soothing, then squeezed sharp as a needle—you hung up there between the nozzles in canvas straps, soaked and limp and wrinkled while the technician enjoyed his toy.

"EeeaaooOOOoommm. . . . Air to ground, air to ground: missile sighted; coming into my sights now. . . ."

Martini bends down and aims over the panel through the ring of nozzles. He closes one eye and peeps through the ring with the other eye.

"On target! Ready . . . Aim . . . Fi—!"

His hands jerk back from the panel and he stands bolt upright, hair flying and both eyes bulging out at the shower booth so wild and scared all the card-players spin around in their chairs to see if they can see it too—but they don't see anything in there but the buckles hanging among the nozzles on stiff new canvas straps.

Martini turns and looks straight at McMurphy. No one else. "Didn't you see thum? Didn't you?"

"See who, Mart? I don't see anything."

"In all those straps? Didn't you?"

McMurphy turns and squints at the shower. "Nope. Not a thing."

"Hold it a minute. They need you to see thum," Martini says.

"Damn you, Martini, I told you I can't see them! Understand? Not a blessed thing!"

"Oh," Martini says. He nods his head and turns from the shower booth. "Well, I didn't see thum either. I's just kidding you."

McMurphy cuts the deck and shuffles it with a buzzing snap. "Well—I don't care for that sort of kiddin', Mart." He cuts to shuffle again, and the cards splash everywhere like the deck exploded between his two trembling hands.

i remember it was a Friday again, three weeks after we voted on TV, and everybody who could walk was herded over to Building One for what they try to tell us is chest X-rays for TB, which I know is a check to see if everybody's machinery is functioning up to par.

We're benched in a long row down a hall leading to a door marked X-RAY. Next to X-ray is a door marked EENT where they check our throats during the winter. Across the hall from us is another bench, and it leads to that metal door. With the line of rivets. And nothing marked on it at all. Two guys are dozing on the bench between two black boys, while another victim inside is getting his treatment and I can hear him screaming. The door opens inward with a whoosh, and I can see the twinkling tubes in the room. They wheel the victim out still smoking, and I grip the bench where I sit to keep from being sucked through that door. A black boy and a white one drag one of the other guys on the bench to his feet, and he sways and staggers under the drugs in him. They usually give you red capsules before Shock. They push him through the door, and the technicians get him under each arm. For a second I see the guy realizes where they got him, and he stiffens both heels into the cement floor to keep from being pulled to the table—then the door pulls shut, phumph, with metal hitting a mattress, and I can't see him any more.

"Man, what they got going on in there?" McMurphy asks Harding.

"In there? Why, that's right, isn't it? You haven't had the pleasure. Pity. An experience no human should be without." Harding laces his fingers behind his neck and leans back to look at the door. "That's the Shock Shop I was telling you about some time back, my friend, the EST, Electro-Shock Therapy. Those fortunate souls in there are being given a free trip to the moon. No, on second thought, it isn't completely free. You pay for the service with brain cells instead of money, and everyone has simply billions of brain cells on deposit. You won't miss a few."

He frowns at the one lone man left on the bench. "Not a very large clientele today, it seems, nothing like the crowds of yesteryear. But then, *c'est la vie*, fads come and go. And I'm afraid we are witnessing the sunset of EST. Our dear head nurse is one of the few with the heart to stand up for a grand old Faulknerian tradition in the treatment of the rejects of sanity: Brain Burning."

The door opens. A Gurney comes whirring out, nobody pushing it, takes the corner on two wheels and disappears smoking up the hall. McMurphy watches them take the last guy in and close the door.

"What they do is"—McMurphy listens a moment—"take some bird in there and shoot *electricity* through his skull?"

"That's a concise way of putting it."

"What the hell *for*?"

"Why, the patient's good, of course. Everything done here is for the patient's good. You may sometimes get the impression, having lived only on our ward, that the hospital is a vast efficient mechanism that would function quite well if the patient were not imposed on it, but that's not true. EST isn't always used for punitive measures, as our nurse uses it, and it isn't pure sadism on the staff's part, either. A number of supposed Irrecoverables were brought back into contact with shock, just as a number were helped with lobotomy and leucotomy. Shock treatment has some advantages; it's cheap, quick, entirely painless. It simply induces a seizure."

"What a life," Sefelt moans. "Give some of us pills to stop a fit, give the rest shock to start one."

Harding leans forward to explain it to McMurphy. "Here's how it came about: two psychiatrists were visiting a slaughterhouse, for God knows what perverse reason, and were watching cattle being killed by a blow between the eyes with a sledgehammer. They noticed that not all of the cattle were killed,

that some would fall to the floor in a state that greatly re-
sembled an epileptic convulsion. 'Ah, *zo*,' the first doctor says.
'Ziz is exactly vot ve need for our patients—zee induced *fit!*'
His colleague agreed, of course. It was known that men coming out of an epileptic convulsion were inclined to be calmer
and more peaceful for a time, and that violent cases completely
out of contact were able to carry on rational conversations after
a convulsion. No one knew why; they still don't. But it was
obvious that if a seizure could be induced in non-epileptics,
great benefits might result. And here, before them, stood a man
inducing seizures every so often with remarkable aplomb."

Scanlon says he thought the guy used a hammer instead of a
bomb, but Harding says he will ignore that completely, and he
goes ahead with the explanation.

"A hammer *is* what the butcher used. And it was here that
the colleague had some reservations. After all, a man wasn't a
cow. Who knows when the hammer might slip and break a
nose? Even knock out a mouthful of teeth? Then where would
they be, with the high cost of dental work? If they were going
to knock a man in the head, they needed to use something
surer and more accurate than a hammer; they finally settled
on electricity."

"Jesus, didn't they think it might do some damage? Didn't
the public raise Cain about it?"

"I don't think you fully understand the public, my friend; in
this country, when something is out of order, then the quickest
way to get it fixed is the best way."

McMurphy shakes his head. "Hoo-*wee!* Electricity through
the head. Man, that's like electrocuting a guy for murder."

"The reasons for both activities are much more closely related than you might think; they are both cures."

"And you say it don't *hurt?*"

"I personally guarantee it. Completely painless. One flash
and you're unconscious immediately. No gas, no needle, no
sledgehammer. Absolutely painless. The thing is, no one ever
wants another one. You . . . change. You forget things. It's
as if"—he presses his hands against his temples, shutting his

eyes—"it's as if the jolt sets off a wild carnival wheel of images, emotions, memories. These wheels, you've seen them; the barker takes your bet and pushes a button. *Chang!* With light and sound and numbers round and round in a whirlwind, and maybe you win with what you end up with and maybe you lose and have to play again. Pay the man for another spin, son, pay the man."

"Take it easy, Harding."

The door opens and the Gurney comes back out with the guy under a sheet, and the technicians go out for coffee. McMurphy runs his hand through his hair. "I don't seem able to get all this stuff that's happening straight in my mind."

"What's that? This shock treatment?"

"Yeah. No, not just that. All this . . ." He waves his hand in a circle. "All these things going on."

Harding's hand touches McMurphy's knee. "Put your troubled mind at ease, my friend. In all likelihood you needn't concern yourself with EST. It's almost out of vogue and only used in the extreme cases nothing else seems to reach, like lobotomy."

"Now lobotomy, that's chopping away part of the brain?"

"You're right again. You're becoming very sophisticated in the jargon. Yes; chopping away the brain. Frontal-lobe castration. I guess if she can't cut below the belt she'll do it above the eyes."

"You mean Ratched."

"I do indeed."

"I didn't think the nurse had the say-so on this kind of thing."

"She does indeed."

McMurphy acts like he's glad to get off talking about shock and lobotomy and get back to talking about the Big Nurse. He asks Harding what he figures is wrong with her. Harding and Scanlon and some of the others have all kinds of ideas. They talk for a while about whether she's the root of all the trouble here or not, and Harding says she's the root of most of it. Most of the other guys think so too, but McMurphy isn't so sure any more. He says he thought so at one time but now he don't know. He says he don't think getting her out of the way would really make much difference; he says that there's something bigger making all this mess and goes on to try to say what he thinks it is. He finally gives up when he can't explain it.

McMurphy doesn't know it, but he's onto what I realized a long time back, that it's not just the Big Nurse by herself, but it's the whole Combine, the nation-wide Combine that's the really big force, and the nurse is just a high-ranking official for them.

The guys don't agree with McMurphy. They say they *know* what the trouble with things is, then get in an argument about that. They argue till McMurphy interrupts them.

"Hell's bells, listen at you," McMurphy says. "All I hear is gripe, gripe, gripe. About the nurse or the staff or the hospital. Scanlon wants to bomb the whole outfit. Sefelt blames the drugs. Fredrickson blames his family trouble. Well, you're all just passing the buck."

He says that the Big Nurse is just a bitter, icy-hearted old woman, and all this business trying to get him to lock horns with her is a lot of bull—wouldn't do anybody any good, especially him. Getting shut of her wouldn't be getting shut of the real deep-down hang-up that's causing the gripes.

"You think not?" Harding says. "Then since you are suddenly so lucid on the problem of mental health, what *is* this trouble? What *is* this deep-down hang-up, as you so cleverly put it."

"I tell you, man, I don't know. I never seen the beat of it." He sits still for a minute, listening to the hum from the X-ray room; then he says, "But if it was no more'n you say, if it was, say, just this old nurse and her sex worries, then the solution to all your problems would be to just throw her down and solve her worries, wouldn't it?"

Scanlon claps his hands. "Hot damn! That's it. You're nominated, Mack, you're just the stud to handle the job."

"Not me. No sir. You got the wrong boy."

"Why not? I thought you's the super-stud with all that whambam."

"Scanlon, buddy, I plan to stay as clear of that old buzzard as I possibly can."

"So I've been noticing," Harding says, smiling. "What's happened between the two of you? You had her on the ropes for a period there; then you let up. A sudden compassion for our angel of mercy?"

"No; I found out a few things, that's why. Asked around some different places. I found out why you guys all kiss her ass so much and bow and scrape and let her walk all over you. I got wise to what you were using me for."

"Oh? That's interesting."

"You're blamed right it's interesting. It's interesting to me that you bums didn't tell me what a risk I was running, twisting her tail that way. Just because I don't like her ain't a sign I'm gonna bug her into adding another year or so to my sentence. You got to swallow your pride sometimes and keep an eye out for old Number One."

"Why, friends, you don't suppose there's anything to this rumor that our Mr. McMurphy has conformed to policy merely to aid his chances of an early release?"

"You know what I'm talking about, Harding. Why didn't you tell me she could keep me committed in here till she's good and ready to turn me loose?"

"Why, I had *forgotten* you were committed." Harding's face folds in the middle over his grin. "Yes. You're becoming sly. Just like the rest of us."

"You damn betcha I'm becoming sly. Why should it be me goes to bat at these meetings over these piddling little gripes about keeping the dorm door open and about cigarettes in the Nurses' Station? I couldn't figure it at first, why you guys were coming to me like I was some kind of savior. Then I just happened to find out about the way the nurses have the big say as to who gets discharged and who doesn't. And I got wise awful damned fast. I said, 'Why, those slippery bastards have *conned* me, snowed me into holding their bag. If that don't beat all, conned ol' R. P. McMurphy.'" He tips his head back and grins at the line of us on the bench. "Well, I don't mean nothing personal, you understand, buddies, but screw that noise. I want out of here just as much as the rest of you. I got just as much to lose hassling that old buzzard as *you* do."

He grins and winks down his nose and digs Harding in the ribs with his thumb, like he's finished with the whole thing but no hard feelings, when Harding says something else.

"No. You've got more to lose than I do, my friend."

Harding's grinning again, looking with that skitterish sideways look of a jumpy mare, a dipping, rearing motion of the head. Everybody moves down a place. Martini comes away from the X-ray screen, buttoning his shirt and muttering, "I wouldn't of believed it if I hadn't saw it," and Billy Bibbit goes to the black glass to take Martini's place.

"You have more to lose than I do," Harding says again. "I'm voluntary. I'm not committed."

McMurphy doesn't say a word. He's got that same puzzled look on his face like there's something isn't right, something he can't put his finger on. He just sits there looking at Harding, and Harding's rearing smile fades and he goes to fidgeting around from McMurphy staring at him so funny. He swallows and says, "As a matter of fact, there are only a few men on the ward who *are* committed. Only Scanlon and—well, I guess some of the Chronics. And you. Not many commitments in the whole hospital. No, not many at all."

Then he stops, his voice dribbling away under McMurphy's eyes. After a bit of silence McMurphy says softly, "Are you bullshitting me?" Harding shakes his head. He looks frightened. McMurphy stands up in the hall and says, "Are you guys *bullshitting* me!"

Nobody'll say anything. McMurphy walks up and down in front of that bench, running his hand around in that thick hair. He walks all the way to the back of the line, then all the way to the front, to the X-ray machine. It hisses and spits at him.

"You, Billy—you *must* be committed, for Christsakes!"

Billy's got his back to us, his chin up on the black screen, standing on tiptoe. No, he says into the machinery.

"Then *why?* *Why?* You're just a young guy! You oughta be out running around in a convertible, bird-dogging girls. All of this"—he sweeps his hand around him again—"why do you stand for it?"

Billy doesn't say anything, and McMurphy turns from him to another couple of guys.

"Tell me why. You gripe, you bitch for *weeks* on end about how you can't stand this place, can't stand the nurse or anything about her, and all the time you ain't committed. I can understand it with some of those old guys on the ward. They're *nuts.* But you, you're not exactly the everyday man on the street, but you're not *nuts.*"

They don't argue with him. He moves on to Sefelt.

"Sefelt, what about you? There's nothing wrong with you but you have fits. Hell, I had an uncle who threw conniptions twice as bad as yours and saw visions from the Devil to boot, but he didn't lock himself in the nuthouse. You could get along outside if you had the guts—"

"Sure!" It's Billy, turned from the screen, his face boiling tears. "Sure!" he screams again. "If we had the g-guts! I could go outside to-today, if I had the guts. My m-m-mother is a good friend of M-Miss Ratched, and I could get an AMA signed this afternoon, if I had the guts!"

He jerks his shirt up from the bench and tries to pull it on, but he's shaking too hard. Finally he slings it from him and turns back to McMurphy.

"You think I wuh-wuh-wuh-*want* to stay in here? You think I wouldn't like a con-convertible and a guh-guh-girl friend? But did you ever have people l-l-laughing at you? No, because you're so b-big and so *tough!* Well, I'm not big and tough. Neither is Harding. Neither is F-Fredrickson. Neither is Suh-Sefelt. Oh—oh, you—you t-talk like we stayed in here because we liked it! Oh—it's n-no use . . ."

He's crying and stuttering too hard to say anything else, and he wipes his eyes with the backs of his hands so he can see. One of the scabs pulls off his hand, and the more he wipes the more he smears blood over his face and in his eyes. Then he starts running blind, bouncing down the hall from side to side with his face a smear of blood, a black boy right after him.

McMurphy turns round to the rest of the guys and opens his mouth to ask something else, and then closes it when he sees how they're looking at him. He stands there a minute with the row of eyes aimed at him like a row of rivets; then he says, "Hell's bells," in a weak sort of way, and he puts his cap back on and pulls it down hard and goes back to his place on the bench. The two technicians come back from coffee and go back in that room across the hall; when the door whooshes open you can smell the acid in the air like when they recharge a battery. McMurphy sits there, looking at that door.

"I don't seem able to get it straight in my mind. . . ."

Crossing the grounds back to the ward, McMurphy lagged back at the tail end of the bunch with his hands in the pockets of his greens and his cap tugged low on his head, brooding over a cold cigarette. Everybody was keeping pretty quiet. They'd got Billy calmed down, and he was walking at the front of the group with a black boy on one side and that white boy from the Shock Shop on the other side.

I dropped back till I was walking beside McMurphy and I wanted to tell him not to fret about it, that nothing could be done, because I could see that there was some thought he was worrying over in his mind like a dog worries at a hole he don't know what's down, one voice saying, Dog, that hole is none of your affair—it's too big and too black and there's a spoor all over the place says bears or something just as bad. And some other voice coming like a sharp whisper out of way back in his breed, not a smart voice, nothing cagey about it, saying, *Sic* 'im, dog, *sic* 'im!

I wanted to tell him not to fret about it, and I was just about to come out and say it when he raised his head and shoved his hat back and speeded up to where the least black boy was walking and slapped him on the shoulder and asked him, "Sam, what say we stop by the canteen here a second so I can pick me up a carton or two of cigarettes."

I had to hurry to catch up, and the run made my heart ring a high, excited pitch in my head. Even in the canteen I still heard that sound my heart had knocked ringing in my head, though my heart had slowed back to normal. The sound reminded me of how I used to feel standing in the cold fall Friday night out on a football field, waiting for the ball to be kicked and the game to get going. The ringing would build and build till I didn't think I could stand still any longer; then the kick would come and it would be gone and the game would be on its way. I felt that same Friday-night ringing now, and felt the same wild, stomping-up-and-down impatience. And I was seeing sharp and high-pitched too, the way I did before a game and the way I did looking out of the dorm window a while back: everything was sharp and clear and solid like I forgot it could be. Lines of toothpaste and shoelaces, ranks of sunglasses and ballpoint pens guaranteed right on them to write a lifetime on butter under water, all guarded against shoplifters by a big-eyed force of Teddy bears sitting high on a shelf over the counter.

McMurphy came stomping up to the counter beside me and hooked his thumbs in his pockets and told the salesgirl to give him a couple of cartons of Marlboros. "Maybe make it three cartons," he said, grinning at her. "I plan to do a lot of smokin'."

The ringing didn't stop until the meeting that afternoon. I'd been half listening to them work on Sefelt to get him to face up to the reality of his problems so he could adjust ("It's the Dilantin!" he finally yells. "Now, Mr. Sefelt, if you're to be helped, you must be honest," she says. "But, it's *got* to be the Dilantin that does it; don't it make my *gums* soft?" She smiles. "Jim, you're forty-five years old . . .") when I happened to catch a look at McMurphy sitting in his corner. He wasn't fiddling with a deck of cards or dozing into a magazine like he had been during all the meetings the last two weeks. And he wasn't slouched down. He was sitting up stiff in his chair with a flushed, reckless look on his face as he looked back and forth from Sefelt to the Big Nurse. As I watched, the ringing went higher. His eyes were blue stripes under those white eyebrows, and they shot back and forth just the way he watched cards turning up around a poker table. I was certain that any minute he was going to do some crazy thing to get him up on Disturbed for sure. I'd seen the same look on other guys before they'd climbed all over a black boy. I gripped down on the arm of my chair and waited, scared it would happen, and, I began to realize, just a little scared it wouldn't.

He kept quiet and watched till they were finished with Sefelt; then he swung half around in his chair and watched while Fredrickson, trying some way to get back at them for the way they had grilled his friend, griped for a few loud minutes about the cigarettes being kept in the Nurses' Station. Fredrickson talked himself out and finally flushed and apologized like always and sat back down. McMurphy still hadn't made any kind of move. I eased up where I'd been gripping the arm of the chair, beginning to think I'd been wrong.

There was just a couple of minutes left in the meeting. The Big Nurse folded up her papers and put them in the basket and set the basket off her lap on the floor, then let her eyes swing to McMurphy for just a second like she wanted to check if he was awake and listening. She folded her hands in her lap and looked down at the fingers and drew a deep breath, shaking her head.

"Boys, I've given a great deal of thought to what I am about to say. I've talked it over with the doctor and with the rest of the staff, and, as much as we regretted it, we all came to the same conclusion—that there should be some manner of punishment meted out for the unspeakable behavior concerning the house duties three weeks ago." She raised her hand and looked around. "We waited this long to say anything, hoping that you men would take it upon yourselves to apologize for the rebellious way you acted. But not a one of you has shown the slightest sign of remorse."

Her hand went up again to stop any interruptions that might come—the movement of a tarot-card reader in a glass arcade case.

"Please understand: We do not impose certain rules and restrictions on you without a great deal of thought about their therapeutic value. A good many of you are in here because you could not adjust to the rules of society in the Outside World, because you refused to face up to them, because you tried to circumvent them and avoid them. At some time—perhaps in your childhood—you may have been allowed to get away with flouting the rules of society. When you broke a rule you knew it. You wanted to be dealt with, *needed* it, but the punishment did not come. That foolish lenience on the part of your parents may have been the germ that grew into your present illness. I tell you this hoping you will understand that it is *entirely for your own good* that we enforce discipline and order."

She let her head twist around the room. Regret for the job she has to do was worked into her face. It was quiet except for that high fevered, delirious ringing in my head.

"It's difficult to enforce discipline in these surroundings. You must be able to see that. What can we do to you? You can't be arrested. You can't be put on bread and water. You must see that the staff has a problem; what *can* we do?"

Ruckly had an idea what they could do, but she didn't pay any attention to it. The face moved with a ticking noise till the features achieved a different look. She finally answered her own question.

"We must take away a privilege. And after careful consideration of the circumstances of this rebellion, we've decided that there would be a certain justice in taking away the privilege of the tub room that you men have been using for your card games during the day. Does this seem unfair?"

Her head didn't move. She didn't look. But one by one everybody else looked at him sitting there in his corner. Even the old Chronics, wondering why everybody had turned to look in one direction, stretched out their scrawny necks like birds and turned to look at McMurphy—faces turned to him, full of a naked, scared hope.

That single thin note in my head was like tires speeding down a pavement.

He was sitting straight up in his chair, one big red finger scratching lazily at the stitchmarks run across his nose. He grinned at everybody looking at him and took his cap by the brim and tipped it politely, then looked back at the nurse.

"So, if there is no discussion on this ruling, I think the hour is almost over . . ."

She paused again, took a look at him herself. He shrugged his shoulders and with a loud sigh slapped both hands down on his knees and pushed himself standing out of the chair. He stretched and yawned and scratched the nose again and started strolling across the day-room floor to where she sat by the Nurses' Station, heisting his pants with his thumbs as he walked. I could see it was too late to keep him from doing whatever fool thing he had in mind, and I just watched, like everybody else. He walked with long steps, too long, and he had his thumbs hooked in his pockets again. The iron in his boot heels cracked lightning out of the tile. He was the logger again, the swaggering gambler, the big redheaded brawling Irishman, the cowboy out of the TV set walking down the middle of the street to meet a dare.

The Big Nurse's eyes swelled out white as he got close. She hadn't reckoned on him doing anything. This was supposed to be her final victory over him, supposed to establish her rule once and for all. But here he comes and he's big as a house!

She started popping her mouth and looking for her black boys, scared to death, but he stopped before he got to her. He stopped in front of her window and he said in his slowest, deepest drawl how he figured he could use one of the smokes he bought this mornin', then ran his hand through the glass.

The glass came apart like water splashing, and the nurse threw her hands to her ears. He got one of the cartons of cigarettes with his name on it and took out a pack, then put it back and turned to where the Big Nurse was sitting like a chalk statue and very tenderly went to brushing the slivers of glass off her hat and shoulders.

"I'm sure *sorry*, ma'am," he said. "Gawd but I am. That window glass was so spick and span I com-*pletely* forgot it was there."

It took just a couple of seconds. He turned and left her sitting there with her face shifting and jerking and walked back across the day room to his chair, lighting up a cigarette.

The ringing that was in my head had stopped.

part 3

after that, McMurphy had things his way for a good long while. The nurse was biding her time till another idea came to her that would put her on top again. She knew she'd lost one big round and was losing another, but she wasn't in any hurry. For one thing, she wasn't about to recommend release; the fight could go on as long as she wanted, till he made a mistake or till he just gave out, or until she could come up with some new tactic that would put her back on top in everybody's eyes.

A good lot happened before she came up with that new tactic. After McMurphy was drawn out of what you might call a short retirement and had announced he was back in the hassle by breaking out her personal window, he made things on the ward pretty interesting. He took part in every meeting, every discussion—drawling, winking, joking his best to wheedle a skinny laugh out of some Acute who'd been scared to grin since he was twelve. He got together enough guys for a basketball team and some way talked the doctor into letting him bring a ball back from the gym to get the team used to handling it. The nurse objected, said the next thing they'd be playing soccer in the day room and polo games up and down the hall, but the doctor held firm for once and said let them go. "A number of the players, Miss Ratched, have shown marked progress since that basketball team was organized; I think it has proven its therapeutic value."

She looked at him a while in amazement. So he was doing a little muscle-flexing too. She marked the tone of his voice for later, for when her time came again, and just nodded and went to sit in her Nurses' Station and fiddle with the controls on her equipment. The janitors had put a cardboard in the frame over her desk till they could get another window pane cut to fit, and she sat there behind it every day like it wasn't even there, just like she could still see right into the day room. Behind that square of cardboard she was like a picture turned to the wall.

She waited, without comment, while McMurphy continued to run around the halls in the mornings in his white-whale shorts, or pitched pennies in the dorms, or ran up and down the hall blowing a nickel-plated ref's whistle, teaching Acutes the fast break from ward door to the Seclusion Room at the other end, the ball pounding in the corridor like cannon shots and McMurphy roaring like a sergeant, "Drive, you puny mothers, *drive!*"

When either one spoke to the other it was always in the most polite fashion. He would ask her nice as you please if he could use her fountain pen to write a request for an Unaccompanied Leave from the hospital, wrote it out in front of her on her desk, and handed her the request and the pen back at the same time with such a nice, "Thank you," and she would look at it and say just as polite that she would "take it up with the staff"—which took maybe three minutes—and come back to tell him she certainly was sorry but a pass was not considered therapeutic at this time. He would thank her again and walk out of the Nurses' Station and blow that whistle loud enough to break windows for miles, and holler, "Practice, you mothers, get that ball and let's get a little sweat rollin'."

He'd been on the ward a month, long enough to sign the bulletin board in the hall to request a hearing in group meeting about an Accompanied Pass. He went to the bulletin board with her pen and put down under TO BE ACCOMPANIED BY: "A twitch I know from Portland named Candy Starr."—and ruined the pen point on the period. The pass request was brought up in group meeting a few days later, the same day, in fact, that workmen put a new glass window in front of the Big Nurse's desk, and after his request had been turned down on the grounds that this Miss Starr didn't seem like the most wholesome person for a patient to go pass with, he shrugged and said that's how she bounces I guess, and got up and walked to the Nurses' Station, to the window that still had the sticker from the glass

company down in the corner, and ran his fist through it again
—explained to the nurse while blood poured from his fingers
that he thought the cardboard had been left out and the frame
was open. "When did they sneak that danged glass in there?
Why that thing is a *menace!*"

The nurse taped his hand in the station while Scanlon and
Harding dug the cardboard out of the garbage and taped it
back in the frame, using adhesive from the same roll the nurse
was bandaging McMurphy's wrist and fingers with. McMurphy
sat on a stool, grimacing something awful while he got his cuts
tended, winking at Scanlon and Harding over the nurse's head.
The expression on her face was calm and blank as enamel, but
the strain was beginning to show in other ways. By the way she
jerked the adhesive tight as she could, showing her remote
patience wasn't what it used to be.

We got to go to the gym and watch our basketball team
—Harding, Billy Bibbit, Scanlon, Fredrickson, Martini, and
McMurphy whenever his hand would stop bleeding long enough
for him to get in the game—play a team of aides. Our two big
black boys played for the aides. They were the best players
on the court, running up and down the floor together like a
pair of shadows in red trunks, scoring basket after basket with
mechanical accuracy. Our team was too short and too slow,
and Martini kept throwing passes to men that nobody but him
could see, and the aides beat us by twenty points. But something happened that let most of us come away feeling there'd
been a kind of victory, anyhow: in one scramble for the ball
our big black boy named Washington got cracked with somebody's elbow, and his team had to hold him back as he stood
straining to where McMurphy was sitting on the ball—not
paying the least bit of heed to the thrashing black boy with
red pouring out of his big nose and down his chest like paint
splashed on a blackboard and hollering to the guys holding
him, "He beggin' for it! The sonabitch jus' *beggin'* for it!"

McMurphy composed more notes for the nurse to find in
the latrine with her mirror. He wrote long outlandish tales about
himself in the log book and signed them Anon. Sometimes

he slept till eight o'clock. She would reprimand him, without heat at all, and he would stand and listen till she was finished and then destroy her whole effect by asking something like did she wear a B cup, he wondered, or a C cup, or any ol' cup at all?

The other Acutes were beginning to follow his lead. Harding began flirting with all the student nurses, and Billy Bibbit completely quit writing what he used to call his "observations" in the log book, and when the window in front of her desk got replaced again, with a big X across it in whitewash to make sure McMurphy didn't have any excuse for not knowing it was there, Scanlon did it in by accidentally bouncing our basketball through it before the whitewashed X was even dry. The ball punctured, and Martini picked it off the floor like a dead bird and carried it to the nurse in the station, where she was staring at the new splash of broken glass all over her desk, and asked couldn't she please fix it with tape or something? Make it well again? Without a word she jerked it out of his hand and stuffed it in the garbage.

So, with basketball season obviously over, McMurphy decided fishing was the thing. He requested another pass after telling the doctor he had some friends at the Siuslaw Bay at Florence who would like to take eight or nine of the patients out deep-sea fishing if it was okay with the staff, and he wrote on the request list out in the hall that this time he would be accompanied by "two sweet old aunts from a little place outside of Oregon City." In the meeting his pass was granted for the next weekend. When the nurse finished officially noting his pass in her roll book, she reached into her wicker bag beside her feet and drew out a clipping that she had taken from the paper that morning, and read out loud that although fishing off the coast of Oregon was having a peak year, the salmon were running quite late in the season and the sea was rough and dangerous. And she would suggest the men give that some thought.

"Good idea," McMurphy said. He closed his eyes and sucked a deep breath through his teeth. "Yes sir! The salt smell o' the poundin' sea, the crack o' the bow against the waves—braving the elements, where men are men and boats are boats. Miss Ratched, you've talked me into it. I'll call and rent that boat this very night. Shall I sign you on?"

Instead of answering she walked to the bulletin board and pinned up the clipping.

The next day he started signing up the guys that wanted to go and that had ten bucks to chip in on boat rent, and the nurse started steadily bringing in clippings from the newspapers that told about wrecked boats and sudden storms on the coast. McMurphy pooh-poohed her and her clippings, saying that his two aunts had spent most of their lives bouncing around the waves in one port or another with this sailor or that, and they both guaranteed the trip was safe as pie, safe as pudding, not a thing to worry about. But the nurse still knew her patients. The clippings scared them more than McMurphy'd figured. He'd figured there would be a rush to sign up, but he'd had to talk and wheedle to get the guys he did. The day before the trip he still needed a couple more before he could pay for the boat.

I didn't have the money, but I kept getting this notion that I wanted to sign the list. And the more he talked about fishing for Chinook salmon the more I wanted to go. I knew it was a fool thing to want; if I signed up it'd be the same as coming right out and telling everybody I wasn't deaf. If I'd been hearing all this talk about boats and fishing it'd show I'd been hearing everything else that'd been said in confidence around me for the past ten years. And if the Big Nurse found out about that, that I'd heard all the scheming and treachery that had gone on when she didn't think anybody was listening, she'd hunt me down with an electric saw, fix me where she *knew* I was deaf and dumb. Bad as I wanted to go, it still made me smile a little to think about it: I had to keep on acting deaf if I wanted to hear at all.

I lay in bed the night before the fishing trip and thought it over, about my being deaf, about the years of not letting on I heard what was said, and I wondered if I could ever act any other way again. But I remembered one thing: it wasn't me that started acting deaf; it was people that first started acting like I was too dumb to hear or see or say anything at all.

It hadn't been just since I came in the hospital, either; people first took to acting like I couldn't hear or talk a long time before that. In the Army anybody with more stripes acted that way toward me. That was the way they figured you were supposed to act around someone looked like I did. And even as far back as grade school I can remember people saying that they didn't think I was listening, so they quit listening to the things I was saying. Lying there in bed, I tried to think back when I first noticed it. I think it was once when we were still living in the village on the Columbia. It was summer. . . .

. . . and I'm about ten years old and I'm out in front of the shack sprinkling salt on salmon for the racks behind the house, when I see a car turn off the highway and come lumbering across the ruts through the sage, towing a load of red dust behind it as solid as a string of boxcars.

I watch the car pull up the hill and stop down a piece from our yard, and the dust keeps coming, crashing into the rear of it and busting in every direction and finally settling on the sage and soapweed round about and making it look like chunks of red, smoking wreckage. The car sits there while the dust settles, shimmering in the sun. I know it isn't tourists with cameras because they never drive this close to the village. If they want to buy fish they buy them back at the highway; they don't come to the village because they probably think we still scalp people and burn them around a post. They don't know some of our people are lawyers in Portland, probably wouldn't believe it if I told them. In fact, one of my uncles became a real lawyer and Papa says he did it purely to prove he could, when he'd rather poke salmon in the fall than anything. Papa says if you don't watch it people will force you one way or the other, into doing what they think you should do, or into just being mule-stubborn and doing the opposite out of spite.

The doors of the car open all at once and three people get

out, two out of the front and one out of the back. They come climbing up the slope toward our village and I see the first two are men in blue suits, and the behind one, the one that got out of the back, is an old white-haired woman in an outfit so stiff and heavy it must be armor plate. They're puffing and sweating by the time they break out of the sage into our bald yard.

The first man stops and looks the village over. He's short and round and wearing a white Stetson hat. He shakes his head at the rickety clutter of fishracks and secondhand cars and chicken coops and motorcycles and dogs.

"Have you ever in all your born days seen the like? Have you now? I swear to heaven, have you *ever?*"

He pulls off the hat and pats his red rubber ball of a head with a handkerchief, careful, like he's afraid of getting one or the other mussed up—the handkerchief or the dab of damp stringy hair.

"Can you imagine people wanting to live this way? Tell me, John, can you?" He talks loud on account of not being used to the roar of the falls.

John's next to him, got a thick gray mustache lifted tight up under his nose to stop out the smell of the salmon I'm working on. He's sweated down his neck and cheeks, and he's sweated clean out through the back of his blue suit. He's making notes in a book, and he keeps turning in a circle, looking at our shack, our little garden, at Mama's red and green and yellow Saturday-night dresses drying out back on a stretch of bedcord—keeps turning till he makes a full circle and comes back to me, looks at me like he just sees me for the first time, and me not but two yards away from him. He bends toward me and squints and lifts his mustache up to his nose again like it's me stinking instead of the fish.

"Where do you suppose his parents are?" John asks. "Inside the house? Or out on the falls? We might as well talk this over with the man while we're out here."

"I, for one, am not going inside that hovel," the fat guy says.

"That hovel," John says through his mustache, "is where the

Chief lives, Brickenridge, the man we are here to deal with, the noble leader of these people."

"Deal with? Not me, not my job. They pay me to appraise, not fraternize."

This gets a laugh out of John.

"Yes, that's true. But someone should inform them of the government's plans."

"If they don't already know, they'll know soon enough."

"It would be very simple to go in and talk with him."

"Inside in that squalor? Why, I'll just bet you anything that place is acrawl with black widows. They say these 'dobe shacks always house a regular civilization in the walls between the sods. And *hot*, lord-a-mercy, I hope to tell you. I'll wager it's a regular oven in there. Look, look how overdone little Hiawatha is here. Ho. Burnt to a fair turn, he is."

He laughs and dabs at his head and when the woman looks at him he stops laughing. He clears his throat and spits into the dust and then walks over and sits down in the swing Papa built for me in the juniper tree, and sits there swinging back and forth a little bit and fanning himself with his Stetson.

What he said makes me madder the more I think about it. He and John go ahead talking about our house and village and property and what they are worth, and I get the notion they're talking about these things around me because they don't know I speak English. They are probably from the East someplace, where people don't know anything about Indians but what they see in the movies. I think how ashamed they're going to be when they find out I know what they are saying.

I let them say another thing or two about the heat and the house; then I stand up and tell the fat man, in my very best schoolbook language, that our sod house is likely to be cooler than any one of the houses in town, *lots* cooler! "I know for a *fact* that it's cooler'n that school I go to and even cooler'n that movie house in The Dalles that advertises on that sign drawn with icicle letters that it's 'cool inside'!"

And I'm just about to go and tell them, how, if they'll come on in, I'll go get Papa from the scaffolds on the falls, when I

see that they don't look like they'd heard me talk at all. They
aren't even looking at me. The fat man is swinging back and
forth, looking off down the ridge of lava to where the men are
standing their places on the scaffolding in the falls, just plaid-
shirted shapes in the mist from this distance. Every so often
you can see somebody shoot out an arm and take a step forward like a swordfighter, and then hold up his fifteen-foot
forked spear for somebody on the scaffold above him to pull
off the flopping salmon. The fat guy watches the men standing in their places in the fifty-foot veil of water, and bats his
eyes and grunts every time one of them makes a lunge for a
salmon.

The other two, John and the woman, are just standing. Not
a one of the three acts like they heard a thing I said; in fact
they're all looking off from me like they'd as soon I wasn't
there at all.

And everything stops and hangs this way for a minute.

I get the funniest feeling that the sun is turned up brighter
than before on the three of them. Everything else looks like
it usually does—the chickens fussing around in the grass on
top of the 'dobe houses, the grasshoppers batting from bush to
bush, the flies being stirred into black clouds around the fish
racks by the little kids with sage flails, just like every other
summer day. Except the sun, on these three strangers, is all of
a sudden way the hell brighter than usual and I can see the . . .
seams where they're put together. And, almost, see the apparatus inside them take the words I just said and try to fit
the words in here and there, this place and that, and when they
find the words don't have any place ready-made where they'll
fit, the machinery disposes of the words like they weren't even
spoken.

The three are stock still while this goes on. Even the swing's
stopped, nailed out at a slant by the sun, with the fat man
petrified in it like a rubber doll. Then Papa's guinea hen wakes
up in the juniper branches and sees we got strangers on the
premises and goes to barking at them like a dog, and the spell
breaks.

The fat man hollers and jumps out of the swing and sidles away through the dust, holding his hat up in front of the sun so's he can see what's up there in the juniper tree making such a racket. When he sees it's nothing but a speckled chicken he spits on the ground and puts his hat on.

"I, myself, sincerely *feel*," he says, "that whatever offer we make on this . . . metropolis will be quite sufficient."

"Could be. I still think we should make some effort to speak with the Chief—"

The old woman interrupts him by taking one ringing step forward. "No." This is the first thing she's said. "No," she says again in a way that reminds me of the Big Nurse. She lifts her eyebrows and looks the place over. Her eyes spring up like the numbers in a cash register; she's looking at Mamma's dresses hung so careful on the line, and she's nodding her head.

"No. We don't talk with the Chief today. Not yet. I think . . . that I agree with Brickenridge for once. Only for a different reason. You recall the record we have shows the wife is not Indian but white? White. A woman from town. Her name is Bromden. He took her name, not she his. Oh, yes, I think if we just leave now and go back into town, and, of course, spread the word with the townspeople about the government's plans so they understand the advantages of having a hydroelectric dam and a lake instead of a cluster of shacks beside a falls, *then* type up an offer—and mail it to the wife, you see, by mistake? I feel our job will be a great deal easier."

She looks off to the men on the ancient, rickety, zigzagging scaffolding that has been growing and branching out among the rocks of the falls for hundreds of years.

"Whereas if we meet now with the husband and make some abrupt offer, we may run up against an un*told* amount of Navaho stubbornness and love of—I suppose we must call it home."

I start to tell them he's *not* Navaho, but think what's the use if they don't listen? They don't care what tribe he is.

The woman smiles and nods at both the men, a smile and a

nod to each, and her eyes ring them up, and she begins to move stiffly back to their car, talking in a light, young voice.

"As my sociology professor used to emphasize, 'There is generally one person in every situation you must never underestimate the power *of*.'"

And they get back in the car and drive away, with me standing there wondering if they ever even *saw* me.

I was kind of amazed that I'd remembered that. It was the first time in what seemed to me centuries that I'd been able to remember much about my childhood. It fascinated me to discover I could still do it. I lay in bed awake, remembering other happenings, and just about that time, while I was half in a kind of dream, I heard a sound under my bed like a mouse with a walnut. I leaned over the edge of the bed and saw the shine of metal biting off pieces of gum I knew by heart. The black boy named Geever had found where I'd been hiding my chewing gum; was scraping the pieces off into a sack with a long, lean pair of scissors open like jaws.

I jerked back up under the covers before he saw me looking. My heart was banging in my ears, scared he'd seen me. I wanted to tell him to get away, to mind his own business and leave my chewing gum alone, but I couldn't even let on I heard. I lay still to see if he'd caught me bending over to peek under the bed at him, but he didn't give any sign—all I heard was the zzzth-zzzth of his scissors and pieces falling into the sack, reminded me of hailstones the way they used to rattle on our tar-paper roof. He clacked his tongue and giggled to himself.

"Um-ummm. Lord gawd amighty. Hee. I wonder how many times this muthuh chewed some o' this stuff? Just as *hard*."

McMurphy heard the black boy muttering to himself and woke and rolled up to one elbow to look at what he was up to at this hour down on his knees under my bed. He watched the black boy a minute, rubbing his eyes to be sure of what he was seeing, just like you see little kids rub their eyes; then he sat up completely.

"I will be a sonofabitch if he ain't in here at eleven-thirty at night, fartin' around in the dark with a pair of scissors and a paper sack." The black boy jumped and swung his flashlight up in McMurphy's eyes. "Now tell me, Sam: what the devil are you collectin' that needs the cover of night?"

"Go back to sleep, McMurphy. It don't concern nobody else."

McMurphy let his lips spread in a slow grin, but he didn't look away from the light. The black boy got uneasy after about half a minute of shining that light on McMurphy sitting there, on that glossy new-healed scar and those teeth and that tattooed panther on his shoulder, and took the light away. He bent back to his work, grunting and puffing like it was a mighty effort prying off dried gum.

"One of the duties of a night aide," he explained between grunts, trying to sound friendly, "is to keep the bedside area cleaned up."

"In the dead of night?"

"McMurphy, we got a thing posted called a *Job* Description, say cleanliness is a *twenty-fo'-hour job!*"

"You might of done your twenty-four hours' worth before we got in bed, don't you think, instead of sittin' out there watching TV till ten-thirty. Does Old Lady Ratched know you boys watch TV most of your shift? What do you reckon she'd do if she found out about that?"

The black boy got up and sat on the edge of my bed. He tapped the flashlight against his teeth, grinning and giggling. The light lit his face up like a black jack o'lantern.

"Well, let me tell you about this gum," he said and leaned close to McMurphy like an old chum. "You see, for years I been wondering where Chief Bromden got his chewin' gum—never havin' any money for the canteen, never havin' anybody give him a stick that I saw, never askin' the Red Cross lady—so I *watched*, and I *waited*. And look here." He got back on his knees and lifted the edge of my bedspread and shined the light under. "How 'bout that? I bet they's pieces of gum under here been used a *thousand* times!"

This tickled McMurphy. He went to giggling at what he saw. The black boy held up the sack and rattled it, and they laughed some more about it. The black boy told McMurphy good night and rolled the top of the sack like it was his lunch and went off somewhere to hide it for later.

"Chief?" McMurphy whispered. "I want you to tell me something." And he started to sing a little song, a hillbilly song, popular a long time ago: " 'Oh, does the Spearmint lose its flavor on the bedpost overnight?' "

At first I started getting real mad. I thought he was making fun of me like other people had.

" 'When you chew it in the morning,' " he sang in a whisper, " 'will it be too hard to bite?' "

But the more I thought about it the funnier it seemed to me. I tried to stop it but I could feel I was about to laugh—not at McMurphy's singing, but at my own self.

" 'This questions got me goin', won't somebody set me right; does the Spearmint lose its flavor on the bedpost o-ver niiiiiite?' "

He held out that last note and twiddled it down me like a feather. I couldn't help but start to chuckle, and this made me scared I'd get to laughing and not be able to stop. But just then McMurphy jumped off his bed and went to rustling through his nightstand, and I hushed. I clenched my teeth, wondering what to do now. It'd been a long time since I'd let anyone hear me do any more than grunt or bellow. I heard him shut the bedstand, and it echoed like a boiler door. I heard him say, "Here," and something lit on my bed. Little. Just the size of a lizard or a snake . . .

"Juicy Fruit is the best I can do for you at the moment, Chief. Package I won off Scanlon pitchin' pennies." And he got back in bed.

And before I realized what I was doing, I told him Thank you.

He didn't say anything right off. He was up on his elbow, watching me the way he'd watched the black boy, waiting for me to say something else. I picked up the package of gum from the bedspread and held it in my hand and told him Thank you.

It didn't sound like much because my throat was rusty and my tongue creaked. He told me I sounded a little out of practice and laughed at that. I tried to laugh with him, but it was a squawking sound, like a pullet trying to crow. It sounded more like crying than laughing.

He told me not to hurry, that he had till six-thirty in the morning to listen if I wanted to practice. He said a man been still long as me probably had a considerable lot to talk about, and he lay back on his pillow and waited. I thought for a minute for something to say to him, but the only thing that came to my mind was the kind of thing one man can't say to another because it sounds wrong in words. When he saw I couldn't say anything he crossed his hands behind his head and started talking himself.

"Ya know, Chief, I was just rememberin' a time down in the Willamette Valley—I was pickin' beans outside of Eugene and considering myself damn lucky to get the job. It was in the early thirties so there wasn't many kids able to get jobs. I got the job by proving to the bean boss I could pick just as fast and clean as any of the adults. Anyway, I was the only kid in the rows. Nobody else around me but grown-ups. And after I tried a time or two to talk to them I saw they weren't for listening to me—scrawny little patchquilt redhead anyhow. So I hushed. I was so peeved at them not listening to me I kept hushed the livelong four weeks I picked that field, workin' right along side of them, listening to them prattle on about this uncle or that cousin. Or if somebody didn't show up for work, gossip about him. Four weeks and not a peep out of me. Till I think by God they forgot I *could* talk, the mossbacked old bastards. I bided my time. Then, on the last day, I opened up and went to telling them what a petty bunch of farts they were. I told each one just how his buddy had drug him over the coals when he was absent. Hooee, did they listen then! They finally got to arguing with each other and created such a shitstorm I lost my quarter-cent-a-pound bonus I had comin' for not missin' a day because I already had a bad reputation around town and the bean boss claimed the disturbance was likely my fault even if he couldn't prove it. I cussed him out too. My shootin' off my mouth that time probably cost me twenty dollars or so. Well worth it, too."

He chuckled a while to himself, remembering, then turned his head on his pillow and looked at me.

"What I was wonderin', Chief, are you biding your time towards the day you decide to lay into them?"

"No," I told him. "I couldn't."

"Couldn't tell them off? It's easier than you think."

"You're . . . lot bigger, tougher'n I am," I mumbled.

"How's that? I didn't get you, Chief."

I worked some spit down in my throat. "You are bigger and tougher than I am. You can do it."

"Me? Are you kidding? Criminy, look at you: you stand a head taller'n any man on the ward. There ain't a man here you couldn't turn every way but loose, and that's a fact!"

"No. I'm way too little. I used to be big, but not no more. You're twice the size of me."

"Hoo boy, you *are* crazy, aren't you? The first thing I saw when I came in this place was you sitting over in that chair, big as a damn mountain. I tell you, I lived all over Klamath and Texas and Oklahoma and all over around Gallup, and I swear you're the biggest Indian I ever saw."

"I'm from the Columbia Gorge," I said, and he waited for me to go on. "My Papa was a full Chief and his name was Tee Ah Millatoona. That means The-Pine-That-Stands-Tallest-on-the-Mountain, and we didn't live on a mountain. He was real big when I was a kid. My mother got twice his size."

"You must of had a real moose of an old lady. How big was she?"

"Oh—big, big."

"I mean how many feet and inches?"

"Feet and inches? A guy at the carnival looked her over and says five feet nine and weight a hundred and thirty pounds, but that was because he'd just *saw* her. She got bigger all the time."

"Yeah? How much bigger?"

"Bigger than Papa and me together."

"Just one day took to growin', huh? Well, that's a new one on me: I never heard of an Indian woman doing something like that."

"She wasn't Indian. She was a town woman from The Dalles."

"And her name was what? Bromden? Yeah, I see, wait a minute." He thinks for a while and says, "And when a town woman marries an Indian that's marryin' somebody beneath her, ain't it? Yeah, I think I see."

"No. It wasn't just her that made him little. Everybody worked on him because he was big, and wouldn't give in, and did like he pleased. Everybody worked on him just the way they're working on you."

"They who, Chief?" he asked in a soft voice, suddenly serious.

"The Combine. It worked on him for years. He was big enough to fight it for a while. It wanted us to live in inspected houses. It wanted to take the falls. It was even in the tribe, and they worked on him. In the town they beat him up in the alleys and cut his hair short once. Oh, the Combine's big—big. He fought it a long time till my mother made him too little to fight any more and he gave up."

McMurphy didn't say anything for a long time after that. Then he raised up on his elbow and looked at me again, and asked why they beat him up in the alleys, and I told him that they wanted to make him see what he had in store for him only worse if he didn't sign the papers giving everything to the government."

"What did they want him to give to the government?"

"Everything. The tribe, the village, the falls . . ."

"Now I remember; you're talking about the falls where the Indians used to spear salmon—long time ago. Yeah. But the way I remember it the tribe got paid some huge amount."

"That's what they said to him. He said, What can you pay for the way a man lives? He said, What can you pay for what a man is? They didn't understand. Not even the tribe. They stood out in front of our door all holding those checks and they wanted him to tell them what to do now. They kept asking him to invest for them, or tell them where to go, or to buy a farm. But he was too little anymore. And he was too drunk, too. The Combine had whipped him. It beats everybody. It'll beat you too. They can't have somebody as big as Papa running around unless he's one of them. You can see that."

"Yeah, I reckon I can."

"That's why you shouldn't of broke that window. They see you're big, now. Now they got to bust you."

"Like bustin' a mustang, huh?"

"No. No, listen. They don't bust you that way; they work on you ways you can't fight! They put things in! They *install* things. They start as quick as they see you're gonna be big and go to working and installing their filthy machinery when you're little, and keep on and on and on till you're *fixed!*"

"Take 'er easy, buddy; shhhh."

"And if you *fight* they lock you someplace and make you stop—"

"Easy, easy, Chief. Just cool it for a while. They heard you."

He lay down and kept still. My bed was hot, I noticed. I could hear the squeak of rubber soles as the black boy came in with a flashlight to see what the noise was. We lay still till he left.

"He finally just drank," I whispered. I didn't seem to be able to stop talking, not till I finished telling what I thought was all of it. "And the last I see him he's blind in the cedars from drinking and every time I see him put the bottle to his mouth he don't suck out of it, it sucks out of him until he's shrunk so wrinkled and yellow even the dogs don't know him, and we had to cart him out of the cedars, in a pickup, to a place in Portland, to die. I'm not saying they kill. They didn't kill him. They did something else."

I was feeling awfully sleepy. I didn't want to talk any more. I tried to think back on what I'd been saying, and it didn't seem like what I'd wanted to say.

"I been talking crazy, ain't I?"

"Yeah, Chief"—he rolled over in his bed—"you been talkin' crazy."

"It wasn't what I wanted to say. I can't say it all. It don't make sense."

"I didn't say it didn't make sense, Chief, I just said it was talkin' crazy."

He didn't say anything after that for so long I thought he'd gone to sleep. I wished I'd told him good night. I looked over at him, and he was turned away from me. His arm wasn't under the covers, and I could just make out the aces and eights tattooed there. It's big, I thought, big as my arms used to be when I played football. I wanted to reach over and touch the place where he was tattooed, to see if he was still alive. He's layin' awful quiet, I told myself, I ought to touch him to see if he's still alive. . . .

That's a lie. I know he's still alive. That ain't the reason I want to touch him.

I want to touch him because he's a man.

That's a lie too. There's other men around. I could touch them.

I want to touch him because I'm one of these queers!

But that's a lie too. That's one fear hiding behind another. If I was one of these queers I'd want to do other things with him. I just want to touch him because he's who he is.

But as I was about to reach over to that arm he said, "Say, Chief," and rolled in bed with a lurch of covers, facing me, "Say, Chief, why don't you come on this fishin' trip with us tomorrow?"

I didn't answer.

"Come on, what do ya say? I look for it to be one hell of an occasion. You know these two aunts of mine comin' to pick us up? Why, those ain't aunts, man, no; both those girls are workin' shimmy dancers and hustlers I know from Portland. What do you say to that?"

I finally told him I was one of the Indigents.

"You're *what?*"

"I'm broke."

"Oh," he said. "Yeah, I hadn't thought of that."

He was quiet for a time again, rubbing that scar on his nose with his finger. The finger stopped. He raised up on his elbow and looked at me.

"Chief," he said slowly, looking me over, "when you were full-sized, when you used to be, let's say, six seven or eight and weighed two eighty or so—were you strong enough to, say, lift something the size of that control panel in the tub room?"

I thought about that panel. It probably didn't weigh a lot more'n oil drums I'd lifted in the Army. I told him I probably could of at one time.

"If you got that big again, could you still lift it?"

I told him I thought so.

"To hell with what you think; I want to know can you *promise* to lift it if I get you big as you used to be? You promise me that, and you not only get my special body-buildin' course for nothing but you get yourself a ten-buck fishin' trip, *free!*" He licked his lips and lay back. "Get me good odds too, I bet."

He lay there chuckling over some thought of his own. When I asked him how he was going to get me big again he shushed me with a finger to his lips.

"Man, we can't let a secret like this out. I didn't say I'd tell you *how*, did I? Hoo boy, blowin' a man back up to full size is a secret you can't share with everybody, be dangerous in the hands of an enemy. You won't even know it's happening most of the time yourself. But I give you my solemn word, you follow my training program, and here's what'll happen."

He swung his legs out of bed and sat on the edge with his hands on his knees. The dim light coming in over his shoulder from the Nurses' Station caught the shine of his teeth and the one eye glinting down his nose at me. The rollicking auctioneer's voice spun softly through the dorm.

"*There* you'll be. It's the Big Chief Bromden, cuttin' down the boulevard—men, women, and kids rockin' back on their heels to peer up at him: 'Well well well, what giant's this *here*, takin' ten feet at a step and duckin' for telephone wires?' Comes stompin' through town, stops just long enough for virgins, the rest of you twitches might's well not even line up 'less you got tits like muskmelons, nice strong white legs long enough to lock around his mighty back, and a little cup of poozle warm and juicy and sweet as butter an' honey. . . ."

In the dark there he went on, spinning his tale about how it would be, with all the men scared and all the beautiful young girls panting after me. Then he said he was going out right this very minute and sign my name up as one of his fishing crew. He stood up, got the towel from his bedstand and wrapped it around his hips and put on his cap, and stood over my bed.

"Oh man, I tell you, I tell you, you'll have women trippin' you and beatin' you to the floor."

And all of a sudden his hand shot out and with a swing of his arm untied my sheet, cleared my bed of covers, and left me lying there naked.

"Look there, Chief. Haw. What'd I tell ya? You growed a half a foot already."

Laughing, he walked down the row of beds to the hall.

two whores on their way down from Portland to take us deep-sea fishing in a boat! It made it tough to stay in bed until the dorm lights came on at six-thirty.

I was the first one up out of the dorm to look at the list posted on the board next to the Nurses' Station, check to see if my name was really signed there. SIGN UP FOR DEEP SEA FISHING was printed in big letters at the top, then McMurphy had signed first and Billy Bibbit was number one, right after Mc-

Murphy. Number three was Harding and number four was Fredrickson, and all the way down to number ten where nobody'd signed yet. My name was there, the last put down, across from the number nine. I was actually going out of the hospital with two whores on a fishing boat; I had to keep saying it over and over to myself to believe it.

The three black boys slipped up in front of me and read the list with gray fingers, found my name there and turned to grin at me.

"Why, who you s'pose signed Chief Bromden up for this foolishness? Inniuns ain't able to write."

"What makes you think Inniuns able to *read?*"

The starch was still fresh and stiff enough this early that their arms rustled in the white suits when they moved, like paper wings. I acted deaf to them laughing at me, like I didn't even know, but when they stuck a broom out for me to do their work up the hall, I turned around and walked back to the dorm, telling myself, The hell with that. A man goin' fishing with two whores from Portland don't have to take that crap.

It scared me some, walking off from them like that, because I never went against what the black boys ordered before. I looked back and saw them coming after me with the broom. They'd probably have come right on in the dorm and got me but for McMurphy; he was in there making such a fuss, roaring up and down between the beds, snapping a towel at the guys signed to go this morning, that the black boys decided maybe the dorm wasn't such safe territory to venture into for no more than somebody to sweep a little dab of hallway.

McMurphy had his motorcycle cap pulled way forward on his red hair to look like a boat captain, and the tattoos showing out from the sleeves of his T-shirt were done in Singapore. He was swaggering around the floor like it was the deck of a ship, whistling in his hand like a bosun's whistle.

"*Hit* the deck, mateys, *hit* the deck or I keelhaul the lot of ye from stock to stern!"

He rang the bedstand next to Harding's bed with his knuckles.

"*Six* bells and *all's* well. Steady as she goes. Hit the deck. Drop your cocks and grab your socks."

He noticed me standing just inside the doorway and came rushing over to thump my back like a drum.

"Look here at the Big Chief; here's an example of a good sailor and fisherman: up before day and out diggin' red worms for bait. The rest of you scurvy bunch o' lubbers'd do well to follow his lead. *Hit* the deck. Today's the day! Outa the sack and into the sea!"

The Acutes grumbled and griped at him and his towel, and the Chronics woke up to look around with heads blue from lack of blood cut off by sheets tied too tight across the chest, looking around the dorm till they finally centered on me with weak and watered-down old looks, faces wistful and curious. They lay there watching me pull on warm clothes for the trip, making me feel uneasy and a little guilty. They could sense I had been singled out as the only Chronic making the trip. They watched me—old guys welded in wheelchairs for years, with catheters down their legs like vines rooting them for the rest of their lives right where they are, they watched me and knew instinctively that I was going. And they could still be a little jealous it wasn't them. They could know because enough of the man in them had been damped out that the old animal instincts had taken over (old Chronics wake up sudden some nights, before anybody else knows a guy's died in the dorm, and throw back their heads and howl), and they could be jealous because there was enough man left to still remember.

McMurphy went out to look at the list and came back and tried to talk one more Acute into signing, going down the line kicking at the beds still had guys in them with sheets pulled over their heads, telling them what a great thing it was to be out there in the teeth of the gale with a he-man sea crackin' around and a goddam yo-heave-ho and a bottle of rum. "C'mon, loafers, I need one more mate to round out the crew, I need one more goddam volunteer. . . ."

But he couldn't talk anybody into it. The Big Nurse had the rest scared with her stories of how rough the sea'd been lately and how many boats'd sunk, and it didn't look like we'd get that last crew member till a half-hour later when George Sorensen came up to McMurphy in the breakfast line where we were waiting for the mess hall to be unlocked for breakfast.

Big toothless knotty old Swede the black boys called Rub-a-dub George, because of his thing about sanitation, came shuffling up the hall, listing well back so his feet went well out in front of his head (sways backward this way to keep his face as far away from the man he's talking to as he can), stopped in front of McMurphy, and mumbled something in his hand. George was very shy. You couldn't see his eyes because they were in so deep under his brow, and he cupped his big palm around most of the rest of his face. His head swayed like a crow's nest on top of his mastlike spine. He mumbled in his hand till McMurphy finally reached up and pulled the hand away so's the words could get out.

"Now, George, what is it you're sayin'?"

"Red worms," he was saying. "I joost don't think they do you no good—not for the Chin-nook."

"Yeah?" McMurphy said. "Red worms? I might agree with you, George, if you let me know what about these red worms you're speaking ot."

"I think joost a while ago I hear you say Mr. Bromden was out digging the red worms for bait."

"That's right, Pop, I remember."

"So I joost say you don't have you no good fortune with them worms. This here is the month with one big Chinook run—su-ure. Herring you need. Su-ure. You jig you some herring and use those fellows for bait, *then* you have some good fortune."

His voice went up at the end of every sentence—for-*chune* —like he was asking a question. His big chin, already scrubbed so much this morning he'd worn the hide off it, nodded up and down at McMurphy once or twice, then turned him around to lead him down the hall toward the end of the line. Mc-Murphy called him back.

"Now, hold 'er a minute, George; you talk like you know something about this fishin' business."

George turned and shuffled back to McMurphy, listing back

so far it looked like his feet had navigated right out from under him.

"You bet, su-ure. Twenty-five year I work the Chinook trollers, all the way from Half Moon Bay to Puget Sound. Twenty-five year I fish—before I get so dirty." He held out his hands for us to see the dirt on them. Everybody around leaned over and looked. I didn't see the dirt but I did see scars worn deep into the white palms from hauling a thousand miles of fishing line out of the sea. He let us look a minute, then rolled the hands shut and drew them away and hid them in his pajama shirt like we might dirty them looking, and stood grinning at McMurphy with gums like brine-bleached pork.

"I had a good troller boat, joost forty feet, but she drew twelve feet water and she was solid teak and solid oak." He rocked back and forth in a way to make you doubt that the floor was standing level. "She was one good troller boat, by golly!"

He started to turn, but McMurphy stopped him again.

"Hell, George, why didn't you say you were a fisherman? I been talking up this voyage like I was the Old Man of the Sea, but just between you an' me and the wall there, the only boat I been on was the battleship *Missouri* and the only thing I know about fish is that I like eatin' 'em better than cleanin' 'em."

"Cleanin' is *easy*, somebody show you how."

"By God, you're gonna be our captain, George; we'll be your crew."

George tilted back, shaking his head. "Those boats awful *dirty* any more—everything *awful* dirty."

"The hell with that. We got a boat specially sterilized fore and aft, swabbed clean as a hound's tooth. You won't get dirty, George, 'cause you'll be the captain. Won't even have to bait a hook; just be our captain and give orders to us dumb landlubbers—how's that strike you?"

I could see George was tempted by the way he wrung his hands under his shirt, but he still said he couldn't risk getting dirty. McMurphy did his best to talk him into it, but George was still shaking his head when the Big Nurse's key hit the lock of the mess hall and she came jangling out the door with her wicker bag of surprises, clicked down the line with automatic smile-and-good-morning for each man she passed. McMurphy noticed the way George leaned back from her and scowled. When she'd passed, McMurphy tilted his head and gave George the one bright eye.

"George, that stuff the nurse has been saying about the bad sea, about how terrible dangerous this trip might be—what about that?"

"That ocean could be awful bad, sure, awful rough."

McMurphy looked down at the nurse disappearing into the station, then back at George. George started twisting his hands around in his shirt more than ever, looking around at the silent faces watching him.

"By golly!" he said suddenly. "You think I let her scare me about that ocean? You think *that?*"

"Ah, I guess not, George. I was thinking, though, that if you don't come along with us, and if there *is* some awful stormy calamity, we're every last one of us liable to be lost at sea, you know that? I said I didn't know nothin' about boating, and I'll tell you something else: these two women coming to get us?, I told the doctor was my two aunts, two widows of fishermen? Well, the only cruisin' either one of them ever did was on solid cement. They won't be no more help in a fix than me. We *need* you, George." He took a pull on his cigarette and asked, "You got ten bucks, by the way?"

George shook his head.

"No, I wouldn't suppose so. Well, what the devil, I gave up the idea of comin' out ahead days ago. Here." He took a pencil out of the pocket of his green jacket and wiped it clean on his shirttail, held it out to George. "You captain us, and we'll let you come along for five."

George looked around at us again, working his big brow over the predicament. Finally his gums showed in a bleached smile and he reached for the pencil. "By golly!" he said and headed off with the pencil to sign the last place on the list

After breakfast, walking down the hall, McMurphy stopped
and printed c-a-p-t behind George's name.

The whores were late. Everybody was beginning to think
they weren't coming at all when McMurphy gave a yell from
the window and we all went running to look. He said that was
them, but we didn't see but one car, instead of the two we
were counting on, and just one woman. McMurphy called to
her through the screen when she stopped on the parking lot,
and she came cutting straight across the grass toward our ward.
She was younger and prettier than any of us'd figured on.
Everybody had found out that the girls were whores instead of
aunts, and were expecting all sorts of things. Some of the re-
ligous guys weren't any too happy about it. But seeing her
coming lightfooted across the grass with her eyes green all the
way up to the ward, and her hair, roped in a long twist at the
back of her head, jouncing up and down with every step like
copper springs in the sun, all any of us could think of was that
she was a girl, a female who wasn't dressed white from head
to foot like she'd been dipped in frost, and how she made her
money didn't make any difference.
She ran right up against the screen where McMurphy was and
hooked her fingers through the mesh and pulled herself against
it. She was panting from the run, and every breath looked like
she might swell right through the mesh. She was crying a little.
"McMurphy, oh, you damned McMurphy . . ."
"Never mind that. Where's Sandra?"
"She got tied up, man, can't make it. But you, damn it, are
you okay?"
"She got tied up!"
"To tell the truth"—the girl wiped her nose and giggled—
"ol' Sandy got *married*. You remember Artie Gilfillian from
Beaverton? Always used to show up at the parties with some
gassy thing, a gopher snake or a white mouse or some gassy
thing like that in his pocket? A real maniac—"
"Oh, sweet Jesus!" McMurphy groaned. "How'm I supposed
to get ten guys in one stinkin' Ford, Candy sweetheart? How'd

Sandra and her gopher snake from Beaverton figure on me swinging *that?*"

The girl looked like she was in the process of thinking up an answer when the speaker in the ceiling clacked and the Big Nurse's voice told McMurphy if he wanted to talk with his lady friend it'd be better if she signed in properly at the main door instead of disturbing the whole hospital. The girl left the screen and started toward the main entrance, and McMurphy left the screen and flopped down in a chair in the corner, his head hanging. "Hell's *bells,*" he said.

The least black boy let the girl onto the ward and forgot to lock the door behind her (caught hell for it later, I bet), and the girl came jouncing up the hall past the Nurses' Station, where all the nurses were trying to freeze her bounce with a united icy look, and into the day room just a few steps ahead of the doctor. He was going toward the Nurses' Station with some papers, looked at her, and back at the papers, and back at her again, and went to fumbling after his glasses with both hands.

She stopped when she got to the middle of the day-room floor and saw she was circled by forty staring men in green, and it was so quiet you could hear bellies growling, and, all along the Chronic row, hear catheters popping off.

She had to stand there a minute while she looked around to find McMurphy, so everybody got a long look at her. There was a blue smoke hung near the ceiling over her head; I think apparatus burned out all over the ward trying to adjust to her come busting in like she did—took electronic readings on her and calculated they weren't built to handle something like this on the ward, and just burned out, like machines committing suicide.

She had on a white T-shirt like McMurphy's only a lot smaller, white tennis shoes and Levi pants snipped off above her knees to give her feet circulation, and it didn't look like that was near enough material to go around, considering what it had to cover. She must've been seen with lots less by lots more men, but under the circumstances she began to fidget around self-consciously like a schoolgirl on a stage. Nobody spoke while they looked. Martini did whisper that you could read the dates of the coins in her Levi pockets, they were so tight, but he was closer and could see better'n the rest of us.

Billy Bibbit was the first one to say something out loud, not really a word, just a low, almost painful whistle that described how she looked better than anybody else could have. She laughed and thanked him very much and he blushed so red that she blushed with him and laughed again. This broke things into movement. All the Acutes were coming across the floor trying to talk to her at once. The doctor was pulling on Harding's coat, asking who *is* this. McMurphy got up out of his chair and walked through the crowd to her, and when she saw him she threw her arms around him and said, "You damned McMurphy," and then got embarrassed and blushed again. When she blushed she didn't look more than sixteen or seventeen, I swear she didn't.

McMurphy introduced her around and she shook everybody's hand. When she got to Billy she thanked him again for his whistle. The Big Nurse came sliding out of the station, smiling, and asked McMurphy how he intended to get all ten of us in one car, and he asked could he maybe *borrow* a staff car and drive a load himself, and the nurse cited a rule forbidding this, just like everyone knew she would. She said unless there was another driver to sign a Responsibility Slip that half of the crew would have to stay behind. McMurphy told her this'd cost him fifty goddam bucks to make up the difference; he'd have to pay the guys back who didn't get to go.

"Then it may be," the nurse said, "that the trip will have to be canceled—and *all* the money refunded."

"I've already rented the boat; the man's got seventy bucks of mine in his pocket right now!"

"Seventy dollars? So? I thought you told the patients you'd need to collect a hundred dollars plus ten of your own to finance the trip, Mr. McMurphy."

"I was putting gas in the cars over and back."

"That wouldn't amount to thirty dollars, though, would it?"

She smiled so nice at him, waiting. He threw his hands in the air and looked at the ceiling.

"Hoo *boy*, you don't miss a chance do you, Miss District Attorney. Sure; I was keepin' what was left over. I don't think any of the guys ever thought any different. I figured to make a little for the trouble I took get—"

"But your plans didn't work out," she said. She was still smiling at him, so full of sympathy. "Your little financial speculations can't *all* be successes, Randle, and, actually, as I think about it now, you've had more than your share of victories." She mused about this, thinking about something I knew we'd hear more about later. "Yes. Every Acute on the ward has written you an IOU for some 'deal' of yours at one time or another, so don't you think you can bear up under this one small defeat?"

Then she stopped. She saw McMurphy wasn't listening to her any more. He was watching the doctor. And the doctor was eying the blond girl's T-shirt like nothing else existed. McMurphy's loose smile spread out on his face as he watched the doctor's trance, and he pushed his cap to the back of his head and strolled to the doctor's side, startling him with a hand on the shoulder.

"By God, Doctor Spivey, you ever see a Chinook salmon hit a line? One of the fiercest sights on the seven seas. Say, Candy honeybun, whyn't you tell the doctor here about deep-sea fishing and all like that. . . ."

Working together, it didn't take McMurphy and the girl but two minutes and the little doctor was down locking up his office and coming back up the hall, cramming papers in a brief case.

"Good deal of paper work I can get done on the boat," he explained to the nurse and went past her so fast she didn't have a chance to answer, and the rest of the crew followed, slower, grinning at her standing in the door of that Nurses' Station.

The Acutes who weren't going gathered at the day-room door, told us don't bring our catch back till it's cleaned, and Ellis pulled his hands down off the nails in the wall and squeezed Billy Bibbit's hand and told him to be a fisher of men.

And Billy, watching the brass brads on that woman's Levis wink at him as she walked out of the day room, told Ellis to hell with that fisher of *men* business. He joined us at the door, and the least black boy let us through and locked the door behind us, and we were out, outside.

The sun was prying up the clouds and lighting the brick front of the hospital rose red. A thin breeze worked at sawing what leaves were left from the oak trees, stacking them neatly against the wire cyclone fence. There were little brown birds occasionally on the fence; when a puff of leaves would hit the fence the birds would fly off with the wind. It looked at first like the leaves were hitting the fence and turning into birds and flying away.

It was a fine woodsmoked autumn day, full of the sound of kids punting footballs and the putter of small airplanes, and everybody should've been happy just being outside in it. But we all stood in a silent bunch with our hands in our pockets while the doctor walked to get his car. A silent bunch, watching the townspeople who were driving past on their way to work slow down to gawk at all the loonies in green uniforms. McMurphy saw how uneasy we were and tried to work us into a better mood by joking and teasing the girl, but this made us feel worse somehow. Everybody was thinking how easy it would be to return to the ward, go back and say they decided the nurse had been right; with a wind like this the sea would've been just too rough.

The doctor arrived and we loaded up and headed off, me and George and Harding and Billy Bibbit in the car with McMurphy and the girl, Candy; and Fredrickson and Sefelt and Scanlon and Martini and Tadem and Gregory following in the doctor's car. Everyone was awfully quiet. We pulled into a gas station about a mile from the hospital; the doctor followed. He got out first, and the service-station man came bouncing out, grinning and wiping his hands on a rag. Then he stopped grinning and went past the doctor to see just what was *in* these cars. He backed off, wiping his hands on the oily rag, frowning. The doctor caught the man's sleeve nervously and took out a ten-dollar bill and tucked it down in the man's hands like setting out a tomato plant.

"Ah, would you fill both tanks with regular?" the doctor asked. He was acting just as uneasy about being out of the hospital as the rest of us were. "Ah, would you?"

"Those uniforms," the service-station man said, "they're from the hospital back up the road, aren't they?" He was looking around him to see if there was a wrench or something handy. He finally moved over near a stack of empty pop bottles. "You guys are from that *asylum.*"

The doctor fumbled for his glasses and looked at us too, like he'd just noticed the uniforms. "Yes. No, I mean. We, they *are* from the asylum, but they are a work crew, not inmates, of course not. A work crew."

The man squinted at the doctor and at us and went off to whisper to his partner, who was back among the machinery. They talked a minute, and the second guy hollered and asked the doctor who we were and the doctor repeated that we were a work crew, and both of the guys laughed. I could tell by the laugh that they'd decided to sell us the gas—probably it would be weak and dirty and watered down and cost twice the usual price—but it didn't make me feel any better. I could see everybody was feeling pretty bad. The doctor's lying made us feel worse than ever—not because of the lie, so much, but because of the truth.

The second guy came over to the doctor, grinning. "You said you wanted the Soo-preme, sir? You bet. And how about us checking those oil filters and windshield wipes?" He was bigger than his friend. He leaned down on the doctor like he was sharing a secret. "Would you believe it: eighty-eight per cent of the cars show by the figures on the road today that they need new oil filters and windshield wipes?"

His grin was coated with carbon from years of taking out spark plugs with his teeth. He kept leaning down on the doctor, making him squirm with that grin and waiting for him to admit he was over a barrel. "Also, how's your work crew fixed for sunglasses? We got some good Polaroids." The doctor knew he had him. But just the instant he opened his mouth, about to give in and say Yes, anything, there was a whirring noise and the top of our car was folding back. McMurphy was fighting and cursing the accordion-pleated top, trying to force it back faster than the machinery could handle it. Everybody could see how mad he was by the way he thrashed and beat at that slowly rising top; when he got it cussed and hammered and wrestled down into place he climbed right out over the girl and over the side of the car and walked up between the doctor and the service-station guy and looked up into the black mouth with one eye.

"Okay now, Hank, we'll take regular, just like the doctor ordered. Two tanks of regular. That's all. The hell with that other slum. And we'll take it at three cents off because we're a goddamned government-sponsored expedition."

The guy didn't budge. "Yeah? I thought the professor here said you weren't patients?"

"Now Hank, don't you see that was just a kindly precaution to keep from *startlin'* you folks with the truth? The doc wouldn't lie like that about just *any* patients, but we ain't ordinary nuts; we're every bloody one of us hot off the criminal-insane ward, on our way to San Quentin where they got better facilities to handle us. You see that freckle-faced kid there? Now he might look like he's right off a *Saturday Evening Post* cover, but he's a insane knife artist that killed three men. The man beside him is known as the Bull Goose Loony, unpredictable as a wild hog. You see that big guy? He's an Indian and he beat six white men to death with a pick handle when they tried to cheat him trading muskrat hides. Stand up where they can get a look at you, Chief."

Harding goosed me with his thumb, and I stood up on the floor of the car. The guy shaded his eyes and looked up at me and didn't say anything.

"Oh, it's a bad group, I admit," McMurphy said, "but it's a planned, authorized, legal government-sponsored excursion, and we're entitled to a legal discount just the same as if we was the FBI."

The guy looked back at McMurphy, and McMurphy hooked his thumbs in his pockets and rocked back and looked up at him across the scar on his nose. The guy turned to check if his buddy was still stationed at the case of empty pop bottles, then grinned back down on McMurphy.

"Pretty tough customers, is that what you're saying, Red? So much we better toe the line and do what we're told, is that what you're saying? Well, tell me, Red, what is it *you're* in for? trying to assassinate the President?"

"Nobody could *prove* that, Hank. They got me on a bum rap. I killed a man in the ring, ya see, and sorta got *taken* with the kick."

"One of these killers with boxing gloves, is that what you're telling me, Red?"

"Now I didn't say that, did I? I never could get used to those pillows you wore. No, this wasn't no televised main event from the Cow Palace; I'm more what you call a back-lot boxer."

The guy hooked his thumbs in his pockets to mock McMurphy. "You are more what I call a back-lot bull-thrower."

"Now I didn't say that bull-throwing wasn't also one of my abilities, did I? But I want you to look here." He put his hands up in the guy's face, real close, turning them over slowly, palm and knuckle. "You ever see a man get his poor old meat-hooks so pitiful chewed up from just throwin' the *bull?* Did you, Hank?"

He held those hands in the guy's face a long time, waiting to see if the guy had anything else to say. The guy looked at the hands, and at me, and back at the hands. When it was clear he didn't have anything else real pressing to say, McMurphy walked away from him to the other guy leaning against the pop cooler and plucked the doctor's ten-dollar bill out of his fist and started for the grocery store next to the station.

"You boys tally what the gas comes to and send the bill to the hospital," he called back. "I intend to use the cash to pick up some refreshments for the men. I believe we'll get that in place of windshield wipes and eighty-eight per cent oil filters."

By the time he got back everybody was feeling cocky as fighting roosters and calling orders to the service-station guys to check the air in the spare and wipe the windows and scratch that bird dropping off the hood if you please, just like we owned the show. When the big guy didn't get the windshield to suit Billy, Billy called him right back.

"You didn't get this sp-spot here where the bug h-h-hit."

"That wasn't a bug," the guy said sullenly, scratching at it with his fingernail, "that was a bird."

Martini called all the way from the other car that it couldn't of been a bird. "There'd be feathers and bones if it was a bird."

A man riding a bicycle stopped to ask what was the idea of all the green uniforms; some kind of club? Harding popped right up and answered him.

"No, my friend. We are lunatics from the hospital up the highway, psycho-ceramics, the cracked pots of mankind. Would you like me to decipher a Rorschach for you? No? You must hurry on? Ah, he's gone. Pity." He turned to McMurphy. "Never before did I realize that mental illness could have the aspect of power, *power*. Think of it: perhaps the more insane a man is, the more powerful he could become. Hitler an example. Fair makes the old brain reel, doesn't it? Food for thought there."

Billy punched a beer can for the girl, and she flustered him so with her bright smile and her "Thank you, Billy," that he took to opening cans for all of us.

While the pigeons fretted up and down the sidewalk with their hands folded behind their backs.

I sat there, feeling whole and good, sipping at a beer; I could hear the beer all the way down me—zzzth zzzth, like that. I had forgotten that there can be good sounds and tastes like the sound and taste of a beer going down. I took another big drink and started looking around me to see what else I had forgotten in twenty years.

"Man!" McMurphy said as he scooted the girl out from under the wheel and tight over against Billy. "Will you just look at the Big Chief slug down on that firewater!"—and slammed the car out into traffic with the doctor squealing behind to keep up.

He'd shown us what a little bravado and courage could accomplish, and we thought he'd taught us how to use it. All the way to the coast we had fun pretending to be brave. When people at a stop light would stare at us and our green uniforms we'd do just like he did, sit up straight and strong and tough-looking and put a big grin on our face and stare straight back at them till their motors died and their windows sunstreaked and they were left sitting when the light changed, upset bad by what a tough bunch of monkeys was just now not three feet from them, and help nowhere in sight.

As McMurphy led the twelve of us toward the ocean.

I think McMurphy knew better than we did that our tough looks were all show, because he still wasn't able to get a real laugh out of anybody. Maybe he couldn't understand why we weren't able to laugh yet, but he knew you can't really be strong until you can see a funny side to things. In fact, he worked so hard at pointing out the funny side of things that I was wondering a little if maybe he was blind to the other side, if maybe he wasn't able to see what it was that parched laughter deep inside your stomach. Maybe the guys weren't able to see it either, just feel the pressures of the different beams and frequencies coming from all directions, working to push and bend you one way or another, feel the Combine at work—but I was able to *see* it.

The way you see the change in a person you've been away from for a long time, where somebody who sees him every day, day in, day out, wouldn't notice because the change is gradual. All up the coast I could see the signs of what the Combine had accomplished since I was last through this country, things like, for example—a *train* stopping at a station and laying a string of full-grown men in mirrored suits and machined hats, laying them like a hatch of identical insects, half-life things coming pht-pht-pht out of the last car, then hooting its electric whistle and moving on down the spoiled land to deposit another hatch.

Or things like five thousand houses punched out identical by a machine and strung across the hills outside of town, so fresh from the factory they're still linked together like sausages, a sign saying "NEST IN THE WEST HOMES—NO DWN. PAYMENT FOR VETS," a playground down the hill from the houses, behind a checker-wire fence and another sign that read "ST. LUKE'S SCHOOL FOR BOYS"—there were five thousand kids in green corduroy pants and white shirts under green pullover sweaters playing crack-the-whip across an acre of crushed gravel. The line popped and twisted and jerked like a snake, and every crack popped a little kid off the end, sent him rolling up against the fence like a tumbleweed. Every crack. And it was always the same little kid, over and over.

All that five thousand kids lived in those five thousand houses, owned by those guys that got off the train. The houses looked so much alike that, time and time again, the kids went home by mistake to different houses and different families. Nobody ever noticed. They ate and went to bed. The only one they noticed was the little kid at the end of the whip. He'd always be so scuffed and bruised that he'd show up out of place wherever he went. He wasn't able to open up and laugh either. It's a hard thing to laugh if you can feel the pressure of those beams coming from every new car that passes, or every new house you pass.

"We can even have a lobby in Washington," Harding was saying, "an organization. NAAIP. Pressure groups. Big billboards along the highway showing a babbling schizophrenic running a wrecking maching, bold, red and green type: 'Hire the Insane.' We've got a rosy future, gentlemen."

We crossed a bridge over the Siuslaw. There was just enough mist in the air that I could lick out my tongue to the wind and taste the ocean before we could see it. Everyone knew we were getting close and didn't speak all the way to the docks.

The captain who was supposed to take us out had a bald gray metal head set in a black turtleneck like a gun turret on a U-boat; the cold cigar sticking from his mouth swept over us. He stood beside McMurphy on the wooden pier and looked out to sea as he talked. Behind him and up a bunch of steps, six or eight men in windbreakers were sitting on a bench along the front of the bait shop. The captain talked loudly, half to the loafers on his one side and half to McMurphy on the other side, firing his copper-jacket voice someplace in between.

"Don't care. Told you specifically in the letter. You don't have a signed waiver clearing me with proper authorities, I don't go out." The round head swiveled in the turret of his sweater, beading down that cigar at the lot of us. "Look there. Bunch like that at sea, could go to diving overboard like rats. Relatives could sue me for everything I own. I can't risk it."

McMurphy explained how the other girl was supposed to get all those papers up in Portland. One of the guys leaning against the bait shop called, "What other girl? Couldn't Blondie there handle the lot of you?" McMurphy didn't pay the guy any mind and went on arguing with the captain, but you could see how it bothered the girl. Those men against the shop kept leering at her and leaning close together to whisper things. All our crew, even the doctor, saw this and got to feeling ashamed that we didn't do something. We weren't the cocky bunch that was back at the service station.

McMurphy stopped arguing when he saw he wasn't getting any place with the captain, and turned around a couple of times, running his hand through his hair.

"Which boat have we got rented?"

"That's it there. The *Lark*. Not a man sets foot on her till I have a signed waiver clearing me. Not a man."

"I don't intend to rent a boat so we can sit all day and watch it bob up and down at the dock," McMurphy said. "Don't you have a phone up there in your bait shack? Let's go get this cleared up."

They thumped up the steps onto the level with the bait

shop and went inside, leaving us clustered up by ourselves, with that bunch of loafers up there watching us and making comments and sniggering and goosing one another in the ribs. The wind was blowing the boats at their moorings, nuzzling them up against the wet rubber tires along the dock so they made a sound like they were laughing at us. The water was giggling under the boards, and the sign hanging over the door to the bait shack that read "SEAMAN'S SERVICE—CAPT BLOCK, PROP" was squeaking and scratching as the wind rocked it on rusty hooks. The mussels that clung to the pilings, four feet out of water marking the tide line, whistled and clicked in the sun.

The wind had turned cold and mean, and Billy Bibbit took off his green coat and gave it to the girl, and she put it on over her thin little T-shirt. One of the loafers kept calling down, "Hey you, Blondie, you like fruitcake kids like that?" The man's lips were kidney-colored and he was purple under his eyes where the wind'd mashed the veins to the surface. "Hey you, Blondie," he called over and over in a high, tired voice, "hey you, Blondie . . . hey you, Blondie . . . hey you, Blondie . . ."

We bunched up closer together against the wind.

"Tell me, Blondie, what've they got *you* committed for?"

"Ahr, she ain't committed, Perce, she's part of the *cure!*"

"Is that right, Blondie? You hired as part of the *cure?* Hey you, Blondie."

She lifted her head and gave us a look that asked where was that hard-boiled bunch she'd seen and why weren't they saying something to defend her? Nobody would answer the look. All our hard-boiled strength had just walked up those steps with his arm around the shoulders of that bald-headed captain.

She pulled the collar of the jacket high around her neck and hugged her elbows and strolled as far away from us down the dock as she could go. Nobody went after her. Billy Bibbit shivered in the cold and bit his lip. The guys at the bait shack whispered something else and whooped out laughing again.

"Ask 'er, Perce—go on."

"Hey, Blondie, did you get 'em to sign a waiver clearing you with proper authorities? Relatives could sue, they tell me, if one of the boys fell in and drown while he was on board. Did you ever think of that? Maybe you'd better stay here with us, Blondie."

"Yeah, Blondie; my relatives wouldn't sue. I promise. Stay here with us fellows, Blondie."

I imagined I could feel my feet getting wet as the dock sank with shame into the bay. We weren't fit to be out here with people. I wished McMurphy would come back out and cuss these guys good and then drive us back where we belonged.

The man with the kidney lips folded his knife and stood up and brushed the whittle shavings out of his lap. He started walking toward the steps. "C'mon now, Blondie, what you want to mess with these bozos for?"

She turned and looked at him from the end of the dock, then back at us, and you could tell she was thinking his proposition over when the door of the bait shop opened and McMurphy came shoving out past the bunch of them, down the steps.

"Pile in, crew, it's all set! Gassed and ready and there's bait and beer on board."

He slapped Billy on the rear and did a little hornpipe and commenced slinging ropes from their snubs.

"Ol' Cap'n Block's still on the phone, but we'll be pulling off as quick as he comes out. George, let's see if you can get that motor warmed up. Scanlon, you and Harding untie that rope there. Candy! What you doing off down there? Let's get with it, honey, we're shoving off."

We swarmed into the boat, glad for anything that would take us away from those guys standing in a row at the bait shop. Billy took the girl by the hand and helped her on board. George hummed over the dashboard up on the bridge, pointing out buttons for McMurphy to twist or push.

"Yeah, these pukers, puke boats, we call them," he said to McMurphy, "they joost as easy like driving the ottomobile."

The doctor hesitated before climbing aboard and looked to-

ward the shop where all the loafers stood milling toward the
steps.

"Don't you think, Randle, we'd better wait . . . until the
captain—"

McMurphy caught him by the lapels and lifted him clear of
the dock into the boat like he was a small boy. "Yeah, Doc,"
he said, "wait till the captain *what?*" He commenced to laugh
like he was drunk, talking in an excited, nervous way. "Wait
till the captain comes out and tells us that the phone number
I gave him is a flophouse up in Portland? You bet. Here,
George, damn your eyes; take hold of this thing and get us out
of here! Sefelt! Get that rope loose and get on. George, come
on."

The motor chugged and died, chugged again like it was clearing its throat, then roared full on.

"*Hoowee!* There she goes. Pour the coal to 'er, George, and
all hands stand by to repel boarders!"

A white gorge of smoke and water roared from the back
of the boat, and the door of the bait shop crashed open and
the captain's head came booming out and down the steps like
it was not only dragging his body behind it but the bodies of
the eight other guys as well. They came thundering down the
dock and stopped right at the boil of foam washing over their
feet as George swung the big boat out and away from the
docks and we had the sea to ourselves.

A sudden turn of the boat had thrown Candy to her knees,
and Billy was helping her up and trying to apologize for the
way he'd acted on the dock at the same time. McMurphy came
down from the bridge and asked if the two of them would like
to be alone so they could talk over old times, and Candy looked
at Billy and all he could do was shake his head and stutter.
McMurphy said in that case that he and Candy'd better go
below and check for leaks and the rest of us could make do
for a while. He stood at the door down to the cabin and saluted and winked and appointed George captain and Harding
second in command and said, "Carry on, mates," and followed
the girl out of sight into the cabin.

The wind lay down and the sun got higher, chrome-plating the east side of the deep green swells. George aimed the boat straight out to sea, full throttle, putting the docks and that bait shop farther and farther behind us. When we passed the last point of the jetty and the last black rock, I could feel a great calmness creep over me, a calmness that increased the farther we left land behind us.

The guys had talked excitedly for a few minutes about our piracy of the boat, but now they were quiet. The cabin door opened once long enough for a hand to shove out a case of beer, and Billy opened us each one with an opener he found in the tackle box, and passed them around. We drank and watched the land sinking in our wake.

A mile or so out George cut the speed to what he called a trolling idle, put four guys to the four poles in the back of the boat, and the rest of us sprawled in the sun on top of the cabin or up on the bow and took off our shirts and watched the guys trying to rig their poles. Harding said the rule was a guy got to hold a pole till he got one strike, then he had to change off with a man who hadn't had a chance. George stood at the wheel, squinting out through the salt-caked windshield, and hollered instructions back how to fix up the reels and lines and how to tie a herring into the herring harness and how far back to fish and how deep:

"And take that number *four* pole and you put you twelve ounces on him on a rope with a breakaway rig—I show you how in joost a minute—and we go after that *big* fella down on the bottom with that pole, by golly!"

Martini ran to the edge and leaned over the side and stared down into the water in the direction of his line. "Oh. Oh, my God," he said, but whatever he saw was too deep down for the rest of us.

There were other sports boats trolling up and down the coast, but George didn't make any attempt to join them; he kept pushing steadily straight on out past them, toward the open sea. "You bet," he said. "We go out with the commercial boats, where the real *fish* is."

The swells slid by, deep emerald on one side, chrome on the other. The only noise was the engine sputtering and humming, off and on, as the swells dipped the exhaust in and out of the water, and the funny, lost cry of the raggedy little black birds swimming around asking one another directions. Everything else was quiet. Some of the guys slept, and the others watched the water. We'd been trolling close to an hour when the tip of Sefelt's pole arched and dived into the water.

"George! Jesus, George, give us a hand!"

George wouldn't have a thing to do with the pole; he grinned and told Sefelt to ease up on the star drag, keep the tip pointed up, *up*, and work hell outa that fella!

"But what if I have a seizure?" Sefelt hollered.

"Why, we'll simply put hook and line on you and use you for a lure," Harding said. "Now work that fella, as the captain ordered, and quit worrying about a seizure."

Thirty yards back of the boat the fish broke into the sun in a shower of silver scales, and Sefelt's eyes popped and he got so excited watching the fish he let the end of his pole go down, and the line snapped into the boat like a rubber band.

"*Up*, I told you! You let him get a straight pull, don't you see? Keep that tip *up* . . . *up!* You had you one big silver there, by golly."

Sefelt's jaw was white and shaking when he finally gave up the pole to Fredrickson. "Okay—but if you get a fish with a hook in his mouth, that's my godblessed fish!"

I was as excited as the rest. I hadn't planned on fishing, but after seeing that steel power a salmon has at the end of a line I got off the cabin top and put on my shirt to wait my turn at a pole.

Scanlon got up a pool for the biggest fish and another for the first fish landed, four bits from everybody that wanted in it, and he'd no more'n got his money in his pocket than Billy drug in some awful thing that looked like a ten-pound toad with spines on it like a porcupine.

"That's no fish," Scanlon said. "You can't win on that."

"It isn't a b-b-bird.

"That there, he's a *ling* cod," George told us. "He's one good eating fish you get all his warts off."

"See there. He is too a fish. P-p-pay up."

Billy gave me his pole and took his money and went to sit up close to the cabin where McMurphy and the girl were, looking at the closed door forlornly. "I wu-wu-wu-wish we had enough poles to go around," he said, leaning back against the side of the cabin.

I sat down and held the pole and watched the line swoop out into the wake. I smelt the air and felt the four cans of beer I'd drunk shorting out dozens of control leads down inside me: all around, the chrome sides of the swells flickered and flashed in the sun.

George sang out for us to look up ahead, that here come just what we been looking for. I leaned around to look, but all I saw was a big drifting log and those black seagulls circling and diving around the log, like black leaves caught up in a dust devil. George speeded up some, heading into the place where the birds circled, and the speed of the boat dragged my line until I couldn't see how you'd be able to tell if you did get a bite.

"Those fellas, those cormorants, they go after a school of *candle* fishes," George told us as he drove. "Little white fishes the size of your finger. You dry them and they burn joost like a candle. They are *food* fish, chum fish. And you bet where there's a big school of them candle fish you find the silver salmon feeding."

He drove into the birds, missing the floating log, and suddenly all around me the smooth slopes of chrome were shattered by diving birds and churning minnows, and the sleek silver-blue torpedo backs of the salmon slicing through it all. I saw one of the backs check its direction and turn and set course for a spot thirty yards behind the end of my pole, where my herring would be. I braced, my heart ringing, and then felt a jolt up both arms as if somebody'd hit the pole with a ball bat, and my line went burning off the reel from under my thumb, red as blood. "Use the star drag!" George yelled at me, but what

I knew about star drags you could put in your eye so I just mashed harder with my thumb until the line turned back to yellow, then slowed and stopped. I looked around, and there were all three of the other poles whipping around just like mine, and the rest of the guys scrambling down off the cabin at the excitement and doing everything in their power to get underfoot.

"Up! Up! Keep the tip up!" George was yelling.

"McMurphy! Get out here and look at this."

"Godbless you, Fred, you got my blessed fish!"

"McMurphy, we need some help!"

I heard McMurphy laughing and saw him out of the corner of my eye, just standing at the cabin door, not even making a move to do anything, and I was too busy cranking at my fish to ask him for help. Everyone was shouting at him to do something, but he wasn't moving. Even the doctor, who had the deep pole, was asking McMurphy for assistance. And McMurphy was just laughing. Harding finally saw McMurphy wasn't going to do anything, so he got the gaff and jerked my fish into the boat with a clean, graceful motion like he's been boating fish all his life. He's big as my leg, I thought, big as a fence post! I thought, He's bigger'n any fish we ever got at the falls. He's springing all over the bottom of the boat like a rainbow gone wild! Smearing blood and scattering scales like little silver dimes, and I'm scared he's gonna flop overboard. McMurphy won't make a move to help. Scanlon grabs the fish and wrestles it down to keep it from flopping over the side. The girl comes running up from below, yelling it's her turn, dang it, grabs my pole, and jerks the hook into me three times while I'm trying to tie on a herring for her.

"Chief, I'll be damned if I ever saw anything so *slow!* Ugh, your thumb's bleeding. Did that monster bite you? Somebody fix the Chief's thumb—hurry!"

"Here we go into them again," George yells, and I drop the line off the back of the boat and see the flash of the herring vanish in the dark blue-gray charge of a salmon and the line go sizzling down into the water. The girl wraps both arms around the pole and grits her teeth. "*Oh* no you don't, dang you! *Oh* no . . . !"

She's on her feet, got the butt of the pole scissored in her crotch and both arms wrapped below the reel and the reel crank knocking against her as the line spins out: "*Oh* no you don't!" She's still got on Billy's green jacket, but that reel's whipped it open and everybody on board sees the T-shirt she had on is gone—everybody gawking, trying to play his own fish, dodge mine slamming around the boat bottom, with the crank of that reel fluttering her breast at such a speed the nipple's just a red blur!

Billy jumps to help. All he can think to do is reach around from behind and help her squeeze the pole tighter in between her breasts until the reel's finally stopped by nothing more than the pressure of her flesh. By this time she's flexed so taut and her breasts look so firm I think she and Billy could both turn loose with their hands and arms and she'd *still* keep hold of that pole.

This scramble of action holds for a space, a second there on the sea—the men yammering and struggling and cussing and trying to tend their poles while watching the girl; the bleeding, crashing battle between Scanlon and my fish at everybody's feet; the lines all tangled and shooting every which way with the doctor's glasses-on-a-string tangled and dangling from one line ten feet off the back of the boat, fish striking at the flash of the lens, and the girl cussing for all she's worth and looking now at her bare breasts, one white and one smarting red—and George takes his eye off where he's going and runs the boat into that log and kills the engine.

While McMurphy laughs. Rocking farther and farther backward against the cabin top, spreading his laugh out across the water—laughing at the girl, at the guys, at George, at me sucking my bleeding thumb, at the captain back at the pier and the bicycle rider and the service-station guys and the five thousand houses and the Big Nurse and all of it. Because he knows you have to laugh at the things that hurt you just to keep yourself in balance, just to keep the world from running you plumb

crazy. He knows there's a painful side; he knows my thumb
smarts and his girl friend has a bruised breast and the doctor
is losing his glasses, but he won't let the pain blot out the humor no more'n he'll let the humor blot out the pain.

I notice Harding is collapsed beside McMurphy and is laughing too. And Scanlon from the bottom of the boat. At their
own selves as well as at the rest of us. And the girl, with her
eyes still smarting as she looks from her white breast to her red
one, she starts laughing. And Sefelt and the doctor, and all.

It started slow and pumped itself full, swelling the men bigger and bigger. I watched, part of them, laughing with them—
and somehow not with them. I was off the boat, blown up off
the water and skating the wind with those black birds, high
above myself, and I could look down and see myself and the
rest of the guys, see the boat rocking there in the middle of
those diving birds, see McMurphy surrounded by his dozen
people, and watch them, us, swinging a laughter that rang out
on the water in ever-widening circles, farther and farther, until
it crashed up on beaches all over the coast, on beaches all over
all coasts, in wave after wave after wave.

The doctor had hooked something off the bottom on the
deep pole, and everybody else on board except George had
caught and landed a fish by the time he lifted it up to where
we could even see it—just a whitish shape appearing, then diving for the bottom in spite of everything the doctor tried to
do to hold it. As soon as he'd get it up near the top again, lifting and reeling at it with tight, stubborn little grunts and refusing any help the guys might offer, it would see the light and
down it would go.

George didn't bother starting the boat again, but came down
to show us how to clean the fish over the side and rip the gills
out so the meat would stay sweeter. McMurphy tied a chunk
of meat to each end of a four-foot string, tossed it in the air,
and sent two squawking birds wheeling off, "Till death do them
part."

The whole back of the boat and most of the people in it were dappled with red and silver. Some of us took our shirts off and dipped them over the side and tried to clean them. We fiddled around this way, fishing a little, drinking the other case of beer, and feeding the birds till afternoon, while the boat rolled lazily around the swells and the doctor worked with his monster from the deep. A wind came up and broke the sea into green and silver chunks, like a field of glass and chrome, and the boat began to rock and pitch about more. George told the doctor he'd have to land his fish or cut it loose because there was a bad sky coming down on us. The doctor didn't answer. He just heaved harder on the pole, bent forward and reeled the slack, and heaved again.

Billy and the girl had climbed around to the bow and were talking and looking down in the water. Billy hollered that he saw something, and we all rushed to that side, and a shape broad and white was becoming solid some ten or fifteen feet down. It was strange watching it rise, first just a light coloring, then a white form like fog under water, becoming solid, alive. . . .

"Jesus God," Scanlon cried, "that's the doc's fish!"

It was on the side opposite the doctor, but we could see by the direction of his line that it led to the shape under the water.

"We'll never get it in the boat," Sefelt said. "And the wind's getting stronger."

"He's a big flounder," George said. "Sometimes they weigh two, three hundred. You got to lift them in with the winch."

"We'll have to cut him loose, Doc," Sefelt said and put his arm across the doctor's shoulders. The doctor didn't say anything; he had sweated clear through his suit between his shoulders, and his eyes were bright red from going so long without glasses. He kept heaving until the fish appeared on his side of the boat. We watched it near the surface for a few minutes longer, then started getting the rope and gaff ready.

Even with the gaff in it, it took another hour to drag the fish into the back of the boat. We had to hook him with all three other poles, and McMurphy leaned down and got a hand in his gills, and with a heave he slid in, transparent white and flat, and flopped down to the bottom of the boat with the doctor.

"That was something." The doctor panted from the floor, not enough strength left to push the huge fish off him. "That was . . . certainly something."

The boat pitched and cracked all the way back to shore, with McMurphy telling grim tales about shipwrecks and sharks. The waves got bigger as we got closer to shore, and from the crests clots of white foam blew swirling up in the wind to join the gulls. The swells at the mouth of the jetty were combing higher than the boat, and George had us all put on life jackets. I noticed all the other sports boats were in.

We were three jackets short, and there was a fuss as to who'd be the three that braved that bar without jackets. It finally turned out to be Billy Bibbit and Harding and George, who wouldn't wear one anyway on account of the dirt. Everybody was kind of surprised that Billy had volunteered, took his life jacket off right away when we found we were short, and helped the girl into it, but everybody was even more surprised that McMurphy hadn't insisted that he be one of the heroes; all during the fuss he'd stood with his back against the cabin, bracing against the pitch of the boat, and watched the guys without saying a word. Just grinning and watching.

We hit the bar and dropped into a canyon of water, the bow of the boat pointing up the hissing crest of the wave going before us, and the rear down in the trough in the shadow of the wave looming behind us, and everybody in the back hanging on the rail and looking from the mountain that chased behind to the streaming black rocks of the jetty forty feet to the left, to George at the wheel. He stood there like a mast. He kept turning his head from the front to the back, gunning the throttle, easing off, gunning again, holding us steady riding the uphill slant of that wave in front. He'd told us before we started the run that if we went over that crest in *front*, we'd surfboard out of control as soon as the prop and rudder broke water, and if we slowed down to where that wave *behind* caught up it would break over the stern and dump ten tons of water into the boat. Nobody joked or said anything funny about the way he kept turning his head back and forth like it was mounted up there on a swivel.

Inside the mooring the water calmed to a choppy surface again, and at our dock, by the bait shop, we could see the captain waiting with two cops at the water's edge. All the loafers were gathered behind them. George headed at them full throttle, booming down on them till the captain went to waving and yelling and the cops headed up the steps with the loafers. Just before the prow of the boat tore out the whole dock, George swung the wheel, threw the prop into reverse, and with a powerful roar snuggled the boat in against the rubber tires like he was easing it into bed. We were already out tying up by the time our wake caught up; it pitched all the boats around and slopped over the dock and whitecapped around the docks like we'd brought the sea home with us.

The captain and the cops and the loafers came tromping back down the steps to us. The doctor carried the fight to them by first off telling the cops they didn't have any jurisdiction over us, as we were a legal, government-sponsored expedition, and if there was anyone to take the matter up with it would have to be a federal agency. Also, there might be some investigation into the number of life jackets that the boat held if the captain really planned to make trouble. Wasn't there supposed to be a life jacket for every man on board, according to the law? When the captain didn't say anything the cops took some names and left, mumbling and confused, and as soon as they were off the pier McMurphy and the captain went to arguing and shoving each other around. McMurphy was drunk enough he was still trying to rock with the roll of the boat and he slipped on the wet wood and fell in the ocean twice before he got his footing sufficient to hit the captain one up alongside of his bald head and settle the fuss. Everybody felt better that that was out of the way, and the captain and McMurphy both went to the bait shop to get more beer while the rest of us worked at hauling our fish out of the hold. The loafers stood on that upper dock, watching and smoking pipes

they'd carved themselves. We were waiting for them to say
something about the girl again, hoping for it, to tell the truth,
but when one of them finally did say something it wasn't about
the girl but about our fish being the biggest halibut he'd ever seen
brought in on the Oregon coast. All the rest nodded that that was
sure the truth. They came edging down to look it over. They
asked George where he learned to dock a boat that way, and we
found out George'd not just run fishing boats but he'd also
been captain of a PT boat in the Pacific and got the Navy
Cross. "Shoulda gone into public office," one of the loafers
said. "Too dirty," George told him.

They could sense the change that most of us were only
suspecting; these weren't the same bunch of weak-knees from
a nuthouse that they'd watched take their insults on the dock
this morning. They didn't exactly apologize to the girl for the
things they'd said, but when they ask to see the fish she'd
caught they were just as polite as pie. And when McMurphy
and the captain came back out of the bait shop we all shared
a beer together before we drove away.

It was late when we got back to the hospital.

The girl was sleeping against Billy's chest, and when she
raised up his arm'd gone dead holding her all that way in such
an awkward position, and she rubbed it for him. He told her
if he had any of his weekends free he'd ask her for a date, and
she said she could come to visit in two weeks if he'd tell her
what time, and Billy looked at McMurphy for an answer. Mc-
Murphy put his arms around both of their shoulders and said,
"Let's make it two o'clock on the nose."

"Saturday afternoon?" she asked.

He winked at Billy and squeezed the girl's head in the crook
of his arm. "No. Two o'clock Saturday night. Slip up and
knock on that same window you was at this morning. I'll talk
the night aide into letting you in."

She giggled and nodded. "You damned McMurphy," she
said.

Some of the Acutes on the ward were still up, standing
around the latrine to see if we'd been drowned or not. They

watched us march into the hall, blood-speckled, sunburned, stinking of beer and fish, toting our salmon like we were conquering heroes. The doctor asked if they'd like to come out and look at his halibut in the back of his car, and we all started back out except McMurphy. He said he guessed he was pretty shot and thought he'd hit the hay. When he was gone one of the Acutes who hadn't made the trip asked how come McMurphy looked so beat and worn out where the rest of us looked red-cheeked and still full of excitement. Harding passed it off as nothing more than the loss of his suntan.

"You'll recall McMurphy came in full steam, from a rigorous life outdoors on a work farm, ruddy of face and abloom with physical health. We've simply been witness to the fading of his magnificent psychopathic suntan. That's all. Today he did spend some exhausting hours—in the dimness of the boat cabin, incidentally—while we were out in the elements, soaking up the Vitamin D. Of course, that may have exhausted him to some extent, those rigors down below, but think of it, friends. As for myself, I believe I could have done with a little less Vitamin D and a little more of his kind of exhaustion. Especially with little Candy as a taskmaster. Am I wrong?"

I didn't say so, but I was wondering if maybe he wasn't wrong. I'd noticed McMurphy's exhaustion earlier, on the trip home, after he'd insisted on driving past the place where he'd lived once. We'd just shared the last beer and slung the empty can out the window at a stop sign and were just leaning back to get the feel of the day, swimming in that kind of tasty drowsiness that comes over you after a day of going hard at something you enjoy doing—half sunburned and half drunk and keeping awake only because you wanted to savor the taste as long as you could. I noticed vaguely that I was getting so's I could see some good in the life around me. McMurphy was teaching me. I was feeling better than I'd remembered feeling since I was a kid, when everything was good and the land was still singing kids' poetry to me.

We'd drove back inland instead of the coast, to go through this town McMurphy'd lived in the most he'd ever lived in one place. Down the face of the Cascade hill, thinking we were lost till . . . we came to a town covered a space about twice the size of the hospital ground. A gritty wind had blown out the sun on the street where he stopped. He parked in some reeds and pointed across the road.

"There. That's the one. Looks like it's propped up outa the weeds—my misspent youth's humble abode."

Out along the dim six-o'clock street, I saw leafless trees standing, striking the sidewalk there like wooden lightning, concrete split apart where they hit, all in a fenced-in ring. An iron line of pickets stuck out of the ground along the front of a tangleweed yard, and on back was a big frame house with a porch, leaning a rickety shoulder hard into the wind so's not to be sent tumbling away a couple of blocks like an empty cardboard grocery box. The wind was blowing a few drops of rain, and I saw the house had its eyes clenched shut and locks at the door banged on a chain.

And on the porch, hanging, was one of those things the Japs make out of glass and hang on strings—rings and clangs in the least little blow—with only four pieces of glass left to go. These four swung and whipped and rung little chips off on the wooden porch floor.

McMurphy put the car back in gear.

"Once, I been here—since way the hell gone back in the year we were all gettin' home from that Korea mess. For a visit. My old man and old lady were still alive. It was a good home."

He let out the clutch and started to drive, then stopped instead.

"My God," he said, "look over there, see a dress?" He pointed out back. "In the branch of that tree? A rag, yellow and black?"

I was able to see a thing like a flag, flapping high in the branches over a shed.

"The first girl ever drug me to bed wore that very same dress. I was about ten and she was probably less, and at the time a lay seemed like such a big deal I asked her if didn't she think, *feel*, we oughta *announce* it some way? Like, say, tell our folks, 'Mom, Judy and me got engaged today.' And I meant what I said, I was that big a fool; I thought if you made it, man, you were legally *wed*, right there on the spot, whether it was something you wanted or not, and that there wasn't any breaking the rule. But this little whore—at the most eight or nine—reached down and got her dress off the floor and said it was mine, said, 'You can hang this up someplace, I'll go home in my drawers, announce it that way—they'll get the idea.' Jesus, nine years old," he said, reached over and pinched Candy's nose, "and knew a lot more than a good many pros."

She bit his hand, laughing, and he studied the mark.

"So, anyhow, after she went home in her pants I waited till dark when I had the chance to throw that damned dress out in the night—but you feel that wind? caught the dress like a kite and whipped it around the house outa sight and the next morning, by God, it was hung up in that tree for the whole town, was how I figured then, to turn out and see."

He sucked his hand, so woebegone that Candy laughed and gave it a kiss.

"So my colors were flown, and from that day to this it seemed I might as well live up to my name—dedicated lover— and it's the God's truth: that little nine-year-old kid out of my youth's the one who's to blame."

The house drifted past. He yawned and winked. "Taught me to love, bless her sweet ass."

Then—as he was talking—a set of tail-lights going past lit up McMurphy's face, and the windshield reflected an expression that was allowed only because he figured it'd be too dark for anybody in the car to see, dreadfully tired and strained and *frantic*, like there wasn't enough time left for something he had to do. . . .

While his relaxed, good-natured voice doled out his life for us to live, a rollicking past full of kid fun and drinking buddies and loving women and barroom battles over meager honors— for all of us to dream ourselves into.

part 4

the Big Nurse had her next maneuver under way the day after the fishing trip. The idea had come to her when she was talking to McMurphy the day before about how much money he was making off the fishing trip and other little enterprises along that line. She had worked the idea over that night, looking at it from every direction this time until she was dead sure it could not fail, and all the next day she fed hints around to start a rumor and have it breeding good before she actually said anything about it.

She knew that people, being like they are, sooner or later are going to draw back a ways from somebody who seems to be giving a little more than ordinary, from Santa Clauses and missionaries and men donating funds to worthy causes, and begin to wonder: What's in it for them? Grin out of the side of their mouths when the young lawyer, say, brings a sack of pecans to the kids in his district school—just before nominations for state senate, the sly devil—and say to one another, *He's* nobody's fool.

She knew it wouldn't take too much to get the guys to wondering just what it was, now that you mention it, that made McMurphy spend so much time and energy organizing fishing trips to the coast and arranging Bingo parties and coaching basketball teams. What pushed him to keep up a full head of steam when everybody else on the ward had always been content to drift along playing pinochle and reading last year's magazines? How come this one guy, this Irish rowdy from a work farm where he'd been serving time for gambling and battery, would loop a kerchief around his head, coo like a teen-ager, and spend two solid hours having every Acute on the ward hoorahing him while he played the girl trying to teach Billy Bibbit to dance? Or how come a seasoned con like this—an old pro, a carnival artist, a dedicated odds-watcher gambling man —would risk doubling his stay in the nuthouse by making more and more an enemy out of the woman who had the say-so as to who got discharged and who didn't?

The nurse got the wondering started by pasting up a statement of the patients' financial doings over the last few months; it must have taken her hours of work digging into records. It showed a steady drain out of the funds of all the Acutes, except one. His funds had risen since the day he came in.

The Acutes took to joking with McMurphy about how it looked like he was taking them down the line, and he was never one to deny it. Not the least bit. In fact, he bragged that if he stayed on at this hospital a year or so he just might be discharged out of it into financial independence, retire to Florida for the rest of his life. They all laughed about that when he was around, but when he was off the ward at ET or OT or PT, or when he was in the Nurses' Station getting bawled out about something, matching her fixed plastic smile with his big ornery grin, they weren't exactly laughing.

They began asking one another why he'd been such a busy bee lately, hustling things for the patients like getting the rule lifted that the men had to be together in therapeutic groups of eight whenever they went somewhere ("Billy here has been talkin' about slicin' his wrists again," he said in a meeting when he was arguing against the group-of-eight rule. "So is there seven of you guys who'd like to join him and make it therapeutic?"), and like the way he maneuvered the doctor, who was much closer to the patients since the fishing trip, into ordering subscriptions to *Playboy* and *Nugget* and *Man* and getting rid of all the old *McCall's* that bloated-face Public Relation had been bringing from home and leaving in a pile on the ward, articles he thought we might be particularly interested in checked with green ink. McMurphy even had a petition in the mail to somebody back in Washington, asking that they look into the lobotomies and electro-shock that were still going on in government hospitals. I just *wonder*, the guys were beginning to ask, what's in it for ol' Mack?

After the thought had been going around the ward a week or so, the Big Nurse tried to make her play in group meeting;

the first time she tried, McMurphy was there at the meeting
and he beat her before she got good and started (she started
by telling the group that she was shocked and dismayed by the
pathetic state the ward had allowed itself to fall into: Look
around, for heaven sakes; actual pornography clipped from
those smut books and pinned on the walls—she was planning,
incidentally, to see to it that the Main Building made an investigation of the *dirt* that had been brought into this hospital.
She sat back in her chair, getting ready to go on and point out
who was to blame and why, sitting on that couple seconds of
silence that followed her threat like sitting on a throne, when
McMurphy broke her spell into whoops of laughter by telling
her to be sure, now, an' remind the Main Building to bring
their leetle *hand* mirrors when they came for the investigation)
—so the next time she made her play she made sure he wasn't
at the meeting.

He had a long-distance phone call from Portland and was
down in the phone lobby with one of the black boys, waiting
for the party to call again. When one o'clock came around
and we went to moving things, getting the day room ready, the
least black boy asked if she wanted him to go down and get
McMurphy and Washington for the meeting, but she said no,
it was all right, let him stay—besides, some of the men here
might like a chance to discuss our Mr. Randle Patrick Mc-
Murphy in the absence of his dominating presence.

They started the meeting telling funny stories about him
and what he'd done, and talked for a while about what a great
guy he was, and she kept still, waiting till they all talked this
out of their systems. Then the other questions started coming
up. What about McMurphy? What made him go on like he
was, do the things he did? Some of the guys wondered if maybe
that tale of him faking fights at the work farm to get sent here
wasn't just more of his spoofing, and that maybe he was crazier
than people thought. The Big Nurse smiled at this and raised
her hand.

"Crazy like a fox," she said. "I believe that is what you're
trying to say about Mr. McMurphy."

"What do you m-m-mean?" Billy asked. McMurphy was his special friend and hero, and he wasn't too sure he was pleased with the way she'd laced that compliment with things she didn't say out loud. "What do you m-m-mean, 'like a fox'?"

"It's a simple observation, Billy," the nurse answered pleasantly. "Let's see if some of the other men could tell you what it means. What about you, Mr. Scanlon?"

"She means, Billy, that Mack's nobody's fool."

"Nobody said he wuh-wuh-wuh-*was!*" Billy hit the arm of the chair with his fist to get out the last word. "But Miss Ratched was im-implying—"

"No, Billy, I wasn't implying anything. I was simply observing that Mr. McMurphy isn't one to run a risk without a reason. You would agree to that, wouldn't you? Wouldn't all of you agree to that?"

Nobody said anything.

"And yet," she went on, "he seems to do things without thinking of himself at all, as if he were a martyr or a saint. Would anyone venture that Mr. McMurphy was a saint?"

She knew she was safe to smile around the room, waiting for an answer.

"No, not a saint *or* a martyr. Here. Shall we examine a cross section of this man's philanthropy?" She took a sheet of yellow paper out of her basket. "Look at some of these *gifts*, as devoted fans of his might call them. First, there was the gift of the tub room. Was that actually his to give? Did he lose anything by acquiring it as a gambling casino? On the other hand, how much do you suppose he made in the short time he was croupier of his little Monte Carlo here on the ward? How much did you lose, Bruce? Mr. Sefelt? Mr. Scanlon? I think you all have some idea what your personal losses were, but do you know what his total winnings came to, according to deposits he has made at Funds? Almost three hundred dollars."

Scanlon gave a low whistle, but no one else said anything.

"I have various other bets he made listed here, if any of you care to look, including something to do with deliberately trying to upset the staff. And all of this gambling was, is, completely against ward policy and every one of you who dealt with him knew it."

She looked at the paper again, then put it back in the basket. "And this recent fishing trip? What do you suppose Mr. Mc-Murphy's profit was on this venture? As I see it, he was provided with a car of the doctor's, even with money from the doctor for gasoline, and, I am told, quite a few other benefits—without having paid a nickel. Quite like a fox, I must say."

She held up her hand to stop Billy from interrupting.

"Please, Billy, understand me: I'm not criticizing this sort of activity as such; I just thought it would be better if we didn't have any delusions about the man's motives. But, at any rate, perhaps it isn't fair to make these accusations without the presence of the man we are speaking of. Let's return to the problem we were discussing yesterday—what was it?" She went leafing through her basket. "What was it, do you remember, Doctor Spivey?"

The doctor's head jerked up. "No . . . wait . . . I think . . ."

She pulled a paper from a folder. "Here it is. Mr. Scanlon; his feelings about explosives. Fine. We'll go into that now, and at some other time when Mr. McMurphy is present we'll return to him. I do think, however, that you might give what was said today some thought. Now, Mr. Scanlon . . ."

Later that day there were eight or ten of us grouped together at the canteen door, waiting till the black boy was finished shop-lifting hair oil, and some of the guys brought it up again. They said they didn't agree with what the Big Nurse had been saying, but, hell, the old girl had some good points. And yet, damn it, Mack's still a good guy . . . really.

Harding finally brought the conversation into the open.

"My friends, thou protest too much to believe the protesting. You are all believing deep inside your stingy little hearts that our Miss Angel of Mercy Ratched is absolutely correct in every assumption she made today about McMurphy. You know she was, and so do I. But why deny it? Let's be honest and give this man his due instead of secretly criticizing his capitalistic talent. What's wrong with him making a little profit? We've all certainly got our money's worth every time he fleeced us, haven't we? He's a shrewd character with an eye out for a quick dollar. He doesn't make any pretense about his motives, does he? Why should we? He has a healthy and honest attitude about his chicanery, and I'm all for him, just as I'm for the dear old capitalistic system of free individual enterprise, comrades, for him and his downright bullheaded gall and the American flag, bless it, and the Lincoln Memorial and the whole bit. Remember the Maine, P. T. Barnum and the Fourth of July. I feel *compelled* to defend my friend's honor as a good old red, white, and blue hundred-per-cent American con man. Good guy, my foot. McMurphy would be embarrassed to absolute *tears* if he were aware of some of the simon-pure motives people had been claiming were behind some of his dealings. He would take it as a direct effrontery to his craft."

He dipped into his pocket for his cigarettes; when he couldn't find any he borrowed one from Fredrickson, lit it with a stagey sweep of his match, and went on.

"I'll admit I was confused by his actions at first. That window-breaking—Lord, I thought, here's a man that seems to actually want to stay in this hospital, stick with his buddies and all that sort of thing, until I realized that McMurphy was doing it because he didn't want to lose a good thing. He's making the most of his time in here. Don't ever be misled by his backwoodsy ways; he's a very sharp operator, level-headed as they come. You watch; everything he's done was done with reason."

Billy wasn't about to give in so easy. "Yeah. What about him teaching me to d-dance?" He was clenching his fists at his side; and on the backs of his hands I saw that the cigarette burns had all but healed, and in their place were tattoos he'd drawn by licking an indelible pencil. "What about that, Harding? Where is he making muh-muh-money out of teaching me to *dance?*"

"Don't get upset, William," Harding said. "But don't get impatient, either. Let's just sit easy and wait—and see how he works it."

It seemed like Billy and I were the only two left who believed in McMurphy. And that very night Billy swung over to Harding's way of looking at things when McMurphy came back from making another phone call and told Billy that the date with Candy was on for certain and added, writing an address down for him, that it might be a good idea to send her a little *bread* for the trip.

"Bread? Muh-money? How muh-muh-much?" He looked over to where Harding was grinning at him.

"Oh, *you* know, man—maybe ten bucks for her and ten—"

"Twenty bucks!" It doesn't cost that muh-muh-much for bus fare down here."

McMurphy looked up from under his hatbrim, gave Billy a slow grin, then rubbed his throat with his hand, running out a dusty tongue. "Boy, oh boy, but I'm terrible dry. Figure to be even drier by a week come Saturday. You wouldn't begrudge her bringin' me a little swallow, would you, Billy Boy?"

And gave Billy such an innocent look Billy had to laugh and shake his head, no, and go off to a corner to excitedly talk over the next Saturday's plans with the man he probably considered a pimp.

I still had my own notions—how McMurphy was a giant come out of the sky to save us from the Combine that was networking the land with copper wire and crystal, how he was too big to be bothered with something as measly as money—but even I came halfway to thinking like the others. What happened was this: He'd helped carry the tables into the tub room before one of the group meetings and was looking at me standing beside the control panel.

"By God, Chief," he said, "it appears to me you growed ten inches since that fishing trip. And lordamighty, look at the size of that foot of yours; big as a flatcar!"

I looked down and saw how my foot was bigger than I'd ever remembered it, like McMurphy's just saying it had blowed it twice its size.

"And that *arm!* That's the arm of an ex-football-playing Indian if I ever saw one. You know what I think? I think you oughta give this here panel a leetle heft, just to test how you're comin'."

I shook my head and told him no, but he said we'd made a deal and I was obligated to give it a try to see how his *growth* system was working. I didn't see any way out of it so I went to the panel just to show him I couldn't do it. I bent down and took it by the levers.

"That's the baby, Chief. Now just straighten up. Get those legs under your butt, there . . . yeah, yeah. Easy now . . . just straighten up. Hooeee! Now ease 'er back to the deck."

I thought he'd be real disappointed, but when I stepped back he was all grins and pointing to where the panel was off its mooring by half a foot. "Better set her back where she came from, buddy, so nobody'll know. Mustn't let anybody know yet."

Then, after the meeting, loafing around the pinochle games, he worked the talk around to strength and gut-power and to the control panel in the tub room. I thought he was going to tell them how he'd helped me get my size back; that would prove he didn't do everything for money.

But he didn't mention me. He talked until Harding asked him if he was ready to have another try at lifting it and he said no, but just because he couldn't lift it was no sign it couldn't be done. Scanlon said maybe it could be done with a crane, but no *man* could lift that thing by himself, and McMurphy nodded and said maybe so, maybe so, but you never can tell about such things.

I watched the way he played them, got them to come around to him and say, *No, by Jesus, not a man alive could lift it*— finally even suggest the bet themselves. I watched how reluctant he looked to bet. He let the odds stack up, sucked them in deeper and deeper till he had five to one on a sure thing from every man of them, some of them betting up to twenty dollars. He never said a thing about seeing me lift it already.

All night I hoped he wouldn't go through with it. And during the meeting the next day, when the nurse said all the men who participated in the fishing trip would have to take special showers because they were suspected of vermin, I kept hoping she'd fix it somehow, make us take our showers right away or something—anything to keep me from having to lift it.

But when the meeting was over he led me and the rest of the guys into the tub room before the black boys could lock it up, and had me take the panel by the levers and lift. I didn't want to, but I couldn't help it. I felt like I'd helped him cheat them out of their money. They were all friendly with him as they paid their bets, but I knew how they were feeling inside, how something had been kicked out from under them. As soon as I got the panel back in place, I ran out of the tub room without even looking at McMurphy and went into the latrine. I wanted to be by myself. I caught a look at myself in the mirror. He'd done what he said; my arms were big again, big as they were back in high school, back at the village, and my chest and shoulders were broad and hard. I was standing there looking when he came in. He held out a five-dollar bill.

"Here you go, Chief, chewin'-gum money."

I shook my head and started to walk out of the latrine. He caught me by the arm.

"Chief, I just offered you a token of my appreciation. If you figure you got a bigger cut comin'—"

"No! Keep your money, I won't have it."

He stepped back and put his thumbs in his pockets and tipped his head up at me. He looked me over for a while.

"Okay," he said. "Now what's the story? What's everybody in this place giving me the cold nose about?"

I didn't answer him.

"Didn't I do what I said I would? Make you man-sized again? What's wrong with me around here all of a sudden? You birds act like I'm a traitor to my country."

"You're always . . . *winning* things!"

"Winning things! You damned moose, what are you accusin' me of? All I do is hold up my end of the deal. Now what's so all-fired—"

"We thought it wasn't to be *winning* things . . ."

I could feel my chin jerking up and down the way it does before I start crying, but I didn't start crying. I stood there in front of him with my chin jerking. He opened his mouth to say something, and then stopped. He took his thumbs out of his pockets and reached up and grabbed the bridge of his nose between his thumb and finger, like you see people do whose glasses are too tight between the lenses, and he closed his eyes.

"Winning, for Christsakes," he said with his eyes closed. "Hoo boy, winning."

So I figure what happened in the shower room that afternoon was more my fault than anybody else's. And that's why the only way I could make any kind of amends was by doing what I did, without thinking about being cagey or safe or what would happen to me—and not worrying about anything else for once but the thing that needed to be done and the doing of it.

Just after we left the latrine the three black boys came around, gathering the bunch of us for our special shower. The least black boy, scrambling along the baseboard with a black, crooked hand cold as a crowbar, prying guys loose leaning there, said it was what the Big Nurse called a *cautionary* cleansing. In view of the company we'd had on our trip we should get cleaned before we spread anything through the rest of the hospital.

We lined up nude against the tile, and here one black boy came, a black plastic tube in his hand, squirting a stinking salve thick and sticky as egg white. In the hair first, then turn around an' bend over an' spread your cheeks!

The guys complained and kidded and joked about it, trying not to look at one another or those floating slate masks working down the line behind the tubes, like nightmare faces in negative, sighting down soft, squeezy nightmare gunbarrels. They kidded the black boys by saying things like "Hey, Washington, what do you fellas do for fun the *other* sixteen hours?" "Hey, Williams, can you tell me what I had for breakfast?"

Everybody laughed. The black boys clenched their jaws and didn't answer; this wasn't the way things used to be before that damned redhead came around.

When Fredrickson spread his cheeks there was such a sound I thought the least black boy'd be blown clear off his feet.

"Hark!" Harding said, cupping his hand to his ear. "The lovely voice of an angel."

Everyone was roaring, laughing and kidding one another, until the black boy moved on and stopped in front of the next man, and the room was suddenly absolutely quiet. The next man was George. And in that one second, with the laughing and kidding and complaining stopped, with Fredrickson there next to George straightening up and turning around and a big black boy about to ask George to lean his head down for a squirt of that stinking salve—right at that time all of us had a good idea about everything that was going to happen, and why it had to happen, and why we'd all been wrong about McMurphy.

George never used soap when he showered. He wouldn't even let somebody hand him a towel to dry himself with. The black boys on the evening shift who supervised the usual Tuesday and Thursday evening showers had learned it was easier to leave it go like this, and they didn't force him to do any different. That was the way it'd been for a long time. All the black boys knew it. But now everybody knew—even George, leaning backward, shaking his head, covering himself with big oakleaf hands—that this black boy, with his nose busted and his insides soured and his two buddies standing behind him waiting to see what he would do, couldn't afford to pass up the chance.

"Ahhhh, bend you head down here, Geo'ge. . . ."

The guys were already looking to where McMurphy stood a couple of men down the line.

"Ahhhh, c'mon, Geo'ge. . . ."

Martini and Sefelt were standing in the shower, not moving. The drain at their feet kept choking short little gulps of air and soapy water. George looked at the drain a second, as if it were speaking to him. He watched it gurgle and choke. He looked back at the tube in the black hand before him, slow mucus running out of the little hole at the top of the tube down over the pig-iron knuckles. The black boy moved the tube forward a few inches, and George listed farther back, shaking his head.

"No—none that stoof."

"You gonna have to do it, Rub-a-dub," the black boy said, sounding almost sorry. "You gonna *have* to. We can't have the place crawlin' with *bugs*, now, can we? For all I know you got bugs on you a good *inch deep!*"

"No!" George said.

"Ahhh, Geo'ge, you jes' don't have no *idea*. These bugs, they very, very teeny—no bigger'n a *pinpoint*. An', man, what they *do* is get you by the short hair an' hang on, an' drill, down inside you, Geo'ge."

"No bugs!" George said.

"Ahhh, let me tell you, Geo'ge: I seen cases where these awful bugs achually—"

"Okay, Washington," McMurphy said.

The scar where the black boy's nose had been broken was a twist of neon. The black boy knew who'd spoken to him, but he didn't turn around; the only way we knew he'd even heard was by the way he stopped talking and reached up a long gray finger and drew it across the scar he'd got in that basketball game. He rubbed his nose a second, then shoved his hand out in front of George's face, scrabbling the fingers around. "A *crab*, Geo'ge, see? See here? Now you know what a *crab* look like, don't you? Sure now, you get crabs on that *fishin'* boat. We can't have crabs drillin' down into you, can we, Geo'ge?"

"*No crabs!*" George yelled. "No!" He stood straight and his brow lifted enough so we could see his eyes. The black boy stepped back a ways. The other two laughed at him. "Somethin' the matter, Washington, my man?" the big one asked. "Somethin' holding up this end of the pro-ceedure, my man?"

He stepped back in close. "Geo'ge, I'm tellin' you: bend down! You either bend down and take this stuff—or I lay my *hand* on you!" He held it up again; it was big and black as a swamp. "Put this black! filthy! stinkin'! hand all over you!"

"No hand!" George said and lifted a fist above his head as if he would crash the slate skull to bits, splatter cogs and nuts and bolts all over the floor. But the black boy just ran the tube up against George's belly-button and squeezed, and George doubled over with a suck of air. The black boy squirted a load in his whispy white hair, then rubbed it in with his hand, smearing black from his hand all over George's head. George wrapped both arms around his belly and screamed.

"No! No!"

"Now turn around, Geo'ge—"

"I said that's enough, buddy." This time the way his voice sounded made the black boy turn and face him. I saw the black boy was smiling, looking at McMurphy's nakedness—no hat or boots or pockets to hook his thumbs into. The black boy grinned up and down him.

"McMurphy," he said, shaking his head. "Y'know, I was beginnin' to think we might never get down to it."

"You goddamned coon," McMurphy said, somehow sounding more tired than mad. The black boy didn't say anything. McMurphy raised his voice. "Goddamned motherfucking nigger!"

The black boy shook his head and giggled at his two buddies. "What you think Mr. McMurphy is drivin' at with that kind of talk, man? You think he wants me to take the *initiative?* Heeheehee. Don't he know we trained to take such awful-soundin' insults from these crazies?"

"Cocksucker! Washington, you're nothing but a—"

Washington had turned his back on him, turning to George again. George was still bent over, gasping from the blow of that salve in his belly. The black boy grabbed his arm and swung him facing the wall.

"Tha's right, Geo'ge, now spread those cheeks."

"*No-o-o!*"

"Washington," McMurphy said. He took a deep breath and stepped across to the black boy, shoving him away from George. "Washington, all right, all right . . ."

Everybody could hear the helpless, cornered despair in McMurphy's voice.

"McMurphy, you forcing me to protect myself. Ain't he forcing me, men?" The other two nodded. He carefully laid down the tube on the bench beside George, came back up with his fist swinging all in the same motion and busting McMurphy across the cheek by surprise. McMurphy nearly fell. He staggered backward into the naked line of men, and the guys caught him and pushed him back toward the smiling slate face. He got hit again, in the neck, before he gave up to the idea that it had started, at last, and there wasn't anything now but get what he could out of it. He caught the next swing blacksnaking at him, and held him by the wrist while he shook his head clear.

They swayed a second that way, panting along with the panting drain; then McMurphy shoved the black boy away and went into a crouch, rolling the big shoulders up to guard his chin, his fists on each side of his head, circling the man in front of him.

And that neat, silent line of nude men changed into a yelling circle, limbs and bodies knitting in a ring of flesh.

The black arms stabbed in at the lowered red head and bull neck, chipped blood off the brow and the cheek. The black boy danced away. Taller, arms longer than McMurphy's thick red arms, punches faster and sharper, he was able to chisel at the shoulders and the head without getting in close. McMurphy kept walking forward—trudging, flatfooted steps, face down and squinting up between those tattooed fists on each side of his head—till he got the black boy against the ring of nude men and drove a fist square in the center of the white, starched chest. That slate face cracked pink, ran a tongue the color of strawberry ice cream over the lips. He ducked away from McMurphy's tank charge and got in another couple of licks before that fist laid him another good one. The mouth flew open wider this time, a blotch of sick color.

McMurphy had red marks on the head and shoulders, but he didn't seem to be hurt. He kept coming, taking ten blows for one. It kept on this way, back and forth in the shower room, till the black boy was panting and staggering and working mainly at keeping out of the way of those clubbing red arms. The guys were yelling for McMurphy to lay him out. McMurphy didn't act in any hurry.

The black boy spun away from a blow on his shoulder and looked quick to where the other two were watching. "Williams . . . Warren . . . damn you!" The other big one pulled the crowd apart and grabbed McMurphy around the arms from behind. McMurphy shook him off like a bull shaking off a monkey, but he was right back.

So I picked him off and threw him in the shower. He was full of tubes; he didn't weigh more'n ten or fifteen pounds.

The least black boy swung his head from side to side, turned, and ran for the door. While I was watching him go, the other one came out of the shower and put a wrestling hold on me—arms up under mine from behind and hands locked behind my neck—and I had to run backward into the shower and mash him against the tile, and while I was lying there in the water trying to watch McMurphy bust some more of Washington's ribs, the one behind me with the wrestling hold went to biting my neck and I had to break the hold. He laid still then, the starch washing from the uniform down the choking drain.

And by the time the least black boy came running back in with straps and cuffs and blankets and four more aides from Disturbed, everybody was getting dressed and shaking my hand and Mc-Murphy's hand and saying they had it coming and what a rip-snorter of a fight it had been, what a tremendous big victory. They kept talking like that, to cheer us up and make us feel better, about what a fight, what a victory—as the Big Nurse helped the aides from Disturbed adjust those soft leather cuffs to fit our arms.

Up on Disturbed there's an everlasting high-pitched machine-room clatter, a prison mill stamping out license plates. And time is measured out by the di-*dock*, di-*dock* of a Ping-pong table. Men pacing their personal runways get to a wall and dip a shoulder and turn and pace back to another wall, dip a shoulder and turn and back again, fast short steps, wearing crisscrossing ruts in the tile floor, with a look of caged thirst. There's a singed smell of men scared berserk and out of control, and in the corners and under the Ping-pong table there's things crouched gnashing their teeth that the doctors and nurses can't see and the aides can't kill with disinfectant. When the ward door opened I smelled that singed smell and heard that gnash of teeth.

A tall bony old guy, dangling from a wire screwed in between his shoulder blades, met McMurphy and me at the door when the aides brought us in. He looked us over with yellow, scaled eyes and shook his head. "I wash my hands of the whole deal," he told one of the colored aides, and the wire drug him off down the hall.

We followed him down to the day room, and McMurphy stopped at the door and spread his feet and tipped his head back to look things over; he tried to put his thumbs in his pockets, but the cuffs were too tight. "It's a scene," he said out of the side of his mouth. I nodded my head. I'd seen it all before.

A couple of the guys pacing stopped to look at us, and the old bony man came dragging by again, washing his hands of the whole deal. Nobody paid us much mind at first. The aides went off to the Nurses' Station, leaving us standing in the day-room door. McMurphy's eye was puffed to give him a steady wink, and I could tell it hurt his lips to grin. He raised his cuffed hands and stood looking at the clatter of movement and took a deep breath.

"McMurphy's the name, pardners," he said in his drawling cowboy actor's voice, "an' the thing I want to *know* is who's the peckerwood runs the poker game in this establishment?"

The Ping-pong clock died down in a rapid ticking on the floor.

"I don't deal blackjack so good, hobbled like this, but I maintain I'm a fire-eater in a stud game."

He yawned, hitched a shoulder, bent down and cleared his throat, and spat something at a wastepaper can five feet away; it rattled in with a *ting* and he straightened up again, grinned, and licked his tongue at the bloody gap in his teeth.

"Had a run-in downstairs. Me an' the Chief here locked horns with two greasemonkeys."

All the stamp-mill racket had stopped by this time, and every-body was looking toward the two of us at the door. McMurphy drew eyes to him like a sideshow barker. Beside him, I found that I was obliged to be looked at too, and with people staring at me I felt I had to stand up straight and tall as I could. That made my back hurt where I'd fallen in the shower with the black boy on me, but I didn't let on. One hungry looker with a head of shaggy black hair came up and held his hand like he figured I had something for him. I tried to ignore him, but he kept running around in front of whichever way I turned, like a little kid, holding that empty hand cupped out to me.

McMurphy talked a while about the fight, and my back got to hurting more and more; I'd hunkered in my chair in the cor-ner for so long that it was hard to stand straight very long. I was glad when a little Jap nurse came to take us into the Nurses' Station and I got a chance to sit and rest.

She asked if we were calm enough for her to take off the cuffs, and McMurphy nodded. He had slumped over with his head hung and his elbows between his knees and looked completely exhausted—it hadn't occurred to me that it was just as hard for him to stand straight as it was for me.

The nurse—about as big as the small end of nothing whittled to a fine point, as McMurphy put it later—undid our cuffs and gave McMurphy a cigarette and gave me a stick of gum. She said she remembered that I chewed gum. I didn't remember her at all. McMurphy smoked while she dipped her little hand full of pink birthday candles into a jar of salve and worked over his cuts, flinching every time he flinched and telling him she was sorry. She picked up one of his hands in both of hers and turned it over and salved his knuckles. "Who was it?" she asked, looking at the knuckles. "Was it Washington or Warren?"

McMurphy looked up at her. "Washington," he said and grinned. "The Chief here took care of Warren."

She put his hand down and turned to me. I could see the little bird bones in her face. "Are you hurt anywhere?" I shook my head.

"What about Warren and Williams?"

McMurphy told her he thought they might be sporting some plaster the next time she saw them. She nodded and looked at her feet. "It's not all like her ward," she said. "A lot of it is, but not all. Army nurses, trying to run an Army hospital. They are a little sick themselves. I sometimes think all single nurses should be fired after they reach thirty-five."

"At least all single *Army* nurses," McMurphy added. He asked how long we could expect to have the pleasure of her hospitality.

"Not very long, I'm afraid."

"Not very long, you're *afraid?*" McMurphy asked her.

"Yes. I'd like to keep men here sometimes instead of sending them back, but she has seniority. No, you probably won't be very long—I mean—like you are now."

The beds on Disturbed are all out of tune, too taut or too loose. We were assigned beds next to each other. They didn't tie a sheet across me, though they left a little dim light on near the bed. Halfway through the night somebody screamed, "I'm starting to spin, Indian! Look me, look me!" I opened my eyes and saw a set of long yellow teeth glowing right in front of my face. It was the hungry-looking guy. "I'm starting to *spin!* Please look me!"

The aides got him from behind, two of them, dragged him laughing and yelling out of the dorm; "I'm starting to spin, Indian!"—then just *laugh.* He kept saying it and laughing all the way down the hall till the dorm was quiet again, and I could hear that one other guy saying, "Well . . . I wash my hands of the whole deal."

"You had you a buddy for a second there, Chief," McMurphy whispered and rolled over to sleep. I couldn't sleep much the rest of the night and I kept seeing those yellow teeth and that guy's hungry face, asking to Look me! Look me! Or, finally, as I did get to sleep, just asking. That face, just a yellow, starved need, come looming out of the dark in front of me, wanting things . . . asking things. I wondered how McMurphy slept, plagued by a hundred faces like that, or two hundred, or a thousand.

They've got an alarm on Disturbed to wake the patients. They don't just turn on the lights like downstairs. This alarm sounds like a gigantic pencil-sharpener grinding up something awful. McMurphy and I both sat bolt upright when we heard it and were about to lie back down when a loudspeaker called for the two of us to come to the Nurses' Station. I got out of bed, and my back had stiffened up overnight to where I could just barely bend; I could tell by the way McMurphy gimped around that he was as stiff as I was.

"What they got on the program for us now, Chief?" he asked. "The boot? The rack? I hope nothing too strenuous, because, man, am I stove up bad!"

I told him it wasn't strenuous, but I didn't tell him anything else, because I wasn't sure myself till I got to the Nurses' Station, and the nurse, a different one, said, "Mr. McMurphy and Mr. Bromden?" then handed us each a little paper cup.

I looked in mine, and there are three of those red capsules. This *tsing* whirs in my head I can't stop.

"Hold on," McMurphy says. "These are those knockout pills, aren't they?"

The nurse nods, twists her head to check behind her; there's two guys waiting with ice tongs, hunching forward with their elbows linked.

McMurphy hands back the cup, says, "No sir, ma'am, but I'll forgo the blindfold. *Could* use a cigarette, though."

I hand mine back too, and she says she must phone and she slips the glass door across between us, is at the phone before anybody can say anything else.

"I'm sorry if I got you into something, Chief," McMurphy says, and I barely can hear him over the noise of the phone wires whistling in the walls. I can feel the scared downhill rush of thoughts in my head.

We're sitting in the day room, those faces around us in a circle, when in the door comes the Big Nurse herself, the two big black boys on each side, a step behind her. I try to shrink down in my chair, away from her, but it's too late. Too many people looking at me; sticky eyes hold me where I sit.

"Good morning," she says, got her old smile back now. Mc-
Murphy says good morning, and I keep quiet even though she
says good morning to me too, out loud. I'm watching the black
boys; one has tape on this nose and his arm in a sling, gray hand
dribbling out of the cloth like a drowned spider, and the other
one is moving like he's got some kind of cast around his ribs.
They are both grinning a little. Probably could of stayed home
with their hurts, but wouldn't miss this for nothing. I grin back
just to show them.

The Big Nurse talks to McMurphy, soft and patient, about
the irresponsible thing he did, the childish thing, throwing a
tantrum like a little boy—aren't you *ashamed?* He says he guesses
not and tells her to get on with it.

She talks to him about how they, the patients downstairs on
our ward, at a special group meeting yesterday afternoon, agreed
with the staff that it might be beneficial that he receive some
shock therapy—unless he realizes his mistakes. All he has to do
is *admit* he was wrong, to indicate, *demonstrate* rational contact,
and the treatment would be canceled this time.

That circle of faces waits and watches. The nurse says it's up
to him.

"Yeah?" he says. "You got a paper I can sign?"

"Well, no, but if you feel it nec—"

"And why don't you add some other things while you're at it
and get them out of the way—things like, oh, me being part of
a plot to overthrow the government and like how I think life on
your ward is the sweetest goddamned life this side of Hawaii—
you know, that sort of crap."

"I don't believe that would—"

"*Then*, after I sign, you bring me a blanket and a package of
Red Cross cigarettes. Hooee, those Chinese Commies could
have learned a few things from you, lady."

"Randle, we are trying to help you."

But he's on his feet, scratching at his belly, walking on past
her and the black boys rearing back, toward the card tables.

"O-kay, well well well, where's this poker table, buddies . . . ?"

The nurse stares after him a moment, then walks into the Nurses' Station to use the phone.

Two colored aides and a white aide with curly blond hair walk us over to the Main Building. McMurphy talks with the white aide on the way over, just like he isn't worried about a thing.

There's frost thick on the grass, and the two colored aides in front trail puffs of breath like locomotives. The sun wedges apart some of the clouds and lights up the frost till the grounds are scattered with sparks. Sparrows fluffed out against the cold, scratching among the sparks for seeds. We cut across the crackling grass, past the digger squirrel holes where I saw the dog. Cold sparks. Frost down the holes, clear out of sight.

I feel that frost in my belly.

We get up to that door, and there's a sound behind like bees stirred up. Two men in front of us, reeling under the red capsules, one bawling like a baby, saying "It's my cross, thank you Lord, it's all I got, thank you Lord. . . ."

The other guy waiting is saying, "Guts ball, guts ball." He's the lifeguard from the pool. And he's crying a little too.

I won't cry or yell. Not with McMurphy here.

The technician asks us to take off our shoes, and McMurphy asks him if we get our pants slit and our heads shaved too. The technician says no such luck.

The metal door looks out with its rivet eyes.

The door opens, sucks the first man inside. The lifeguard won't budge. A beam like neon smoke comes out of the black panel in the room, fastens on his cleat-marked forehead and drags him in like a dog on a leash. The beam spins him around three times before the door closes, and his face is scrambled fear. "Hut *one*," he grunts. "Hut *two!* Hut *three!*"

I hear them in there pry up his forehead like a manhole cover, clash and snarl of jammed cogs.

Smoke blows the door open, and a Gurney comes out with the first man on it, and he rakes me with his eyes. That face. The Gurney goes back in and brings the lifeguard out. I can hear the yell-leaders spelling out his name.

The technician says, "Next group."

The floor's cold, frosted, crackling. Up above the light whines, tube long and white and icy. Can smell the graphite salve, like the smell in a garage. Can smell acid of fear. There's one window, up high, small, and outside I see those puffy sparrows strung up on a wire like brown beads. Their heads sunk in the feathers against the cold. Something goes to blowing wind over my hollow bones, higher and higher, air raid! air raid!

"Don't holler, Chief. . . ."

Air raid!

"Take 'er easy. I'll go first. My skull's too thick for them to hurt me. And if they can't hurt me they can't hurt you."

Climbs on the table without any help and spreads his arms out to fit the shadow. A switch snaps the clasps on his wrists, ankles, clamping him into the shadow. A hand takes off his wrist-watch, won it from Scanlon, drops it near the panel, it springs open, cogs and wheels and the long dribbling spiral of spring jumping against the side of the panel and sticking fast.

He don't look a bit scared. He keeps grinning at me.

They put the graphite salve on his temples. "What is it?" he says. "Conductant," the technician says. "Anointest my head with conductant. Do I get a crown of thorns?"

They smear it on. He's singing to them, makes their hands shake.

" 'Get Wildroot Cream Oil, Cholly. . . .' "

Put on those things like headphones, crown of silver thorns over the graphite at his temples. They try to hush his singing with a piece of rubber hose for him to bite on.

" 'Mage with thoothing lan-o-lin.' "

Twist some dials, and the machine trembles, two robot arms pick up soldering irons and hunch down on him. He gives me the wink and speaks to me, muffled, tells me something, says something to me around that rubber hose just as those irons get close enough to the silver on his temples—light arcs across, stiffens him, bridges him up off the table till nothing is down but his wrists and ankles and out around that crimped black rubber hose a sound like *hooeee!* and he's frosted over completely with sparks.

And out the window the sparrows drop smoking off the wire.

They roll him out on a Gurney, still jerking, face frosted white. Corrosion. Battery acid. The technician turns to me.

Watch that other moose. I know him. Hold him!

It's not a will-power thing any more.

Hold him! Damn. No more of these boys without Seconal.

The clamps bite my wrists and ankles.

The graphite salve has iron filings in it, temples scratching. He said something when he winked. Told me something. Man bends over, brings two irons toward the ring on my head. The machine hunches on me.

AIR RAID.

Hit at a lope, running already down the slope. Can't get back, can't go ahead, look down the barrel an' you dead dead dead.

We come up outa the bullreeds run beside the railroad track. I lay an ear to the track, and it burns my cheek.

"Nothin' either way," I say, "a *hundred* miles. . . ."

"Hump," Papa says.

"Didn't we used to listen for buffalo by stickin' a knife in the ground, catch the handle in our teeth, hear a herd way off?"

"Hump," he says again, but he's tickled. Out across the other side of the track a fencerow of wheat chats from last winter. Mice under that stuff, the dog says.

"Do we go up the track or down the track, boy?"

"We go across, is what the ol' dog says."

"That dog don't heel."

"He'll do. There's birds over there is what the ol' dog says."

"Better hunting up the track bank is what your ol' man says."

"Best right across in the chats of wheat, the dog tells me."

Across—next thing I know there's people all over the track, blasting away at pheasants like anything. Seems our dog got too far out ahead and run all the birds outa the chats to the track.

Dog got three mice.

. . . man, Man, MAN, MAN . . . broad and big with a wink like a star.

Ants again oh Jesus and I got 'em bad this time, prickle-footed bastards. Remember the time we found those ants tasted like dill pickles? Hee? You said it wasn't dill pickles and I said it was, and your mama kicked the living tar outa me when she heard: Teachin' a kid to eat *bugs!*

Ugh. Good Injun boy should know how to survive on anything he can eat that won't eat him first.

We ain't Indians. We're civilized and you remember it.

You told me Papa When I die pin me up against the sky. Mama's name was Bromden. Still is Bromden. Papa said he was born with only one name, born smack into it the way a calf drops out in a spread blanket when the cow insists on standing up. Tee Ah Millatoona, the Pine-That-Stands-Tallest-on-the-Mountain, and I'm the biggest by God Injun in the state of Oregon and probly California and Idaho. Born right into it.

You're the biggest by God fool if you think that a good Christian woman takes on a name like Tee Ah Millatoona. You were born into a name, so okay, I'm born into a name. Bromden. Mary Louise Bromden.

And when we move into town, Papa says, that name makes gettin' that Social Security card a lot easier.

Guy's after somebody with a riveter's hammer, get him too, if he keeps at it. I see those lightning flashes again, colors striking.

Ting. Tingle, tingle, tremble toes, she's a good fisherman, catches hens, puts 'em inna pens . . . wire blier, limber lock, three geese inna flock . . . one flew east, one flew west, one flew over the cuckoo's nest . . . O-U-T spells out . . . goose swoops down and plucks *you* out.

My old grandma chanted this, a game we played by the hours, sitting by the fish racks scaring flies. A game called Tingle Tingle Tangle Toes. Counting each finger on my two outspread hands, one finger to a syllable as she chants.

Tingle, ting-le, tang-le toes (seven fingers) she's a good fisherman, catches hens (sixteen fingers, tapping a finger on each beat with her black crab hand, each of my fingernails looking up at her like a little face asking to be the *you* that the goose swoops down and plucks out).

I like the game and I like Grandma. I don't like Mrs. Tingle Tangle Toes, catching hens. I don't like her. I do like that goose flying over the cuckoo's nest. I like him, and I like Grandma, dust in her wrinkles.

Next time I saw her she was stone cold dead, right in the middle of The Dalles on the sidewalk, colored shirts standing around, some Indians, some cattlemen, some wheatmen. They cart her down to the city burying ground, roll red clay into her eyes.

I remember hot, still electric-storm afternoons when jackrabbits ran under Diesel truck wheels.

Joey Fish-in-a-Barrel has twenty thousand dollars and three Cadillacs since the contract. And he can't drive none of 'em.

I see a dice.

I see it from the inside, me at the bottom. I'm the weight, loading the dice to throw that number one up there above me. They got the dice loaded to throw a snake eyes, and I'm the load, six lumps around me like white pillows is the other side of the dice, the number six that will always be down when he throws. What's the other dice loaded for? I bet it's loaded to throw one too. Snake eyes. They're shooting with crookies against him, and I'm the load.

Look out, here comes a toss. Ay, lady, the smokehouse is empty and baby needs a new pair of opera pumps. Comin' at ya. *Faw!*

Crapped out.

Water. I'm lying in a puddle.

Snake eyes. Caught him again. I see that number one up above me: he can't whip frozen dice behind the feedstore in an alley—in Portland.

The alley is a tunnel it's cold because the sun is late afternoon. Let me . . . go see Grandma. Please, Mama.

What was it he said when he winked?

One flew east one flew west.

Don't stand in my way.

Damn it, nurse, don't stand in my way Way WAY!

My roll. *Faw*. Damn. Twisted again. Snake eyes.

The schoolteacher tell me you got a good head, boy, be something. . . .

Be what, Papa? A rug-weaver like Uncle R & J Wolf? A basket-weaver? Or another drunken Indian.

I say, attendant, you're an Indian, aren't you?

Yeah, that's right.

Well, I must say, you speak the language quite well.

Yeah.

Well . . . three dollars of regular.

They wouldn't be so cocky if they knew what me and the *moon* have going. No damned regular Indian . . .

He who—what was it?—walks out of step, hears another drum.

Snake eyes again. Hoo boy, these dice are *cold*.

After Grandma's funeral me and Papa and Uncle Running-and-Jumping Wolf dug her up. Mama wouldn't go with us; she never heard of such a thing. Hanging a corpse in a *tree*! It's enough to make a person sick.

Uncle R & J Wolf and Papa spent twenty days in the drunk tank at The Dalles jail, playing rummy, for Violation of the Dead.

But she's our goddanged mother!

It doesn't make the slightest difference, boys. You shoulda left her buried. I don't know when you blamed Indians will learn. Now, where is she? you'd better tell.

Ah go fuck yourself, paleface, Uncle R & J said, rolling himself a cigarette. I'll never tell.

High high high in the hills, high in a pine tree bed, she's tracing the wind with that old hand, counting the clouds with that old chant: . . . three geese in a flock . . .

What did you say to me when you winked?

Band playing. Look—the *sky*, it's the Fourth of July.

Dice at rest.

They got to me with the machine again . . . I wonder . . .

What did he say?

. . . wonder how McMurphy made me big again.

He said Guts ball.

They're out there. Black boys in white suits peeing under the door on me, come in later and accuse me of soaking all six these pillows I'm lying on! Number six. I thought the room was a dice. The number one, the snake eye up there, the circle, the white *light* in the ceiling . . . is what I've been seeing . . . in this little square room . . . means it's after dark. How many hours have I been out? It's fogging a little, but I won't slip off and hide in it. No . . . never again . . .

I stand, stood up slowly, feeling numb between the shoulders. The white pillows on the floor of the Seclusion Room were soaked from me peeing on them while I was out. I couldn't remember all of it yet, but I rubbed my eyes with the heels of my hands and tried to clear my head. I worked at it. I'd never worked at coming out of it before.

I staggered toward the little round chicken-wired window in the door of the room and tapped it with my knuckles. I saw an aide coming up the hall with a tray for me and knew this time I had them beat.

there had been times when I'd wandered around in a daze for as long as two weeks after a shock treatment, living in that foggy, jumbled blur which is a whole lot like the ragged edge of sleep, that gray zone between light and dark, or between sleeping and waking or living and dying, where you know you're not unconscious any more but don't know yet what day it is or who you are or what's the use of coming back at all—for two weeks. If you don't have a reason to wake up you can loaf around in that gray zone for a long, fuzzy time, or if you want to bad enough I found you can come fighting right out of it. This time I came fighting out of it in less than a day, less time than ever.

And when the fog was finally swept from my head it seemed like I'd just come up after a long, deep dive, breaking the surface after being under water a hundred years. It was the last treatment they gave me.

They gave McMurphy three more treatments that week. As quick as he started coming out of one, getting the click back in his wink, Miss Ratched would arrive with the doctor and they would ask him if he felt like he was ready to come around and face up to his problem and come back to the ward for a cure. And he'd swell up, aware that every one of those faces on Disturbed had turned toward him and was waiting, and he'd tell the nurse he regretted that he had but one life to give for his country and she could kiss his rosy red ass before he'd give up the goddam ship. *Yeh!*

Then stand up and take a couple of bows to those guys grinning at him while the nurse led the doctor into the station to phone over to the Main Building and authorize another treatment.

Once, as she turned to walk away, he got hold of her through the back of her uniform, gave her a pinch that turned her face red as his hair. I think if the doctor hadn't been there, hiding a grin himself, she would've slapped McMurphy's face.

I tried to talk him into playing along with her so's to get out of the treatments, but he just laughed and told me Hell, all they was doin' was chargin' his battery for him, free for nothing. "When I get out of here the first woman that takes on ol' Red McMurphy the ten-thousand-watt psychopath, she's gonna light up like a pinball machine and pay off in silver dollars! No, I ain't scared of their little battery-charger."

He insisted it wasn't hurting him. He wouldn't even take his capsules. But every time that loudspeaker called for him to forgo breakfast and prepare to walk to Building One, the muscles in his jaw went taut and his whole face drained of color, looking thin and scared—the face I had seen reflected in the windshield on the trip back from the coast.

I left Disturbed at the end of the week and went back to the ward. I had a lot of things I wanted to say to him before I went, but he'd just come back from a treatment and was sitting following the ping-pong ball with his eyes like he was wired to it. The colored aide and the blond one took me downstairs and let me onto our ward and locked the door behind me. The ward seemed awful quiet after Disturbed. I walked to our day room and for some reason stopped at the door; everybody's face turned up to me with a different look than they'd ever given me before. Their faces lighted up as if they were looking into the glare of a sideshow platform. "Here, in fronta your very eyes," Harding spiels, "is the *Wild*man who broke the arm . . . of the black boy! Hey-ha, lookee, lookee." I grinned back at them, realizing how McMurphy must've felt these months with these faces screaming up at him.

All the guys came over and wanted me to tell them everything that had happened; how was he acting up there? What was he doing? Was it true, what was being rumored over at the gym, that they'd been hitting him every day with EST and he was shrugging it off like water, makin' book with the technicians on how long he could keep his eyes open after the poles touched.

I told them all I could, and nobody seemed to think a thing about me all of a sudden talking with people—a guy who'd been considered deaf and dumb as far back as they'd known him, talking, listening, just like anybody. I told them everything that they'd heard was true, and tossed in a few stories of my own. They laughed so hard about some of the things he'd said to the nurse that the two Vegetables under their wet sheets on the Chronics' side grinned and snorted along with the laughter, just like they understood.

When the nurse herself brought the problem of Patient McMurphy up in group the next day, said that for some unusual

reason he did not seem to be responding to EST at all and that
more drastic means might be required to make contact with
him, Harding said, "Now, that is possible, Miss Ratched, yes—
but from what I hear about your dealings upstairs with Mc-
Murphy, he hasn't had any difficulty making contact with
you."

She was thrown off balance and flustered so bad with everybody in the room laughing at her, that she didn't bring it up
again.

She saw that McMurphy was growing bigger than ever while
he was upstairs where the guys couldn't see the dent she was
making on him, growing almost into a legend. A man out of
sight can't be made to look weak, she decided, and started
making plans to bring him back down to our ward. She figured
the guys could see for themselves then that he could be as
vulnerable as the next man. He couldn't continue in his hero
role if he was sitting around the day room all the time in a
shock stupor.

The guys anticipated this, and that as long as he was on the
ward for them to see she would be giving him shock every time
he came out of it. So Harding and Scanlon and Fredrickson
and I talked over how we could convince him that the best
thing for everybody concerned would be his escaping the ward.
And by the Saturday when he was brought back to the ward—
footworking into the day room like a boxer into a ring, clasping
his hands over his head and announcing the champ was back—
we had our plan all worked out. We'd wait until dark, set a
mattress on fire, and when the firemen came we'd rush him
out the door. It seemed such a fine plan we couldn't see how he
could refuse.

But we didn't think about its being the day he'd made a date
to have the girl, Candy, sneak onto the ward for Billy.

They brought him back to the ward about ten in the morning— "Fulla piss an' vinegar, buddies; they checked my plugs
and cleaned my points, and I got a glow on like a Model T
spark coil. Ever use one of those coils around Halloween time?
Zam! Good clean fun." And he batted around the ward bigger

than ever, spilled a bucket of mop water under the Nurses' Station door, laid a pat of butter square on the toe of the least black boy's white suede shoes without the black boy noticing, and smothered giggles all through lunch while it melted to show a color Harding referred to as a "most suggestive yellow," —bigger than ever, and each time he brushed close by a student nurse she gave a yip and rolled her eyes and pitter-patted off down the hall, rubbing her flank.

We told him of our plan for his escape, and he told us there was no hurry and reminded us of Billy's date. "We can't disappoint Billy Boy, can we, buddies? Not when he's about to cash in his cherry. And it should be a nice little party tonight if we can pull it off; let's say maybe it's my going-away party."

It was the Big Nurse's weekend to work—she didn't want to miss his return—and she decided we'd better have us a meeting to get something settled. At the meeting she tried once more to bring up her suggestion for a more drastic measure, insisting that the doctor consider such action "before it is too late to help the patient." But McMurphy was such a whirligig of winks and yawns and belches while she talked, she finally hushed, and when she did he gave the doctor and all the patients fits by agreeing with everything she said.

"Y'know, she might be right, Doc; look at the good that few measly volts have done me. Maybe if we *doubled* the charge I could pick up channel eight, like Martini; I'm tired of layin' in bed hallucinatin' nothing but channel four with the news and weather."

The nurse cleared her throat, trying to regain control of her meeting. "I wasn't suggesting that we consider more shock, Mr. McMurphy—"

"Ma'am?"

"I was suggesting—that we consider an operation. Very simple, really. And we've had a history of past successes eliminating aggressive tendencies in certain hostile cases—"

"Hostile? Ma'am, I'm friendly as a pup. I haven't kicked the tar out of an aide in nearly two weeks. There's been no cause to do any cuttin', now, has there?"

She held out her smile, begging him to see how sympathetic she was. "Randle, there's no cutting involv—"

"Besides," he went on, "it wouldn't be any use to lop 'em off; I got another pair in my nightstand."

"Another—pair?"

"One about as big as a baseball, Doc."

"Mr. McMurphy!" Her smile broke like glass when she realized she was being made fun of.

"But the other one is big enough to be considered normal."

He went on like this clear up to the time we were ready for bed. By then there was a festive, county-fair feeling on the ward as the men whispered of the possibility of having a party if the girl came with drinks. All the guys were trying to catch Billy's eye and grinning and winking at him every time he looked. And when we lined up for medication McMurphy came by and asked the little nurse with the crucifix and the birthmark if he could have a couple of vitamins. She looked surprised and said she didn't see that there was any reason why not and gave him some pills the size of birds' eggs. He put them in his pocket.

"Aren't you going to swallow them?" she asked.

"Me? Lord no, I don't need vitamins. I was just gettin' them for Billy Boy here. He seems to me to have a peaked look of late—tired blood, most likely."

"Then—why don't you give them to Billy?"

"I will, honey, I will, but I thought I'd wait till about midnight when he'd have the most need for them"—and walked to the dorm with his arm crooked around Billy's flushing neck, giving Harding a wink and me a goose in the side with his big thumb as he passed us, and left that nurse pop-eyed behind him in the Nurses' Station, pouring water on her foot.

You have to know about Billy Bibbit: in spite of him having wrinkles in his face and specks of gray in his hair, he still looked like a kid—like a jug-eared and freckled-faced and buck-toothed kid whistling barefoot across one of those calendars, with a string of bullheads dragging behind him in the dust—and yet he was nothing like this. You were always surprised to find when he stood up next to one of the other men he was just as tall as anyone, and that he wasn't jug-eared or freckled or buck-toothed at all under a closer look, and was, in fact, thirty-some years old.

I heard him give his age only one time, overheard him, to tell the truth, when he was talking to his mother down in the lobby. She was receptionist down there, a solid, well-packed lady with hair revolving from blond to blue to black and back to blond again every few months, a neighbor of the Big Nurse's, from what I'd heard, and a dear personal friend. Whenever we'd go on some activity Billy would always be obliged to stop and lean a scarlet cheek over that desk for her to dab a kiss on. It embarrassed the rest of us as much as it did Billy, and for that reason nobody ever teased him about it, not even McMurphy.

One afternoon, I don't recall how long back, we stopped on our way to activities and sat around the lobby on the big plastic sofas or outside in the two-o'clock sun while one of the black boys used the phone to call his bookmaker, and Billy's mother took the opportunity to leave her work and come out from behind her desk and take her boy by the hand and lead him outside to sit near where I was on the grass. She sat stiff there on the grass, tight at the bend with her short round legs out in front of her in stockings, reminding me of the color of bologna skins, and Billy lay beside her and put his head in her lap and let her tease at his ear with a dandelion fluff. Billy was talking about looking for a wife and going to college someday. His mother tickled him with the fluff and laughed at such foolishness.

"Sweetheart, you still have scads of time for things like that. Your whole life is ahead of you."

"Mother, I'm th-th-thirty-one years old!"

She laughed and twiddled his ear with the weed. "*Sweet*heart, do I look like the mother of a middle-aged man?"

She wrinkled her nose and opened her lips at him and made a kind of wet kissing sound in the air with her tongue, and I had to admit she didn't look like a mother of any kind. I didn't believe myself that he could be thirty-one years old till later when I edged up close enough to get a look at the birth date on his wristband.

At midnight, when Geever and the other black boy and the nurse went off duty, and the old colored fellow, Mr. Turkle, came on for his shift, McMurphy and Billy were already up, taking vitamins, I imagined. I got out of bed and put on a robe and walked out to the day room, where they were talking with Mr. Turkle. Harding and Scanlon and Sefelt and some of the other guys came out too. McMurphy was telling Mr. Turkle what to expect if the girl did come,—reminding him, actually, because it looked like they'd talked it all over beforehand a couple of weeks back. McMurphy said that the thing to do was let the girl in the *window*, instead of risking having her come through the lobby, where the night supervisor might be. And to unlock the Seclusion Room then. Yeah, won't that make a fine honeymoon shack for the lovers? Mighty secluded. ("Ahhh, McM-murphy," Billy kept trying to say.) And to keep the lights out. So the supervisor couldn't see in. And close the dorm doors and not wake up every slobbering Chronic in the place. And to keep *quiet*; we don't want to disturb them.

"Ah, come on, M-M-Mack," Billy said.

Mr. Turkle kept nodding and bobbing his head, appearing to fall half asleep. When McMurphy said, "I guess that pretty well covers things," Mr. Turkle said, "No—not en-tiuhly," and sat there grinning in his white suit with his bald yellow head floating at the end of his neck like a balloon on a stick.

"Come on, Turkle. It'll be worth your while. She should be bringin' a couple of bottles."

"You gettin' closer," Mr. Turkle said. His head lolled and bobbled. He acted like he was barely able to keep awake. I'd heard he worked another job during the day, at a race track. McMurphy turned to Billy.

"Turkle is holdin' out for a bigger contract, Billy Boy. How much is it worth to you to lose your ol' cherry?"

Before Billy could stop stuttering and answer, Mr. Turkle shook his head. "It ain' *that*. Not money. She bringin' more than the bottle with her, though, ain't she, this sweet thing?

You people be sharing more'n a bottle, won't you." He grinned around at the faces.

Billy nearly burst, trying to stutter something about not Candy, not *his* girl! McMurphy took him aside and told him not to worry about *his* girl's chastity—Turkle'd likely be so drunk and sleepy by the time Billy was finished that the old coon couldn't put a carrot in a washtub.

The girl was late again. We sat out in the day room in our robes, listening to McMurphy and Mr. Turkle tell Army stories while they passed one of Mr. Turkle's cigarettes back and forth, smoking it a funny way, holding the smoke in when they inhaled till their eyes bugged. Once Harding asked what manner of cigarette they were smoking that smelled so provocative, and Mr. Turkle said in a high, breath-holding voice, "Jus' a plain old cigarette. Hee hee, yes. You want a toke?"

Billy got more and more nervous, afraid the girl might not show up, afraid she might. He kept asking why didn't we all go to bed, instead of sitting out here in the cold dark like hounds waiting at the kitchen for table scraps, and we just grinned at him. None of us felt like going to bed; it wasn't cold at all, and it was pleasant to relax in the half-light and listen to McMurphy and Mr. Turkle tell tales. Nobody acted sleepy, or not even very worried that it was after two o'clock and the girl hadn't showed up yet. Turkle suggested maybe she was late because the ward was so dark she couldn't *see* to tell which one to come to, and McMurphy said that was the obvious truth, so the two of them ran up and down the halls, turning on every light in the place, were even about to turn on the big overhead wake-up lights in the dorm when Harding told them this would just get all the other men out of bed to share things with. They agreed and settled for all the lights in the doctor's office instead.

No sooner did they have the ward lit up like full daylight than there came a tapping at the window. McMurphy ran to the window and put his face to it, cupping his hands on each side so he could see. He drew back and grinned at us.

"She walks like beauty, in the night," he said. He took Billy by the wrist and dragged him to the window. "Let her in, Turkle. Let this mad stud at her."

"Look, McM-M-M-Murphy, wait." Billy was balking like a mule.

"Don't you mamamamurphy me, Billy Boy. It's too late to back out now. You'll pull through. I'll tell you what: I got five dollars here says you burn that woman down; all right? Open the window, Turkle."

There were two girls in the dark, Candy and the other one that hadn't shown up for the fishing trip. "Hot dog," Turkle said, helping them through, "enough for ever'body."

We all went to help: they had to lift their tight skirts up to their thighs to step through the window. Candy said, "You damn McMurphy," and tried so wild to throw her arms around him that she came near to breaking the bottles she held by the neck in each hand. She was weaving around quite a bit, and her hair was falling out of the hairdo she had piled on top of her head. I thought she looked better with it swung at the back like she'd worn it on the fishing trip. She gestured at the other girl with a bottle as she came through the window.

"Sandy came along. She just up and left that maniac from Beaverton that she married; isn't that wild?"

The girl came through the window and kissed McMurphy and said, "Hello, Mack. I'm sorry I didn't show up. But that's over. You can take just so many funsies like white mice in your pillowcase and worms in your cold cream and frogs in your bra." She shook her head once and wiped her hand in front of her like she was wiping away the memory of her animal-loving husband. "Cheesus, what a maniac."

They were both in skirts and sweaters and nylons and barefoot, and both red-cheeked and giggling. "We had to keep asking for directions," Candy explained, "at every bar we came to."

Sandy was turning around in a big wide-eyed circle. "Whooee, Candy girl, what are we in *now*? Is this real? Are we in an asylum? *Man!*" She was bigger than Candy, and maybe five years older, and had tried to lock her bay-colored hair in a stylish bun at the back of her head, but it kept stringing down around her broad milk-fed cheekbones, and she looked like a cowgirl trying to pass herself off as a society lady. Her shoulders and breasts and hips were too wide and her grin too big and open for her to ever be called beautiful, but she was pretty and she was healthy and she had one long finger crooked in the ring of a gallon of red wine, and it swung at her side like a purse.

"How, Candy, how, how, how do these wild things happen to us?" She turned around once more and stopped, with her bare feet spread, giggling.

"These things don't happen," Harding said to the girl solemnly. "These things are fantasies you lie awake at night dreaming up and then are afraid to tell your analyst. You're not *really* here. That wine isn't real; *none* of this exists. Now, let's go on from there."

"Hello, Billy," Candy said.

"Look at that stuff," Turkle said.

Candy straight-armed one of the bottles awkwardly toward Billy. "I brought you a present."

"These things are Thorne Smithian daydreams!" Harding said.

"Boy!" the girl named Sandy said. "What have we got ourselves into?"

"Shhhh," Scanlon said and scowled around him. "You'll wake up those other bastards, talking so loud."

"What's the matter, stingy?" Sandy giggled, starting to turn in her circle again. "You scared there's not enough to go around?"

"Sandy, I mighta known you'd bring that damn cheap port."

"Boy!" She stopped her turning to look up at me. "Dig this one, Candy. A Goliath—fee, fi, fo, fum."

Mr. Turkle said, "Hot dog," and locked the screen back, and Sandy said, "Boy," again. We were all in an awkward little cluster in the middle of the day room, shifting around one another, saying things just because nobody knew what else to do yet—never been up against a situation like it—and I don't

know when this excited, uneasy flurry of talk and giggling and
shuffling around the day room would've stopped if that ward
door hadn't rung with a key knocking it open down the hall—
jarred everybody like a burglar alarm going off.

"Oh, Lord God," Mr. Turkle said, clapping his hand on the
top of his bald head, "it's the soo-pervisor, come to fire my
black ass."

We all ran into the latrine and turned out the light and
stood in the dark, listening to one another breathe. We could
hear that supervisor wander around the ward, calling for Mr.
Turkle in a loud, half-afraid whisper. Her voice was soft and
worried, rising at the end as she called, "Mr. Tur-kull? Mis-tur
Turkle?"

"Where the hell is he?" McMurphy whispered. "Why don't
he answer her."

"Don't worry," Scanlon said. "She won't look in the can."

"But why don't he answer? Maybe he got too high."

"Man, what you talkin'? I don't get too high, not on a little
middlin' joint like that one." It was Mr. Turkle's voice somewhere in the dark latrine with us.

"Jesus, Turkle, what are you doing in here?" McMurphy was
trying to sound stern and keep from laughing at the same time.
"Get out there and see what she wants. What'll she think if
she doesn't find you?"

"The end is upon us," Harding said and sat down. "Allah be
merciful."

Turkle opened the door and slipped out and met her in the
hall. She'd come over to see what all the lights were on about.
What made it necessary to turn on every fixture in the ward?
Turkle said every fixture wasn't on; that the dorm lights were
off and so were the ones in the latrine. She said that was no
excuse for the other lights; what possible reason could there be
for all this light? Turkle couldn't come up with an answer for
this, and during the long pause I heard the bottle being passed
around near me in the dark. Out in the hall she asked him
again, and Turkle told her, well, he was just cleanin' up, policing
the areas. She wanted to know why, then, was the latrine, the

place that his job description called for him to have clean, the only place that was dark? And the bottle went around again while we waited to see what he'd answer. It came by me, and I took a drink. I felt I needed it. I could hear Turkle swallowing all the way out in the hall, umming and ahing for something to say.

"He's skulled," McMurphy hissed. "Somebody's gonna have to go out and help him."

I heard a toilet flush behind me, and the door opened and Harding was caught in the hall light as he went out, pulling up his pajamas. I heard the supervisor gasp at the sight of him and he told her to pardon him, but he hadn't seen her, being as it was so dark."

"It isn't dark."

"In the latrine, I meant. I always switch off the lights to achieve a better bowel movement. Those mirrors, you understand; when the light is on the mirrors seem to be sitting in judgment over me to arbitrate a punishment if everything doesn't come out right."

"But Aide Turkle said he was cleaning in there . . ."

"And doing quite a good job, too, I might add—considering the restrictions imposed on him by the dark. Would you care to see?"

Harding pushed the door open a crack, and a slice of light cut across the latrine floor tile. I caught a glimpse of the supervisor backing off, saying she'd have to decline his offer but she had further rounds to make. I heard the ward door unlock again up the hall, and she let herself off the ward. Harding called to her to return soon for another visit, and everybody rushed out and shook his hand and pounded his back for the way he'd pulled it off.

We stood there in the hall, and the wine went around again. Sefelt said he'd as leave have that vodka if there was something to mix it with. He asked Mr. Turkle if there wasn't something on the ward to put in it and Turkle said nothing but water. Fredrickson asked what about the cough sirup? "They give me a little now and then from a half-gallon jug in the drug room. It's not bad tasting. You have a key for that room, Turkle?"

Turkle said the supervisor was the only one on nights who had a key to the drug room, but McMurphy talked him into letting us have a try at picking the lock. Turkle grinned and nodded his head lazily. While he and McMurphy worked at the lock on the drug room with paper clips, the girls and the rest of us ran around in the Nurses' Station opening files and reading records.

"Look here," Scanlon said, waving one of those folders. "Talk about complete. They've even got my first-grade report card in here. Aaah, miserable grades, just miserable."

Bill and his girl were going over his folder. She stepped back to look him over. "All these things, Billy? Phrenic this and pathic that? You don't look like you have all these things."

The other girl had opened a supply drawer and was suspicious about what the nurses needed with *all* those hot-water bottles, a million of 'em, and Harding was sitting on the Big Nurse's desk, shaking his head at the whole affair.

McMurphy and Turkle got the door of the drug room open and brought out a bottle of thick cherry-colored liquid from the ice box. McMurphy tipped the bottle to the light and read the label out loud.

"Artificial flavor, coloring, citric acid. Seventy per cent inert materials—that must be water—and twenty per cent alcohol— that's fine—and ten per cent codeine Warning Narcotic May Be Habit Forming." He unscrewed the bottle and took a taste of it, closing his eyes. He worked his tongue around his teeth and took another swallow and read the label again. "Well," he said, and clicked his teeth together like they'd just been sharpened, "if we cut it a leetle bit with the vodka, I think it'll be all right. How are we fixed for ice cubes, Turkey, old buddy?"

Mixed in paper medicine cups with the liquor and the port wine, the sirup had a taste like a kid's drink but a punch like the cactus apple wine we used to get in The Dalles, cold and soothing on the throat and hot and furious once it got down. We turned out the lights in the day room and sat around drinking it. We threw the first couple of cups down like we were taking our medication, drinking it in serious and silent doses and looking one another over to see if it was going to kill anybody. McMurphy and Turkle switched back and forth from the drink to Turkle's cigarettes and got to giggling again as they discussed how it would be to lay that little nurse with the birthmark who went off at midnight.

"I'd be scared," Turkle said, "that she might go to whuppin' me with that big ol' cross on that chain. Wun't that be a fix to be in, now?"

"*I'd* be scared," McMurphy said, "that just about the time I was getting my jollies she'd reach around behind me with a thermometer and take my temperature!"

That busted everybody up. Harding stopped laughing long enough to join the joking.

"Or worse yet," he said. "Just lie there under you with a dreadful concentration on her face, and tell you—oh Jesus, listen —tell you what your *pulse* was!"

"Oh don't . . . oh my Gawd . . ."

"Or even worse, just lie there and be able to calculate your pulse and temperature both—sans instruments!"

"Oh Gawd, oh please don't . . ."

We laughed till we were rolling about the couches and chairs, choking and teary-eyed. The girls were so weak from laughing they had to try two or three times to get to their feet. "I gotta . . . go tinkle," the big one said and went weaving and giggling toward the latrine and missed the door, staggered into the dorm while we all hushed one another with fingers to the lips, waiting, till she gave a squeal and we heard old Colonel Matterson roar, "The pillow is . . . a *horse!*"—and come whisking out of the dorm right behind her in his wheelchair.

Sefelt wheeled the colonel back to the dorm and showed the girl where the latrine was personally, told her it was generally used by males only but he would stand at the door while she was in there and guard against intrusions on her privacy, defend it against all comers, by gosh. She thanked him solemnly and shook his hand and they saluted each other and while she was inside here came the colonel out of the dorm in his wheel-chair again, and Sefelt had his hands full keeping him out of the latrine. When the girl came out of the door he was trying to ward off the charges of the wheelchair with his foot while we stood on the edge of the fracas cheering one guy or the other. The girl helped Sefelt put the colonel back to bed, and then the two of them went down the hall and waltzed to music nobody could hear.

Harding drank and watched and shook his head. "It isn't happening. It's all a collaboration of Kafka and Mark Twain and Martini."

McMurphy and Turkle got to worrying that there might still be too many lights, so they went up and down the hall turning out everything that glowed, even the little knee-high night lights, till the place was pitch black. Turkle got out flashlights, and we played tag up and down the hall with wheelchairs from storage, having a big time till we heard one of Sefelt's convulsion cries and went to find him sprawled twitching beside that big girl, Sandy. She was sitting on the floor brushing at her skirt, looking down at Sefelt. "I never experienced anything like it," she said with quiet awe.

Fredrickson knelt beside his friend and put a wallet between his teeth to keep him from chewing his tongue, and helped him get his pants buttoned. "You all right, Seef? Seef?"

Sefelt didn't open his eyes, but he raised a limp hand and picked the wallet out of his mouth. He grinned through his spit. "I'm all right," he said. "Medicate me and turn me loose again."

"You really need some medication, Seef?"

"Medication."

"Medication," Fredrickson said over his shoulder, still kneeling. "Medication," Harding repeated and weaved off with his flashlight to the drug room. Sandy watched him go with glazed eyes. She was sitting beside Sefelt, stroking his head in wonderment.

"Maybe you better bring me something too," she called drunkenly after Harding. "I never experienced anything to come even *close* to it."

Down the hall we heard glass crash and Harding came back with a double handful of pills; he sprinkled them over Sefelt and the woman like he was crumbling clods into a grave. He raised his eyes toward the ceiling.

"Most merciful God, accept these two poor sinners into your arms. And keep the doors ajar for the coming of the rest of us, because you are witnessing the end, the absolute, irrevocable, fantastic end. I've finally realized what is happening. It is our last fling. We are doomed henceforth. Must screw our courage to the sticking point and face up to our impending fate. We shall be all of us shot at dawn. One hundred cc's apiece. Miss Ratched shall line us all against the wall, where we'll face the terrible maw of a muzzle-loading shotgun which she has loaded with Miltowns! Thorazines! Libriums! Stelazines! And with a wave of her sword, *blooie!* Tranquilize all of us completely out of existence."

He sagged against the wall and slid to the floor, pills hopping out of his hands in all directions like red and green and orange bugs. "Amen," he said and closed his eyes.

The girl on the floor smoothed down her skirt over her long hard-working legs and looked at Sefelt still grinning and twitching there under the lights beside her, and said, "Never in my life experienced anything to come even *halfway* near it."

Harding's speech, if it hadn't actually sobered people, had at least made them realize the seriousness of what we were doing. The night was getting on, and some thought had to be given to the arrival of the staff in the morning. Billy Bibbit and his girl mentioned that it was after four o'clock and, if it was all right, if people didn't mind, they'd like to have Mr. Turkle unlock the Seclusion Room. They went off under an arch of flashlight beams, and the rest of us went into the day room to see what we could decide about cleaning up. Turkle was all but passed out when he got back from Seclusion, and we had to push him into the day room in a wheel chair.

As I walked after them it came to me as a kind of sudden surprise that I was drunk, actually drunk, glowing and grinning and staggering drunk for the first time since the Army, drunk

along with half a dozen other guys and a couple of girls—
right on the Big Nurse's ward! Drunk and running and laughing and carrying on with women square in the center of the
Combine's most powerful stronghold! I thought back on the
night, on what we'd been doing, and it was near impossible to
believe. I had to keep reminding myself that it had *truly* happened, that we had made it happen. We had just unlocked a
window and let it in like you let in the fresh air. Maybe the
Combine wasn't all-powerful. What was to stop us from doing
it again, now that we saw we could? Or keep us from doing
other things we wanted? I felt so good thinking about this that
I gave a yell and swooped down on McMurphy and the girl
Sandy walking along in front of me, grabbed them both up,
one in each arm, and ran all the way to the day room with them
hollering and kicking like kids. I felt that good.

Colonel Matterson got up again, bright-eyed and full of lessons, and Scanlon wheeled him back to bed. Sefelt and Martini and Fredrickson said they'd better hit the sack too. Mc-
Murphy and I and Harding and the girl and Mr. Turkle stayed
up to finish off the cough sirup and decide what we were going
to do about the mess the ward was in. Me and Harding acted
like we were the only ones really very worried about it; Mc-
Murphy and the big girl just sat there and sipped that sirup
and grinned at each other and played hand games in the
shadows, and Mr. Turkle kept dropping off to sleep. Harding
did his best to try to get them concerned.

"All of you fail to compren' the complexities of the situation," he said.

"Bull," McMurphy said.

Harding slapped the table. "McMurphy, Turkle, you fail to
realize what has occurred here tonight. On a mental ward. Miss
Ratched's ward! The reekerputions will be . . . devastating!"

McMurphy bit the girl's ear lobe. Turkle nodded and opened
one eye and said, "Tha's true. She'll be on tomorrow, too."

"I, however, have a plan," Harding said. He got to his feet.
He said McMurphy was obviously too far gone to handle the
situation himself and someone else would have to take over.

As he talked he stood straighter and became more sober. He spoke in an earnest and urgent voice, and his hands shaped what he said. I was glad he was there to take over.

His plan was that we were to tie up Turkle and make it look like McMurphy'd snuck up behind him, tied him up with oh, say, strips of torn sheet, and relieved him of his keys, and after getting the keys had broken into the drug room, scattered drugs around, and raised hell with the files just to spite the nurse—she'd believe *that* part—then he'd unlocked the screen and made his escape.

McMurphy said it sounded like a television plot and it was so ridiculous it couldn't help but work, and he complimented Harding on his clear-headedness. Harding said the plan had its merits; it would keep the other guys out of trouble with the nurse, and keep Turkle his job, and get McMurphy off the ward. He said McMurphy could have the girls drive him to Canada or Tiajuana, or even Nevada if he wanted, and be completely safe; the police never press too hard to pick up AWOLs from the hospital because ninety per cent of them always show back up in a few days, broke and drunk and looking for that free bed and board. We talked about it for a while and finished the cough sirup. We finally talked it to silence. Harding sat back down.

McMurphy took his arm from around the girl and looked from me to Harding, thinking, that strange, tired expression on his face again. He asked what about us, why didn't we just up and get our clothes on and make it out with him?

"I'm not quite ready yet, Mack," Harding told him.

"Then what makes you think I am?"

Harding looked at him in silence for a time and smiled, then said, "No, you don't understand. I'll be ready in a few weeks. But I want to do it on my own, by myself, right out that front door, with all the traditional red tape and complications. I want my wife to be here in a car at a certain time to pick me up. I want them to know I was *able* to do it that way."

McMurphy nodded. "What about you, Chief?"

"I figure I'm all right. Just I don't know where I want to go yet. And somebody should stay here a few weeks after you're gone to see that things don't start sliding back."

"What about Billy and Sefelt and Fredrickson and the rest?"

"I can't speak for them," Harding said. "They've still got their problems, just like all of us. They're still sick men in lots of ways. But at least there's that: they are sick *men* now. No more rabbits, Mack. Maybe they can be well men someday. I can't say."

McMurphy thought this over, looking at the backs of his hands. He looked back up to Harding.

"Harding, what is it? What happens?"

"You mean all this?"

McMurphy nodded.

Harding shook his head. "I don't think I can give you an answer. Oh, I could give you Freudian reasons with fancy talk, and that would be right as far as it went. But what you want are the reasons for the reasons, and I'm not able to give you those. Not for the others, anyway. For myself? Guilt. Shame. Fear. Self-belittlement. I discovered at an early age that I was—shall we be kind and say different? It's a better, more general word than the other one. I indulged in certain practices that our society regards as shameful. And I got sick. It wasn't the practices, I don't think, it was the feeling that the great, deadly, pointing forefinger of society was pointing at me— and the great voice of millions chanting, 'Shame. Shame. Shame.' It's society's way of dealing with someone different."

"I'm different," McMurphy said. "Why didn't something like that happen to me? I've had people bugging me about one thing or another as far back as I can remember but that's not what—but it didn't drive me crazy."

"No, you're right. That's not what drove you crazy. I wasn't giving my reason as the sole reason. Though I used to think at one time, a few years ago, my turtleneck years, that society's chastising was the sole force that drove one along the road to crazy, but you've caused me to re-appraise my theory. There's something else that drives people, strong people like you, my friend, down that road."

"Yeah? Not that I'm admitting I'm down that road, but what is this something else?"

"It is us." He swept his hand about him in a soft white circle and repeated, "Us."

McMurphy half heartedly said, "Bull," and grinned and stood up, pulling the girl to her feet. He squinted up at the dim clock. "It's nearly five. I need me a little shut-eye before my big getaway. The day shift doesn't come on for another two hours yet; let's leave Billy and Candy down there a while longer. I'll cut out about six. Sandy, honey, maybe an hour in the dorm would sober us up. What do you say? We got a long drive to-morrow, whether it's Canada or Mexico or wherever."

Turkle and Harding and I stood up too. Everybody was still weaving pretty much, still pretty drunk, but a mellow, sad feel-ing had drifted over the drunk. Turkle said he'd boot McMurphy and the girl out of bed in an hour.

"Wake me up too," Harding said. "I'd like to stand there at the window with a silver bullet in my hand and ask 'Who *wawz* that'er masked man?' as you ride—"

"The hell with that. You guys both get in bed, and I don't want to ever see hide nor hair of you again. You get me?"

Harding grinned and nodded but he didn't say anything. Mc-Murphy put his hand out, and Harding shook it. McMurphy tipped back like a cowboy reeling out of a saloon and winked.

"You can be bull goose loony again, buddy, what with Big Mack outa the way."

He turned to me and frowned. "I don't know what you can be, Chief. You still got some looking to do. Maybe you could get you a job being the bad guy on TV rasslin'. Anyway, take 'er easy."

I shook his hand, and we all started for the dorm. McMurphy told Turkle to tear up some sheets and pick out some of his favorite knots to be tied with. Turkle said he would. I got into my bed in the graying light of the dorm and heard Mc-Murphy and the girl get into his bed. I was feeling numb and warm. I heard Mr. Turkle open the door to the linen room out in the hall, heave a long, loud, belching sigh as he pulled the door closed behind him. My eyes got used to the dark, and I could see McMurphy and the girl snuggled into each other's shoulders, getting comfortable, more like two tired little kids than a grown man and a grown woman in bed together to make love.

And that's the way the black boys found them when they came to turn on the dorm lights at six-thirty.

i 've given what happened next a good lot of thought, and I've come around to thinking that it was bound to be and would have happened in one way or another, at this time or that, even if Mr. Turkle had got Mc-Murphy and the two girls up and off the ward like was planned. The Big Nurse would have found out some way what had gone on, maybe just by the look on Billy's face, and she'd have done the same as she did whether McMurphy was still around or not. And Billy would have done what he did, and McMurphy would have heard about it and come back.

Would have *had* to come back, because he could no more have sat around outside the hospital, playing poker in Carson City or Reno or someplace, and let the Big Nurse have the last move and get the last play, than he could have let her get by with it right under his nose. It was like he'd signed on for the whole game and there wasn't any way of him breaking his contract.

As soon as we started getting out of bed and circulating around the ward, the story of what had taken place was spreading in a brush fire of low talk. "They had a *what?*" asked the

ones who hadn't been in on it. "A *whore?* In the dorm? Jesus."
Not only a whore, the others told them, but a drunken blast
to boot. McMurphy was planning to sneak her out before the
day crew came on but he didn't wake up. "Now what kind of
crock are you giving us?" No crock. It's every word gospel. I
was in on it.

Those who had been in on the night started telling about it
with a kind of quiet pride and wonder, the way people tell
about seeing a big hotel fire or a dam bursting—very solemn
and respectful because the casualties aren't even counted yet
—but the longer the telling went on, the less solemn the fellows got. Everytime the Big Nurse and her hustling black boys
turned up something new, such as the empty bottle of cough
sirup or the fleet of wheelchairs parked at the end of the hall
like empty rides in an amusement park, it brought another
part of the night back sudden and clear to be told to the
guys who weren't in on it and to be savored by the guys who
were. Everybody had been herded into the day room by the
black boys, Chronics and Acutes alike, milling together in
excited confusion. The two old Vegetables sat sunk in their
bedding, snapping their eyes and their gums. Everybody was
still in pajamas and slippers except McMurphy and the girl;
she was dressed, except for her shoes and the nylon stockings,
which now hung over her shoulder, and he was in his black
shorts with the white whales. They were sitting together on a
sofa, holding hands. The girl had dozed off again, and Mc-
Murphy was leaning against her with a satisfied and sleepy grin.

Our solemn worry was giving way, in spite of us, to joy
and humor. When the nurse found the pile of pills Harding
had sprinkled on Sefelt and the girl, we started to pop and
snort to keep from laughing, and by the time they found Mr.
Turkle in the linen room and led him out blinking and groaning, tangled in a hundred yards of torn sheet like a mummy
with a hangover, we were roaring. The Big Nurse took our
good humor without so much as a trace of her little pasted
smile; every laugh was being forced right down her throat
till it looked as if any minute she'd blow up like a bladder.

McMurphy draped one bare leg over the edge of the sofa and pulled his cap down to keep the light from hurting his reddened eyes, and he kept licking out a tongue that looked like it had been shellacked by that cough syrup. He looked sick and terrifically tired, and he kept pressing the heels of his hands against his temples and yawning, but as bad as he seemed to feel he still held his grin and once or twice went so far as to laugh out loud at some of the things the nurse kept turning up.

When the nurse went in to call the Main Building to report Mr. Turkle's resignation, Turkle and the girl Sandy took the opportunity to unlock that screen again and wave good-by to all and go loping off across the grounds, stumbling and slipping on the wet, sun-sparkled grass.

"He didn't lock it back up," Harding said to McMurphy. "Go on. Go on after them!"

McMurphy groaned and opened one eye bloody as a hatching egg. "You kidding me? I couldn't even get my *head* through that window, let alone my whole body."

"My friend, I don't believe you fully comprehend—"

"Harding, goddam you and your big words; all I fully comprehend this morning is I'm still half drunk. And sick. Matter of fact, I think you're still drunk too. Chief, how about you; are you still drunk?"

I said that my nose and cheeks didn't have any feeling in them yet, if this could be taken to mean anything.

McMurphy nodded once and closed his eyes again; he laced his hands across his chest and slid down in his chair, his chin settling into his collar. He smacked his lips and smiled as if he were napping. "Man," he said, "everybody is still drunk."

Harding was still concerned. He kept on about how the best thing for McMurphy to do was get dressed, quickly, while old Angel of Mercy was in there calling the doctor again to report the atrocities she had uncovered, but McMurphy maintained that there wasn't anything to get so excited about; he wasn't any worse off than before, was he? "I've took their best punch," he said. Harding threw up his hands and went off, predicting doom.

One of the black boys saw the screen was unlocked and locked it and went into the Nurses' Station for the big flat ledger, came back out running his finger down the roll and lipping the names he read out loud as he sighted the men that matched up with them. The roll is listed alphabetically backwards to throw people off, so he didn't get to the Bs till right at the last. He looked around the day room without taking his finger from that last name in the ledger.

"Bibbit. Where's Billy Bibbit?" His eyes were big. He was thinking Billy'd slipped out right under his nose and would he ever catch it. "Who saw Billy Bibbit go, you damn goons?"

This set people to remembering just where Billy was; there were whispers and laughing again.

The black boy went back into the station, and we saw him telling the nurse. She smashed the phone down in the cradle and came out the door with the black boy hot after her; a lock of her hair had broken loose from beneath her white cap and fell across her face like wet ashes. She was sweating between her eyebrows and under her nose. She demanded we tell her where the Eloper had gone. She was answered with a chorus of laughter, and her eyes went around the men.

"So? He's not gone, is he? Harding, he's still here—on the ward, isn't he? Tell me. Sefelt, tell me!"

She darted the eyes out with every word, stabbing at the men's faces, but the men were immune to her poison. Their eyes met hers; their grins mocked the old confident smile she had lost.

"Washington! Warren! Come with me for room check."

We rose and followed as the three of them went along, unlocking the lab, the tub room, the doctor's office. . . . Scanlon covered his grin with his knotty hand and whispered, "Hey, ain't it gonna be some joke on ol' Billy." We all nodded. "And Billy's not the only one it's gonna be a joke on, now that I think about it; remember who's in there?"

The nurse reached the door of the Seclusion Room at the end of the hall. We pushed up close to see, crowding and craning to peep over the Big Nurse and the two black boys as she unlocked it and swung it open. It was dark in the windowless room. There was a squeak and a scuffle in the dark, and the nurse reached out, flicked the light down on Billy and the girl where they were blinking up from that mattress on the floor like two owls from a nest. The nurse ignored the howl of laughter behind her.

"William Bibbit!" She tried so hard to sound cold and stern. "William . . . Bibbit!"

"Good morning, Miss Ratched," Billy said, not even making any move to get up and button his pajamas. He took the girl's hand in his and grinned. "This is Candy."

The nurse's tongue clucked in her bony throat. "Oh, Billy Billy Billy—I'm so ashamed for you."

Billy wasn't awake enough to respond much to her shaming, and the girl was fussing around looking under the mattress for her nylons, moving slow and warm-looking after sleep. Every so often she would stop her dreamy fumbling and look up and smile at the icy figure of the nurse standing there with her arms crossed, then feel to see if her sweater was buttoned, and go back to tugging for her nylon caught between the mattress and the tile floor. They both moved like fat cats full of warm milk, lazy in the sun; I guessed they were still fairly drunk too.

"Oh, Billy," the nurse said, like she was so disappointed she might break down and cry. "A woman like *this*. A cheap! Low! Painted—"

"Courtesan?" Harding suggested. "Jezebel?" The nurse turned and tried to nail him with her eyes, but he just went on. "Not Jezebel? No?" He scratched his head in thought. "How about Salome? She's notoriously evil. Perhaps 'dame' is the word you want. Well, I'm just trying to *help*."

She swung back to Billy. He was concentrating on getting to his feet. He rolled over and came to his knees, butt in the air like a cow getting up, then pushed up on his hands, then came to one foot, then the other, and straightened. He looked pleased with his success, as if he wasn't even aware of us crowding at the door teasing him and hoorahing him.

The loud talk and laughter swirled around the nurse. She

looked from Billy and the girl to the bunch of us behind her. The enamel-and-plastic face was caving in. She shut her eyes and strained to calm her trembling, concentrating. She knew this was it, her back to the wall. When her eyes opened again, they were very small and still.

"What worries me, Billy," she said—I could hear the change in her voice—"is how your poor mother is going to take this."

She got the response she was after. Billy flinched and put his hand to his cheek like he'd been burned with acid.

"Mrs. Bibbit's always been so proud of your discretion. I know she has. This is going to disturb her terribly. You know how she is when she gets disturbed, Billy; you know how ill the poor woman can become. She's very sensitive. Especially concerning her son. She always spoke so proudly of you. She al—"

"Nuh! Nuh!" His mouth was working. He shook his head, begging her. "You d-don't n-n-need!"

"Billy Billy Billy," she said. "Your mother and I are old friends."

"No!" he cried. His voice scraped the white, bare walls of the Seclusion Room. He lifted his chin so he was shouting at the moon of light in the ceiling. "N-n-*no!*"

We'd stopped laughing. We watched Billy folding into the floor, head going back, knees coming forward. He rubbed his hand up and down that green pant leg. He was shaking his head in panic like a kid that's been promised a whipping just as soon as a willow is cut. The nurse touched his shoulder to comfort him. The touch shook him like a blow.

"Billy, I don't want her to believe something like this of you—but what am I to think?"

"Duh-duh-don't t-tell, M-M-M-Miss Ratched. Duh-duh-duh—"

"Billy, I have to tell. I hate to believe you would behave like this, but, really, what else can I think? I find you alone, on a mattress, with this sort of woman."

"No! I d-d-didn't. I was—" His hand went to his cheek again and stuck there. "She did."

"Billy, this girl could not have pulled you in here forcibly."
She shook her head. "Understand, I would like to believe something else—for your poor mother's sake."

The hand pulled down his cheek, raking long red marks. "She
d-did." He looked around him. "And M-M-McMurphy! He did.
And Harding! And the-the-the rest! They t-t-teased me, *called*
me things!"

Now his face was fastened to hers. He didn't look to one
side or the other, but only straight ahead at her face, like there
was a spiraling light there instead of features, a hypnotizing
swirl of cream white and blue and orange. He swallowed and
waited for her to say something, but she wouldn't; her skill,
her fantastic mechanical power flooded back into her, analyzing
the situation and reporting to her that all she had to do was
keep quiet.

"They m-m-made me! Please, M-Miss Ratched, they may-
may-MAY—!"

She checked her beam, and Billy's face pitched downward,
sobbing with relief. She put a hand on his neck and drew his
cheek to her starched breast, stroking his shoulder while she
turned a slow, contemptuous look across the bunch of us.

"It's all right, Billy. It's all right. No one else is going to
harm you. It's all right. I'll explain to your mother."

She continued to glare at us as she spoke. It was strange
to hear that voice, soft and soothing and warm as a pillow, coming out of a face hard as porcelain.

"All right, Billy. Come along with me. You can wait over
here in the doctor's office. There's no reason for you to be sub-
mitted to sitting out in the day room with these . . . friends
of yours."

She led him into the office, stroking his bowed head and
saying, "Poor boy, poor little boy," while we faded back down
the hall silently and sat down in the day room without looking at one another or speaking. McMurphy was the last one
to take a seat.

The Chronics across the way had stopped milling around and
were settling into their slots. I looked at McMurphy out of

the corner of my eye, trying not to be obvious about it. He was in his chair in the corner, resting a second before he came out for the next round—in a long line of next rounds. The thing he was fighting, you couldn't whip it for good. All you could do was keep on whipping it, till you couldn't come out any more and somebody else had to take your place.

There was more phoning going on in the Nurses' Station and a number of authorities showing up for a tour of the evidence. When the doctor himself finally came in, every one of these people gave him a look like the whole thing had been planned by him, or at least condoned and authorized. He was white and shaky under their eyes. You could see he'd already heard about most of what had gone on here, on his ward, but the Big Nurse outlined it for him again, in slow, loud details so we could hear it too. Hear it in the proper way, this time, solemnly, with no whispering or giggling while she talked. The doctor nodded and fiddled with his glasses, batting eyes so watery I thought he must be splashing her. She finished by telling him about Billy and the tragic experience we had put the poor boy through.

"I left him in your office. Judging from his present state, I suggest you see him right away. He's been through a terrible ordeal. I shudder to think of the damage that must have been done to the poor boy."

She waited until the doctor shuddered too.

"I think you should go see if you can speak with him. He needs a lot of sympathy. He's in a pitiful state."

The doctor nodded again and walked off toward his office. We watched him go.

"Mack," Scanlon said. "Listen—you don't think any of us are being taken in by this crap, do you? It's bad, but we know where the blame lies—we ain't blaming you."

"No," I said, "none of us blame you." And wished I'd had my tongue pulled out as soon as I saw the way he looked at me.

He closed his eyes and relaxed. Waiting, it looked like. Harding got up and walked over to him and had just opened his mouth to say something when the doctor's voice screaming down the hall smashed a common horror and realization onto everybody's face.

"Nurse!" he yelled. "Good lord, *nurse!*"

She ran, and the three black boys ran, down the hall to where the doctor was still calling. But not a patient got up. We knew there wasn't anything for us to do now but just sit tight and wait for her to come to the day room to tell us what we all had known was one of the things that was bound to happen.

She walked straight to McMurphy.

"He cut his throat," she said. She waited, hoping he would say something. He wouldn't look up. "He opened the doctor's desk and found some instruments and cut his throat. The poor miserable, misunderstood boy killed himself. He's there now, in the doctor's chair, with his throat cut."

She waited again. But he still wouldn't look up.

"First Charles Cheswick and now William Bibbit! I hope you're finally satisfied. Playing with human lives—gambling with human lives—as if you thought yourself to be a *God!*"

She turned and walked into the Nurses' Station and closed the door behind her, leaving a shrill, killing-cold sound ringing in the tubes of light over our heads.

First I had a quick thought to try to stop him, talk him into taking what he'd already won and let her have the last round, but another, bigger thought wiped the first thought away completely. I suddenly realized with a crystal certainty that neither I nor any of the half-score of us could stop him. That Harding's arguing or my grabbing him from behind, or old Colonel Matterson's teaching or Scanlon's griping, or all of us together couldn't rise up and stop him.

We couldn't stop him because we were the ones making him do it. It wasn't the nurse that was forcing him, it was our need that was making him push himself slowly up from sitting, his big hands driving down on the leather chair arms, pushing him up, rising and standing like one of those moving-picture zombies, obeying orders beamed at him from forty masters. It was us that had been making him go on for weeks, keeping him standing long after his feet and legs had given out, weeks of making him wink and grin and laugh and go on with his act long after his humor had been parched dry between two electrodes.

We made him stand and hitch up his black shorts like they were horsehide chaps, and push back his cap with one finger like it was a ten-gallon Stetson, slow, mechanical gestures—and when he walked across the floor you could hear the iron in his bare heels ring sparks out of the tile.

Only at the last—after he'd smashed through that glass door, her face swinging around, with terror forever ruining any other look she might ever try to use again, screaming when he grabbed for her and ripped her uniform all the way down the front, screaming again when the two nippled circles started from her chest and swelled out and out, bigger than anybody had ever even imagined, warm and pink in the light—only at the last, after the officials realized that the three black boys weren't going to do anything but stand and watch and they would have to beat him off without their help, doctors and supervisors and nurses prying those heavy red fingers out of the white flesh of her throat as if they were her neck bones, jerking him backward off of her with a loud heave of breath, only then did he show any sign that he might be anything other than a sane, willful, dogged man performing a hard duty that finally just had to be done, like it or not.

He gave a cry. At the last, falling backward, his face appearing to us for a second upside down before he was smothered on the floor by a pile of white uniforms, he let himself cry out:

A sound of cornered-animal fear and hate and surrender and defiance, that if you ever trailed coon or cougar or lynx is like the last sound the treed and shot and falling animal makes as the dogs get him, when he finally doesn't care any more about anything but himself and his dying.

I hung around another couple of weeks to see what was to come. Everything was changing. Sefelt and Fredrickson signed out together Against Medical Advice, and two days later another three Acutes left, and six more transferred to another ward. There was a lot of investigation about the party on the ward and about Billy's death, and the doctor was informed that his resignation would be accepted, and he informed them that they would have to go the whole way and can him if they wanted him out.

The Big Nurse was over in Medical for a week, so for a while we had the little Jap nurse from Disturbed running the ward; that gave the guys a chance to change a lot of the ward policy. By the time the Big Nurse came back, Harding had even got the tub room back open and was in there dealing blackjack himself, trying to make that airy, thin voice of his sound like McMurphy's auctioneer bellow. He was dealing when he heard her key hit the lock.

We all left the tub room and came out in the hall to meet her, to ask about McMurphy. She jumped back two steps when we approached, and I thought for a second she might run. Her face was bloated blue and out of shape on one side, closing one eye completely, and she had a heavy bandage around her throat. And a new white uniform. Some of the guys grinned at the front of it; in spite of its being smaller and tighter and more starched than her old uniforms, it could no longer conceal the fact that she was a woman.

Smiling, Harding stepped up close and asked what had become of Mack.

She took a little pad and pencil from the pocket of her uniform and wrote, "He will be back," on it and passed it around. The paper trembled in her hand. "Are you sure?" Harding wanted to know after he read it. We'd heard all kinds of things, that he'd knocked down two aides on Disturbed and taken their keys and escaped, that he'd been sent back to the work farm —even that the nurse, in charge now till they got a new doctor, was giving him special therapy.

"Are you quite positive?" Harding repeated.

The nurse took out her pad again. She was stiff in the joints, and her more than ever white hand skittered on the pad like one of those arcade gypsies that scratch out fortunes for a penny. "Yes, Mr. Harding," she wrote. "I would not say so if I was not positive. He will be back."

Harding read the paper, then tore it up and threw the pieces at her. She flinched and raised her hand to protect the bruised side of her face from the paper. "Lady, I think you're full of so much bullshit," Harding told her. She stared at him, and her hand wavered over the pad a second, but then she turned and walked into the Nurses' Station, sticking the pad and pencil back down in the pocket of her uniform.

"Hum," Harding said. "Our conversation was a bit spotty, it seemed. But then, when you are told that you are full of bullshit, what kind of written comeback *can* you make?"

She tried to get her ward back into shape, but it was difficult with McMurphy's presence still tromping up and down the halls and laughing out loud in the meetings and singing in the latrines. She couldn't rule with her old power any more, not by writing things on pieces of paper. She was losing her patients one after the other. After Harding signed out and was picked up by his wife, and George transferred to a different ward, just three of us were left out of the group that had been on the fishing crew, myself and Martini and Scanlon.

I didn't want to leave just yet, because she seemed to be too sure; she seemed to be waiting for one more round, and I wanted to be there in case it came off. And one morning, after McMurphy'd been gone three weeks, she made her last play.

The ward door opened, and the black boys wheeled in this Gurney with a chart at the bottom that said in heavy black letters, MC MURPHY, RANDLE P. POST-OPERATIVE. And below this was written in ink, LOBOTOMY.

They pushed it into the day room and left it standing against the wall, along next to the Vegetables. We stood at the foot of the Gurney, reading the chart, then looked up to the other end at the head dented into the pillow, a swirl of red hair over a face milk-white except for the heavy purple bruises around the eyes.

After a minute of silence Scanlon turned and spat on the floor. "Aaah, what's the old bitch tryin' to put over on us anyhow, for crap sakes. That ain't him."

"*Nothing* like him," Martini said.

"How stupid she think we are?"

"Oh, they done a pretty fair job, though," Martini said, moving up alongside the head and pointing as he talked. "See. They got the broken nose and that crazy scar—even the sideburns."

"Sure," Scanlon growled, "but *hell!*"

I pushed past the other patients to stand beside Martini. "Sure, they can do things like scars and broken noses," I said. "But they can't do that *look*. There's nothin' in the face. Just like one of those store dummies, ain't that right, Scanlon?"

Scanlon spat again. "Damn right. Whole thing's, you know, too *blank*. Anybody can see that."

"Look here," one of the patients said, peeling back the sheet, "tattoos."

"Sure," I said, "they can do tattoos. But the arms, huh? The arms? They couldn't do those. His arms were *big!*"

For the rest of the afternoon Scanlon and Martini and I ridiculed what Scanlon called that crummy sideshow fake lying there on the Gurney, but as the hours passed and the swelling began subsiding around the eyes I saw more and more guys strolling over to look at the figure. I watched them walk by acting like they were going to the magazine rack or the drinking fountain, so they could sneak another look at the face. I watched and tried to figure out what he would have done. I was only sure of one thing: he wouldn't have left something like that sit there in the day room with his name tacked on it for twenty or thirty years so the Big Nurse could use it as an example of what can happen if you buck the system. I was sure of that.

I waited that night until the sounds in the dorm told me everybody was asleep, and until the black boys had stopped making their rounds. Then I turned my head on the pillow so I could see the bed next to mine. I'd been listening to the breathing for hours, since they had wheeled the Gurney in and lifted the stretcher onto the bed, listening to the lungs stumbling and stopping, then starting again, hoping as I listened they would stop for good—but I hadn't turned to look yet.

There was a cold moon at the window, pouring light into

the dorm like skim milk. I sat up in bed, and my shadow fell across the body, seeming to cleave it in half between the hips and the shoulders, leaving only a black space. The swelling had gone down enough in the eyes that they were open; they stared into the full light of the moon, open and undreaming, glazed from being open so long without blinking until they were like smudged fuses in a fuse box. I moved to pick up the pillow, and the eyes fastened on the movement and followed me as I stood up and crossed the few feet between the beds.

The big, hard body had a tough grip on life. It fought a long time against having it taken away, flailing and thrashing around so much I finally had to lie full length on top of it and scissor the kicking legs with mine while I mashed the pillow into the face. I lay there on top of the body for what seemed days. Until the thrashing stopped. Until it was still a while and had shuddered once and was still again. Then I rolled off. I lifted the pillow, and in the moonlight I saw the expression hadn't changed from the blank, dead-end look the least bit, even under suffocation. I took my thumbs and pushed the lids down and held them till they stayed. Then I lay back on my bed.

I lay for a while, holding the covers over my face, and thought I was being pretty quiet, but Scanlon's voice hissing from his bed let me know I wasn't.

"Take it easy, Chief," he said. "Take it easy. It's okay."

"Shut up," I whispered. "Go back to sleep."

It was quiet a while; then I heard him hiss again and ask, "Is it finished?"

I told him yeah.

"Christ," he said then, "she'll know. You realize that, don't you? Sure, nobody'll be able to prove anything—anybody coulda kicked off in post-operative like he was, happens all the time—but her, she'll know."

I didn't say anything.

"Was I you, Chief, I'd breeze my tail outa here. Yessir. I tell you what. You leave outa here, and I'll say I saw him up and moving around after you left and cover you that way. That's the best idea, don't you think?"

"Oh, yeah, just like that. Just ask 'em to unlock the door and let me out."

"No. He showed you how one time, if you think back. That very first week. You remember?"

I didn't answer him, and he didn't say anything else, and it was quiet in the dorm again. I lay there a few minutes longer and then got up and started putting on my clothes. When I finished dressing I reached into McMurphy's nightstand and got his cap and tried it on. It was too small, and I was suddenly ashamed of trying to wear it. I dropped it on Scanlon's bed as I walked out of the dorm. He said, "Take it easy, buddy," as I walked out.

The moon straining through the screen of the tub-room windows showed the hunched, heavy shape of the control panel, glinted off the chrome fixtures and glass gauges so cold I could almost hear the click of it striking. I took a deep breath and bent over and took the levers. I heaved my legs under me and felt the grind of weight at my feet. I heaved again and heard the wires and connections tearing out of the floor. I lurched it up to my knees and was able to get an arm around it and my other hand under it. The chrome was cold against my neck and the side of my head. I put my back toward the screen, then spun and let the momentum carry the panel through the screen and window with a ripping crash. The glass splashed out in the moon, like a bright cold water baptizing the sleeping earth. Panting, I thought for a second about going back and getting Scanlon and some of the others, but then I heard the running squeak of the black boys' shoes in the hall and I put my hand on the sill and vaulted after the panel, into the moonlight.

I ran across the grounds in the direction I remembered seeing the dog go, toward the highway. I remember I was taking huge strides as I ran, seeming to step and float a long ways before my next foot struck the earth. I felt like I was flying. Free. Nobody bothers coming after an AWOL, I knew, and Scanlon could handle any questions about the dead man—no need to be running like this. But I didn't stop. I ran for miles before

I stopped and walked up the embankment onto the highway.

I caught a ride with a guy, a Mexican guy, going north in a truck full of sheep, and gave him such a good story about me being a professional Indian wrestler the syndicate had tried to lock up in a nuthouse that he stopped real quick and gave me a leather jacket to cover my greens and loaned me ten bucks to eat on while I hitchhiked to Canada. I had him write his address down before he drove off and I told him I'd send him the money as soon as I got a little ahead.

I might go to Canada eventually, but I think I'll stop along the Columbia on the way. I'd like to check around Portland and Hood River and The Dalles to see if there's any of the guys I used to know back in the village who haven't drunk themselves goofy. I'd like to see what they've been doing since the government tried to buy their right to be Indians. I've even heard that some of the tribe have took to building their old ramshackle wood scaffolding all over that big million-dollar hydroelectric dam, and are spearing salmon in the spillway. I'd give something to see that. Mostly, I'd just like to look over the country around the gorge again, just to bring some of it clear in my mind again.

I been away a long time.

The Author and His Work

❀◇

TOM WOLFE

Tom Wolfe, author of *The Kandy-Kolored Tangerine-Flake Stream-line Baby* and *The Pump House Gang,* wrote the first extended account of Kesey and his group, the Merry Pranksters. A freelance journalist, Wolfe has contributed many essays to such publications as the *New York Magazine,* the *London Weekend Telegraph,* the *New York World Journal Tribune,* and *Esquire.*

WHAT DO YOU THINK OF
MY BUDDHA?

A considerable new message . . . The current fantasy . . . Fantasy is a word Kesey has taken to using more and more, for all sorts of plans, ventures, world views, ambitions. It is a good word. It is ironic and it isn't. It refers to everything from getting hold of a pickup truck—"that's our fantasy for this weekend"—to some scary stuff out on the raggedy raggedy edge. . . . But how to tell it? . . . It has never been possible, has it, truly, just to come out and announce the current fantasy, not even in days gone by, when it seemed so simple. . . .

Even back on Perry Lane, where everyone was young and intellectual and analytical, and the sky, supposedly, was the limit—there was no way he could just come right out and say: Come in a little closer, friends . . . They had their own fantasy for him: he was a "diamond in the rough." Wellllll, that was all right, being a diamond in the rough. He had gone to Stanford University in 1958 on a creative-writing fellowship, and they had taken him in on Perry Lane because he was such a swell diamond in the rough. Perry Lane was Stanford's bohemian quarter. As bohemias go, Perry Lane was Arcadia, Arcadia just off the Stanford golf course. It was a cluster of two-room cottages with weathery wood shingles in an oak forest, only not just amid trees and greenery, but amid vines, honey-suckle tendrils, all buds and shoots and swooping tendrils and twitterings like the best of Arthur Rackham and *Honey Bear*. Not only that, it had true cultural cachet. Thorstein Veblen had lived there. So had two Nobel Prize winners everybody knew about though the names escaped them. The cottages rented for just sixty dollars a month. Getting into Perry Lane was like getting into a club. Everybody who lived there had known somebody else who lived there, or they would never have gotten in, and naturally they got to know each other very closely too, and there was always something of an atmosphere of communal living. Nobody's door was ever shut on Perry Lane, except when they were pissed off.

It was sweet. Perry Lane was a typical 1950s bohemia. Everybody sat around shaking their heads over America's tail-fin, housing-development civilization, and Christ, in Europe, so what if the plumbing didn't work, they had mastered the art of living. Occasionally somebody would suggest an orgy or a three-day wine binge, but the model was always that old Zorba the Greek romanticism of sandals and simplicity and back to first principles. Periodically they would take pilgrimages forty miles north to North Beach to see how it was actually done.

The main figures on Perry Lane were two novelists, Robin White, who had just written the Harper Prize novel, *Elephant Hill*, and Gwen Davis, a kind of West Coast Dawn Powell. In any case, all the established Perry Laners could see Kesey coming a mile away.

He had Jack London Martin Eden Searching Hick, the hick with intellectual yearnings, written all over him. He was from Oregon—who the hell was ever from Oregon?—and he had an Oregon country drawl and too many muscles and calluses on his hands and his brow furrowed when he was thinking hard, and it was perfect.

White took Kesey under his wing and got him and his wife Faye a cottage on Perry Lane. The Perry Lane set liked the idea at once. He could always be counted on to do *perfect* things. Like the time they were all having dinner—there was a lot of communal dining—and some visitor was going on about the ineffable delicacy of James Baldwin's work, and Kesey keeps eating but also trying to edge a word in saying, well, bub, I dunno, I cain't exactly go along with you there, and the fellow puts down his knife and fork very carefully and turns to the others and says,

"I'll be delighted to listen to what*ever* Mr. Kesey has to say—as soon as he learns to eat from a plate without holding down his meat with his thumb."

Perfect! He had been voted "most likely to succeed" at his high school in Springfield, Oregon, and had graduated from the University of Oregon, where he was all involved in sports and fraternities, the All-American Boy bit. He had been a star wrestler in the 174-pound class and a star actor in college plays. He had even gone to Los Angeles after he finished college, and knocked around Hollywood for a while with the idea of becoming a movie star. But the urge to write, to create, had burst up through all this thick lumpy All-American crap somehow, like an unaccountable purslane blossom, and he had started writing, even completing a novel about college athletics, *End of Autumn*. It had never been published, and probably never would be, but he had the longing to do this thing. And his background—it was great, too. Somehow the Perry Lane set got the idea that his family were Okies, coming out of the Dust Bowl during the Depression, and then up to

Oregon, wild, sodden Oregon, where they had fought the land and shot bears and the rivers were swift and the salmon leaped silver in the spring big two-hearted rivers.

His wife Faye—she was from the same kind of background, only she came from Idaho, and they had been high-school sweethearts in Springfield, Oregon, and had run off and gotten married when they were both freshmen in college. They once made a bet as to which of them had been born in the most Low Rent, bottomdog shack, his old place in La Junta, or hers in Idaho. He was dead sure there was no beating La Junta for Rundown until they got to Idaho, and she sure as hell did win that one. Faye was even more soft-spoken than Kesey. She hardly spoke at all. She was pretty and extremely sweet, practically a madonna of the hill country. And their cottage on Perry Lane—well, everybody else's cottage was run-down in a careful bohemian way, *simplicity*, Japanese paper lamp globes and monk's cloth and blond straw rugs and Swedish stainless steel knives and forks and cornflowers sticking out of a hand-thrown pot. But theirs was just plain Low Rent. There was always something like a broken washing machine rusting on the back porch and pigweed, bladderpods, scoke, and scurf peas growing ragged out back. Somehow it was . . . *perfect* . . . to have him and Faye on hand to *learn* as the Perry Lane sophisticates talked about life and the arts.

Beautiful! . . . the current fantasy . . . But how to tell them? —about such arcane little matters as Captain Marvel and The Flash . . . and *The Life*—and the very *Superkids*—

". . . a considerable new message . . . the blissful counterstroke . . ."

—when they had such a nice clear picture of him as the horny-nailed son of the Western sod, fresh from Springfield, Oregon. It was true that his father, Fred Kesey, had started him and his younger brother, Joe, known as Chuck, shooting and fishing and swimming as early as they could in any way manage it, also boxing, running, wrestling, plunging down the rapids of the Willamette and the McKenzie Rivers, on inner-tube rafts, with a lot of rocks and water and sartin' death foamin' down below. But it was not so they could tame animals, forests, rivers, wild upturned convulsed Oregon. It was more to condition them to do more of what his father had already done a pretty good job of—claim whatever he can rightly get by being man enough to take it, and not on the frontier, either. . . . Kesey Sr. had been part of the 1940s migration from the Southwest—not of "Okies" but of Protestant entrepreneurs who looked to the West Coast as a land of business opportunity. He started out in the Willamette Valley with next to nothing and founded a marketing cooperative for dairy farmers, the Eugene Farmers Cooperative, and built it into the biggest dairy operation in the area, retailing under the name of Darigold. He was one of the big postwar success stories in the Valley—and ended up not in an old homestead with wood sidings and lightning rods but in a modern home in the suburbs, lowslung and pastel, on a street called Debra Lane. The incredible postwar American electro-pastel surge into the suburbs!—it was sweeping the Valley, with superhighways, dreamboat cars, shopping centers, soaring thirty-foot Federal Sign & Signal Company electric supersculptures— Eight New Plexiglas Display Features!—a surge of freedom and mobility, of cars and the money to pay for them and the time to enjoy them and a home where you can laze in a rich pool of pale wall-to-wall or roar through the technological wonderworld in motor launches and, in the case of men like his father, private planes—

The things he would somehow suddenly remember about the old home town—over here, for example, is the old white clapboard house they used to live in, and behind it, back a ways, is the radio tower of station KORE with a red light blinking on top—and at night he used to get down on his knees to say his prayers and there would be the sky and the light blinking—and he always kind of thought he was praying to that red light. And the old highway used to take a bend

right about here, and it seemed like there was always somebody driving through about three or four in the morning, half
asleep, and they would see the lights over there in town where
it was getting built up and they'd think the road headed
straight for the lights and they'd run off the bend and Kesey
and his dad would go out to see if they could help the guy
draggle himself out of the muck—chasing street lights!—praying to the red beacon light of KORE!—and a little run-in at
Gregg's Drive-In, as it used to be called, it is now Speck's, at
Franklin Boulevard at the bridge over the river. That was the
big high-school drive-in, with the huge streamlined sculpted
pastel display sign with streaming streamlines superslick A-22
italic script, floodlights, clamp-on trays, car-hop girls in floppy
blue slacks, hamburgers in some kind of tissuey wax paper
steaming with onions pressed down and fried on the grill and
mustard and catsup to squirt all over it from out plastic squirt
cylinders. Saturday nights when everybody is out cruising—
some guy was in his car in the lot at Gregg's going the wrong
way, so nobody could move. The more everybody blew the
horns, the more determined the guy got. Like *this* was the
test. He rolls up the windows and locks the doors so they can't
get at him and keeps boring in. This guy vs. Kesey. So Kesey
goes inside and gets a potato they make the french fries with
and comes out and jams it over the guy's exhaust pipe, which
causes the motor to conk out and you ain't going *any* which
way now, bub. The guy brings charges against Kesey for ruining his engine and Kesey ends up in juvenile court before a
judge and tries to tell him how it is at Gregg's Drive-In on a
Saturday night: the Life—that *feeling*—The Life—the late
1940s early 1950s American Teenage Drive-In Life was
precisely what it was all about—but how could you tell anyone about it?

But of course!—the *feeling*—out here at night, free, with
the motor running and the adrenaline flowing, cruising in the
neon glories of the new American night—it was very Heaven
to be the first wave of the most extraordinary kids in the his-

tory of the world—only fifteen, sixteen, seventeen years old, dressed in the *haute couture* of pink Oxford shirts, sharp pants, snaky half-inch belts, fast shoes—with all this Straight-6 and V-8 power underneath and all this neon glamour overhead, which somehow tied in with the technological superheroics of the jet, TV, atomic subs, ultrasonics—Postwar American suburbs—glorious world! and the hell with the intellectual badmouthers of America's tailfin civilization . . . They couldn't know what it was like or else they had it cultivated out of them—the feeling—to be very Superkids! the world's first generation of the little devils—feeling immune, beyond calamity. One's parents remembered the sloughing common order, War & Depression—but Superkids knew only the emotional surge of the great payoff, when nothing was common any longer—The Life! A glorious place, a glorious age, I tell you! A very Neon Renaissance— And the myths that actually touched you at that time—not Hercules, Orpheus, Ulysses, and Aeneas—but Superman, Captain Marvel, Batman, The Human Torch, The Sub-Mariner, Captain America, Plastic Man, The Flash—but of course! On Perry Lane, what did they think it was—quaint?—when he talked about the comic-book Superheroes as the honest American myths? It was a fantasy world *already*, this electro-pastel world of Mom&Dad&Buddy&Sis in the suburbs. There they go, in the family car, a white Pontiac Bonneville sedan—*the family car!*—a huge crazy god-awful-powerful fantasy creature to begin with, 327-horsepower, shaped like twenty-seven nights of lubricious luxury brougham seduction—*you're already there, in Fantasyland,* so why not move off your snug-harbor quilty-bed dead center and cut loose—go ahead and say it—Shazam!—juice it up to what it's already aching to be: 327,000 horsepower, a whole superhighway long and *soaring, screaming* on toward . . . Edge City, and ultimate fantasies, current and future. . . . Billy Batson said *Shazam!* and turned into Captain Marvel. Jay Garrick inhaled an experimental gas in the research lab . . .

. . . and began traveling and thinking at the speed of light as . . . The Flash . . . the current fantasy. Yes. The Kesey diamond-in-the-rough fantasy did not last very long. The most interesting person on Perry Lane as far as he was concerned was not any of the novelists or other literary intellectuals, but a young graduate student in psychology named Vik Lovell. Lovell was like a young Viennese analyst, or at least a California graduate-school version of one. He was slender with wild dark hair and very cool intellectually and wound-up at the same time. He introduced Kesey to Freudian psychology. Kesey had never run into a system of thought like this before. Lovell could point out in the most persuasive way how mundane character traits and minor hassles around Perry Lane fit into the richest, most complex metaphor of life ever devised, namely, Freud's. . . . And a little experimental gas . . . Yes. Lovell told him about some experiments the Veterans Hospital in Menlo Park was running with "psychomimetic" drugs, drugs that brought on temporary states resembling psychoses. They were paying volunteers seventy-five dollars a day. Kesey volunteered. It was all nicely calcimined and clinical. They would put him on a bed in a white room and give him a series of capsules without saying what they were. One would be nothing, a placebo. One would be Ditran, which always brought on a terrible experience. Kesey could always tell that one coming on, because the hairs on the blanket he was under would suddenly look like a field of hideously diseased thorns and he would put his finger down his throat and retch. But one of them—the first thing he knew about it was a squirrel dropped an acorn from a tree outside, only it was tremendously loud and sounded like it was not outside but right in the room with him and not actually a sound, either, but a great suffusing presence, visual, almost tactile, a great impacting of . . . *blue* . . . all around him and suddenly he was in a realm of consciousness he had never dreamed of before and it was not a dream or a delirium but part of his awareness. He looks at the ceiling. It begins moving. Panic—and yet there is no panic. The ceiling is moving—not in a crazed swirl but along its own planes its own planes of light and shadow and surface not nearly so nice and smooth as plasterer Super Plaster Man intended with infallible carpenter level bubble sliding in dim honey Karo syrup tube not so foolproof as you thought, bub, little lumps and ridges up there, bub, and lines, lines like spines on crests of waves of white desert movie sand each one with MGM shadow longshot of the ominous A-rab coming up over the next crest for only the sinister Saracen can see the road and you didn't know how many subplots you left up there, Plaster Man, trying to smooth it *all* out, *all* of it, with your bubble in a honey tube carpenter's level, to make us all down here look up and see nothing but ceiling, because we all know ceiling, because it has a *name*, ceiling, therefore it is nothing but a ceiling—no room for A-rabs up there in Level Land, eh, Plaster Man. Suddenly he is like a Ping-pong ball in a flood of sensory stimuli, heart beating, blood coursing, breath suspiring, teeth grating, hand moving over the percale sheet over those thousands of minute warfy woofings like a brush fire, sun glow and the highlight on a stainless-steel rod, quite a little movie you have going on in that highlight there, Hondo, Technicolors, pick each one out like fishing for neon gumballs with a steam shovel in the Funtime Arcade, a Ping-pong ball in a flood of sensory stimuli, all quite ordinary, but . . . *revealing* themselves for the first time and happening . . . Now . . . as if for the first time he has entered a moment in his life and known exactly what is happening to his senses now, at this moment, and with each new discovery it is as if he has entered into all of it himself, is *one* with it, the movie white desert of the ceiling becomes something rich, personal, his, beautiful beyond description, like an orgasm behind the eyeballs, and his A-rabs—A-rabs behind the eyelids, eyelid movies, room for them and a lot more in the five billion thoughts per second stroboscope synapses—his A-rab heroes, fine Daily Double horsehair mustaches wrapped about the Orbicularis Oris of their mouths—

Face! The doctor comes back in and, marvelous, poor tight cone ass, doc, Kesey can now see *into him*. For the first time he notices that the doctor's lower left lip is trembling, but he more than *sees* the tremor, he understands it, he can—almost seen!—see each muscle fiber decussate, pulling the poor jelly of his lip to the left and the fibers one by one leading back into infrared caverns of the body, through transistor-radio innards of nerve tangles, each one on Red Alert, the poor ninny's inner hooks desperately trying to make the little writhing bastards *keep still in there*, I am Doctor, this is a human specimen before me—the poor ninny has his own desert movie going on inside, only each horsehair A-rab is a threat—if only his lip, his face, would stay level, level like the honey bubble of the Official Plaster Man assured him it would—

Miraculous! He could truly *see into people* for the first time—

And yes, that little capsule sliding blissly down the gullet was LSD.

Very soon it was already time to push on beyond another fantasy, the fantasy of the Menlo Park clinicians. The clinicians' fantasy was that the volunteers were laboratory animals that had to be dealt with objectively, quantitatively. It was well known that people who volunteered for drug experiments tended to be unstable anyway. So the doctors would come in in white smocks, with the clipboards, taking blood pressures and heart rates and urine specimens and having them try to solve simple problems in logic and mathematics, such as adding up columns of figures, and having them judge time and distances, although they did have them talk into tape recorders, too. But the doctors were *so out of it*. They never took LSD themselves and they had absolutely no comprehension, and it couldn't be put into words anyway.

Sometimes you wanted to paint it huge—Lovell is under LSD in the clinic and he starts drawing a huge Buddha on the wall. It somehow encompasses the whole—White Smock comes in and doesn't even look at it, he just starts asking the old questions on the clipboard, so Lovell suddenly butts in:

"What do you think of my Buddha?"

White Smock looks at it a moment and says, "It looks very feminine. Now let's see how rapidly you can add up this column of figures here . . ."

Very feminine. Deliver us from the clichés that have locked up even these so-called experimenters' brains like the accordion fences in the fur-store window—and Kesey was having the same problem with his boys. One of them was a young guy with a lie-down crewcut and the straightest face, the straightest, blandest, most lineless awfulest Plaster Man honey bubble levelest face ever made, and he would come in and open his eyes wide once as if to make sure this muscular hulk on the bed were still *rational* and then get this smug tone in his voice which poured out into the room like absorbent cotton choked in chalk dust from beaten erasers Springfield High School.

"Now when I say 'Go,' you tell me when you think a minute is up by saying, 'Now.' Have you got that?"

Yeah, he had that. Kesey was soaring on LSD and his sense of time was *wasted*, and thousands of thoughts per second were rapping around between synapses, fractions of a second, so what the hell is a minute—but then one thought stuck in there, held . . . ma-*li*-cious, *de*-li-cious. He remembered that his pulse had been running seventy-five beats a minute every time they took it, so when Dr. Fog says "Go," Kesey slyly slides his slithering finger onto his pulse and counts up to seventy-five and says:

"Now!"

Dr. Smog looks at his stop watch. "Amazing!" he says, and walks out of the room.

You said it, bub, but like a lot of other people, you don't even know.

LSD; how can—now that those big fat letters are babbling out on coated stock from every newsstand . . . But this was late 1959, early 1960, a full two years before Mom&Dad&Buddy& Sis heard of the dread letters and clucked because Drs. Timothy Leary and Richard Alpert were french-frying the brains of Harvard boys with it. It was even before Dr. Humphrey Osmond had invented the term "psychodelic," which was later amended to "psychedelic" to get rid of the nuthouse connotation of "psycho" . . . LSD! It was quite a little secret to have stumbled onto, a hulking supersecret, in fact—the triumph of the guinea pigs! In a short time he and Lovell had tried the whole range of the drugs, LSD, psilocybin, mescaline, peyote, IT-290 the superamphetamine, Ditran the bummer, morning-glory seeds. They were onto a discovery that the Menlo Park clinicians themselves never—mighty fine irony here: the White Smocks were supposedly using *them*. Instead the White Smocks had handed them the very key itself. *And you don't even know, bub . . . with these drugs your perception is altered enough that you find yourself looking out of completely strange eyeholes. All of us have a great deal of our minds locked shut. We're shut off from our own world. And these drugs seem to be the key to open these locked doors.* How many?—maybe two dozen people in the world were on to this incredible secret! One was Aldous Huxley, who had taken mescaline and written about it in *The Doors of Perception*. He compared the brain to a "reducing valve." In ordinary perception, the senses send an overwhelming flood of information to the brain, which the brain then filters down to a trickle it can manage for the purpose of survival in a highly competitive world. Man has become so rational, so utilitarian, that the trickle becomes most pale and thin. It is efficient, for mere survival, but it screens out the most wondrous part of man's potential experience without his even knowing it. *We're shut off from our own world*. Primitive man once experienced the rich and sparkling flood of the senses fully. Children experience it for a few months—until "normal" training, conditioning, close the doors on this other world, usually for good. Somehow, Huxley had said, the drugs opened these ancient doors. And through them modern man may at last go, and rediscover his divine birthright—

But these are *words*, man! *And you couldn't put it into words*. The White Smocks liked to put it into words, like *hallucination* and *dissociative phenomena*. They could understand the visual skyrockets. Give them a good case of an ashtray turning into a Venus flytrap or eyelid movies of crystal cathedrals, and they could groove on that, *Kluver, op cit., p. 43n.* That was swell. *But don't you see?*—the visual stuff was just the décor with LSD. In fact, you might go through the whole experience without any true hallucination. The whole thing was . . . *the experience* . . . this certain indescribable *feeling* . . . Indescribable, because words can only jog the memory, and if there is no memory of . . . The *experience* of the barrier between the subjective and the objective, the personal and the impersonal, the *I* and the *not-I* disappearing . . . that *feeling!* . . . Or can you remember when you were a child watching someone put a pencil to a sheet of paper for the first time, to draw a picture . . . and the line begins to grow— into a nose! and it is not just a pattern of graphite line on a sheet of paper but the very miracle of creation itself and your own dreams flowed into that magical . . . growing . . . line, and it was not a picture but a *miracle* . . . an *experience* . . . and now that you're soaring on LSD that *feeling* is coming on again—only now the creation is of the entire universe—

Meanwhile, over on Perry Lane, this wasn't precisely the old Searching Hick they all knew and loved. Suddenly Kesey —well, he was soft-spoken, all right, but he came on with a lot of vital energy. Gradually the whole Perry Lane thing was gravitating around Kesey. Volunteer Kesey gave himself over to science over at the Menlo Park Vets hospital—and somehow drugs were getting up and walking out of there and over to Perry Lane, LSD, mescaline, IT-290, mostly. Being hip on

Perry Lane now had an element nobody had ever dreamed about before, wild-flying, mind-blowing drugs. Some of the old Perry Lane luminaries' *cool* was tested and they were found wanting. Robin White and Gwen Davis were against the new drug thing. That was all right, because Kesey had had about enough of them, and the power was with Kesey. Perry Lane took on a kind of double personality, which is to say, Kesey's. Half the time it would be just like some kind of college fraternity row, with everybody out on a nice autumn Saturday afternoon on the grass in the dapple shadows of the trees and honey suckle tendrils playing touch football or basketball. An hour later, however, Kesey and his circle would be hooking down something that in the entire world only they and a few avant-garde neuropharmacological researchers even knew about, drugs of the future, of the neuropharmacologists' centrifuge utopia, the coming age of . . .

Well shee-ut. An' I don't reckon we give much of a damn any more about the art of living in France, either, boys, every frog ought to have a little paunch, like Henry Miller said, and go to bed every night in pajamas with collars and piping on them—just take a letter for me and mail it down to old Morris at Morris Orchids, Laredo, Texas, boys, tell him about enough peyote cactus to mulch all the mouldering widows' graves in poor placid Palo Alto. Yes. They found out they could send off to a place called Morris Orchids in Laredo and get peyote, and one of the new games of Perry Lane—goodbye Robin, goodbye Gwen—got to be seeing who was going down to the Railway Express at the railroad station and pick up the shipment, since possession of peyote, although not of LSD, was already illegal in California. There would be these huge goddamned boxes of the stuff, one thousand buds and roots seventy dollars; buds only—slightly higher. If they caught you, you were *caught*, because there was no excuse possible. There was no other earthly reason to have these goddamned fetid plants except to get high as a coon. And they would all set about cutting them into strips and putting them out to dry, it took days, and then grinding them up into powder and packing them in gelatin capsules or boiling it down to a gum and putting it in the capsules or just making a horrible goddamned broth that was so foul, so unbelievably vile, you had to chill it numb to try to kill the taste and fast for a day so you wouldn't have anything on your stomach, just to keep eight ounces of it down. But then—*soar*. Perry Lane, Perry Lane.

    Miles
        Miles
            Miles
                Miles
                    Miles
                        Miles
                            Miles
                                under all that good
vegetation from Morris Orchids and having visions of
    Faces
        Faces
            Faces
                Faces
                    Faces
                      Faces
                        Faces

                                so many faces
rolling up behind the eyelids, faces he has never seen before, complete with spectral cheekbones, pregnant eyes, stringy wattles, and all of a sudden: Chief Broom. For some reason peyote does this . . . Kesey starts getting eyelid movies of faces, whole galleries of weird faces, churning up behind the eyelids, faces from out of nowhere. He knows nothing about Indians and has never met an Indian, but suddenly here is a full-blown Indian—Chief Broom—the solution, the whole mothering key, to the novel . . .

He hadn't even meant to write this book. He had been working on another one, called *Zoo* about North Beach. Lovell had suggested why didn't he get a job as night attendant on the psychiatric ward at Menlo Park. He could make some money, and since there wasn't much doing on the ward at night, he could work on *Zoo*. But Kesey got absorbed in the life on the psychiatric ward. The whole system—if they set out to invent the perfect Anti-cure for what ailed the men on this ward, they couldn't have done it better. Keep them cowed and docile. Play on the weakness that drove them nuts in the first place. Stupefy the bastards with tranquilizers and if they still get out of line haul them up to the "shock shop" and punish them. Beautiful—

Sometimes he would go to work high on acid. He could *see into their faces*. Sometimes he wrote, and sometimes he drew pictures of the patients, and as the lines of the ball-point greasy creased into the paper the lines of their faces, he could —the *interiors* of these men came into the lines, the ball-point crevasses, it was the most incredible feeling, the anguish and the pain came right out front and flowed in the crevasses in their faces, and in the ball-point crevasses, the same—*one!*— crevasses now, black starling nostrils, black starling eyes, blind black starling geek cry on every face: "Me! Me! Me! Me! I am —Me!"—he could see clear into them. And—how could you tell anybody about this? they'll say you're a nut yourself—but afterwards, not high on anything, he could *still see into people.*

The novel, *One Flew Over the Cuckoo's Nest*, was about a roustabout named Randle McMurphy. He is a big healthy animal, but he decides to fake insanity in order to get out of a short jail stretch he is serving on a work farm and into what he figures will be the soft life of a state mental hospital. He comes onto the ward with his tight reddish-blond curls tumbling out from under his cap, cracking jokes and trying to get some action going among these deadasses in the loony bin.

They can't resist the guy. They suddenly want to *do* things. The tyrant who runs the place, Big Nurse, hates him for weakening . . . Control, and the System. By and by, many of the men resent him for forcing them to struggle to act like men again. Finally, Big Nurse is driven to play her trump card and finish off McMurphy by having him lobotomized. But this crucifixion inspires an Indian patient, a schizoid called Chief Broom, to rise up and break out of the hospital and go sane: namely, run like hell for open country.

Chief Broom. The very one. From the point of view of craft, Chief Broom was his great inspiration. If he had told the story through McMurphy's eyes, he would have had to end up with the big bruiser delivering a lot of homilies about his down-home theory of mental therapy. Instead, he told the story through the Indian. This way he could present a schizophrenic state the way the schizophrenic himself, Chief Broom, feels it and at the same time report the McMurphy Method more subtly.

Morris Orchids! He wrote several passages of the book under peyote and LSD. He even had someone give him a shock treatment, clandestinely, so he could write a passage in which Chief Broom comes back from "the shock shop." Eating Laredo buds—he would write like mad under the drugs. After he came out of it, he could see that a lot of it was junk. But certain passages—like Chief Broom in his schizophrenic fogs— it was true *vision*, a little of what you could see if you opened the doors of perception, friends . . .

Right after he finished *One Flew Over the Cuckoo's Nest*, Kesey sublet his cottage on Perry Lane and he and Faye went back up to Oregon. This was in June 1961. He spent the summer working in his brother Chuck's creamery in Springfield to accumulate some money. Then he and Faye moved into a little house in Florence, Oregon, about fifty miles west of Springfield, near the ocean, in logging country. Kesey started gathering material for his second novel, *Sometimes a*

Great Notion, which was about a logging family. He took to riding early in the morning and at night in the "crummies." These were pickup trucks that served as buses taking the loggers to and from the camps. At night he would hang around the bars where the loggers went. He was Low Rent enough himself to talk to them. After about four months of that, they headed back to Perry Lane, where he was going to do the writing.

One Flew Over the Cuckoo's Nest was published in February 1962, and it made his literary reputation immediately:

"A smashing achievement"—*Mark Schorer*
"A great new American novelist"—*Jack Kerouac*
"Powerful poetic realism"—*Life*
"An amazing first novel"—*Boston Traveler*
"This is a first novel of special worth"—New York *Herald Tribune*
"His storytelling is so effective, his style so impetuous, his grasp of characters so certain, that the reader is swept along. . . . His is a large, robust talent, and he has written a large, robust book"—*Saturday Review*

And on the Lane—all this was a confirmation of everything they and Kesey had been doing. For one thing there was the old Drug Paranoia—the fear that this wild uncharted drug thing they were into would gradually . . . *rot your brain.* Well, here was the answer. Chief Broom!

And McMurphy . . . but of course. The current fantasy . . . he was a McMurphy figure who was trying to get them to move off their own snug-harbor dead center, out of the plump little game of being ersatz daring and ersatz alive, the middle-class intellectual's game, and move out to . . . Edge City . . . where it was scary, but people were whole people. And if drugs were what unlocked the doors and enabled you to do this thing and realize all this that was in you, then so let it be . . .

KEN KESEY

This draft of the opening scene is no doubt the one referred to when Kesey says he "choked down eight of the little cactus plants" and "wrote the first three pages." A comparison with the final version, however, indicates that Kesey made significant revisions, especially after he had decided upon the novel's point of view.

AN EARLY DRAFT OF THE
OPENING SCENE OF
ONE FLEW OVER THE
CUCKOO'S NEST

I think it way time to let somebody in on it, if they can stand it I can. I think I can. You must read about it in those advances those sheets you get every morning which have what they desire you to know. You got that same part that makes them a dime a sheet. Nothing else. I think it way time one of us tried to tell you and let you see what truely happened.

The basic story is this: one of us is dead, and it don't make much difference which one because you won't even remember and you just read it this morning at the bottom of the last page of that sheet you get. One dead. He dead. A man dead. Died in hospital. Died of Pnemonia. Exhasstion. Recent, once long ago, sometime way back, a Colenel in Europe. Oh yes.

Courtesy of The University of Oregon Library. Reprinted by permission of Ken Kesey.

That you get in you sheet and go right on with you business, runniing a tunge around a coffee cup edge. That much you can digest and puke not back up. But I think it way time somebody, me, told you. I have decided I can stand it if you can.

Let's go back to when he came in.

Let's go back to before he came in, the morning, so you can look around. It's all part of the filthy machinery and combine, anyway.

They out there. Black boys in white suits, up before I am to commit sex acts in the hall and get it mopped up before I can get up to catch them. They are mopping when I come out of the dorm and they all look up at me, eyes out of a vacuum tube. They stick a mop at me and motion which way they figure me to go today, and I go. Behind me I can hear them humming hate and other death; they always hum it out loud around me, not because they hate me special, but because I don't talk and can't tell about it.

The big ward door is a funnel's bottom. We keep it locked so all the backlog won't come pouring in on us and sufficate us like ants in the bottom of an hourglass. When the big nurse comes through she close it quick behind her bacause they're out their pincing at her ass. She locks it with a sigh and swings a load of clanking bottles off her shoulder; she always keep them their in a fresh laundried pillow case and is inclined and grab one out at the tiniest provokation and administer to you right where you stand. For that reason I try to be on the good side of her and let the mop push me back to the wall as she goes by. "Home at last," I hear her say as she drags past and tosses her pillowcase into a corner where it crashes, mixing everything. "What a night, what a night." She wipes her face and eyes like she dipping her hands in cold water. "What a relief to get back home," is what she say near me, because I don't talk.

Then she sight the colored boys. Wheoo, that's something different! She goes into a croach and advances on them where

—

they huddled at the end of the corridor. My god, she gonna tear them black limb from limb! She swole till her back splitting out the white uniform, she let her arms get long enough to wrap around them five six times, like hairy tenticles. I Hide behind the mob and think My god, this time they're gonna tear each other clean apart and leave us alone. But just she starts mashing them and they start ripping at her belly with mop handles all the patients come pouring out of the dorms to check on the hullabaloo and the colored boys fall in line behind the nurse, and smiling, they herd the patients down to shave. I hide in the mop closet and listen to the shriek and grind of shaver as it tears the hide off one then another; I hide there, but after a while one colored boy just opens out his nostrils like the big black ends of two funnells and snuffs me right into his belly. There he hold me wrapped in black guts while two other black bastards in white in white go at my face with one of the murder combines. I scream when they touch my temples. I can control the screaming until they get to the temples and start screwing the electrodes in, then I always scream and the last thing I hear that morning is the big nurse whooping a laughing and scuttling up the hall while she crash patients out of her way with the pillowcase of broken glass and pills. They hold me down while she jams pillowcase and all into my mouth and shoves it down with a mophandle.

KEN KESEY

The correspondence between Kesey and his close friend, Ken Babbs, provides fascinating insights into Kesey's creative process. This letter was written during the early stages of *Cuckoo's Nest's* composition while Kesey was experimenting with peyote and other drugs and working nights at the Menlo Veterans Hospital.

LETTER TO KEN BABBS:
["PEYOTE AND
POINT OF VIEW"]

Babbs.

. . . Nature clings to you. All over me are little bits of leaf, dirt, ants, bugs, crushed moth wings and various bits of other flora and fauna that is taking place generaly unnoticed around us. But suddenly you communicate with the ways of nature and it with you; so it clings to you. I have twigs in my hair and mud between my toes. I can remember the feeling of being three years old. This is one of the good things about it, this return to childhood.

Another thing; it is a desert drug, a warm drug, a thing of the Indians. I had a class one time that tought that the geometric shapes used by the American Indians was their way of standing up to a chaotic world of nature, without order, with-

Courtesy of the University of Oregon Library. Reprinted by permission of Ken Kesey.

out control. They wished to show that they could *control* and did so with shape, with line, with the orderly zig-zag of ten thousand dusty pots in ten thousand dusty museums.

Wrong.

The Indians had Peoti, or something like it first. All these shapes when I close my eyes are indian blanket shapes of intricate geometric perfection. I can work them if I wish, into a scatter of broken colored glass, a stepped-on rainbow, but they swarm back to shape. Hexagons of green and red and neon blue; triangles of magenta and flame orange. This is what the indians saw. And wanted to paint because it was pretty. This is why our natives did not creat like the natives of africa or china, who were belly to belly with a Nature just as chaotic as it was here on the American continent. But our aztecs and Navahos and Mescal Indians had a drug which worked a universal pattern on the inside of their eyeballs, a message from the gods in code, and they painted it. Nothing very highflown. Just a bunch of Indians highoutoftheirminds on a handful of evil-tasting cactus that also happed to be a drug that effected the rods and cones of their eyes.

Enough thinking. This is a drug of the viscera anyway. I would like to screw if I thought I could take the troubel. As it stands, I feel I might become very infatuated with some womans second-from-the-end toe, and never get any further. Such a *fascinating* toesy!

The typewriter is cold to my cheek. The back of the chair is insistant. I received a letter from Malcolm Cowly who says "some of the most brilliant scenes I have ever read" and "passion like I've not run across in you young writers before" and, to sum it all up, no.

So as soon as the baby situation settles I think it might probably that we come ma-maing and da-daing out or down that way, because I've got to see new scenes and get new prospectives; the scene here is so over pouring that to write about it while being in it is somewhat like a drowning man in a hidious maelstrom of broken limbs and shambled lives and mashed egos, being sucked deeper and deeper, into something that he feels (in spite of the way it looks) is truely *good*, being whirled and sucked, and flailed and dashed about with salt water in his nose and ears and nothing solide to brace against other than a passing prow wich splatters the side of his head from time to time—and all the while trying to describe it calmly and objectively. Too much love and too much hurt, all at the same time, constantly—with people who are gigantic in character and goodness that is strange to them and cruelty that is not—and I've got to get away to see it better.

This might be the end of the letter. I don't know. I leave it open and consider the possibility that it might simply be the bottome of the last page.

Much later a cat on 5-c-4 is banging his life away in measured beats against a lath and plaster wall. He has been carrying on this way since I came on at eleven thirty, shaking the whole hospital with the steady drum of his skull. Leave him alone for thirty years and he could bring it all down about us in an avalanche of plaster dust and plumbing.

I laid down at six and tried to sleep, but I was still too high; my mind was overrun with a thumming of moth wings that dusted grey powder in my eyes, with larva hatching, maggots pulsating along, white and translucent as wax in the moonlight, ants storming the turrents of my mind, rattling their antenni and giving off fierce odors of formic acid.

I'll discuss point of view for a time now. I am beginning to agree with Stegner, that it truely is the most important problem in writing. The book I have been doing on the lane is a third person work, but something was lacking; I was not free to impose my perception and bizzare eye on the god-author who is supposed to be viewing the scene, so I tried something that will be extremely difficult to pull off, and, to my knowledge, has never been tried before—the narrator is going to be a character. He will not take part in the action, or ever speak as I, but he will be a character to be influenced by the events that take place, he will have a position and personallity, and a character that is not essentially mine (though it may, by chance, be). Think of this: I, me ken kesey, is stepped back another step and am writing about a third person auther writing about something. Fair makes the mind real, don't it?

I am swinging around to an idea that I objected strongly to at first; that the novelist to be at last true and free must be a diarist. Have you read Trocchi's work for Evergreen, *Cain's Book*? Some of the best prose going. Almost as good as *Naked Lunch*. Both have power and honesty, but lack something I plan to try to add—control. I need to take the spew of the diary mind, study it for a drift, and re-work it to emphisise this drift without giving the prose the appearance of being re-worked.

Near time to end this letter and buff some halls; here are some tag ends: use your I T 290, and I mean use it. Don't worry about it. Get your tape recorder out and ramble into it and send me the ramblings. These things can be keys, no more. Not crutches as I once feared. There is harm in them and guilt in using them and you pay (You never get something for nothing, Mailer says about his prose under pot). This is true, you do pay, in critical judgment, fear and money —but what you get is worth just exactly what you [letter ends].

❖◈❖

KEN KESEY

This letter to Babbs, reprinted here in its entirety, describes the originals of many *Cuckoo's Nest* characters, confirming Kesey's statement that "real people and situations inspired the novel's secondary characters."

LETTER TO KEN BABBS:
["PEOPLE ON THE WARD"]

Babbss:

Can you believe it? Working full time for the first time in two *years!* The depths to which I have sunk are undescernable.

Right now—or from 7:30 to 4—we are completing the four weeks of training at the hospital, with discarded texts and disregarded nurses. The first two weeks were spent on what is called the circle wards, or the *better* wards, wards where the men have enough marbles left to choose up sides and play the game, but these last two weeks we are being subjected to the vegetables, the geriatrics, the organs eating and organs shitting and pissing and moaning and coming on in religious tongues, creatures of demands that needs spooned puree and pablum, infants growing backwards, away from civilization and rationalization, back to complete dependence, to darkness, the womb, the seed. . . .

Courtesy of the University of Oregon Library. Reprinted by permission of Ken Kesey.

Around the day room. All twisted out of shape by so many years. Ellis: with whatever it was that frightened him absolutely *out* of his mind, standing right before his aghast eyes, still gaping, horrified, outraged and farting in his fear. Bewick: his face showing only a gnawed dissatisfaction, gnawed so deeply that he is finally and forever even dissatisfied with that, and only whimpers tearlessly. Pete: grinning, shaking his happy old head, limping spryly about in his pajamas, answering only one question; —"Why'd you quit driving the truck, Pete?" "I was *ty-urd*. Fo' twenny eight years, then I got *ty-urd*."

Like old Buckly, who asserts, or answers when asked: "We had some fun, didn't we? Sure, we gone have lots of fun."

Or old Chartes, whose trigger-question is "How is you're wife?" and whose screamed anser is *"F-f-f-uh thuh wife! F-f-f-k theu wife!"*

You get to know them by their bits.

Maternick is tidy, is his bit. No one can touch him. He won't touch an object another has touched. He strips if a towel touches him. He rubbed the hide off the end of his nose after running it up against a patient who had stopped to quickly. He is tall, stooped, eyes lost under a cliff of a brow, rubbing his hands forever together, looks like an old time wrestler I saw once called the "Swedish Angel." And he coughs violently whenever he smokes his daily alloted cigarette—"The smoke . . . *dirty!*" But beggs continually for cigarettes.

You know Kramer because he carries his hand tight over his appendex, ready for a quick draw. And has a mean left hook for a feeble octogenarian. You know Camino because he figures he'll eat anything that don't eat him first. You know Moses because it takes two men to shower him and four men to dress him and when you grasp his arm it is like a metal bedstead. You know Libby because every thirty seconds, with clocklike regularity, he is struck by some hilarious incident out of his seventy year potluck past, and he roars with toothless laughter. Bechi you know before you see him, for the atrocity photographs brought back from the boneyards of Buechenwald, Aushwatze, a skeleton dipped in yellow wax . . .

Some you don't know by name, only by the number of times you have to shuck down their pajamas and swab out their mustard-colored crotches, (why does the butt deteriorate so with years? become flaps, folds?) or by the length of his rootlike cock as you tape on a cathiter tube. You know them by the empty eyes, like the eyes are holes spiked in the shell and all you can see inside are the delapidated organs, grinding through their organ duties out of loyalty? instinct? habit? You know them by the fingernails you clip, the skulls you oil, the noses you blow. No names; smells, cheesy skins, crudded eyes, cheekbones like shoulder blades, differnt chairs where different assimilations of these attributes sit. You could mix them up—put a long cock on where a short one was, a tight, bald scalp over a head of white thread hair—and probably never notice the difference.

Some you find are quite diffinately people and you can talk to them. Some have been fashioned into more-than-human genuses of time and age. One is Papa George.

Papa is old, but he is in no way senile or physically impaired. He sits alone in a padded chair with his arms wrapped about his drawn up knees, and looks at the scene around him with glum disgust. His hair is white and his nose and chin are growing closer together now that the fence of teeth have disappeared, and his eyes are as pale and blue as watered milk. He seldom moves or shouts or demands attention, and when you ask him a question you can see he damn well understands it. His answer, however, is another matter.

The glumness fades and his eyes are no longer pale; he twinkles with a mischief so innocent you expect him to gurgle like a baby. Instead he begins a low, intoned song that is tuned to a thousand half-recalled hymns from long past Sundays.

The words are being improvised as he goes along; they always rhyme:

> I sang because I'm happy,
> Because I'm full of love,
> Because I saw the Jesus Christ
> Jack-off in a tub.
> And I shit upon the mule's back
> And my piss came dribbling down
> And both of us farted together
> With a godalmighty sound . . .

. . . on and on as long as you sit and listen, until he finally busts up with laughter that is not at himself, or at the song, but at the man fool enough to sit there and listen to such drivvel.

They call Papa George a Schizophrenic and lock him up because who knows what eager, pink, ten-year old ear might sometimes fall prey to one of his devistating ditties?

Another of Time's creations is Mellanson. He is my favorite, and I would spend the day with him if I could get away with it. He is tall, bony with bones that you know were once straight and useful. He sits in his wheelchair at attention, with his hands on the balls of his calcified knees. His face is brown as a saddle and his hair is full and the color of a bay horse. Under his black brows his eyes have appearence of calm authority, kindness that is kind because it is right. The palms of his hands are a tome of wrinkles, and holding them before him he reads them like the scriptures.

"Now you, you are to go to Washington, down to Congress," he says with patient authority. He explains it softly so you can preform your duty with the least amount of trouble. "You will go first into San Francisco, with . . . with Bob Beer and Giant Logan . . . and all three of you are to go to Van Ness street and catch a bus to Washington. Now . . . you will all pay the bus driver two dollars and when you get to Washington you will get out and go to Congress. Now . . . you will get your orders there. I don't know what they will be, but I think you will go to New York. Bob and Giant Logan will go on to Fort Riley."

He pauses to wait for questions. Do we understand, me and the two ghosts beside me? Then he goes on, dispatching personal all over the world, giving calm, patient orders that he is certain will be carried out because somewhere in his grab-bag memory he knows they already have been carried out, by Bob or Giant or some other shadowy attache, in some other year.

Sometimes he is kind enough to take time away from his duties to explain to us about how things are; there is not a hint of egotism in his knowledge, he explains merely because he *knows* and he feels I would like to know also, and he likes me well enough to take the trouble.

"Now . . ." he starts, reading from one scriptured palm with a long, sensitive finger, ". . . the Flag is England. The stars are the people. The stripes are . . . a watermellon." (You can see the associations when they click into place, and they are *right*) "And the watermelon is America. The peach, the plum, the pear are all also America. The brown nut is Mexico. The strawberry is America. The pecan is Mexico."

This information is all written there in that palm.

At times the information is poetic: "Florida is where the sunshine goes for the winter." At times, ironic: "The Clown . . . is America. The Clown is . . . the plum, the diaper, the telephone, the automobile. The Clown is . . . the people."

His voice is without intentional drama, but it is deep, sonorous and specific—like Sandburg's voice.

Sometimes his words sketch out bits of his past: "Nineteen and . . . twenty. They put them all on boxcars. The bastards were down from Washington. They ordered it. Haveler Kennicut and . . . Grant Smith loaded them. The bastards watched. They put them on the boxcars and took them all to Fort Riley. Some were shot. They took the others to Fort Riley."

His hands manipulate the reins, undo the cinch, lift the saddle from the last of the United States Cavalry.

Only one time did he look at me and see the white suit I was wearing. He was scribbling names, dates, numbers on a little scrap of paper and I had been watching over his shoulder. He looked at me, then indicated the wardful of patients with his pencil. "These must be the people in my world now," he confided. He showed me the paper. "These are the notes I take on my life."

Kesey

McMurphy frowned at me a minute, then asked. "Yeah? She got bigger...
How big?"

"Bigger'n pappy an' me together."

"Just took to growin', huh? How come her to swell up that way. I
never heard of a Indian woman doing somethin' like that..."

"She ~~was a Mexican woman~~" *wasn't Indian She was from The Dalles, a town woman.*

Yeah... sure,

"And her name was what? Sanchez?" ~~And when a Mex~~ *town woman* marries an Indian
somebody the whites that's marryin', ~~beneath~~ her, ~~don't~~ *aint* it? So...If ~~I got it right...she made~~ *Yeah, I think I see.*
~~you daddy get littler because, well, on account of he was an Indian and~~
~~she was a Mexican?"~~

I nodded, then told him,

"Because she was a woman, too. But it wasn't just her. Everybody
worked on him."

"Why?"

"Because he was too big. He...wouldn't give in. And everybody worked
on him, just the way they're working on you. They can't have somebody ~~that~~
big runnin' round...unless he's one of them. You can see that."

"Yeah, I reckon I can."

should'a & "That's why you ~~gotta~~ quit lettin' 'em see ~~you~~ ~~be~~ big. ~~if they see~~ *that you're they thought*
for a while you was little . Then you showed 'em you was big and
~~it they'll bust you"~~ *now they got to bust you."*

"Like ~~bustin~~ bustin' a mustang, huh?"

"No. *or listen,* They don't bust you that way; they work on you ways you can't
fight! They put things in! They install things. They start as quick as
they see you're gonna be ~~g~~ big and go to fixin' you to where you can't
work right! ~~If~~ If you're too big you might turn out to be dangerous,
a Communist, or a fiend, or a ~~mani-fighter!~~ *gangster!* So they start installing
their filthy machinery when you're little, *and keep on and on* till your fixed...!"

These two pages from the first draft show the extensive revisions Kesey
made. Compare pp. 208f in the text. The handwritten page, beginning
with 1, is actually the verso of the page noted as 195. (Courtesy of the
University of Oregon Library. Reprinted by permission of Ken Kesey.)

① "Who's they?"

"The Combine. It worked on him for years. He was big enough to fight it for a while. He fought it in the village and he fought the ~~whole~~ part of it that drove out from town to make us live in inspected houses, and he fought the part that wanted the dam and the money and ~~wanted to beat him up in the alleys.~~
He fought it a long time till my mother made him to little."

Mr. Murphy looked at me a while, ~~thinking~~ by raining over what I'd told him. Then he asked, "Why did somebody want to beat him up in the village?" and I told him that they wanted to beat him into giving up, even some of our people, they were in on it. They tried to beat him up.

"Because— let me see— they wanted your old man to give in about something?"

"That's what they said. They wanted him to sell the rights to the falls." ~~to~~

"You're talking about the Columbia falls where the Indians used to spear salmon. Yeah, I remember something about that. The land made it all a lake."

"He gave up."

"~~They~~ got paid good, did ~~they~~ you? I remember it was something like—"

"What can you say for the way somebody lives? They stood in the fire when he ~~told them~~ and looked at him and they were all holding those checks and they wanted him to give them something else. They didn't know where to go. They wanted him to tell them but he was too little. And he was too drunk, too. The Combine had beat him. It always does. It'll beat you, too.

347

KEN KESEY

AN IMPOLITE INTERVIEW
WITH KEN KESEY

Q. Okay. Let's start off with a simple one. How would you distinguish between freedom and insanity?

A. True freedom and sanity spring from the same spiritual well, already mixed, just add incentive. Insanity, on the other hand, is dependent on *material* fad and fashion, and the weave of one's prison is of that material. "But I didn't weave it," I hear you protest. "My parents, their parents, *generations* before me wove it!"

Could be, but when you're a prisoner, the task is not to shout epithets at the warden, but to *get out*. . . .

Q. It's no accident that the initials of your protagonist in One Flew Over the Cuckoo's Nest *are R.P.M.—Revolutions Per Minute—and that you don't take that word lightly, but where is your vision of revolution in relation to both Ho Chi Minh and Charles Reich?*

A. Chuck and Ho? Naturally I can't hope to under the circumstances with reference to each of their personal visions huh?

This interview was first published in *The Realist*, number 90, May–June, 1971, and appears in full in *Kesey's Garage Sale*. It is reprinted by permission of The Viking Press and Ken Kesey.

Q. I'm talking about the spectrum from Chuckie's bell-bottoms to Ho's anti-aircraft.

A. Ah. I see. Well, I think that either sticking a leg in a pair of bell-bottoms or loading a canister into an anti-aircraft weapon may or may not be a revolutionary act. This is only known at the center of the man doing the act. And *there* is where the revolution must lie, at the *seat of the act's impetus,* so that finally every action, every thought and prayer, springs from this committed center.

Q. You've said, regarding the media, that if you follow the wires, they all lead to the Bank of America. Would you expand on that?

A. When you've had a lot of microphones poked at you with questions like—"Mr. Kesey, would you let your daughter take acid with a black man?" "Mr. Kesey, do you advocate the underwear of the Lennon Sisters?" "Mr. Kesey, how do you react to the findings of the FAD indicating that patoolee oil causes cortizone damage?"—you get so you can follow the wires back to their two possible sources. Perhaps one wire out of a thousand leads to one of the sources, to the heart of the man holding the microphone, while the other nine hundred and ninety-nine go through a bramble of ambition, ego, manipulation and desire, sparking and hissing and finally joining into one great coaxial cable that leads out of this snarl and plugs straight into the Bank of America. . . .

This is the story of Freddy Schrimpler:

As part of his training, a psychiatric aide must spend at least two weeks working the geriatric wards, or "shit pits" as they were called by the other aides. These wards are concrete barns built, not for attempted cures or even for attempted treatments of the herds of terminal humanity that would otherwise be roaming the streets, pissing and drooling and disgusting the healthy citizenry, but for nothing more than shelter and sustenance, waiting rooms where old guys spend ten, twenty, sometimes thirty years waiting for their particular opening in the earth. At eight in the morning they are herded and wheeled into showers, then to Day Rooms where they are fed a tooth-less goo, then are plunked into sofas ripe with decades of daily malfunctions of worn-out sphincters, then fed again, and washed again, and their temperatures taken if they're still warm enough to register, and their impacted bowels dug free in the case of sphincters worn-out in the other direction, and their hair and cheesy old fingernails clipped (the clippings swept into a little pink and grey pile), and fed again and washed again, and then usually left alone through the long afternoons.

Some of these derelicts still have a lot going and enjoy trap-ping flies and other such morsels in the snare of their baited hands, and some engage in contented and garrulous conversa-tions with practically anything, and some watch TV, but most of them lie motionless on the plastic covered sofas or in gurney beds, little cots of barely-breathing bones and skin under the government sheets. Even the doctors call them vegetables.

In caring for these men something becomes immediately obvious to all the young aides undergoing their first real brush with responsibility. The thought is very explicit. After the first meal squeezed into a slack mouth, or after the first diaper change or catheter taping, every one of the trainees have thought this thought, and some have spoken it:

"Without our help these guys would *die!*"

And, after the hundredth feeding and diapering and chang-ing, the *next* thought, though never spoken, is: "Why don't we just *let* them die?"

An awful question to find in your head, because even young aides know that age can happen to anyone. "This could I someday be!" But even fear of one's own future can't stop the asking: Why *don't* we just let them die? What's wrong with letting nature take its own corpse? Why do humans feel they have the right to forestall the inevitable fate of others? Freddy Schrimpler helped me find my answer:

Freddy was seventy or eighty years old and had been on the Geriatrics Ward for close to twenty years. From morning until bedtime he lay in the dayroom in a gurney bed against the wall, on his side under a sheet, his little head covered with a faint silver gossamer that seemed too delicate to be human hair—it looked more like a fungus mycilium joining the head to the pillow—and his mouth drooling a continual puddle at his cheek. Only his eyes moved, pale and bright blue they followed the activity in the ward like little caged birds. The only sound he made was a muffled squeaking back in his throat when he had dirtied his sheets and, since his bowels were usually impacted, like most of the inmates who couldn't move, this sound was made but rarely and even then seemed to exhaust him for hours.

One afternoon, as I made my rounds to probe with rectal thermometer at the folds of wasted glutinus maximus of these gurney bed specimens—hospital policy made it clear that the temperature of anything breathing, even vegetables, had to be logged once a month—I heard this stifled squeak. I looked up; it was Freddy's squeak but since it was his temperature I was attempting to locate I knew that he hadn't shit his sheets. I resumed my probing, somewhat timidly, for the flesh of these men is without strength and a probe in the wrong direction can puncture an intestine. The squeak came again, slower, and sounding remarkably like speech! I moved closer to the pink and toothless mouth, feeling his breath at my ear.

"Makes you . . . Kinda nervous . . . don't it?" he squeaked. The voice was terribly strained and faltering, but even through the distortion you could clearly make out the unmistakable tone of intelligence and awareness and, most astonishingly, humor.

In the days that followed I brought my ear to that mouth as often as the nurses let me get away with it. He told me his story. A stroke years ago had suddenly clipped all the wires leading from the brain to the body. He found that while he could hear and see perfectly, he couldn't send anything back out to the visitors that dropped by his hospital bed more and more infrequently. Finally they sent him to the VA, to this

ward where, after years of effort, he had learned to make his
little squeak. Sure, the doctors and nurses knew he could talk,
but they were too busy to shoot the breeze and didn't really
think he should exhaust himself by speaking. So he was left on
his gurney to drift alone in his rudderless vessel with his short-
wave unable to send. He wasn't crazy; in fact the only difference that I could see between Freddy and Buddha was in the
incline of their lotus position. As I got to know him I spoke of
the young aides' thought.

"Let a man die for his own good?" he squeaked, incredulous.
"Never believe it. When a man . . . when anything . . . is ready
to stop living . . . it stops. You watch . . ."

Before I left the ward, two of the vegetables died. They
stopped eating and died, as though a decision of the whole
being was reached and nothing man or medicine could do
would turn this decision. As though the decision was cellularly
unanimous (I remember a friend telling me about her
attempted suicide; she lay down and placed a rag soaked in
carbon tetrachloride over her face. But just before she went
out completely there was a sudden clamor from all the rest of
her: "Hey! Wait! What about us? Why weren't we consulted!?" And being a democratic girl at heart she rallied over
mind's presumptuous choice. "Our mind has no right to kill our
body," she told me after the attempt. "Not on the grounds of
boredom, anyway . . .") and met with the satisfaction of all
concerned. . . .

Q. *Jack Kerouac once stated his philosophy as: "I don't
know, I don't care, and it doesn't make any difference." And
yet his widow said he died a lonely man. Was he deceiving
himself, or what?*

A. I feel bad about Kerouac. He was a prophet and we let
him die from us. He *did* know, and he *did* care, and the letters
of praise that I composed in my head to him *would have* made
a difference had I, and all the others who felt the same respect,
mailed them. Sometimes polemics and fashion get so thick that
we can't make out a clear call for help from a friend.

Q. You've referred to Neal Cassady as one of the hippest people you've ever known, and yet if it's true that he died while walking along the railroad tracks counting the ties—and his last words were "Sixty-four thousand, nine hundred twenty-eight"—it seems more compulsive than hip?

A. Long before his death Cassady has passed that point where being hip or compulsive had any relative meaning to him. His was the yoga of a man driven to the cliffedge by the grassfire of an entire nation's burning material madness. Rather than be consumed by this burn he jumped, choosing to sort things out in the fast-flying but smogfree moments of a life with no retreat. In this commitment he placed himself irrevocably beyond category. Once, when asked why he wouldn't at least *try* to be cool, he said: "Me trying to be cool would be like James Joyce trying to write like Herb Gold."

Q. How did Cassady respond the time you told him you feared you were losing your sense of humor?

A. With great concern and sympathy, as though I had told him that I had cancer of the lymphthf.

Q. How did you regain it?

A. The lymphthf? It came back of its own, after I dropped a five gallon jar of mayonnaise on my foot.

Q. No, I mean how did you regain your sense of humor?

A. Oh, that. I never did, I guess. Rehabilitation, as my counselor up at the Sheriff's Honor Camp used to tell me, is a two way street. . . .

Q. Your favorite metaphor seems to be that the human race is involved in some sort of drama. But since there's no script, do you have any predictions as to developments in the plot?

A. The Good Guys will win. The consciousness now being forged will hang, tempered and true, in the utility closet alongside old and faithful tools like Mercy and Equality and Will Rogers. The accolades will be tremendous. Even Hitler, going through the gates only a few steps in front of Old Scratch himself, will get a terrific hand. And finally, God willing, the mortgage on this wad of woe will be fully paid off. . . .

Q. *Would you care to elaborate a little on the relationship between dope and faith?*

A. Or, what to do with your hands when the fuses blow. Sometimes we have to take steps to keep our right hand from knowing what our left hand is doing—break up their alliance and turn your palms allward and wait for the spark of creation!—and other times we need to fold our fingers in prayer. So I hereby recommend, if you feel ready to turn palms allward and spread your arms and a-gallivanting go, I recommend LSD-25 and/or psyloscibin if you can be sure it's good stuff (Where do you get this good stuff? Beats me; I don't have any. The first and best I ever got came to me by the very reliable way of the Federal Government. They gave me mine—paid me and quite a few other rats both white and black twenty dollars a session in fact to test it for them, *started it* so to speak, then, when they caught a glimpse of what was coming down in that little room full of guinea pigs, they snatched the guinea pigs out, slammed the door, locked it, barred it, dug a ditch around it, set two guards in front of it, and gave the hapless pigs a good talking to and warned them—on threat of worse than death—to *never* go in that door again—and if you still think they should give you yours after careful examination of the rot-minded, chromosome damaged results of these little experiments begun ten years ago [check the records of Dr. Leo Hollister from early '60s file of Menlo Park and Palo Alto V.A. hospital], then I think you should demand they either give you yours or award all those poor guinea pigs the Purple Heart, the Distinguished Service Cross, and full disability benefits for them and all their offspring as well. . . .) And for the times when you've had enough spoils and gallivanting, and you're weary and blistered with the wind, I recommend let the hands join (after a little tequila, or far better, a *Dilatin*) and close your eyes and focus both the *right side of you* and the *left side of you* on the ONE BEYOND YOU . . . then drink some tea and smoke a joint and throw the *Ching* and get to work or whatever you let go to weed during your gallivant and *don't hang out,* every inch of hanging out you do past the point of knowing what needs to be done becomes more a drag, a drain, and an amalgamated lie. *Too much hanging out without a doubt will warp your spine and turn off half your mind,* the memory half, which gets tired of supplying the speech half with information squandered in rap fest *bons mots* and says, "Fuck it; if that's all he's doing with his mouth I think I'll go to sleep."

Then, after a week or so of this—"cleaning up," Cassady called it—spread those hands again and open a place for something to happen. I know of no other way to Faith; it can't be bought; it can't be learned; and it can't be muscled in. Faith doesn't come from security. It comes from survival. . . .

Q. What do you think our kids are going to do that will shock and dismay us as much as the things we've been doing have shocked and dismayed our parents?

A. Nothing. Ever. If our efforts have been sincere. Are Grape Nuts as hard to chew as they were when you were a kid?

Q. Oh, is THAT what you were supposed to do with them? . . . But how come you wouldn't let your kids read Zap Comics?

A. Once, on our way to film *Atlantis Rising,* we were encamped at Ed McClanahan's amid a mighty passle of kids: my kids, Babbs' kids, Ed's kids, Chuck's kids . . . and as they played in the backyard us grown folks rested ourselves on the back porch and smoked, drank, shot the shit, and read of the new crop of *Zap* and Zap style comics that Ed had brought from his office. Fierce stuff, gory and righteously disturbing stuff, the only stuff I'd seen with any of the real raw excitement that you feel from when art is in there dealing with the issues, since I'd first come across Rob Boise's work of statues screwing. Fascinating stuff . . .

Because, in some of the comics of that period particularly, along with the art, there was often something else in the works of even geniuses like Crumb and Wilson and Shelton, speed-trip-like digressions where you could see the artists working to exercise their own personal demons by, however unintentionally, casting them into whatever swine happened to be succeptible, which wasn't us grown folks because we were either full up with our own demons or had the defense built up by our own exorcising, so we were safe. I wasn't so sure about the kids.

It's like this: I've got nothing against my kids watching a couple make love but having them watch a flagellant is something different. But that doesn't explain it either. I've got it: it's the *consciousness the artist is communicating* that I'm concerned with; not the activity the art is depicting. I've always brought city stuff back from the city for my kids, *Zap* included (so I actually *do* let them read *Zap*; as a matter of fact, I can't recall any of the *Zaps* that I ever withheld; it was mostly the *Zap* spinoffs), some stuff even to read aloud to them because it was so fine you know that the consciousness producing it must have been unimpeachable, *whatever* the subject matter or how luridly it was dealt with, stuff like Lenore Goldberg, and Captain Pissgums, and Fritz the Cat and Mr. Natural and Wonder Warthog and, Lord, *most* of the ones that everybody reads—but I now read them through first to try to plumb the *consciousness* serving as the impetus, and some I withhold.

I mean, W. C. Fields was a great artist but would we ask him to babysit when he was working off a bad hangover? . . .

Q. *There was a student rebel poster during the 1968 uprising in France that said: "Psychology aims at the systematic subordination of individual behavior to false social norms"— do you see any change in terms of encounter groups and psychodrama?*

A. Once, at Esalen, I happened in on the end of a week's dance therapy. There were the graduates, all aglow with a week's total encounter and breakthrough, recapping their recent victories. Fritz Perls was there too. "Vait!" he said. . . .

"Vait!" Fritz protested. "Vhere are you the *rest* of the veeks?"

"Vwat—I mean *what* do you mean?" asked the dance therapist, cautiously.

"He means," I interjected helpfully, "what does Superman do between phone booths?"

"I mean," Fritz answered for himself, "you are dividing your lives between *this veek* . . . and *all other veeks!*"

Which means to me that the idea of "sessions" may insure failure of psychology aims, that to avoid a schizophrenic dichotomy we must either (1) let psychodrama push back the rest of our lives, or (2) let the rest of our lives push back the psychodrama, or (3) live the drama without benefit of Alfred Hitchcock.

I mean, I heard the fatality report for the weekend in Lane County: A girl was killed when her horse fell on her. A guy crashed in his single engine plane. A guy drowned waterskiing. A mountain climber killed falling down a mountain. It's when you take a break that you stumble, and psychodrama is a vacation, a luxury. Look at the cars driven by the participants, at the houses they live in. Could Bobby Seale afford psychodrama? Does he need it? Does he even have *room* for it? . . .

But, I'll tell you, Paul, these are hard questions. I don't like the sound of me answering too-hard questions. I sound oracular, like I know more than I do. My words have a disproportionate weight. Like, I got a long letter from a Ph.D. in biology about the article in the *Last Supplement* on cancer, and another about the article on immunization, asking essentially: Are we certain we have looked into such things as cancer and smallpox vaccination enough to allow statements about things as important as some old lady who might go for the Leitrile cure instead of going to a doctor, or some kid's future with smallpox? No! We are not qualified! This isn't to say that we couldn't be if we put our full energies into these areas and stopped trying to live like rock stars, but right now, no, I'm not qualified. No more than I'm qualified to make judgments regarding other people's karmic state or depth of their revolutionary commitment. But I'm easy; some kid with big eyes and a notepad could come up and ask me how the universe was created and if he looks like he thinks I know pretty soon *I* think I know and I'm running it down to him like the gospel. I'm easy but in *no fucking way qualified*!

KEN KESEY

"KEN KESEY WAS A
SUCCESSFUL DOPE FIEND"

KESEY: Neal Cassady one time, he was driving in down-town
Santa Cruz, he was just so wired, he made a U-turn in front of a
bookstore. See, you're doing a thing like *Have you quit beating
your wife . . . answer yes or no.* So this cop stops him, comes up
and says, what are you high on? And Cassady says, *Obitrol,
officer, obitrol.* And the cop says, Alright, get out. So Cassady
got out, and he starts to search Cassady, and Cassady reaches
into his pockets and both pockets were full of pills. He
grabbed the pills in his hands in the bottom of his pockets, and
pulled them out, and the change spread everywhere, and he
shoved the pills back in there, and began to pick up the change
and run around. Until finally he just kind of faded away.
There's no sense in going against it. It's a look in your eyes
and a tone in your voice, man. The revolution is getting away
from that. It's getting so that whenever you go up to anybody
what comes off with you is a good feeling, so that there's nothing for them to poke against.

ARGUS: *Do you think policemen and Richard Nixon and the
rich people who run the country relate to that?*

This interview was published in The Whole Earth Catalogue and
appears in full in Kesey's Garage Sale. It is reprinted by permission of The
Viking Press, Ken Kesey and Stewart Brand.

KESEY: They're people, man, and as soon as you draw the line and say they aren't people, then you . . .

ARGUS: *Who's drawing the line? Who's putting people in jail? Who's killing people in the streets?*

KESEY: What difference does it make?

ARGUS: *You don't make any distinction between oppressor and oppressed?*

KESEY: You're talking about *shoulds,* and you're talking about where things ought to be, instead of where we are as where we got to work from. It's where we are.

ARGUS: *Don't you have any vision?*

KESEY: You ask me if I've got any vision. I've got three kids. I mean I'm invested in this world. I prune my trees even though I'm not going to have fruit for two years in a row. Because I'm doing all I can to try to build a better world. All the time . . .

ARGUS: *I can dig it, but the thing that means . . .*

KESEY: The thing that you want is something that you're going to have to go find somebody else to get it from, because I can't give it to you.

ARGUS: *I ain't asking for it from you, I'm asking . . .*

KESEY: You're damn near demanding it.

ARGUS: *I'm demanding answers, because I think you have information and I think people can relate to that. And I think that personal liberation is fine, but it has to be related to liberating everybody on the planet.*

KESEY: No, listen, what this country needs is sanity. Individual sanity, and all the rest will come true.

ARGUS: *Bullshit.*

KESEY: You can't do it any other way. You work from the heart out, you don't work from the issue down.

ARGUS: *You don't think it's a heartfelt thing, making a revolution. You don't think that means anything?*

KESEY: Not when it tightens your stomach like that.

ARGUS: *I can dig that we shouldn't have tight stomachs, man, but who's giving us a tight stomach?*

KESEY: I had to spend six months in jail, taking all the stuff that you're talking about, firsthand, over and over, until you realize that what they want you to do is what you're doing. You're going for the fried ice cream, as they call it. And as long as that action is taking place, as long as you take the gauntlet, you'll have somebody to slap you.

ARGUS: *To make an analogy, John Sinclair, when he started out in 1964, was all peace and love, good vibes, one of the first hippies in Detroit. He didn't want to slap anybody down.*

KESEY: Cassady served eighteen months for two joints. He never mentioned it. There was no bitterness. There was no complaint about it at all. It was unjust and everybody knew that and accepted that and just worked from there. . . .

ARGUS: *There should be something you have to say to everybody in our culture that wants to try to relate to you.*

KESEY: There was a wise man who lived up in the mountains and all these people wanted him to drop into the mosque and give them the word on Sunday, so he said all right. He showed up on Sunday and there was this huge crowd of people and he got up there and he says, *Good people, do you know what I'm going to talk to you about?*, and they all shouted back No and he says *Ignorant People,* and he turns around and he leaves. And so they go back up and say *Wait a minute, man, you came through too fast for us, drop in again next Sunday* . . . and he says all right. So next Sunday he's down there and he starts, *Good people, do you know what I'm going to talk to you about?* and this time they're ready for him and they all yell *Yes* and he says *Good!* and he turns around and he leaves. And so finally they say, *Look, man, just one more time, cause somehow it's slipping past us.* So he comes down the third time and starts up there, *Good people,* and this time they're ready for him . . . *Some of us do and some of us don't. Good! Let those who do communicate their knowledge with those who do not.*

ARGUS: *Well, let's do that. Communicate your knowledge with those who do not.*

KESEY: I just did it. It's true, man, it's all I've got, I mean, I know more about my brother's creamery than I do about the revolution. You can't expect me to know stuff about . . . I don't know that stuff.

I live out there in a tiny little town. My wife goes to school twice a week. She's a librarian. We have a team of Springfield Creamery Jugs. It started out and it was the laughingstock of the basketball league because there's all these long-haired freaks and spades with Afro cuts who were getting called by the ref. And when the ref calls, too much of his fascism shows for him to be comfortable about it. He points the finger and then realizes he's held his finger out there too long and all the spades see it and everybody sees it and as soon as they go against him and play against him, they get their good game . . . but as soon as they get ahead they fold: *Resist not evil.* As soon as you resist evil, as soon as it's gone, you fold, because it's what you're based on. Finally, the spades realized that the ref wasn't just calling the fouls on them but on the whole team, on the whole idea of the team, on the way we moved. Every time we'd get out there and play these guys who were against us, we played against them in their own style of game, you know . . . it has to do with the way a person stands and the way he moves . . . instead of just bopping out there in the field, on the court . . . as soon as that movement took place out there in the court we'd win; but when we got angry, and got against them, they were better at it than we were.

The guys that you're opposing in this revolution thing, it's not a revolution, it's ancient.

ARGUS: *If you resent it, and you think it limits you so much, why did you let Tom Wolfe write the book* [The Electric Kool-Aid Acid Test]? *Did that inhibit you at all, because obviously that turned on millions of other people who otherwise wouldn't have heard about it.*

KESEY: I'll tell you a little story. Wolfe was there and this was towards the end of the time he was hanging around. We were up at my brother's farm, Space-Heater House, and we were moving this statue up onto the wall, and he had painted it with pigment, he hadn't used the right stuff, so the paint had never dried. Tom Wolfe was out there, and he had his notepad, and me and Ramrod were trying to move this thing up on the wall, and obviously we needed help. And there was only the three of us, and Tom Wolfe was out there, and he was dressed the way he always dresses, in his blue suit, and we finally said, *Goddammit, Tom, give us a hand.* So he put his notepad down, and he went to put it up there, and he got this swatch of red paint on the side of his coat, of oil pigment. We stood there, in this moment of realization, and I told him, *you just can't expect to fool with it without getting it on you.* And that's the last time I ever saw Tom Wolfe. But I love him.

III

Literary Criticism

✿◇

JACK F. McCOMB

Jack F. McComb, a captain in the United States Air Force, has
been a combat pilot and jet fighter instructor. This parody was
written while he was a student at the United States Air Force
Academy.

THE RPM

OLD TESTICLE

THE BOOK OF GENITALS

Chapter I

1. In the beginning Mac was the heaven and the asylum and
all that was.

2. Mac was the form and the essence; He created and created
and procreated. Everything came from Mac and was Mac.

3. In His creation He made Chief Bromden and from him the
house known as Chronic. Bromden begat Ellis and Ellis begat
Col. Matterson and Matterson begat Ruckly and Old Pete.
From the son of Pete came all the Wheelers and Walkers and
Vegetables.

4. Mac saw no color except black and white and created
another house.

5. This was the house of Acute. Harding, the father, begat
Bibbit and Cheswick. Bibbit begat Martini, etc.

By permission of Jack F. McComb.

Chapter II

1. Mac reigned over all except the Combine. The Combine was the Big Nurse and all her niggers and machines and arch-niggers and arch-machines in the bowels of the asylum and everywhere.

2. The asylum was because Mac was not paying attention. Time passed with fear and hatred; no love was to be found.

3. The Big Nurse perpetrated and mechanized and cast fear on Acutes and Chronics alike.

4. The houses of Mac existed in nothingness under the wrath of the Combine.

THE BOOK OF PERVERTS

Chapter I

1. In the reign of the Combine, Taber the soothsayer, brought the word of the coming of Mac, and he was screwed.

2. Later, an old cretin called Pete of the Railroad told of the wonder of Mac and how the Combine operated. The strain was too much for the live miscarriage and he fizzled and was tired.

NEW TESTICLES

EPISTLES OF ST. KESEY

THE COMING

Chapter I

1. Mac was a product of passion, copulation, and bawdiness. He lived in the town of Everywhere, South of the Columbia.

2. The infant Mac got Himself laid and learned to love and flew His yellow banner high.

3. There is a time for laying and a time for loving, a time for fighting and a time for conning. Mac picked the wrong time and got Himself thrown in the cooler.

4. Fighting some more, He was committed. Mac, being human, could not send a son to earth and also, being human, couldn't see evil until He stepped in it.

Chapter II

1. And all the asylum was without happiness and all was fear and order. No laughter or love was to be found.

2. The Spirit of Mac moved into the scene. Mac said, "Let there be love and laughter," and the Big Nurse said, "NO."

3. Mac saw the lack and was sorely pissed.

EPISTLES OF ST. BROMDEN

THE GOING

Chapter I

1. All the asylum except the Big Nurse rejoiced at the new Admission. Mac gave hope where no hope existed.

2. Mac was a hero. He bucked the Nurse and the Combine. He was strong and bull-headed and innocent.

Chapter II

1. Mac wanted to get out and started looking out for ole number one and hope left the asylum. St. Cheswick died of despair.

2. Mac journeyed to the X-ray clinic and talked with the inmates. His questions astounded them with His common sense. He learned of the common despair and the inner fear. Mac learned the ropes.

3. Mac re-enlisted and smashed His hand through a plate glass window.

Chapter III

1. Hope returned and Mac continued to buck the Big Nurse, who was biding her time, which she had and Mac didn't.

2. Things were rosy, so Mac, knowing His lack of time,

gathered up Twelve of His buddies and headed for the sea to fish.

3. On the way, Mac had to con the gas station money-grubbers. They used fear and shame to sell their wares. Mac conjured up a big lie and beat them about the head and shoulders with it.

4. On the ocean, they drank and loved and learned to laugh.

Chapter IV

1. When the crew returned, the Big Nurse said they had the crabs and decreed that a sanitation program be instituted to persecute them.

2. The arch-nigger Williams scared one of Mac's children and He and Chief Bromden cleaned the devils good.

Chapter V

1. Mac was faced with giving up or suffering and he went to the electrodes and suffered for his kindness.

2. Bromden and Mac were given EST, Bromden once and Mac many times.

3. Mac triumphed and the Big Nurse retreated.

THE GONE

Chapter I

1. Mac returned to the ward and all was rosy except Mac knew His time was short.

2. A gala going away party was planned for Billy's cherry and Mac.

3. Whores and booze and laughter slipped in during the night and a good time was had by all.

4. Mac was caught because the Good Negro forgot to wake him.

5. Mac forgave the Good Negro because he knew he could not escape anyway.

Chapter II

1. The Big Nurse caught Billy and Billy's whore. She shamed Billy and brought back the old fear.

2. Billy stole a scalpel and cut his throat. Billy could not live in Mac's world.

3. The Nurse's insinuations caused Billy's death and Mac knew what He must do. The Nurse tried to shame Mac and He unveiled her boobs in their human splendor and then choked her. Aides and Officials pulled Mac off her and he knew he was to die.

Chapter III

1. The Big Nurse sent Mac to the Main Building for a lobotomy, so He would no longer be free and strong. The pious Dr. Spivey, a half-hearted supporter of Mac, did not stop the lobotomy.

2. The physical form of Mac became a shell of nothingness, placed in the ward to create fear in the hearts of all.

3. All Mac's people saw this and knew Mac's physical being must be destroyed so that others might live.

4. Mac's people, through the hand of his most devoted disciple, St. Bromden, snuffed out His life with a pillow.

5. All the fishing crew scattered to the ends of the earth and Pious Spivey bucked the Nurse.

Chapter IV

1. Mac once again became the form and the essence. His fishing Buddies and Whores all over the earth are laughing and loving and bucking the Combine.

2. Someday the hum of the Combine's machinery will be drowned out by laughter and all will be free from the fear within and love and disorder shall reign.

LESLIE A. FIEDLER

Leslie Fiedler is one of the best-known literary critics in the United States. Among his books are *Love and Death in the American Novel*, *No! in Thunder*, and *An End to Innocence*. In addition, he has written two novels and has received many awards for his works. He is currently Professor of English at the State University of New York, Buffalo.

THE HIGHER SENTIMENTALITY

. . . Nothing in the seventeenth century compares in scope and avowed seriousness even with the literature of the nineteenth century Drug Cult (centered around opiates, and therefore implicated in the myth of an Absolute East rather than a Polar West), from Poe and Coleridge and DeQuincy to Baudelaire—much less with the prose and verse being composed now on, or in the name of, "pot." Certainly it is hard to identify a tobacco-style, as one can an opium-style, and even a marijuana (or, as we come to synthesize a Super-West of our own, an LSD) one.

In Cohen's *Beautiful Losers*, for instance, the sort of vision evoked by psychedelics, or bred by the madness toward which their users aspire, is rendered in a kind of prose appropriate to that vision—a prose hallucinated and even, it seems to me, hallucinogenic: a style by which it is possible to be actually turned on, though only perhaps (judging by the critical resistance to Cohen's book) if one is already tuned in to the times. Yet even he felt a need for an allegiance to the past as well as the future, to memory as well as madness—or perhaps more accurately a need to transmute memory into madness, dead legend into living hallucination; and for him the myth of Catherine Tekakwitha served that purpose.

For us, however, on the other side of a border that is religious as well as political, mythological as well as historical, her story will not work; and what we demand in its place is the archetypal account of no analogous girl (for us women make satisfactory devils, but inadequate saints), but the old, old fable of the White outcast and the noble Red Man joined together against home and mother, against the female world of civilization. This time, however, we require a new setting, at once present and archaic—a setting which Ken Kesey discovered in the madhouse: *our* kind of madhouse, which is to say, one located in the American West, so that the Indian can make his reappearance in its midst with some probability, as well as real authenticity.

Perhaps it was necessary for Kesey to come himself out of Oregon, one of our last actual Wests (just as it was necessary for him to have been involved with one of the first experiments with the controlled use of LSD), since for most Americans after Mark Twain, the legendary colored companion of the white fugitive had been turned from Red to Black. Even on the most naïve levels, the Negro has replaced the Indian as the natural enemy of Woman; as in the recent film *The Fortune Cookie*, for instance, the last scene of which fades out on a paleface *schlemiel* (delivered at last from his treacherous whore of a white wife) tossing a football back and forth with his Negro buddy in a deserted football stadium. Similarly, in such sophisticated fiction as James Purdy's *Cabot Wright Begins*, the color scheme demanded by the exigencies of current events is observed, though in this case, the relationship has become overtly and explicitly homosexual:

. . . His dark-skinned prey seated himself under the street-lamp and Bernie, more desperate by the moment, seated himself next to him, then almost immediately introduced himself.

His new friend accepted the introduction in the manner in which it was meant. They exchanged the necessary information about themselves, Bernie learning that his chance acquaintance was Winters Hart, from a town in the Congo. . . . Taking Winters Hart's left hand in his, Bernie held his friend's dark finger on which he wore a wedding-ring, and pressed the finger and the hand.

Far from being annoyed at this liberty, Winters Hart was, to tell the truth, relieved and pleased. Isolation in a racial democracy, as he was to tell Bernie later that night, as they lay in Bernie's bed together, isolation, no thank you.

The title of the chapter from Purdy's book from which this passage comes is "One Flew East, One Flew West"—referring, I suppose, to the two sexual choices open to men; but it reminds us of the title of Kesey's archetypal Western, *One Flew Over the Cuckoo's Nest*, which represents a third possibility of White transcendence: madness itself. . . .

[Kesey's] novel opens with an obviously psychotic "I" reflecting on his guards, one of whom identifies him almost immediately, speaking in a Negro voice: "Here's the Chief. The *soo*-pah Chief, fellas. Ol' Chief Broom. Here you go, Chief Broom. . . ." Chief Bromden is his real name, this immense schizophrenic, pretending he is deaf-and-dumb to baffle "the Combine," which he believes controls the world: "Look at him: a giant janitor. There's your Vanishing American, a six-foot-six sweeping machine, scared of its own shadow. . . ." Or rather Bromden is the name he has inherited from his white mother, who subdued the full-blooded Chief who sired him and was called "The-Pine-That-Stands-Tallest-on-the-Mountain." "He fought it a long time," the half-breed son comments at one point, "till my mother made him too little to fight any more and he gave up."

Chief Bromden believes he is little, too, what was left in him of fight and stature subdued by a second mother, who presides over the ward in which he is confined ("She may be a mother, but she's big as a damn barn and tough as knife metal . . .") and, at one point, had given him two hundred successive shock treatments. Not only is Mother II big, however, especially in the breasts; she is even more essentially *white:* "Her face is smooth, calculated, and precision-made, like an expensive baby doll, skin like flesh-colored enamel, blend of white and cream and baby-blue eyes . . ." and her opulent body is bound tight in a starched white uniform. To understand her in her full mythological significance, we must recall that seventeenth century first White Mother of Us All, Hannah Duston, and her struggle against the Indians who tried to master her.

Hannah has represented from the start those forces in the American community—soon identified chiefly with the female and maternal—which resist all incursions of savagery, no matter what their course. But only in the full twentieth century is the nature of Hannah's assault made quite clear, first in Freudian terms and then in psychedelic ones. "No, buddy," Kesey's white hero, Randle Patrick McMurphy, comments on the Big Nurse. "She ain't pecking at your *eyes.* That's not what she's peckin' at." And when someone, who really knows but wants to hear spoken aloud what he is too castrated to say, asks at *what,* then, R. P. McMurphy answers, "At your balls, buddy, at your ever-lovin' *balls.*" Yet toward the close of the book, McMurphy has to be told by the very man who questioned him earlier the meaning of his own impending lobotomy at the hands of Big Nurse ("Yes, chopping away the brain. Frontal-lobe castration. I guess if she can't cut below the belt she'll do it above the eyes"), though by this time he understands why he, as well as the Indian (only victim of the original Hannah's blade), has become the enemy of the White Woman.

In his own view, McMurphy may be a swinger, and in the eyes of his Indian buddy an ultimate Westerner, the New American Man: "He walked with long steps, too long, and he had his thumbs hooked in his pockets again. The iron in his boot

heels cracked lightning out of the tile. He was the logger again,
the swaggering gambler . . . the cowboy out of the TV set walking down the middle of the street to meet a dare."

But to Big Nurse—and the whole staff of the asylum whom,
White or Black, male or female, she has cowed—he is only a
"psychopath," not less sick for having chosen the nuthouse in
which he finds himself to the work-farm to which his society
had sentenced him. And she sees the purpose of the asylum as
being precisely to persuade men like him to accept and function
in the world of rewards and punishments which he has rejected
and fled.

To do this, however, she must persuade him like the rest that
he is only a "bad boy," *her* bad boy, quite like, say Huckleberry
Finn. But where Huck's substitute mothers demanded that he
give up smoking, wear shoes, go to school, she asks (it is the last
desperate version of "sivilisation") that he be sane: "All he has
to do is *admit* he was wrong, to indicate, *demonstrate* rational
contact and the treatment would be cancelled this time."

The choice is simple: either sanity abjectly accepted, or sanity
imposed by tranquilizers, shock treatments, finally lobotomy
itself. But McMurphy chooses instead if not madness, at least
aggravated psychopathy and an alliance with his half-erased,
totally schizophrenic Indian comrade—an alliance with all that
his world calls unreason, quite like that which bound Henry to
Wawatam, Natty Bumppo to Chingachgook, even Ishmael to
Queequeg (that versatile Polynesian, who, at the moment of
betrothal, whips out a tomahawk pipe, quite as if he were a
real Red Man). And this time, the alliance is not merely explicitly, but quite overtly directed against the White Woman,
which is to say, Hannah Duston fallen out of her own legend
into that of Henry and Wawatam.

For a while, the result seems utter disaster, since McMurphy,
driven to attempt the rape of his tormentor, is hauled off her
and duly lobotomized, left little more than a vegetable with "a
face milk-white except for the heavy purple bruises around the
eyes." Whiter than the White Woman who undid him, white as

mother's milk: this is McMurphy at the end, except that Chief Bromden will not let it be the end, will not let "something like that sit there in the day room with his name tacked on it for twenty or thirty years so the Big Nurse could use it as an example of what can happen if you buck the system. . . ."

Therefore in the hush of the first night after the lobotomy, he creeps into the bed of his friend for what turns out to be an embrace—for only in a caricature of the act of love can he manage to kill him: "The big, hard body had a tough grip on life. . . . I finally had to lie full length on top of it and scissor the kicking legs with mine. . . . I lay there on top of the body for what seemed like days. . . . Until it was still a while and had shuddered once and was still again."

It is the first real *Liebestod* in our long literature of love between white man and colored, and the first time, surely, that the Indian partner in such a pair has outlived his White brother. Typically, Chingachgook had predeceased Natty, and Queequeg, Ishmael; typically, Huck had been younger than Jim, Ike than Sam Fathers. Everyone who has lived at the heart of our dearest myth knows that it is the white boy-man who survives, as the old Indian, addressing the Great Spirit, prepares to vanish. Even so recent a novel as Berger's *Little Big Man* has continued to play it straight, closing on the traditional dying fall, as Old Lodge Skins subsides after a final prayer, and his white foster son says:

> He laid down then on the damp rocks and died right away. I descended to the treeline, fetched back some poles, and built him a scaffold. Wrapped him in the red blanket and laid him thereon. Then after a while I started down the mountain in the fading light.

But on the last page of *One Flew Over the Cuckoo's Nest*, Chief Bromden is on his way back to the remnants of his tribe who "have took to building their old ramshackle wood scaffolding all over the big million-dollar . . . spillway." And his very last words are: "I been away a long time."

It is, then, the "Indian" in Kesey himself, the undischarged refugee from a madhouse, the AWOL Savage, who is left to boast: *And I only am escaped alone to tell thee.* But the "Indian" does not write books; and insofar as Kesey's fable can be read as telling the truth about himself as well as about all of us, it prophesies silence for him, a silence into which he has, in fact, lapsed, though not until he had tried one more Gutenberg-trip in *Sometimes a Great Notion.*

It is a book which seems to me not so much a second novel as a first novel written (or, perhaps, only published) second: a more literary, conventionally ambitious, and therefore *strained* effort—for all its occasional successes, somehow an error. *One Flew Over the Cuckoo's Nest* works better to the degree that it is dreamed or hallucinated rather than merely written—which is to say, to the degree that it, like its great prototype *The Leatherstocking Tales,* is Pop Art rather than *belles lettres*—the dream once dreamed in the woods, and now redreamed on pot and acid.

Its very sentimentality, good-guys bad-guys melodrama, occasional obviousness and thinness of texture, I find—like the analogous things in Cooper—not incidental flaws, but part of the essential method of its madness. There is a phrase which reflects on Kesey's own style quite early in the book, defining it aptly, though it pretends only to represent Chief Bromden's vision of the world around him: "Like a cartoon world, where the figures are flat and outlined in black, jerking through some kind of goofy story that might be real funny if it weren't for the cartoon figures being real guys. . . ."

Everywhere in Kesey, as a matter of fact, the influence of comics and, especially, comic books is clearly perceptible, in the mythology as well as in the style; for like those of many younger writers of the moment, the images and archetypal stories which underlie his fables are not the legends of Greece and Rome, not the fairy tales of Grimm, but the adventures of Captain Marvel and Captain Marvel, Jr., those new-style Supermen who, sometime just after World War II, took over the fantasy of the young, What Western elements persist in Kesey are, as it were, first translated back into comic-strip form, then turned once more into words on the conventional book page. One might, indeed, have imagined Kesey ending up as a comic book writer, but since the false second start of *Sometimes a Great Notion*, he has preferred to live his comic strip rather than write or even draw it.

The adventures of Psychedelic Superman as Kesey had dreamed and acted them, however—his negotiations with Hell's Angels, his being busted for the possession of marijuana, his consequent experiences in court and, as a refugee from the law, in Mexico—all this, like the yellow bus in which he used to move up and down the land taking an endless, formless movie, belongs to hearsay and journalism rather than to literary criticism, challenging conventional approaches to literature even as it challenges literature itself. But *One Flew Over the Cuckoo's Nest* survives the experiments and rejections which followed it; and looking back five years after its initial appearance, it seems clear that in it for the first time the New West was clearly defined: the West of Here and Now, rather than There and Then—the West of Madness.

The Westering impulse which Europe had begun by regarding as blasphemous (as, for instance, in Dante's description of Ulysses sailing through the Pillars of Hercules toward "the world without people"), it learned soon to think of as crazy, mocking Columbus and his dream of a passage to India, and condemning as further folly each further venture into a further West after the presence of America had been established (think, for example, of Cabeza de Vaca walking into the vast unknown and becoming, on his impossible adventure, a god to those savages whose world he penetrated).

It is only a step from thinking of the West as madness to regarding madness as the true West, but it took the long years between the end of the fifteenth century and the middle of the twentieth to learn to take that step. There is scarcely a New Western among those I have discussed which does not in some way flirt with the notion of madness as essential to the New World; but only in Leonard Cohen (though Thomas Berger comes close) and in Kesey is the final identification made, and in Kesey at last combined with the archetype of the love that binds the lonely white man to his Indian comrade—to his *mad* Indian comrade, perhaps even to the *madness* of his Indian comrade, as Kesey amends the old tale.

We have come to accept the notion that there is still a territory unconquered and uninhabited by palefaces, the bearers of "civilization," the cadres of imperialist reason; and we have been learning that into this territory certain psychotics, a handful of "schizophrenics," have moved on ahead of the rest of us— unrecognized Natty Bumppos or Huck Finns, interested not in claiming the New World for any Old God, King, or Country, but in becoming New Men, members of just such a New Race as D. H. Lawrence foresaw. (How fascinating, then, that R. D. Laing, leading exponent among contemporary psychiatrists of the theory that some schizophrenics have "broken through" rather than "broken down," should, despite the fact that he is an Englishman, have turned to our world and its discovery in search of an analogy; he suggests that Columbus's stumbling upon America and his first garbled accounts of it provide an illuminating parallel to the ventures of certain madmen into the regions of extended or altered consciousness, and to their confused version, once they are outside of it, of the strange realm in which they have been.)

Obviously, not everyone is now prepared, and few of us ever will be, to make a final and total commitment to the Newest West via psychosis; but a kind of tourism into insanity is already possible for those of us not yet ready or able to migrate permanently from the world of reason. We can take, as the New Westerns suggest, what is already popularly called—in the aptest of metaphors—a "trip," an excursion into the unknown with the aid of drugs. The West has seemed to us for a long time a place of recreation as well as of risk; and this is finally fair enough, for all the ironies implicit in turning a wilderness into a park. After all, the West remains always in some sense true to itself, as long as the Indian, no matter how subdued, penned off, or costumed for the tourist trade, survives—as long as we can confront there a creature radically different from the old self we seek to recreate in two weeks' vacation.

And while the West endures, the Western demands to be written—that form which represents a traditional and continuing dialogue between whatever old selves we transport out of whatever East, and the radically different other whom we confront in whatever West we attain. That other is the Indian still, as from the beginning, though only vestigially, nostalgically now; and also, with special novelty and poignancy, the insane.

If a myth of America is to exist in the future, it is incumbent on our writers, no matter how square and scared they may be in their deepest hearts, to conduct with the mad just such a dialogue as their predecessors learned long ago to conduct with the aboriginal dwellers in the actual Western Wilderness. It is easy to forget, but essential to remember, that the shadowy creatures living scarcely imaginable lives in the forests of Virginia once seemed as threatening to all that good Europeans believed as the acid-head or the borderline schizophrenic on the Lower East Side now seems to all that good Americans have come to believe in its place.

TERRY G. SHERWOOD

Terry Sherwood is an American who teaches English literature at the University of Victoria, British Columbia. In 1969, he received his Ph.D. from Berkeley, where he was interested primarily, and still is, in sixteenth- and seventeenth-century English literature.

ONE FLEW OVER THE CUCKOO'S NEST AND THE COMIC STRIP

Although first published in 1962, Ken Kesey's *One Flew Over the Cuckoo's Nest* still enjoys a wide readership. Kesey's "hippy" reputation and the book's unusual expression of anti-Establishment themes, ranging from rebellion against conformity to pastoral retreat, would explain its current popular appeal. The critics' response to the book is less understandable. A warm reception by reviewers has been followed by relatively little critical interest. The book deserves more attention as an imaginative expression of a moral position congenial to an important segment of the American population and as a noteworthy use of Popular culture in a serious novel. This essay will demonstrate the central importance of the nexus between Kesey's aesthetic, informed by comic strip principles, and his moral vision, embodying simple, elemental truths. Kesey's references to comic strip materials are not just casual grace notes but clear indica-

Reprinted with permission from *Critique*, XIII, 1 (1971), 96–109.

tions of his artistic stance. Significantly, the importance of the comic strip to Kesey has been confirmed by Leslie Fiedler,[1] the one major critic discussing the novel at length, although he neither affirms such a high degree of artistic consciousness in Kesey nor examines certain essential details.

The climactic ward party ends with reference to the comic strip hero, the Lone Ranger. Harding asks to be awakened for McMurphy's escape. "I'd like to stand there at the window with a silver bullet in my hand and ask 'Who wawz that'er masked man?' as you ride—."[2] The insightful Harding clearly recognizes that McMurphy, like the comic strip savior, whose silver bullet annihilates Evil, has freed the inmates from the clutches of the monster Big Nurse. The Lone Ranger reference underlines an aesthetic set out clearly in the novel. Briefly, Kesey's method embodies that of the caricaturist, the cartoonist, the folk artist, the allegorist. Characterization and delineation of incident are inked in bold, simple, exaggerated patterns for obvious but compelling statement. As in the comic strip, action in Kesey's novel turns on the mythic confrontation between Good and Evil: an exemplary he-man versus a machine-tooled, castrating matriarch ever denied our sympathies. Both are bigger than life; both are symbolic exaggerations of qualities; neither is "realistic." Bromden's description of the inmates' and ward attendants' stylized behavior is instructive. "Like a cartoon world, where the figures are flat and outlined in black, jerking through some kind of goofy story that might be real funny if it weren't for the cartoon figures being real guys" (34). Characters and incidents are types, bound by set characteristics, before they are uniquely individual. In demonstrating the centrality of such comic strip elements, I will indicate first how they are reinforced by other materials from Popular culture

---

[1] Leslie A. Fiedler, *The Return of the Vanishing American* (New York, 1968), pp. 179–185.
[2] Ken Kesey, *One Flew Over the Cuckoo's Nest* (New York, 1962), p. 258. Subsequent page references are given parenthetically within the text.

sharing similar techniques, then more explicitly how they shape character and incident, and finally how Kesey's failure to heed the dangers of his mode is symptomatic of the book's moral flaws and central to critical evaluation.

Kesey draws from one form of Popular culture, the folk song, in his initial characterization of McMurphy. We hear lines from "The Roving Gambler" and "The Wagoner's Lad" in McMurphy's exuberant solo on his first morning in the asylum. Both songs treat a typical opposition between the wanderer and society in terms of romantic love. With characteristic bravado the gambler McMurphy sings, "She took me to her parlor, and coo-oo-ooled me with her fan"—I can hear the whack as he slaps his bare belly—"whispered low in her mamma's ear, I luh-uhvv that gamblin' man" (97). The town-bred girl is inevitably drawn to the rover living by the uncertainties of the card game, not the genteel stability and sexual constriction of the matriarchal parlor. Despite McMurphy's resonating exuberance, the second song is more darkly intoned, with the harshness of fare-well and the settled community's stony resistance, thereby predicting McMurphy's unalterable battle with Big Nurse. The lad's poverty and way of life ensure parental disapproval. "Oh, your parents don't like me, they say I'm too po-o-or; they say I'm not worthy to enter your door. . . . Hard livin's my pleas-ure, my money's my o-o-wn, an' them that don't like me, they can leave me alone" (92). Like the comic strip, a method of the folk song is presentation of simple, typical behavioral patterns, while eschewing introspection and highly subtle characterization. Simple details express typical patterns. The town girl's fan cools the heat of the wanderer's movement, and the wagoner's lad expresses proud opposition to economic bigotry by refusing the girl's offer of hay for his horses. Murphy's brief medley is self-characterization—foot-loose virility, uncompromised independence, gambler's whim, acceptance of harsh physical effort, and resistance to society worked out within the easily understood boundaries of folk art.

Kesey further mines Popular culture in frequent references to

McMurphy as the cowboy hero. When McMurphy approaches to break the nurses' window, Bromden says, "He was the logger again, the swaggering gambler, the big red-headed brawling Irishman, the cowboy out of the TV set walking down the middle of the street to meet a dare" (189). Elsewhere, McMurphy speaks in his "drawling cowboy actor's voice" (264). The television "western" intersects the Lone Ranger and folk song references to emphasize frontier values. Kesey uses the stereotyped cowboy hero for precisely the reasons he is often attacked: unrelenting selfhood and independence articulated with verbal calmness and defended by physical valor and ready defiance of opposition. Stock "western" formulae constitute a convenient reservoir of popular literary associations for depicting McMurphy in easily definable terms.

Kesey's mode of simplification voices a moral vision rooted in clear-cut opposition between Good and Evil, between natural man and society, between an older mode of existence honoring masculine physical life and a modern day machine culture inimical to it, between the Indian fishing village and the hydroelectric dam. Modern society standardizes men and straitjackets its misfits; it causes the illness which it quarantines. The spiritual residue of the American Old West opposes the machine culture; but the West, as such, is doomed like McMurphy. For Kesey, Popular culture's hardened simplicity of detail expresses continuing American values and problems, etched deeply in the American consciousness. Modern machine culture is the most recent manifestation of society's threat to the individual, perhaps the most threatening.

Thus, Kesey turns to the comic strip, a more recent aspect of Popular culture, for his literary materials. Here he finds the method of exaggeration basic to his aesthetic.[3] In *The Electric*

---

[3] It is likely that Kesey has the "tall tale" in mind, particularly the Paul Bunyan stories, as indicated by McMurphy's logging experience. However, Kesey's explicit references are to the comic strip. In any event, the modes are similar.

Kool-Aid Acid Test Tom Wolfe delineates Kesey's attention to comic strips. For Kesey, the comic book superheroes (Captain Marvel, Superman, Plastic Man, the Flash, *et al.*) were the true mythic heroes of his contemporary adolescent generation. Kesey was interested significantly in this comic strip world during his Stanford University, Perry Lane days, the gestation period of *One Flew Over the Cuckoo's Nest*.[4] He realized this interest most spectacularly later in Merry Prankster days by affecting the superhero's costume to image transcendent human possibility (witness his Flash Gordon–like garb at a Vietnam teach-in in 1965[5] and his cape and leotards at the LSD graduation in 1966).[6] The longevity of his interest, antedating his first novel and lasting after his Mexican exile, affirms its personal significance. Wolfe's book colors in the authorial consciousness behind the Lone Ranger reference and Bromden's belief that McMurphy, despite his wardmates' fear of his self-aggrandizement, was a "giant come out of the sky to save us from the Combine" (255). The Lone Ranger's mask mysteriously separates him from other men, his origin is uncertain, and his silver bullet has supernatural powers; that is, he has divine characteristics. Bromden's vision of McMurphy as a saving giant recalls airborne superheroes like Superman and Captain Marvel, miraculously aiding others in one fell swoop; also, we are hereby conditioned for the depiction of McMurphy as Christ, sacrificed on the cross-shaped electroshock table on behalf of the ward. For Kesey, the heavenly Christ and the supernatural comic book hero stand on common mythic ground as images of human potential. McMurphy's self-regarding and independent pursuit of physical pleasure, inspirited by defiant laughter and gambler's unconcern for security, make him superior to other men and free him from society; his power of miracle is transmitting his

---

[4] Tom Wolfe, *The Electric Kool-Aid Acid Test* (Toronto, 1968), pp. 32–35.
[5] Wolfe, p. 196.
[6] Wolfe, p. 352.

traits to others. He can do the impossible by executing the fishing trip against Big Nurse's wishes and healing sick men with his fists. He has the superhero's efficacious physical power but, like Christ, the magnitude of his threat to society forces his crucifixion.

The comic strip also inspires the characterization of Big Nurse. The Combine, a machine culture which harvests and packages men, is modern Evil; and Big Nurse, its powerful agent. She shares the comic strip villain's control over modern technology; her glass-enveloped nurses' cubicle is the ward's electronic nerve center, and she punishes on the electroshock table. She is Miss Ratched—the ratchet—essential cog in ward machinery (also the ratchet wrench, adjusting malfunctioning inmates?). Her giantism is expressed in her nickname, Big Nurse, and frequently in descriptions of her. "She's too big to be beaten. She covers one whole side of the room like a Jap statue. There's no moving her and no help against her" (109). "Her nostrils flare open, and every breath she draws she gets bigger, as big and tough-looking's I seen her get over a patient since Taber was here—I can smell the hot oil and magneto spark when she goes past, and every step hits the floor she blows up a size bigger, blowing and puffing, roll down anything in her path" (93). Kesey scales her to match the giant of the sky, McMurphy. Like the comic strip villain, she never enjoys our sympathies, even when rendered voiceless and physically weak by McMurphy's uncavalier assault following Billy Bibbit's suicide.

Our lack of sympathy is tied to her static nature as a principle, not a human being. The comic strip is essentially a pictorial representation of stereotyped moral and psychological truths for unsophisticated readers. The Lone Ranger's mask, the image of his mysterious separateness, and Freddy Freeman's crutch, the image of his mortal half, pictorially express constants in their natures. Kesey's characterizations of McMurphy and Big Nurse emphasize similar repeated details. In McMurphy's motorcyclist's cap we see the stereotyped antisocial belligerence of cycle gangs; in his scarred fists, his ready valor and worker's energy; in his red hair, the Irishman's volatility; in the scar on his nose, an emblem of wounds bravely received in aggressive assertion of self; in his white whale underpants, his untamed and socially destructive natural vitality. A hard shell of plastic, starch, and enamel encases Big Nurse's humanity. The impenetrable surface of her "doll's face and doll's smile" (151) iconographically represents her stunted feelings. The militaristic, stiff nurse's uniform constrains the sexual and maternal potential of her admirable bosom. She is part of a machine attempting to level even sexual differences. The stable lines in Kesey's characterization of the two antagonists stress their essential natures.

Imaginative variations of comic strip principles show Kesey's sophisticated manipulation of his mode, as in Bromden's metamorphosis through McMurphy's influence. Bromden's rejuvenation is the gauge of McMurphy's savior's power and is Kesey's promise of hope. Bromden escapes, not McMurphy. The modern world cannot accommodate the freewheeling Irishman. The freedom of the Old West is gone; its spirit resides only in myth; the Irish minority has been assimilated. McMurphy is hounded into a prison farm and, despite delusions of freely choosing the asylum, drawn fatalistically into the showdown with Big Nurse. Gradually, he understands his Messianic role: "We made him stand and hitch up his black shorts like they were horsehide chaps, and push back his cap with one finger like it was a ten-gallon Stetson, slow, mechanical gestures—and when he walked across the floor you could hear the iron in his bare heels ring sparks out of the tile" (305). He cannot remain in a conformist world in which men no longer share the ecstasy of violence and the gambler's defiance of fate; but, by sacrificing himself, he can infuse the spirit of rebellion and selfhood into those able to combine it with other strengths. His diminishing strength transfers to Bromden. McMurphy cannot lift the tub room control panel, but, possessing the "secret" power of "blowin' a man back up to full size" (211), can empower

Bromden to make the symbolic gesture of throwing the panel through the asylum wall, of turning the machine upon itself. The doomed giant can create another giant. Shazam. The six foot, eight inch "Vanishing American" (67), the first man in the ward, has been deflated by a racist society which bulldozes its Indian villages and, after using the tribesmen to fight crippling wars, incarcerates them in asylums to clean floors for white inmates. Kesey looks to dormant Indian values, represented *in potentia* by Bromden's size, for answers to problems of modern culture. Residual Indian pastoralism and regard for physical life, plus a yet strong sense of community, represent a possibility for life in defiance of the Combine; but these values need inspiration, inflation by McMurphy's Spirit. Kesey's central image is the superhero's metamorphosis from mortal weakness to supernatural strength.

The relationship between the white McMurphy and the Indian Bromden is further delineated in Kesey's strategic Lone Ranger reference. Bromden is McMurphy's Tonto, the silent but loyal Indian companion under auspices of his white spiritual guide. Equation of McMurphy and the "masked man" not only stresses McMurphy's savior role in "western" terms, but also sums up the previous relationship between McMurphy and Bromden in order to overturn the traditional expectation of Indian subservience. The Lone Ranger and Tonto become, respectively, the sacrificial Christ and his independent disciple, a writer of Holy Scripture carrying Good News composed of both men's values. Only Tonto leaves the asylum: Bromden's Indian values imbued with McMurphy's Spirit are Kesey's final answer to the questions asked by the book. Strategic use of the Lone Ranger, just before McMurphy's demise and Bromden's complete metamorphosis, crystallizes the book's pivotal racial relationship before redefining it. Again, a skillful hand adapts the comic strip materials.

Different kinds of comic strips serve the author's purpose. Although the showdown with Big Nurse most obviously expresses modern man's resistance against a crippling society, she expresses only locally a general condition delineated in part by strokes of Kesey's animal cartoonist's pen. As noted earlier, Kesey borrows frequently from other forms of Popular culture, using techniques similar to the comic strip's. He modulates between forms with considerable finesse. Appalled by the predatory group therapy, McMurphy discusses this "peckin' party" (55) with the ineffectual Harding. The discussion takes its cue from McMurphy's homespun metaphor. Despite his fastidious complaint about McMurphy's metaphorical mixture ("bitch," "ballcutter," "chicken") Harding spins out variations on the animal imagery to articulate his latent antagonism against Big Nurse. Initial denial that she is a "giant monster of the poultry clan, bent on sadistically pecking out our eyes" (57) yields to his own categorization of her as wolf and the men as rabbits. "All of us here are rabbits of varying ages and degrees, hippity-hopping through our Walt Disney world" (62). Animal metaphors depicting static human traits, a common device in folk literature, are frequent in the novel, *e.g.*, Williams, the black attendant, "crawls" to Big Nurse "like a dog to a whipping" (94). To invoke Disney is to translate the animal metaphors into modern cartoon terms especially appropriate to a modern standardized world. Harding's remark at the end of the book— "No more rabbits, Mack" (294)—is to be seen in this more appropriate modern context.

Bromden's first extended description of the conformist ward weds the cartoon to similar literary forms. After depicting the ward inmates and attendants as cartoon figures "flat and outlined in black" (31) locked irrevocably into set behavior and speaking "cartoon comedy speech" (33), he shifts to a similar mode. "The technicians go trotting off, pushing the man on the Gurney, like cartoon men—or like puppets, mechanical puppets in one of those Punch and Judy acts where it's supposed to be funny to see the puppet beat up by the Devil and swallowed headfirst by a smiling alligator" (35). The puppet show reaches out with one hand through the alligator image to Kesey's animal metaphors and with the other to the "dreamy doll faces of the workmen" (84) in Bromden's hallucination and the doll faces of Billy Bibbit (130) and Big Nurse (26). (The standardized world includes even Big Nurse, who in her stunted emotional development, is victim as well as victimizer.) Kesey deftly shifts from the cartoon to the puppet show to toys, changing terms within his aesthetic frame without altering it.

The same principle governs in a less obvious way McMurphy's white whale underpants, a gift, he tells us, from a co-ed "Literary major" who thought him a "symbol" (81). This is one of the few times when Kesey goes beyond popular culture *per se*, but Melville is readily adaptable for his purpose. We are reminded that McMurphy is not a "realistic" character, but a representation of certain qualities shared by Moby Dick— natural vitality, strength, immortality, anti-social destructiveness. However, this is a caricature white whale, emblazoned on the Irishman's black underpants to emphasize his sexually intoned vitality, and bearing a devilish red eye linked to McMurphy's red hair and volatile Irish nature. This is a cartoon Moby Dick, minus the cosmic horror and mystery, precise in its suggestions and domesticated for Kesey's purposes.

Designating McMurphy a "symbol" is a clear statement of Kesey's aesthetic, as are the "flat and outlined" cartoon men. But to demonstrate the presence of this aesthetic, as done hereto, is not to elucidate its ultimate moral significance for Kesey. In this regard, Harding is absolutely central for through him Kesey guides our response to important elements in the novel. Harding has concealed his homosexuality, at least bisexuality, behind insincere sexual bravado and, more importantly, behind his considerable learning. He is the modern intellectual avoiding simple realities. Unlike the co-ed, who could appreciate McMurphy's vitality and sexuality while labeling him with terms from her academic vocabulary, Harding initially rejects McMurphy's homely "analogy" of the "peckin' party," clouding the truth with modern psychological cant. Yet, besides Bromden, he is the most aware character and not prevented by snobbish scorn of McMurphy's "TV-cowboy stoicism" (77) from seeing in McMurphy's deliberate affectation of cowboy drawl an affirmation of "western" values. McMurphy instructs him, not *vice versa*, and his identification of McMurphy and the Lone Ranger is a final measure of new knowledge, expressed significantly in Popular cultural terms. No longer "Perfessor Harding" defeated in the symbolic blackjack game by another queen (77), he has the vision of wisdom to see Big Nurse as Evil Monster.

Harding is closest to the intended reader, college educated and uprooted from moral values of Popular culture by academic prejudices. Like the reader, he can recognize the comic strip aesthetic but is unwilling to admit its moral truths. The novel offers simple truths in a simplified mode, taunting the reader for his literary condescension and related moral weakness. Like McMurphy we must turn to our "cartoon magazine" (160) and television "westerns" for a rudimentary vision of human values, and away from a specious notion of moral complexity in the modern world. Kesey encourages anti-intellectualism, at least anti-academicism. Significantly, Harding is not cured of homosexual impulses, just his fear of admitting them; far removed from the springs of fully realized physical existence, the intellectual can learn self-consciously from those who drink directly. Harding's change is paradigmatic for the intended effect on the educated reader aware of the nature of Kesey's aesthetic, but lacking the moral perception lying behind it.

Of course, given that moral problems tend toward more complexity and not less, this necessary link between moral vision and literary mode causes us uneasiness. The book lures us in the wrong direction. Even the reader recognizing the self-indulgence in exaggerating the modern world's complexity may deny that moral problems are simple or that a frontier defiance dependent upon physical courage and raw individuality can solve them. McMurphy lacks the introspective self-irony and spiritual wisdom which could enrich and humanize his readiness to act in a physical world. In my judgment the book's major weakness lies partially in a wavering treatment of Mc-Murphy as "symbol." Kesey rejects the profounder symbolism of Melville, frightening in its incomprehensible mysteriousness, for the delimited symbolism of the comic strip superhero. Our sympathy with these "unrealistic" and superhuman heroes is always reserved. We cannot expect psychological fullness from them. Kesey wishes to shorten partially this aesthetic distance to increase our sympathy with McMurphy, the human opposite to the plastic monstrosity Big Nurse. Kesey risks the simplification of his statement. Unfortunately, he does not manage to have it both ways: as he rounds out the character McMurphy, we rightly expect a fuller range of human response than necessary for a "symbolic" representation of masculine physical vitality. But our expectations remain unsatisfied. The rebel McMurphy resembles the prankish schoolboy against the schoolmarm or the naughty boy against the mother. Although the book recommends laughter as necessary therapy against absurdity (227), there is a euphoric tone of boyish escapism and wish-fulfillment to McMurphy's humor too often reminiscent of the bathroom or locker room. The euphoria at times embarrasses, as in the maudlin, communal warmth of the fishing boat trip and the ward party. In sum, the novel too often shares the wish-fulfillment of the comic strip without preserving the hard lines of its mythic representation.

Admittedly, other attempts to humanize McMurphy also reveal Kesey's awareness of the problems posed by his "symbolic" characterization, however unsuccessful his solutions. The brawler McMurphy uncharacteristically paints pictures and writes letters in a "beautiful flowing hand" (153). His upset caused by a return letter suggests an emotional softness complementary to more typical behavior, as does his sensitivity to the personal loss necessitated by his savior's responsibilities. The visit to McMurphy's old home emphasizes his fatigue and "frantic" anticipation of that loss. The dress flapping in the tree commemorates his first act of love, freely given by the nine-year-old "little whore," and thereby keynotes his loving but defiantly anti-Social relationships with his prostitute lovers (244–45). We are asked to believe that the sensitive and anguished letter writer, the energetic lover, and the tavern warrior are at bottom the same character apotheosized in his savior's role; his "psychopathic" sexuality and violence are really the human feeling and zest for life in which his Calling is grounded. As the Lone Ranger acting outside Society on behalf of humanity, he protects those qualities from extinction in others. Accordingly, his self-sacrifice is consistent with the lesson in gratuitous love taught by his childhood lover. Despite these attempts to fill in the simple comic strip outline of McMurphy's character, such details are too incidental, too hastily appended, to modify substantially our more limited version of him.

Kesey's handling of sex suffers from a failure to consider all implications of his materials, comic strip included. According to Leslie Fiedler, the love between McMurphy and Bromden expresses mythically an escape from the values of a white civilization ruled by women;[7] but Fiedler overlooks the inadvertent blurring of Kesey's mythology caused by the unclear status of sex, both before and after McMurphy's death. The "symbolic" McMurphy is the blatantly sexual doctor of "whambam" seeing the inmates' sexual inadequacies as important expressions of psychological debility. Bringing prostitutes into the asylum is saving therapy which, contrary to Kesey's intents, fails to save. Neither of the Irishman's two principal disciples, Harding and Bromden, is fully heterosexual. Sefelt's prodigious sexual powers are merely adjunct to his epilepsy and Billy Bibbit's sexual initiation brings suicide. Despite McMurphy's joking estimate of Bromden's sexual potential (212), the Indian is asexual; he embraces only the lobotomized body of McMurphy in defense of the Spirit; this murderous act of love could even be seen as homosexual in nature if it were not for the book's overt heterosexuality. Bromden's sexuality simply is not restored with his physical power. McMurphy's Spiritual influence is un-

---

[7] Fiedler, p. 180 f.

sexed further by its comic strip ties: the superhero lives in a boys' escape world in which sexuality is released in muscular athleticism or violence; the Lone Ranger and Tonto are above sexuality, if not innocently homosexual; likewise the TV cowboy is rarely sexual. The meaning of McMurphy's physical assault on Big Nurse, a public exposure of inherent femininity in a figurative rape of machine morality, is eroded by Kesey's failure to free McMurphy from such inadvertent implications of asexuality in the comic strip characterization, and by the failure to provide a convincing heterosexual disciple for McMurphy. The book seems at times an unwitting requiem for heterosexuality, most ironically sounded in the innocent child's embrace of McMurphy and the prostitute Sandy after the ward party. However, we must conclude only that Kesey fails to harness the potential allusiveness of his materials.

We are left with a somewhat sentimentalized over-simplification of moral problems. Admittedly, Kesey's opposition of Good and Evil is less bald and the victory of Good less clear than might seem. The superhero McMurphy is sacrificed to the machine culture and Big Nurse remains in the ward. There is little hope that the Combine can be defeated. Only limited defiance is possible, for Harding by accepting his homosexual inclinations, for Bromden by escaping from the asylum. Moreover, such defiance is perhaps imaginary: Bromden begins his narration *in* the asylum, recalling *past* events concerning McMurphy and breaking a long-held silence. "But, please. It's still hard for me to have a clear mind thinking on it. But it's truth *even if it didn't happen*" [my italics] (8). Perhaps Bromden's story is like the comic strip, a world only as it ought to be. After all, McMurphy must die and Bromden's interpretation of his future is euphoric, without convincing evidence of further satisfaction. Whether he finds his fellow tribesmen (perhaps drunk or widely disseminated) or fishes atop the hydroelectric dam (that others do so is only hearsay) or flees to Canada (also Combine territory?), he must remain outside Combine society (311). Perhaps the only escape from modern life is the tenuous-ness of hallucination. Kesey's irony compromises the victory of Good, suggesting that things may be more difficult than they seem.[8]

However, these notes in a minor key do not really discolor the euphoric ending. The book's beginning is too easily forgotten and we are pushed along by Bromden's optimism. We are to hope, not despair, and, more importantly, not define the line between. Kesey believes in the comic strip world in spite of himself. This is the moral ground on which critical faultfinding must begin. Kesey has not avoided the dangers of a simplistic aesthetic despite his attempts to complicate it. He forgets that the comic strip world is not an answer to life, but an escape from it. The reader finds Kesey entering that world too uncritically in defense of the Good.

---

[8] Fiedler contends that the frontier in the "New Western" is the mind itself, that Bromden's schizophrenia symbolizes the new reality, and that McMurphy is attracted to Bromden because of his madness. However, the book itself will not bear the weight of such an argument, since McMurphy strives to save Bromden from his schizophrenia, not enter into it himself. Fiedler's argument could have been strengthened had he recognized the ambiguity of Bromden's whereabouts at the book's end and asserted that *all* events in the book are hallucinations.

JAMES E. MILLER, JR.

James E. Miller, Jr., is Professor of English at the University of Chicago. He has written extensively on Melville and Whitman and has edited works by both authors. He has also been a Guggenheim Fellow and a Fulbright Lecturer.

THE HUMOR IN THE HORROR

. . . Though all the ingredients of modern fiction look like the ingredients of stark tragedy, they turn out most frequently, when mixed with heavy dashes of the modern ironic sensibility, to be the ingredients of a kind of comedy of outrage, often hilarious. Near the end of Salinger's *Catcher in the Rye*, after Holden Caulfield has seemingly tried and found locked all the doors that might lead him out of his terrible predicament, he attempts to preoccupy himself by reading a magazine he finds on a park bench: "But this damn article I started reading made me feel almost worse. It was all about hormones. It described how you should look, your face and eyes and all, if your hormones were in good shape, and I didn't look that way at all. I looked exactly like the guy in the article with lousy hormones. So I started getting worried about my hormones. Then I read this other article about how you can tell if you have cancer or not. It said if you had any sores in your mouth that didn't heal pretty quickly, it was a sign that you probably had cancer. I'd

Reprinted from *Quests Surd and Absurd,* © 1968 by the University of Chicago Press.

had this sore on the inside of my lip for about *two weeks*. So I figured I was getting cancer. That magazine was some little cheerer upper." This is but one instance in a multitude in the book in which an episode of crucial seriousness is alleviated—or intensified—by a comic mode. Wright Morris repeatedly injects the absurd in his serious novels, as when in *The Field of Vision* he has Gordon Boyd shake a bottle of pop and squirt the supercharged liquid into the face of a bull in the middle of the bull fight, or when, in *Ceremony in Lone Tree*, he portrays the mailman Bud Momeyer, arrayed in Indian feathers, shooting an arrow through Colonel Ewing's pet bulldog, which has been insured for ten thousand dollars. The comic tone filters through all of the grotesqueries of Flannery O'Connor: near the end of *Wise Blood*, Haze Motes has blinded himself and begins to indulge in other means of self-torture, such as wrapping barbed wire around his chest in preparation for sleep; his landlady Mrs. Flood exclaims, "There's no reason for it. People have quit doing it"; he answers with stoic logic: "They ain't quit doing it as long as I'm doing it." Absurdity abounds everywhere in such surrealists and satirists as James Purdy (from *Malcolm* to *Cabot Wright Begins*) and Terry Southern (from *Candy* to *The Magic Christian*). And even in so sober a novelist as Saul Bellow, *Herzog* is structurally based on an essentially comic device, the protagonist's mad letter-writing to everyone ranging from his enemies to the classic philosophers and even to God—copiously quoted letters which are never sent anywhere, except to the reader.

As the comic doomsday vision has come to dominate the fiction of the post–World War II period, it has recently acquired the title of "black humor." And although it is not difficult to find pre–World War II examples (as in William Faulkner's *Sanctuary* or *As I Lay Dying*, or Herman Melville's *Bartleby* or *Confidence Man*), never before in our literature, perhaps, has the blackness been so bleak or the comedy so savage. Recent examples which loom largest, all novels of the 1960s, are Joseph Heller's *Catch-22*, Ken Kesey's *One Flew Over the Cuckoo's*

Nest, and Thomas Pynchon's *V.* If, for example, we read Kesey's *Cuckoo's Nest* as a paradigm of the predicament of modern man, we find the entire world a nuthouse, with Big Nurse in her stiff, starched white, imposing her power through the use of all her gleaming, glittering, flashing machinery; and her power completes the degradation and dehumanization of her victims, who are efficiently divided into two groups: the "hopeful" Acutes, who "move around a lot. They tell jokes to each other and snicker in their fists . . . and they write letters with yellow, runty, chewed pencils"; and the hopeless Chronics, who are the culls of the Acutes—the "Chronics are in for good . . . [and] are divided into Walkers . . . and Wheelers and Vegetables." The great fear of the Acute is to become a Chronic, as has happened to one Ellis, who came back from the "brain-murdering room," or the "Shock Shop," "nailed against the wall in the same condition they lifted him off the table for the last time, in the same shape, arms out, palms cupped, with the same horror on his face. He's nailed like that on the wall, like a stuffed trophy. They pull the nails when it's time to eat. . . ." Ellis may be one version of modern man, hopeless, helpless, self-crucified, committed for life to a super-efficient asylum that destroys what it cannot dehumanize.

The nightmare world, alienation and nausea, the quest for identity, and the comic doomsday vision—these are the four elements that characterize recent American fiction. But a fifth element should be added, not as one of the central or dominant ingredients, but, as I place it here, as a kind of afterthought, or postscript. It is—

A Thin, Frail Line of Hope   It would be misleading, if only slightly so, to imply that all is despair in the contemporary novel. There is, in fact, some measure of affirmation in nearly all of the contemporary novelists, slender in some, robust in others. In the novelists who are, in some complex sense, religious novelists, such as J. D. Salinger, Flannery O'Connor, or John Updike, the affirmation tends to be expressed in some kind of spiritually transcendental terms, however vague or faint.

In such surrealistic novelists as James Purdy, John Hawkes, or William Burroughs, the hope, if it is there, appears only occasionally and faintly in the tone of voice emerging from behind the pages of the novels. Perhaps most characteristic of the thin, frail line of hope in contemporary fiction is the kind of affirmation found in such novels as Heller's *Catch-22* and Kesey's *One Flew Over the Cuckoo's Nest*—the defiant assertion of one's humanity in the face of overwhelming forces that dehumanize and destroy. . . .

❀◇

JOSEPH J. WALDMEIR

Joseph J. Waldmeir has taught literature in Denmark and, as a
Fulbright Lecturer, in Finland. He is at present at Michigan State
University. He has written and edited numerous essays on American
literature.

TWO NOVELISTS OF THE ABSURD:
HELLER AND KESEY[1]

Only twice since the Second World War, in Joseph Heller's
Catch-22 and in Ken Kesey's *One Flew Over the Cuckoo's
Nest,* have serious American novelists made a conscious effort
to transport the novel into the realm of the absurd—up to now
the realm occupied principally by European dramatists and
novelists (such as Genet and Kafka) and by Albee and Kopit in
the United States. Certain American novels, among them Saul
Bellow's *Henderson the Rain King,* Norman Mailer's *Barbary
Shore,* and Ralph Ellison's *Invisible Man,* have sidled to the
threshold only to be caught up short before they could cross it
—apparently by the novelists' allegiance to tradition in form
and content. But Heller and Kesey plunge enthusiastically
across, hopefully enhancing or redirecting tradition, clearly in
the belief that they can more easily reach their audience by

From *Wisconsin Studies in Contemporary Literature,* V, 3 (1964),
192–204. Copyright © 1964 by the Regents of the University of Wisconsin.
[1] This paper was read at a meeting of the Modern Language Association
of Finland, at the University of Helsinki, Helsinki, Finland, in Spring, 1964.

chopping away at its preconceptions of order both in life and in art. The popular as well as critical success of both novels is evidence enough that Heller and Kesey may be right, and certainly justifies a critical examination of each novel in terms of its effort to reduce the world to, and reconstruct it as, absurdity. The examination is the more justified since one effort has been a brilliant success while the other remains a magnificent failure.

Catch-22 is a disconcerting book; it alternately attracts and repels, delights and bores. "If I were a major critic," Norman Mailer has written with becoming modesty, "it would be a virtuoso performance to write a definitive piece on *Catch-22*. It would take ten thousand words or more." But Mailer proceeded to devote only about a thousand words to the one elaborate joke (Do you walk to work or carry your lunch?) upon which the novel is built; and a close reading of the text in terms of texture and tone reveals only that its complexity is superficial, that its variety is only apparent, that its apparent repetitiveness is unfortunately only too real.

The novel proceeds from Heller's discovery that everything in the modern world is up for grabs; that nothing—and therefore, ipso facto, everything—makes coherent, logical sense. By the ancient comic device of portraying the preposterous as normal, it is possible to make of this discovery something delightfully, often uproariously, funny, and Heller is superb at the creation of this kind of comedy.

Nearly everything and everybody in *Catch-22* is outlandish, wacky. There is Lt. Scheisskopf, whose monomaniacal love for dress parades finally earns him promotion to General. There is ex-PFC Wintergreen, who, for all practical purposes, runs the war from his clerk's desk by manipulating orders and memoranda. There is the Major named Major Major Major, who got his rank through an understandable IBM error, who doesn't want the rank nor know how to use it, and who consequently flees his office through a window whenever he is about to be approached with a problem. And there are others, equally wacky, but in a far more vicious, deadly sense. There is Captain Black, who, out of jealousy of Major Major, institutes the Glorious Loyalty Oath Crusade in order to prove that Major Major is a Communist by the simple device of refusing to let him sign the Oath (" 'You never heard him denying it until we began accusing him, did you?' "). There is Col. Cathcart, who is most upset to learn that enlisted men pray to the same God as officers (recall the famous Mauldin cartoon of the sunset) and that God listens to them; whose one great dream is to be immortalized in a feature story in the *Saturday Evening Post*, and who, to achieve this end, keeps upping the number of missions his squadron must fly until he has tripled the required number. There is Cpl. Whitcomb, the Chaplain's assistant, who devises a form letter to take care of the growing casualties resulting from Col. Cathcart's policy; the letter reads in part: "Dear Mrs., Mr., Miss, or Mr. and Mrs.: Words cannot express the deep personal grief I experienced when your husband, son, father, or brother was killed, wounded, or reported missing in action." And finally —though there are many others who could and some readers would argue should be mentioned—there is Milo Minderbinder, angle-shooter extraordinary, caricature of the American businessman. He forms a syndicate, M & M Enterprises, dealing in everything imaginable from Lebanese cedar to Dutch tulips, Swiss cheeses, Spanish oranges, and Egyptian cotton. He insists that he operates a legitimate business in the American way, for each member of the squadron is a shareholder in the syndicate; and, since business is above quarrels between nations, there are English, French, German, and Italian partners in the syndicate as well—all of which makes very little difference since the profits are all plowed back into the business anyway, and there are no holds to share. Milo sells petroleum and ball bearings to the Germans and even contracts with them, in a major coup for the syndicate, to bomb and strafe his own airfield with planes of its own squadron. And because he is successful in the American tradition—that is, because his books show a substantial profit—Milo is admired and respected by the American people;

even, though somewhat grudgingly, by those who lost loved ones in the bombing and strafing.

Lt. John Yossarian, a bomber pilot from whose point of view we observe most of the action, is one of the few even moderately "normal" characters in the novel. The others—the Chaplain, Doc Daneeka, Major Danby, each a friend and confidant of Yossarian—are all caught up to some degree in the prevailing absurdity. But Yossarian is not. Each of his actions, preposterous, indeed crazy though it might be, is carefully calculated both to protest the absurdity and to get him out of combat if not clean out of the service. He complains of a non-existent liver pain in order to be hospitalized to await the pain's becoming jaundice so that it can be treated. (The first variation of the elaborate joke: the doctors can cure jaundice, but a simple pain in the liver they cannot cure, whether the pain exists or not.) Yossarian censors enlisted men's mail by editing the letters unmercifully, sometimes deleting all modifiers and articles, sometimes blacking out all but the salutation and close; and he signs as the name of the censoring officer either Washington Irving or Irving Washington. He either goes to sleep or behaves boorishly at briefing sessions. On the day that he is to be awarded a medal he appears in ranks totally nude, protesting that his uniform is covered with the blood of the man whose death earned him the medal. But his counter-absurdity campaign is fruitless, the world being what it is. In the first place, Yossarian is not considered crazy by his superiors but simply insubordinate, and therefore eligible not for a Section-8, but for flying more combat missions. In the second place, there is the magnificently absurd logic of *Catch-22* "Which specified that a concern for one's own safety in the face of dangers that were real and immediate was the process of a rational mind." All one must do to be grounded for mental reasons, Doc Daneeka explains to Yossarian, is to ask; but asking is proof that one is not crazy. Put in another way: "If he flew [more missions] he was crazy and didn't have to; but if he didn't want to he was sane and had to."

The novel moves by fits and starts toward Yossarian's eventual desertion, but this is not a forward movement. It really does not go anywhere that it has not already been in its first few pages, albeit with slight variations in situation and character. In addition, there is no clearly juxtapositional relationship among its episodes; they are by and large interchangeable—so much so that many of them could actually be removed without in the least marring the novel's structure. In fact, since Heller tends to tell the same joke and laugh the some ironic laugh over and over again, removing some of the episodes could cut down the repetitiveness, the redundancy, and improve the novel considerably. Plotless really, the book is unified by the pattern of absurdity established at its outset. But this is a tenuous unity at best; and it is here, faced with chaotic structure and endless repetition of episodes which individually are often quite funny, that one begins to feel doubt and dissatisfaction about the novel. Somehow, one feels, it would have been better if it had been better made.

In one sense, this criticism may seem rather picayune; after all, the novel remains brilliantly comic, episodic or not. But in another, higher sense, the criticism is of major seriousness, for the episodic flaw is symptomatic of the novel's failure—and most importantly, of its failure *on its own terms*: as absurd. The artist must have a position, a point of view, some awareness of what things should or could be in order to be aware of the absurdity of things as they are. Without such an awareness, he really has nothing to portray—and the portrayal of nothing as absurd equals the portrayal of nothing as nothing. And (here Heller is hoist by his own petard, *Catch-22* itself) all of the absurd episodes imaginable cannot turn his work into something—above all, cannot make it absurd.

Heller could have used Milo Minderbinder, the soldier-businessman who profits so heavily from the non-sense of war, to crystallize a direction and purpose for the book. The anonymous writer who reviewed the novel for *Daedalus* (which review was reprinted as a feature in the *National Observer*) apparently had this possibility in mind when he wrote that "*Catch-22* is immoral because it follows a fashion in spitting indiscriminately at business and the professions, at respectability, at ideals, at all visible tokens of superiority. It is a leveling book in the worst sense, leveling everything and everyone downward." However, Milo is far too outlandish a character, far too preposterous and overdrawn to contribute to any sort of social criticism, let alone to the leftist-nihilism suggested in the review. Milo is the only character who can support the reviewer's conclusion, yet the conclusion is hardly inescapable; the evidence in fact would seem as justifiably to indicate that Heller is conservative, that by means of reducing Milo to the ridicule of caricature, he has reduced social criticism itself, especially of businessmen, to the same level. Still, it is difficult to believe that either conclusion is accurate. It seems most reasonable to believe that Heller consciously and intentionally failed to use Milo as any sort of social critical foil, that he feared that doing so would impose a seriousness upon the novel the responsibility for which he did not wish to assume.

Yet finally, as if he were suddenly convinced that the novel needed some direction and purpose—needed, so to speak, to be rescued from itself—Heller invests Yossarian with idealism and nobility of motive. In a scene recognized even by Robert Brustein in his extremely favorable review as "an inspirational sequence which is the weakest thing in the book," Yossarian justifies his imminent desertion against an appeal to his patriotism and his anti-Nazi conscience: " 'Christ, Danby,' " he argues; " 'I earned that medal I got. . . . I've flown seventy goddam combat missions. Don't talk to me about fighting to save my country. I've been fighting all along to save my country. . . . The Germans will be beaten in a few months. And Japan will be beaten a few months after that. If I were to give up my life now, it wouldn't be for my country.' " The weakness of the sequence is of course that it is totally unconvincing. There is nothing wrong with an American novelist being in favor of the Second World War; Heller would in fact be unique if he opposed it. But since he appears to be opposed to it throughout the novel, there is something wrong with Yossarian, even as Heller's spokesman, mouthing pro-war sentiments. The statement constitutes a reversal of intention almost as flagrant as Wouk's in *The Caine Mutiny*; it really negates or denies the novel. One might forgive it if Heller could see it as even moderately integral, if the novel had prepared the way for it. But such is not the case; the sequence is not added up to, it is simply added on, an afterthought, as if Heller were saying: "You see? This has all been a joke—good, clean fun with overtones of the macabre to titillate. But underneath there has really been something deep and important going on." Unfortunately, however, there hasn't been.[2]

One Flew Over the Cuckoo's Nest is as tightly organized and directed as *Catch-22* is loose and unfocused. It has few wasted moments or scenes; it has no wasted characters. The novel's greatest strength lies in Kesey's refusal to throw his people away for the sake of comic effect. Most of the characters in the novel, all of the principal ones, are connected with a madhouse, as either confinees or keepers. This is a situation made to order for the kind of comedy at which Heller excels, but Kesey expands it, enlarges it. His people are funny, but not in the same way as Heller's. They are not truly mad, for one thing—nearly all of them are voluntarily committed—they are "touched,"

---

[2] A propos of this discussion, in an interview with Ken Barnard for the *Detroit News* "Sunday Magazine," September 13, 1970, Heller suggests a different interpretation: "I see *Catch-22* as not about World War II. It certainly does not reflect my attitude toward that war. For everybody after Pearl Harbor, it was a war we wanted to fight—a war we knew had to be won. . . . An important point in the book is that the war in Europe is drawing to a close as the danger to Yossarian from his own superiors intensifies. He was able to say in the end of the book that the war against Germany is just about over and the country's not in danger any more, but he is. It's essentially a conflict between people—American officers and their own government. They are the antagonists of *Catch-22*—much more so than the Germans and Hitler, who are scarcely mentioned."

tipped toward differentness by idiosyncrasy or physical disability. And while on the surface the differentness is preposterous, hence comical, as one digs beneath the surface he becomes uneasily aware that the differentness is really normality aggravated and extended. In other words, the seeds of the madness of Kesey's characters are in each one of us, sublimated, dormant, but waiting disconcertingly close to the surface.

There is neither a Scheisskopf nor a Major Major here—no sort of innocent wackiness. Neither is there a Capt. Black, or Col. Cathcart, or Milo Minderbinder—no vicious innocents whose potentiality for evil is vitiated by their utter outlandishness. There is Dale Harding, intellectual, incipient homosexual, who married a very sexy woman in order to assert a manhood which he did not possess, and who, by accusation and innuendo, has forced his wife into acts the awareness of which has driven him into the institution. Harding is master of a highly literate nastiness when referring to his wife; the other side of his coin is Ruckly, whose mind has been so scrambled by an attendant's error in administering electro-therapy that he can only react to the word "wife," and whose reaction is always a violent " 'Ffffuck da wife!' " the only three words he can say. There is Martini, who sees things, including Ruckly's wife (" 'Oh. Her? Yeah, I see here. *Yeah*.' "), and whose participation in a Monopoly game (" 'What's thum other things? Hold it a minute. What's thum other things *all* over the board?' ") makes for a crazily comic scene. But Martini's tendency to complete pictures is nightmarish as well as comic: when he sees straps, his imagination supplies men to be bound by them. There is Billy Bibbit, thirty-one-year-old virgin, who stutters out of an impotence which is incurable because he stutters; and who answers when he is asked when he first stuttered: " 'Fir-first stutter? First stutter? The first word I said I st-stuttered: m-m-m-m-mamma.' " There is the senile Colonel Matterson who lifts the nurses' skirts with his cane, and who continually lectures from an imaginary text in his hand:

" 'America is . . . tell-ah-vision. . . . The But-ter . . . is the Re-pub-li-can party.' " And there is Chief Bromden, from whose paranoic point of view we see much of the action and receive much of the commentary on it. The Chief is a giant American Indian who has been driven into a terror-stricken depression by his contacts with the white world, especially the white business world. He pretends to be a deaf mute in order to avoid all human contact. He believes that time and all events and all men's actions are guided from an enormous control panel hidden in the nurses' office. He is given to hallucinations in which pain and death figure prominently, and when these become too real, he escapes by retreating entirely within himself; but he sees his retreat as an engulfment by fog from a gigantic Army surplus fog-machine installed in the vents of the ward by the same authorities who built the control panel. He fights back at authority by collecting wads of chewing gum, chewing them soft again, and sticking them under his bed.

Funny? Yes and no. We may laugh, but the laughter is not the same as that which we give to *Catch-22*. It has echoes; it is brittle. Any feeling that we might have had on beginning the book that Kesey has cheated, has taken the downhill road toward a portrayal of the absurdly comic—as, for example, Jacobean dramatists often did by setting scenes in Bedlam—is obviated by the wryness of our laughter. But even more importantly, it is obviated by the fact that Kesey shapes his unique cast of characters into a society, close-knit, functioning; a society in which the norm is differentness—a society of disaffiliates. But the characters are strange disaffiliates, aware of their differentness and only occasionally defensive, and seldom angry, about it. " 'All of us here are rabbits of varying ages and degrees, hippity-hopping through our Walt Disney world,' " Harding says. " 'Oh, don't misunderstand me, we're not in here *because* we are rabbits—we'd be rabbits wherever we were—we're all in here because we can't *adjust* to our rabbithood.' " The mirror then which they hold up to life is warped both horizontally and vertically, and the image we see in it is and is not ourselves, is—and is not—comic.

Set against this society is Miss Ratched, called Big Nurse by the patients. Except for a tremendous mammalian development, she is a quite ordinary-looking, fifty-year-old woman. In the eyes of the outside world, she is absolutely normal; indeed, she is a perfect representative of a standardized, conformist, correct outside world, whose elemental desire is to protect itself against non-conformity or incorrectness either by conversion (that is, by cure) or by exile (that is, by incarceration). Chief Bromden sees the nurse as a representative of "the 'Combine' . . . a huge organization that aims to adjust the Outside as well as . . . the Inside." He sees her as the operator of the control panel, wielding

> a sure power that extends in all directions on hairlike wires too small for anybody's eyes but mine; I see her sit in this web of wires like a watchful robot, tend her work with mechanical insect skill, know every second which wire runs where and just what current to send up to get the results she wants. . . . What she dreams of there in the center of those wires is a world of precision, efficiency and tidiness like a pocket watch with a glass back, a place where the schedule is unbreakable and all the patients who aren't Outside, obedient under her beam, are wheelchair Chronics with catheter tubes run direct from every pantleg to the sewer under the floor.

But the nurse's power depends not upon the Outside but upon the society of the Inside. " 'We *need* a good strong wolf like the nurse to teach us our place,' " Harding continues. " 'I simply need her to make me *happy* with my role [as a rabbit].' " Ironically then, if that need should be destroyed, the nurse would lose her power and her control. Consequently, the nurse's response to every threat to her control, real or imagined, is the exertion of more power. She has surrounded herself with a staff which she controls absolutely and which in turn can exert maximum control over the inmates. Her three orderlies are frightened semi-sadists who relish their permission to tyrannize the patients as a compensation for their fear of the nurse and their strong feelings of inferiority—it is neither accident nor racism that Kesey makes them Negroes or that one of them, a dwarf, is the result of his mother's rape by a white man. She controls the selection of the psychiatrist for her ward simply by being there before him, by having rigidly established policies, and by her attitude, that is, her willingness or unwillingness to cooperate, which can either make or break his usefulness. Dr. Spivey, her psychiatrist at the time of the novel, is a meek ineffectual theorizer who sympathizes with the actual problems of the patients, but has no real understanding of them and is made so uncomfortable by them that his tendency, somewhat akin to Major Major's, is to run away from them, down to his office to draw on graphs.

Into this cuckoo's nest drops Randle Patrick McMurphy who, by beating up fellow convicts on a prison farm, had contrived to have the state commit him to the easy life of the nest for diagnosis and treatment as a potentially dangerous psychopath. Drunk, brawler, gambler, ladies' man, hell-raiser extraordinary, McMurphy is the only true misfit, the only true disaffiliate in the nest; and he brings into it an independence, a self-confidence, and a hatred of authority destined to upset the delicate balance of preposterousnesses and tip the scales toward absurdity.

In small and large ways, he makes a shambles of the routine, the procedures, the fixed positions, the *order* of the nest. He refuses to remove his cap, day or night. He dashes about wearing only black undershorts with red-eyed white whales emblazoned on them (" 'From a co-ed at Oregon State . . . a Literary major. . . . She gave them to me because she said I was a symbol' "). He asks the Big Nurse if she has ever measured the distance from nipple to nipple of her enormous breasts; and, as latrine orderly, he pastes small slips of paper with obscenities written backward on them under the lips of the bowls so that the nurse will see them when she inspects, first-sergeant fashion, with a mirror. He promotes the setting up of a game room, then wins all of the other patients' money at blackjack and poker. He organizes the patients into a basketball team and has them practice dribbling and passing up and down the ward while he shouts instructions and blows shrilly on a whistle.

These are only a few examples of the sort of guerrilla warfare McMurphy conducts against the nurse's authority. On a more significant level, he forces the theoretical democracy of the ward, under which the patients had always voted on policy which the Big Nurse had actually dictated, into a true democracy, by campaigning, lobbying, cajoling the electorate. The patients vote to watch the World Series on television over the nurse's strenuous objection that doing so would interfere with occupational therapy; and when she vetoes their vote by cutting off the power which feeds the television set, the patients, following McMurphy's lead, simply pretend to watch it, laughing at and cheering the blank screen while the nurse explodes. The patients vote, again overriding the nurse's protest, to accompany McMurphy on a deep-sea fishing trip arranged by his "aunt," a golden-hearted prostitute named Candy. The trip is delightfully comic; everyone relaxes, especially McMurphy, who spends most of his time in the cabin with Candy, and Dr. Spivey, whom McMurphy had conned into accompanying the group as its legal attendant, and who catches the largest fish.

The immediate motive for McMurphy's antics, in addition to a simple sense of fun and a straightforward lust for life, complemented by a hatred and fear of authority and discipline (early in the novel, he identifies the Big Nurse as a " 'ball-cutter,' " one of those people " 'who try to make you weak so they can get you to toe the line . . . to live like they want you to' " by " 'going for your vitals' ") is a hard-headed self-interest. McMurphy enters the nest to get out of hard work, teaches the patients to gamble in order to win their money, and pursues his wild course partly at least because he had bet the patients that he could cause the nurse to lose her icy composure by means of it—a bet which he wins as she screams at them watching the blank television screen.

As long as these remain his sole motivations, McMurphy is in magnificent control of the situation in the nest. But slowly, gradually his self-interest begins to expand, and a new motive subsumes the other three: a feeling of responsibility to and for the other inmates of the nest, a desire, a need, to protect their vitals from the nurse's shears. And with the strengthening of the new motive, McMurphy begins to lose control and to expose his own vitals. He continues to harass the nurse long after he has collected the bet, long after he learns that she dictates the length of his confinement, not the court-imposed sentence to the prison farm. And when the new motivation leads him to defend another patient from one of the ward attendants and a violent fight ensues, the Big Nurse starts to snip away. McMurphy is strait-jacketed and hauled off for a calming electrotherapy treatment.

Three successive shocks fail to castrate McMurphy, though they roughen his composure and blunt his exuberance sufficiently that, when he is returned to the ward, his hell-raising gaiety is less spontaneous, more forced. And, of course, he overcompensates. Before his sentence to electro-therapy, he had planned a little midnight party in the ward the main purpose of which was to be the destruction of Billy Bibbit's virginity by "Aunt" Candy. But now, as McMurphy struggles to reassert control, the party develops into a wild bacchanalian wing-ding, the climax of all the harrassment, all the antics, all the anti-authoritarian nose-thumbing. The party appears at first reading to be the weakest episode in the novel; both its humor and its point are blurred at about the time the patients break into the supply room to drink cherry-flavored alcohol-and-codeine cough syrup. But perhaps Kesey may be forgiven for overdoing the episode, since he is trying to show that the form of protest which the party represents will no longer work; that it is at best sterile and at worst destructive; that a man, once committed, cannot by any means, but especially by a reductio ad absurdum, postpone his rush toward destiny—though that destiny itself be the ultimate absurdity.

On the surface, the party is a huge success, with everyone getting happily drunk, the ward being satisfactorily demolished, and McMurphy sleeping with Candy's friend, Sandy. It is climaxed the following morning as Big Nurse discovers the now non-virginal, non-stuttering Billy Bibbit wrapped peacefully in Candy's arms. But with one quick snip, the nurse turns success to failure, manhood to whimpering despair. She tells Billy that it is her duty to inform his mother of his actions, and he suddenly stutters so badly that he cannot even protest. Distracted, cowering, Billy is taken to await the doctor's arrival, and while alone in the office, he commits suicide by cutting his throat with a scalpel.

Immediately the nurse turns her weapon on McMurphy, charging him with driving Billy to his death. And with his defenses dissipated by the party's nightmare ending, McMurphy finds himself face to face with *Catch*-22, uncluttered, pin-point sharp—a thin absurd line stretched tautly between the comic and the tragic. Either to deny or to accept responsibility for Billy's death is to admit that he is mad, and is to negate all that his weeks of struggle have achieved, is in fact to make futile the death itself. For the death to be meaningful McMurphy must win, must be free, must live; but in order to win he must lose, in order to be free he must bind himself inextricably, in order to live he must be destroyed. The only alternative is to desert the struggle, and, his motive crystallized by the nurse's accusation, McMurphy rejects it. " 'We couldn't stop him,' " says Chief Bromden:

> because we were the ones making him do it. It wasn't the nurse that was forcing him, it was our need that was making him push himself slowly up from sitting, his big hands driving down on the leather chair arms, pushing him up, rising and standing like one of those moving-picture zombies, obeying orders beamed at him

from forty masters. It was us that had been making him go on for weeks, keeping him standing long after his feet and legs had given out, weeks of making him wink and grin and laugh and go on with his act long after his humor had been parched dry between two electrodes.

Hitching up his black shorts, McMurphy rips the nurse's uniform down the front so that "the two nippled circles started from her chest and swelled out and out, bigger than anybody had ever imagined, warm and pink in the light," and knocking her backward, crawls atop her and sinks his fingers into her throat.

Before he can complete the murder, McMurphy is dragged away, back to disturbed, back to the completion of his castration, the price he must pay for his victory. For he does win; with the sacrifice of his own manhood he buys back the manhood of most of the other inmates. One by one the Acutes, the walking wounded, leave the nest, until only three are left when McMurphy is wheeled back in, no longer McMurphy, his arms thin and helpless, his face chalky and blank except for the purple bruises around his eyes which are the after-effects of a lobotomy. Among those remaining is Chief Bromden, determined that McMurphy shall not be made to lose any more than his life, shall not be forced to pay with his dignity as well as his manhood for the freedom of the inmates. In the night, he consummates McMurphy's symbolic sacrifice by smothering what is left of him with a pillow. Then the Chief too, a giant once more, whole and unafraid, strides away from the nest.

Everything in *One Flew Over the Cuckoo's Nest* drives inexorably toward this denouement, and therein rests the novel's strength. There is no waste; there are no loose ends tied together by after-the-fact, jerry-built rationalizations. The conflict between McMurphy the disaffiliate—pushing and being pushed into a commitment which, Kesey implies, only the disaffiliate can choose to make—and Big Nurse—Milo Minderbinder focused and pointed, society, order, the Combine-syndicate—begins from an almost philosophic necessity and proceeds inevitably to McMurphy's "victory" through self-sacrifice. In addition, without harming the tightness of the novel, Kesey writes on the figurative as well as on the literal level, enriching the novel's texture and at the same time clarifying its conflict. Thus the nurse's tremendous bust, coupled with her essential asexuality ("'I couldn't get it up over [her] even if she had the beauty of Marilyn Monroe,'" says McMurphy, the self-confessed whambam man), label the social pressure of the Combine as matriarchal, and underscore the tragedy of Billy Bibbit as the motivating force behind McMurphy's self-destructive violent attack on her. And the bust, in conjunction with the whales emblazoned on McMurphy's shorts, set her forth as Ahab's nemesis, the evil in good which Ahab must destroy and be destroyed by; and, of course, McMurphy is Ahab, good in evil, driving beyond hope of return toward guilt and expiation. Even more appropriately, considering the selfish-altruistic duality of McMurphy's motivation, Kesey draws freely from Christian symbolism to reinforce his points. So, for example, the electrotherapy table is shaped like a crucifix, McMurphy is hung upon it three times, and he asks "'Do I get a crown of thorns?'" just before the dials are twisted. And Kesey integrates the symbolism perfectly, carrying the Christian parallel to its logical conclusion by causing Chief Bromden, McMurphy's biographer, his priest, to murder the already dead victor-victim, thus partaking of the sacrifice in order that he may live whole, renewed, a man again.

Kesey creates finally in McMurphy a modern un-hero or anti-hero who expands himself, through a gradual shift in his concern from himself to those around him, into the role of the traditional hero. It is a strange and preposterous role, the more preposterous since McMurphy retains his anti-heroic qualities throughout the transition—the prostitute Candy emphasizes the strangeness by calling him *a* McMurphy, as if he were a condition or a state of being. In the modern world, such a hero, individualistic to the point of disaffiliation but at the same time

altruistic to the point of self-sacrifice, is by definition absurd;
and all people and actions touched by such heroism are tinted
by its absurdity. Accordingly, such heroes must end in tragedy,
like Ahab or Jesus, or, and this comparison seems yet more
fruitful, like Kafka's Joseph K., who is caught in the same
absurd situation as McMurphy, who battles the Combine as
stubbornly as McMurphy, who is pursued by the furies of responsibility as relentlessly as McMurphy, and who dies, as all
McMurphys must die, figuratively driving the knife into his own
throat.

There are flaws in *One Flew Over the Cuckoo's Nest*—
Kesey shifts point of view frequently, largely because of the
undependability of Chief Bromden as an observer; some of the
Chief's introspection, though interesting enough, drags a bit;
and the possibility that the climactic party scene may be somewhat overdone has already been mentioned. But the flaws are
minor; they are the sort that often serve to make first novels
even more interesting because they result from the novelist's
serious and sincere hard work. There is no flabbiness, there are
no episodic loose ends in *One Flew Over the Cuckoo's Nest* as
there so obviously are in *Catch-22*. Kesey's book is controlled,
tight; it moves forward with the inevitability of great argument.
And as we have seen, perhaps paradoxically, the successful
portrayal of absurdity, because it requires a tightness rather
than a looseness of form, also requires argument, the positing of
directions from which and toward which and around which
the action and the characters may move—requires, if you will,
at least the potential existence of the Court or Godot or the
Rhinoceros or an American Dream or a Combine. If the argument should control the novel; if, for example, Kesey had allowed his work to be dominated by the Big Nurse–Combine
equation or by anti-electro-therapy propaganda, then the novel
would have slipped toward the documentary and failed for
precisely the opposite reasons that *Catch-22* fails: because it
would contain too much something rather than too much noth-

ing. But Kesey maintains control; though his positions and his allegiances are never in doubt, his arguments are not dominant but integral, and *One Flew Over the Cuckoo's Nest* thus becomes the first truly successful American novel of the absurd since World War II.

❀◆

JOHN A. BARSNESS

John Barsness was chairman of the English department at Boise State
College. He also held offices in the Western American Literature
Association and in the Rocky Mountain American Studies Association. His publications include articles in *Western American Literature*
and *New Mexico Review*. Professor Barsness died in 1969.

KEN KESEY: THE HERO IN

MODERN DRESS

In American literature, it has been virtually impossible to distinguish between the serious and the popular hero. On the one
hand, he may appear as Melville's Handsome Sailor, "with no
perceptible trace of the vainglorious about him, rather with the
offhand unaffectedness of natural regality . . . mighty boxer . . .
on every suitable occasion foremost";[1] on the other, he may be
as familiar as Owen Wister's Virginian, "a slim, young giant,
more beautiful than pictures . . . no dinginess . . . or shabbiness
. . . could tarnish the splendor that radiated from his youth and
strength."[2] Either figure is interchangeable with the other, a
peculiarly native and primordial image arising primarily out of
nineteenth-century notions of the democratic frontiersman,
made virtuous and pure by the beneficial influences of nature,

---

Reprinted from *Bulletin of the Rocky Mountain Modern Language
Association*, XXIII, 1 (March 1969) 27–33.

[1] Herman Melville, "Billy Budd," *The Portable Melville* (New York,
1964), pp. 638–9.
[2] Owen Wister, *The Virginian* (New York, 1911), p. 4.

absolutely free physically and morally from the debilitating corruptions of European civilization. He flourishes best among the innocent ideals of the Jeffersonian landscape, that well-groomed pastoral panorama, populated with peaceful, hardworking, independent yeomen, roused to instant action by any threat to their independence.

In such surroundings, the American hero was adored for over a hundred years. He has had less success in the twentieth century, except in his best-known native form as the cowboy, where he lingers on in popular literature in multiple versions of the Virginian, more and more stylized, farther and farther from the nineteenth-century pastoral conviction. But it has become increasingly difficult to maintain that rugged frontiersman as hero, particularly since at midcentury the society approaches an overwhelming urbanization, and contemporary literature seems totally preoccupied with non-heroes whose landscapes are concrete and steel and whose primary characteristics are fixed upon failure. In such surroundings, faced with such assumptions, the hero is an anachronism, out of scale and out of kilter with contemporary standards of truth.

That is why it is so surprising to meet a pair of Western heroes in contemporary American literature, the protagonists of two novels by Ken Kesey: Randle McMurphy in *One Flew Over the Cuckoo's Nest* (1962) and Hank Stamper in *Sometimes a Great Notion* (1964). Even more surprisingly, both of these heroes have received contemporary praise and survived contemporary criticism, possibly because they are so cleverly concealed in the jungle of contemporary standards which Kesey nourishes around them. McMurphy is a patient in an Oregon mental hospital; Hank Stamper is so surrounded by Freudian implications, complicated fraternal relationships, and sexual rivalries that it is nearly impossible to catch a glimpse of his shining armor. Yet heroes both are, and they dwell, as their ancestors did, in the Virgin Land, victims like all their kind of the pastoral dream in which civilization is a dirty word and

Jeffersonian democracy is both the shape of the golden past and the definition of the utopian ideal.

It is an attractive dream, a familiar and simple myth in the Western novel, where the good guys always triumph over the bad guys; or it is a complicated fable in a novel like *The Adventures of Huckleberry Finn*, where the heroes of the river glide forever past the slack corruption of the town. In essence, any version of the story is a transcendental one. Central to it is the hero, more Jacksonian than Jeffersonian man, intuitive in action, non-intellectual in habit, anti-social, anti-urban, and full of the freedom and strength inherent in nature. The enemy he fights is society, artificial, complex, institutionalized—civilization, if you will, the enemy of Randle McMurphy and Hank Stamper as it was of the Virginian and Huckleberry Finn. Oppressive, conformist, regulatory, civilization is the suppressor of individual freedom and the mindless slave of a material goal. Opposed to it, the hero becomes the ultimate idealist, sacrificial but triumphant, intuitively sensitive to a higher and more spiritual good, and, in spite of the trappings of reality with which his author may surround him, the central figure of a romance.

In *One Flew Over the Cuckoo's Nest*, it seems difficult to believe, since Randle McMurphy is, as we have seen, a man who has committed himself to a state mental hospital in order to avoid the physical labor of a prison farm. But in spite of this we recognize him immediately as the hero: "voice loud and full of hell . . . redheaded with long red sideburns and a tangle of curls . . . broad across the jaw and shoulders, a broad white devilish grin . . . hard . . ."[3] And from that moment he takes over, quite naturally, the world of the hospital ward. Almost immediately be becomes the "Bull Goose Loony"—the leader of the patients—standing up staunchly to Big Nurse Ratched, matriarchal symbol, destroyer of manhood, rule-maker, civilizer,

---

[3] Ken Kesey, *One Flew Over the Cuckoo's Nest* (New York, 1962), p. 16; Viking Compass edition, p. 11.

and devil. The conflict thereafter is simple: Hero McMurphy vs. Villainess Ratched, he, like all heroes, alone except for the passive and undependable patients; she, supported by all the resources of the hospital and its staff. Nobly, altruistically, McMurphy sets out singlehandedly to rescue his wardmates from oppressive, regimented civilization—the world *inside* the hospital. Outside is freedom; *outside*, therefore, they must go, figuratively or literally. At first it is only figuratively—small victories over regimentation, a card game in an empty room. Later, there is even a temporary excursion into nature itself—a carefree trip on a fishing boat, a high point in the rising action, set off by small demonstrations of the power of Big Nurse. That McMurphy overcomes this power is part of the romance; that he ultimately goes down to defeat is inevitable. The climax is touched off by a wild night when the ward itself becomes the *outside*, complete with whisky and whores. But before McMurphy can escape discovery, *order* and *authority*, in all their nightmarish power, force the suicide of one of the patients. In a last defiant gesture, McMurphy rips the uniform from Big Nurse, exposing her as mere woman, and is led away captive to lobotomy to become a mindless vegetable.

This "defeat" along with Kesey's faultless portrayal of institutionalized and aberrant minds, has as much as anything else concealed the heroic fable which is the foundation for this black comedy. But it is not defeat. This hero is too much of an individual, too powerful, actually too successful for that. Though he does not escape, his ally, the Columbia Indian Chief Broom does, and in him the natural man ultimately triumphs. For it is Chief Broom, the Indian pretending dumbness in the face of civilization's blind indifference to him, who rescues McMurphy's mindless body by choking it to death, and goes over the hill to his own freedom among the wild fields and the flowing rivers—the natural world—of his childhood. McMurphy has set him free, first by returning his hulk to life, then by pointing the way to escape and destroying himself for the sake of the only other truly human figure in the novel. It is McMurphy who eventually shapes and dominates *One Flew Over the Cuckoo's Nest*. Thus he becomes the familiar sacrificial figure; like Robert Jordan protecting the flight of Maria, or Sidney Carton at the guillotine, he imitates the Christian martyr, demonstrating virtue by the manner of his death.

Hank Stamper, on the other hand, survives. In shape, Hank is almost identical to McMurphy, big, lusty, physically and personally so vibrant as to dominate his surroundings—and just as much a loner. As hero, his triumph is demonstrated by his survival, and his quarrel is even more clearly with civilization than was McMurphy's, for Hank Stamper is fighting the whole community, represented by the loggers' union and the town of Wakonda, Oregon. Living across the river from them, he is as isolated from this community philosophically as he is physically, for he is wildcatting logs for the big lumber company against whom the town is striking. Indeed, the only community Hank Stamper seems to have any feeling for is his nuclear family: cousin Joe Ben (with wife and children), father Henry, wife Viv, and half-brother Lee, who is his major antagonist outside the town. Hank's task is obvious—he must complete the order for logs in spite of total community opposition and the Freudian conflict with his eastern, college-bred half-brother, who is determined to sleep with his wife in revenge for the seduction of his mother by her stepson Hank. The novel has an extraordinarily complicated structure, stylistically and psychologically, and this, as in *One Flew Over the Cuckoo's Nest*, is the means by which Kesey camouflages his romance as a contemporary black comedy.

But in spite of such deviations from earlier, simpler, and more Victorian patterns, the hero, as Kesey draws him, is even more obvious in *Sometimes a Great Notion* than in *One Flew Over the Cuckoo's Nest*. Just as the classic tradition demands that the hero have a supreme goal to which all other heroic values except honor may be sacrificed, so too does the American version demand that the hero's will and character be the primary means by which he attains his goal.

So it is with Hank. The family business—hence the family living—is being kept alive by his decision to log for the larger company and, in effect, to act as strike-breaker for them. From the beginning it is obvious that it is not the business but the independence which it represents that is of supreme importance to Hank, particularly as it gives him the necessary state of freedom without which no hero can survive. More significantly, it is Hank alone who wills this action; in order to protect this independence and the natural existence from which it stems, he will even defy all the orthodox assumptions of contemporary society. In this his character is clearly that of the nineteenth-century hero, responsible to no one but himself, viewing social cooperation as a sign of weakness, opposition to his will as immoral. Possessed of such a single-minded will, it is no trick at all to justify the part he plays as enemy of the livelihood of the families of Wakonda. Conventional liberal ideals simply don't work for this hero. The furthest he can go toward such loyalties is to that nuclear family—or, as a sop to traditional Christian ethics, to justifying individual success as the key to general human success. Not humanity but the goal becomes holy: delivering the completed booms of logs into the hands of the company becomes Hank's righteous passion. The resultant action is arranged like the classic plot—a series of sharp little conflicts arranged along a rising curve of intensity through Hank's apparent defeat by death, weather, and the union to the final resounding climax of his decision to defy all the forces arrayed against him and get his logs to market. Along the way a host of traditional obstacles litter his path: the growing hostility of the community, the magical hexes of the whore Indian Jenny, the fight with Big Newton, and the inevitably successful seduction of his wife by his half-brother which finishes the destruction of even his family in the pursuit of victory.

Along the way he has stamped his way back and forth over the town, demonstrated the superiority of his commonsensical nature over the fairy intellectualism of his brother (in spite of that seduction), and shown in word and deed his intuitive symbiosis with nature. But even when he is taking a physical beating, he is the hero. It is not really surprising, in the end, that he should set out implacably to accomplish his end, his only allies a boy and his half-brother Lee, whose Hellenic revenge, as well as his civilized intellectual mask, are finally submerged in the primitive floodtide of their mutual Stamper blood. The victory of the hero in this novel is complete. Hank Stamper not only triumphs over all the forces of evil (the town, the corrupted institutionalized society, black civilization itself), but also over his own temptation to give in to overwhelming despair.

At the end, he has reclaimed his individuality, defying tide, temptation, and the town to deliver his logs to the company and prove his heroic righteousness again. Like the ancient Greek warriors, he rises above his obvious humanness to super-human heights; like Natty Bumppo, he demonstrates the natural sources of his virtue and like Randle McMurphy, he holds unswervingly to his predestined goal.

Thus it remains apparent that both of Kesey's heroes are more peculiarly American than European, drawing their strength from the American myth rather than the classic one. They both are virtuous, hardworking yeomen and Jacksonian images of the central American figure, from whose agrarian roots all the democratic values are drawn. In their strength they are kin to Mike Fink and Paul Bunyan rather than to Gargantua; in their practical ambition they adhere to Henry Ford or John D. Rockefeller rather than Robin Hood; and in their moral structure, in spite of their earthiness, they imitate the Virginian or John Alden rather than Lancelot.

What amazes one about these two novels is the deceptiveness with which such heroism is displayed. There is no real trace here of the grandiloquence with which a Walter Scott portrays an Ivanhoe, or even, in spite of previous remarks, of the simple-mindedness of Natty Bumppo. Kesey, perhaps more than any contemporary American writer, has the touch of actuality—of a landscape that has been seen, a dialogue which has

been heard, an action which in spite of its heroic qualities is to
be believed. He knows how the *outside* looks to one who is
fettered *inside*; he knows not only how the rainsoaked forest
of coastal Oregon looks, he knows how it feels to endure whole
seasons of rain. He knows the language of the working people
about whom he writes; he is one of the few writers who can set
down the incessantly obscene talk of the working stiff without
sounding as though he's done it to offend.

But more than that, Kesey is capable of interplaying a wide
variety of characters in their proper roles without missing a
beat. One comes to believe in the mist-enclosed mind of Chief
Broom as he comes to believe in the communal unity of the
whole mad ward upon which McMurphy descends. But he
equally comes to believe in the communal world of the Snag
and the normal madnesses of that proprietal bar. It is impossible
not to believe in the presence of these human beings in their
several locations and actions. What frustrates one is the seeming
necessity of also viewing them as types: the hero and his lesser
lights combatting the forces of evil. It is still the good guys
against the bad guys, even if all the scenes are engagingly
different. One comes inevitably up against the thematic questions: is the side of good always that of the American Hero?
Does an engaging personality, physical superiority, love of nature in her many moods, unswerving loyalty to the ideal of
individuality, automatically range one on the side of righteousness? Are ordinary folk in their tired confusion and their puerile
actions to be so contemptuously brushed aside? Is civilization
always the corruptive betrayer?

That, of course, is the way the myth defines it, heroic America cutting herself off from corrupt and civilized Europe, sending her faithful yeomen into the wilderness to hack paradise out
of the limitless forests. That is the rhetorical way in which the
American has always enacted the role. That Kesey's heroes seem
to carry out that old-fashioned dream in an atmosphere of contemporary confusion does not lessen the traditional and

romantic structure underlying it. Indeed, the central comic thread of madness in *One Flew Over the Cuckoo's Nest* and the theme of fraternal conflict in *Sometimes a Great Notion* are ultimately so much a part of the essential heroic action that their blackness is only orthodox villainy rather than avant-garde comedy. One cannot help but empathize with the tragicomedy of Billy Bibbit in *One Flew Over the Cuckoo's Nest*, driven to suicide by the organized incomprehension designed to "cure" him, or with the fondly drawn protrait of religio-superstitious Joe Ben in *Sometimes a Great Notion*, helpless for all his signs and portents before the indifferent accident of a rising tide. That Billy cures himself for one brief sexual moment and that Joe Ben literally laughs himself to death are ironic touches, but they are only incidental to the essential plot: the hero, though he may not survive, will triumph. It is a little like John Steinbeck's sardonic separation of a cast of characters into white hats, black hats, and gray hats. The white hats are the heroes; the black hats are the villains; and the gray hats are all the subordinate characters who will turn good if they are bad and bad if they are good. A little educated guessing will arrange Kesey's characters into types and sub-types of these basic groups, in spite of the vividness with which they are drawn. A few examples will suffice: Chief Broom is a white hat, for all his reluctance to become a hero (indeed, his relation to McMurphy is singularly reminiscent of Leslie Fielder's basic duo: Natty Bumppo and Chingachgook, the Lone Ranger and Tonto); the Negro ward-boys are as obviously black hats as they are black figures; Dr. Spivey is patently a gray hat, as are one or two puzzling nurses. Lee Stamper is a gray hat, who switches from independent black hat to white hat as he throws off his sexual victory and joins his brother in defying the world; Joe Ben is a white hat, a Loyal Companion like Chingachgook or Chief Broom, though not dark; Evenwrite, Draeger, even Big Newton, are black hats of varying degrees of villainy. It is an interesting game, and it would be no more than that if it were not for the way the action of each story arranges black hat against white hat, hero against villain, until in the end it is plain to see that Ken Kesey, individualist and rebel, has written in these two novels what his native region always seems to induce: a pair of Westerns.

❖◇

IRVING MALIN

Irving Malin teaches at the City College of New York. In addition
to a number of essays, he has published *William Faulkner: An Interpretation*, *New American Gothic*, and *Jews and Americans*.

KEN KESEY: *ONE FLEW*
OVER THE CUCKOO'S NEST

In "Writing American Fiction," an article which appeared in
the March 1961 issue of *Commentary*, Philip Roth states: "the
American writer in the middle of the twentieth century has his
hands full in trying to understand, and then describe, and then
make *credible* much of the American reality." He thinks that
this reality is "even a kind of embarrassment to one's own
meager imagination." There is an urgent artistic problem: How
can the writer deal with such "stupefying," crazy events, our
"universal descent into unreality" (Benjamin DeMott's phrase)?

One answer is the Gothic. New American Gothic disrupts
our "rational" world view or pictures our unreal concerns; it
gives us violent juxtapositions, distorted vision, even prophecy,
without becoming completely private. When it seeks to present
a "social" situation, to proclaim Truth, it lacks authority.

What are the irrational forces Gothic presents? It is primarily
concerned with love, knowing that—as Leslie Fiedler has said—
"there can be no terror without the hope for love and love's

Reprinted from *Critique*, V, 2 (1962), 81–84.

defeat." The typical hero is a weakling. The only way he can escape from the anxiety which plagues him is through a compulsive design. He "loves" this plan, and he compels others to fit into it. His concern for them is not benevolent; it is narcissistic. Narcissism, compulsion, cruel abstractionism—these are found in *Other Voices, Other Rooms, Reflections in a Golden Eye, The Cannibal, Malcolm,* and *The Violent Bear It Away.*

New American Gothic usually deals with a microcosm because the "buried life" does not need a large area of society in which to reveal itself. We have in the novels listed above: Skulley's Landing, an army post in peacetime, a rooming house in Germany, a Chateau, and the backwoods. The private world, however, displays the "big" tensions of contemporary America: "unnatural" self-love and disintegration of order.

New American Gothic is "poetic," using a great deal of imagery. Three images are especially important: haunted houses (imprisonment), violent journeys, and distorted reflections. Because Gothic deals with a narrow view of personality and a microcosm, it creates an intensive, vertical world—one best created in the story or short novel. Perhaps the most successful examples of new American Gothic are "The Headless Hawk," *Reflections in a Golden Eye, The Cannibal,* "The Displaced Person" and 63: *Dream Palace.*

One Flew Over the Cuckoo's Nest by Ken Kesey is a Gothic novel. It employs the themes and images already mentioned, but it does so in a new way. It is not simply imitative. The important theme is, again, the compulsive design. The "Big Nurse" —as the narrator calls her—is an authoritarian, middle-aged woman who tries to impose her will upon her lunatics—she must make them fear and respect her so that she can feel superior. She exerts power not to help others but to help herself: her compulsive design cannot stop—except through violence—because it is all she has.

The "Big Nurse" is no longer a woman—she has become a Frankenstein monster. All of her gestures, commands, feelings, and possessions are mechanized: "there's no compact or lipstick or woman stuff, she's got that bag full of a thousand parts she aims to use in her duties today—wheels and gears, cogs polished to a hard glitter, tiny pills that gleam like porcelain, needles, forceps. . . ." She is "precise, automatic." But God has played a trick on her: the Big Nurse cannot flee from nature. Although she is monstrous, she is still partially female—and the more she tries to exert her "will to power," the more she desperately wants (unconsciously) sex—some kind of affection. She is torn between two worlds.

Obviously, Mr. Kesey must offer us others who combat the design of Big Nurse (and her helpers). There are two. The narrator, an inmate of the asylum, lives in a kind of fog, but he is able to recognize that the authoritarian ruler is more insane than he—after all, he has some kind of affection for his "papa," an Indian chief, who used to take him hunting. He has pity for himself and the other "Acutes" and "Chronics." The narrator senses the faults of the "Combine"—that whole rigid routine, of which Big Nurse is only one cog. Although he always thinks of plots, fiendish motives—a paranoid pattern, in fact—the narrator is praised by Kesey. The insane do *see*; they are less innocent than the slaves of the Combine—such people as silly Red Cross helpers, corrupt government officials, TV viewers. In the upside-down world, the "cuckoo's nest," "insane" and "sane" are meaningless words—words the Combine imposes. Thus the absurd scene in which the hospital staff debates whether an inmate is "negatively Oedipal," or "psychopathic," or "schizophrenic," neglecting the fact that he is *human*.

The narrator cannot resurrect himself; he cannot triumph over Big Nurse. He seeks a guide in the new inmate, McMurphy. This con-man enters laughing: "You boys don't look so crazy to me." Soon McMurphy begins to see that he must assert his will if he is to remain a happy man, and not become a machine. He *plays* with Big Nurse, irritating her smooth order by breaking a window, by not doing his appointed job, by asking for outrageous things. His play inspires the other inmates, especially the narrator, who regain some of their laughing, fighting vitality. But the Combine finally squeezes McMurphy: it makes him a *thing* by performing a lobotomy on him (after he tries to kill Big Nurse). The narrator cannot bear this transformation; mercifully he kills McMurphy and then runs away from the institution.

Mr. Kesey is less concerned with ideas than he should be. There are the "good guys" and the "bad guys." The Combine is dismissed quickly, but we wonder whether it is enough to proclaim the insanity of the system—after all, there are some "rational" adults who realize its falseness and still function in it. Nature—the woods, the streams, sex, the family—is praised without philosophical probing. What if we don't fish? Can we still be human? Of course, Mr. Kesey is not "simple-minded"—he does show us that life contains many terrifying ambiguities. Big Nurse tries to fool the Acutes into thinking McMurphy is a charlatan, who cares less about them than *she* does. For a moment we believe that the benevolent "father" may be a fake. Black and white change to gray.

Mr. Kesey impressively uses imagery—he is a poet, not a philosopher. He employs a consistent range of images to express his almost manic condemnation of the system—we accept these more easily than his "message." And the images *are* the real meaning of his novel.

Several images represent the values of the Combine: imprisonment, mechanization, unreality. On the very first page we see that people are locked-up—in the institution and in the inhumanity of designs. The narrator refers to the henchmen of Big Nurse—their "eyes glittering out of the black faces like the hard glitter of radio tubes out of the back of an old radio." The image brilliantly arranges the scene: not only does this tell us that the narrator is slightly "mad"—it prepares us for the compulsive, automatic actions of the attendants, which help to make them unreal. Here are some other Combine-images: Big Nurse is "precision-made, like an expensive baby doll. . . ." She has made herself into a product, an almost "perfect work."

She tries to "manufacture" others: "Big Nurse puts a thousand pounds down me." The Chronics are "machines with flaws inside that can't be repaired." The literal facts of hospital life—of shock treatments, of operations, of the daily routine—become "symbolic." Mr. Kesey is so adept at stating these images that he needs only to *describe*, not to *explain*. Thus when Mc-Murphy returns after his operation, the narrator says: "There's nothin' in the face. Just like one of those store dummies. . . ." We remember the Nurse as doll, the henchmen as "cartoon figures."

Opposed to these images of the Combine are natural images—free movement, warmth, pastoral. McMurphy is presented this way: "He stands looking at us, rocking back in his boots, and he laughs and laughs." He does not feel trapped; he shakes with humanity. Play is crucial. His carnival idea, his card games, his fishing expedition, his "marriage" of the whore and Billy—all these demonstrate that his capricious spirit is not mechanized. But Mr. Kesey realizes that such "openness" is never completely achieved in the Combine-world. McMurphy *can only be natural by violence*. He has to smash windows, break through imprisonment. The narrator remembers the woods, but he thinks: the "bird breaks, feathers springing, jumps out of the cedar into the birdshot from Papa's gun." The movement must be cataclysmic, after being inhibited for such a long time. Also the body cannot be "romantically" soft, constantly threatened as it is by automation. McMurphy's hand contains carbon, scars, and cuts; the narrator sees himself at first as deaf-and-dumb. (He joins the mutes in *The Heart Is a Lonely Hunter* and "Raise High the Roof Beam, Carpenters.") Mr. Kesey maintains that the Combine and nature interact—we have horrifying oppositions.

But this dialectic also produces humor: "you have to laugh at the things that hurt you just to keep yourself in balance, just to keep the world from running you plumb crazy." "Humor blots out the pain." Mr. Kesey gives us many amusing scenes which are "black"—Big Nurse for example, informs Billy, the whore's betrothed, that she is going to tell his mother!—but he knows that if we can laugh at the unreality around us, we retain our humanity. Gothic and comedy are Janus-faced. *One Flew Over the Cuckoo's Nest* is an honest, claustrophobic, stylistically brilliant first novel which makes us shiver as we laugh—paradoxically, it keeps us "in balance" by revealing our madness.

❀◇

ROBERT BOYERS

Robert Boyers teaches English at Skidmore College in Saratoga
Springs, New York. He is the editor-in-chief of *Salmagundi*, a
quarterly of the arts and social sciences, and has edited a collection
of essays on Robert Lowell.

PORNO-POLITICS

There is no lack of conviction in Ken Kesey's *One Flew Over
the Cuckoo's Nest,* but neither is there an attempt to deal with
human sexuality as a complex phenomenon. Kesey's novel is
wholly successful as an indictment of modern society, and as an
exploration into the kind of subtly repressive mechanisms we
help to build into the fabric of our daily lives. Kesey's solution
to our common problem is the opening of floodgates, the releasing of energies which have too long lain unused or forgotten. Chief among these are the twin resources of laughter
and uninhibited sexuality, the linkage between which Kesey
manages to clarify in the course of his novel.

The novel is set in a mental institution which is, in many
respects, a microcosm of the society-at-large. It is to Kesey's
credit that he never strains to maintain the parallel at any
cost—it is a suggested parallel at most, and, where it suits his
novelistic purposes, Kesey lets it go completely. His protagonist

---

Reprinted with permission from an essay entitled "Attitudes toward Sex
in American 'High Culture,'" *The Annals of the American Academy of
Political and Social Sciences,* 376 (March 1968), 36–52.

is one Randle Patrick McMurphy, pronounced psychopathic by
virtue of being "overzealous in [his] sexual relations." His purpose in the institution, as in life apparently, is both to have a
hell of a good time, and to defy "ball cutters," defined by Mc-
Murphy himself as "people who try to make you weak so they
can get you to toe the line, to follow their rules, to live like they
want you to." McMurphy is a truly monumental character—a
gambler, a braggart, a fantastic lover, and a gadfly who insults
and goads those who resist his charismatic injunctions. While
he is something of a sensualist who dwells regularly on the
ecstasies of sexual transport, and even goes so far as to bring his
whores into the hospital to restore the vitality of his moribund
fellow-psychopaths, McMurphy feels himself and his comrades
the victims of women, not their lords and masters as his rhetoric
would have it. His techniques of resistance and defiance are
mostly pathetic, as they can achieve what are at best pyrrhic
victories. One is never tempted to question the validity, the
nobility, or even the necessity of McMurphy's defiance, but no
mature reader will be convinced that his techniques can realis-
tically accomplish what Kesey claims for them at the novel's
end—the reclamation of numerous human beings who had
grown passive and torpid before McMurphy's arrival.

At one point, McMurphy characterizes the inmates of the
hospital as "victims of a matriarchy." In Kesey's view, modern
society is a reflection of womanish values—archetypically responsible, cautious, repressive, deceitful, and solemn. One must
look to the spirit of the whore if one would know what is best
in women, and what can best bring out what is vital in men.
There is no doubt that Kesey labors under a most reactionary
myth, involving the mystique of male sexuality, which sees men
as intrinsically better than women in terms of the dynamism
and strength they can impart to the universe. Unable rationally
to account for the disparity between such a projection and the
puny reality of our male lives, Kesey waxes fatalistic, though
never submissive, and sees "ball cutters" everywhere. It is a kind
of paranoid, conspiratorial view of things, not without its meas-

ure of accuracy, but it somehow evades the crucial issues which Kesey and others have raised.

At the heart of Kesey's notion of what is possible for modern liberated man is a phenomenon which one may call porno-politics. It is a phenomenon which resides primarily in the imagination of a few thousand people, most of them young and bright, and which is occasionally manifested in the hysterical behavior of certain radical partisans of unpopular causes, a behavior which, by the way, many would call resolutely anti-political, for all its pretensions to the contrary. Advocates of porno-politics are usually utopian socialists who lack the vision and patience to realize their goals politically: that is, they are youthful dreamers who are frustrated by the customary routines through which men achieve power or influence in order to alter the political relations which obtain in their society. Frequently, the retreat into varieties of porno-politics results from people relying too heavily on the flexibility of a given political system, and on the sheer magnetism of their own sincerity, which they and their associates had always considered irresistible. When the erstwhile utopian realizes how restrictive and closed the political structure of his society is, despite its aggressive disclaimers, and when he is made aware of the basic indifference to his ideals and to his attractiveness among the masses of people, he is suffused by a kind of anger and dread. As the society affords him virtually no outlet for these feelings, which rarely become specific enough to fix legitimate targets anyway, the befuddled utopian permits his vision of the possible to undergo a remarkable transformation. Unable to affect masses of men or to move political and social institutions, he transfers the burden of realizing a perfectly harmonious society to sex.

In Kesey's novel, we have what seemingly amounts to a *reductio ad absurdum* of familiar Freudian propositions. It is repressed sexuality which ostensibly lies behind every psychosis, and which is responsible for the acquiescence of all men in the confining conventions of Western society. It is in the spirit of random and thoroughly abandoned sexuality that Kesey's Mc-

Murphy would remake men, and subsequently the world. What is a little frightening in a novel like this, though, is that such a projection does not at all operate on a metaphorical level. Sex is not here a mere metaphor for passion, nor for any positive engagement with one's fellow human beings. There is a literalism in Kesey's suggestions of sexual apocalypse, with its unavoidable ramifications into a political and social context, which cannot be lightly taken. Other talented people are caught up in such projections, and are delivering gospels of sexual salvation with a hysterical dogmatism that is, for many of us, laughable and pathetic. This is so particularly for those who have observed the failure of libertarian sexual experimentation and random coupling to affect substantially the pettiness and self-absorption even of those who are most easily committed to libertarian modes and who have no need perpetually to justify such commitments ideologically. How futile it is for intelligent people seriously to expect their sexual programs and practices to have a liberating effect on masses of men, when what these people want is to be left alone to enjoy what they have. What porno-politics essentially amounts to is a form of entertainment for a middle-class audience, which alternatively writhes and applauds before the late-night news, and welcomes the opportunity to indulge and express postures it considers intrinsic to its worth as modern men: tolerance and righteous indignation.

Kesey's brilliance is evidenced by his ability to be seduced by porno-political utopianism, and yet not to yield to it entirely. What save him are his sense of the ridiculous and his understanding of men as fundamentally dishonest and irresolute. Kesey wants to believe that the source of all terror and passivity is somehow sexual, that the liberation of sexual energies in the form of primal fantasies will enable men to conceive of themselves as more passionate and autonomous individuals. But his intelligence forces him, as it were, against his will, to tell a truth which is more complex and disheartening. He recounts a group therapy session which had taken place in the institution some years before McMurphy's arrival. Unlike the usual dispirited proceedings, this particular session stood out for the violent release of confessions that it evoked from the habitually desultory and tight-lipped inmates. Once the momentum is established, the inmates begin shouting confessions: "I lied about trying. I did take my sister!"/ "So did I! So did I!"/ "And me! And me!"

At first, all of this seems satisfying, at least from a conventionally clinical point of view: repressed memories are rising to the surface, where they can be handled therapeutically. But, almost immediately, we are shown that not only did such events never occur in the lives of these men; they do not even represent their fantasy lives. Such "confessions" have nothing at all to do with the wish-fulfillment that is a strong component of compulsive fantasies. What the inmates have done is simply to exploit certain readily available clichés issuing from standard interpretations of modern man as the perennial victim of sexual repression. The inmates are victims of something much more embracing and diversified than simple sexual guilt or repression, though the sexual element may be particularly significant in the case of two or three inmates among many. What is sickening is their desire to please the therapists by revealing what they are supposed to, rather than what is really inside them. Finally, they are shamed by the resounding announcement of hopeless old Pete: "I'm tired," he shouts—a confession so simple and true that it puts an abrupt end to the rampant dishonesty of the others. Kesey loves McMurphy, and identifies with his aspirations—he wants men to be free, to laugh the authorities down, to refuse to be manipulated. He wants, moreover, to go along with McMurphy's sexual orientation, and to be as optimistic as McMurphy about the effects of sexual liberation on the reigning political and social atmosphere. But McMurphy is not a mask for Kesey, nor is any single character in the novel. In fact, as much as Kesey admires McMurphy's stratagems for outwitting the matriarch *par excellence* who goes under the title Big Nurse, we are never quite certain whether to laugh at McMurphy as well as with him. Big Nurse, as the personification of

"the system" at its most callow, repressive, yet ostensibly enlightened, represents a tendency toward antiseptic desexualiza-
tion which is abhorrent. We want McMurphy to bewilder her,
to kill her with his charming nonchalance and boyish exuberance, and to parade his own aggressive sexuality before her. We
want her to be teased and tempted so that she will be provoked
to try to castrate McMurphy, if not actually, then symbolically,
as she has successfully whipped the other inmates. We want to
see McMurphy put to the test of the vitality and resilience he
proudly proclaims, as if he could redeem us from any misgivings
we might have about our own potency.

And yet, throughout this novel, we know that nothing Mc-
Murphy does, or encourages his comrades to do, will make any
substantive difference to the system that we all despise. Mc-
Murphy, through an ideological predisposition, which in his
case is more instinctive than learned, attributes to sex what
even he knows it cannot accomplish. His is a heroic endeavor
in every way, but McMurphy is at bottom a little lost boy who
gets into the big muddy way up over his head. The picture of
him, in bed with his whore at last, almost at the end of the
novel, is utterly revealing: ". . . more like two tired little kids
than a grown man and a grown woman in bed together to make
love." McMurphy can behave as brashly as he likes, and speak
with utter abandon of sex, but for him it has still an element of
mystery, of vows exchanged, even if only for a brief duration.
His libertarian apocalyptism is sincere, but in McMurphy's own
character we can see that a libertarian sexual orientation ultimately has little to do with making men free as political and
social beings. McMurphy needs no sexual swagger to be free,
though, in his case, it is a believable accouterment of his personality. What is indispensable in McMurphy's character is his
propensity to laugh, in his lucid moments to see himself as
something of a spectacle, not wholly detached nor different
from the other inmates who have failed to retain their resilience.
When he loses his laugh, he grows desperate, and places upon
sex that burden of hope for transcendence which the reality of

sexual experience must frustrate. When, at the very conclusion of the book, McMurphy rips open Big Nurse's hospital uniform, revealing, for all to see, her prodigious breasts, we see where McMurphy's porno-political vision has led him. Unable to affect a world that victimizes him, a civilization which, in the words of the British psychoanalyst R. D. Laing "... represses not only 'the instincts,' not only sexuality, but any form of transcendence," McMurphy is driven to rape the reality incarnated in Big Nurse. In his fear and frustration, he does not see what, of all things, should be most obvious to him: that he cannot make another human being aware of his humanity by destroying or suppressing those elements of his own humanity that have made McMurphy a beautiful person. By his action, he demonstrates the original futility of his project, the necessary brutalization of his sexual ethic, and the dehumanization implicit in the act of invoking an *Eros* which is imperfectly understood and crudely employed.

HAROLD CLURMAN

Harold Clurman has been a distinguished actor and stage director
for many years, as well as being the drama critic for *The Nation*
magazine. He was awarded the George Jean Nathan Drama Criticism
award in 1961, and since 1963 has been Executive Consultant for
the Lincoln Center Repertory Theatre.

REVIEW OF THE PLAY

Certain plays are more memorable for the reaction they pro-
voke in their audiences than for their intrinsic qualities. One
would think that the audiences had written them. Such is the
case of Dale Wasserman's dramatization of a novel by Ken
Kesey, *One Flew Over the Cuckoo's Nest* (Mercer-Hansberry
Theatre: 240 Mercer Street).

I did not see an earlier dramatization of the novel, produced
some years ago with Kirk Douglas, nor have I read the book.
The present adaptation, said to be more streamlined than the
former, is a gruesome soap opera, but the audience is delighted.
It laughs, applauds, and at times shouts its approval. At least
that is what occurred at a (sold-out) preview I attended. The
play was literally a howling success and may very well continue
to be so, especially with the kind of young folk I saw at the
performance just mentioned.

The scene is a ward in a state mental hospital. Most of the
patients are "voluntary." A young man, Billy Bibbit, has

Reprinted with permission from *The Nation*, April 5, 1971.

endured a subjection to his mother that has caused in him a lamentable and permanent stutter; a married man is tormented by fear of sexual deficiency; several others display behavior that is merely feeble-willed or wildly eccentric. Then there are the "committed" patients: one, Chief Bromden, half Indian, has apparently lost the powers of speech and hearing; another has undergone an operation referred to as "a castration of the mind." Over all these unfortunates—who prefer the "protection" of the asylum to the horrors of outside—rules the efficient and rigorous Nurse Ratched, in whose official solicitude and severe discipline one suspects sadism.

Into this brood comes Patrick McMurphy, a rambunctious roustabout, guilty of assault and rape. His laughing defiance of Nurse Ratched, his friendliness to the other inmates and his encouragement of infraction of the regulations ordered by the hospital staff leads to "insurrection." In fact, McMurphy's insubordination helps Chief Bromden overcome his condition as a deaf-mute, a state induced by the humiliation of his father and race on the part of government and real estate interests. When McMurphy, outraged by one of Nurse Ratched's most unfeeling ploys, tries to strangle her, she vengefully orders a lobotomy for him. This turns him into something less than a man. Now rid of his physical disabilities, Chief Bromden, after a mercy killing of his savior, McMurphy, makes a dash for freedom: he it is who flies over the cuckoo's nest.

One might suppose all this to be quite grim, but there is only a dab of sentiment and lots of fun in the telling. What arouses the audience's mirth is the show's derision of vested authority, the comeuppance of rule and order. Nurse Ratched, who even browbeats her medical adviser, is less a character than a stand-in for external power, of which the most common symbol is the police. Prohibited drinking, smoking of pot, crude fornication are joyfully viewed as signs of happy release from oppression.

I choose one example of the play's process and the effect on its audience. McMurphy wishes to help Billy, the young man

whose mother has so intimidated him that he has remained a
virgin as well as the victim of a lifelong speech affliction. At a
midnight party, a girl is brought in to provide the uninitiated
youth with his first "experience." When Nurse Ratched's entrance interrupts this adventure and she upbraids him and asks
if he is not ashamed of himself, his answer (for once unimpeded
by a stutter) indicates that he is immensely pleased by what has
happened. The audience responds with a scream of satisfaction.
This is followed by the nurse's threat to tell the boy's mother of
his misbehavior. After stuttering once more in helpless fear, he
runs off stage in panic. A moment later we learn that he has
cut his throat. The audience quickly forgets this only to cheer
once more when McMurphy rises to strangle the woman for her
villainy.

All this is swift and summary: the trite canon of hand-me-
down psychoanalysis, the ready acquiescence in and indeed the
celebration of facile rebelliousness and a wretched "idealism" or
"revolution" without pain—automatic, mindless, cheaply triumphant, popular—are the hallmarks of the occasion. This state of
being is real in the audience and thus gives substance to the
play's sham.

The production is effective in its own vein, and the cast
headed by William Devane, Janet Ward, Jack Aaron, Lawrie
Driscoll and William Burns does its work very well.

❀◇

WALTER KERR

Walter Kerr is the drama critic for *The New York Times*. He has written three plays and a number of books on the American theater.

. . . AND THE YOUNG FLEW
OVER THE CUCKOO'S NEST

A few weeks ago I expressed some surprise that members of the younger generation should find themselves so heartily enjoying a Broadway comedy as conventional as "Butterflies Are Free." Shortly thereafter a press agent called me to suggest that conventional comedy was by no means the only thing the younger generation was ready to enjoy. If I wanted to find out for myself how else the land might lie I could drop down to the Mercer-Hansberry and see "One Flew Over the Cuckoo's Nest."

I'd missed the Off Broadway revival when it opened and, having disliked the earlier production uptown, was obviously dragging my feet. But this new mounting had caught on enough to have run for a good six months now, it was obviously appealing to *some* audience in substantial numbers, and it was plainly my business to go. I went. The press agent, so far from simply trying to engineer a plug for his show, was quite right. The audience for "One Flew Over the Cuckoo's Nest" is almost entirely composed of the very young, teeners, early twen-

ties at most—not of people the age of Ken Kesey, who wrote
the novel, or of Dale Wasserman, who made a play of it.

They were all about me—seas of golden hair, wave-crests of
sunny laughter, buckets of applause. They weren't far-out kids,
particularly; no ostentatious sloppiness. They were the young as
the young have always been. But with a difference. The difference was in the play, and in the meanings they took from it.

You may or may not remember that "One Flew Over the
Cuckoo's Nest" takes place in a ward in a state mental hospital,
presided over by a rabbity doctor and a much stronger, at first
sweetly solicitous nurse. One of the patients is apparently catatonic, the son of an Indian chief whose manhood had been
destroyed; another fastens himself to the blank white walls in a
crucifixion posture; most are as near-normal as the prim and
bespectacled chap in a bathrobe who cheerfully divides his
companions into "the curables, the chronics, and the
vegetables."

There are group therapy sessions. It soon becomes apparent
—too soon for my dramatic taste, but let that wait—that Nurse
Ratched is not so much engaged in a process of relieving the
guilt feelings her crippled patients may have as she is determined to fix her charges forever in doubly guilt-ridden states.
A boy who probably loves his mother and is hounded by fear of
failing her is persuaded that he really loathes her and has become ill as a means of punishing her. Our prim friend, patently
as sound of mind and spirit as anyone walking the streets of
today's cities, is persuaded that he is effeminate or has been
emasculated by his wife. The therapy is geared to make the
psychosis permanent. One and all are being conditioned to
regard themselves as helpless.

A swaggering fellow named Randle Patrick McMurphy ar-
rives, simian grin at the ready when he isn't solemnly chewing
gum. He has escaped the drudgery of a prison sentence at a
work farm by shamming mental illness and though he isn't very
bright—he hasn't realized, for instance, that in having himself
committed to an institution he has extended his term of con-

finement indefinitely, become a prisoner until medical rather than legal authorities decide to let him out—he is quite bright enough to see through the whole sorry operation. He immediately decides to lead a revolt against it.

His revolt takes various forms: he runs a kind of gambling syndicate despite regulations against gambling, he conducts a campaign for longer television hours, he secretly helps the Indian to overcome his therapy-induced muteness and deafness, he takes bets that he can best Nurse Ratched in open conflict.

With each bravura challenge to the "system," with each bracing thrust of the shoulders to throw off "conditioning," the present audience breaks into delighted cheers and applause. I don't think the rather awkward dramaturgy of the play bothers them in the least. Mr. Wasserman's adaptation still seems to me jaggedly put together; episodes don't build upon one another but jerk back and forth, with trivial developments following larger ones as puzzling anticlimaxes; everything is arranged for the author's convenience, including McMurphy's capacity for quickly detecting the truth. Nor does it help to tell me, in a program note, that the play is in some sense a cartoon; it is not consistently a cartoon. No matter. Dramaturgy, I think, is the last thing these young men and women have come for.

They have come to attend to an image of what they most fear in their lives, perhaps with some hope of exorcising it by the energy of their applause. What they most fear is just that "conditioning" which is the central action of the play. They are afraid that they are conditioned, will be conditioned, have been conditioned. They have been taught to make responses that are not their own, and have so been robbed of identity.

The fear is not entirely new, of course. In the introduction to his fascinating study of American fiction during the past twenty years, "City of Words," Tony Tanner has pointed out that a tension has always existed in American life between the concept of freedom and the concept of social form, of shape or contour. Unlimited freedom has been sought as a good; to find it the shackles of social shape must be thrown off, but once they are all thrown off man may have no shape at all, may end as a jelly-fish, without identity. Conversely if he accepts existing social contours in order to give himself an identity through shape, the imposed contours may make him rigid and false to himself, thus destroying identity again. A constantly recurring problem for the prototypical American hero has been, in Mr. Tanner's question: "Can he find a freedom which is not a jelly, and can he establish an identity which is not a prison?" The setting here is a prison, and we see how it functions.

But there is something more there, something closer to the once extravagant science-fiction speculations of Kurt Vonnegut Jr.'s "Sirens of Titan" and to the now soberly proposed recommendations of scientist B. F. Skinner. We are already beyond choice, beyond the tension of options. Somebody has got hold of the machinery and no matter how much we rebel or struggle or defy or cry out we can always be conditioned a little further.

Nurse Ratched is the key to the piece, its prime force and ultimate symbol. I do not like her as a character in a play because I grew up in a humanistic tradition, was trained in a humanistic theater, and therefore like my characters to be recognizably human. Nurse Ratched isn't human. She is entirely malevolent, without any saving softnesses or familiar margins for error. She is herself a computer. And she is all-powerful.

When McMurphy gets a bit out of hand, and is having rather too much success in restoring their identities to his companions, he is whisked to the laboratory and given shock treatments. When the shock treatments do not tranquilize him ("Sin while you may," the fellow in the bathrobe cries, "for tomorrow we shall be tranquilized!"), he is subjected to a frontal lobotomy. Nurse Ratched, with the controls at her finger-tips, has made him a vegetable.

But who is Nurse Ratched, and why does the young audience believe in her (I assume that it does)? Why is she a woman? (There are other such women in the background of the play: the Indian's father has had his manhood destroyed by a white wife.) Where did she get her absolute power and what, in the end, is her motive? Why does she wish to condition all living things to her will?

Perhaps she is simply the mythical "they" who are always out to get us, in which case any audience's belief in her is apt to be a bit paranoid. But the boys and girls I sat with and watched certainly did not seem paranoid. They seemed amused and, after a certain point, resigned. I wanted answers to my questions. I don't think they did. Are they, then, persuaded that we are all already manipulated by some unidentifiable hostile force, without power to comprehend the "system" let alone do battle with it? Scary, if you think of it that way.

Well, at least they cheered McMurphy on in his lost battle. The production at the Mercer-Hansberry, by the way, is superior at every turn to the original Broadway mounting.

✿◈✿

MARCIA L. FALK

Marcia L. Falk, who teaches literature and writing at Stanford
University, is a poet and translator who is presently working on a
verse translation of the Biblical "Song of Songs." Her primary concern is the relationship between the art and the societal attitudes
they express and help create.

LETTER TO THE EDITOR OF
THE NEW YORK TIMES

To the Editor:

In response to Walter Kerr's belated review of "One Flew Over
the Cuckoo's Nest": I too saw the show after it had been running for quite a while, in San Francisco. I was shocked at what
I saw (though I should have known better, having read the
book) because, in the long time the play had been running,
never once had I read a review which warned me of the
blatant sexism I was to witness onstage, or even asked some of
the most obvious questions about the political statements of the
play.

Kerr finally raised the key question: Why is Nurse Ratched,
the omnipotent, omni-malevolent villain of the play, a woman?
Kerr didn't speculate why, but he did note parenthetically that
"There are other such women in the background of the play."

The truth is that *every* woman in the background is such a demonic figure, and the play is full of false yet dangerous clichés about their power over men.

The most striking example is Chief Bromden's mother: she has made his father small, she has grown to twice his size. It is largely because of her power to threaten male virility that the Chief is now in a mental institution. Of course, she is *only a symbol*; as a white woman married to an Indian man, her emasculation of her husband only *represents* the White Man's brutal destruction of all cultures other than his own.

Why is white racism depicted in these terms? It should be remembered that this white woman's singular unforgivable act was her refusal to take on her husband's name! Somehow, in the confused vision of the author and playwright, the refusal of women, an oppressed class, to utterly submit to male-oriented social structures is identified with the attack of white men, the oppressor class, on peoples of color.

The whole play is constructed from such a muddled vision. It pretends to challenge all the reactionary institutions in our society—prisons, mental hospitals and the Federal Government itself, which has destroyed the Indian reservations. But it never once challenges the completely inhuman sexist structure of society, nor does it make any attempt to overthrow sexist or racist stereotypes. The only blacks in the play are stupid and malicious hospital orderlies. And the only right-on women in the play are mindless whores. In fact, in this play, if a woman is *not* totally mindless, she is a direct threat to (male) life.

Thus the play offers us this basic sexist dichotomy: women are either dumb and silly (like the quivering young nurse, terrified of McMurphy; like the squealing, wiggling prostitutes who come to build up the men's egos) or they are shrewd, conniving, and malicious (castrating wives, dominating mothers, and a super-powerful domineering nurse). Every man in the play has been psychologically mutilated by a woman, from the guilt-ridden Billy Bibbit, whom his mother and Nurse

Ratched are in cahoots to destroy, to the cynical Harding, whose "wife's ample bosom at times gives him a feeling of inferiority."

It goes without saying that, just as there are no positive, fully human female figures to identify with, there are likewise no strong, healthy male figures. Of course, we are *supposed* to believe in McMurphy, the super-male macho hero who equates strength with sexual parts and whose solution to every problem is sex. We laugh and cheer as McMurphy humiliates the young nurse by sticking a banana up her skirt, manhandles his girlfriends as he passes them around (confident of his masculinity, he can afford to be generous), and generally bullies everyone in his social sphere.

If *that* represents the healthy exercise of the human spirit, then the White Man too was healthy as he stole from the Indians everything they had, raping their culture and treating them as objects not worthy of human respect.

Kerr points out that "Cuckoo's Nest" is a play about conditioning in this society, and that young people identify with it because it exposes that threat to human freedom. This play is not *about* conditioning nearly so much as it *is* a dangerous piece of conditioning itself. With a pseudo-radical posture, it swallows whole hog all the worst attitudes toward women prevalent in our society and delivers the pig right back to us, suitably decorated and made righteous.

If you do not perceive exactly how destructive this work is, imagine for a moment the effect it must have on a girl child watching it. Who, in this play, can *she* grow up to be? Where is *her* place in the struggle for human freedom? At best she can mature into a good sex object, equipped to build the egos of emotionally crippled men by offering a "liberated" attitude toward sex! Above all, she learns from viewing this play that any aggressiveness, intelligence, strength, or potency on the part of the female is always dangerous, evil, and ugly. She learns to hate women who dare to try to be as powerful as men. She learns to squelch her own potential for strength, or she learns to hate herself. She is, after all, destined to become a woman, and women are hateful and fearful things.

The answer to Kerr's question seems to be that Nurse Ratched is a woman because Ken Kesey hates and fears women. And apparently Dale Wasserman, along with everyone else who helped adapt Kesey's novel and engineer it into a piece of theater, are so thoroughly conditioned by the basic sexist assumptions of our society that they never even noticed, or cared to question, the psychic disease out of which the book's vision was born.

Stanford, Calif.

[Ms. Falk has requested that her original wording be noted here. In paragraph 7, lines 5 and 6, "balls, should be substituted for "sexual parts" and "to get a good fuck" for "sex." Likewise, in the penultimate paragraph, line 5, "sex object" originally read "piece of ass."]

IV

Analogies and Perspectives

DALE WASSERMAN

Dale Wasserman is a playwright who has received numerous awards for his stage, television, and motion picture scripts. Of these, *Man of La Mancha* (1965) was perhaps his most popular. In addition to his successful adaptations of prose works, he has also written original plays and short stories.

FROM HIS PLAY

ONE FLEW OVER THE

CUCKOO'S NEST

ACT III

(In the darkness the clock chimes eleven; then LIGHTS FADE into Night Lighting. AIDE TURKLE *enters the deserted room from the outer corridor. Crooning a shapeless tune, he goes about his duties: straightening up furniture, check-*

---

ing locked doors, etc. CHESWICK *pops his head out of the dormitory.*)

CHESWICK. Ssssssssst!

TURKLE. (*Startled, turns his flashlight on* CHESWICK'S *face.*) Lord he'p me, I thought you was a snake!

CHESWICK. (*In an excited whisper.*) She showed up yet?

TURKLE. She who?

CHESWICK. Candy!

TURKLE. (*Blandly.*) I don' know nothin' 'bout no candy.

CHESWICK. (*Dismayed.*) Mac said he made a deal with you.

TURKLE. I ain't got the slightest inclination what you talkin' 'bout.

CHESWICK. Don't go away! (*Disappears back within the dormitory.* TURKLE *continues his puttering about. In a few moments* McMURPHY *emerges with* CHESWICK *at his shoulder.*)

McMURPHY. Turkey, ol' boy! What's the beef?

TURKLE. Ain't no beef.

McMURPHY. So?

TURKLE. Ain't no money changed hands, neither.

McMURPHY. (*Digs in his pocket for a wad of bills.*) There y'are. Begged, borrowed and stole.

TURKLE. (*Taking it, mournfully.*) You know, they fin' out 'bout this they fire my ass.

McMURPHY. She's bringin' liquor, Turkey.

TURKLE. (*Brightening.*) Yeah?

McMURPHY. Bottle of Scotch and one of vodka. Which d'you want?

TURKLE. (*Deliberating.*) Sorta like 'em both.

McMURPHY. Hey, what're *we* supposed to drink?

10036, or 7623 Sunset Blvd., Hollywood, Calif., or if in Canada to Samuel French (Canada) Ltd., at 27 Grenville St., Toronto, Ont.

Copies of this play, in individual paper covered acting editions, are available from Samuel French, Inc., 25 W. 45th St., New York, N.Y. or 7623 Sunset Blvd., Hollywood, Calif. or in Canada Samuel French, (Canada) Ltd., 26 Grenville St., Toronto, Ont.

TURKLE. (*Morally.*) You ain't supposed to drink at *all*.

McMURPHY, (*To* CHESWICK, *who is at the window.*) Any sign?

CHESWICK. Nary sign.

McMURPHY. (*Slaps his forehead.*) Hoo boy, am I stupid! How they gonna find the right window in the dark? (*To* TURKLE.) Turn on the lights.

TURKLE. Hey, now, tha's *dangerous*. Miz Ratched, she see the ward lit up—

McMURPHY. Come on, Turkey, she's asleep.

TURKLE. (*Grumbling as he finds the key.*) That ol' shitepoke *never* sleep. (*The LIGHTS GO ON and* HARDING *and the other* ACUTES *come piling out of the dormitory.*)

HARDING. Is she here?

McMURPHY. Shhh! (*To* TURKLE.) Gimme the window key.

TURKLE. I ain't s'pose to let these keys off'n—

McMURPHY. *Gimme*.

TURKLE. (*Muttering as he removes it from the ring.*) Tha' better be *good* liquor.

McMURPHY. (*Tossing the key to* HARDING.) Keep an eye on the window, huh? Cheswick, watch out down the hall. (*To* FREDERICKS.) And close the doors 'fore we wake up every slobberin' Chronic in the place!

HARDING. (*At the window.*) Ssst! She walks in beauty!

McMURPHY. Well, let 'er in! Let this mad stud at her!

BILLY. (*As* HARDING *unlocks the screen.*) Look, McM-M-Murphy, wait—

McMURPHY. Don't you mama-murphy me, Billy Boy, it's too late to back out now.

(CANDY *is climbing through the window, helped by* HARDING *and* SCANLON, *impeded by the bottles she carries in each hand. She's barefoot and quite tipsy.*)

CANDY. (*Charging at* McMURPHY.) You damned McMurphy! (*She flings her arms about him to kiss him, and* TURKLE *adroitly snatches the bottle of Scotch.*) Hey, what the hell—!

McMurphy. That's okay, baby. (*Inspecting the half-full bottle of vodka.*) But what happened to this one?

Candy. (*Giggling, patting her stomach.*) We got the rest of it right here.

McMurphy. We?

Candy. Oh, lordy, I forgot, Sandra's out there!

Sandra. (*Is struggling through the window with Harding's help, showing a lot of leg.*) These goddam tight skirts.

Scanlon. *Hot* dog!

McMurphy. Sandy, baby!

Sandra. Hiya, Mac! (McMurphy *lifts her to her feet and kisses her.* Sandra *is a big, earthy wench with bay-colored hair. Like* Candy, *she is barefoot and a little drunk.*)

McMurphy. What'd you do with your husband?

Sandra. (*As* Harding *locks the screen and pockets the key.*) That creep!

Candy. (*Giggling.*) She up and left him. Ain't that a gasser?

Sandra. Lissen, you can take just so many funsies like worms in your cold cream and frogs down your bra. Cheesus, what a creep!

Candy. (*With warmth.*) Hello, Billy!

Billy. (*Bashfully.*) Hello, C-C-C-C—

Candy. Never mind. (*She kisses him.*)

Cheswick. (*Charging in, excitedly.*) Somebody's coming!

(*There is a wild rush for cover.* Candy, Billy *and some of the men dash into the dormitory.* McMurphy *drags* Sandra *into the latrine, followed by* Scanlon *and others.* Harding *dives into the broom closet.* Turkle *starts to follow in a dazed way and is pushed back out. He remembers to cork the Scotch and shove it out of sight.*)

Martini. (*Entering from dormitory.*) Oh, boy, where's the party? (McMurphy's *hand reaches out from the latrine and yanks him out of sight just as* Nurse Ratched *enters.*)

NURSE RATCHED. Mr. Turkle?

TURKLE. (*Turning to face her.*) Evenin', Miz Ratched.

NURSE RATCHED. (*Her eyes busy.*) Why are these lights on?

TURKLE. (*As she prowls* D. *to look around the corner of the Station.*) Well, ma'am, I was cleanin'.

NURSE RATCHED. With what?

TURKLE. (*At a loss.*) With . . . with . . . (*A hand comes out of the broom closet and shoves a mop in* TURKLE's *hand.*)

NURSE RATCHED. (*Turning back* U.) Yes, Turkle? (TURKLE *holds the mop out wordlessly.*) According to Job Description the only room you're supposed to mop is the latrine.

TURKLE. Yes, ma'am, that's where I was.

NURSE RATCHED. (*Pointing.*) Then why is that the only place that's dark?

TURKLE. (*At a loss again.*) Well, I . . . I . . .

(NURSE RATCHED *marches toward the latrine door. There is the sound of a toilet flushing.* MCMURPHY *comes out of the door, buttoning up his uniform.*)

MCMURPHY. Oh, 'scuse me, I didn't know there was ladies present!

NURSE RATCHED. (*Narrowly.*) What were you doing in there?

MCMURPHY. (*With innocent puzzlement.*) Well, ma'am . . .

NURSE RATCHED. In the *dark*?

MCMURPHY. Oh, I always switch off the lights when I go in there. On account of the mirrors.

NURSE RATCHED. The mirrors?

MCMURPHY. When the light's on I seem to see faces peerin' out of 'em. Thing like that could make ya constipated.

NURSE RATCHED. Aide Turkle said he was cleaning in there!

MCMURPHY. Yes, ma'am, and doin' a damn good job considerin'. (*Shoving the door open a little.*) Like to see?

NURSE RATCHED. Go to bed, Mr. McMurphy. (MCMURPHY *trots into the dormitory, whistling. To* TURKLE:) And turn these lights off *now*. (*Turns and marches out as* TURKLE *hastens to comply. He listens for the sound of the ward door closing.*)

TURKLE. (*Hissing.*) Okay!

HARDING. (*Emerging from the broom closet, meets* McMUR-PHY *coming out of the dormitory; shakes his hand.*) Simply brilliant.

McMURPHY. You done pretty well yourself! (*To* SANDRA.) Ya okay, baby?

SANDRA. (*Darkly, eyeing* MARTINI.) Somebody pinched my ass.

McMURPHY. Gimme your keys, Turkey.

TURKLE. *Now* what?

McMURPHY. I gotta find somethin' for us to drink! (*Takes the keys and opens the Nurses' Station.* CHESWICK, MARTINI *and* SCANLON *follow.* SANDRA *goes circling, looking over the men.*)

SANDRA. Whooee, Candy girl, is this for real? I mean, are we in an *asylum*? (*To* HARDING.) Tell the truth, are you really nuts?

HARDING. Absolutely, madam. We are psycho-ceramics, the cracked pots of humanity. Would you like me to decipher a Rorschach?

McMURPHY. (*On microphone from Station, wearing a nurse's cap.*) Behave yourself, boys! (*All dive for cover momentarily. Then* SCANLON *pops up out of the window seat, scaring* SANDRA.)

SANDRA. How, Candy, how, how, how do these wild things happen to us? (*Discovering* CHIEF BROMDEN.) Boy, look at this one, a regular Goliath! (*Wiggling her fingers at him.*) Fee, fie, fo, fum! (*The* CHIEF *retreats in alarm.*)

CHESWICK. (*Bursting out of the now-open Station where* McMURPHY *is going through the drug cabinet.*) Hey, here's our files! I always wanted to know what they said about me. (*Reading, as others grab and open folders.*) Gosh, I'm in *terrible* shape.

SCANLON. They even got my first-grade report card here. Aah, miserable grades, just miserable.

CANDY. (*Looking over* BILLY's *folder with him.*) All these things, Billy? Phrenic this and pathic that? You don't look like you've got all those things.

MARTINI. (*Reading, indignantly.*) They're *crazy.*

McMURPHY. (*On microphone.*) Medication! (*Comes out of Station laden with jugs and bottles of medicine.*) Find me somethin' to shake these up in. (CHESWICK *brings a hot water bottle with tube attached, to hang on a stand.*)

HARDING. (*Reading the label on a jug of cherry-colored liquid.*) Artificial coloring, citric acid. Sixty percent inert materials.

FREDERICKS. What's inert materials?

HARDING. Water.

McMURPHY. (*Pointing out a line.*) Twenty-two percent alcohol. (*Is pouring liquids into the hot water bottle.*)

HARDING. (*Reading the next label.*) Ten percent codeine, Warning: May Be Habit Forming.

McMURPHY. (*Seizing it.*) Nothin' like a good bad habit.

HARDING. (*Next bottle.*) Tincture of nux vomica.

McMURPHY. (*Emptying it in.*) That'll give it body.

CHESWICK. (*Returning from the Station.*) Here's some ice cubes. (*Drops them in cups.*)

McMURPHY. (*Shakes up the cocktail with professional dexterity. Tastes it. Clicks his teeth together loudly.*) If we cut it a *leetle* bit . . . (*Pours the remaining vodka into the shaker and shakes it up.*)

SANDRA. (*Giggling.*) Jeez, what a shindy. Is this really happening?

HARDING. No, ma'am. The whole thing is a collaboration between Franz Kafka and Mark Twain.

McMURPHY. (*Pouring.*) Bar's open!

HARDING. (*Tasting.*) Dee-licious!

CANDY. (*Taking a sip.*) Tastes like cough medicine.

SANDRA. (*Getting to her feet.*) 'Scuse me, I gotta tinkle. (*She goes weaving* U.)

HARDING. You know this stuff gives one the feeling of—of—

MᴄMᴜʀᴘʜʏ. (*Grinning.*) No more rabbits?

Hᴀʀᴅɪɴɢ. Old friend, you have taught me that mental illness can have the aspect of *power*. Perhaps the more insane a man is the more powerful he can become.

Sᴄᴀɴʟᴏɴ. Sure—Hitler!

Hᴀʀᴅɪɴɢ. Fair makes the old brain reel!

MᴄMᴜʀᴘʜʏ. Say, what if we were to organize?

Cʜᴇsᴡɪᴄᴋ. A lobby in Washington!

Fʀᴇᴅᴇʀɪᴄᴋs. Pressure groups!

Hᴀʀᴅɪɴɢ. Oh, excellent! We'll call it the N-Double-A-I-P. (*As the others look puzzled.*) National Association for the Advancement of Insane Persons. We could have billboards along the highway, showing a babbling schizophrenic running a wrecking machine.

Cʜᴇsᴡɪᴄᴋ. And a slogan! Gotta have a slogan!

MᴄMᴜʀᴘʜʏ "Hire the Insane!" (*There is a scream, and* Sᴀɴᴅʀᴀ *comes running from the dormitory with* Cᴏʟ. Mᴀᴛᴛᴇʀsᴏɴ *wheeling in pursuit.*)

Cᴏʟ. Mᴀᴛᴛᴇʀsᴏɴ. The night—is a woman!

MᴄMᴜʀᴘʜʏ. (*Leaps up to block the* Cᴏʟᴏɴᴇʟ *as* Sᴀɴᴅʀᴀ *cowers behind him.*) Colonel, ain't you *ashamed?* (Sᴄᴀɴʟᴏɴ *wheels the* Cᴏʟᴏɴᴇʟ *back into the dormitory.*)

Sᴀɴᴅʀᴀ. This damn place is dangerous!

Cʜᴇsᴡɪᴄᴋ. (*Leads her to the latrine.*) Went the wrong way, lady. (Mᴀʀᴛɪɴɪ *is in the Station, fiddling with the tape machine. Now it comes on: MUSIC.*)

MᴄMᴜʀᴘʜʏ. Oh, God, not *that* stuff!

Mᴀʀᴛɪɴɪ. How about backwards? (*He reverses the tape.*)

Hᴀʀᴅɪɴɢ. Now, that is *music*.

Cᴀɴᴅʏ. C'mon, Billy! (*Pulls him to his feet and they dance, cheek to cheek. The men fall back from them as they hold each other closely, moving more slowly . . . and they are looking into each other's eyes as* Mᴀʀᴛɪɴɪ *obligingly softens the music.*)

MᴄMᴜʀᴘʜʏ. (*Dangling* Tᴜʀᴋʟᴇ's *keys.*) How about the Seclusion Room?

CHESWICK. (*Happily.*) Sure, the place is one big mattress!

HARDING. One moment! Shall we send them off without benefit of ceremony? Come, children—here, before me. (*Mounts a chair as* BILLY *and* CANDY *link hands before him and the group forms up in rough semblance of a wedding.*) Dearly beloved, we are gathered in the sight of Freud to celebrate the end of innocence and cheer on its demise. Who stands sponsor for the benedict?

McMURPHY. (*Moving to* BILLY'S *side.*) R. P. McMurphy.

HARDING. And for the bride?

SANDRA. (*Coming to* CANDY'S *side.*) Me!

HARDING. Very well, then. Do you, Candy Starr, take this man to love and cherish for such brief time as rules and regulations may allow?

CANDY. I do.

HARDING. Do you, Billy Bibbit, take this woman to have and hold until the night shift changes and our revels end?

BILLY. I duh-duh-duh—I duh—

McMURPHY. Hell, yes!

HARDING. Most merciful God, we ask that You accept these two into Your kingdom with Your well-known compassion. And keep the door ajar for all the rest of us, for this may be our final fling and we are doomed, henceforth, to the terrible burden of sanity. As comes the dawn we shall most assuredly be lined up against the wall and fired upon with bullets of Miltown! Librium! Thorazine! Go, my children—sin while ye may, for tomorrow we shall be tranquilized.

(CANDY *and* BILLY *kiss.* MARTINI *brings up the music and* McMURPHY *strews pills over the couple as they exit.* SANDRA *is sniffling.*)

McMURPHY. (*Touched.*) Sandra, baby!

SANDRA. It was so damn beautiful. Hell of a lot nicer than *my* wedding. (McMURPHY *hugs her.*)

HARDING. (*With a sigh.*) Mac, we're sure going to miss you.

McMURPHY. So why don't you all come along? Chief?

CHIEF BROMDEN. What would I do on the outside?

McMURPHY. You could be the bad guy on TV rasslin'. Harding, how about you?

HARDING. Oh, I'll be going soon, but I've got to do it my own way. Sign the papers, call my wife and say "Pick me up at a certain time." You understand?

McMURPHY. Sure, but . . . what is it with you guys? What happens?

HARDING. You mean what drove us here in the first place? Oh, I don't know . . . a lot of theories . . . but I do know what drives people like you—strong people—crazy.

McMURPHY. Okay, what?

HARDING. Us.

McMURPHY. (*Uncertainly.*) Bull.

HARDING. Oh, yes, my friend.

McMURPHY. Hey, what's happening to the party? Drink up! Drink up, you mother-lovin' loonies, this is Big Mac tendin' bar, and when he pours let no man—! (CHIEF BROMDEN, *having tossed down his drink, lets out a wild whoop, startling everyone.*) Chief, was that you?

CHIEF BROMDEN. (*Equally startled.*) I guess so.

McMURPHY. What ya doin', declarin' war?

CHIEF BROMDEN. My tribe never made war on nobody. Maybe that was our mistake. We should of! (*Whoops again, pleased with the sound, then goes into a shuffling war dance, accompanying himself with chanted Indian gutturals. The others fall delighted into line and it becomes a snake-dance, weaving its noisy way around the room.*)

(COL. MATTERSON *comes wheeling in and joins the line.* NURSE RATCHED *enters from the corridor and stands frozen in incredulity. She is there some moments before anyone becomes aware.*)

McMurphy. Hiya, kid! We got room for one more. (Nurse Ratched *turns and flees. The dance continues, then* Harding *pulls out of line.*)

Harding. (*Yelling.*) Stop! Quiet! Shut *up*, everybody. (*With delayed horror.*) Was that . . . did I see . . . ?

McMurphy. (*Aggrieved.*) I assed her to stay.

Harding. Oh, God, she went to get help. (*Hurrying to the window.*) Mac, you've got to get out of here.

McMurphy. (*Cheerfully tipsy.*) Okay, soon's I say g'bye to my buddies.

Harding. (*Swinging open the grille.*) In a *hurry*.

Turkle. I don' know 'bout him—but *I* am gonna run like hell. (*Climbs onto the sill, tumbles out of sight.*)

Harding. Sandy!

Sandra. You coming, Mac?

McMurphy. (*Shaking hands with the men.*) Best damned buddies I ever had!

Harding. (*As* Sandra *climbs through the window.*) Don't hang *around* . . . !

McMurphy. (*To* Bromden.) You gonna be all right? 'Cause if you ain't I'll hear about it, and I'll come bustin' back inta this place, and—

Harding. (*Crossing to him.*) Come *on*, Mac.

McMurphy. Okay, all *right*, I just wanta be certain—

(Warren *and* Williams, *not quite fully dressed, come in fast.* Nurse Ratched *is close behind.*)

Nurse Ratched. (*Snapping it.*) Stand still, everyone. Just remain right where you are. (*Switches on the lights. The men blink confusedly.*) Warren. Room check. (Warren *races off.*) Williams—

Williams. (*Pointing.*) The window!

Nurse Ratched. (*Sharply, stopping him.*) No. Let him go. (*To* McMurphy.) Go on, McMurphy. You've made your profit. Get out while the going's good.

McMurphy. (*Scornfully.*) Oh, very smart. Tryin' to bug me till I blow my top. Well, shove it, sister, 'cause I'm hip. And I'm leavin'—(*Singing as he moves jauntily across the stage.*)— " 'Cause my horses ain't hungry, they won't eat your hay, So fare thee well, darlin', I'm goin' my—" (Warren *pushes* Billy *and* Candy *onstage. They are disheveled and bewildered, covering their eyes against the light.* McMurphy *stops dead at the window.*)

Nurse Ratched. Where were they?

Warren. (*Grinning.*) Seclusion Room. On the floor.

Nurse Ratched. William—Bibbit. Oh, Billy, I'm so ashamed!

Billy. (*Defiantly.*) I'm not.

McMurphy. Thassit, Billy—!

Nurse Ratched. You be silent! Oh, Billy . . . a woman like *this*.

Billy. Like what?

Nurse Ratched. A cheap—low—painted—

Billy. She is not! She's good, and sweet, and—!

McMurphy. (*Delightedly.*) Attaboy, Billy!

Nurse Ratched. (*Dragging* Candy *forward.*) Look at her.

Candy. (*Fleeing to* McMurphy.) Mac—!

Billy. (*Simultaneously.*) You leave her alone!

Nurse Ratched. Billy, have you thought how your poor mother is going to take this? She's always been so proud of your decency. You know what this is going to do to her. You know, don't you?

Billy. No. No. You don't nuh-need—

Nurse Ratched. Don't need to tell her? How could I not?

Billy. (*Beginning to crumble.*) Duh-duh-don't tell her, Miss Ratched. Duh-duh—

Nurse Ratched. Billy, dear, I *have* to. I have to tell her that you were found on the floor of the Seclusion Room . . . with this woman. That you and she—

Billy. No! I d-d-didn't! I mean, she m-made me do it!

NURSE RATCHED. I can't believe she pulled you in there *forcibly.*

BILLY. (*Wildly.*) It was the others. They m-made fun of me. Thuh-they—

NURSE RATCHED. Who, Billy?

BILLY. All of them. Thuh-thuh—

NURSE RATCHED. Who, Billy?

BILLY. (*Clutching her knees, sobbing.*) McMuh-Mur-phy. It was him. He teased me. He c-called me things. . . .

McMURPHY. (*In dismay.*) Billy . . .

BILLY. McMurphy!

NURSE RATCHED. (*Stroking* BILLY's *head; eyes on* MC-MURPHY.) Well, Randle, are you satisfied? Playing with human lives as if you thought you were God?

HARDING. (*Blocking the way as he sees* McMURPHY's *intention.*) No, Mac, it's what she wants!

McMURPHY. (*In helpless fury, knocking* HARDING *aside.*) Don'tcha think I know it?

NURSE RATCHED. (*Signaling the* AIDES *not to interfere; smilingly, as* McMURPHY *crosses toward her.*) Come on, Mr. Mc-Murphy. Mister brave . . . tough . . . *masculine* . . . (*He reaches out and rips her uniform open down the front. Her knee comes up viciously, and* McMURPHY *barely eludes it.* NURSE RATCHED *screams, the scream cut off as his hands lock about her throat.*)

(*Then the* AIDES *are upon* McMURPHY, *clubbing him to the floor with brutal rabbit-punches. He yells—once—an animal cry of defiance and despair as they club him into insensibility. The cry is caught up and continued in* CHIEF BROM-DEN's *throat as he spins away to* D.R. *A single light stabs down at him as all other lights BLACK OUT. There is a hissing sound, a great continued exhalation.*)

CHIEF BROMDEN. The fog. It's comin' in again. Snowin' down so thick I'm wet all over. (*He moans.*) Papa, they got to me again. Some way they got the wires on me and they're givin' orders. Go right. Go left. Do this. Do that. Sign the papers twenty times and don't step on the grass. Get up. Lay down. Be sick. Get well. Take out a license, go to hell. Where can I run? How can I get away? Papa, there's no place to hide no more. No place to hide!

(*LIGHTS UP on the Day Room. It is post-supper; night. The* CHRONICS *have already been put to bed; the* ACUTES *are all present with the exception of* BILLY *and* McMURPHY. CHIEF BROMDEN *is in position as at the beginning of the play—back to the audience, hunched in catatonic stance.* NURSE NAKAMURA *is seated in the Station working on reports.* HARDING *is at the card table dealing blackjack to* CHESWICK, SCANLON, FREDERICKS, *and* MARTINI.)

HARDING. (*Imitating* McMURPHY's *style.*) Hey-a, hey-a, come on, suckers, the game is twenty-one, you hit or you sit. Hit, the gentleman says, coming at you, *faw*. All right, I'm waiting, *whups*, he wants another card, *faw*, it's a ten, too bad, my friend, and the dealer drags it down. Ay there, the smokehouse is empty and baby needs new opera pumps, what do you do, Scanlon?

SCANLON. Oh, I wasn't payin' any mind.

HARDING. Well, pay some mind.

SCANLON. (*Getting up restlessly.*) Gosh, if we only *knew*. Where they got him. What they're doin'. Damn near a whole *week* now.

CHESWICK. Hey, you know what a guy down at the dining room told me? He says McMurphy knocked out two aides and took their keys away from them and escaped!

FREDERICKS. (*Hopefully.*) That *sounds* like Mac.

HARDING. What ward was your informant from?

CHESWICK. Disturbed.

MARTINI. Somebody told *me* they'd caught him and sent him back to the Work Farm.

HARDING. (*Wearily.*) And a loony down in Occupational

Therapy told *me* that McMurphy had sprouted wings and was last seen soaring in lazy circles overhead, defecating on the hospital.

MARTINI. (*Open-mouthed.*) Honest?

(HARDING *throws up his hands in disgust. The phone in the Station rings.* NURSE NAKAMURA *answers it as the men come to attention, although her words cannot be heard. She picks up her bag and comes out of the Station.*)

CHESWICK. Was that something about McMurphy?

NURSE NAKAMURA. (*Cheerfully.*) That was my walking papers. Back to Disturbed for Yours Truly.

FREDERICKS. Miss Ratched's coming back?

NURSE NAKAMURA. The next key you hear in the lock. Better put the cards away, she doesn't know about our little gambling hell.

SCANLON. Nurse, did ya hear *anything* about McMurphy?

NURSE NAKAMURA. Look, fellow, I don't want to tell you lies. . . . (*Smiles at them.*) Going to miss me?

SCANLON. (*Sincerely.*) You been a real gentleman!

NURSE NAKAMURA. Well, thanks!

(WARREN *enters, harbinger for* NURSE RATCHED *who is close behind.* NURSE RATCHED *wears a bandage around her throat. Her manner has changed: warier, and her eyes are nervous.*)

NURSE RATCHED. (*Her voice husky.*) Isn't it past bedtime?

NURSE NAKAMURA. I let them stay up to welcome you. (*As she exits.*) So long, guys!

CHESWICK. (*Advancing.*) Miss Ratched— (NURSE RATCHED *takes a quick step backward.*)—what we want to know—

NURSE RATCHED. About Billy? He's in the Medical Ward. He tried to kill himself, you know.

HARDING. Is McMurphy coming back? I think we have a right—

NURSE RATCHED. I agree, Mr. Harding.

HARDING. Well?

NURSE RATCHED. He will be back.

CHESWICK. When?

NURSE RATCHED. Don't you believe me?

SCANLON. (*Deliberately.*) Lady, we think you are full of bull.

NURSE RATCHED. (*A pause; calmly.*) I assure you, McMurphy will be back. Now I think it's time you were in bed? (*She faces them steadily, and the men file silently into the dormitory. Only* CHIEF BROMDEN, *unnoticed and unmoving, remains* D. R. *To* WARREN.) Bring him in. (WARREN *exits.* NURSE RATCHED *uses her little key to switch off the main lights.* WARREN *and* WILLIAMS *wheel in a Gurney bed upon which* McMURPHY *lies covered by a blanket. He is immobile. Following* NURSE RATCHED'S *signals the* AIDES *position the bed.*) That's fine, boys. (*The* AIDES *exit silently on their rubber shoes.* NURSE RATCHED *feels* McMURPHY'S *pulse a moment, straightens the blanket. Softly, looking down at him:*) That's just fine. (*She exits.*)

(CHIEF BROMDEN *turns his head, crosses slowly to the bed, stands there studying the motionless figure. From the dormitory* CHESWICK *enters. Then* SCANLON, MARTINI *and* FREDERICKS. *They range themselves about the bed, not too close.* CHESWICK, *at the foot, lifts the chart that hangs there and holds it to the feeble light.*)

SCANLON. What's it say?

CHESWICK. McMurphy, Randle Patrick. Postoperative. Prefrontal lobotomy.

FREDERICKS. Lobotomy.

SCANLON. So they done it to 'im.

CHIEF BROMDEN. (*Voice low and harsh.*) That ain't McMurphy.

SCANLON. (*Surprised.*) No?

CHIEF BROMDEN. Some dummy they rigged up.

CHESWICK. (*Startled.*) You think so?

CHIEF BROMDEN. Factory-made.

MARTINI. Hey, I bet he's right!

SCANLON. Sure! What're they trying to put over on us?

CHESWICK. (*Dubiously.*) They did a pretty fair job, though. See? The busted nose.

FREDERICKS. That crazy scar.

CHESWICK. Even the sideburns. (*Pulls the blanket back a little.*) Look. Tattoos.

CHIEF BROMDEN. They can do tattoos.

SCANLON. That's right, they can do anything.

MARTINI. Look, its eyes is open!

FREDERICK. (*As they bend over, peering.*) All smoked up.

CHESWICK. Nobody inside.

CHIEF BROMDEN. (*Contemptuously.*) Eyes. Couple a burnt-out fuses.

CHESWICK. That settles it.

SCANLON. How stupid does that ol' bitch think we are? (CHIEF BROMDEN *slides a pillow out from under* McMURPHY's *head.*)

MARTINI. Whatcha doin', Chief?

CHIEF BROMDEN. You think Mac would want this thing sittin' around the Day Room twenty-thirty years with his name stuck on it?

MARTINI. (*Wistfully, as with tacit unanimity the men turn away from the* CHIEF, *ignoring what he is doing.*) Gee, I wish McMurphy would come back.

CHESWICK. (*Brightly.*) Hey, you remember that time he pinched Miss Ratched on the butt and said he was just trying to stay in contact?

SCANLON. (*Chortling.*) And them things he'd write in the Log Book? "Madam, do you wear a B cup or a C cup or any old cup at all?" (*The laughter becomes general.* U. *of them* CHIEF BROMDEN *is pressing the pillow down on* McMURPHY's *face.*)

FREDERICKS. And that time in the dining room when he flipped a piece of butter on the wall and bet it would reach the floor by seven-thirty?

MARTINI. And he *won!* (*The glee rises higher.*)

CHESWICK. D'you remember the time that little nurse—

SCANLON. The one that wears a cross!

CHESWICK.—she dropped a pill down the front of her uniform, and McMurphy tries to help her get it out, and she hollers—

FREDERICKS. (*Falsetto.*)—"Don't touch me, I'm a *Catholic!*" (*They are whooping with laughter, pounding each other's backs.* HARDING *enters from the dormitory. He has changed to his pajamas.*)

HARDING. (*Irritably.*) What in the hell is going on? You guys are supposed to be . . . to be in . . . (*Becomes aware of the tableau. The men fall silent. He gasps.*) Chief! (*He flings himself on* BROMDEN.) Chief, let go. Help me, boys! (*The men don't move.*) Chief . . . let go. Let—go. (*Pulls with all his strength, and finally* CHIEF BROMDEN *stumbles away. Flings aside the pillow. Feels for pulse in* MCMURPHY'S *neck. In soft horror:*) Oh, Christ Jesus . . . (*Turns to face* CHIEF BROMDEN. *The* CHIEF *begins to cry. He sinks down, childlike, crying.* HARDING *turns from him and races into the dormitory.*)

CHESWICK. It's okay, Chief, take it easy.

SCANLON. Sure, take it easy.

(*The* CHIEF'S *huge body shakes with sobs.* HARDING *re-enters at a run, crossing to the windows.*)

FREDERICKS. (*Curiously.*) What're you doing?

HARDING. I've still got the key! (*He unlocks the grille, swings it open.*) All right, Chief. Get going.

SCANLON. Hey, wait a minute—

HARDING. Chief, do you hear me?

SCANLON. Why you hollerin' at him?

HARDING. If he's gone they can't prove anything!

MARTINI. He didn't do nothin' wrong!

HARDING. I know.

CHESWICK. Anybody can die, postoperative. Happens all the time.

HARDING. I know.

FREDERICKS. *We'll* never tell.

HARDING. I know. But he *will*. (*He kneels, gripping* CHIEF BROMDEN *by the shoulders.*) Chief, d'you understand? She'll take hold of you. The Big Nurse. She'll look you in the eyes. And you'll *talk*.

CHIEF BROMDEN. (*It penetrates. Quaveringly.*) What should I do?

HARDING. Beat it!

CHIEF BROMDEN. Out . . . there?

HARDING. Flag a ride on the highway. Head north, up into Canada. You'll be okay.

CHESWICK. That's right, Chief, they never go after AWOLs.

SCANLON. Sure, and we'll say he was alive *after* you busted out.

CHIEF BROMDEN. I'm afraid.

HARDING. Chief—

CHIEF BROMDEN. I can't do it. I'm not big enough!

HARDING. You're as big as you're ever going to get!

CHIEF BROMDEN. No. No, McMurphy said . . . he says . . . (*His eyes turn to the panel at the foot of the Station.*)

HARDING. (*A wail.*) Chief, what are you *doing*?

CHIEF BROMDEN. (*Knocking* HARDING *aside.*) McMurphy said . . . (*He crosses to the panel, heaves upward on it. Nothing happens. He takes a deep breath, tries again. There comes a cracking sound, a screech and ripping as the panel pulls loose. Electrical cables snap; there are blue-white pops of light and puffs of smoke. The night-lights and the lights in the Station go out.*)

SCANLON. (*Awed.*) Great God Almighty. (*Somewhere in a far corridor an alarm bell sets up a clamor.*)

HARDING. Oh, Christ, they'll come down with an army. (*To the men.*) Play it cool! (*The four men scurry to the card table.*)

CHIEF BROMDEN. (*Dazedly.*) I done it. (*Exulting, lifting* HARDING *off his feet.*) I done it, Harding, I'm full size again!

HARDING. Okay, Chief, *out.* Remember, north to Canada.

CHIEF BROMDEN. (*Being propelled to the window.*) They got waterfalls in Canada!

HARDING. That's it, find yourself a waterfall.

CHIEF BROMDEN. (*Holding out his hand.*) G'bye, Harding.

HARDING. (*As they grip hands.*) It's going to be good out there.

CHIEF BROMDEN. Yeah. . . . (*Looks out into the moonlit world, and smiles.*) I been away a long, long time. (*Slides through the window and is gone.*)

HARDING. (*Closes the grille, drops the key outside. Joins the men at the table, takes the cards from* CHESWICK. HARDING, *singing as he deals.*)

"My horses ain't hungry, they won't eat your hay,
So fare thee well, darlin', I'm gone on my way. . . ."
ALL. (*Joining in, singing.*)
"My wagons are loaded, my whip's in my hand. . . ."
(*Etc. . . . as:*)

THE CURTAIN FALLS
THE END

❖◇

MARY FRANCES ROBINSON,
Ph.D., and
WALTER FREEMAN,
M.D., Ph.D., F.A.C.P.

Mary Frances Robinson is a clinical psychologist at the Missouri State Hospital in St. Louis, and the author of various articles on psychosurgery. She received her Ph.D. from the University of Chicago and was chairman of the Department of Psychology at St. Joseph Junior College from 1948 to 1957.

Walter Freeman was a psychiatrist and neurologist who pioneered the use of prefrontal and transorbital lobotomies as a treatment for severe mental illness, performing the first lobotomy in the United States in 1936. He was Professor of Neurology at George Washington University from 1927 to 1954 and a president of the American Association of Neuropathologists. His publications include *Neuropathology* (1933) and *The Psychiatrist* (1967). He died in 1972 at the age of seventy-six.

GLIMPSES OF POSTLOBOTOMY
PERSONALITIES

The problem of this study [is] to investigate the essential nature of the change brought about by psychosurgery that results in the relief of a patient's symptoms and the alteration of some aspects of his personality.

From *Psychosurgery and the Self*, pp. 15–32, copyright © 1954 by Grune and Stratton, Inc. New York. Reprinted by permission.

Actually, of course, changing the personality is the avowed purpose of psychosurgery, just as it is the purpose of all types of psychotherapy, but the dramatic speed with which the operative procedure succeeds in cases where all other therapy has failed highlights the changes. Without the long, painful process of developing insight in the patients, psychosurgery somehow relieves them of their sufferings and makes it possible for them to go back to their homes and to survive in the very environment in which their disorders developed. That changes have taken place in them is obvious; much less obvious is the exact nature of those changes. When one studies patients after psychosurgery, he is faced with something new. He cannot appeal to the authority of a revered psychiatrist or psychologist or school of thought. Extensive batteries of established tests have produced little of importance.

The work methods that led to the present hypothesis are unconventional in an experimental study and need explanation. They were entirely inductive and essentially the methods that a psychotherapist uses in trying to understand a patient during early interviews. They included a calm warmth of manner toward the patient to make talking easy for him, along with intense watching, listening, and empathic sharing as he talked. In this instance, however, the interviews led to objectives not mainly therapeutic but investigative. What each patient said was recorded and studied, protocols were frequently compared, and tentative generalizations were formulated.

The hypothesis that ultimately appeared plausible may be stated here quite simply. Psychosurgery changes the structure of the self through reducing the capacity for the feeling of self-continuity.

The purpose of the present chapter is to share with the reader some of the observations and insights that led to the hypothesis by giving sketches of some of the patients whose characteristics were especially significant. No full case histories will be reported; only the most pertinent matter will be given, and where possible given in the patient's own words. Each patient is referred to by number—the number under which his papers are filed in the clinic records.

It must be understood that the material which follows has been selected, not with the idea of presenting a fair picture of representative post-psychosurgical patients, but with the deliberate purpose of pointing up attitudes and ideas found in *some* people after lobotomy that are not characteristic of neurotic, psychotic, or normal individuals.

The Postlobotomy Syndrome

Critics of psychosurgery have made much of the cluster of symptoms known as the postlobotomy syndrome. It seems suitable to present first a patient exhibiting that syndrome, in order to show the reader most strikingly and instructively the worst effects of the operation and to clarify thus the basis for the hypothesis.

Case 187 had stopped school at the beginning of the eighth grade and had been a practical nurse before her marriage. She was always irritable and highstrung and became much disturbed emotionally during the period of the menopause. She complained of aches and pains all over her body, felt frantic during her sleepless nights, and was very eager for the operation, which was performed in 1943. She made a quick recovery and soon returned home from the hospital. Four years after operation, she was a vigorous-looking woman with strong features and thick gray hair brushed straight back from her face. Her conversation was jerky, profuse, and rambling. "I never think about the past; it's too long ago. I keep house after a fashion; don't care how it looks. I smoke too much. Can't sit still long enough to listen to the radio, but I go to church regular—yes, ma'am! And to the movies whenever I can get the money out of my husband. My son asked me 'What will you do if Dad dies?' I said, 'I'll go live with you!'" She threw her head back and laughed uproariously. "I'll tell you one thing—I'll never get married again!" When asked if she were unhappy with her husband, she laughed again and shouted, "No, I beat the devil out of him!"

It is evident that this woman had retained some of her premorbid characteristics. Her restlessness, talkativeness, and self-
assertiveness, preserved through illness, were merely exaggerated
by the operation. Of her illness itself there seemed to be no
trace. She was certainly neither hypochondriacal nor complaining nor torn by anxiety. Prefrontal lobotomy had relieved her of
those symptoms and had produced others. She had become
euphoric, boisterous, and tactless, and seemed to have lost all
capacity for restraint and sympathy. It is easy to understand
that she was a trial to her family, yet to an outsider there
was something disarming and even engaging in her objectivity,
in her amused recognition of her own outrageousness. Along
with her other postoperative characteristics, this peculiar objectivity needs to be explained and perhaps related to the reason-
ing indicated in the first sentence quoted from her monologue,
"I never think about the past; it's too long ago."

Case 187 is the only exemplar of the lobotomy syndrome in
the series of fifty-one cases. In some patients, schizophrenic
deterioration has blurred the picture, in several a few symptoms
(e.g., euphoria) are present, in others no grossly unfavorable
results of psychosurgery are apparent. It is thus necessary to look
for changes less obvious than these cited, subtle indications that
these people, who are quite diverse as individuals, are markedly
different from the rest of us and different from their former
selves, yet somehow like each other. As a thread upon which to
string the introductory observations, it is convenient to use the
interval after surgery, for most patients follow much the same
pattern.

Postsurgical Picture

No matter how delusional or desperate or violent the patient
may have been when he entered the hospital, almost at once
after the operation he becomes relaxed and quiescent, though
not asleep. He can recognize his relatives but shows no particular interest in their presence. He follows directions with a fair
degree of cooperation but is too inert to talk. During the first

twenty-four hours he is frequently nauseated. For the first day or two and sometimes for a week or weeks, he may be quite incontinent, and entirely without shame about it, even though he admits he does not like the feel of wet sheets. One girl was especially troublesome. One night her mother found her bed soaked and asked her how it happened. "Were you awake?" "Yes, I was awake." "Didn't you know you had to urinate?" "Yes, of course." "Then why didn't you go to the toilet in the bathroom?" "Well, mother, because I was in bed!" Many children have nocturnal enuresis, but they are not likely to use this type of logic in explaining their behavior.

Patients are usually disoriented in all spheres immediately after prefrontal lobotomy. Recognition of people comes first, usually within a few hours. Orientation to place comes next. They often confuse the hospital and town with others that they may have known earlier, but they get them straightened out in a day or two. Orientation in time is much more difficult. At first they are confused as to the time of day. As was related in *Psychosurgery*, Case 281 insisted that it was afternoon, and was not convinced of his error, even though he could remember that his last meal consisted of cereal, toast, bacon, and coffee.

The most profound disorientation occurs in the area of the self. After operation these people are much interested in satisfying their desires, but they seem to be entirely uninterested in themselves as persons. A few disclaim changes in themselves after the operation. Case 465, a doctor (formerly brilliant and suicidal), who was well acquainted with the literature on psychosurgery, denied that the operation had been performed. "You didn't go on operating. You just closed up and put the bandages on. You couldn't have operated on me because I am just the same as I was before, and there would be some change if you had operated on me."

Case 478, reported in *Psychosurgery*, Second Edition, was asked by the psychologist how she was feeling. "Oh, just the same as I ever did," she said. "But," she was told, "look at those scars on your wrist. You tried to kill yourself, didn't you?" "Oh, that! Well, I must have been crazy then." "Then you must feel differently now, don't you?" "No, I told you. I feel just the same."

Why did these people not recognize in themselves changes that were so obvious to others? Why was suicide no longer necessary to them?

Characteristics During Convalescence

After return home from the hospital, patients go through a period of varying length that is particularly difficult for their relatives. Their wants are vivid, their tempers uncertain, and the whim of the moment tends to rule them. They sometimes exhibit "echo symptoms" in the form of depression or delusion, and then may suddenly become placid again or perhaps euphoric. They are overresponsive to any sympathy or hostility they feel in the people around them, hence their environment is of crucial importance. A calm but firm expectation of conformity to family routine can hardly fail to produce results different from those produced by emotional overindulgence, and the effects of both of these will be different from continuance in hospital wards. Case 601 came of a family of teachers who were much aware of adjustment problems. She showed no untoward symptoms.

Case 607, on the other hand, was overindulged, though her relatives tried to carry out the psychiatrist's directions as regards training. "My family thinks I should get a job; I don't want to because my philosophy does not include work. I went to college in order to learn how to live, not how to make a living. However, if it will make my father happy, I'm willing to get a job. I would like to get a job in a glamorous night club where I could see handsome young men in evening dress. I don't care at all to see the women. However, there is one difficulty about getting such a job. I am afraid of the dark, and the trip home would be a problem."

This romantic hangover might be expected to subside as the four-month postoperative interval lengthened to a year or two.

It is quoted here largely as an example of the odd objectivity which has been mentioned before, but which will be discussed later. She did not "care at all to see the women" and hence said so.

Case 154 had a mother who "couldn't bear to make her do things since she had been through so much." She had worked hard and anxiously, studying for her Master's degree in chemistry, and then suffered from a love affair that turned out badly for her. Schizophrenia, which soon developed, was terminated by prefrontal lobotomy. After she returned from the hospital, and for quite a period afterward, she chose to take only one or two baths a month. She would often turn the water into the tub and after a few minutes let it out again, telling her mother gaily that she hadn't felt like taking off her clothes.

Inertia is a common symptom after operation and may last for weeks or months. Quickness of movement is usually recovered first in the eyes, then in the throat and face muscles, and last in the big muscles of the back and legs.

Case 500 (age thirty-seven) is a striking example. She had suffered from agitated depression, worrying about everything, and feeling powerless to get anything done. A year after prefrontal lobotomy, she was free of worry and had made a good recovery, except for indolence. She could not be induced to do anything about housekeeping. Her mother called the psychologist at 11 o'clock one morning and suggested that a telephone call might induce her to keep her 2 o'clock appointment. This conversation took place. "You are coming in at 2 o'clock, aren't you?" "Well, if I can get ready, I am." "What do you have to do?" "Well, I have to eat my breakfast and get dressed and call a cab." "Won't three hours give you time enough for that?" "Well, I'll try." She arrived at 4:00 and explained that she couldn't manage it any earlier, though she had tried hard, because she had had to eat her breakfast and get dressed and answer the phone twice. "You know *you* called once!"

No other appointment was kept so promptly. She usually telephoned at 5 o'clock and said she was afraid she was too late to start. After several such postponements, she called up one day at 3:00 to say that she was all ready and just had to call her cab. She arrived at 7:45. She was not apologetic but asked a little querulously, "What I want to know is when will I get over being so slow?" She clearly did not consider herself responsible for her tardiness.

It is evident that, in this early period, actual training rather than psychotherapy is needed, with perhaps some goodnatured pulling and pushing to motivate the patient toward conformity.

Case 276 is especially instructive, since he went through several periods of change postoperatively. He had suffered from obsessive tension for some fifteen years. He was extremely articulate and self-analytical during this period, and, with the help of his wife, to whom he was devoted, wrote a long account of the development of his illness. When he was thirty-six, he became so desperate that prefrontal lobotomy seemed the only alternative to suicide. Postoperatively he went through most of the characteristic phases. Echo symptoms were prominent for a while, and he had much to say about counterfeit money. Then he became profane and instead of showing affection for his wife, he became clumsily abusive. Later he showed inertia. A couple of months after the operation, his wife went to bed one night at 9 o'clock, leaving him shaving in the bathroom. Hours later when she awoke, he was still standing in front of the mirror with a razor in his hand and dried lather on one cheek. He recovered from this inertia before long and then went through a restless phase, which diminished but did not disappear during the next three years. Before his illness became acute, he had helped design apparatus for research in physics. After the operation he could not do that work, but he was quite efficient at a more routine government job, which paid a good salary. He liked to talk with the men in the office and to play practical jokes of a rather juvenile sort. Largely through his wife's insistence, he enrolled in a university class in modern physics. When he received notice that he had failed, he laughed gaily. Nothing concerned him deeply. He talked readily about his illness and related tales of his obsession with considerable amusement. During his illness he had been devoted to his wife and dependent upon her, and for a period shortly after operation he was quite passionate for a while.

After three years he said, "Oh, I like my wife all right, but I don't need her any more." Yet prefrontal lobotomy had not only saved this man from suicide; it had enabled him to hold a job and to get considerable satisfaction out of his daily life. The change it made in him was fundamental indeed.

Postconvalescent Personality

It is not possible to state positively the length of convalescence, for it varies with the individual. In rare cases it may last only a few months; in other patients improvement may continue for several years. In general, however, a period of relative stability appears to be reached two or three years after the operation. (This interval is far longer, of course, than that allowed by most investigators when they make their appraisals of psychosurgery.) It seems practicable to consider these relatively stable cases here under three informal and somewhat overlapping categories: levels of ambition, general motivation, and detachment of self-judgment.

LEVELS OF AMBITION

Many observers have noted that following prefrontal lobotomy people seem satisfied with levels of achievement lower than those that they had demanded of themselves prior to illness. In Partridge's phrase, "They do not seem on tiptoe any more." Landis, Zubin, and Mettler comment on their lack of "zeal."

It may be that this lowered achievement is the result of lessened ability to plan and to give prolonged attention, as will be indicated by the tests described in Chapter IV; it may reflect merely lessened motivation, or quite possibly a combination of the two. Perhaps some day tests will be devised to detect the part played by each factor. The evidence to be presented in this chapter comes not from test results but from the types of jobs held by the patients, from the types of interest shown by them, and from their own self-judgments.

Case 196, who had held the same well-paid job in one of the government offices for a three-year period since his operation, remarked, "Mentally I am ambitious, but I don't seem to do anything about it." Few individuals have gone back to the more arduous professions which demand a high degree of skill in interpersonal relations. A physician said he was just as much interested in medicine as ever but did not care to practice it again; he might like to take up photography, but thought he preferred to read novels. A former interior decorator in the series is a saleswoman in a wallpaper shop. A nurse said that looking after her plants gave her enough to do.

One of the few rather ambitious persons is Case 76, one of the lawyers mentioned earlier. He is the most analytical of any in the entire series. Though he had been the leader of his classes in college and law school, he was able to practice law only for a short time because of the development of a severe obsessive tension which lasted for years. Following operation, he was idle for a year and then obtained a position of considerable responsibility in one of the government agencies, which he has continued to hold. In response to a question about operative effects, he said, "Yes, prefrontal lobotomy changed me—very fortunately for all concerned! Oh, I think I have suffered some intellectual loss. My briefs seem to lack something of the sweet articulation that they once had. But there are compensations. There is a great deal of competition among the lawyers in my agency. The other people in our building call our corridor 'Ulcer Gulch.' I think my work is perhaps a little below average in quality—but I do not have an ulcer!"

Other patients less able than Case 76 were occasionally confronted by failure but seemed quite unconcerned by it. When Case 276 (mentioned above) reported that he had failed his physics course, he was asked, "Did you perhaps not study enough?" He roared with laughter. "Well, evidently *not*," he said.

Many postlobotomy patients are discharged from the first jobs they get, less because of actual incompetence than because they won't bestir themselves to try hard enough to please their employers. They often admit the justice of their dismissal (another instance of detached attitude) and seldom seem depressed by it. After they reach a period of stability, however, and find jobs for which they are fitted, many of them settle down to steady work and do it well. If they are not "on tiptoe," neither are they distracted by yearning for "the distant hills."

Although after psychosurgery patients are like children in certain respects (which will be discussed later), they are not at all childlike in their attitudes toward work or recreation. After the first postoperative days they have neither the tastes nor enthusiasms of children. They lack the creative curiosity of which Murphy speaks. They rarely throw themselves wholeheartedly into any activity. With few exceptions, those who care to read prefer magazines and newspapers to books. They show no special eagerness for games, and few care to participate in any kind of sport. Even watching ball games is enjoyed most through motion picture shows and television. In this age of spectator pleasures, these facts are neither remarkable nor restricted to psychosurgery patients, but it is interesting to note that to most of these people simple inactivity is not at all displeasing.

Such evidence as has been presented here certainly does not rule out the possibility that psychosurgery reduces some types of intellectual ability, but makes evident the fact that in any case some nonintellective factors have changed, such as initiative and enthusiasm.

MOTIVATION

There seems to be no doubt about changes having taken place in the field of motivation. The important point for research is to ascertain the kinds of changes. Discussion here will range from physiological drives through emotions and interests to ethical standards.

Some of the primary or physiological drives seem especially strong in these patients. Sleep and rest seem to have a more positive attraction than is usual, and many patients go to bed early, not so much because they are tired as because going to bed

₃omething they like to do. On the other hand, there are occasional patients who are restless and seem to like activity for activity's sake, as for example Case 187. The neurological explanation for this contrast is yet to be found; psychologically, it suffices to note that in both kinds of cases immediate pleasure rather than longtime satisfaction is sought.

Many patients have excellent appetites far past the postoperative period and become much overweight because they are unwilling to diet. Case 22, who is so fat that her neck has disappeared into her featherbed body, said, "What I like best to do is to get big bags of popcorn and candy and sit right on the front row of a movie and enjoy myself." Case 479, who is practically globular, admitted, "I could get into my clothes better, with less exertion, if I was thinner. It would be nice, but I don't do anything about it." Obviously for these two women immediate pleasure outweighs future satisfaction.

At first glance the situation as regards sex is ambiguous. In some cases, especially among the formerly neurotic who had been inhibited by jealousies and anxieties, sexual expression is freer and more normal than before. In other cases, formerly obsessed with sex, the drive is definitely weaker. It is evident that in both types of case the same factor is really operating—morbid anticipation is gone. Without such anticipation, the strength of the drive can be more appropriate to the immediate situation.

In general after psychosurgery, patients' emotions, though quite appropriate, tend to be more vivid and labile and less persistent than before. Their prevailing mood is cheerful. They show affection frequently, less often love, and only rarely grief. Occasionally a patient will comment on his own lack of emotional intensity. Case 327 said, "When I lost my father I was upset, but not so much. I don't have the deep, sincere feeling that I used to have. I used to feel so deeply I'd throw up."

Case 403, a fat, comfortable-looking country woman, was

extremely loquacious, and most of her talk about herself. She said, "I used to be awful easy to feel bad and awful easy to cry, but now I feel so good I hardly ever cry. I told my sister, 'Sister,' I said, 'I won't cry now, whomever passes out.' 'Oh, Sister,' she said, 'won't you cry if I pass out?' 'Well, Sister,' I said, 'I'll think a good long time before I do!' " She laughed in enjoyment of her own cleverness.

Patients often become irritated and angry, especially with their relatives; but they seldom retain resentments for long. Case 189 said, "My husband scolds me because I don't keep house better. It makes me mad." "Then do you try harder to make the house look nice?" "No, of course not. But I don't like him to criticize me." Before operation she had been quite literally unable to bear his criticism.

Many of these patients preoperatively had suffered agonies of anxiety and fear. Psychosurgery relieves them almost completely. A frequent comment is, "I never worry about anything any more." Such worries as they do express seem to have no bite to them.

Money, often a potent source of worry in our society, is seldom mentioned by these people. One woman who was asked what changes she would like to make in herself answered, "I'd like to have more money so I could go more places and buy more things," but there was nothing special she wanted to buy. None of the women of whom the inquiry was made said she liked to go shopping. Apparently possessions, including money, have little prestige value for most people after psychosurgery, though Case 437 speaks proudly of his first editions. Future security concerns them only moderately, in some cases not at all. Many of them earn money and save it, but they are not preoccupied by it.

Sustained remorse, so characteristic of a morbid state, was not encountered in any patient in the series. In fact these patients seemed incapable of remorse or of embarrassment over past deeds. They were rarely disconcerted by any situation, even when their shortcomings were pointed out in the presence of a group. Case 143 said, "It's right hard for me to be embarrassed; but sometimes I embarrass other people."

They are gregarious rather than genuinely social, and in a group have little to say. With one person, however, they become expansive and even garrulous. They often laugh heartily, especially over what they say themselves, and seem to invite others to laugh with them. They seldom listen carefully enough to note the effect their words are having upon others. And when they are told that they have been tactless or have hurt someone's feelings, they are cheerfully unconcerned.

Yet in spite of their careless chatter and their indifference to other people's opinions, these people seldom do anything really objectionable from an ethical point of view. Early training, so potent as shown by Dollard and Miller and Cameron and Magaret, as well as their past experiences, which seem to mean so little to them now, nevertheless established habits and attitudes in the premorbid period which still control their behavior. No patient in the series has had a record of lawbreaking. Only one (Case 50) drank to excess, and he had developed the habit in high school, long before operation. Case 57 sponged on her family (and perhaps on other people) but she too was merely carrying out a well-established habit. Four or five patients, including 187, who was mentioned earlier, were disagreeable within the family circle, and several were hard to manage; but they all behaved within the limits set by conventional standards. They seemed to have no tendency toward theft or lying. Indeed, telling the *whole* truth is one of their characteristics that has proved most annoying to their families. They showed no tendency toward sexual abnormalities, as has been noted, and no preoccupation with sex; they discussed their sex life easily and naturally, as they did their other experiences.

Good habits and attitudes are just as persistent as bad ones after lobotomy, and moral training still holds. Case 55 wanted very much to be married. "But," she complained to the psychologist, "I have such bad luck with my boy friends! I liked the last one I had a lot, but do you know, the last time I was with him, he wanted to do something that was not nice; it was not a *bit* nice. Of course I wouldn't let him. He said, 'If you won't let me do what I want to, I won't every come to see you any more.' 'Well,' I said, 'don't ever think I *want* you to!' " Her indignation was unmistakably sincere. Apparently her "Superego" has not been "amputated."

Two patients were mothers of young children. Both seemed to try hard to carry through each day's many tasks but found difficulty in planning ahead. Case 189 said she could never manage to get the children to Sunday School on time.

Several patients attended church with some regularity, but none of them showed depth of religious feeling. Not one of the group indicated that any aspiration was a force in his life, religious, educational, scientific, artistic, social. Not one of them was more creative than Case 215, who enjoyed planning and giving dinner parties. None of them seemed to reach forward toward the distant future. Case 327 said, "No, I never plan for the future. When tomorrow comes it will be time enough to decide what picture show I want to go to then."

The evidence (and much more might be adduced) points to a very significant change in motivation brought about by the operation. It indicates that psychosurgical patients, though they have the usual variety of motives, experience them and are governed by them only as they affect the present and immediate future. It is in this respect, especially, that they seem childlike.

In his analysis of the constitutional psychopath, Bakan has coined the descriptive term "presentization of the individual." The term fits this aspect of lobotomy patients very well. Though these people may remember the past without difficulty, they seem able to make very little use of it in interpreting the present and future. They "learn from experience" less readily than most of us. In these respects they are like the psychopaths as Sullivan describes them, but in other respects they are different, and the differences are important. The constitutional psychopaths have had their disabilities from childhood, while their personalities were being shaped, and they become thoroughly selfish people, often antisocial. Psychosurgical patients, on the other hand, grew up for the most part as sensitive, conforming individuals, and after the operation they are still likable.

DETACHMENT OF SELF-JUDGMENT

A strange, naïve, complacent detachment about the self is one of the most interesting and significant characteristics displayed after psychosurgery.

Most of us, as observers of our own behavior, occasionally at least, don't like what we see and feel disturbed about it. If we are oversensitive and maladjusted, we are likely to magnify our blunders and to brood over them remorsefully. If we are better adjusted, we are likely to try to make amends to the person we think we have offended; perhaps we apologize, or we try to make light of what we have done, or we try to explain our acts and excuse them to ourselves. In any event, we try not to make those particular mistakes again. The attitude of the postlobotomy patients is rather different from this. They see their faults and weaknesses and vices clearly enough and recognize them for what they are, but far from privately brooding over them, they seem to regard them as interesting topics for comment. They often say, "That's the way I am." Petrie cites an especially good instance. Her patient said, "I know I am moody, but after all, that's me, like the color of my eyes." They evince no anxiety about criticism and little responsibility for making amends or for reform.

As was mentioned above, Case 500 asked, "When will I get over being so slow?" Case 55, gentle and charming in the clinic, said dolefully one day, "I feel so sorry for my family; I say just dreadful things to them." "Why do you say them?" "Oh, I don't know; I just do." "And then do you feel sorry you've said them?" "No, I am not sorry I said them; I am just sorry they have to put up with me."

There is no rationalizing here—no feeling of a need for

rationalizing. Defense and escape mechanisms, as commonly described, are seldom if ever encountered in these people—not once in our records of 51 patients.

Case 196 has already been mentioned as having held the same good job for four years since the operation. He was a good-looking man in the middle thirties, with a pleasing manner. In a rambling talk a few days after taking the tests, he revealed a good deal about his attitudes toward his wife. "I blow up sometimes and make her very unhappy. I'm a lot less considerate than I used to be. When I hurt her, I feel bad for a minute, but I get over it. I am ashamed that I don't feel worse, but I just don't. . . . It's difficult for me to be interested in anything; things don't make much of an impression on me . . . my wife says I have a cold personality. I sometimes take pleasure in arguing with her, and then I throw salt in the wound. I seem to take some sadistic pleasure in it. . . . When my wife says sharp things to me, I start arguing but my feelings aren't really hurt. Before the operation, an unkind remark would upset me for days. . . . I should make an effort to stop arguing, but I don't." Though he said he felt ashamed, there was no evidence of it as he spoke. He seemed quite complacent about his behavior, and obviously enjoyed talking about it.

Case 154, who was also in the middles thirties, was less complacent than the previous case and was more critical of herself than was anyone else in the series. In that respect she was not typical of the group, yet much that she said was highly significant and perhaps has wide application. It will be remembered that she was mentioned above as being reluctant about bathing. She appeared for the test with grimy face and hands and wore an elaborate white linen dress that was soiled from neck to hem. Yet her lively intelligence made her somehow attractive. She said, "I don't like anything inside myself. I'm a hopeless mess." Then her face crinkled into laughter and she appeared to invite her listener to laugh, too. "I think I have the wrong viewpoint about things; I don't seem able to get along with people. Maybe I ought to be ashamed of myself, but I'm not." She laughed again. She is complex enough to condemn her behavior and then to condemn

…ue toward her behavior. But she is quite unemotional …u even unregretful about it all. "I resent authority. I wonder if that is because of my father. He dominated everybody. I always fought back. My grandmother is eighty-nine, senile, alcoholic, and man-crazy. I know she is not responsible, but I forget that instantly and go into a towering rage." She laughed hard. "I'm a mess. What's the matter with me? Don't I want to grow up?" She seemed to recognize some contradictions in herself and to wonder about them, but did not feel any regret or any responsibility about changing.

In all these cases and in many others not cited, there is a recognition of personal shortcoming that is quite different from insight. It is a rather complacent recognition that includes acceptance but not responsibility. The individual pronounces judgment upon himself but is not concerned emotionally in the verdict.

SUMMARY

A study of individual cases shows that any hypothesis, to be adequate, must take into consideration a number of observations. It must be remembered that the generalizations which follow are by no means applicable to every patient. In some cases, many of the characteristics may be lacking, in others, existent only as trends. Listed here starkly, without the modifying effects of the total personalities in which they are embedded, they constitute not so much a picture as a caricature of the postlobotomy personality. Sometimes, however, a caricature is useful.

1. In a very short time (a few hours or days at most) psychosurgery, if successful, frees patients of their morbid symptoms, in most cases permanently, at least in so far as the experience of a decade and a half will permit us to judge. The past, once unbearably painful, is now powerless to hurt. It has not been forgotten, it has not been assimilated through psychotherapy, it has simply ceased to matter.

2. Patients are childish in their behavior during their first postoperative days, are lazy and even inert, and need careful training to insure personal cleanliness and conformity to a household routine. They are unconcerned about themselves as persons and are usually oblivious to changes that have taken place in themselves.

3. After convalescence, their premorbid personalities emerge, with an overlay of characteristics that seem attributable to the operation. Their intellectual achievement fails to reach the former level, perhaps because of insufficient motivation; their motivation in general seems to be of a short-term variety. Their wants are imperative but concern the present only. Their emotions flare up quickly and are appropriate to the occasion but rather shallow and fleeting. The prevailing mood is cheerful, with few expressions of anxiety. They are open and candid, and sometimes their frankness has a disconcerting quality. It is unshaded, somehow, and in extreme cases may be merciless and unashamed, as though the speaker could not enter imaginatively into the effects his words might have. ("I like my wife all right, but I don't need her any more.") In such cases, lobotomy patients seem lacking in both sympathy and empathy. They are quite objective in viewing their own faults and seldom rationalize or make excuses for themselves. They seem incapable of feeling embarrassment or remorse over past mistakes. Lacking in subtle appreciations, but also in ulterior motives, they are likable, complacent, and natural—unnaturally natural.

It is evident that these people are different from most of our friends and neighbors, and even from themselves before illness, in curious but definite ways. They are certainly different from the tortured selves they were preoperatively. They seem to be cut off from those selves and cut off, too, from apprehension of future consequences. They appear to be living completely within a quite comfortable here and now, and they are remarkably self-consistent, that is, their behavior is largely predictable. Their personalities seem to be simplified and singularly without depth.

HYPOTHESIS

Scientists work mainly with concepts—terms that sum up similarities among objects of thought. Many psychological terms are used so often in common speech that we forget their conceptual nature. Personality, intelligence, originality, schizophrenia, emotion, the self—none of these terms describes entities; they are simply useful concepts, perhaps better called constructs.

The construct of the self, of rather recent popularity in psychological literature, is used somewhat loosely to designate the more subjective aspects of the personality. Though it is becoming the focus of a good deal of present-day psychological theory, its structure has not yet been much analyzed. Observation of postlobotomy patients compels that analysis, for the changes in personality appear to be in the sphere of the self, and especially in the more subtle aspects of the self.

The hypothesis of this study has already been stated. Psychosurgery alters the structure of the self through reducing capacity for the feeling of self-continuity.

The term self-continuity was not one of the writer's concepts when this study was begun. It emerged from recognition of what seemed to be lacking in these patients that the rest of us have—the feeling of somehow going on in time—the feeling of being essentially the same individual as one was yesterday and will be tomorrow, but recognizing that one has changed since childhood and may go on changing. This feeling is seldom put into words by any of us except possibly when we fear the end of the self, as in death, but it is implicit in our looking back over the past and forward to the future. Our pasts and futures are living realities to us, and the present often seems most significant, not for itself, but for the way it enables us or forces us to reach forward. Hence we want self-respect and self-enhancement. Hence we are concerned with the approval or disapproval of others.

Postlobotomy patients appear different from us and like each

other in just this respect. They appear to lack (though in varying degrees, to be sure) any strong feeling of self-continuity.

It will be noted that the phrase used in the hypothesis is
"capacity for the feeling of self-continuity," much as one would
say, "capacity for the feeling of strong emotion." These capacities may be interrelated in some complex fashion.

❖◈❖

ARTHUR P. NOYES, M.D., and
LAWRENCE C. KOLB, M.D.

Doctor Kolb is Professor and Chairman, Department of Psychiatry, College of Physicians and Surgeons, Columbia University, and is Director, New York State Psychiatric Institute and Psychiatric Service, Presbyterian Hospital of New York.

Doctor Noyes is Director, Psychiatric Education, Pennsylvania Department of Public Welfare and has been Superintendent of the Norristown State Hospital, Norristown, Pennsylvania.

SHOCK AND OTHER
PHYSICAL THERAPIES

The employment of the so-called shock therapies dates from 1933 when Manfred Sakel, then working in the Clinic of the University of Vienna, reported that deep hypoglycemic states produced by large doses of insulin produced a beneficial effect on the course of schizophrenia. With the subsequent introduction of other forms of shock therapy, attempts were made to establish a common denominator of action in them all. Not yet, however, has a theory been presented that satisfactorily explains the therapeutic action in any one of the forms of shock therapy, much less one that applies to all forms. There is now available a number of important follow-up studies that describe

From *Modern Clinical Psychiatry*, 6th edition, 538–42. Reprinted by permission of Lawrence C. Kolb and W. B. Saunders Co.

and delineate the nature of the therapeutic effect of these procedures over long periods of time, a necessity for the understanding of any treatment offered in the field of psychiatric therapy.

Electric Convulsive Therapy

In 1938 Cerletti and Bini described a method of producing convulsions by electricity and began its use in the treatment of schizophrenia.

The apparatus operates on 110-volt, 60-cycle, alternating current and contains mainly a variable transformer, ohm, volt, and ampere meters, and an automatic timer. The combined voltage and time settings constitute the "dose." Applications may range from 70 to 130 volts continuing from 0.1 to 0.5 second. Usually one starts with 80 volts for 0.2 second. If this fails to produce a convulsion, the voltage may be increased to 90 or 100 volts and the period of application increased. If this does not result in a seizure, no further application should be made until the following day. Only generalized seizures are productive of desired results. The operator will find that the dose must be determined by the convulsive threshold of the individual patient. This threshold is higher in female than in male patients, and higher in middle-aged than in younger persons. The threshold is raised after the first seizure.

The patient becomes unconscious immediately after the current is applied, even if no seizure follows. He will have no memory of a "shock." The convulsion conforms closely to those of spontaneous origin, with a tonic phase continuing for approximately 10 seconds followed by a clonic phase of somewhat longer duration. The convulsion is accompanied by apnea.

TECHNIQUE AND RESPONSES

In addition to the usual physical examination, including blood pressure, before the patient receives electric convulsive therapy, a roentgenogram should be made of the chest and of the lateral aspect of the spine; there should also be an electro-cardiogram. An electroencephalogram is recommended. If the patient is to be treated in the morning, he receives either no breakfast or a glass of fruit juice and one slice of toast two hours before treatment. The patient should void, and dentures should be removed before treatment. If the patient suffers from nausea following the seizure, he may be given 50 mg. of Dramamine prior to the next treatment. He may receive the treatment either on a well-padded table or on a bed, the springs of which are supported by a board between spring and mattress. Compression fractures of vertebrae are occasional complications. Formerly it was believed that their frequency would be reduced if the spine were slightly overextended either by placing a firm pillow under the small of the back or by placing the patient on a Gatch bed during the treatment. This overextension is no longer generally recommended.

The patient is placed in a comfortable dorsal position, or the spine may be slightly flexed. The shoulders and arms are held lightly by a nurse to prevent extreme movements of the latter. Usually a restraint sheet is sufficient for the thighs, but if they are held, the control should not be too rigid lest fractures of an acetabulum or of a femur result. A padded tongue depressor or other resilient mouth gag is placed between the teeth to prevent biting the tongue or other injury. The assistant who holds the mouth gag in place holds the patient's chin firmly upon the gag so that the jaw cannot open too far and become dislocated. Electrode paste is rubbed into the skin on both sides of the forehead, and the electrodes, previously soaked in saturated salt solution, are applied to the prepared areas. The apparatus button is pressed and the patient becomes instantly unconscious. Following the clonic phase, there is a phase of muscular relaxation with stertorous respiration. It is well to roll the patient on his side to prevent inhalation of saliva. The patient remains unconscious for about five minutes, then slowly rouses during the next five to ten minutes.

After the treatment there is a period of confusion, during

which the patient should be watched lest he fall out of bed. He should usually be permitted to lie for one-half to one hour after treatment. If left undisturbed, he may sleep an hour or more. In most cases there is no postconvulsive excited state, but a patient who is subject to this disturbance should receive $3\frac{3}{4}$ grains of sodium amytal intravenously just prior to application of the electricity.

There is insufficient evidence to show that unidirectional or brief stimuli techniques or the use of other types of currents or variant methods of application are superior to the ordinary form of treatment just described.

FREQUENCY

Treatments are usually given three times a week. The period for which treatment should be continued depends largely upon the results obtained and upon the nature of the disorder treated. In depressive reactions, the patient may have received the maximum benefit after five to ten treatments. In disorders in which the patient is slowly but definitely improving, treatment may continue to 25 or 30 applications followed, if desirable, by maintenance treatments. Two treatments per day may be given for two or three successive days in the case of acutely disturbed patients who are threatened by psychotic exhaustion.

INDICATIONS

The greatest usefulness of electroconvulsive therapy is in depression. Its most frequent use, therefore, is in the treatment of involutional melancholia and of the depressive phase of manic-depressive psychosis. In case depression is an associated symptom in other disorders, this form of therapy may be followed by beneficial results. It is frequently used as a substitute for insulin shock therapy in acute and subacute schizophrenia reactions. Its use as a "maintenance" treatment in chronically disturbed schizophrenics and in the manic phase of manic-depressive psychosis is discussed in another section.

As experience with electroconvulsive shock therapy has increased, conditions regarded as contraindications have decreased. *Age*, in itself, is not considered a contraindication. The aged patient should, of course, be very carefully examined for physical abnormalities. Although the condition of the *cardiovascular system* should be carefully evaluated before electric convulsive therapy is given, the strain of the convulsion on that system has probably been exaggerated. Hypertension, abnormal electrocardiograms, or a history of angina pectoris or of coronary thrombosis are not in themselves contraindications to treatment if the patient has a good cardiac reserve.

Cardiac decompensation usually debars electroconvulsive therapy. The presence of aortic aneurysm also excludes the use of this treatment. If hypertension is largely caused by emotional factors, it need not be a cause for rejection of treatment but, on the contrary, may be an indication for its use. Vascular accidents as a result of electroconvulsive therapy are exceedingly rare. The use of electric convulsive therapy in the presence of myocardial disease depends upon its seriousness and the urgency of the need for treatment. If agitation is producing a constant strain on the heart, convulsive treatment may be used.

Generally speaking, *tuberculosis*, if there is a history of recent hemorrhage or evidence of high activity, excludes treatment, but the patient who is a feeding problem is often benefited through the resulting gain of weight. Latent tuberculosis is rarely activated. Except for recent fractures, *bone disease* is not a frequent contraindication to treatment. *Pregnancy* is not usually considered a contraindication. Electric shock is a safer form of therapy than insulin in the psychoses of pregnancy.

COMPLICATIONS

Impairment of Memory. Scarcely to be called a complication is the almost constant impairment of memory that accompanies electroconvulsive therapy. It may vary from a mild tendency to forget names to a severe confusion of the Korsakoff type. At first it tends to cover a long period prior to treatment, then gradually to diminish to events immediately before treatment. It is often distressing to the patient and may continue to some degree for several weeks or a few months following the termination of treatment. Full return of memory finally occurs. Psychological investigations indicate that electric convulsive therapy is not followed by any intellectual impairment.

Fractures and Dislocations. The most frequent complications in electroconvulsive therapy are fractures and dislocations caused by muscular contraction. The fracture occurring most often is a *compression fracture of vertebrae,* in the dorsal area between the second and eighth, usually the third, fourth, or fifth vertebrae. Approximately 20 per cent of the patients suffer this injury, which occurs twice as frequently among men as among women. Apparently a majority of the fractures occur early in the course of treatment. They are not of major clinical importance and do not require special treatment. Many are found only on roentgenologic examination. Back pain may persist for a few days or weeks. Fractures of the femur, of the acetabulum, and of the neck of the humerus may occur. Dislocation of the jaw is frequent unless pressure is applied to prevent the opening of the mouth at the onset of the tonic phase.

Apnea. Apnea occurs physiologically in any general convulsive seizure, but in electroconvulsive therapy the respiratory arrest may be disturbingly prolonged. Some therapists use artificial respiration immediately after the convulsion as a safety measure. If apnea persists, artificial respiration should be continued. A metal airway should be available to prevent the tongue from falling back and to lead air through accumulations of saliva and mucus. Deaths as a result of electroconvulsive therapy are exceedingly uncommon.

"SOFTENING" OF SEIZURES

In order to avoid fractures or dislocations and to diminish the risk in elderly or infirm patients, convulsions may be modified by means of curare and other drugs. Curare inhibits the action of acetylcholine at neuromuscular junctions and softens the muscular contractions.

In recent years succinylcholine dichloride (Anectine) has largely supplanted curare preparations as a muscle relaxant because of less risk of respiratory paralysis attending its use. From 10 to 40 mg. of succinylcholine dichloride may be mixed in the same syringe with 0.8 mg. of atropine and 2 ml. of pentothal. At the end of the convulsion, oxygen under positive pressure is administered until the patient breathes spontaneously.

In approximately one in a thousand patients, prolonged apnea may occur after the use of succinylcholine. It has been suggested that those sensitive to this drug and its diethyl derivative, suxethonium, have inherited a less active variant of the enzyme pseudocholinesterase so that the drug action persists an undue length of time.

Usually a period of controlled respiration will terminate the apnea. Coramine (1 to 2.5 gm. in 4 to 10 ml.) may be given intravenously to counteract excessive barbiturate. If apnea persists for a half hour, edrophonium (Tensilon) should then be tried, and if this is unsuccessful, neostigmine (1.0 to 1.5 mg.) preceded by atropine (0.4 to 0.6 mg.) should be administered.

RESULTS OF TREATMENT

In the depressions of involutional melancholia and of manic-depressive psychosis, the improvement following electroconvulsive shock therapy is striking. In 80 per cent or more of these disorders, five to ten treatments are followed by full or social recovery. Prior to the treatment of involutional melancholia by electric shock therapy, protracted depression, sometimes lasting for years, was the rule. Early treatment of this disorder and of the depressions of manic-depressive psychosis by shock therapy will save many patients who would otherwise commit suicide.

Electroconvulsive shock therapy has no influence on the recurrence of manic-depressive episodes. Guilt and self-punishing, and self-accusatory trends are usually rapidly alleviated. In less than half of the cases of the paranoid type of involutional psychosis is treatment followed by much improvement, even though the maximum number of convulsions is induced. Senile depressions are usually relieved unless arteriosclerotic or senile brain changes have been important determinants.

The results of treatment of the manic phase of manic-depressive psychosis are less favorable than of the depressive phase but have been greatly improved by the practice of giving treatments more frequently. Best results are secured by giving two treatments a day for the first two or three days. These are usually followed by much confusion, but as this clears, the patient is found to be definitely improved.

The effectiveness of electroconvulsive treatment of schizophrenia has been the subject of much discussion. It is generally agreed that this form of treatment is beneficial in a large percentage of schizophrenics with affective features. It is also helpful in hastening a remission in early, acute forms of the disorder. It is of little value in hebephrenia or when the onset has been of a prolonged, insidious nature. The best results are secured in catatonic excitement. As with other shock therapies, this treatment is not followed by material improvement in the chronic, disorganized schizophrenic.

Electroconvulsive therapy is of little value in the treatment of psychoneuroses except in those manifesting depressive features and perhaps the anxiety states associated with gross stress reaction.

✿◇

RALPH ELLISON

Ralph Ellison's *Invisible Man* won the National Book Award in
1953. Since then, he has traveled and lectured widely on American
Negro attitudes and culture, as well as having taught creative
writing at many universities. He is currently working on another
novel.

From *INVISIBLE MAN*

CHAPTER 11

I was sitting in a cold, white rigid chair and a man was looking
at me out of a bright third eye that glowed from the center of
his forehead. He reached out, touching my skull gingerly, and
said something encouraging, as though I were a child. His
fingers went away.

"Take this," he said. "It's good for you." I swallowed. Suddenly my skin itched, all over. I had on new overalls, strange
white ones. The taste ran bitter through my mouth. My fingers
trembled.

A thin voice with a mirror on the end of it said, "How is he?"

"I don't think it's anything serious. Merely stunned."

"Should he be sent home now?"

"No, just to be certain we'll keep him here a few days.
Want to keep him under observation. Then he may leave."

Now I was lying on a cot, the bright eye still burning into

mine, although the man was gone. It was quiet and I was numb. I closed my eyes only to be awakened.

"What is your name?" a voice said.

"My head . . ." I said.

"Yes, but your name. Address?"

"My head—that burning eye . . ." I said.

"Eye?"

"Inside," I said.

"Shoot him up for an X-ray," another voice said.

"My head . . ."

"Careful!"

Somewhere a machine began to hum and I distrusted the man and woman above me.

They were holding me firm and it was fiery and above it all I kept hearing the opening motif of Beethoven's *Fifth*—three short and one long buzz, repeated again and again in varying volume, and I was struggling and breaking through, rising up, to find myself lying on my back with two pink-faced men laughing down.

"Be quiet now," one of them said firmly. "You'll be all right." I raised my eyes, seeing two indefinite young women in white, looking down at me. A third, a desert of heat waves away, sat at a panel arrayed with coils and dials. Where was I? From far below me a barber-chair thumping began and I felt myself rise on the tip of the sound from the floor. A face was now level with mine, looking closely and saying something without meaning. A whirring began that snapped and cracked with static, and suddenly I seemed to be crushed between the floor and ceiling. Two forces tore savagely at my stomach and back. A flash of cold-edged heat enclosed me. I was pounded between crushing electrical pressures; pumped between live electrodes like an accordion between a player's hands. My lungs were compressed like a bellows and each time my breath returned I yelled, punctuating the rhythmical action of the nodes.

"Hush, goddamit," one of the faces ordered. "We're trying to get you started again. Now shut up!"

The voice throbbed with icy authority and I quieted and tried to contain the pain. I discovered now that my head was encircled by a piece of cold metal like the iron cap worn by the occupant of an electric chair. I tried unsuccessfully to struggle, to cry out. But the people were so remote, the pain so immediate. A faced moved in and out of the circle of lights, peering for a moment, then disappeared. A freckled, red-haired woman with gold nose-glasses appeared; then a man with a circular mirror attached to his forehead—a doctor. Yes, he was a doctor and the women were nurses; it was coming clear. I was in a hospital. They would care for me. It was all geared toward the easing of pain. I felt thankful.

I tried to remember how I'd gotten here, but nothing came. My mind was blank, as though I had just begun to live. When the next face appeared I saw the eyes behind the thick glasses blinking as though noticing me for the first time.

"You're all right, boy. You're okay. You just be patient," said the voice, hollow with profound detachment.

I seemed to go away; the lights receded like a tail-light racing down a dark country road. I couldn't follow. A sharp pain stabbed my shoulder. I twisted about on my back, fighting something I couldn't see. Then after a while my vision cleared.

Now a man sitting with his back to me, manipulating dials on a panel. I wanted to call him, but the *Fifth Symphony* rhythm racked me, and he seemed too serene and too far away. Bright metal bars were between us and when I strained my neck around I discovered that I was not lying *on* an operating table but *in* a kind of glass and nickel box, the lid of which was propped open. Why was I here?

"Doctor! Doctor!" I called.

No answer. Perhaps he hadn't heard, I thought, calling again and feeling the stabbing pulses of the machine again and feeling myself going under and fighting against it and coming up to hear voices carrying on a conversation behind my head. The static sounds became a quiet drone. Strains of music, a Sunday air, drifted from a distance. With closed eyes, barely breathing I

warded off the pain. The voices droned harmoniously. Was it a
radio I heard—a phonograph? The *vox humana* of a hidden
organ? If so, what organ and where? I felt warm. Green hedges,
dazzling with red wild roses appeared behind my eyes, stretching with a gentle curving to an infinity empty of objects, a
limpid blue space. Scenes of a shaded lawn in summer drifted
past; I saw a uniformed military band arrayed decorously in
concert, each musician with well-oiled hair, heard a sweet-voiced
trumpet rendering "The Holy City" as from an echoing distance, buoyed by a choir of muted horns; and above, the
mocking obbligato of a mocking bird. I felt giddy. The air
seemed to grow thick with fine white gnats, filling my eyes,
boiling so thickly that the dark trumpeter breathed them in and
expelled them through the bell of his golden horn, a live white
cloud mixing with the tones upon the torpid air.

I came back. The voices still droned above me and I disliked
them. Why didn't they go away? Smug ones. Oh, doctor, I
thought drowsily, did you ever wade in a brook before breakfast? Ever chew on sugar cane? You know, doc, the same fall
day I first saw the hounds chasing black men in stripes and
chains my grandmother sat with me and sang with twinkling
eyes:

> "Godamighty made a monkey
> Godamighty made a whale
> And Godamighty made a 'gator
> With hickeys all over his tail . . ."

Or you, nurse, did you know that when you strolled in pink
organdy and picture hat between the rows of cape jasmine,
cooing to your beau in a drawl as thick as sorghum, we little
black boys hidden snug in the bushes called out so loud that
you daren't hear:

> "Did you ever see Miss Margaret boil water?
> Man, she hisses a wonderful stream,
> Seventeen miles and a quarter,
> Man, and you can't see her pot for the steam . . ."

But now the music became a distinct wail of female pain. I opened my eyes. Glass and metal floated above me.

"How are you feeling, boy?" a voice said.

A pair of eyes peered down through lenses as thick as the bottom of a Coca-Cola bottle, eyes protruding, luminous and veined, like an old biology specimen preserved in alcohol.

"I don't have enough room," I said angrily.

"Oh, that's a necessary part of the treatment."

"But I need more room," I insisted. "I'm cramped."

"Don't worry about it, boy. You'll get used to it after a while. How is your stomach and head?"

"Stomach?"

"Yes, and your head?"

"I don't know," I said, realizing that I could feel nothing beyond the pressure around my head and on the tender surface of my body. Yet my senses seemed to focus sharply.

"I don't feel it," I cried, alarmed.

"Aha! You see! My little gadget will solve everything!" he exploded.

"I don't know," another voice said. "I think I still prefer surgery. And in this case especially, with this, uh . . . background, I'm not so sure that I don't believe in the effectiveness of simple prayer."

"Nonsense, from now on do your praying to my little machine. I'll deliver the cure."

"I don't know, but I believe it a mistake to assume that solutions—cures, that is—that apply in, uh . . . primitive instances, are, uh . . . equally effective when more advanced conditions are in question. Suppose it were a New Englander with a Harvard background?"

"Now you're arguing politics," the first voice said banteringly.

"Oh, no, but it *is* a problem."

I listened with growing uneasiness to the conversation fuzzing away to a whisper. Their simplest words seemed to refer to something else, as did many of the notions that unfurled through my head. I wasn't sure whether they were talking about me or someone else. Some of it sounded like a discussion of history . . .

"The machine will produce the results of a prefrontal lobotomy without the negative effects of the knife," the voice said. "You see, instead of severing the prefrontal lobe, a single lobe, that is, we apply pressure in the proper degrees to the major centers of nerve control—our concept is Gestalt—and the result is as complete a change of personality as you'll find in your famous fairy-tale cases of criminals transformed into amiable fellows after all that bloody business of a brain operation. And what's more," the voice went on triumphantly, "the patient is both physically and neurally whole."

"But what of his psychology?"

"Absolutely of no importance!" the voice said. "The patient will live as he has to live, and with absolute integrity. Who could ask more? He'll experience no major conflict of motives, and what is even better, society will suffer no traumata on his account."

There was a pause. A pen scratched upon paper. Then, "Why not castration, doctor?" a voice asked waggishly, causing me to start, a pain tearing through me.

"There goes your love of blood again," the first voice laughed. "What's that definition of a surgeon, 'A butcher with a bad conscience'?"

They laughed.

"It's not so funny. It would be more scientific to try to define the case. It has been developing some three hundred years—"

"Define? Hell, man, we know all that."

"Then why don't you try more current?"

"You suggest it?"

"I do, why not?"

"But isn't there a danger . . . ?" the voice trailed off.

I heard them move away; a chair scraped. The machine droned, and I knew definitely that they were discussing me and steeled myself for the shocks, but was blasted nevertheless. The pulse came swift and staccato, increasing gradually until I fairly danced between the nodes. My teeth chattered. I closed my eyes and bit my lips to smother my screams. Warm blood filled my mouth. Between my lids I saw a circle of hand and faces, dazzling with light. Some were scribbling upon charts.

"Look, he's dancing," someone called.

"No, really?"

An oily face looked in. "They really do have rhythm, don't they? Get hot, boy! Get hot!" it said with a laugh.

And suddenly my bewilderment suspended and I wanted to be angry, murderously angry. But somehow the pulse of current smashing through my body prevented me. Something had been disconnected. For though I had seldom used my capacities for anger and indignation, I had no doubt that I possessed them; and, like a man who knows that he must fight, whether angry or not, when called a son of a bitch, I tried to *imagine* myself angry—only to discover a deeper sense of remoteness. I was beyond anger. I was only bewildered. And those above seemed to sense it. There was no avoiding the shock and I rolled with the agitated tide, out into the blackness.

When I emerged, the lights were still there. I lay beneath the slab of glass, feeling deflated. All my limbs seemed amputated. It was very warm. A dim white ceiling stretched far above me. My eyes were swimming with tears. Why, I didn't know. It worried me. I wanted to knock on the glass to attract attention, but I couldn't move. The slightest effort, hardly more than desire, tired me. I lay experiencing the vague processes of my body. I seemed to have lost all sense of proportion. Where did my body end and the crystal and white world begin? Thoughts evaded me, hiding in the vast stretch of clinical whiteness to which I seemed connected only by a scale of receding grays. No sounds beyond the sluggish inner roar of the blood. I couldn't open my eyes. I seemed to exist in some other dimension, utterly alone; until after a while a nurse bent down and forced a warm fluid between my lips. I gagged, swallowed, feeling the fluid course slowly to my vague middle. A huge iridescent bubble seemed to enfold me. Gentle hands moved

over me, bringing vague impressions of memory. I was laved
with warm liquids, felt gentle hands move through the indefinite limits of my flesh. The sterile and weightless texture of a
sheet enfolded me. I felt myself bounce, sail off like a ball
thrown over the roof into mist, striking a hidden wall beyond a
pile of broken machinery and sailing back. How long it took, I
didn't know. But now above the movement of the hands I
heard a friendly voice, uttering familiar words to which I could
assign no meaning. I listened intensely, aware of the form and
movement of sentences and grasping the now subtle rhythmical
differences between progressions of sound that questioned and
those that made a statement. But still their meanings were lost
in the vast whiteness in which I myself was lost.

Other voices emerged. Faces hovered above me like inscru-
table fish peering myopically through a glass aquarium wall. I
saw them suspended motionless above me, then two floating
off, first their heads, then the tips of their finlike fingers, moving
dreamily from the top of the case. A thoroughly mysterious
coming and going, like the surging of torpid tides. I watched
the two make furious movements with their mouths. I didn't
understand. They tried again, the meaning still escaping me. I
felt uneasy. I saw a scribbled card, held over me. All a jumble
of alphabets. They consulted heatedly. Somehow I felt responsible. A terrible sense of loneliness came over me; they seemed
to enact a mysterious pantomime. And seeing them from this
angle was disturbing. They appeared utterly stupid and I didn't
like it. It wasn't right. I could see smut in one doctor's nose; a
nurse had two flabby chins. Other faces came up, their mouths
working with soundless fury. But we are all human, I thought,
wondering what I meant.

A man dressed in black appeared, a long-haired fellow, whose
piercing eyes looked down upon me out of an intense and
friendly face. The others hovered about him, their eyes anxious
as he alternately peered at me and consulted my chart. Then he
scribbled something on a large card and thrust it before my
eyes:

WHAT IS YOUR NAME?

A tremor shook me; it was as though he had suddenly given a name to, had organized the vagueness that drifted through my head, and I was overcome with swift shame. I realized that I no longer knew my own name. I shut my eyes and shook my head with sorrow. Here was the first warm attempt to communicate with me and I was failing. I tried again, plunging into the blackness of my mind. It was no use; I found nothing but pain. I saw the card again and he pointed slowly to each word:

WHAT . . . IS . . . YOUR . . . NAME?

I tried desperately, diving below the blackness until I was limp with fatigue. It was as though a vein had been opened and my energy syphoned away; I could only stare back mutely. But with an irritating burst of activity he gestured for another card and wrote:

WHO . . . ARE . . . YOU?

Something inside me turned with a sluggish excitement. This phrasing of the question seemed to set off a series of weak and distant lights where the other had thrown a spark that failed. Who am I? I asked myself. But it was like trying to identify one particular cell that coursed through the torpid veins of my body. Maybe I was just this blackness and bewilderment and pain, but that seemed less like a suitable answer than something I'd read somewhere.

The card was back again:

WHAT IS YOUR MOTHER'S NAME?

Mother, who *was* my mother? Mother, the one who screams when you suffer—but who? This was stupid, you always knew your mother's name. Who was it that screamed? Mother? But the scream came from the machine. A machine my mother? . . . Clearly, I was out of my head.

He shot questions at me: *Where were you born? Try to think of your name.*

I tried, thinking vainly of many names, but none seemed to fit, and yet it was as though I was somehow a part of all of them, had become submerged within them and lost.

You must remember, the placard read. But it was useless. Each time I found myself back in the clinging white mist and my name just beyond my fingertips. I shook my head and watched him disappear for a moment and return with a companion, a short, scholarly-looking man who stared at me with a blank expression. I watched him produce a child's slate and a piece of chalk, writing upon it:

WHO WAS YOUR MOTHER?

I looked at him, feeling a quick dislike and thinking, half in amusement, I don't play the dozens. And how's *your* old lady today?

THINK

I stared, seeing him frown and write a long time. The slate was filled with meaningless names.

I smiled, seeing his eyes blaze with annoyance. Old Friendly Face said something. The new man wrote a question at which I stared in wide-eyed amazement:

WHO WAS BUCKEYE THE RABBIT?

I was filled with turmoil. Why should he think of *that*? He pointed to the question, word by word. I laughed, deep, deep inside me, giddy with the delight of self-discovery and the desire to hide it. Somehow *I* was Buckeye the Rabbit . . . or had been, when as children we danced and sang barefoot in the dusty streets:

Buckeye the Rabbit
Shake it, shake it
Buckeye the Rabbit
Break it, break it . . .

Yet, I could not bring myself to admit it, it was too ridiculous —and somehow too dangerous. It was annoying that he had hit upon an old identity and I shook my head, seeing him purse his lips and eye me sharply.

BOY, WHO WAS BRER RABBIT?

He was your mother's back-door man, I thought. Anyone knew they were one and the same: "Buckeye" when you were very young and hid yourself behind wide innocent eyes; "Brer," when you were older. But why was he playing around with these childish names? Did they think I was a child? Why didn't they leave me alone? I would remember soon enough when they let me out of the machine. . . . A palm smacked sharply upon the glass, but I was tired of them. Yet as my eyes focused upon Old Friendly Face he seemed pleased. I couldn't understand it, but there he was, smiling and leaving with the new assistant.

Left alone, I lay fretting over my identity. I suspected that I was really playing a game with myself and that they were taking part. A kind of combat. Actually they knew as well as I, and I for some reason preferred not to face it. It was irritating, and it made me feel sly and alert. I would solve the mystery the next instant. I imagined myself whirling about in my mind like an old man attempting to catch a small boy in some mischief, thinking, Who am I? It was no good. I felt like a clown. Nor was I up to being both criminal and detective—though why criminal I didn't know.

I fell to plotting ways of short-circuiting the machine. Perhaps if I shifted my body about so that the two nodes would come together—No, not only was there no room but it might electrocute me. I shuddered. Whoever else I was, I was no Samson. I had no desire to destroy myself even if it destroyed the machine; I wanted freedom, not destruction. It was exhausting, for no matter what the scheme I conceived, there was one constant flaw—myself. There was no getting around it. I could no more escape than I could think of my identity. Perhaps, I thought, the two things are involved with each other. When I discover who I am, I'll be free.

It was as though my thoughts of escape had alerted them. I looked up to see two agitated physicians and a nurse, and thought, It's too late now, and lay in a veil of sweat watching them manipulate the controls. I was braced for the usual shock, but nothing happened. Instead I saw their hands at the lid, loosening the bolts, and before I could react they had opened the lid and pulled me erect.

"What's happened?" I began, seeing the nurse pause to look at me.

"Well?" she said.

My mouth worked soundlessly.

"Come on, get it out," she said.

"What hospital is this?" I said.

"It's the factory hospital," she said. "Now be quiet."

They were around me now, inspecting my body, and I watched with growing bewilderment, thinking, what is a *factory* hospital?

I felt a tug at my belly and looked down to see one of the physicians pull the cord which was atttached to the stomach node, jerking me forward.

"What is this?" I said.

"Get the shears," he said.

"Sure," the other said. "Let's not waste time."

I recoiled inwardly as though the cord were part of me. Then they had it free and the nurse clipped through the belly band and removed the heavy node. I opened my mouth to speak but one of the physicians shook his head. They worked swiftly. The nodes off, the nurse went over me with rubbing alcohol. Then I was told to climb out of the case. I looked from face to face, overcome with indecision. For now that it appeared that I was being freed, I dared not believe it. What if they were transferring me to some even more painful machine? I sat there, refusing to move. Should I struggle against them?

"Take his arm," one of them said.

"I can do it," I said, climbing fearfully out.

I was told to stand while they went over my body with the stethoscope.

"How's the articulation?" the one with the chart said as the other examined my shoulder.

"Perfect," he said.

I could feel a tightness there but no pain.

"I'd say he's surprisingly strong, considering," the other said.

"Shall we call in Drexel? It seems rather unusual for him to be so strong."

"No, just note it on the chart."

"All right, nurse, give him his clothes."

"What are you going to do with me?" I said. She handed me clean underclothing and a pair of white overalls.

"No questions," she said. "Just dress as quickly as possible."

The air outside the machine seemed extremely rare. When I bent over to tie my shoes I thought I would faint, but fought it off. I stood shakily and they looked me up and down.

"Well, boy, it looks as though you're cured," one of them said. "You're a new man. You came through fine. Come with us," he said.

We went slowly out of the room and down a long white corridor into an elevator, then swiftly down three floors to a reception room with rows of chairs. At the front were a number of private offices with frosted glass doors and walls.

"Sit down there," they said. "The director will see you shortly."

I sat, seeing them disappear inside one of the offices for a second and emerge, passing me without a word. I trembled like a leaf. Were they really freeing me? My head spun. I looked at my white overalls. The nurse said that this was the factory hospital. . . . Why couldn't I remember what kind of factory it was? And why a *factory* hospital? Yes . . . I did remember some vague factory; perhaps I was being sent back there. Yes, and he'd spoken of the director instead of the head doctor; could they be one and the same? Perhaps I was in the factory already. I listened but could hear no machinery.

Across the room a newspaper lay on a chair, but I was too concerned to get it. Somewhere a fan droned. Then one of the doors with frosted glass was opened and I saw a tall austere-looking man in a white coat, beckoning to me with a chart.

"Come," he said.

I got up and went past him into a large simply furnished office, thinking, *Now, I'll know. Now.*

"Sit down," he said.

I eased myself into the chair beside his desk. He watched me with a calm, scientific gaze.

"What is your name? Oh here, I have it," he said, studying the chart. And it was as though someone inside of me tried to tell him to be silent, but already he had called my name and I heard myself say, "Oh!" as a pain stabbed through my head and I shot to my feet and looked wildly around me and sat down and got up and down again very fast, remembering. I don't know why I did it, but suddenly I saw him looking at me intently, and I stayed down this time.

He began asking questions and I could hear myself replying fluently, though inside I was reeling with swiftly changing emotional images that shrilled and chattered, like a sound-track reversed at high speed.

"Well, my boy," he said, "you're cured. We are going to release you. How does that strike you?"

Suddenly I didn't know. I noticed a company calendar beside a stethoscope and a miniature silver paint brush. Did he mean from the hospital or from the job? . . .

"Sir?" I said.

"I said, how does that strike you?"

"All right, sir," I said in an unreal voice. "I'll be glad to get back to work."

He looked at the chart, frowning. "You'll be released, but I'm afraid that you'll be disappointed about the work," he said.

"What do you mean, sir?"

"You've been through a severe experience," he said. "You aren't ready for the rigors of industry. Now I want you to rest, undertake a period of convalescence. You need to become re-adjusted and get your strength back."

"But, sir—"

"You mustn't try to go too fast. You're glad to be released, are you not?"

"Oh, yes. But how shall I live?"

"Live?" his eyebrows raised and lowered. "Take another job," he said. "Something easier, quieter. Something for which you're better prepared."

"Prepared?" I looked at him, thinking, Is he in on it too? "I'll take anything, sir," I said.

"That isn't the problem, my boy. You just aren't prepared for work under our industrial conditions. Later, perhaps, but not now. And remember, you'll be adequately compensated for your experience."

"Compensated, sir?"

"Oh, yes," he said. "We follow a policy of enlightened humanitarianism; all our employees are automatically insured. You have only to sign a few papers."

"What kind of papers, sir?"

"We require an affidavit releasing the company of responsi-bility," he said. "Yours was a difficult case, and a number of specialists had to be called in. But, after all, any new occupa-tion has its hazards. They are part of growing up, of becoming adjusted, as it were. One takes a chance and while some are prepared, others are not."

I looked at his lined face. Was he doctor, factory official, or both? I couldn't get it; and now he seemed to move back and forth across my field of vision, although he sat perfectly calm in his chair.

It came out of itself: "Do you know Mr. Norton, sir?" I said.

"Norton?" His brows knitted. "What Norton is this?"

Then it was as though I hadn't asked him; the name sounded strange. I ran my hand over my eyes.

"I'm sorry," I said. "It occurred to me that you might. He was just a man I used to know."

"I see. Well"—he picked up some papers—"so that's the way it is, my boy. A little later perhaps we'll be able to do something. You may take the papers along if you wish. Just mail them to us. Your check will be sent upon their return. Meanwhile, take as much time as you like. You'll find that we are perfectly fair."

I took the folded papers and looked at him for what seemed to be too long a time. He seemed to waver. Then I heard myself say, "Do you know him?" my voice rising.

"Who?"

"Mr. Norton," I said. "Mr. Norton!"

"Oh, why, no."

"No," I said, "no one knows anybody and it was too long a time ago."

He frowned and I laughed. "They picked poor Robin clean," I said. "Do you happen to know Bled?"

He looked at me, his head to one side. "Are these people friends of yours?"

"Friends? Oh, yes," I said, "we're all good friends. Buddies from way back. But I don't suppose we get around in the same circles."

His eyes widened. "No," he said. "I don't suppose we do. However, good friends are valuable to have."

I felt light-headed and started to laugh and he seemed to waver again and I thought of asking him about Emerson, but now he was clearing his throat and indicating that he was finished.

I put the folded papers in my overalls and started out. The door beyond the rows of chairs seemed far away.

"Take care of yourself," he said.

"And you," I said, thinking, it's time, it's past time.

Turning abruptly, I went weakly back to the desk, seeing him

looking up at me with his steady scientific gaze. I was overcome
with ceremonial feelings but unable to remember the proper
formula. So as I deliberately extended my hand I fought down
laughter with a cough.

"It's been quite pleasant, our little palaver, sir," I said. I
listened to myself and to his answer.

"Yes, indeed," he said.

He shook my hand gravely, without surprise or distaste. I
looked down, he was there somewhere behind the lined face
and outstretched hand.

"And now our palaver is finished," I said, "Good-bye."

He raised his hand. "Good-bye," he said, his voice non-
committal.

Leaving him and going out into the paint-fuming air I had
the feeling that I had been talking beyond myself, had used
words and expressed attitudes not my own, that I was in the
grip of some alien personality lodged deep within me. Like the
servant about whom I'd read in psychology class who, during a
trance, had recited pages of Greek philosophy which she had
overheard one day while she worked. It was as though I were
acting out a scene from some crazy movie. Or perhaps I was
catching up with myself and had put into words feelings which
I had hitherto suppressed. Or was it, I thought, starting up the
walk, that I was no longer afraid? I stopped, looking at the
buildings down the bright street slanting with sun and shade. I
was no longer afraid. Not of important men, not of trustees and
such; for knowing now that there was nothing which I could
expect from them, there was no reason to be afraid. Was that
it? I felt light-headed, my ears were ringing. I went on.

Along the walk the buildings rose, uniform and close together. It was day's end now and on top of every building the
flags were fluttering and diving down, collapsing. And I felt that
I would fall, had fallen, moved now as against a current sweeping swiftly against me. Out of the grounds and up the street I
found the bridge by which I'd come, but the stairs leading

back to the car that crossed the top were too dizzily steep to climb, swim or fly, and I found a subway instead.

Things whirled too fast around me. My mind went alternately bright and blank in slow rolling waves. We, he, him—my mind and I—were no longer getting around in the same circles. Nor my body either. Across the aisle a young platinum blonde nibbled at a red Delicious apple as station lights rippled past behind her. The train plunged. I dropped through the roar, giddy and vacuum-minded, sucked under and out into late afternoon Harlem.

❖❖❖❖❖❖❖❖❖❖❖❖❖❖❖❖❖❖❖❖❖❖❖❖❖❖❖❖❖❖❖❖❖❖❖❖

ROBERT PENN WARREN

Robert Penn Warren has been one of the most influential men of
letters in modern American literature. Currently Professor of English
at Yale University, he has written many novels, essays, and poems,
for which he has received the Bollingen Prize, the National Book
Award, and two Pulitzer Prizes.

From ALL THE KING'S MEN

It was June, and hot. Every night, except those nights when I
went to sit in an air-conditioned movie, I went to my room after
dinner and stripped buck-naked and lay on the bed, with an electric fan burring and burrowing away into my brain, and read a
book until the time when I would become aware that the sound
of the city had sunk off to almost nothing but the single hoot
of a taxi far off or the single lost clang and grind of a streetcar,
an owl car heading out. Then I would reach up and switch off
the light and roll over and go to sleep with the fan still burring
and burrowing.

I did see Adam a few times in June. He was more deeply
involved than before in the work of the medical center, more
grimly and icily driving himself. There was, of course, some
letup in the work at the University with the end of term, but
whatever relief was there, was more than made up for by an
increase in his private practice and work at the clinic. He said

---

he was glad to see me when I went to his apartment, and maybe he was, but he didn't have much to say, and as I sat there he would seem to be drawing deeper and deeper into himself until I had the feeling that I was trying to talk to somebody down a well and had better holler if I wanted to be understood. The only time he perked up was one night when, after he had remarked on the fact that he was to perform an operation the next morning, I asked about the case.

It was a case of catatonic schizophrenia, he said.

"You mean he is a nut?" I asked.

Adam grinned and allowed that that wasn't too far wrong.

"I didn't know you cut on folks for being nutty," I said. "I thought you just humored and gave them cold baths and let them make raffia baskets and got them to tell you their dreams."

"No," he said, "you can cut on them." Then he added, almost apologetically, "A prefrontal lobectomy."

"What's that?"

"You remove a piece of the frontal lobe of the brain on each side," he said.

I asked would the fellow live. He said you never could tell for sure, but if he did live he would be different.

I asked how did he mean, different.

"Oh, a different personality," he replied.

"Like after you get converted and baptized?"

"That doesn't give you a different personality," he said. "When you get converted you still have the same personality. You merely exercise it in terms of a different set of values."

"But this fellow will have a different personality?"

"Yes," Adam said. "The way he is now he simply sits on a chair or lies on his back on a bed and stares into space. His brow is creased and furrowed. Occasionally he utters a low moan or an exclamation. In some such cases we discover the presence of delusions of persecution. But always the patient seems to experience a numbing, grinding misery. But after we are through with him he will be different. He will be relaxed and cheerful and friendly. He will smooth his brow. He will

sleep well and eat well and will love to hang over the back
fence and compliment the neighbors on their nasturtiums and
cabbages. He will be perfectly happy."

"If you can guarantee results like that," I said, "you ought to
do a land-office business. As soon as the news gets round."

"You can't ever guarantee anything," Adam said.

"What happens if it doesn't come out according to Hoyle?"

"Well," he said, "there have been cases—not mine, thank God
—where the patient didn't become cheerfully extroverted but
became completely and cheerfully amoral."

"You mean he would throw the nurses down right on the
floor in broad daylight?"

"About that," Adam said. "If you'd let him. All the ordinary
inhibitions disappeared."

"Well, if your guy tomorrow comes out like that he will
certainly be an asset to society."

Adam grinned sourly, and said, "He won't be any worse than
a lot of other people who haven't been cut on."

"Can I see the cutting?" I asked. I felt all of a sudden that I
had to see it. I had never seen an operation. As a newspaper-
man, I had seen three hangings and one electrocution, but they
are different. In a hanging you do not change a man's personality. You just change the length of his neck and give him a quiz-
zical expression, and in an electrocution you just cook some
bouncing meat in a wholesale lot. But this operation was going
to be more radical even than what happened to Saul on the
road to Damascus. So I asked could I see the operation.

"Why?" Adam asked, studying my face.

I told him it was plain curiosity.

He said, all right, but it wouldn't be pretty.

"It will be as pretty as a hanging, I guess," I replied.

Then he started to tell me about the case. He drew me pictures and he got down books. He perked up considerably and
almost talked my ear off. He was so interesting that I forgot to
ask him a question which had flitted through my mind earlier
in our conversation. He had said that in the case of a religious

conversion the personality does not change, that it is merely exercised in terms of a different set of values. Well, I had meant to ask him how, if there was no change in personality, how did the person get a different set of values to exercise his personality in terms of? But it slipped my mind at the time.

Anyway, I saw the operation.

Adam got me rigged up so I could go right down in the pit with him. They brought in the patient and put him on the table. He was a hook-nosed, sour-faced, gaunt individual who reminded me vaguely of Andrew Jackson or a back-country evangelist despite the white turban on his head made out of sterile towels. But that turban was pushed pretty far back at a jaunty angle, for the front part of his head was exposed. It had been shaved. They put the mask on him and knocked him out. Then Adam took a scalpel and cut a neat little cut across the top of the head and down at each temple, and then just peeled the skin off the bone in a neat flap forward. He did a job that would have made a Comanche brave look like a tyro with a scalping knife. Meanwhile, they were sopping up the blood, which was considerable.

Then Adam settled down to the real business. He had a contraption like a brace and bit. With that he drilled five or six holes—burr holes they call them in the trade—on each side of the skull. Then he started to work with what he had told me earlier was a Gigli saw, a thing which looked like a coarse wire. With that he sawed on the bone till he had a flap loose on each side of the front of the head and could bend the flap down and get at the real mechanism inside. Or could as soon as he had cut the pale little membrane which they call the meninges.

By that time it had been more than an hour, or so it seemed to me, and my feet hurt. It was hot in there, too, but I didn't get upset, even with the blood. For one thing, the man there on the table didn't seem real. I forgot that he was a man at all, and kept watching the high-grade carpenter work which was going on. I didn't pay much attention to the features of the process which did indicate that the thing on the table was a man. For instance, the nurse kept on taking blood-pressure readings and now and then she would mess with the transfusion apparatus—for they were giving the patient a transfusion all the time out of a bottle rigged up on a stand with a tube coming down.

I did fine until they started the burning. For taking out the chunks of brain they use an electric gadget which is nothing but a little metal rod stuck in a handle with an electric cord coming out of the handle. The whole thing looks like an electric curling iron. In fact, all the way through I was struck by the notion that all the expensive apparatus was so logical and simple and homey, and reminded me so completely of the stuff around any well-equipped household. By ransacking the kitchen and your wife's dressing table you can get together in five minutes enough of a kit to set up in business for yourself.

Well, in the process of electrocautery this little rod does the trick of cutting, or rather burning. And there is some smoke and quite a lot of odor. At least, it seemed like a lot to me. At first it wasn't so bad, but then I knew where I had smelled an odor like that before. It was the night, long back when I was a kid, when the old livery stable had burned down at the Landing and they hadn't managed to get all the horses out. The smell of the cooking horses was on the still, damp, ripe night air and you couldn't forget it, even after you didn't hear any more the shrieks the horses had made. As soon as I realized that the burning brain had a smell like the burning horses, I didn't feel good.

But I stuck it out. It took a long time, hours more, for they can't cut but a little bit of brain at a time, and have to keep working deeper and deeper. I stuck it out until Adam had sewed up the meninges and had pulled the skull flaps back into place and had drawn up the flap of skin and laced it down all shipshape.

Then the little pieces of brain which had been cut out were put away to think their little thoughts quietly somewhere among the garbage, and what was left inside the split-open skull of the gaunt individual was sealed back up and left to think up an entirely new personality.

When Adam and I went out, and he was washing up and we were getting our white nightshirts off, I said to him, "Well, you forgot to baptize him."

"Baptize him?" Adam asked, sliding out of the white nightshirt.

"Yeah," I said, "for he is born again and not of woman. I baptize thee in the name of the Big Twitch, the Little Twitch, and the Holy Ghost. Who, no doubt, is a Twitch, too."

"What the hell are you talking about?" he demanded.

"Nothing," I said, "I was just trying to be funny."

Adam put on a faint, indulgent smile, but he didn't seem to think it was very funny. And looking back on it, I can't find it very funny myself. But I thought it was funny at the time. I thought it would bust a gut. But that summer from the height of my Olympian wisdom, I seemed to find a great many things funny which now do not appear quite as funny.

KEN KESEY

One should compare this sketch with the portrait of Dean Moriarty which follows.

NEAL CASSADY

—dum de dum de dum goes the old head most of the time just plain old ordinary what-else-is-new? dum de dum de dum all the time it's no big thing because it's always gone dum de dum de dum and even when it seems to be going dum de diddle it's actually still going dum de dum de dum under that particular curlicue, still going dum de dum de dum and none would ever be the wiser if it wasn't for certain undomesticated mind fuckers come humming past with a dum de dum de train too late mate—step lively now; don't wait!—you're on the wrong tracks anyhow *particularly* considering that that dum de dum clinker in fact done *quit* choo-chooing past this station when MacArthur left Bataan in '42 so I'm steering you straight, mate; best thing is just keep on truckin' nimble always out there on the tip of your *own treacherous tongue*, right?

Such minstrels are among our most rare and precious tools. Tongues free-flapping and frictionless; consciousnesses without stashes. No need to edit. Nothing is nothing to lose so it's never kept back. Who needs a snakey little editor got his nails

From *The Last Supplement to the Whole Earth Catalogue*, 1971, 83–84, and appears in *Kesey's Garage Sale*. Reprinted by permission of Ken Kesey, Stewart Brand, and The Viking Press.

gnawed to the quick, checking the comode? It's all good shit whatso'mever aint it? and if it aint how else we gonna get it out to work on it? Meditation? Yeah, yeah but you ever try meditation with a case of crabs? Cutting and pasting, Burrough's fashion? You, maybe, but if what you really crave is the good clean thrills and delight and completely dedicated positive— if, perhaps, ah um, yas, possibly just a *leetle bit* wired (speed? horrors!)—energy then climb in, hang on—watch that idiot microbus!—but even, granted, speeding a leetle bit nothing that can't be—whup! whazoop? Watch it, idiot!—most adequately handled if that frizzled right front don't rupture round this *full left!*—full left it is, sir—*full ninety degree left* ("trick is, chief, to zig when they zag.") into full tilt satori. . . .

He was far out, folks. I realize more and more just how far out he was as the years pass since his death and each time I penetrate what I thought was virgin territory I find Neal's familiar restless footprints messing through the choicest glens. I mean, friends and neighbors, I mean he was *far out,* just one hell of a hero and the tales of his exploits will always be blowing around us (one night in the dark Grant Avenue pavements an ebullient Cassady raps circles around a Lennie Bruce too strung-out to appreciate that this t-shirted maniac weaving words like a carpet before him was paying Lennie his own respect . . .) or: a muni court judge once made the mistake of asking, "Mr. Cassady, how is it *possible* for one man to incur *twenty-seven Moving Violation Citations* in the course of one month!?!", and Neal duly launched into response, detailing precisely how the first came about when he was ticketed for not stopping at a stop sign, which, y'understand, was later proved in previous court action—you'll find it on the Dec. '67 records for Marin County, yer honor, if you care to check—had been knocked down by a pole truck a few minutes previous to the ticket in question, and, though innocent proven, the license was suspended in the interim foul-up of red tape and the *next ticket* led to subsequent puncture of the right rear as the patrol officer pulled us over into an A&W parking lot on I think it was the corner of Grove and University, the lot being strewn with broken beer bottles—not faulting the officer, of course; it was dark—and this puncture drew the third citation for impeding traffic in as the puncture didn't manifest itself until an hour later in the going-to-work Bay Bridge traffic . . ." and on and on, through debacle after debacle, calling all the proper dates, times, street numbers, officer's names casually to mind for the judge's edification (Cassady had read all nine volumes of Proust's *Remembrance of Things Past* and could quote long machinegunning bursts when tempted) as the judge leaned further and further over the bench to gape at this feat ("T'weren't nuthin', Chief," Cassady later confided, "even a bad dog won't bite if you talk to him right") in amazement. When Neal finished there was nothing for the judge to do but grant complete dismissal but the stories really veer one from the mark Neal had in mind. Only through the actual speed-shifting grind and gasp and zoom of his high compression voice do you get the sense of the urgent sermon that Neal was driving madcap into every road-blocked head he came across.

◈◆◈

JACK KEROUAC

Jack Kerouac was the prophet and spokesman for the Beat Generation, a term which he coined to describe the attitudes and life
styles of many people during the late 1940s and 1950s. After *On
the Road* (1957), he published ten novels in the next six years, as
well as poetry and a book of philosophy. He died in 1969. The
model for Dean Moriarty was his good friend, Neal Cassady.

FROM *ON THE ROAD*

I first met Dean not long after my wife and I split up. I had
just gotten over a serious illness that I won't bother to talk
about, except that it had something to do with the miserably
weary split-up and my feeling that everything was dead. With
the coming of Dean Moriarty began the part of my life you
could call my life on the road. Before that I'd often dreamed of
going West to see the country, always vaguely planning and
never taking off. Dean is the perfect guy for the road because
he actually was born on the road, when his parents were passing
through Salt Lake City in 1926, in a jalopy, on their way to Los
Angeles. First reports of him came to me through Chad King,
who'd shown me a few letters from him written in a New
Mexico reform school. I was tremendously interested in the
letters because they so naïvely and sweetly asked Chad to teach
him all about Nietzsche and all the wonderful intellectual

things that Chad knew. At one point Carlo and I talked about
the letters and wondered if we would ever meet the strange
Dean Moriarty. This is all far back, when Dean was not the way
he is today, when he was a young jailkid shrouded in mystery.
Then news came that Dean was out of reform school and was
coming to New York for the first time; also there was talk that
he had just married a girl called Marylou.

One day I was hanging around the campus and Chad and
Tim Gray told me Dean was staying in a cold-water pad in
East Harlem, the Spanish Harlem. Dean had arrived the night
before, the first time in New York, with his beautiful little
sharp chick Marylou; they got off the Greyhound bus at 50th
Street and cut around the corner looking for a place to eat and
went right in Hector's, and since then Hector's cafeteria has
always been a big symbol of New York for Dean. They spent
money on beautiful big glazed cakes and creampuffs.

All this time Dean was telling Marylou things like this:
"Now, darling, here we are in New York and although I haven't
quite told you everything that I was thinking about when we
crossed Missouri and especially at the point when we pass the
Booneville reformatory which reminded me of my jail problem,
it is absolutely necessary now to postpone all those leftover
things concerning our personal lovethings and at once begin
thinking of specific worklife plans . . ." and so on in the way
that he had in those early days.

I went to the cold-water flat with the boys, and Dean came
to the door in his shorts. Marylou was jumping off the couch;
Dean had dispatched the occupant of the apartment to the
kitchen, probably to make coffee, while he proceeded with his
loveproblems, for to him sex was the one and only holy and
important thing in life, although he had to sweat and curse to
make a living and so on. You saw that in the way he stood
bobbing his head, always looking down, nodding, like a young
boxer to instructions, to make you think he was listening to
every word, throwing in a thousand "Yeses" and "That's rights."
My first impression of Dean was of a young Gene Autry—trim,

thin-hipped, blue-eyed, with a real Oklahoma accent—a side-burned hero of the snowy West. In fact he'd just been working on a ranch, Ed Wall's in Colorado, before marrying Marylou and coming East. Marylou was a pretty blonde with immense ringlets of hair like a sea of golden tresses; she sat there on the edge of the couch with her hands hanging in her lap and her smoky blue country eyes fixed in a wide stare because she was in an evil gray New York pad that she'd heard about back West, and waiting like a longbodied emaciated Modigliani surrealist woman in a serious room. But, outside of being a sweet little girl, she was awfully dumb and capable of doing horrible things. That night we all drank beer and pulled wrists and talked till dawn, and in the morning, while we sat around dumbly smoking butts from ashtrays in the gray light of a gloomy day, Dean got up nervously, paced around, thinking, and decided the thing to do was to have Marylou make break-fast and sweep the floor." In other words we've got to get on the ball, darling, what I'm saying, otherwise it'll be fluctuating and lack true knowledge or crystallization of our plans." . . .

All my other current friends were "intellectuals"—Chad the Nietzschean anthropologist, Carlo Marx and his nutty surrealist low-voiced serious staring talk, Old Bull Lee and his critical anti-everything drawl—or else they were slinking criminals like Elmer Hassel, with that hip sneer; Jane Lee the same, sprawled on the Oriental cover of her couch, sniffing at the *New Yorker*. But Dean's intelligence was every bit as formal and shining and complete, without the tedious intellectualness. And his "criminality" was not something that sulked and sneered; it was a wild yea-saying overburst of American joy; it was Western, the west wind, an ode from the Plains, something new, long prophesied, long a-coming (he only stole cars for joy rides). Besides, all my New York friends were in the negative, night-mare position of putting down society and giving their tired bookish or political or psychoanalytical reasons, but Dean just raced in society, eager for bread and love; he didn't care one way or the other, "so long's I can get that lil ole gal with that lil sumpin down there tween her legs, boy," and "so long's we can *eat*, son, y'ear me? I'm *hungry*, I'm *starving*, let's *eat right now!*"—and off we'd rush to *eat*, whereof, as saith Ecclesiastes, "It is your portion under the sun."

A western kinsman of the sun, Dean. Although my aunt warned me that he would get me in trouble, I could hear a new call and see a new horizon, and believe it at my young age; and a little bit of trouble or even Dean's eventual rejection of me as a buddy, putting me down, as he would later, on starving sidewalks and sickbeds—what did it matter? I was a young writer and I wanted to take off.

Somewhere along the line I knew there'd be girls, visions, everything; somewhere along the line the pearl would be handed to me. . . .

I left everybody and went home to rest. My aunt said I was wasting my time hanging around with Dean and his gang. I knew that was wrong, too. Life is life, and kind is kind. What I wanted was to take one more magnificent trip to the West Coast and get back in time for the spring semester in school. And what a trip it turned out to be! I only went along for the ride, and to see what else Dean was going to do, and finally, also, knowing Dean would go back to Camille in Frisco, I wanted to have an affair with Marylou. We got ready to cross the groaning continent again. I drew my GI check and gave Dean eighteen dollars to mail to his wife; she was waiting for him to come home and she was broke. What was on Marylou's mind I don't know. Ed Dunkel, as ever, just followed. . . .

It was drizzling and mysterious at the beginning of our journey. I could see that it was all going to be one big saga of the mist. "Whooee!" yelled Dean. "Here we go!" And he hunched over the wheel and gunned her; he was back in his element, everybody could see that. We were all delighted, we all realized we were leaving confusion and nonsense behind and performing our one and noble function of the time, *move*. And we moved! We flashed past the mysterious white signs in the night somewhere in New Jersey that say SOUTH (with an arrow) and WEST (with an arrow) and took the south one. New Orleans! It burned in our brains. From the dirty snows of "frosty fagtown New York," as Dean called it, all the way to the greeneries and river smells of old New Orleans at the washed-out bottom of America; then west. Ed was in the back seat; Marylou and Dean and I sat in front and had the warmest talk about the goodness and joy of life. Dean suddenly became tender. "Now dammit, look here, all of you, we all must admit that everything is fine and there's no need in the world to worry, and in fact we should realize what it would mean to us to UNDERSTAND that we're not REALLY worried about ANYTHING. Am I right?" We all agreed. "Here we go, we're all together . . . What did we do in New York? Let's forgive." We all had our spats back there. "That's behind us, merely by miles and inclinations. Now we're heading down to New Orleans to dig Old Bull Lee and ain't that going to be kicks and listen will you to this old tenorman blow his top"—he shot up the radio volume till the car shuddered—"and listen to him tell the story and put down true relaxation and knowledge."

We all jumped to the music and agreed. The purity of the road. The white line in the middle of the highway unrolled and hugged our left front tire as if glued to our groove. Dean hunched his muscular neck, T-shirted in the winter night, and blasted the car along. He insisted I drive through Baltimore for traffic practice; that was all right, except he and Marylou insisted on steering while they kissed and fooled around. It was crazy; the radio was on full blast. Dean beat drums on the dashboard till a great sag developed in it; I did too. The poor Hudson—the slow boat to China—was receiving her beating.

"Oh man, what kicks!" yelled Dean. "Now Marylou, listen really, honey, you know that I'm hotrock capable of everything at the same time and I have unlimited energy—now in San Francisco we must go on living together. I know just the place for you—at the end of the regular chain-gang run—I'll be home just a cut-hair less than every two days and for twelve hours at a stretch, and *man*, you know what we can do in twelve hours, darling. Meanwhile I'll go right on living at Camille's like nothin, see, she won't know. We can work it, we've done it before." It was all right with Marylou, she was really out for Camille's scalp. The understanding had been that Marylou would switch to me in Frisco, but I now began to see they were going to stick and I was going to be left alone on my butt at the other end of the continent. But why think about that when all the golden land's ahead of you and all kinds of unforeseen events wait lurking to surprise you and make you glad you're alive to see? . . .

We began rolling in the foothills before Oakland and suddenly reached a height and saw stretched out ahead of us the fabulous white city of San Francisco on her eleven mystic hills with the blue Pacific and its advancing wall of potato-patch fog beyond, and smoke and goldenness in the late afternoon of time. "There she blows!" yelled Dean. "Wow! Made it! Just enough gas! Give me water! No more land! We can't go any further 'cause there ain't no more land! Now Marylou, darling, you and Sal go immediately to a hotel and wait for me to contact you in the morning as soon as I have definite arrangements made with Camille and call up Frenchman about my railroad watch and you and Sal buy the first thing hit town a paper for the want ads and workplans." And he drove into the Oakland Bay Bridge and it carried us in. The downtown office buildings were just sparkling on their lights; it made you think of Sam Spade. When we staggered out of the car on O'Farrell Street and sniffed and stretched, it was like getting on shore after a long voyage at sea; the slopy street reeled under our feet; secret chop sueys from Frisco Chinatown floated in the air. We took all of our things out of the car and piled them on the sidewalk.

Suddenly Dean was saying good-by. He was bursting to see Camille and find out what had happened. Marylou and I stood dumbly in the street and watched him drive away. "You see what a bastard he is?" said Marylou. "Dean will leave you out in the cold any time it's in his interest."

"I know," I said, and I looked back east and sighed. . . .

Dean found me when he finally decided I was worth saving. He took me home to Camille's house. "Where's Marylou, man?"

"The whore ran off." Camille was a relief after Marylou; a well-bred, polite young woman, and she was aware of the fact that the eighteen dollars Dean had sent her was mine. But O where went thou, sweet Marylou? I relaxed a few days in Camille's house. From her living-room window in the wooden tenement on Liberty Street you could see all of San Francisco burning green and red in the rainy night. Dean did the most ridiculous thing of his career the few days I was there. He got a job demonstrating a new kind of pressure cooker in the kitchens of homes. The salesman gave him piles of samples and pamphlets. The first day Dean was a hurricane of energy. I drove all over town with him as he made appointments. The idea was to get invited socially to a dinner party and then leap up and start demonstrating the pressure cooker. "Man," cried Dean excitedly, "this is even crazier than the time I worked for Sinah. Sinah sold encyclopedias in Oakland. Nobody could turn him down. He made long speeches, he jumped up and down, he laughed, he cried. One time we broke into an Okie house where everybody was getting ready to go to a funeral. Sinah got down on his knees and prayed for the deliverance of the deceased soul. All the Okies started crying. He sold a complete set of encyclopedias. He was the maddest guy in the world. I wonder where he is. We used to get next to pretty young daughters and feel them up in the kitchen. This afternoon I had the gonest housewife in her little kitchen—arm around her, demonstrating. Ah! Hmm! Wow!"

"Keep it up, Dean," I said. "Maybe someday you'll be mayor of San Francisco." He had the whole cookpot spiel worked out; he practiced on Camille and me in the evenings.

One morning he stood naked, looking at all San Francisco out the window as the sun came up. He looked like someday he'd he the pagan mayor of San Francisco. But his energies ran out. One rainy afternoon the salesman came around to find out what Dean was doing. Dean was sprawled on the couch. "Have you been trying to sell these?"

"No," said Dean, "I have another job coming up."

"Well, what are you going to do about all these samples?"

"I don't know." In a dead silence the salesman gathered up his sad pots and left. I was sick and tired of everything and so was Dean. . . .

What I accomplished by coming to Frisco I don't know. Camille wanted me to leave; Dean didn't care one way or the other. I bought a loaf of bread and meats and made myself ten sandwiches to cross the country with again; they were all going to go rotten on me by the time I got to Dakota. The last night Dean went mad and found Marylou somewhere downtown and we got in the car and drove all over Richmond across the bay, hitting Negro jazz shacks in the oil flats. Marylou went to sit down and a colored guy pulled the chair out from under her. The gals approached her in the john with propositions. I was approached too. Dean was sweating around. It was the end; I wanted to get out.

At dawn I got my New York bus and said good-by to Dean and Marylou. They wanted some of my sandwiches. I told them no. It was a sullen moment. We were all thinking we'd never see one another again and we didn't care. . . .

Before I knew it, once again I was seeing the fabled city of San Francisco stretched on the bay in the middle of the night. I ran immediately to Dean. He had a little house now. I was burning to know what was on his mind and what would happen now, for there was nothing behind me any more, all my bridges were gone and I didn't give a damn about anything at all. I knocked on his door at two o'clock in the morning.

He came to the door stark naked and it might have been the President knocking for all he cared. He received the world in the raw. "Sal!" he said with genuine awe. "I didn't think you'd actually do it. You've finally come to *me*."

"Yep," I said. "Everything fell apart in me. How are things with you?"

"Not so good, not so good. But we've got a million things to talk about. Sal, the time has *fi-nally* come for us to talk and get with it." We agreed it was about time and went in. My arrival was somewhat like the coming of the strange most evil angel in the home of the snow-white fleece, as Dean and I began talking excitedly in the kitchen downstairs, which brought forth sobs from upstairs. Everything I said to Dean was answered with a wild, whispering, shuddering *"Yes!"* Camille knew what was going to happen. Apparently Dean had been quiet for a few months; now the angel had arrived and he was going mad again. . . .

That night Galatea, Dean, and I went to get Marie. This girl had a basement apartment, a little daughter, and an old car that barely ran and which Dean and I had to push down the street as the girls jammed at the starter. We went to Galatea's, and there everybody sat around—Marie, her daughter, Galatea, Roy Johnson, Dorothy his wife—all sullen in the overstuffed furniture as I stood in a corner, neutral in Frisco problems, and Dean stood in the middle of the room with his balloon-thumb in the air breast-high, giggling. "Gawd damn," he said, "we're all losing our fingers—hawr-hawr-hawr."

"Dean, why do you act so foolish?" said Galatea. "Camille called and said you left her. Don't you realize you have a daughter?"

"He didn't leave her, she kicked him out!" I said, breaking my neutrality. They all gave me dirty looks; Dean grinned. "And with that thumb, what do you expect the poor guy to do?" I added. They all looked at me; particularly Dorothy Johnson lowered a mean gaze on me. It wasn't anything but a sewing circle, and the center of it was the culprit, Dean—responsible, perhaps, for everything that was wrong. I looked out the window at the buzzing night-street of Mission; I wanted to get going and hear the great jazz of Frisco—and remember, this was only my second night in town.

"I think Marylou was very, very wise leaving you, Dean," said Galatea. "For years now you haven't had any sense of responsibility for anyone. You've done so many awful things I don't know what to say to you."

And in fact that was the point, and they all sat around looking at Dean with lowered and hating eyes, and he stood on the carpet in the middle of them and giggled—he just giggled. He made a little dance. His bandage was getting dirtier all the time; it began to flop and unroll. I suddenly realized that Dean, by virtue of his enormous series of sins, was becoming the Idiot, the Imbecile, the Saint of the lot.

"You have absolutely no regard for anybody but yourself and your damned kicks. All you think about is what's hanging between your legs and how much money or fun you can get out of people and then you just throw them aside. Not only that but you're silly about it. It never occurs to you that life is serious and there are people trying to make something decent out of it instead of just goofing all the time."

That's what Dean was, the HOLY GOOF.

"Camille is crying her heart out tonight, but don't think for a minute she wants you back, she said she never wanted to see you again and she said it was to be final this time. Yet you stand here and make silly faces, and I don't think there's a care in your heart."

This was not true; I knew better and I could have told them all. I didn't see any sense in trying it. I longed to go and put my arm around Dean and say, Now look here, all of you, remember just one thing: this guy has his troubles too, and another thing, he never complains and he's given all of you a damned good time just being himself, and if that isn't enough for you then send him to the firing squad, that's apparently what you're itching to do anyway . . .

Nevertheless Galatea Dunkel was the only one in the gang who wasn't afraid of Dean and could sit there calmly, with her face hanging out, telling him off in front of everybody. There were earlier days in Denver when Dean had everybody sit in the dark with the girls and just talked, and talked, and talked, with a voice that was once hypnotic and strange and was said to make the girls come across by sheer force of persuasion and the content of what he said. This was when he was fifteen, sixteen. Now his disciples were married and the wives of his disciples had him on the carpet for the sexuality and the life he had helped bring into being. I listened further.

"Now you're going East with Sal," Galatea said, "and what do you think you're going to accomplish by that? Camille has to stay home and mind the baby now you're gone—how can she keep her job?—and she never wants to see you again and I don't blame her. If you see Ed along the road you tell him to come back to me or I'll kill him."

Just as flat as that. It was the saddest night. I felt as if I was with strange brothers and sisters in a pitiful dream. Then a complete silence fell over everybody; where once Dean would have talked his way out, he now fell silent himself, but standing in front of everybody, ragged and broken and idiotic, right under the lightbulbs, his bony mad face covered with sweat and throbbing veins, saying, "Yes, yes, yes," as though tremendous revelations were pouring into him all the time now, and I am convinced they were, and the others suspected as much and were frightened. He was BEAT—the root, the soul of Beatific. What was he knowing? He tried all in his power to tell me what he was knowing, and they envied that about me, my position at his side, defending him and drinking him in as they once tried to do. Then they looked at me. What was I, a stranger, doing on the West Coast this fair night? I recoiled from the thought.

"We're going to Italy," I said, I washed my hands of the whole matter. Then, too, there was a strange sense of maternal satisfaction in the air, for the girls were really looking at Dean the way a mother looks at the dearest and most errant child, and he with his sad thumb and all his revelations knew it well, and that was why he was able, in tick-tocking silence, to walk out of the apartment without a word, to wait for us downstairs as soon as we'd made up our minds about *time*. This was what we sensed about the ghost on the sidewalk. I looked out the window. He was alone in the doorway, digging the street. Bitterness, recriminations, advice, morality, sadness—everything was behind him, and ahead of him was the ragged and ecstatic joy of pure being.

"Come on, Galatea, Marie, let's go hit the jazz joints and forget it. Dean will be dead someday. Then what can you say to him?"

"The sooner he's dead the better," said Galatea, and she spoke officially for almost everyone in the room.

"Very well, then," I said, "but now he's alive and I'll bet you want to know what he does next and that's because he's got the secret that we're all busting to find and it's splitting his head wide open and if he goes mad don't worry, it won't be your fault but the fault of God."

They objected to this; they said I really didn't know Dean; they said he was the worst scoundrel that ever lived and I'd find out someday to my regret. I was amused to hear them protest so much. Roy Johnson rose to the defense of the ladies and said he knew Dean better than anybody, and all Dean was, was just a very interesting and even amusing con-man. I went out to find Dean and we had a brief talk about it.

"Ah, man, don't worry, everything is perfect and fine." He was rubbing his belly and licking his lips . . . .

Mission Street that last day in Frisco was a great riot of construction work, children playing, whooping Negroes coming home from work, dust, excitement, the great buzzing and vibrating hum of what is really America's most excited city—and overhead the pure blue sky and the joy of the foggy sea that always rolls in at night to make everybody hungry for food and further excitement. I hated to leave; my stay had lasted sixty-odd hours. With frantic Dean, I was rushing through the world without a chance to see it. In the afternoon we were buzzing toward Sacramento and eastward again.

The car belonged to a tall, thin fag who was on his way home to Kansas and wore dark glasses and drove with extreme care; the car was what Dean called a "fag Plymouth"; it had no pickup and no real power. "Effeminate car!" whispered Dean in my ear. There were two other passengers, a couple, typical halfway tourists who wanted to stop and sleep everywhere. The first stop would have to be Sacramento, which wasn't even the faintest beginning of the trip to Denver. Dean and I sat alone in the back seat and left it up to them and talked. "Now, man, that alto man last night had IT—he held it once he found it; I've never seen a guy who could hold so long." I wanted to know what "IT" meant. "Ah well"—Dean laughed—"now you're asking me impon-de-rables—ahem! Here's a guy and everybody's there, right? Up to him to put down what's on everybody's mind. He starts the first chorus, then lines up his ideas, people, yeah, yeah, but get it, and then he rises to his fate and has to blow equal to it. All of a sudden some where in the middle of the chorus he *gets it*—everybody looks up and knows; they listen; he picks it up and carries. Time stops. He's filling empty space with the substance of our lives, confessions of his bellybottom strain, remembrance of ideas, rehashes of old blowing. He has to blow across bridges and come back and do it with such infinite feeling soul-exploratory for the tune of the moment that everybody knows it's not the tune that counts but IT—" Dean could go no further; he was sweating telling about it.

Then I began talking, I never talked so much in all my life. I told Dean that when I was a kid and rode in cars I used to imagine I held a big scythe in my hand and cut down all the trees and posts and even sliced every hill that zoomed past the window. "Yes! Yes!" yelled Dean. "I used to do it too only different scythe—tell you why. Driving across the West with the long stretches my scythe had to be immeasurably longer and it had to curve over distant mountains, slicing off their tops, and reach another level to get at further mountains and at the same time clip off every post along the road, regular throbbing poles. For this reason—O man, I have to tell you, NOW, I have IT—I have to tell you the time my father and I and a pisspoor bum from Larimer Street took a trip to Nebraska in the middle of the depression to sell flyswatters. And how we made them, we bought pieces of ordinary regular old screen and pieces of wire that we twisted double and little pieces of blue and red cloth to sew around the edges and all of it for a matter of cents in a five-and-ten and made thousands of flyswatters and got in the old bum's jalopy and went clear around Nebraska to every farmhouse and sold them for a nickel apiece—mostly for charity the nickels were given us, two bums and a boy, apple pies in the sky, and my old man in those days was always singing 'Hallelujah, I'm a bum, bum again.' And man, now listen to this, after two whole weeks of incredible hardship and bouncing around and hustling in the heat to see these awful make-shift flyswatters they started to argue about the division of the proceeds and had a big fight on the side of the road and then made up and bought wine and began drinking wine and didn't stop for five days and five nights while I huddled and cried in the background, and when they were finished every last cent was spent and we were right back where we started from, Larimer Street. And my old man was arrested and I had to plead at court to the judge to let him go cause he was my pa and I had no mother. Sal, I made great mature speeches at the age of eight in front of interested lawyers . . ." We were hot; we were going east; we were excited.

"Let me tell you more," I said, "and only as a parenthesis within what you're saying and to conclude my last thought. As a child lying back in my father's car in the back seat I also had a vision of myself on a white horse riding alongside over every possible obstacle that presented itself: this included dodging posts, hurling around houses, sometimes jumping over when I looked too late, running over hills, across sudden squares with traffic that I had to dodge through incredibly—"

"Yes! Yes! Yes!" breathed Dean ecstatically. "Only difference with me was, I myself ran, I had no horse. You were a Eastern kid and dreamed of horses; of course we won't assume such things as we both know they are really dross and literary ideas, but merely that I in my perhaps wilder schizophrenia actually *ran* on foot along the car and at incredible speeds sometimes ninety, making it over every bush and fence and farmhouse and sometimes taking quick dashes to the hills and back without losing a moment's ground . . ."

We were telling these things and both sweating. We had completely forgotten the people up front who had begun to wonder what was going on in the back seat. At one point the driver said, "For God's sakes, you're rocking the boat back there." Actually we were; the car was swaying as Dean and I both swayed to the rhythm and the IT of our final excited joy in talking and living to the blank tranced end of all innumerable riotous angelic particulars that had been lurking in our souls all our lives.

"Oh, man! man! man!" moaned Dean. "And it's not even the beginning of it—and now here we are at last going east together, we've never gone east together, Sal, think of it, we'll dig Denver together and see what everybody's doing although that matters little to us, the point being that we know what IT is and we know TIME and we know that everything is really FINE." Then he whispered, clutching my sleeve, sweating, "Now you just dig them in front. They have worries, they're counting the miles, they're thinking about where to sleep tonight, how much money for gas, the weather, how they'll get there—and all the time they'll get there anyway, you see. But they need to worry and betray time with urgencies false and otherwise, purely anxious and whiny, their souls really won't be at peace unless they can latch on to an established and proven worry and having once found it they assume facial expressions to fit and go with it, which is, you see, unhappiness, and all the time it all flies by them and they know it and that *too* worries them no end. Listen! Listen! 'Well now,'" he mimicked, "'I don't know—maybe we shouldn't get gas in that station. I read recently in *National Petroffious Petroleum News* that this kind of gas has a great deal of O-Octane *gook* in it and someone once told me it even had semi-official high-frequency *cock* in it, and I don't know, well I just don't feel like it anyway . . .' Man, you dig all this." He was poking me furiously in the ribs to understand. I tried my wildest best. Bing, bang, it was all Yes! Yes! Yes! in the back seat and the people up front were mopping their brows with fright and wishing they'd never picked us up at the travel bureau. It was only the beginning, too. . . .

We left Sacramento at dawn and were crossing the Nevada desert by noon, after a hurling passage of the Sierras that made the fag and the tourists cling to each other in the back seat. We were in front, we took over. Dean was happy again. All he needed was a wheel in his hand and four on the road. He talked about how bad a driver Old Bull Lee was and to demonstrate—"Whenever a huge big truck like that one coming loomed into sight it would take Bull infinite time to spot it, 'cause he couldn't *see*, man, he can't *see*." He rubbed his eyes furiously to show. "And I'd say, 'Whoop, look out, Bull, a truck,' and he'd say, 'Eh? what's that you say, Dean?' 'Truck! truck!' and at the *very* last *moment* he would go right up to the truck like this—" And Dean hurled the Plymouth head-on at the truck roaring our way, wobbled and hovered in front of it a moment, the truckdriver's face growing gray before our eyes, the people in the back seat subsiding in gasps of horror, and swung away at the last moment. "Like that, you see, exactly like that, how bad he was." I wasn't scared at all; I knew Dean. The people in the back seat were speechless. In fact they were afraid to complain: God knew what Dean would do, they thought, if they should ever complain. He balled right across the desert in this manner, demonstrating various ways of how not to drive, how his father used to drive jalopies, how great drivers made curves, how bad drivers hove over too far in the beginning and had to scramble at the curve's end, and so on. It was a hot, sunny afternoon. Reno, Battle Mountain, Elko, all the towns along the Nevada road shot by one after another, and at dusk we were in the Salt Lake flats with the lights of Salt Lake City infinitesimally glimmering almost a hundred miles across the mirage of the flats, twice showing above and below the curve of the earth, one clear, one dim. I told Dean that the thing that bound us all together in this world was invisible, and to prove it pointed to long lines of telephone poles that curved off out of sight over the bend of a hundred miles of salt. His floppy bandage, all dirty now, shuddered in the air, his face was a light. "Oh yes, man, dear God, yes, yes!" Suddenly he stopped the car and collapsed. I turned and saw him huddled in the corner of the seat, sleeping. His face was down on his good hand, and the bandaged hand automatically and dutifully remained in the air.

The people in the back seat sighed with relief. I heard them whispering mutiny. "We can't let him drive any more, he's absolutely crazy, they must have let him out of an asylum or something."

I rose to Dean's defense and leaned back to talk to them. "He's not crazy, he'll be all right, and don't worry about his driving, he's the best in the world."

"I just can't stand it," said the girl in a suppressed, hysterical whisper. I sat back and enjoyed nightfall on the desert and waited for poorchild Angel Dean to wake up again. We were on a hill overlooking Salt Lake City's neat patterns of light and he opened his eyes to the place in this spectral world where he was born, unnamed and bedraggled, years ago.

"Sal, Sal, look, this is where I was born, think of it! People change, they eat meals year after year and change with every meal. *EE!* Look!" He was so excited it made me cry. Where would it all lead? The tourists insisted on driving the car the rest of the way to Denver. Okay, we didn't care. We sat in the back and talked. But they got too tired in the morning and Dean took the wheel in the eastern Colorado desert at Craig. We had spent almost the entire night crawling cautiously over Strawberry Pass in Utah and lost a lot of time. They went to sleep. Dean headed pellmell for the mighty wall of Berthoud Pass that stood a hundred miles ahead on the roof of the world, a tremendous Gibraltarian door shrouded in clouds. He took Berthoud Pass like a June bug—same as at Tehachapi, cutting off the motor and floating it, passing everybody and

never halting the rhythmic advance that the mountains themselves intended, till we overlooked the great hot plain of Denver again—and Dean was home.

It was with a great deal of silly relief that these people let
us off the car at the corner of 27th and Federal. Our battered
suitcases were piled on the sidewalk again; we had longer ways
to go. But no matter, the road is life. . . .

The last time I saw him it was under sad and strange circumstances. Remi Boncoeur had arrived in New York after having gone around the world several times in ships. I wanted him
to meet and know Dean. They did meet, but Dean couldn't
talk any more and said nothing, and Remi turned away. Remi
had gotten tickets for the Duke Ellington concert at the
Metropolitan Opera and insisted Laura and I come with him
and his girl. Remi was fat and sad now but still the eager and
formal gentleman, and he wanted to do things the *right way*,
as he emphasized. So he got his bookie to drive us to the concert in a Cadillac. It was a cold winter night. The Cadillac
was parked and ready to go. Dean stood outside the windows
with his bag, ready to go to Penn Station and on across the
land.

"Goody-by, Dean," I said. "I sure wish I didn't have to go to
the concert."

"D'you think I can ride to Fortieth Street with you?" he
whispered. "Want to be with you as much as possible, m'boy,
and besides it's so durned cold in this here New Yawk . . ." I
whispered to Remi. No, he wouldn't have it, he liked me but
he didn't like my idiot friends. I wasn't going to start all over
again ruining his planned evenings as I had done at Alfred's in
San Francisco in 1947 with Roland Major.

"Absolutely out of the question, Sal!" Poor Remi, he had a
special necktie made for this evening; on it was painted a replica
of the concert tickets, and the names Sal and Laura and Remi
and Vicki, the girl, together with a series of sad jokes and some
of his favorite sayings such as "You can't teach the old maestro
a new tune."

So Dean couldn't ride uptown with us and the only thing I could do was sit in the back of the Cadillac and wave at him. The bookie at the wheel also wanted nothing to do with Dean. Dean, ragged in a motheaten overcoat he brought specially for the freezing temperatures of the East, walked off alone, and the last I saw of him he rounded the corner of Seventh Avenue, eyes on the street ahead, and bent to it again. Poor little Laura, my baby, to whom I'd told everything about Dean, began almost to cry.

"Oh, we shouldn't let him go like this. What'll we do?"

Old Dean's gone, I thought, and out loud I said, "He'll be all right." And off we went to the sad and disinclined concert for which I had no stomach whatever and all the time I was thinking of Dean and how he got back on the train and rode over three thousand miles over that awful land and never knew why he had come anyway, except to see me.

So in America when the sun goes down and I sit on the old broken-down river pier watching the long, long skies over New Jersey and sense all that raw land that rolls in one unbelievable huge bulge over to the West Coast, and all that road going, all the people dreaming in the immensity of it, and in Iowa I know by now the children must be crying in the land where they let the children cry, and tonight the stars'll be out, and don't you know that God is Pooh Bear? the evening star must be drooping and shedding her sparkler dims on the prairie, which is just before the coming of complete night that blesses the earth, darkens all rivers, cups the peaks and folds the final shore in, and nobody, nobody knows what's going to happen to anybody besides the forlorn rags of growing old, I think of Dean Moriarty, I even think of Old Dean Moriarty the father we never found, I think of Dean Moriarty.

Topics

for Discussion and Papers

THEMES AND MEANINGS

1. Does Kesey suggest that the psychiatric ward, in *One Flew Over the Cuckoo's Nest*, is in some ways a reduced image of the world outside the asylum? Should the reader attach some value—if only a metaphorical one—to Chief Bromden's notion that ward and world are both ruled by "the Combine"?

2. If the ward is indeed presented as a microcosm, what seems to be Kesey's notion of the relation between individuals and modern society? Should they adjust to it, or revolt against "the Combine," or try to escape?

3. Does the novel reveal a bias against women? (Besides noting the character of Big Nurse, the discussion of this question should include the reported behavior of the wives and mothers of various patients.)

4. Is *Cuckoo's Nest* a novel of the absurd, as Joseph J. Waldmeir claims in his paper? In this category is it a better book than *Catch-22*, as Waldmeir also claims? Do Chief Bromden and Yossarian (in Joseph Heller's novel) flee for the same reason, that is, as the only possible way of escaping from a hopeless situation?

5. Is it fair to say, as some critics have done, that *Cuckoo's Nest* falls into the pattern of Western movies, with black hats, white hats, and a golden-hearted prostitute? Or should we follow Leslie A. Fiedler, who—see the extract in this volume—calls it a novel of "the new West . . . the West of Madness"?

6. In what respects, if any, does *Cuckoo's Nest* reveal the influence of comic books such as *Captain Marvel, Flash Gordon,* and *The Lone Ranger*? (See especially Terry G. Sherwood's paper.)

7. Sherwood says that the author becomes sentimental in his account of the fishing trip and of the big party at the hospital. Robert Boyers accuses him of "porno-politics," that is, of the notion that uninhibited sexuality will solve social problems. To what extent are these criticisms justified?

8. Is *Cuckoo's Nest* a tragedy in any accepted sense of the term, for example, Aristotle's? (For a brief definition, see the article on Tragedy in *The Columbia Encyclopedia*.)

9. The extremely large sale of the novel has been in paperback editions and has been largely, it would appear, to readers under thirty. The play based on the novel was a failure on Broadway, where audiences are likely to be middle-aged, but it has been a lasting success with the younger audiences of off-Broadway theaters—in spite of being condemned by middle-aged critics (as note the reviews in this volume by Harold Clurman and Walter Kerr). How should we explain the special appeal of novel and play to the new generation?

THE CHARACTERS

1. Randle Patrick McMurphy: Does he suggest the hero of many Western stories, the lone cowboy coming into a corrupt little town to set things straight? He starts by looking out for Number One, but at some point in the novel—at what point, exactly?—he begins working to save the other inmates of the ward. In the end does he become in his own way a Christ figure?

2. Chief Bromden: Is his schizophrenia persuasively rendered in the first half of the novel? Is his at least partial cure by McMurphy also rendered persuasively? Do we accept his killing McMurphy as an act of love? What is the symbolic value of his

tearing loose the heavy control panel after McMurphy had failed to do so? What do you think will happen to Chief Bromden after his escape from the hospital?

3. Big Nurse Ratched: Does she represent in exaggerated form what Kesey (or rather Harding) in one place calls "the matriarchy"? Does she suggest other characters in American fiction (for example, Aunt Sally in *Huckleberry Finn*)? Is there any ground for saying, as some have said, that she too is a victim of "the Combine" and, in a special sense, one more among the patients in the ward? What did Kesey mean when he said in an interview that "The Big Nurse murdered President Kennedy"?

4. Billy Bibbit: His stutter suggests that of the hero in Melville's *Billy Budd,* a book to which Kesey has acknowledged an indebtedness. Is there a sense in which Bibbit's death is another tragedy of innocence?

5. The Minor Characters: Do any of these represent familiar types in American society (and fiction)? If so, does the stereotyping of some characters detract from their believability? Do the patients in the ward sometimes function together as members of a Greek chorus, offering comments on the action? In that case, who is the choral leader?

6. Who is the real hero of the novel—McMurphy or Bromden?

7. It is said that truth often comes from the mouths of Shakespeare's fools and madmen. Does the statement apply to Kesey's madmen as well?

8. Neal Cassady was a person admired by the Beats and the Hippies. For Jack Kerouac he served as the original in life of Dean Moriarty, a leading character in *On the Road* (see the extract from the novel reprinted in this volume). Kesey has paid two tributes to Cassady: besides the one reprinted from *Garage Sale,* there is a passage about him in "An Impolite Interview." Compare his personality as depicted in those extracts with that of R. P. McMurphy.

STYLE AND STRUCTURE

1. This volume contains much relevant information about the writing of *One Flew Over the Cuckoo's Nest,* especially in the Tom Wolfe chapter, "What Do You Think of My Buddha?" and in Kesey's two letters to Ken Babbs. Briefly, Kesey had been working as night attendant in the psychiatric ward of the Menlo Park Veterans Administration Hospital and had been deeply moved by some of the patients. He started to write a novel about them, in the third person. Then he had his inspiration, after choking down eight peyote buds, and began telling the story from the point of view of a schizophrenic patient in the ward. All this, expanded and buttressed by quotations, might be the substance of a paper.

2. Then a question based on those briefly mentioned circumstances: Does Kesey's account of the writing place too much emphasis on inspiration (or peyote) and not enough on his intelligent work in revising the novel? Compare his early draft with the opening scene of the novel as published, and also examine the two pages of holograph revisions in the manuscript. In what specific ways did his changes add force to the story?

3. And another question, this one based on Kesey's statement to Babbs about the importance of point of view: What are the advantages (not omitting the opportunity for picturesque writing) and what are the limitations of using Chief Bromden as the center of consciousness?

4. There are various literary and religious allusions in the characters, the events, and the themes of *Cuckoo's Nest.* Identify as many of these as you can and discuss their function.

5. Does the writing of the novel reveal any indebtedness to Faulkner or to Hemingway, two authors whom Kesey admires (each for special qualities)?

6. Kesey had been a student in the drama at the University of Oregon. Can you mention scenes in the novel that are "staged," as it were, with dramatic objectivity?

7. It was Dale Wasserman, a professional playwright, who adapted *One Flew Over the Cuckoo's Nest* for the stage. Obviously he felt that some of the characters had to be simplified to make them actable and that some of the sequences had to be changed. Compare his version of the final scenes, as reprinted here, with the same scenes in the novel (pp. 282–311). What are the principal changes he made? Did he dramatize the text effectively or melodramatize it?

THE PSYCHIATRIC ASPECT

1. Kesey does not lay claim to any special knowledge of psychiatry; he is a novelist, not a physician. Nevertheless he presents a picture of what is wrong, in general, with "acute" patients in a psychiatric ward, and in the case of some patients —Harding, Bibbit, Bromden—he offers an explanation of how they came to be psychotic. Are his explanations persuasive?

2. Kesey also suggests what might be called the Randle P. McMurphy system of practical psychotherapy and depicts it as being amazingly successful in some cases (though it leads to poor Billy Bibbit's being destroyed by Big Nurse). Can you describe the system and, once again, does Kesey make a persuasive plea for it?

3. Kesey is opposed to electric-shock treatments. He tells us that, if the doctor or the attendant makes a mistake, they can reduce a patient to idiocy, and he charges that shocks can be used by a sadistic head nurse as a form of punishment. Does he seem to overstate the case? Compare his account with the medical statement in this volume by Arthur P. Noyes and Lawrence C. Kolb. But note that Kolb reports in a later article ("Psychiatry," *Encyclopedia Britannica*, Vol. 18, p. 717), "Electroconvulsive therapy, like insulin shock, declined in use after the tranquilizing drugs were introduced."

4. Kesey makes clear his belief that the effect of prefrontal lobotomy, or "psychosurgery," is utterly to destroy the human personality. Again, does he overstate the case? To judge by

their medical paper reprinted in this volume, Mary Robinson and Walter Freeman obviously do not share his belief, but they do report some disturbing effects of the operation. Still more disturbing effects have been noted by others. "Prefrontal lobotomy," Kolb says in his *Encyclopedia Britannica* article, "has come to be generally regarded as a radical procedure to be followed only after all other forms of treatment have proved ineffective." The use of the procedure in prisons has been hotly attacked and defended. Most authorities would agree, however, that performing a lobotomy on R. P. McMurphy was a surgical crime.

5. Compare Kesey's account of electric-shock treatments and prefrontal lobotomy with the passages reprinted in this volume from *Invisible Man,* by Ralph Ellison, and *All the King's Men,* by Robert Penn Warren.

TOPICS FOR RESEARCH

1. Read Kesey's other novel, *Sometimes a Great Notion,* and his shorter pieces collected in *Garage Sale.* A paper might discuss the ideas or general attitudes that are implicit in all his published work.

2. The first-person narrator: Compare Kesey's use of this device with its use by earlier American novelists, as notably Hawthorne (*The Blithedale Romance*), Mark Twain (*Huckleberry Finn*), Hemingway (*The Sun Also Rises*), and Faulkner (*As I Lay Dying* and Benjy's stream of consciousness in the first section of *The Sound and the Fury*).

3. The man nobody listens to: Compare Chief Bromden and the narrator of *Invisible Man.*

4. In some respects Kesey's picture of life in a psychiatric ward resembles the bleak pictures of the future presented in Orwell's 1984 and Aldous Huxley's *Brave New World.* Read these two counter-Utopian novels and write a comparison.

5. Several of the famous American novels present the relation between a white hero and a dark-skinned companion: Natty

Bumppo and Uncas (*The Last of the Mohicans*), Ishmael and Queequeg (*Moby-Dick*), Huckleberry Finn and Nigger Jim, Isaac McCaslin and Sam Fathers ("The Bear"). How does the relation of McMurphy and Chief Bromden differ from those others? (See also the discussion of the four earlier works in Leslie A. Fiedler, *Love and Death in the American Novel*.)

6. Read *The American Adam*, by R. W. B. Lewis. Does *Cuckoo's Nest* follow the pattern established in that important critical work? (Another book by Lewis is *The Picaresque Saint*, a title that aptly describes R. P. McMurphy.)

7. (For students with a background in psychology.) The original purpose of the officially sponsored research into the effects of psychedelic drugs, at Menlo Park V.A. Hospital and elsewhere, was to find drugs that induced a temporary state of schizophrenia as a means of finding other drugs that might cure schizophrenia. Find whether the results of such experiments have been recorded in published papers. Was Kesey's experience with the program in any way typical?

Selected Bibliography

Works by Ken Kesey

NOVELS

One Flew Over the Cuckoo's Nest, 1962.
Sometimes a Great Notion, 1964.

COLLECTION

Kesey's Garage Sale, 1973.

Criticism and Commentary

BOOKS

Fiedler, Leslie A. *The Return of the Vanishing American.* New York: Stein and Day, 1968.

Klein, Marcus, ed. *The American Novel since World War II.* Greenwich, Conn.: Fawcett, 1969.

Miller, James E., Jr. *Quests Surd and Absurd.* Chicago: The University of Chicago Press, 1968.

Reich, Charles A. *The Greening of America.* New York: Random House, 1970.

Tanner, Tony. *City of Words: American Fiction 1950–1970.* New York: Harper & Row, 1971.

Wolfe, Tom. *The Electric Kool-Aid Acid Test.* New York: Farrar Straus & Giroux, 1968.

ARTICLES

Barsness, John A. "Ken Kesey: The Hero in Modern Dress." *Bulletin of the Rocky Mountain Modern Language Association,* XXIII, 1 (March 1969), 27–33.

Beards, Richard D. "Stereotyping in Modern American Fiction: Some Solitary Swedish Madmen." *Moderna Sprak*, LXIII, 4 (1969), 329–37.

Boyers, Robert. "Attitudes toward Sex in American 'High Culture.' " *The Annals of the American Academy of Political and Social Sciences*, 376 (March 1968), 36–52.

Fiedler, Leslie A. "The New Mutants." *Partisan Review*, XXXII, 4 (Fall 1965), 505–29.

Hauck, Richard B. "The Comic Christ and the Modern Reader." *College English*, XXXI, 5 (February 1970), 498–506.

Malin, Irving. "Ken Kesey: *One Flew Over the Cuckoo's Nest*." *Critique*, V, 2 (1962), 81–84.

Schopf, William. "Blindfolded and Backwards: Promethean and Bemushroomed Heroism in *One Flew Over the Cuckoo's Nest* and *Catch-22. Bulletin of the Rocky Mountain Modern Language Association*, x, xvi, 3 (Fall 1972), 89–97.

Sherwood, Terry. "*One Flew Over the Cuckoo's Nest* and the Comic Strip." *Critique*, XIII, 1 (1971), 96–109.

Sutherland, Janet. "A Defense of Ken Kesey's *One Flew Over the Cuckoo's Nest*," *English Journal*, LXI, 1 (January 1972), 28–36.

Waldmeir, Joseph J. "Only an Occasional Rutabaga: American Fiction since 1945." *Modern Fiction Studies*, XV, 4 (1969–70), 467–81.

———. "Two Novelists of the Absurd: Heller and Kesey." *Wisconsin Studies in American Literature*, V, 3 (1964), 192–204.

AUDIOTAPE

Widmer, Kingsley. "*One Flew Over the Cuckoo's Nest*," in *The Twentieth Century American Novel* series. Deland, Florida: Everett/Edwards, Inc., 1970 (running time: 37 minutes).